Robert Burns, Robert Chambers

Life and works. Edited by Robert Chambers. Rev. by William

Wallace

Volume II.

Robert Burns, Robert Chambers

Life and works. Edited by Robert Chambers. Rev. by William Wallace
Volume II.

ISBN/EAN: 9783337021474

Printed in Europe, USA, Canada, Australia, Japan

Cover: Foto ©Raphael Reischuk / pixelio.de

More available books at **www.hansebooks.com**

THE

LIFE AND WORKS

OF

ROBERT BURNS

EDITED BY ROBERT CHAMBERS

REVISED BY

WILLIAM WALLACE

IN FOUR VOLUMES

VOLUME II.

W. & R. CHAMBERS, Limited

EDINBURGH AND LONDON

1896

PREFATORY NOTE.

THE second volume of Dr Chambers's *Life and Works of Robert Burns* has, like the first, been partly recast, and almost completely rewritten, to admit of the inclusion of new biographical material and letters which have been discovered since 1851. Fresh light is thrown upon Burns's religious views. To the proper understanding of the correspondence between Sylvander and Clarinda, it is necessary that the letters of both should be studied. Accordingly, Mrs M'Lehose's are now introduced, in their entirety, into the biography. The views of Burns taken by such of his more notable contemporaries as met him in Edinburgh are given at much greater length than they have hitherto been. With a view to showing the extent of his reading, an attempt has been made to trace to their sources the more important quotations from writers, both in prose and verse, which are to be found in his numerous letters. My thanks are due to Mr J. Parker Smith, M.P., Mr H. A. Webster of the Edinburgh University Library, Mr Hew Morrison of the Edinburgh Public Library, Mr George Gray, Town Clerk of Rutherglen, and other gentlemen, for the facilities they have afforded me in examining and collating manuscripts in their possession.   W. W.

CONTENTS—VOL. II.

CHAPTER I.

EDINBURGH (NOVEMBER 1786—APRIL 1787).

CHAPTER II.

EDINBURGH—TOURS—MAUCHLINE (APRIL TO AUGUST 1787).

The second edition of the *Poems* issued—The 'Dedication'—Subscribers—The question of copyright—Letters to Ballantine, Reid,
Dr Moore, Mrs Dunlop, Dunbar, and Dr Blair—Robert Ainslie—

CHAPTER III.

HIGHLAND TOUR—EDINBURGH (JULY TO DECEMBER 1787).

CHAPTER IV.

EDINBURGH—'CLARINDA' (1787-1788).

CHAPTER V.

THE ISLE (JUNE—DECEMBER 1788).

APPENDICES.

LIST OF ILLUSTRATIONS.

LIFE AND WORKS

OF

ROBERT BURNS.

CHAPTER I.

BURNS set out on the 27th November from Mossgiel for the Scottish capital—a journey of about sixty miles. Currie states that he travelled on foot ; but it appears from a note of correction sent to him by Gilbert Burns,[*] but not used, that the poet rode a pony which he borrowed from a friend. An incident of the journey which was related by Mr Archibald Prentice, founder and editor of the *Manchester Times*, confirms Gilbert's note. It appears that, through an Ayrshire friend, George Reid of Barquharie, near Ochiltree, Burns had been made acquainted with Mr Prentice's father,[†] the farmer of Covington-Mains, near Biggar, in Lanarkshire—a zealous admirer of the poet, as is amply testified by his name being set down in the list of sub-scribers to the second edition for twenty copies. According to Mr Prentice :[‡] 'It was arranged by Mr Reid that Burns should, on his journey to Edinburgh, make the farmhouse at Covington-Mains his resting-place on the first night. All the farmers in the parish had read with delight the poet's then published works, and were

---

[*] *Life of Dr Currie*, by his son, 2 vols.

[†] The Archibald Prentice referred to was a son of the farmer. He settled in Manchester in 1815, took an active part in public affairs, and died there in 1857. He was not living at the time of Burns's visit to Covington-Mains. It is interesting to find that a nephew of the farmer was founder and editor of the *Glasgow Chronicle*.

[‡] Letter of Mr Prentice to Professor Wilson, dated March 8, 1841, and published in the *Edinburgh Intelligencer*.

anxious to see him. They were all asked to meet him at a late
dinner, and the signal of his arrival was to be a white sheet
attached to a pitchfork, and put on the top of a cornstack in the
barnyard. The parish is a beautiful amphitheatre, with the Clyde
winding through it, with Wellbrae Hill to the west, Tinto and the
Culter Falls to the south, and the pretty, green, conical hill,
Quothquan Law, to the east. My father's stackyard, lying in the
centre, was seen from every house in the parish. At length
Burns arrived, mounted on a *pownie* borrowed of [the George Reid
already mentioned].* Instantly was the white flag hoisted, and
as instantly were the farmers seen issuing from their houses, and
converging to the point of meeting. A glorious evening, or rather
night, which borrowed something from the morning, followed, and
the conversation of the poet confirmed and increased the admiration created by his writings. On the following morning, he
breakfasted with a large party at the next farmhouse, tenanted by
James Stodart, brother to the Stodarts, the pianoforte-makers of
London ;† took lunch also with a large party at the Bank, in the
parish of Carnwath, with John Stodart, my mother's father, and
rode into Edinburgh that evening on the *pownie*, which he
returned to the owner a few days afterwards by John Samson,
the brother of the immortalised "TAM." Mr Samson took with
him a letter to Mr Reid, in which the poet expressed the great
pleasure he had experienced in meeting his friends at Covington.'

TO MR GEORGE REID, BARQUHARIE.

MY DEAR SIR—John Samson begged your pownie in such a manner,
seconded by Mr Dalrymple of Orangefield, that I hope you will forgive
my not returning it by the carrier.

I left Mr Prentice's on Monday night. There was a most agreeable

---

* Mr Prentice stated here the name of 'a Mr Dalrymple, near Ayr.' That he was in
error is proved by the letter from Burns to George Reid.

† 'I have heard James Stodart's son, a James Stodart also, say, when nearly eighty, that
he remembered when passing the Mains that morning with other companions on his way
to school. The pony was waiting at the door for the owner to start on his journey. The
stalwart "Bauldy" came out and ordered him and the other boys to stop and haud the
stirrup for the man that was to mount, adding "You 'll boast of it till your dying day."
The boys said, "We 'll be late, and we 're fear'd for the maister." "Stop and haud
the stirrup; I 'll settle wi' the maister." They took courage, as well they might, for
Prentice was six feet three, and the dominie but an ordinary mortal. That boy Stodart,
almost an octogenarian at the time he spoke to me, said : "I think I 'm prouder of that
forenoon frae the schule than a' the days I was at it."—From *George Square, Glasgow,* by
Rev. Thomas Somerville, a great-grandson of Mr Prentice, who entertained Burns.

little party in the evening; a Mr Lang,* a dainty body of a clergyman; a Mr and Mrs Stodart—a glorious fellow, with a still more glorious wife, with whom I breakfasted, along with Mr Prentice, next morning. For Mr Prentice, no words can do him justice. Sound sterling sense and plain warm hospitality are truly his. R. B.

EDINBURGH, 29th November 1786.

'My father,' adds Mr Prentice, 'was exactly the sort of man to draw forth all the higher powers of Burns's mind. He combined physical and moral strength in an extraordinary degree; had a great deal of practical knowledge; had read and thought much; had a high relish for *manly* poetry; much benevolence; much indignation at oppression, which nobody dared to exercise within his reach; and no mean conversational powers. Such was the person to appreciate Burns—ay, and to reverence the man who penned "The Cotter's Saturday Night;" and accordingly, though a strictly moral and religious man himself, he always maintained that the virtues of the poet greatly predominated over his faults. I once heard him exclaim with hot wrath, when somebody was quoting from an *Apologist!* "What! do *they* apologise for *him?* One-half of his good, and all his bad, divided amang a score o' them, would make them a' better men!"

'When a lad of seventeen, in the year 1809, I resided for a short time in Ayrshire, in the hospitable house of my father's friend Reid, and surveyed with a strong interest such visitors as had known Burns. I soon learned how to anticipate their representations of his character. The men of strong minds and strong feelings were invariable in their expressions of admiration; but the prosy consequential *bodies* all disliked him as exceeding dictatorial. The men whose religion was based on intellect and high moral sentiment all thought well of him: but the mere professors, with their "twa-mile prayers and half-mile graces," denounced him as "worse than an infidel."'

Burns reached Edinburgh on the 28th November, a day remarkable in the history of the city as the date of the starting of Palmer's mail-carriages, by which letters were to be conveyed between the two capitals of the island in the then surprisingly

* Who the 'Mr Lang' referred to was, does not appear. From Scott's *Fasti*, we learn that there were at that time two Church of Scotland clergymen of the name of Lang—Gilbert Lang, of Largs; and William Lang, of Arngask (Presbytery of Perth). Probably it was the latter who was of the 'party.'

brief period of sixty hours! He came, he says, without a single letter of introduction, and, there is very good reason to believe, with very little money in his pocket. With the exception of Professor Dugald Stewart, he had scarcely a single acquaintance among the inhabitants of Edinburgh. There was, however, one friend whom he could readily approach. This was John Richmond, formerly clerk to Gavin Hamilton. He was now in a writer's (lawyer's) office in the city. He occupied a humble room in Baxter's Close, Lawnmarket, for which he paid three shillings a week.* Into this lodging he willingly received his friend, giving him a share of his bed—of which Burns stood so much in need from indisposition that he stayed in it the whole of the day after his arrival.

According to Allan Cunningham, Burns's first proceedings in Edinburgh were aimless. 'Though he had taken a stride from the furrowed-field into the land of poetry, and abandoned the plough for the harp, he seemed for some days to feel, as in earlier life, unfitted with an aim, and wandered about looking down from Arthur's Seat, surveying the Palace, gazing at the Castle, or contemplating the windows of the booksellers' shops, where he saw all works save the poems of the Ayrshire Ploughman. He found his way to the lowly grave of Fergusson, and kneeling down, kissed the sod; he sought out the house of Allan Ramsay, and on entering it took off his hat; and when he was afterwards introduced to Creech, the bibliopole remembered that he had before heard him inquiring if this had been the shop of the author of the "Gentle Shepherd."' His subsequent proceedings in connection with Fergusson's tomb render it quite possible that Cunningham's story is largely imaginative.

During the preceding summer, Burns had become acquainted with Mr James Dalrymple of Orangefield, near Ayr—a warm-hearted man, an enthusiastic Freemason, a too enthusiastic sportsman, and an occasional writer of verses. As he had been concerned with Mr John Ballantine in laying the foundation-stone of the 'new brig' with masonic honours, we may surmise that it was through that loyal friend of the poet that the introduction was effected. In the earlier half of the eighteenth

---

* According to notes now in the Laing collection of manuscripts in the Edinburgh University Library, and purporting to be communications from Richmond, he paid half-a-crown a week before Burns joined him, and three shillings afterwards.

century, there had lived in Ayr a poor musician or 'violer,'* named Hugh M'Guire. A friendless lad, named Macrae, to whom he had shown some kindness, went abroad, rose in the world, and came home as the retired governor of Madras, with a large fortune. Having no family of his own, Governor Macrae, from a feeling of gratitude, adopted that of M'Guire. To the son, who took his name, he gave a large estate. The eldest daughter, with a handsome dowry, was married in 1744 to William, Earl of Glencairn, father of the well-known friend and patron of the poet. The second became the wife of Lord Alva, a judge of the Court of Session. The fourth was wedded in 1750 to Charles Dalrymple of Orangefield, Sheriff-clerk of Ayrshire, elder brother of the Dr William Dalrymple who baptised Burns, and father of his masonic friend. Thus it happened that the then Earl of Glencairn, Mr Dalrymple of Orangefield, and a certain hot-headed Captain Macrae of Holmains, all distinguished members of society in Edinburgh, were cousins-german through a common descent from the Ayr violer, Hugh M'Guire. The daughter of the violer, now Dowager-Countess of Glencairn, resided at Coates House, near Edinburgh; she was noted for her religious zeal in an age not much noted for pietism. A connection had been established between this group and another of equal local distinction, by the union in 1785 of the Hon. and Rev. John Cunninghame, the younger brother of Lord Glencairn, to Lady Isabella Erskine, sister to the Earl of Buchan and to the Hon. Henry Erskine, Dean of the Faculty of Advocates, both of whom were leading members of Edinburgh society. Having, through Mr Dalrymple, the means of introduction to this 'set,' Burns could not be said to enter Edinburgh quite friendless. Lord Glencairn, too, was already prepared to befriend the Ayrshire poet, having had his attention drawn to the Kilmarnock volume by Mr Dalziel, factor on his Ayrshire estate.

William Creech,† at this time the leading publisher in Edin-

---

* He seems also to have done work as a joiner or carpenter.

† William Creech was born on 21st April 1745 in Newbattle, of which parish his father was minister. His father having died while he was an infant, he was brought up by his mother, and studied at the University of Edinburgh with a view to becoming a doctor. He was induced, however, to accept a position in the shop of Messrs Kincaid & Bell, printers. This he left to become travelling tutor to Lord Kilmaurs (afterwards Earl of Glencairn), who had for some time boarded in his mother's house. He returned to Edinburgh, however, and in 1771, on the dissolution of the firm of Kincaid & Bell, became Mr Kincaid's partner. Two years later his partner retired, and he conducted the business, which now embraced publishing as well as bookselling and printing, alone for forty-four years.

burgh, had in early life acted as tutor to the Earl of Glencairn. The Earl was, therefore, well qualified to introduce Burns to his notice, and recommend to him the publication of the proposed second edition of the Poems. Creech, who was a well-educated man, and himself not without literary abilities of a sort, must have instantly appreciated the genius thus brought under his notice. Apparently, however, he did not at once resolve upon undertaking any risk that might be involved in the proposed edition.

According to a curious record,* Burns was present on the evening of the 7th of December at a meeting of the Canongate Kilwinning Lodge of Freemasons, at its place of assemblage in St John's Street, and there Mr Dalrymple introduced him to the *Past-Master*, the famous advocate, whig, and wit, Henry Erskine. He was peculiarly disposed to befriend such an example of native genius as Burns. This single lodge-night seems to have been enough to make the poet feel as if Erskine were already an old and trusty friend. Burns was now in the prime of his physical and mental powers. Yet, rather singularly, none of the men whom he now met has left on record an account of his personal appearance. The nearest approach to a photograph in words is that which after his death was 'compiled' by Dr Currie from accounts given by John Syme, Alexander Cunningham, and other associates of the poet :

Burns was nearly five feet ten inches in height, and of a form that indicated agility as well as strength. His well-raised forehead, shaded with black curling hair, indicated extensive capacity. His eyes were large, dark, full of ardour and intelligence. His face was well formed, and his countenance uncommonly interesting and expressive. His mode of dressing, which was often slovenly, and a certain fulness and bend in his shoulders, characteristic of his original profession, disguised in some degree the natural symmetry and elegance of his form. The external appearance of Burns was most strikingly indicative of the character of his mind. On a first view, his physiognomy had a certain air of coarseness, mingled, however, with an expression of deep penetration, and of calm thoughtfulness, approaching to melancholy. . . . His dark and haughty countenance easily relaxed into a look of good-will, of pity, or of tenderness ; and as the various emotions succeeded each other in his mind, assumed with equal ease the expression of the broadest humour, of the most extravagant mirth, of the deepest melancholy, or of the most sublime emotion. †

    * *A Winter with Robert Burns*, by James Marshall. (Edinburgh, 1846.)
    † This view is supplemented and confirmed by a sketch of Burns, which was written

Burns, of course, had many enemies who were willing to injure him in Edinburgh, as in Ayrshire, by traducing his character and raking up against him the story of his connection with Jean Armour. Learning from his friend M'Kenzie, of Mauchline, that he had been defended by Sir John Whitefoord, he wrote this letter:

TO SIR JOHN WHITEFOORD, BART.

EDIN., 1st Decr. [1786].

SIR—Mr M'Kenzie, in Mauchline, my very warm and worthy friend, has informed me how much you are pleased to interest yourself in my fate as a man, and, (what to me is incomparably dearer) my fame as a poet. I have, Sir, in one or two instances, been patronized by those of your character in life, when I was introduced to their notice by social friends to them, and honored acquaintances to me; but you are the first gentleman in the country whose benevolence and goodness of heart has interested him for me, unsolicited and unknown. I am not master enough of the etiquette of these matters to know, nor did I stay to inquire, whether formal duty bade, or cold propriety disallowed, my thanking you in this manner, as I am convinced, from the light in which you kindly view me, that you will do me the justice to believe this letter is not the manœuvre of the needy, sharping author, fastening on those in upper life, who honor him with a little notice of him or his works. Indeed the situation of poets is generally such, to a proverb, as may, in some measure, palliate that prostitution of heart and talents they have at times been guilty of. I do not think prodigality is, by any means, a necessary concomitant of a poetic turn, but I believe a careless, indolent inattention to economy is almost inseparable from it; then there must be in the heart of every bard of Nature's making a certain modest sensibility, mixed with a kind of pride, which will ever keep him out of the way of those windfalls of fortune, which frequently light on hardy impudence and foot-licking servility. It is not easy to imagine a more helpless state than his, whose poetic fancy unfits him for the world, and whose character as a scholar gives him some pretensions to the politesse of life—yet is as poor as I am.

For my part, I thank Heaven my star has been kinder; learning never

after his death by Mrs Maria Riddell: 'His figure certainly bore the authentic impress of his birth and original station in life; it seemed moulded by Nature for the rough exercises of agriculture, rather than the gentler cultivation of *belles lettres.* His features were stamped with the hardy character of independence, and the firmness of conscious though not arrogant pre-eminence. I believe no man was ever gifted with a larger portion of the *vivida vis animi;* the animated expressions of his countenance were almost peculiar to himself. The rapid lightnings of his eyes were always the harbingers of some flash of genius, whether they darted the fiery glances of insulted and indignant superiority, or beamed with the impassioned sentiment of fervent and impetuous affections. His voice alone could improve upon the magic of his eye; sonorous, replete with the finest modulation, it alternately captivated the ear with the melody of poetic numbers, the perspicuity of nervous reasoning, or the ardent sallies of enthusiastic patriotism.'

elevated my ideas above the peasant's shed, and I have an independent fortune at the plough-tail.

I was surprised to hear that any one who pretended in the least to the manners of the gentleman should be so foolish, or worse, as to stoop to traduce the morals of such a one as I am, and so inhumanly cruel, too, as to meddle with that late most unfortunate, unhappy part of my story. With a tear of gratitude, I thank you, Sir, for the warmth with which you interposed in behalf of my conduct. I am, I acknowledge, too frequently the sport of whim, caprice, and passion—but reverence to God, and integrity to my fellow-creatures, I hope I shall ever preserve. I have no return, Sir, to make you for your goodness, but one—a return which, I am persuaded, will not be unacceptable—the honest, warm wishes of a grateful heart for your happiness, and every one of that lovely flock who stand to you in a filial relation. If ever calumny aim the poisoned shaft at them, may friendship be by to ward the blow !   R. B.

Sir John's reply may be given, both because it indicates the respect in which Burns was held by his aristocratic acquaintances in Ayrshire, and because it foreshadows the use to which he subsequently put the profits from the second edition of his poems.

SIR JOHN WHITEFOORD TO ROBERT BURNS.

EDINBURGH, 4th December 1786.

SIR—I received your letter a few days ago. I do not pretend to much interest, but what I have I shall be ready to exert in procuring the attainment of any object you have in view. Your character as a man (forgive my reversing your order) as well as a poet, entitle you, I think, to the assistance of every inhabitant of Ayrshire. I have been told you wished to be made a gauger ; I submit it to your consideration, whether it would not be more desirable, if a sum could be raised by subscription for a second edition of your poems, to lay it out in the stocking of a small farm. I am persuaded it would be a line of life much more agreeable to your feelings, and in the end more satisfactory. When you have considered this, let me know, and whatever you determine upon, I will endeavour to promote as far as my abilities will permit. With compliments to my friend the doctor, I am, Your friend and well wisher,

JOHN WHITEFOORD.

P.S.—I shall take it as a favour when you at any time send me a new production.

TO GAVIN HAMILTON, ESQ., MAUCHLINE.

EDINBURGH, Dec. 7, 1786.

HONORED SIR—I have paid every attention to your commands, but can only say what perhaps you will have heard before this reach you, that Muirkirklands were bought by a John Gordon, W.S., but for whom I know not; Mauchlands, Haugh Miln, &c., by a Frederick Fotheringham, supposed to be for Ballochmyle Laird, and Adamhill and Shawwood were bought for Oswald's folks. This is so imperfect an account, and will be so late ere it reach you, that were it not to discharge my conscience I would not trouble you with it; but after all my diligence I could make it no sooner nor better.*

For my own affairs, I am in a fair way of becoming as eminent as Thomas à Kempis or John Bunyan; and you may expect henceforth to see my birth-day inserted among the wonderful events, in the Poor Robin's and Aberdeen Almanacks,† along with the Black Monday, and the battle of Bothwell Bridge. My Lord Glencairn and the Dean of Faculty, Mr H. Erskine, have taken me under their wing; and by all probability I shall soon be the tenth worthy, and the eighth wise man of the world. Through my lord's influence it is inserted in the records of the Caledonian Hunt, that they universally, one and all, subscribe for the 2d edition. My subscription bills come out to-morrow, and you shall have some of them next post. I have met in Mr Dalrymple, of Orangefield, what Solomon emphatically calls 'A friend that sticketh closer than a brother.' The warmth with which he interests himself in my affairs is of the same enthusiastic kind which you, Mr Aiken, and the few patrons that took notice of my earlier poetic days, shewed for the poor unlucky devil of a poet.

I always remember Mrs Hamilton and Miss Kennedy‡ in my poetic prayers, but *you* both in prose and verse.

> May cauld ne'er catch you but a hap,   cold—without
> Nor hunger but in plenty's lap!   —covering
>
>   Amen!   R. B.

Meanwhile, powerful influence was at work on Burns's behalf. Dugald Stewart, on leaving Catrine, at the beginning of November, to commence his winter's work at the university, carried with

---

* The lands of Mauchline Mains, East, West, and South Mossgavil, Haugh-Miln, and some others in Ayrshire, which the Loudon family was at this time forced to part with, were advertised to be sold in the Exchange Coffeehouse, Edinburgh, on the 5th of December. Burns seems to have been commissioned by Gavin Hamilton to send him early intelligence of the result of the sale. The Earl of Loudon had committed suicide, on account of financial troubles, in the preceding April.

† Burns alludes here to two prophetical almanacs, the chief of which, *Poor Robin's*, existed from 1664 to 1823. The Aberdeen Almanac (or *Prognostication*, as it was commonly called) was among the first of the kind issued in Scotland. It was founded in 1623 by Edward Raban, Aberdeen's first printer, enjoyed a long life, and acquired an almost proverbial celebrity. It had an immense circulation, accounted for by the fact that Aberdeen had for long a monopoly (in Scotland) of the sale of almanacs. 'Black Monday,' so termed from its extraordinary coldness and the darkness that prevailed, was Easter Monday, 14th April 1360. The battle of Bothwell Brig, in which the Covenanters were defeated by Monmouth, was fought in 1679.

‡ Mrs Hamilton's sister.

him a copy of the Kilmarnock volume, which he brought under the notice of Henry Mackenzie, the well-known author of *The Man of Feeling*, who was now conducting a periodical, entitled *The Lounger*, published in Edinburgh by Creech. Mackenzie read and admired the poems, and lost no time in writing a generous review, which appeared in *The Lounger* of 9th December.* This pronouncement of the highest critical tribunal in the country at once established the reputation of Burns in Scotland as a true poet; all lesser judges accepted it as confirming the favourable appreciation which their feelings had already prompted.

Mackenzie boldly waived all claim for notice to Burns on the score of his humble position in society. He pronounced him 'a genius of no ordinary rank.' That genius's birth and education might excite wonder at his productions; 'but his poetry, considered abstractedly, and without the apologies arising from his situation, seems to me fully entitled to command our feelings, and to obtain our applause.' After quoting some stanzas from 'The Vision,' and the whole of the 'Mountain Daisy,' as specimens of the moral and tender, the critic continues : 'The power of genius is not less admirable in tracing the manners, than in painting the passions, or in drawing the scenery of Nature. That intuitive glance with which a writer like Shakespeare discerns the characters of men, with which he catches the many-changing hues of life, forms a sort of problem in the science of mind, of which it is easier to see the truth than to assign the cause. Though I am very far from meaning to compare our rustic bard to Shakespeare, yet whoever will read his lighter and more humorous poems, his Dialogue of the Dogs, his Dedication to G[avin] H[amilton], Esq., his Epistles to a Young Friend, and to W[illiam] S[imson], will perceive with what uncommon penetration and sagacity this Heaven-taught ploughman, from his humble and unlettered station, has looked upon men and manners.'

Mackenzie further claimed for him the generous support of his country. 'Burns,' he said, 'possesses the spirit as well as the fancy

---

* 'Even to Scotsmen, we may suspect (or rather we pretty well know from the way in which Robertson and Blair, Hume and Mackenzie write) this burst of genial racy humour from the *terræ filius* of Kilmarnock must have been somewhat startling; and it speaks volumes for the amiable author of *The Man of Feeling* that in the very periodical where he was wont to air his mild Addisonian hobbies he should have warmly commended the Ayrshire ploughman.'—PROFESSOR GEORGE SAINTSBURY in *A History of Nineteenth-century Literature, 1780-1895* (Macmillan & Co., 1896).

of a poet. That honest pride and independence of soul which are sometimes the Muse's only dower, break forth on every occasion in his works. It may be, then, I shall wrong his feelings while I indulge my own, in calling the attention of the public to his situation and circumstances. That condition, humble as it was, in which he found content, and wooed the Muse, might not have been deemed uncomfortable ; but grief and misfortune have reached him there ; and one or two of his poems hint, what I have learnt from some of his countrymen, that he has been obliged to form the resolution of leaving his native land, to seek under a West Indian clime that shelter and support which Scotland has denied him. But I trust means may be found to prevent this resolution from taking place ; and that I do my country no more than justice, when I suppose her ready to stretch out her hand to cherish and retain this native Poet, whose "wood-notes wild" possess so much excellence. To repair the wrongs of suffering or neglected merit ; to call forth genius from the obscurity in which it had pined indignant, and place it where it may profit or delight the world ; these are exertions which give to wealth an enviable superiority, to greatness and to patronage a laudable pride.'*

Burns now tells his own story in letters to his friends :

TO THE REVD. MR GREENFIELD,† INCLOSING TWO SONGS, THE COMPOSITION OF TWO AYRSHIRE MECHANICS.

REVD. SIR—On raking the recesses of my memory the other day, I stumbled on two Songs which I here inclose you as a kind of curiosity

---

* Burns was appreciated in London as well as in Edinburgh. The December (1786) number of *The Monthly Review or Literary Journal* contains an estimate of his works : 'His simple strains, artless and unadorned, seem to flow without effort from the native feelings of the heart. They are always nervous, sometimes inelegant, often natural, simple, and sublime. The objects that have obtained the attention of the author are humble ; for he himself, born in a low station, and following a laborious employment, has had no opportunity of observing scenes in the higher walks of life ; yet his verses are sometimes struck off with a delicacy and artless simplicity that charms like the bewitching though irregular touches of a Shakespeare.'

† Rev. William Greenfield had been translated in 1784 from Wemyss to St Andrew's Church, Edinburgh. This position he held until February of 1787, when he was appointed colleague to Dr Hugh Blair of the High Church. The Poet seems to have met, and liked, Greenfield soon after his arrival in Edinburgh, for he mentions in his letter of 15th December 1786 to Muir of Kilmarnock, that he is got under the patronage of, among others, Professor Greenfield. (He was then, also, professor of Rhetoric in the University of Edinburgh.) Other references to him are found in the Poet's letters, while he is accorded a panegyric in the second Common-place Book. His name appears as a subscriber (for two copies) to the Edinburgh edition of the *Poems*. He was Almoner to the king, 1789-98 ; had

to a Professor of the Belle lettres de la Nature ; which, allow me to say,
I look upon as an additional merit of yours ; a kind of bye-Professorship,
not always to be found among the systematic Fathers and Brothers of
Scientific Criticism. They were the work of Bards such as I lately was ;
and such as, I believe I had better still have been.

Never did Saul's armour sit so heavy on David when going to encounter Goliah, as does the encumbering robe of public notice with
which the friendship and patronage of some 'names dear to fame' have
invested me. I do not say this in the ridiculous idea of seeming self-
abasement and affected modesty ; I have long studied myself, and I
think I know pretty exactly what ground I occupy, both as a Man and
a Poet ; and however the world, or a friend, may sometimes differ from
me in that particular, I stand for it, in silent resolve, with all the
tenaciousness of property. I am willing to believe that my abilities
deserved a better fate than the veriest shades of life ; but to be dragged
forth, with all my imperfections on my head, to the full glare of learned
and polite observation, is what, I am afraid, I shall have bitter reason
to repent.

I mention this to you, once for all, merely, in the Confessor Style,
to disburthen my conscience, and that—' When proud fortune's ebbing
tide recedes '—you may bear me witness, when my buble of fame was
at the highest, I stood, unintoxicated, with the inebriating cup in my
hand looking forward, with rueful resolve, to the hastening time when
the stroke of envious Calumny, with all the eagerness of vengeful
triumph, should dash it to the ground.—I am ever, &c.

[ROBT. BURNS.]*

December, 1786.

TO JOHN BALLANTINE, ESQ., AYR.

EDINBURGH, 13th Dec. 1786.

MY HONORED FRIEND—I would not write you till I could have it in
my power to give you some account of myself and my matters, which

---

the degree of D.D. conferred on him, 1796 ; and the same year was elected Moderator of the
General Assembly. In December 1798 he suddenly demitted his charge and fled the
country.   The Presbytery of Edinburgh, on the 27th of that month, deposed and ex-
communicated him on account (*Scots Magazine*, December 1798) of 'certain flagrant reports
concerning his conduct, which his desertion seemed to preclude the Presbytery from considering as groundless.' The University degraded him from his degrees of A.M. and D.D.
He lived in the North of England, till his death in 1827, under an assumed name. He was
author of several works, the chief being *Essays on the Sources of the Pleasures received
from Literary Compositions* (issued anonymously, 1809 ; second edition, 1813).

* This letter, several phrases in which are identical with passages in a letter of Burns to
Mrs Dunlop, January 15, 1787, forms part of the Laing Collection in the Edinburgh
University Library. It is endorsed, 'Burns : Letters to several persons. Sent to Lady
H. Don, 26th March 1787.' Although in the handwriting of Burns, it is not signed by him.
It may be assumed, therefore, to be a copy of the letter actually sent to Dr Greenfield.
Unless Burns misdated the letter when copying it, it is of considerable value as indicating
that, almost from the moment of his arrival in Edinburgh, he had a presentiment of the
evanescence of his popularity there.

by the bye is often no easy task. I arrived here on Tuesday was se'n-
night,* and have suffered ever since I came to town with a miserable headache and stomach complaint, but am now a good deal better. I have
found a worthy warm friend in Mr Dalrymple, of Orangefield, who introduced me to Lord Glencairn, a man whose worth and brotherly kindness
to me I shall remember when time shall be no more. By his interest it
is passed in the Caledonian Hunt, and entered in their books, that they
are to take each a copy of the second edition, for which they are to pay
one guinea.† I have been introduced to a good many of the *Noblesse*, but
my avowed patrons and patronesses are the Duchess of Gordon—The
Countess of Glencairn, with my Lord, and Lady Betty‡—The Dean of
Faculty—Sir John Whitefoord. I have likewise warm friends among the
literati ; Professors Stewart, Blair, and Mr Mackenzie—the Man of
Feeling. An unknown hand left ten guineas for the Ayrshire bard with
Mr Sibbald, which I got. I since have discovered my generous unknown friend to be Patrick Miller, Esq., brother to the Justice Clerk ;
and drank a glass of claret with him by invitation at his own house
yesternight. I am nearly agreed with Creech to print my book, and I
suppose I will begin on Monday. I will send a subscription bill or two,
next post ; when I intend writing my first kind patron, Mr Aiken. I
saw his son to-day and he is very well.

Dugald Stewart, and some of my learned friends, put me in the
periodical paper called *The Lounger*, a copy of which I here enclose you.
I was, sir, when I was first honored with your notice, too obscure ; now
I tremble lest I should be ruined by being dragged too suddenly into the
glare of polite and learned observation.

I shall certainly, my ever honored patron, write you an account of my
every step ; and better health and more spirits may enable me to make
it something better than this stupid matter-of-fact epistle. I have the
honor to be, Good Sir, Your ever grateful humble servant,

ROBERT BURNS.

If any of my friends write me, my direction is, care of Mr Creech,
bookseller.

TO MR ROBERT MUIR, KILMARNOCK.

EDINBURGH, 15th Dec. 1786.

MY DEAR SIR—I delayed writing you till I was able to give you some
rational account of myself and my affairs. I am got under the patronage of the Duchess of Gordon, Countess Dowager of Glencairn, Sir John
Whitefoord, the Dean of Faculty, Professors Blair, Stewart, Greenfield,
and several others of the noblesse and literati. I believe I shall begin at
Mr Creech's as my publisher. I am still undetermined as to the future ;

---

* *Se'nnight*, a mistake. He had arrived on *Tuesday was fourteen days*.
† Burns must have heard an erroneous report to this effect. The club subscribed for 100
copies, but at *subscription price*.
‡ Lady Betty Cunningham, an unmarried sister of the Earl.

and, as usual, never think of it. I have now neither house nor home that I can call my own, and live on the world at large. I am just a poor wayfaring Pilgrim on the road to Parnassus, a thoughtless wanderer and sojourner in a strange land. I received a very kind letter from Mr A. Dalziel, for which please return my thanks; and tell him I will write him in a day or two. Mr Parker, Charles, Dr Corsan, and honest John, my *quondam* printer, I remember in my prayers when I pray in rhyme. To all of whom, till I have an opportunity [of saluting them in person, present my warmest remembrances].*

In this letter Burns rather curiously says, 'I believe I shall begin at Mr Creech's as my publisher.' As a matter of fact, Creech had, on the day before the letter was written, advertised the Poems as 'in the press, to be published by subscription for the sole benefit of the Author.' Next day the Poet wrote that the matter had been finally settled.

TO MR ROBERT AIKEN, AYR.

DEAR PATRON OF MY VIRGIN MUSE—I wrote Mr Ballantine at large all my operations and 'eventful story,' since I came to town. I have found in Mr Creech, who is my agent forsooth, and Mr Smellie, who is to be my printer, that honor and goodness of heart which I always expect in Mr Aiken's friends. Mr Dalrymple of Orangefield I shall ever remember: my Lord Glencairn I shall ever pray for. The Maker of man has great honor in the workmanship of his Lordship's heart. May he find that patronage and protection in his guardian angel that I have found in him! His Lordship has sent a parcel of subscription bills to the Marquis of Graham, with downright orders to get them filled up with all the first Scottish names about Court. He has likewise wrote to the Duke of Montague and is about to write to the Duke of Portland for their Graces' interest in behalf of the Scotch Bard's subscription.

You will very probably think, my honored friend, that a hint about the mischievous nature of intoxicated vanity may not be unseasonable; but, alas! you are wide of the mark. Various concurring circumstances have raised my fame as a Poet to a height which I am absolutely certain I have not merits to support; and I look down on the future as I would into the bottomless pit.

You shall have one or two more bills when I have an opportunity of a Carrier. I am ever, with the sincerest gratitude, Honored Sir, Your most devoted humble servt., ROBERT BURNS.

EDINR, 16th Dec. 1786.

* MS. torn here: the words within brackets were supplied by Dr Hately Waddell.

TO MR ROBERT MUIR, KILMARNOCK.

EDINBURGH, *Dec. 20th*, 1786.

MY DEAR FRIEND—I have just time for the carrier, to tell you that I received your letter; of which I shall say no more but what a lass of my acquaintance said of her bastard wean; she said she 'did na ken wha was the father exactly, but she suspected it was some o' thae bony blackguard smugglers, for it was like them.' So I only say your obliging epistle was like you. I enclose you a parcel of subscription bills. Your affair of sixty copies * is also like you; but it would not be like me to comply.

Your friend's notion of my life has put a crotchet in my head of sketching it in some future epistle to you. My compliments to Charles and Mr Parker. R. B.

The Caledonian Hunt was an association of the Scottish nobility and gentry, whose chief tie was their common interest in field sports. The promptitude and liberality of its patronage to Burns is beyond all question. The clever, kind-hearted, and eccentric Jane, Duchess of Gordon, was now the acknowledged leader of Edinburgh society. She enjoyed the poetry of Burns, and was eager to see him. The friendship of Henry Erskine has been already alluded to. By the literary men of the city, generally, Burns was cordially received. The period was, however, the evening of the first heyday of Edinburgh letters. A few years before, Burns would perhaps have found an even warmer welcome and a more just appreciation; he would certainly have met, at least, one man intellectually his peer in the Select Society and the Poker Club. But David Hume had, in 1786, been dead half a score of years; Lord Kames was gone; and the majority of their more or less brilliant contemporaries were long past their prime. Adam Smith, as will afterwards be seen, was too ill to see Burns. William Robertson had only seven years to live; Tytler and Lord Hailes even less. It was, in short, the interregnum between Hume and Scott. Burns himself was the man of the age. It strikes us of this day as almost ludicrous that he should have been patronised by men of the undoubted though second-rate capacity of Dugald Stewart, Hugh Blair, and Henry Mackenzie.

* Robert Muir actually subscribed for forty copies of the second edition. He had subscribed for seventy-two copies of the Kilmarnock edition.

In the circle, of which he was made free, nothing made a greater impression upon his mind than the exquisite beauty and grace of Eliza Burnet,* the daughter of Lord Monboddo. To her he makes special allusion in his 'Address to Edinburgh,' rating her among the wonders of the city.

* 'Miss Elizabeth Burnet, second daughter of Lord Monboddo, is frequently mentioned by Burns with great admiration, and most justly, for she was remarkably handsome and a very amiable young woman. She had one great personal defect, however—her teeth were much decayed and discoloured—but fortunately she had a very small mouth, and took care not to open it much in mixed company. She was, moreover, what is not noticed (either by the Poet or his Biographers), herself a poetess and a very clever woman. She always accompanied her father on horseback to and from Monboddo. Their journey lying thro' the village of Laurencekirk, erected in Kincardineshire by his friend and brother judge, Lord Gardenston, who was nearly, if not altogether, as eccentric a man as Lord M. himself. This village was Lord Gardenston's hobby-house. He introduced many manufactures into it, and amongst others the snuff-boxes known by the name of the village, and still much admired. In the inn which he established here a large album was kept, which was frequently enriched by quotations and donations from his own pen. Miss Burnet in an idle hour took occasion to insert a short address to his Lordship, imitated from the prologue to "The Rehearsal :"

> " We well might call this bloated book of yours
> A poesy of weeds, and not of flowers ;
> Yet such have been presented to our noses,
> And some there are, I fear, who've thought them roses."

' Lord Gardenston, who frequently inspected his album, was very irritable, and, taking offence at the above imitation, wrote below it with his own tremulous hand : "This plagiary writer censures without sense ; for tho' there are some things improper, yet every person will reap much entertainment from the variety of quotations." Which produced from the fair lady the following Philippic :

> " My Lord, do not growl
> 'Cause the verses are stole,
>   Altho' you smart under their lash ;
> Should you purge your chaste Olio
> Of each borrowed folio,
>   I fear you'd leave little but trash.
>
> Yet your Lordship should know,
> That a dangerous blow
>   From no such a fair arm could come,
> For the stroke of a wand
> From a Lady's soft hand
>   Is a compliment paid your album.
>
> Then don't take it ill
> That a feminine quill
>   Has ventured to tickle your Toby ;
> 'But allow her to urge,
> That, if you will purge,
>   You first should consult Dr Boby."'

—From 'MSS. Recollections of Burns and Others, written by Alexander Young, Esq., of Harburn, W.S., Edinburgh,' contained in the Laing Collection, Edinburgh University Library. The writer of the 'Recollections' notes that Dr Boby was 'Dr Robert Stewart of Fiddes, an eminent physician in Laurencekirk.'

ADDRESS TO EDINBURGH.

Edina ! Scotia's darling seat !
   All hail thy palaces and tow'rs
Where once beneath a Monarch's feet
   Sat Legislation's sov'reign pow'rs !
From marking wildly-scatt'red flow'rs,
   As on the banks of Ayr I stray'd,
And singing, lone, the ling'ring hours,
   I shelter in thy honor'd shade.

Here Wealth still swells the golden tide,
   As busy Trade his labours plies ;
There Architecture's noble pride
   Bids elegance and splendor rise ;
Here Justice, from her native skies,
   High wields her balance and her rod ;
There Learning, with his eagle eyes,
   Seeks Science in her coy abode.

Thy sons, Edina, social, kind,
   With open arms the Stranger hail ;
Their views enlarg'd, their lib'ral mind,
   Above the narrow, rural vale :
Attentive still to Sorrow's wail,
   Or modest Merit's silent claim ;
And never may their sources fail !
   And never Envy blot their name !

Thy Daughters bright thy walks adorn,
   Gay as the gilded summer sky,
Sweet as the dewy, milk-white thorn,
   Dear as the raptur'd thrill of joy !
Fair Burnet strikes th' adoring eye,
   Heav'n's beauties on my fancy shine ;
I see the Sire of Love on high,
   And own His work indeed divine !

There, watching high the least alarms,
　　Thy rough, rude Fortress gleams afar;
Like some bold Vet'ran, gray in arms,
　　And mark'd with many a seamy scar:
The pond'rous wall and massy bar
　　Grim-rising o'er the rugged rock,
Have oft withstood assailing War,
　　And oft repell'd th' Invader's shock.

With awe-struck thought and pitying tears
　　I view that noble, stately Dome,
Where Scotia's kings of other years,
　　Fam'd heroes! had their royal home:
Alas, how chang'd the times to come!
　　Their royal Name low in the dust!
Their hapless Race wild-wand'ring roam!
　　Tho' rigid Law cries out ''twas just!'

Wild-beats my heart to trace your steps
　　Whose ancestors, in days of yore,
Thro' hostile ranks and ruin'd gaps
　　Old Scotia's bloody lion bore:
Ev'n I who sing in rustic lore,
　　Haply my Sires have left their shed,
And fac'd grim Danger's loudest roar,
　　Bold-following where your Fathers led!

Edina! Scotia's darling seat!
　　All hail thy palaces and tow'rs
Where once beneath a Monarch's feet
　　Sat Legislation's sov'reign pow'rs!
From marking wildly-scatter'd flow'rs,
　　As on the banks of Ayr I stray'd,
And singing, lone, the lingering hours,
　　I shelter in thy honor'd shade.

On 20th December there appeared, as 'never before published,' in the columns of the *Caledonian Mercury,* a much more

G. O. Reid A.R.S.A.

Fair fa' your honest, sonsie face,
(Great chieftain o' the puddin-race!)

F. Jenkins Heliog. Paris

characteristic production of Burns than the 'Address to Edinburgh.' This was the immortal address

TO A HAGGIS.*

Fair fa' your honest, sonsie face,   *Fair fall = Good luck to*
Great Chieftain o' the Puddin-race !   *— jolly, well-favoured*
Aboon them a' ye tak your place,   *Above*
      Painch, tripe, or thairm :   *paunch—intestines*
Weel are ye wordy o' a grace   *worthy*
      As lang 's my arm.

The groaning trencher there ye fill,
Your hurdies like a distant hill,   *buttocks*
Your pin † wad help to mend a mill   *would*
      In time o' need,
While thro' your pores the dews distil
      Like amber bead.

His knife see Rustic-labour dight,   *clean, wipe*
An' cut you up wi' ready sleight,
Trenching your gushing entrails bright
      Like onie ditch ;   *any*
And then, O what a glorious sight,
      Warm-reekin, rich !   *steaming*

Then, horn for horn they stretch an' strive,   *horn-spoon*
Deil tak the hindmost, on they drive,   *last*
Till a' their weel-swall'd kytes belyve   *swelled stomachs*
      Are bent like drums;   *by and by*
Then auld Guidman, maist like to rive,   *almost—burst*
      'Bethankit' hums.   *murmurs 'God be thanked'*

Is there that owre his French *ragout*,   *over*
Or *olio* that wad staw a sow,   *would surfeit*
Or *fricassee* wad mak her spew
      Wi' perfect sconner,   *disgust*
Looks down wi' sneering, scornfu' view
      On sic a dinner?   *such*

---

* 'Haggice' is the spelling in the *Caledonian Mercury*.
 † The wooden pin used to fix the opening in the bag. The haggis is a dish composed of minced offal of mutton, mixed with oatmeal and suet, and boiled in a sheep's stomach.

Poor devil! see him owre his trash,
As feckless as a wither'd rash,   feeble—rush
His spindle shank a guid whip-lash,   thin leg—good
      His nieve a nit;   closed fist—nut
Thro' bluidy flood or field to dash,   bloody
      O how unfit!

But mark the Rustic, haggis-fed,
The trembling earth resounds his tread
Clap in his walie nieve a blade,   large fist
      He 'll mak it whissle;   whistle
An' legs, an' arms, an' heads will sned   lop off
      Like taps o' thrissle.   tops of thistles

Ye Pow'rs wha mak mankind your care
And dish them out their bill o' fare,
Auld Scotland wants nae skinking ware   thin stuff
      That jaups in luggies;   splashes in bowls
But if ye wish her gratefu' prayer,
      Gie her a Haggis!*   Give

Notwithstanding the strong interest awakened in Burns so soon after his arrival in Edinburgh, and the influence exerted in his favour, it appears that he did not at once surmount all the obstacles which stood in the way of his proposed second edition. John Moir, a well-known Edinburgh printer, used to relate

---

* In the *Caledonian Mercury*, and in the *Scots Magazine* for January 1787, in the Poet's Corner of which it also appeared, the last verse ran thus:

      'Ye Powers wha gie us a' that's gude,   give
      Still bless Auld Caledonia's brood
      Wi' great John Barleycorn's heart's blude
        In staups and luggies;   stoups and bowls
      And on our board that King o' food,
        A glorious Haggis.'

There are various traditions as to the origin of the poem. One is that Burns produced it almost in its entirety when at dinner in the house of his friend, Andrew Bruce, merchant, Castlehill, Edinburgh. Another is that the original last verse was given by Burns as a 'grace' to a dinner, of which a haggis formed a part, in the house of a friend, said to be a Mr Morison, cabinet-maker, in Mauchline. But that a haggis was in these days regarded as a luxury to be sighed for, may be gathered from this allusion in the Life of Dr Lawson of Selkirk: 'If I were a king, I do not know that I should live very much differently from what I do—only, perhaps, I would have a haggis oftener to dinner.'—*Life and Times of George Lawson, D.D.*, by the Rev. John Macfarlane, LL.D. (Edinburgh, 1862.)

that he was then serving his apprenticeship with a well-known typographer in the High Street. 'One day a plain-looking man, of rustic appearance, who afterwards proved to be Robert Burns, came to inquire about the printing of a volume of poems. Unluckily the master took his visitor for some poor crack-brained versifier, who might give him a good deal of trouble, but was not likely to yield much solid return in the way of business. He therefore received the application with marked coldness; spoke of being a good deal engaged at present, and of his habit of requiring effective guarantees of payment from any strangers for whom he worked. The visitor, manifestly offended, went away, but not till he had taken occasion to pull out and show a quantity of money sufficient to convince the printer that, if more favourably received, he might have proved a good customer. This was not an end of the typographer's mortifications; for, being vexed at missing so good a job as the printing of Burns's poems, he resolved to lose no second customer of that sort who might come in his way, and accordingly took the risk, soon after, of printing the productions of a poet from Aberdeenshire, which proved a complete failure, so that he lost fully as much by the one concern as he might have gained by the other.'

TO MR WILLIAM CHALMERS, WRITER, AYR.

EDINBURGH, *Dec.* 27, 1786.

MY DEAR FRIEND—I confess I have sinned the sin for which there is hardly any forgiveness—ingratitude to friendship—in not writing you sooner; but of all men living, I had intended to send you an entertaining letter; and by all the plodding, stupid powers, that in nodding, conceited majesty, preside over the dull routine of business—A heavily-solemn oath this!—I am, and have been, ever since I came to Edinburgh, as unfit to write a letter of humor, as to write a commentary on the Revelation of St. John the Divine, who was banished to the Isle of Patmos, by the cruel and bloody Domitian, son to Vespasian and brother to Titus, both emperors of Rome, and who was himself an emperor, and raised the second or third persecution, I forget which, against the Christians, and after throwing the said Apostle John, brother to the Apostle James, commonly called James the Greater, to distinguish him from another James, who was, on some account or other, known by the name of James the Less, after throwing him into the caldron of

boiling oil, from which he was miraculously preserved, he banished the
poor son of Zebedee to a desert island in the Archipelago, where he was
gifted with the second sight, and saw as many wild beasts as I have seen
since I came to Edinburgh; which, a circumstance not very uncommon
in story-telling, brings me back to where I set out.

To make you some amends for what, before you reach this paragraph,
you will have suffered, I enclose you two poems* I have carded and spun
since I passed Glenbuck.†

One blank in the 'Address to Edinburgh'—'Fair B——,' is heavenly
Miss Burnet, daughter of Lord Monboddo,‡ at whose house I have had
the honor to be more than once. There has not been any thing nearly
like her, in all the combinations of beauty, grace, and goodness, the Great
Creator has formed, since Milton's Eve on the first day of her existence.

I have sent you a parcel of subscription-bills, and have written to
Mr Ballantine and Mr Aiken to call on you for some of them, if they
want them. My direction is—care of Andrew Bruce,§ merchant, Bridge-
Street.

TO LORD MONBODDO, ST. JOHN STREET.

I shall do myself the honor, Sir, to dine with you tomorrow, as you
obligingly request.

My conscience twitting me with having neglected to send Miss Eliza a
song which she once mentioned to me as a song she wished to have—I
inclose it for her; with one or two more, by way of a peace-offering.—
I have the honor to be, my Lord, your very humble servt.,

                                          ROBT. BURNS.

Saturday eve. [30th Dec.]

Here may be recorded an incident which, although it seems
trifling in itself, is of interest both as showing how Burns, in spite
of his new and brighter surroundings, did not forget his Ayrshire
friends—even those who were not influential enough to have
assisted in shaping his career—and as indicating how he kept himself in touch with the formative literature of the period in which

---

* The 'Address to Edinburgh' and, in all probability, the verses 'To a Haggis.'

† 'Glenbuck,' alluded to in 'The Brigs o' Ayr,' is the name of the last spot of Ayrshire
over which Burns passed before he entered Lanarkshire on his way to Edinburgh.

‡ James Burnett (spelled 'Burnet' by Burns), born in 1714 at Monboddo, Kincardine-
shire, the residence of his father; educated at Marischal College, Aberdeen, and Edinburgh
University; called to the Scottish bar in 1737; married in 1760 a Miss Farquharson, by
whom he had one son and two daughters, the second of whom, celebrated by Burns, died
in 1790, at the age of twenty-five; raised to the bench as Lord Monboddo in 1767; published (1773-1792) *The Origin and Progress of Language*, and (1779-1799) *Antient Metaphysics*,
in the former of which he to some extent anticipated the conclusions of Darwin and
modern anthropologists; died in Edinburgh in 1799.

§ There is reason to believe that Burns was introduced to Andrew Bruce by a Kilmarnock acquaintance.

he lived. On the 20th December he sent as a present to his old friend, Tennant of Glenconner, whose advice he subsequently took in the choice of a farm in Dumfriesshire, a little volume* of less than three hundred pages, dealing with those theological questions which had interested him ever since he listened to the Moderate preaching of Dr Dalrymple and Dr M'Gill. The title reads: 'Letters concerning the Religion essential to Man ; as it is Distinct from what is merely an Accession to it. In two parts. Translated from the French. Glasgow : Printed for Robert Urie. 1761.' The next page bears the inscription : 'A paltry Present from Robt. Burns the Scotch Bard to his own friend and his Father's friend John Tennant in Glenconner.—20th Dec. 1786.'

The importance and popularity of this anonymous book may be judged by the fact that it is thus referred to by Mr John Morley in his Monograph on Rousseau : 'The leader of the movement in Geneva—that is, of an attempt to pacify the Christian churches on the basis of some such Deism as was shortly to find its passionate expression in the Savoyard vicar's Confession of Faith, was John Alphonse Turretini (1661–1737). . . . His eloquent exposition of rationalistic ideas aroused the usual cry of heresy from the people who justly insist that Deism is not Christianity. There was much stir for many years, but he succeeded in holding his own and in finding many considerable followers. For example, some three years or so after his death a work appeared in Geneva, under the title of *La Religion Essentielle à l' Homme*, showing that faith in the existence of a God suffices, and treating with contempt the belief in the inspiration of the Gospels.' The book is, in fact, a lucid and popularly written manual of the mild Deism which was then prevalent in Europe. There is no evidence that Burns took any of his theological opinions—such, for example, as he subsequently confessed to Clarinda—from this volume. He would, however, to a certainty be attracted by the writer's insistence all through his book that true religion consists less in the holding of a special set of opinions, than in the sincerity with which they are held. Burns would certainly have subscribed to the closing passage of the book : 'In reality, what can the Author of my being require of me, unless it be to employ the free and intelligent capacity which

* The volume is now in the possession of John Tennant's great-grandson, Sir Charles Tennant of The Glen, Innerleithen.

I have received from Him by sincerely acquiescing in everything
that appears to me to be truth. This being supposed, it may
happen that I shall not always be able to discover in the Scripture
whatever another person thinks he discovers in it. But, however,
if that other person acts with sincerity in his enquiry, he fulfils
his task by acquiescing in what appears to him to be evident, and
I, too, fulfil mine by suspending my judgment as to what appears
to me to be doubtful. It is enough, in short, if he and I believe
everything we can believe to be true, and if we act accordingly.
This, I think, is a religion which no controversy can shake.' It is
certainly of considerable significance as a sign of the times, that
Burns should have thought a book containing such opinions as
these a suitable gift for an old Ayrshire farmer. It gives support
to the evangelical contention that moderatism was the thin end
of the wedge of Socinianism, if not synonymous with it.

It has already been mentioned (as probable) how Burns, while
still lingering in Ayrshire, had been gratified by a perusal of the
October number of the *Edinburgh Magazine*, containing a favourable notice of his *Poems*. The two succeeding numbers—
November and December—contained additional notices of, and
extracts from, the *Poems*. Burns thus expressed his gratitude to
Mr James Sibbald,* publisher of the *Magazine*:

TO MR JAMES SIBBALD, BOOKSELLER.

LAWNMARKET, [*Jan.* 1787].

SIR—So little am I acquainted with the modes and manners of the
more public and polished walks of life, that I often feel myself much
embarrassed how to express the feelings of my heart, particularly
gratitude.

> —— Rude am I in speech,
> And little blest in the set, polish'd phrase;
> For since these arms of mine had seven years' pith,
> Till now—some nine moons wasted—they have used
> Their dearest efforts in the rural field;
> And therefore, little can I grace my cause
> In speaking for myself.†

* James Sibbald, son of a farmer in Roxburghshire, was born in 1747. In early life he
was engaged in farm work, but, removing to Edinburgh, he obtained a situation in the
shop of Charles Elliot, bookseller. Finally he started in business on his own account, and
in 1783 commenced the publication of the *Edinburgh Magazine*, to which he contributed
many antiquarian articles. In 1792 he undertook the editorship of the *Edinburgh Herald.*
He died at Leith in 1803. His best-known work is the *Chronicle of the Poetry of Scotland*,
published the year before his death.

† Shakespeare's *Othello*, Act I., scene iii.

The warmth with which you have befriended an obscure man, and young Author in your three last Magazines—I can only say, Sir, I feel the weight of the obligation, and wish I could express my sense of it. In the meantime accept of this conscious acknowledgement from, Sir, Your obliged Servant, ROBERT BURNS.

TO GAVIN HAMILTON, ESQ.

. . . To tell the truth among friends, I feel a miserable blank in my heart, with want of her, and I don't think I shall ever meet with so delicious an armful again. She has her faults; and so have you and I; and so has everybody:

> Their tricks and craft hae put me daft;   mad
> They've ta'en me in and a' that;   taken
> But clear your decks, and here's 'The Sex!'
> I like the jads for a' that: jades
> For a' that and a' that,
> And twice as muckle 's a' that, &c.   much

I have met with a very pretty girl, a Lothian farmer's daughter, whom I have almost persuaded to accompany me to the west country, should I ever return to settle there. By the by, a Lothian farmer is about an Ayrshire Squire of the lower kind; and I had a most delicious ride from Leith to her house yesternight, in a hackney-coach, with her brother and two sisters, and brother's wife. We had dined all together at a common friend's house in Leith, and danced, drank, and sang till late enough. The night was dark, the claret had been good, and I thirsty. . . .
ROBT. BURNS.

EDINBURGH, 7th Jan. 1787.

This letter is interesting as showing that Burns still thought kindly of Jean, but did not contemplate marriage with her. The name of the 'Lothian farmer's daughter,' whom he had 'almost persuaded' to marry him, has not been discovered.

While spending his evenings with beauty, rank, and talent, Burns was content to share John Richmond's room and bed.*

* 'In the first stair on the left hand, on entering the close [Baxter's Close, Lawnmarket], and on the first floor of the house, is the poet's lodging. The tradition of his residence there has passed through very few hands—the predecessor of the present tenant having learned it from Mrs Carfrae [Richmond's landlady], and the poet's room is pointed out with its window looking into Lady Stair's Close. The land [tenement] is an ancient and very substantial building, with large and neatly-moulded windows, retaining the marks of having been finished with stone mullions. . . . From this ancient dwelling Burns issued to dine or sup with the magnates of the land. . . . The poet's lodging is a large and well-proportioned room, neatly panelled with wood, according to a fashion then by no means antiquated.'—WILSON's *Memorials of Edinburgh* (1848; vol. i., p. 166). The house in

Richmond subsequently averred that he used to help his friend to transcribe his poems for the press, and when he came in of a night, jaded, would read to him till he fell asleep. Richmond testified also that Burns kept good hours, and lived soberly. After a brief residence in town, his plain rustic dress was exchanged for a suit of blue and buff, the livery of Fox, with buckskins and top-boots. He continued to wear his hair tied behind, and spread upon his forehead, but without the powder which was then nearly universal. On the whole, his appearance was modest and becoming. It was remarked that he showed no sign of embarrassment in refined society, and that he took his part in conversation with freedom and energy, but without the least forwardness. Principal Robertson declared that he had 'scarcely ever met with any man whose conversation displayed greater vigour than that of Burns.' His poems had, the historian acknowledged, surprised him; his prose compositions appeared even more wonderful; but his conversation surpassed both.

TO MISS LOGAN,*

WITH BEATTIE'S POEMS FOR A NEW-YEAR'S GIFT, JAN. 1, 1787.

Again the silent wheels of time
   Their annual round have driv'n,
And you, tho' scarce in maiden prime,
   Are so much nearer Heav'n.

No gifts have I from Indian coasts
   The infant year to hail;
I send you more than India boasts,
   In Edwin's simple tale.

Our Sex with guile and faithless love,
   Is charg'd, perhaps too true;
But may, dear Maid, each Lover prove
   An Edwin still to you.

Baxter's Close in which Burns lodged no longer exists. The Edinburgh Pen and Pencil Club have placed a large bronze tablet on a new 'land' at the head of Lady Stair's Close, bearing the inscription—'In a house on the east side of this Close Robert Burns lived during his first visit to Edinburgh, 1786.'

  * The 'sentimental sister Susie' of Major Logan, to whom the poet had addressed an epistle on the 30th October of the preceding year.

Mrs Dunlop had written to Dr John Moore,* author of the once popular novel of *Zeluco*, and father of the British commander who fell at Corunna, regarding Burns, and that cultured and kind-hearted man had taken an opportunity of pointing out to the Earl of Eglinton what a genius was now claiming the friendly patronage of all good Scotsmen. The earl immediately sent to Burns, to bespeak the new edition of his poems, and present him with a sum of money by way of subscription.

TO THE EARL OF EGLINTON.†

EDINBURGH, *January* 11, 1787.

MY LORD—As I have but slender pretensions to philosophy, I cannot rise to the exalted ideas of a citizen of the world at large; but have all those national prejudices, which I believe glow peculiarly strong in the breast of a Scotsman. There is scarcely any thing to which I am so feelingly alive as the honor and welfare of old Scotia; and, as a poet, I have no higher enjoyment than singing her sons and daughters. Fate had cast my station in the veriest shades of life; but never did a heart pant more ardently, than mine, to be distinguished; though, till very lately, I looked on every side for a ray of light in vain. It is easy then to guess how supremely I was gratified to be honoured with the countenance and approbation of one of my dear lov'd country's most illustrious sons, when Mr Wauchope‡ called on me yesterday on the part of your lordship. Your munificence, my Lord, certainly deserves my very grateful acknowledgments; but your patronage is a bounty peculiarly suited to my feelings. I am not master enough of the etiquette of life to know, whether there be not some impropriety in troubling your Lordship with my thanks in this manner, but my heart whispered me to do it. From the emotions of my inmost soul I do it. Selfish ingratitude I hope I am incapable of; and mercenary servility I trust, I shall ever have so much honest pride as to detest. I have the honour to be

R. B.

---

* Dr Moore was the son of an Episcopalian clergyman in Stirling, and was born there in 1730. He was trained for the medical profession, and practised as a doctor in Glasgow for some years. In 1778 he removed to London, and gave himself up almost exclusively to literary work. *Zeluco*, the first of his novels, was not published till 1789; but before that he had written *A View of Society and Manners in France* (1779), to which Burns alludes in a letter to Mrs Dunlop, and other works, including *Medical Sketches* (1786). Dr Moore died in 1802.

† Archibald, eleventh Earl of Eglinton, born in 1726, succeeded to the earldom in 1769, and died in 1796.

‡ Mr John Wauchope, W.S.

TO MR MACKENZIE, SURGEON, MAUCHLINE.

MY DEAR SIR—Yours gave me something like the pleasure of an old friend's face. I saw *your* friend and *my* honoured patron, Sir John Whitefoord, just after I read your letter, and gave him your respectful compts. He was pleased to say many handsome things of you, which I heard with the more satisfaction, as I knew them to be just.

His son John, who calls very frequently on me, is in a fuss to-day like a coronation. This is the great day—the Assembly and Ball of the Caledonian Hunt; and John has had the good luck to pre-engage the hand of the beauty-famed, and wealth-celebrated MISS M'ADAM,* our country-woman. Between friends, John is desperately in for it there, and I am afraid will be desperate indeed.

I am sorry to send you the last speech and dying words of *The Lounger.*†

A gentleman waited on me yesterday, and gave me, by Lord Eglinton's order, ten guineas by way of subscription for a brace of copies of my 2nd edition.

I met with Lord Maitland ‡ and a brother of his to-day at breakfast. They are exceedingly easy, accessible, agreeable fellows, and seemingly pretty clever.—I am ever, My Dr Sir, Yours,   ROBT. BURNS.

EDINR., *11th Jan.* 1787.

TO JOHN BALLANTINE, ESQ.

MY HONORED FRIEND—It gives me a secret comfort to observe in myself that I am not yet so far gone as Willie Gaw's Skate, 'past redemption '§; for I have still this favorable symptom of grace, that when my Conscience, as in the case of this letter, tells me that I am leaving something undone that I ought to do, it teases me eternally till I do it.

---

* One of the daughters of John M'Adam of Craigen-Gillan, to whom, as has already been seen, Burns addressed a rhyming epistle.

† Burns here alludes to the demise of *The Lounger*, in its 101st number, on January 6, 1787. Its career was short, having been started on February 5, 1785. Creech was its publisher, and many Scottish men of letters of the day contributed to it. Henry Mackenzie, however, was its mainstay. He wrote fifty-seven of its numbers.

‡ James Maitland, afterwards eighth Earl of Lauderdale. He was almost exactly the same age as Burns, having been born on 29th January 1759, and at the time he met the poet represented Malmesbury as a supporter of Fox. He succeeded to the earldom in 1789, but still retained his almost revolutionary opinions. On one occasion he appeared in the House of Lords in the dress of a Jacobin. He was made a Baron of the United Kingdom in 1806, was for a time Keeper of the Great Seal, and attempted a diplomatic mission to France in the interests of peace. He died at his seat, Thirlstane, in 1839.

§ This is one of a great number of old saws that Burns, when a lad, had picked up from his mother, of which that good old woman had a vast collection.—CROMEK.

I am still 'dark as was Chaos' in respect to Futurity. My generous friend, Mr Peter [Patrick] Miller,[*] brother to the Justice Clerk, has been talking with me about a lease of some farm or other in an estate called Dasswinton [sic] which he has lately bought near Dumfries. Some life-rented, embittering Recollections whisper me that I will be happier any-where than in my old neighbourhood, but Mr Miller is no Judge of land; and though I dare say he means to favour me, yet he may give me, in his opinion, an advantageous bargain that may ruin me. I am to take a tour by Dumfries as I return and have promised to meet Mr Miller on his lands some time in May.

I went to a Mason-lodge[†] yesternight where the Most Worshipful Grand Master Charters [Charteris],[‡] and all the Grand lodge of Scotland visited. The meeting was most numerous and elegant; all the different Lodges about town were present in all their pomp. The Grand Master who presided with great solemnity, and honor to him-self as a Gentleman and Mason, among other general toasts gave, 'Caledonia and Caledonia's Bard, brother B——' which rung through the whole Assemby with multiplied honors and repeated acclamations. As I had no idea such a thing would happen, I was downright thunder struck, and trembling in every nerve made the best return in my power. Just as I finished, some of the Grand Officers said so loud as I could hear, with a most comforting accent, 'Very well indeed,' which set me something to rights again. I have just now had a visit from my Landlady, who is a staid, sober, piously-disposed, sculdudery-abhoring widow, coming on her grand climacterick. She is at present in sore tribulation respecting some 'Daughters of Belial' who are on the floor immediately above. My Landlady who, as I said, is a flesh-disciplining, godly Matron, firmly believes her husband is in Heaven; and having been very happy with him on earth, she vigorously and perseveringly practises some of the most distinguishing Christian virtues, such as, attending Church, railing against vice, &c., that she may be qualified to meet her dear quondam Bedfellow in that happy place where the unclean and the ungodly shall

---

* Patrick Miller, third son of William Miller of Glenlee, and brother of Sir Thomas Miller, president of the Court of Session, was born in 1731. After a somewhat adventurous career, in the course of which he had served as a common sailor, he made sufficient money as a banker in Edinburgh—in 1767 he was made a director of the Bank of Scotland —to buy, in 1785, the estate of Dalswinton, on the Nith, near Dumfries. Patrick Miller's relations with Burns will be dealt with at length later.

† This was St Andrew's Lodge, and the meeting took place on Friday, 12th January. It happened to be one of a series of Grand Visitations that were being made at that time. The Grand Master was accompanied by Alexander Fergusson, of Craigdarroch, Provincial Grand Master of the Southern District.

‡ Francis Charteris, younger of Amisfield (1749–1808), was thirty-sixth Grand Master-Mason of Scotland, 1786–87. He belonged to the Lodge Haddington St John, and was also an affiliated member of Canongate Kilwinning. On the succession of his father to the Earldom of Wemyss (1787) he became Lord Elcho. But he did not live to become Earl Wemyss: he predeceased his father by ten months. His name appears (for four copies) in the list of subscribers to the Edinburgh edition of the Poems.

never enter. This, no doubt, requires some strong exertions of Self-
denial in a hale, well-kept Widow of forty-five; and as our floors are low
and ill-plaistered, we can easily distinguish our laughter-loving, night-
rejoicing neighbors—when they are eating, when they are drinking, when
they are singing, &c., my worthy Landlady tosses sleepless and unquiet,
'looking for rest but finding none,' the whole night. Just now she told
me, though by the by she is sometimes dubious that I am, in her own
phrase, 'but a rough an' roun' Christian,' that 'We should not be uneasy
and envious because the Wicked enjoy the good things of this life; for
these base jades who, in her own words, lie up gandy-going with their
filthy fellows, drinking the best of wines, and singing abominable songs,
they shall one day lie in hell, weeping and wailing and gnashing their
teeth over a cup of God's wrath!'

I have to-day corrected my 152d page. My best good wishes to Mr
Aitken [sic]. I am ever, Dr Sir, Your much indebted humble servt.

ROBT. BURNS.

EDR., 14th Jan., 1787.*

In reference to Mrs Dunlop's late intercession with Dr John
Moore, Burns now addressed her as follows:

TO MRS DUNLOP, OF DUNLOP.

EDINBURGH, 15th January 1787.

MADAM—Yours of the 9th current, which I am this moment honor'd
with, is a deep reproach to me for ungrateful neglect. I will tell you
the real truth, for I am miserably awkward at a fib. I wished to have
written to Dr Moore, before I wrote to you; but though every day since
I received yours of Dec. 30th the idea, the wish, to write to him
has constantly pressed on my thoughts, yet I could not for my soul set
about it. I know his fame and character, and I am one of 'the sons of
little men.' To write him a mere matter-of-fact affair, like a merchant's
order, would be disgracing the little character I have; and to write the
author of 'The View of Society and Manners' a letter of sentiment—I
declare every artery runs cold at the thought. I shall try, however, to
write to him to-morrow or next day. His kind interposition in my
behalf I have already experienced, as a gentleman waited on me the
other day, on the part of Lord Eglinton, with ten guineas by way of
subscription for two copies of my next edition.

The word you object to in the mention I have made of my glorious
countryman and your immortal ancestor, is indeed borrowed from Thomson; but it does not strike me as an improper epithet.† I distrusted my
own judgment on your finding fault with it, and applied for the opinion

---

* Internal evidence shows that this letter was begun on Saturday, 13th January, and
finished on the 14th—Sunday.

† 'Great, unhappy Wallace' heart' in 'The Cotter's Saturday Night.' In spite of his
defence of the 'improper epithet,' he altered it, in 1793, to 'Wallace's undaunted heart.'

of some of the literati here, who honor me with their critical strictures, and they all allow it to be proper. The song you ask I cannot recollect, and I have not a copy of it. I have not composed any thing on the great Wallace, except what you have seen in print; and the inclosed, which I will print in this edition.* You will see I have mentioned some others of the name. When I composed my 'Vision' long ago, I had attempted a description of Kyle, of which the additional stanzas are a part, as it originally stood. My heart glows with a wish to be able to do justice to the merits of the 'Saviour of his Country,' which sooner or later I shall at least attempt.

You are afraid I shall grow intoxicated with my prosperity as a poet: alas! Madam, I know myself and the world too well. I do not mean any airs of affected modesty; I am willing to believe that my abilities deserve some notice; but in a most enlightened, informed age and nation, when poetry is and has been the study of men of the first natural genius, aided with all the powers of polite learning, polite books, and polite company—to be dragged forth to the full glare of learned and polite observation, with all my imperfections of awkward rusticity, and crude unpolished ideas on my head—I assure you, Madam, I do not dissemble when I tell you I tremble for the consequences. The novelty of a poet in my obscure situation, without any of those advantages which are reckoned necessary for that character, at least at this time of day, has raised a partial tide of public notice which has borne me to a height, where I am absolutely, feelingly certain, my abilities are inadequate to support me; and too surely do I see that time when the same tide will leave me, and recede perhaps as far below the mark of truth. I do not say this in the ridiculous affectation of self-abasement and modesty. I have studied myself, and know what ground I occupy; and, however a friend or the world may differ from me in that particular, I stand for my own opinion, in silent resolve, with all the tenaciousness of property. I mention this to you, once for all, to disburthen my mind, and I do not wish to hear or say more about it. But,

When proud fortune's ebbing tide recedes,

you will bear me witness, that when my bubble of fame was at the highest, I stood unintoxicated with the inebriating cup in my hand, looking forward with rueful resolve to the hastening time, when the blow of Calumny should dash it to the ground, with all the eagerness of vengeful triumph. . . .

Your patronizing me and interesting yourself in my fame and character as a poet, I rejoice in; it exalts me in my own idea; and whether you can or cannot aid me in my subscription is a trifle. Has a paltry subscription-bill any charms to the heart of a bard, compared with the patronage of the descendant of the immortal Wallace?   R. B.

---

* Stanzas in 'The Vision,' beginning, 'By stately tower or palace fair,' and ending with the first duan.

TO DR JOHN MOORE, LONDON.

EDINBURGH, 17th *January* 1787.

SIR—Mrs Dunlop has been so kind as to send me extracts of letters she has had from you, where you do the rustic bard the honor of noticing him and his works. Those who have felt the anxieties and solicitudes of authorship can only know what pleasure it gives to be noticed in such a manner, by judges of the first character. Your criticisms, sir, I receive with reverence; only I am sorry they mostly came too late: a peccant passage or two that I would certainly have altered were gone to the press.

The hope to be admired for ages is, in by far the greatest part of those even who are authors of repute, an unsubstantial dream. For my part, my first ambition was, and still my strongest wish is, to please my compeers, the rustic inmates of the hamlet, while ever-changing language and manners shall allow me to be relished and understood. I am very willing to admit that I have some poetical abilities; and as few, if any, writers, either moral or poetical, are intimately acquainted with the classes of mankind among whom I have chiefly mingled, I may have seen men and manners in a different phasis from what is common, which may assist originality of thought. Still I know very well the novelty of my character has by far the greatest share in the learned and polite notice I have lately had; and in a language where Pope and Churchill have raised the laugh, and Shenstone and Gray drawn the tear; where Thomson and Beattie have painted the landscape, and Lyttleton and Collins described the heart, I am not vain enough to hope for distinguished poetic fame.   R. B.

To this letter Dr Moore sent the following answer:

CLIFFORD-STREET, *January* 23d, 1787.

SIR—I have just received your letter, by which I find I have reason to complain of my friend Mrs Dunlop, for transmitting to you extracts from my letters to her, by much too freely and too carelessly written for your perusal. I must forgive her, however, in consideration of her good intention, as you will forgive me, I hope, for the freedom I use with certain expressions, in consideration of my admiration of the poems in general. If I may judge of the author's disposition from his works, with all the other good qualities of a poet, he has not the *irritable* temper ascribed to that race of men by one of their own number, whom you have the happiness to resemble in ease and *curious felicity* of expression. Indeed the poetical beauties, however original and brilliant, and lavishly scattered, are not all I admire in your works: the love of your native country, that feeling sensibility to all the objects of humanity, and the independent spirit which breathes through the whole, give me a most favourable impression of the poet, and have made me often regret that I did not see the poems, the certain effect of which would have been my seeing the author, last summer, when I was longer in Scotland than I have been for many years.

I rejoice very sincerely at the encouragement you receive at Edinburgh, and I think you peculiarly fortunate in the patronage of Dr Blair, who I am informed interests himself very much for you. I beg to be remembered to him; nobody can have a warmer regard for that gentleman than I have, which, independent of the worth of his character, would be kept alive by the memory of our common friend, the late Mr George B[annatin]e.*

Before I received your letter, I sent, inclosed in a letter to Mrs Dunlop, a sonnet by Miss Williams, a young poetical lady,† which she wrote on reading your 'Mountain Daisy;' perhaps it may not displease you:

> While soon 'the garden's flaunting flowers' decay,
>   And scatter'd on the earth neglected lie,
> The 'Mountain Daisy,' cherish'd by the ray
>   A poet drew from heav'n, shall never die.

> Ah, like that lonely flower the poet rose!
>   'Mid penury's bare soil and bitter gale;
> He felt each storm that on the mountain blows,
>   Nor ever knew the shelter of the vale.

> By genius in her native vigor nurst,
>   On nature with impassion'd look he gazed;
> Then through the cloud of adverse fortune burst
>   Indignant, and in light unborrow'd blazed.

> SCOTIA! from rude affliction shield thy bard,
>   His heav'n-taught numbers fame herself will guard.

I have been trying to add to the number of your subscribers, but find many of my acquaintance are already among them. I have only to add, that, with every sentiment of esteem, and the most cordial good wishes, I am, Your obedient humble servant,   J. MOORE.

The now generally-accepted belief that Dr Blacklock's letter of

---

* George Bannatine, minister of Craigie Parish, Ayrshire, 1744–64, and afterwards of the West Parish (now St George's), Glasgow, 1764 till his death in 1769.

† Miss Helen Maria Williams, a well-known contributor to both the poetical and the political literature of the period, was born in London in 1762, and spent the earlier years of her life in Berwick. She settled in Paris about 1790, was imprisoned as a partisan of the Gironde, released on the fall of Robespierre, and died at Paris, December 1827. Although at first 'a violent female devotee of the French Revolution,' in her latter political writings, Miss Williams appeared as a friend of the Bourbons, and an enemy of the Revolution.' She published *Julia*, a novel, in 1790; translated *Paul and Virginia;* wrote several books on France, and for several years the portion of the *Annual Register* relating to that country. Her verse—smooth, flowing, and essentially conventional—includes *Edwin and Elfrida* (1782), a legendary tale, and *The Slave Trade* (1788).

the preceding September to Mr Lawrie was not even the prime
cause of Burns's visit to Edinburgh, is supported by the fact that
Burns allowed several weeks to elapse before he called on the blind
poet.   About the 11th or 12th of December, Blacklock wrote to Mr
Lawrie, to recommend that Mackenzie's criticism should be prefixed
to the new edition of the *Poems*, instead of his letter, which had all
the disadvantages of an extempore effusion.   He added : ' By the
by, I hear that Mr Burns is, and has been, some time in Edinburgh.
These news I am sorry to have heard at second-hand ; they would
have come much more welcome from the bard's own mouth.   I
have, however, written to Mr Mackenzie, the Man of Feeling,* to
beg the favour that he would bring us together.'   On Friday, the
22d December, Mr Lawrie informed Burns that he had had a letter
from Dr Blacklock, expressing a desire to see him.   ' I write this
to you,' says Lawrie, ' that you may lose no time in waiting upon
him, should you not yet have seen him.'†   Burns appears to have
now hastened to visit Blacklock ; yet he allowed several weeks to
elapse before answering Mr Lawrie's letter—a circumstance that
fits the view we take of the immediate causes of the poet's journey
from Ayrshire :

TO THE REVD. MR GEORGE LAWRIE,
NEWMILLS, BY KILMARNOCK.‡

REVD AND DR SIR—When I look at the date of your kind letter,
my heart reproaches me severely with ingratitude in neglecting so long
to answer it.   I will not trouble you with any account, by way of
apology, of my hurried life and distracted attention : do me the justice
to believe that my delay by no means proceeded from want of respect.
I feel, and ever shall feel, for you the mingled sentiments of esteem for a
friend and reverence for a father.

I thank you, Sir, with all my soul for your friendly hints ; though I do
not need them so much as my friends are apt to imagine.   You are
dazzled with news-paper accounts and distant reports, but in reality I

---

* *The Man of Feeling* was published anonymously in 1771, when Henry Mackenzie was
twenty-six years of age.   It was followed by *The Man of the World* in 1773, and *Julia de
Roubigné* in 1777.   Mackenzie, who was a solicitor by business and man of letters by inclination, was appointed Comptroller of Taxes for Scotland in 1804.   He died, 14th January
1831, at the age of eighty-six.

† Currie's edition (1800).   General Correspondence, Letter xii.

‡ Through the kindness of Mr J. Parker Smith, M.P., we have had the opportunity of
collating the original MS., now in his possession.   It may be noted that Burns spells
' Lowrie ' throughout.

have no great temptation to be intoxicated with the cup of prosperity. Novelty may attract the attention of mankind a while ; to it I owe my present *éclat ;* but I see the time not distant far when the popular tide which has borne me to a height of which I am perhaps unworthy, shall recede with silent celerity, and leave me a barren waste of sand, to descend at my leisure to my former station. I do not say this in the affectation of modesty ; I see the consequence is unavoidable and am prepared for it.——I had been at a good deal of pains to form a just, impartial estimate of my intellectual powers before I came here ; I have not added, since I came to Edinburgh, any thing to the account, and I trust I shall take every atom of it back to my shades, the coverts of my unnoticed, early years.

In Dr Blacklock, whom I see very often, I have found what I would have expected in our friend, a clear head and an excellent heart.

By far the most agreeable hours I spend in Edinburgh must be placed to the account of Miss Lawrie and her Pianoforte. I cannot help repeating to you and Mrs Lawrie a compliment that Mr M'Kenzie, the celebrated 'Man of Feeling,' paid to Miss Christie the other night at the Concert. I had come in at an interlude and sat down by him, till I saw Miss Lawrie in a seat not very distant, and went up to pay my respects to her. On my return to Mr M'Kenzie, he asked me who she was ; I told him 'twas the daughter of a reverend friend of mine in the West country. He returned there was something very striking to his idea in her appearance. On my desiring to know what it was, he was pleased to say, ' She has a great deal of the elegance of a well-bred Lady about her, with all the sweet simplicity of a Country girl.'

My Complmts. to all the happy Inmates of Saint Margaret's, I am, Dr. Sir, Yours most gratefully, ROBT. BURNS.

EDINR., *5th Feb.* 1787.

TO JAMES DALRYMPLE, ESQ., OF ORANGEFIELD, ON RECEIVING A RHYMING EPISTLE FROM HIM.

DR. SIR—I suppose the devil is so elated at his success with you that he is determined by a *coup de main* to effect his purposes on you all at once in making you a Poet. I broke open the letter ; hummed over the rhymes ; and as I saw they were extempore, said to myself they were very well : but when I saw at the bottom, a name that I shall ever value with grateful respect, 'I gapit wide but naething spak.' I was nearly as much struck as the three friends of Job, of affliction-bearing memory, when ' they sat down with him seven days and seven nights and spake not a word ;' or, to go farther back, as the brave but unfortunate Jacobite Clans who, as John Milton tells us, after their unhappy Culloden in Heaven, lay ' nine times the space that measures day and night in oblivious astonishment, prone-weltering on the fiery Surge.' I am naturally of a superstitious cast, and so soon as my wonder-scared imagination regained its consciousness and resumed its functions, I cast about in my pericranium what this might portend. My foreboding ideas had the wide stretch of Possibility; and several events, great in their magnitude and important in their consequences, recurred to my fancy. The downfall of the Conclave, or the crushing of the Cork-rumps;[*] a ducal coronet to Lord George[†] and the Protestant interest, or Saint Peter's keys to the h-ll-mouthing John Russell;[‡] Family-prayers in the house of Orangefield, or another brace of bantlings to a certain Bard already overcharged with a numerous issue.

You want to know how I come on. I am just *in statu quo*, or, not to insult a gentleman with my Latin, in auld use and wont. The noble Earl of Glencairn took me by the hand to-day, and interested himself in my concerns, with a goodness like that benevolent Being whose image he so richly bears. 'Oubliez moi, grand Dieu, si jamais je l'oublie!' He is a stronger proof of the immortality of the Soul than any that Philosophy has ever produced. A Mind like his can never die. Let the Wpfull. Squire Hugh Logan, or Mass James M'Kindlay,[§] go into their primitive nothing. At best they are but ill-digested lumps of Chaos, only one of them strongly tinged with bituminous particles and sulphureous effluvia. But my noble Patron, eternal as the heroic swell of Magnanimity and the generous throb of Benevolence, shall look on with princely eye.

> Unhurt amid the war of elements,
> The wrecks of Matter, and the crash of Worlds.

For the blind, mischief-making, little urchin of a Deity you mention, he and I have been sadly at odds ever since some dogtricks he play'd me not half a century ago.

I have compromised matters with his godship of late by uncoupling my heart and fancy, for a slight chace, after a certain Edinr. Belle. My devotions proceed no further than a forenoon's walk, a sentimental conversation, now and then a squeeze of the hand or interchanging an

---

[*] *A Panegyric on Cork Rumps*, an anonymous doggerel poem published at Bath in 1777, describes an outing on the Severn, interrupted by rain, wind, and the capsizing of the boat, which might have had serious issues for the ladies but for the dress-improvers then in use. Luckily—

> ' The enormous cork rumps saved our females from sinking,
> But their cork-pated beaus were reduced once to thinking.'

[†] Burns had in mind, no doubt, the 'No Popery' riots of 1780, of which Lord George Gordon (b. 1751, d. 1793) was the leader. But in 1786 public interest in Lord George had been to some extent revived by his refusal to come forward as a witness in a court of law, and his consequent excommunication for contempt by the Archbishop of Canterbury. The following year he was convicted for issuing a pamphlet reflecting on the laws and criminal justice of the country, and for publishing a libel on Marie Antoinette and the French ambassador in London. To evade imprisonment, he went to Holland, but was sent back to England. There he was apprehended and committed to Newgate, in which he died.

[‡] See Vol. I., p. 171 *et seq.*

[§] See 'The Ordination,' Vol. I., pp. 298-303.

œillade, and when peculiar good humor and sequestered propriety allow
—'Brethren, salute one another with a holy kiss.'—PAUL.

> Kissin is the key o' love,
> An' clappin is the lock,
> An' makin o' 's the best thing
> That ere a young thing got.
> —*An auld Sang o' my Mither's.*

—I have the honour to be, &c.   [ROBERT BURNS.]
  EDINR., *Feb.* [1787.] *

Among the incidents of Burns's 'hurried life' at this time was
his admission into one of the most popular of the masonic lodges
of Edinburgh, on a visit to which, in December, he had met
Henry Erskine (see page 14). The following 'Minute of the
Canongate Kilwinning Lodge (No. 2) of Freemasons, Edinburgh,'
speaks for itself :

1st February 1787.—There being no meeting in January, the lodge met
this evening. The following gentlemen were entered apprentices : Mr
Burns, Mr Spied, Captain Bartlet, Mr Haig, G. Douglas, Esq., E. B.
Clive, Esq., Mr Maule, Mr Wotherspoon, Mr Moir, Mr Lindsay Carnegie,
Mr Archibald Millar, and Mr James Buchan. There were also initiated :
Colonel Dalrymple of Inveresk, Captain Hammond of Marchfield, Cra-
mond, and J. Hammond, Esq.

The R. W. Master having observed that Brother Burns was at present
in the Lodge, who is well known as a great poetic writer, and for a late
publication of his works, which have been universally commended, submitted that he should be assumed a member of this Lodge, which was
unanimously agreed to, and he was assumed accordingly. Having spent
the evening in a very social manner, as the meetings of the Lodge always
have been, it was adjourned till next monthly meeting.

                                   ALEX. FERGUSON, *M.*
JO. MILLAR, *J. W.*   CHAS. MORE, *D.M.*

It is a popular tradition in masonic circles that the poet was at
a subsequent meeting formally inaugurated as laureate of the lodge.
The truth of this tradition has recently been questioned by Mr
David Murray Lyon, the historian of Scottish Freemasonry, and
the whole of the evidence for, and the arguments against, its
validity are now accessible.†

---

   * This letter has hitherto been printed, no doubt on account of the allusion in it to Lord
Glencairn, as a production of Nov. 30 or Dec. 10, 1786. The unsigned copy of it in the Laing
collection in the Edinburgh University Library bears in Burns's handwriting 'Edinr.,
Feb.'

   † See Appendix, No. I.

About this time, in all probability, Burns had brought under his notice a criticism, which was not an unmixed eulogium of his *Poems*, in a London monthly magazine. The February number of *The English Review* (J. Murray, 32 Fleet Street) contained an elaborate criticism of the poems included in the Kilmarnock volume, the character of which may be judged from the fact that the writer praises 'The Cotter's Saturday Night,' and depreciates 'Halloween.' He warns Burns that he 'seems to possess too great a facility of composition, and is too easily satisfied with his own production!' On the other hand, it is allowed that 'he is better acquainted with the English poets than most authors that have come under our review. He possesses the genuine characteristics of a poet—a vigorous mind, a lively fancy, a surprising knowledge of human nature, and an expression fresh, various, and abundant.' By way of general judgment upon Burns, the critic writes: 'Although he is by no means such a poetical prodigy as some of his *malicious* friends have represented, he has a genuine title to the attention and approbation of the public as a *natural*, though a *legitimate* son of the Muses.'

David Stuart Erskine, eleventh Earl of Buchan,* was a very different person from either of his two brothers, Henry, whose introduction to Burns has already been mentioned, and Thomas, who became Lord Chancellor of England. Of but mediocre abilities, he was vain, eccentric, and parsimonious, yet ambitious to be regarded as a patron of literature. He sent Burns† some of those counsels which he thought his rank entitled him to offer to one in the situation of 'the Ayrshire Ploughman.'

EDINBURGH, *February* 1, 1787.

MR BURNS—I have redd with great pleasure several of your poems, and have subscribed in Lady Glencairn's list for six copies of your book for myself, and two for Lady Buchan.

These little doric pieces of yours in our provincial dialect are very beautiful, but you will soon be able to diversify your language, your Rhyme and your subject, and then you will have it in your power to show the extent of your genius and to attempt works of greater magnitude, variety and importance. Take care, however, that you do not suffer the wings of your Pegasus to be sullied or curtailed by the grosser or more polished invaders of your genuine Invention, but let him fly with the rein,

---

* Born in 1742, succeeded to the title in 1767, and died in 1829.

† This letter is now in the Burns Monument at Edinburgh.

but not the curb. Keep your Eye upon Parnassus and drink deep of the fountains of Helicon, but beware of the Joys that is dedicated to the Jolly God of wine.

Go and visit my Parnassus on the banks of the Tweed, and visit the birth place of Thomson on the Water of Rule; feed your Muse with Ethereal mildness when the spring first opens the primrose on the steep verdant margin of *his* parent stream; fire her in Summer with the view of Flodden Field from the summit of Mount Eildon; ripen her in Autumn with the placid chearfull scenes of harvest and the snowey fleece yielding to the happy hands of the contented shepherd; and in Winter sit on the ruins of Dryburgh, and with the history of your country full in your memory and in your heart, call upon her genius to inspire you with the Majesty of Song; and may the Apollo of my Nypa who sits on the fork of Eildon enable you to produce the genuine offspring of Genius, sentiment, and skill—never to die.

I am, Mr Burns, with great justice to your merits, your wellwisher
BUCHAN.

Burns replied thus:

TO THE EARL OF BUCHAN.

MY LORD—The honor your Lordship has done me by your notice and advice in yours of the 1st Inst., I shall ever gratefully remember.—

> Praise from thy lips 'tis mine with joy to boast,
> They best can give it who deserve it most.

Your Lordship touches the darling chord of my heart when you advise me to fire my Muse at Scottish story and Scottish scenes. I wish for nothing more than to make a leisurely pilgrimage through my native country; to sit and muse on those once hard-contended fields where Caledonia, rejoicing, saw her bloody lion borne through broken ranks to victory and fame; and catching the inspiration, to pour the deathless Names in Song. But, my Lord, in the midst of these delighting enthusiastic Reveries, a long-visaged, dry, moral-looking Phantom strides across my imagination, and with the frigid air of a declaiming Preacher, sets off with a text of Scripture—'I, Wisdom, dwell with Prudence. Friend, I do not come to open the ill-closed wounds of your Follies and Misfortunes, merely to give you pain; I wish through these wounds to imprint a lasting impression on your heart! I will not mention how many of my salutary advices you have despised. I have given you line upon line, precept upon precept; and while I was chalking you out the straight way to Wealth and Character, with audacious effrontery, you have zigzagged across the path, contemning me to my face. You know the consequences. It is not yet three months since Home was so hot for you, that you were on the wing for the western shore of the Atlantic; not to make a fortune, but to hide your disgrace.

'Now that your dear-lov'd Scotia puts it in your power to return to the situation of your forefathers, will you follow these will-o'-wisp meteors of Fancy and Whim, till they bring you once more to the brink of ruin? I grant the utmost ground you can occupy is but half a step from the veriest Poverty, but still it is half a step from it. If all that I can urge is ineffectual, let Her who seldom calls to you in vain, let the call of Pride prevail with you. You know how you feel at the iron grip of ruthless Oppression: you know how you bear the galling sneer of contumelious Greatness. I hold you out the conveniences, the comforts of life, independence and character, in the one hand; I tender you servility, dependence and wretchedness, in the other: I will not insult your Common sense by bidding you make a choice.'

This, my Lord, is an unanswerable harangue. I must return to my rustic station, and in my wonted way woo my rustic Muse at the Ploughtail. Still, my Lord, while the drops of life, while the sound of Caledonia, warm my heart; gratitude to that dear-priz'd country in which I boast my birth, and gratitude to those her distinguished Names who have honored me so much with their Approbation and Patronage, shall, while stealing through my humble Shades, ever distend my bosom, and at times, as now, draw forth the swelling tear. I have the honor to be, with the highest respect, My Lord, your much indebted, humble ser[vant,]   ROBERT BURNS.

LAWNMARKET, *Feb.* 7, 1787.

During the first blaze of Burns's reputation in Edinburgh, numerous rhyming epistles were addressed to him, publicly and privately—generally of no value except as showing how enormously he excelled his contemporaries, even in the mere technique of verse-making. One, however, from Mrs Scot of Wauchope (in Roxburghshire), a niece to Mrs Cockburn, the author of 'I've seen the smiling of Fortune beguiling,'* was effective. To it Burns replied.

THE GUIDWIFE OF WAUKHOPE-HOUSE
TO ROBERT BURNS, THE AYRSHIRE BARD.

Feb. 1787.

My canty, witty, rhyming ploughman,	jolly
I hafflins doubt it is na true, man,	half
That ye between the stilts was bred,	at the plough
Wi' ploughmen schooled, wi' ploughmen fed.	

---

* Mrs Scot, daughter of Mr David Rutherford, 'counsellor' in Edinburgh, was born there in 1729. She was 'rather advanced' in life, says a biographer, when she married Walter Scot, a country gentleman in Roxburghshire. She died in 1789. Under the title of *Alonzo and Cora, with other Original Poems,* her literary remains were published in 1801. The volume contained her epistle to Burns, and also the Poet's reply.

I doubt it sair, ye 've drawn your knowledge   *much*
Either frae grammar-school or college.
Guid troth, your saul and body baith   *In truth—soul—both*
War better fed, I 'd gie my aith,   *Were—oath*
Than theirs who sup sour milk and parritch,   *porridge*
An' bummil through the single Caritch.   *blunder—Shorter Catechism*
Whaever heard the ploughman speak,
Could tell gif Homer was a Greek?   *if*
He 'd flee as soon upon a cudgel,
As get a single line of Virgil.
An' then sae slee ye crack your jokes   *so slyly*
O' Willie Pitt and Charlie Fox.
Our great men a' sae weel descrive,   *so well describe*
An' how to gar the nation thrive,   *make*
Ane maist wad swear ye dwalt amang them,   *One almost would—dwelt*
An' as ye saw them, sae ye sang them.   *so*
But be ye ploughman, be ye peer,
Ye are a funny blade, I swear;
An' tho' the cauld I ill do bide,   *cold—endure*
Yet twenty miles, an' mair, I 'd ride   *more*
O'er moss an' muir, an' never grumble,
Tho' my auld yad should gie a stumble,   *old horse—give*
To crack a winter-night wi' thee,   *talk*
An' hear thy sangs and sonnets slee.   *ingenious*
A guid saut herring an' a cake,   *good salt*
Wi' sic a cheel a feast wad make,   *fine fellow*
I 'd rather scour your rumming yill,   *drink—foaming ale*
Or eat o' cheese an' bread my fill,
Than wi' dull lairds on turtle dine,
An' farlie at their wit and wine.   *wonder*
O, gif I kenn'd but whare ye baide,   *if I knew—resided*
I 'd send to you a marled plaid;   *chequered*
'Twad haud your shoulders warm and braw,   *keep*
An' douce at kirk or market shaw;   *decent*
Far south, as weel as north, my lad,
A' honest Scotsmen loe the 'maud':   *All—love the plaid*
Right wae that we 're sae far frae ither;   *sorrowful—other*
Yet proud I am to ca' ye brither.   *brother*

               Your most obed., E. S.

TO MRS SCOT,

GUIDWIFE OF WAUKHOPE-HOUSE, ROXBURGHSHIRE.

GUIDWIFE,

    I mind it weel in early date,   *well*
    When I was beardless, young and blate,   *bashful*

An' first cou'd thresh the barn,
Or haud a yokin at the pleugh—   *do a day's ploughing*
An' tho' forfoughten sair eneugh,   *fatigued sore enough*
    Yet unko proud to learn :   *very*
When first amang the yellow corn
    A man I reckon'd was,
An' with the lave ilk merry morn   *rest—each*
    Could rank my rig and lass :*   *strip of land*
      Still shearing and clearing
        The tither stookèd raw,   *one row of stooks or shocks after another*
      With clavers and haivers   *gossip and nonsense*
        Wearing the time awa :   *away*

Ev'n then a wish (I mind its pow'r)—
A wish that to my latest hour
    Shall strongly heave my breast :
That I for poor auld Scotland's sake
Some useful plan or book could make,
    Or sing a sang at least.   *song*
The rough bur-thistle spreading wide   *spear-thistle*
    Amang the bearded bear,
I turn'd my weeding heuk aside,   *hook*
    An' spar'd the symbol dear :
      No nation, no station
        My envy e'er could raise :
      A Scot still, but blot still,   *without dishonour*
        I knew nae higher praise.   *no*

But still the elements o' sang
In formless jumble, right an' wrang,
    Wild floated in my brain ;
'Till, on that harste I said before,   *harvest*
My partner † in the merry core,   *company*
    She rous'd the forming strain :
I see her yet, the sonsy quean,   *buxom lass*
    That lighted up my jingle,   *rhyme*
Her pauky smile, her kittle e'en   *artful—fascinating eyes*
    That gar'd my heartstrings tingle :   *made*

* When he was allotted a 'rig' to 'shear' and a girl to 'gather' after him.
† 'Handsome Nell.'

So tichèd, bewitchèd,   'ticed = enticed
  I rav'd ay to mysel ;
But bashing and dashing,   abashed—cast down
  I kenn'd na how to tell.   knew not

Health to the sex ! ilk guid chiel says,   each good fellow
Wi' merry dance in winter-days,
  An' we to share in common ;
The gust o' joy, the balm of woe,   spice
The saul o' life, the heav'n below,   soul
  Is rapture-giving woman.
Ye surly sumphs who hate the name,   fools
  Be mindfu' o' your mither :   mother
She, honest woman, may think shame
  That ye 're connected with her :
    Ye 're wae men, ye 're nae men   woful (poor creatures)—no
    That slight the lovely dears :
  To shame ye, disclaim ye,
    Ilk honest birkie swears.   Each—fellow

For you, na bred to barn and byre,   not—cow-house
Wha sweetly tune the Scottish lyre,
  Thanks to you for your line :
The marled plaid ye kindly spare   chequered
By me should gratefully be ware—   worn
  'Twad please me to the Nine.
I 'd be mair vauntie o' my hap   more proud—wrap
  Douce hingin owre my curple,   Decently hanging over—haunches
Than ony ermine ever lap,   any—hung in folds
  Or proud imperial purple.
    Fareweel then, lang heal' then   long health
    An' plenty be your fa' ;   lot
  May losses and crosses
    Ne'er at your hallan ca'.   door call

          R. BURNS.

March 1787.

Meanwhile the preparation of the new edition was proceeding rapidly in the printing-office of William Smellie. Smellie himself, at this time a man of forty-six, aspired to a literary reputation. Somewhat rough in manner, he had a vast fund of knowledge, shrewdness, and talent.* In his office, at the foot of the Anchor Close, he had printed for Gilbert Stuart, Robert Fergusson, William Robertson, Hugo Arnot, Adam Smith, and many others of the literati of that age in Scotland, all of whom had been his personal friends. His son Alexander well remembered the visits of the poet to the composing-room. 'Burns would walk up and down the room three or four times, cracking a whip which he carried, to the no small surprise of the men. He paid no attention to any of his own *copy* that might be in hand, but looked at any other which he saw lying on the cases. One day he asked a man how many languages he was acquainted with. "Indeed, sir," replied the man, "I've enough ado wi' my *ain*." Burns remarked that behind there was one of his companions setting up a Gaelic Bible, and another composing from a Hebrew Grammar. "These two," said the compositor, "are the greatest dolts in the house." Burns seemed amused by the remark, and said he would make a note of it.'

Alexander Smellie also related the following anecdote : 'There was a particular stool in the office which Burns uniformly occupied while correcting his proof-sheets ; as he would not sit on any other, it always bore the name of Burns's Stool. In 1814 it was still in the office, and in the same situation where it was when Burns sat on it. At this time Sir John Dalrymple was printing in Mr Smellie's office an *Essay on the Properties of Coal Tar*. One day it happened that Sir John occupied the stool when Burns came into the correcting-room looking for his favourite seat. It was known that what Burns wanted was the stool ; but before saying anything to Sir John on the subject, Burns was requested to walk into the composing-room. The opportunity was taken in his absence to request of Sir John to indulge the bard with his favourite seat, but without mentioning his name. Sir John said : "I will not give up my seat to yon impudent

---

* William Smellie was born at Pleasance, Edinburgh, in 1740. He was apprenticed to a firm of Edinburgh printers in 1752, and nineteen years later set up in business. An omnivorous, if not very careful, reader, he took an interest in such widely different subjects as Hebrew, Botany, and Scottish Antiquities, edited and wrote articles for the first edition of the *Encyclopædia Britannica*, combated the views of Linnæus, and, in 1773, along with Dr Gilbert Stuart, started the *Edinburgh Magazine*.

staring fellow." Upon which it was replied: "Do you not know that that staring fellow, as you call him, is Burns the poet?" Sir John instantly left the stool, exclaiming: "Good gracious! Give him all the seats in your house!" Burns was then called in, took possession of his stool, and commenced the reading of his proofs.'

Burns was introduced by his printer to one of those convivial clubs which then abounded in Edinburgh—almost every one being founded upon some whim or conceit which gave a distinctive character to its proceedings. This particular club (founded by Smellie himself) assumed the name of the Crochallan Fencibles, from a composite cause. The landlord of the tavern—in the Anchor Close, a land off the High Street—in which the Club met, Daniel Douglas, was noted for singing a beautiful Gaelic song called 'Crochallan' (properly, *Cro Chalein*—that is, Colin's Cattle). The other half of the club's title was taken from those fencible regiments which were raised to protect the country while the regular army was chiefly engaged in fighting the American colonists. It was customary to subject a new entrant to a severe ordeal of raillery, by way of proving his temper; and Burns declared that, on his installation, he was 'thrashed' in a style beyond all his experience. Burns met at the club several of the men whose acquaintance he had previously made at the Canongate Kilwinning Lodge, among them William Dunbar, who at night appeared as *Colonel of the Crochallans*, but in daylight sobriety practised as a Writer to the Signet, from which position he ultimately attained the position of Inspector-general of Stamp-duties for Scotland.* Smellie has been thus described by Burns:

Shrewd Willie Smellie to Crochallan came;
The old cock'd hat, the brown surtout the same;
His grisly beard just bristling in its might,
('Twas four long nights and days from shaving-night;)

---

* William Dunbar was the third son of Alexander Dunbar, of Boath, Nairnshire. He was year after year appointed the representative elder of the Nairn Town Council to the General Assembly. It is said that 'a faggot vote was created for him in Nairnshire, but being a conscientious man he "would not swear"—namely, take the trust oath that the qualification was genuine, and he renounced.'—BAIN's *History of Nairnshire*. He died unmarried in 1807. His elder brother, James, became professor of Philosophy in King's College, Aberdeen, and an LL.D.

His uncomb'd, hoary locks, wild-staring, thatch'd
A head for thought profound and clear unmatch'd
Yet, tho' his caustic wit was biting rude,
His heart was warm, benevolent and good.

Dunbar was commemorated in verses of a different strain.   There
was an old rough Border ditty referring to a certain 'Rattlin,
Roaring Willie,' of great celebrity in his day as a wandering
violer.   To this Burns added a stanza, which we are to take
as a picture of the Colonel in his place of command and at the
moment of his highest exultation:

RATTLIN, ROARING WILLIE.

As I cam by Crochallan,
   I cannily keekit ben,   *cautiously looked in*
Rattlin, roarin Willie
   Was sitting at yon boord-en',   *end of the table*
Sitting at yon boord-en',
   And amang guid companie;   *good*
Rattlin, roarin Willie,
   Ye're welcome hame to me.

Dunbar, who presented Burns with a copy of Spenser, is elsewhere described by him as 'one of the worthiest fellows in the
world.'

During the printing of the new edition of the *Poems*, a proposal
to insert, as frontispiece to the volume, a portrait of the poet was
made.   But there was then in the Scottish capital no portrait-
painter of reputation.   Creech, however, was acquainted with a
young landscape-painter, named Alexander Nasmyth,* whom he
thought likely to produce a likeness, if induced to try.   He, accordingly, brought Nasmyth to his house to breakfast with Burns,† calculating that the artist would be inspired with such an interest in
the bard as would dispose him to do his very best with his brush.

* Alexander Nasmyth was born in Edinburgh in 1757, and apprenticed in London to
Allan Ramsay, a portrait-painter, and son of the poet.   After studying in Italy, he settled in
Edinburgh.   He died in 1840.
† Nasmyth, according to his son James, was first introduced to Burns by Patrick Miller
at Dalswinton.

ROBERT BURNS

F Jenkins delin. Pinxt

The plan was successful, and the poet gave sittings to the artist at his lodgings in Wardrop's Court. Nasmyth worked *con amore*, and having attained a point at which he thought the likeness good, stopped, so that the painting was never finished. It is believed that he generously refused to accept any remuneration for his work.[*] An engraver named John Beugo[†] transferred the likeness to copper, on the same terms. He took the greatest possible pains with the face, being assisted by several sittings from the poet for the purpose of retouching the plate.[‡]

After a sitting for the painting, Nasmyth and the poet sometimes took a walk, their destination being frequently the King's Park, where Burns delighted to climb Arthur's Seat, and, lying on the summit, gaze at the panorama of twelve of the principal Scottish counties. Once, after a convivial meeting in a High Street tavern which lasted till an early hour in the morning, they agreed not to go home at all, but to start on an excursion to the Pentland Hills. Passing a cottage a few miles out of town, they heard a loud noise within, and, entering to learn what was the matter, found that the sounds proceeded from a poor man whose reason had given way. Nasmyth used afterwards to describe the appalling exclamations of the lunatic, and the effect which they had upon Burns. The two friends continued their walk to the hills, and came down to Roslin to breakfast. The poet found the cheer in Mrs David Wilson's little inn so good that, in gratitude, he scrawled a couple of verses on the reverse side of a wooden platter :

> My blessings on you, sonsy wife ;   buxom
>   I ne'er was here before ;
> You 've gi'en us walth for horn and knife,   wealth
>   Nae heart could wish for more.

---

[*] At a late period of life, Nasmyth prepared a full-length sketch of Burns, from memory, for Lockhart's *Life of Burns*, in which it appears on the title-page.

[†] John Beugo, engraver (1759–1841), also engraved notes for Scottish banks, and is credited with having trained Robert Charles Bell, a more famous engraver than himself. He issued anonymously (1797) *Poetry, Miscellaneous and Dramatic*, by an Artist. He is buried in Old Greyfriars Churchyard.

[‡] 'I used to think Beugo's engraving from Nasmyth's picture shewed more character and expression than the picture itself ; but it was the first likeness of my brother I had seen, not having seen the picture till long after, and perhaps the impression then made upon my mind may have made me partial to the engraving.'—*Gilbert Burns to George Thomson*, *July 2*, 1821.

Heaven keep you free frae care and strife,   from
    Till far ayont fourscore ;   beyond
And while I toddle on thro' life,   walk
    I 'll ne'er gang by your door.*   go

TO DR MOORE.

EDINBURGH, 15th February 1787.

REVERED SIR—Pardon my seeming neglect in delaying so long to
acknowledge the honour you have done me in your kind notice of me,
January 23d. Not many months ago I knew no other employment than
following the plough, nor could boast any thing higher than a distant
acquaintance with a country clergyman. Mere greatness never embar-
rasses me ; I have nothing to ask from the great, and I do not fear their
judgment : but genius, polished by learning, and at its proper point of
elevation in the eye of the world, this of late I frequently meet with, and
tremble at its approach. I scorn the affectation of seeming modesty to
cover self-conceit. That I have some merit I do not deny ; but I see
with frequent wringings of heart, that the novelty of my character, and
the honest national prejudice of my countrymen, have borne me to a
height altogether untenable to my abilities.

For the honor Miss Williams has done me, please, Sir, return her in
my name my most grateful thanks. I have more than once thought of
paying her in kind, but have hitherto quitted the idea in hopeless

---

* From information derived many years ago from the late Matthew Stobie, Kirklandhill,
Haddingtonshire, who lived in Roslin at the time. James Nasmyth, the artist's youngest
son, and famous as the inventor of the steam-hammer, gives the following account of this
incident in his autobiography, which was published in 1885 under the editorship of Dr
Samuel Smiles : 'A visit which the two paid to Roslin Castle is worthy of commemoration.
On one occasion my father and a few choice spirits had been spending a "nicht wi' Burns."
The place of resort was a tavern in the High Street, Edinburgh. As Burns was a brilliant
talker, full of spirit and humour ; time fled until the " wee sma' hours ayont the twal' "
arrived. The party broke up about three o'clock. At that time of the year (the 13th of
June) the night is very short, and morning comes early. Burns, on reaching the street,
looked up to the sky. It was perfectly clear, and the rising sun was beginning to brighten
the mural crown of St Giles' Cathedral. Burns was so much struck with the beauty of the
morning, that he put his hand on my father's arm and said, " It 'll never do to go to bed in
such a lovely morning as this ! Let 's awa' to Roslin Castle." No sooner said than done.
The poet and painter set out. Nature lay bright and lovely before them in that delicious
summer morning. After an eight-miles' walk they reached the castle at Roslin. Burns
went down under the great Norman arch, where he stood rapt in speechless admiration of
the scene. The thought of the eternal renewal of youth and freshness of nature, contrasted
with the crumbling decay of man's efforts to perpetuate his work, even when founded upon
a rock, as Roslin Castle is, seemed greatly to affect him. My father was so much impressed
with the scene that, while Burns was standing under the arch, he took out his pencil and
paper, and made a hasty sketch of the subject. This sketch was highly treasured by my
father, in remembrance of what must have been one of the most memorable days in his
life.'

despondency. I had never before heard of her; but the other day I got her poems, which for several reasons, some belonging to the head, and others the offspring of the heart, give me a great deal of pleasure. I have little pretensions to critic lore; there are, I think, two characteristic features in her poetry—the unfettered wild flight of native genius, and the querulous, *sombre* tenderness of ' time settled sorrow.'

I only know what pleases me, often without being able to tell why.

R. B.

Dr Moore answered :

CLIFFORD-STREET, *28th February* 1787.

DEAR SIR—Your letter of the 15th gave me a great deal of pleasure. It is not surprising that you improve in correctness and taste, considering where you have been for some time past. And I dare swear there is no danger of your admitting any polish which might weaken the vigour of your native powers.

I am glad to perceive that you disdain the nauseous affectation of decrying your own merit as a poet, an affectation which is displayed with most ostentation by those who have the greatest share of self-conceit, and which only adds undeceiving falsehood to disgusting vanity. For you to deny the merit of your poems would be arraigning the fixed opinion of the public.

As the new edition of my *View of Society* is not yet ready, I have sent you the former edition, which I beg you will accept as a small mark of my esteem. It is sent by sea to the care of Mr Creech, and, along with these four volumes for yourself, I have also sent my *Medical Sketches*, in one volume, for my friend Mrs Dunlop of Dunlop : this you will be so obliging as to transmit, or if you chance to pass soon by Dunlop, to give to her.

I am happy to hear that your subscription is so ample, and shall rejoice at every piece of good fortune that befalls you. For you are a very great favorite in my family;* and this is a higher compliment than perhaps you are aware of. It includes almost all the professions, and of course is a proof that your writings are adapted to various tastes and situations. My youngest son, who is at Winchester school, writes to me that he is translating some stanzas of your ' Halloween ' into Latin verse, for the benefit of his comrades. This union of taste partly proceeds, no doubt, from the cement of Scottish partiality, with which they are all somewhat tinctured. Even *your translator*, who left Scotland too early in life for recollection, is not without it. . . . I remain with great sincerity, Your obedient servant,
J. MOORE.

* ' . . . I have been much pleased with the poems of the Scottish ploughman. His " Cotter's Saturday Night " has much of the same kind of merit as "The Schoolmistress ;" and " The Daisy " and "The Mouse," which I believe you have had in the papers, I think are charming. The endearing diminutives, and the Doric rusticity of the dialect, suit such subjects extremely. . . .'—*From a letter of Mrs Barbauld to her father, John Aikin, D.D., dated* 31st *January* 1787.

TO JOHN BALLANTINE, ESQ.

MY HONORED FRIEND—I will soon be with you now 'in guid black prent;' in a week or ten days at farthest. I am obliged, against my own wish, to print subscribers' names, so if any of my Ayr friends have subscription-bills, they must be sent in to Creech directly. I am getting my phiz done by an eminent engraver; and if it can be ready in time, I will appear in my book, looking, like other *fools*, to my title page.—I have the honor to be, Ever your grateful   ROBT. BURNS.

Before this time Burns had gratified his own generous feelings by an act of piety towards his unfortunate precursor Fergusson. The first step he took in the matter is fully told in an excerpt from the session-records of the parish of Canongate :

Session-house, within the Kirk of Canongate, the twenty second day of February, one thousand seven hundred eighty seven years.
Sederunt of the Managers of the Kirk and Kirkyard Funds of Canongate.

Which day, the treasurer to the said funds produced a letter from Mr Robert Burns, of date the sixth current, which was read and appointed to be engrossed in their sederunt book, and of which letter the tenor follows :

'To the honourable bailies of Canongate, Edinburgh.* Gentlemen, I am sorry to be told that the remains of Robert Fergusson, the so justly celebrated poet, a man whose talents for ages to come will do honor to our Caledonian name, lie in your church-yard among the ignoble dead, unnoticed and unknown.

'Some memorial to direct the steps of the lovers of Scottish song, when they wish to shed a tear over the "narrow house" of the bard who is no more, is surely a tribute due to Fergusson's memory : a tribute I wish to have the honor of paying.

'I petition you then, gentlemen, to permit me to lay a simple stone over his revered ashes, to remain an unalienable property to his deathless fame. I have the honor to be, gentlemen, your very humble servant, (*sic subscribitur*)   'ROBERT BURNS.'

Thereafter the said managers, in consideration of the laudable and disinterested motion of Mr Burns, and the propriety of his request, did, and hereby do, unanimously, grant power and liberty to the said Robert

* Burns had addressed himself to the Canongate Magistrates, instead of to the Managers of the Kirk and Kirkyard Funds.

Burns, to erect a headstone at the grave of the said Robert Fergusson, and to keep up and preserve the same to his memory in all time coming. Extracted forth of the records of the managers by

WILLIAM SPROTT, *Clerk.*

TO MR PETER STUART.

[EDINBURGH, *February* 1787.]

MY DEAR SIR—You may think, and too justly, that I am a selfish, ungrateful fellow, having received so many repeated instances of kindness from you, and yet never putting pen to paper to say, thank you; but if you knew what a devil of a life my conscience has led me on that account, your good heart would think yourself too much avenged. By the bye, there is nothing in the whole frame of man, which seems to me so unaccountable as that thing called conscience. Had the troublesome yelping cur powers efficient to prevent a mischief, he might be of use; but at the beginning of the business, his feeble efforts are to the workings of passion as the infant frosts of an autumnal morning to the unclouded fervor of the rising sun : and no sooner are the tumultuous doings of the wicked deed over, than, amidst the bitter native consequences of folly, in the very vortex of our horrors, up starts conscience and harrows us with the feelings of the damned.

I have inclosed you, by way of expiation, some verse and prose, that, if they merit a place in your truly entertaining miscellany, you are welcome to. The prose extract is literally as Mr Sprott sent it me.

The inscription on the stone is as follows :

HERE LIES ROBERT FERGUSSON, POET.

BORN, SEPTEMBER 5th, 1751—DIED, 16th OCTOBER 1774.

No sculptur'd marble here, nor pompous lay,
 'No storied urn nor animated bust,'
This simple stone directs pale SCOTIA'S way
 To pour her sorrows o'er her POET'S dust.*

On the other side of the stone is as follows :

By special grant of the managers to Robert Burns, who erected this stone, this burial-place is to remain for ever sacred to the memory of Robert Fergusson.

R. B.

The person to whom this letter was addressed was Peter Stuart, subsequently founder and editor of the *Star* newspaper in London, a well-known contributor, on the side of the Government, to the

---

* This epitaph, showing some variations, is entered, with two additional verses, in the second Common-place Book. See *supra.*

daily press during the first decade of the present century. Stuart
appears to have known Fergusson in his early youth, and to
have entertained a warm admiration for his talents and amiability.
His reply, dated 8th March, to this letter of Burns contains a
very absurd tirade against the poor Canongate magistrates,
as if they had been concerned in starving the poet whose
grave they now allowed Burns to adorn. The letter, however,
is of some value as showing us what was commonly believed
about Burns's position and doings in Edinburgh. 'Next week,'
says the writer, 'I hope to have the pleasure of seeing you in
Edinburgh, and, as my stay will be for eight or ten days, I wish
you or ***** would take a snug well-aired bedroom for me, where I
may have the pleasure of seeing you over a morning cup of tea.
But by all accounts it will be a matter of some difficulty to see
you at all, unless your company is bespoke a week beforehand.
There is a great rumour here concerning your great intimacy with
the Duchess of [Gordon] and other ladies of distinction. I am
really told that "cards to invite fly by thousands each night;"
and if you had one, I suppose there would also be "bribes to
your old secretary." '*

The keen sympathy felt by Burns for Fergusson was expressed
on many occasions. Very soon after making arrangements regarding the tombstone, he presented (March 19, 1787)† a copy of

---

* These are quotations from a curious ballad then fashionable.

† This interesting volume, which was for some time in the Edinburgh Select Subscription
Library, is now in the possession of the Earl of Rosebery. On the fly-leaves at the end
there are given in Burns's handwriting, 'A Tragic Fragment' and 'A Prayer under the
Pressure of Bitter (sic) Anguish' (see Vol. I., pp. 54, 82). On a fly-leaf at the front of
the volume, and immediately before the portrait, is written, also in Burns's handwriting,
'This copy of Ferguson's poems is presented as a mark of esteem, friendship, and regard,
to Miss R. Carmichael, poetess, by Robert Burns. Edinburgh, 19th March, 1787.' This
was not the only copy of Fergusson that Burns possessed, or in which he wrote some
of his verses. He presented another to Mrs Dalzel, wife of Andrew Dalzel, professor of Greek in Edinburgh University. On the first blank-leaf he inscribed the
lines beginning, 'Ah, woe is me, my mother dear,' which have already been given
(see Vol. I., pp. 63-4). That copy is now in the Edinburgh Free Public Library. In 1846
Mary Dalzel, Professor Dalzel's daughter, presented the volume to the late Mr J. T. Gibson
Craig, Edinburgh. On the second fly-leaf of the volume these notes are inscribed : 'This
volume of Ferguson's poems was given by Burns to Mrs Dalzel, my mother, some time
about the year 1788.—Mary Dalzel. Presented by me to Mr J. T. Gibson Craig, 26 June
1846.—M. Dalzel.' On the sale of the second portion of Mr Gibson Craig's library in London
in 1888, this volume, along with Burns's copy of Allan Ramsay's 'Gentle Shepherd'
(with Allan's illustrations), which had been presented to him by his friend, Alexander
Cunningham, was bought by Mr William M'Ewan, M.P. for the Central Division of Edinburgh. Both volumes were presented by Mr M'Ewan to the Edinburgh Free Public
Library.

the works of the Edinburgh poet to Miss Rebekah Carmichael,
a young poetess,* and, under the portrait which served for a
frontispiece, wrote the following

VERSES.

Curse on ungrateful man, that can be pleas'd
And yet can starve the author of the pleasure.
O thou, my elder brother in misfortune,
By far my elder brother in the muse,†
With tears I pity thy unhappy fate!
Why is the bard unfitted for the world,‡
Yet has so keen a relish of its pleasures?

TO THE EARL OF GLENCAIRN.

My Lord—I wanted to purchase a profile of your Lordship which I
was told was to be got in town; but I am truly sorry to see that a
blundering Painter has spoilt a 'human face divine.' The inclosed
stanzas I intended to have written below a picture, or profile shade, of
your Lordship, could I have been so happy as to procure one with any
thing of a likeness.

As I will soon return to my shades, I wanted to have something like a
material object for my gratitude; I wanted to have it in my power to
say to a friend 'There is my noble Patron, my generous Benefactor.'
Allow me, my Lord, to offer my warm request, to be permitted to publish
these verses. I conjure your Lordship by the honest throe of gratitude,
by the generous wish of benevolence, by all the powers and feelings
which compose the magnanimous mind, do not deny me this my darling
petition. I owe much, very much indeed, to your Lordship; and, what
has not in some other instances always been the case with me, the
weight of the obligation is a pleasing load. I trust I have a heart as
independent as your Lordship's, than which I can say nothing more; and
I would not be beholden to favours which would crucify my feelings.
Your dignified character in life, and manner of supporting that character,
are flattering to my pride; and I would be jealous of the purity of my

---

* In 1790 appeared ' Poems by Miss Carmichael. Edinburgh, Printed for the Author, and
sold by Peter Hill.' The five hundred subscribers to the volume include ' Mr Robert Burns,
two copies.' Miss Carmichael became Mrs Hay.

†"Variation—' Muses.'

‡ Variation—' Unpitied by.' This appears in most versions of these lines, but ' unfitted for'
obviously expresses Burns's meaning much better.

grateful attachment, where I was under the patronage of one of the much-favored sons of Fortune. Almost every Poet has celebrated his Patrons, particularly when they were names dear to Fame, and illustrious in their country: allow me then, my Lord, if you think the verses have intrinsic merit, to tell the world how much I have the honor to be, Your Lordship's highly indebted and ever grateful, humble servt.,

ROBT. BURNS.

EDINBURGH, *Feb.* 1787.

VERSES INTENDED TO BE WRITTEN BELOW A NOBLE EARL'S PICTURE.

Whose is that noble, dauntless brow?
    And whose that eye of fire?
And whose that generous, Princely mien
    Ev'n rooted Foes admire?

Stranger, to justly show that brow,
    And mark that eye of fire,
Would take *His* hand, whose vernal tints
    His other Works inspire.*

Bright as a cloudless Summer-sun,
    With stately port he moves;
His guardian Seraph eyes with awe
    The noble Ward he loves.

Among th' illustrious Scottish Sons,
    That Chief thou may'st discern,
Mark Scotia's fond-returning eye,
    It dwells upon GLENCAIRN.

It would appear that the earl refrained from giving permission, for the verses remained in manuscript till long afterwards.

In the new edition Burns inserted a considerable number of pieces either written since the first edition was published, or excluded from it. He now let 'Death and Dr Hornbook' go forth, also 'The Ordination,' and the 'Address to the Unco Guid,' which

---

* The MS. of this is now in the Museum of the City Chambers, Edinburgh. The last word of stanza second is 'admire:' it is probable that the Poet intended to write 'inspire.'

various considerations had formerly induced him to repress. The 'Brigs of Ayr,' 'Tam Samson's Elegy,' and the 'Address to Edinburgh' were the principal new pieces in the volume. He also included some juvenile pieces of less moment: 'John Barleycorn,' a 'Paraphrase of the First Psalm,' 'A Prayer, under the pressure of Violent Anguish,' besides three or four songs. There may be included in this group a political ballad, entitled 'A Fragment,' dealing with the American War, in the quaintly familiar language of a rustic, and the rough draft of which, it has been conjectured, was written so early as the spring of 1784.

BALLAD ON THE AMERICAN WAR.

TUNE—*Killiecrankie.*

When Guilford * good our Pilot stood,
 An' did our hellim thraw, man,   *helm turn*
Ae night, at tea, began a plea   *lawsuit*
 Within America, man :
Then up they gat the maskin-pat,†
 And in the sea did jaw, man,   *dash*
An' did nae less, in full Congress,
 Than quite refuse our law, man.

Then thro' the lakes Montgomery ‡ takes,
 I wat he was na slaw, man,   *slow*
Down Lowrie's Burn § he took a turn,
 And Carleton did ca', man :   *drive*
But yet, whatreck, he, at Quebec, *notwithstanding*
 Montgomery-like ‖ did fa', man,   *fall*
Wi' sword in hand, before his band,
 Amang his en'mies a', man.

---

* Frederick North, second Earl of Guilford, better known as Lord North.
† Ten-pot. Mask=brew. The allusion is to the Boston tea-riots of 1773.
‡ General Richard Montgomery invaded Canada (autumn 1775) and took Montreal, the British commander, Sir Guy Carleton, retiring before him. In an attack on Quebec he was less fortunate, being killed while leading his men.
§ 'Lowrie's Burn,' a name for the St Lawrence.
‖ A compliment to the Montgomeries of Coilsfield.

Poor Tammy Gage within a cage
    Was kept at Boston-ha', man,*
Till Willie Howe took o'er the knowe   *went over the hill*
    For Philadelphia,† man :
Wi' sword an' gun he thought a sin
    Guid Christian bluid to draw, man ;   *blood*
But at New-York, wi' knife an' fork,
    Sir Loin he hackèd sma',‡ man.   *small*

Burgoyne gaed up like spur an' whip,   *went*
    Till Fraser brave did fa', man ;
Then lost his way, ae misty day,   *one*
    In Saratoga shaw,§ man.   *wood*
Cornwallis fought as lang 's he dought,   *dared*
    An' did the Buckskins claw, man ;‖   *Virginians beat*
But Clinton's glaive, frae rust to save,   *sword — from*
    He hung it to the wa', man.

Then Montague, an' Guilford too,
    Began to fear a fa', man ;
And Sackville doure, wha stood the stoure   *grimly deter-*
         mined—brunt
    The German Chief¶ to thraw, man :   *of the struggle*
         thwart
For Paddy Burke, like ony Turk,
    Nae mercy had at a', man ;
An' Charlie Fox threw by the box,
    An' lows'd his tinkler jaw, man.   *loosed*

Then Rockingham took up the game ;
    Till Death did on him ca', man ;   *call*
When Shelburne meek held up his cheek
    Conform to Gospel law, man :

---

* General Gage, governor of Massachusetts, was cooped up in Boston by General Washington during the latter part of 1775 and early part of 1776. In consequence of his inefficiency, he was replaced in October of that year by General Howe.

† General Howe removed his army from New York to Philadelphia in the summer of 1777.

‡ Alluding to a *razzia* made by orders of Howe at Peekskill, March 1777, when a large quantity of cattle belonging to the Americans was destroyed.

§ General Burgoyne surrendered his army to General Gates, at Saratoga, on the Hudson, October 1776.

‖ Alluding to the active operations of Lord Cornwallis in Virginia, in 1780, which ended, however, in the surrender of his army at Yorktown, October 1781, while vainly hoping for reinforcement from General Clinton at New York.

¶ The commander of the Hessian auxiliaries.

Saint Stephen's boys, wi' jarring noise,
 They did his measures thraw, man,   *thwart*
For North an' Fox united stocks,
 An' bore him to the wa', man.*

Then Clubs an' Hearts were Charlie's cartes: *cards*
 He swept the stakes awa', man,
Till the Diamond's Ace, of Indian race,
 Led him a sair *faux pas*, man†:
The Saxon lads, wi' loud placads,   *cheers*
 On Chatham's Boy did ca', man;
An' Scotland drew her pipe, an' blew
 'Up, Willie,‡ waur them a', man!'   *vanquish*

Behind the throne, then, Granville's gone,
 A secret word or twa, man;
While slee Dundas§ arous'd the class   *astute*
 Be-north the Roman wa', man:
An' Chatham's wraith, in heav'nly graith,   *ghost's garb*
 (Inspirèd Bardies saw, man,)
Wi' kindling eyes, cry'd 'Willie, rise!
 Would I hae fear'd them a', man?'

But, word an' blow, North, Fox and Co.
 Gowff'd‖ Willie like a ba', man,   *Struck*
Till Suthron raise, an' coost their claise   *cast off—clothes*
 Behind him in a raw, man: *row*

* Lord North's administration was succeeded by that of the Marquis of Rockingham, March 1782. On the death of the latter, in the succeeding July, Lord Shelburne became prime-minister, and Fox resigned his secretaryship. Under Shelburne, peace was restored, January 1783. By an alliance between Lord North and Fox, however, he was soon after forced to resign in favour of his rivals, the heads of the celebrated Coalition.

† Fox's famous India Bill, by which his ministry was brought to destruction, December 1783.

‡ 'Up an' waur them a', Willie,' a Jacobite song on the battle of Sheriffmuir, was then popular in Scotland.

§ Henry Dundas, afterwards Viscount Melville, was at this period accounted Pitt's 'Grand Vizier for Scotland.'

‖ This is the only line in Burns which can be construed as an allusion to the now universally popular game of golf.

TO GAVIN HAMILTON, ESQ.

Edinburgh, *March 8th*, 1787.

DEAR SIR—Yours came safe, and I am, as usual, much indebted to your goodness. Poor Captain Montgomerie is cast. Yesterday it was tried whether the husband could proceed against the unfortunate lover without first divorcing his wife, and their Gravities on the Bench were unanimously of opinion that Maxwell may prosecute for damages directly, and need not divorce his wife at all if he pleases ; and Maxwell is immediately, before the Lord Ordinary, to prove, what I dare say will not be denied, the *Crim Con*—then their Lordships will modify the damages, which I suppose will be pretty heavy, as their Wisdoms have expressed great abhorrence of my gallant Right Worshipful Brother's * conduct.

O, all ye powers of love unfortunate, and friendless woe, pour the balm of sympathizing pity on the grief-torn, tender heart of the hapless Fair One !

My two songs on Miss W. Alexander and Miss P. Kennedy† were likewise tried yesterday by a jury of literati, and found defamatory libels against the fastidious powers of Poesy and Taste ; and the author forbidden to print them under pain of forfeiture of character. I cannot help almost shedding a tear to the memory of two songs that had cost me some pains, and that I valued a good deal, but I must submit.

My most respectful compliments to Mrs Hamilton and Miss Kennedy.

My poor unfortunate Songs come again across my memory. D——n the pedant, frigid soul of Criticism for ever and ever ! I am ever, Dear Sir, Your obliged ROBERT BURNS.

The Faculty Decisions, under date March 7, 1787, report the judgment of the Court of Session in a case in which a legal point arose between Mr Maxwell Campbell of Skerrington, in Ayrshire, and Captain James Montgomerie, late of the 93d Foot, as to whether the former could prosecute the latter for the dishonour of his wife, without previously divorcing her. It appears that Mrs Maxwell Campbell was heiress, in her own right, of Skerrington, that she had had two children by her husband, and that she left his house in June 1783, in company with Captain Montgomerie, to whom she bore a child in November of the subsequent year. Burns's expressions would seem to indicate a

---

* Captain Montgomerie was a member of the Eglintoun family, and a 'brother' of Burns in the Masonic sense.

† These songs were, in all probability, 'The Lass o' Ballochmyle,' and 'Young Peggy blooms, our bonicst lass.'

popular belief in Scotland that there were extenuating circumstances in the conduct of the lady, and that the policy of the husband in abstaining from a process of divorce, which would have deprived him of an estate, did not meet with general approval.

Burns could scarcely but take an interest in the proceedings of the supreme civil court, always an object of peculiar respect to the country folk of Scotland. As a result of his visits to Parliament House, we have well-drawn sketches of the two leading advocates of that day—the Dean of Faculty, Harry Erskine, and the Lord Advocate, Mr Ilay Campbell* (subsequently Lord President).

EXTEMPORE IN THE COURT OF SESSION.

TUNE—*Killiecrankie.*

LORD ADVOCATE.

He clench'd his pamphlets in his fist,	
He quoted and he hinted,	
Till, in a declamation-mist,	
His argument he tint it :	lost
He gapèd for 't, he grapèd for 't,	groped
He fand it was awa, man ;	found—away
But what his common sense came short,	
He ekèd out wi' law, man.	

MR ERSKINE.

Collected, Harry stood a wee,	for a short time
Then open'd out his arm, man ;	
His lordship sat wi' ruefu' e'e,	eye
And ey'd the gathering storm, man :	
Like wind-driv'n hail it did assail,	
Or torrents owre a lin, man ;	over—waterfall
The BENCH sae wise lift up their eyes,	
Half-wauken'd wi' the din, man.	wakened

---

* Henry Erskine, second son of Henry David, tenth Earl of Buchan, born in Edinburgh in 1746 ; called to the bar in 1768 ; Lord Advocate in 1783 ; Dean of Faculty in 1786 ; Dean of Faculty and member for the Dumfries Burghs in 1806-1807 ; died at his seat of Amondell, West Lothian, in 1817.—Sir Ilay Campbell, son of Archibald Campbell of Succoth, clerk of session, born in 1734 ; called to the bar in 1757 ; Solicitor-general for Scotland in 1783 ; Lord Advocate and M.P. for Glasgow in 1784 ; appointed Lord President of the Court of Session in 1789 ; resigned office and made a baronet in 1808 ; died at Garscube, near Glasgow, in 1823.

TO MR JAMES CANDLISH,[*]

STUDENT IN PHYSIC, COLLEGE, GLASGOW.

EDINBURGH, *March* 21, 1787.

MY EVER DEAR OLD ACQUAINTANCE—I was equally surprised and pleased at your letter; though I dare say you will think, by my delaying so long to write to you, that I am so drowned in the intoxication of good fortune as to be indifferent to old and once dear connections. The truth is, I was determined to write a good letter, full of argument, amplification, erudition, and, as Bayes[†] says, *all that*. I thought of it, and thought of it, but for my soul I cannot; and lest you should mistake the cause of my silence, I just sit down to tell you so. Don't give yourself credit, though, that the strength of your logic scares me : the truth is, I never mean to meet you on that ground at all. You have shewn me one thing which was to be demonstrated; that strong pride of reasoning, with a little affectation of singularity, may mislead the best of hearts. I, likewise, since you and I were first acquainted, in the pride of despising old women's stories, ventured in 'the daring path Spinoza[‡] trod;' but experience of the weakness, not the strength, of human powers, made me glad to grasp at revealed religion.

I must stop, but don't impute my brevity to a wrong cause. I am still, in the Apostle Paul's phrase, 'The old man with his deeds,' as when we were sporting about the lady-thorn. I shall be four weeks here yet, at least; and so I shall expect to hear from you—welcome sense, welcome nonsense. I am, with the warmest sincerity, My dear old friend, Yours,

ROBT. BURNS.

TO MRS DUNLOP.

EDINBURGH, *March* 22d, 1787.

MADAM—I read your letter with watery eyes. A little, very little while ago, *I had scarce a friend but the stubborn pride of my own bosom;* now I am distinguished, patronised, befriended by you. Your friendly

---

[*] This is the same James Candlish (or M'Candlish), whom, as has already been seen, Burns first met as a boy in Dalrymple, who married Miss Smith, one of the Mauchline belles, became a lecturer on medicine in Edinburgh, and died in 1806. His son, Dr Robert Smith Candlish, was the well-known Principal of the Free Church College, Edinburgh.

[†] Bayes—*i.e.* Dryden, as satirised in Buckingham's *Rehearsal*—interlards his conversation with 'and all that.' Thus in Act V.: 'I'l make 'em know what it is to injure a person who does 'em the honour to write for 'em, and all that; a company of proud, conceited, humorous, cross-grain'd persons, and all that. I gad, I'l make 'em the most contemptible, despicable, inconsiderable persons, and all that.'

[‡] Spinoza's name was at this time a vague synonym for atheism or infidelity. 'Dauntless pursues the path Spinoza trod' occurs in John Brown's (1715-66) 'Essay on Satire' prefixed by Warburton to the *Essay on Man* in his edition of Pope.

advices, I will not give them the cold name of criticisms, I receive with reverence. I have made some small alterations in what I before had printed. I have the advice of some very judicious friends among the literati here, but with them I sometimes find it necessary to claim the privilege of thinking for myself. The noble Earl of Glencairn, to whom I owe more than to any man, does me the honor of giving me his strictures : his hints, with respect to impropriety or indelicacy, I follow implicitly.

You kindly interest yourself in my future views and prospects ; there I can give you no light. It is all

> Dark as was Chaos ere the infant sun
> Was roll'd together, or had try'd his beams
> Athwart the gloom profound.

The appellation of a Scottish bard is by far my highest pride ; to continue to deserve it is my most exalted ambition. Scottish scenes and Scottish story are the themes I could wish to sing. I have no dearer aim than to have it in my power, unplagued with the routine of business, for which heaven knows I am unfit enough, to make leisurely pilgrimages through Caledonia ; to sit on the fields of her battles ; to wander on the romantic banks of her rivers ; and to muse by the stately towers or venerable ruins, once the honored abodes of her heroes.

But these are all Utopian thoughts : I have dallied long enough with life ; 'tis time to be in earnest. I have a fond, an aged mother to care for ; and some other bosom-ties perhaps equally tender. Where the individual only suffers by the consequences of his own thoughtlessness, indolence or folly, he may be excusable ; nay, shining abilities, and some of the nobler virtues may half sanctify a heedless character ; but where God and nature have entrusted the welfare of others to his care ; where the trust is sacred, and the ties are dear, that man must be far gone in selfishness, or strangely lost to reflection, whom these connexions will not rouse to exertion.

I guess that I shall clear between two and three hundred pounds by my authorship ; with that sum I intend, so far as I may be said to have any intention, to return to my old acquaintance, the plough, and, if I can meet with a lease by which I can live, to commence farmer. I do not intend to give up poetry : being bred to labour, secures me independence, and the muses are my chief, sometimes have been my only, enjoyment. If my practice second my resolution, I shall have principally at heart the serious business of life ; but while following my plough, or building up my shocks, I shall cast a leisure glance to that dear, that only feature of my character, which gave me the notice of my country, and the patronage of a Wallace.

Thus, honored madam, I have given you the bard, his situation, and his views, native as they are in his own bosom. . . .

ROBT. BURNS.

TO MRS DUNLOP.

EDINBURGH, 15th *April* 1787.

MADAM—There is an affectation of gratitude which I dislike. The periods of Johnson and the pauses of Sterne may hide a selfish heart. For my part, madam, I trust I have too much pride for servility, and too little prudence for selfishness. I have this moment broken open your letter, but

> Rude am I in speech,
> And therefore little can I grace my cause
> In speaking for myself— *

so I shall not trouble you with any fine speeches and hunted figures. I shall just lay my hand on my heart, and say, I hope I shall ever have the truest, the warmest, sense of your goodness.

I come abroad, in print, for certain on Wednesday. Your orders I shall punctually attend to ; only, by the way, I must tell you that I was paid before for Dr Moore's and Miss Williams's copies, through the medium of Commissioner Cochrane in this place, but that we can settle when I have the honor of waiting on you.

Dr Smith † was just gone to London the morning before I received your letter to him. R. B.

'The Ayrshire Ploughman'—as he was generally styled—was the lion of the season in Edinburgh. On the strength of his volume he was received into the highest circles of society. Here, by his demeanour, and the fascination of his conversation, he greatly deepened the interest which his poetry had awakened. Only the autumn before Burns had been labouring on a small Ayrshire farm. He was now entertained and treated as an equal by the remnant of that brilliant circle of Scottish men of letters who adorned the later half of the eighteenth century. He was courted and treated with sincere respect by such members of the

---

* Shakespeare's *Othello*, Act I., scene iii.

† Author of the *Wealth of Nations*. Although Adam Smith (b. 1723, d. 1790) was only sixty-three years of age at the time of Burns's visit to Edinburgh, and was living there as Commissioner of Customs for Scotland, failing health accounts for the fact that he, the greatest of David Hume's contemporaries, took comparatively little interest in the poet. 'The winter of 1786-1787,' says his latest biographer (*Life of Adam Smith*, by John Rae.—Macmillan & Co., 1895), 'laid him so low with a chronic obstruction of the bowels that Robertson wrote to Gibbon that they were in great danger of losing him.' As soon as he recovered he went to London, to consult his friend John Hunter. A somewhat similar reason may be given for the comparative indifference of William Robertson (1721-1793), the historian, ecclesiastical leader, and Principal of Edinburgh University, who was then sixty-five, and whose life-work was virtually over.

aristocracy as lived in Edinburgh during winter. 'Elegant society' in Edinburgh formed in those days, as it does still, a limited circle. From the large infusion of the professions of law and medicine, and of the class connected with the university, it had a tone of undoubted, if somewhat cold, enlightenment and refinement. At this particular time its calm was disturbed in no small degree by the grace, gaiety, and irrepressible energy of the Duchess of Gordon. A letter written by Drummond, a member of the Scottish bar, to a friend in India in the February preceding Burns's arrival in Edinburgh, contains a striking account of the habits of the Duchess. 'The good town,' he says, 'is uncommonly crowded and splendid at present. The example of dissipation set by her Grace the Duchess of Gordon* is far from showing vice her own image. It is really astonishing to think what effect a single person will have on public manners, when supported by high rank and great address. She is never absent from a public place, and the later the hour, so much the better. It is often four o'clock in the morning before she goes to bed, and she never requires more than five hours' sleep. Dancing, cards, and company occupy her whole time.' Such was the leader of society in Edinburgh at the period when Burns was plunged into it.

The general tone of middle-class life at this epoch was convivial. Lawyers of good repute, merchants, well-to-do tradesmen, teachers of the High School, were either Freemasons or members of social clubs, and frequented taverns in the evening for the sake of pleasures which they had not yet learned to enjoy under the more decorous auspices of the home circle. Men dined early in those days, and worked till about eight o'clock, when they considered themselves free to devote the rest of the day to enjoyment. Either a private supper-party invited them, with their wives, or they knew of some comfortable snuggery, such as John Dowie's† or Daniel Douglas's tavern, in certain alleys of the High Street, where they could calculate upon meeting congenial spirits, with whom to spend three or four hours over ale or

---

* The eccentric and fascinating Jane, Duchess of Gordon, is believed to have been born in 1749. She was the second daughter of Sir William Maxwell of Monreith in Wigtownshire, and married in 1767 Alexander, fourth Duke of Gordon. She died in 1812. Her husband survived her, dying in 1827 at the age of eighty-two.

† John Dowie's tavern stood in Liberton's Wynd (demolished in 1834). He always affected the old costume—cocked hat, and buckles at the knees and shoes. He died in 1817.

punch. Into these coteries Burns was often drawn by his social temper and good-nature.

It really does not appear, however, that Burns's character was either spoiled by the aristocracy and gentry, or debauched by the tradesmen and clerks. On the contrary, the tone of his letters all through this spring is remarkable for soberness in every sense of the word. He coolly surveyed his present position and his prospects, estimated at their due weight the flatteries bestowed upon him, and prepared, with a full share of the foresight which is generally regarded as a characteristic of Scotsmen, for the struggle which he was to encounter as soon as he should have to apply his literary gains to eking out a livelihood. The traditions of Edinburgh supply no evidence that sheer bacchanalianism was ever indulged in by Burns. Every insinuation of such a nature, when carefully inquired into, vanishes into air. Dugald Stewart, writing with reference to the summer of 1787, says: 'Notwithstanding various reports I heard during the preceding winter of Burns's predilection for convivial and not very select society, I should have concluded in favour of his habits of sobriety from all of him that fell under my own observation. He told me, indeed, himself that the weakness of his stomach was such as to deprive him entirely of any merit in his temperance.' The allusion to 'not very select society' looks at first somewhat startling; but it should be borne in mind that Stewart, who lived a quiet academic life, would be apt to lump with the plebeian and coarse men who were far from being either vicious or of inferior social position to himself. He probably alludes to such men as Smellie, Dunbar, William Nicol of the High School, Alexander Cunningham, and others, who, though not members of Professor Stewart's 'set,' and though perhaps of somewhat convivial habits, were yet men of honourable character and respectable standing in Edinburgh. Amongst them Burns felt himself at home. He found in them kindliness and good-humour, rollicking joviality, not a little wit and cleverness, and a hearty appreciation of his own talents. It is not surprising that he entered into and enjoyed their society. There is, however, no reason to believe that Burns was thus exposed to any demoralising influence but what would have been found in middle-class society in every country town in Scotland.

Josiah Walker, who saw Burns frequently at this period, is

entitled to be heard upon this subject. After remarking that
Burns, in good society, never struggled to put on for a moment a
better manner than was natural to him, he goes on to say :
'Though he took his full share in conversation, not only from a
perception that it was expected, but from a consciousness that it
would gratify expectation, yet he did so in a manner that was
dignified and manly, and altogether remote from petulant vanity
or offensive exultation in an importance so new to him. His
deportment was plain without vulgarity, and though it had little
softness, and showed him ready to repel any insult with decision
at least, if not with roughness, yet he soon made it evident that
those who behaved to him with propriety were in no danger of
any unprovoked or boorish rudeness.'

Walker first met Burns at breakfast in Dr Blacklock's house.
'I was not much struck with his first appearance, as I had previously heard it described. His person, though strong and well
knit, and much superior to what might be expected in a ploughman,
was still rather coarse in its outline. His stature, from want of
setting up, appeared to be only of the middle size, but was rather
above it. His motions were firm and decided, and though without
any pretensions to grace, were at the same time so free from
clownish constraint, as to show that he had not always been confined to the society of his profession. His countenance was not of
that elegant cast which is most frequent among the upper ranks,
but it was manly and intelligent, and marked by a thoughtful
gravity which shaded at times into sternness. In his large, dark
eye the most striking index of his genius resided. It was full of
mind, and would have been singularly expressive, under the
management of one who could employ it with more art, for the
purpose of expression.

'He was plainly, but properly dressed, in a style midway
between the holiday-costume of a farmer and that of the company
with which he now associated. His black hair, without powder,
at a time when it was very generally worn, was tied behind, and
spread upon his forehead. Upon the whole, from his person,
physiognomy, and dress, had I met him near a seaport, and been
required to guess his condition, I should have probably conjectured
him to be the master of a merchant-vessel of the most respectable
class.

'In no part of his manner was there the slightest degree of affectation; nor could a stranger have suspected, from anything in his behaviour or conversation, that he had been for some months the favourite of all the fashionable circles of a metropolis.

'In conversation he was powerful. His conceptions and expression were of corresponding vigour, and on all subjects were as remote as possible from commonplaces. Though somewhat authoritative, it was in a way which gave little offence, and was readily imputed to his inexperience in those modes of smoothing dissent and softening assertion which are important characteristics of polished manners. After breakfast, I requested him to communicate some of his unpublished pieces. . . . I paid particular attention to his recitation, which was plain, slow, articulate, and forcible, but without any eloquence or art. He did not always lay the emphasis with propriety, nor did he humour the sentiment by the variations of his voice. He was standing, during the time, with his face towards the window, to which, and not to his auditors, he directed his eye; thus depriving himself of any additional effect which the language of his composition might have borrowed from the language of his countenance. In this he resembled the generality of singers in ordinary company, who, to shun any charge of affectation, withdraw all meaning from their features, and lose the advantage by which vocal performers on the stage augment the impression and give energy to the sentiment of the song.

'The day after my first introduction to Burns, I supped in company with him at Dr Blair's. The other guests were very few, and as each had been invited chiefly to have an opportunity of meeting with the poet, the doctor endeavoured to draw him out, and to make him the central figure of the group. Though he therefore furnished the greatest proportion of the conversation, he did no more than what he saw evidently was expected. Men of genius have often been taxed with a proneness to commit blunders in company, from that ignorance or negligence of the laws of conversation which must be imputed to the absorption of their thoughts in a favourite subject, or to the want of that daily practice in attending to the petty modes of behaviour which is incompatible with a studious life. From singularities of this sort Burns was unusually free; yet on the present occasion he made a more

awkward slip than any that are reported of the poets or mathe-
maticians most noted for absence. Being asked from which of the
public places he had received the greatest gratification, he named
the High Church, but gave the preference as a preacher to the
colleague* of our worthy entertainer, whose celebrity rested on his
pulpit eloquence, in a tone so pointed and decisive as to throw the
whole company into the most foolish embarrassment. The doctor,
indeed, with becoming self-command, endeavoured to relieve the
rest by cordially seconding the encomium so injudiciously introduced; but this did not prevent the conversation from labouring
under that compulsory effort which was unavoidable, while the
thoughts of all were full of the only subject on which it was
improper to speak. Of this blunder Burns must instantly have
been aware, but he shewed the return of good sense by making no
attempt to repair it. His secret mortification was indeed so great
that he never mentioned the circumstance until many years after,
when he told me that his silence had proceeded from the pain
which he felt in recalling it to his memory.'

Only one fault of manner has been charged against Burns at
this period, and it was one that he never got rid of—and, perhaps,
never seriously tried to get rid of. Like Carlyle, in many respects
his successor, he was prone to give his opinion on any subject
under discussion with more decision than was consistent with
conventional politeness. The greatest breach of decorum which
has been laid to his charge is recorded by Cromek. It has often
been brought forward as characteristic of Burns at this period,
with as much justice one might ascribe bad temper to a man
who once gives way to passion : 'At a private breakfast-party, in a
literary circle of Edinburgh,† the conversation turned on the
poetical merit and pathos of Gray's "Elegy," a poem of which he
was enthusiastically fond. A clergyman present,‡ remarkable for

---

* The Rev. William Greenfield already alluded to.

† This incident, which is now fully told in the biography of Burns for the first time,
occurred at the house of Alexander Christison, one of the teachers of the High School. He
was born about 1753; educated at a parish school in Berwickshire; became a schoolmaster;
in 1785 was appointed Master in the High School of Edinburgh, from which, in 1806, he
obtained the professorship of Humanity in the University. This post he held till his death
in 1820. He is said to have been a 'most conscientious professor.' One of his sons was Sir
Robert Christison, the eminent physician, chemist, and professor of Medical Jurisprudence
and Materia Medica.

‡ Said to have been the Rev. William Robb, minister of Tongland, Kirkcudbrightshire,
from 1769 to his death in 1797.

his love of paradox and for his eccentric notions upon every subject, distinguished himself by an injudicious and ill-timed attack on this exquisite poem, which Burns, with generous warmth for the reputation of Gray, manfully defended. As the gentleman's remarks were rather general than specific, Burns urged him to bring forward the passages which he thought exceptionable. He made several attempts to quote the poem, but always in a blundering, inaccurate manner. Burns bore all this for a good while with his usual good-natured forbearance, till at length, goaded by the fastidious criticisms and wretched quibblings of his opponent, he roused himself, and with an eye flashing contempt and indignation, and with great vehemence of gesticulation, he thus addressed the cold critic : " Sir, I now perceive a man may be an excellent judge of poetry by square and rule, and after all be a d—— blockhead !" ' A man of warm and sensitive nature might on occasion be goaded into an outburst of this kind ; but that is a totally different thing from a habit of outraging propriety in conversation. Besides, Cromek has omitted to tell the whole of the story that has been so often quoted to Burns's discredit. Mrs Christison, beside whom he was sitting, had an infant upon her knee. Immediately after crushing the clergyman, he turned to the child and said softly, ' I beg your pardon, my little dear.'

Amongst those of Burns's contemporaries who have recorded their views of him as he appeared at this time is Dugald Stewart. ' The attentions he received during his stay in town from all ranks and descriptions of persons, were such as would have turned any head but his own. I cannot say that I could perceive any unfavourable effect which they left on his mind. He retained the same simplicity of manners and appearance which had struck me so forcibly when I first saw him in the country ; nor did he seem to feel any additional self-importance from the number and rank of his new acquaintance. His dress was perfectly suited to his station—plain and unpretending, with a sufficient attention to neatness.

' The variety of his engagements, while in Edinburgh, prevented me from seeing him so often as I could have wished. In the course of the spring he called on me once or twice, at my request, early in the morning, and walked with me to Braid Hills, in the neighbourhood of the town, when he charmed me still more by his private conversation than he had ever done in company. He was passionately fond of the beauties of nature ; and I recollect once he told me, when I was admiring a distant prospect in one of our morning walks, that the sight of so many smoking cottages gave a pleasure to his mind, which none could understand who had not witnessed, like himself, the happiness and the worth which they contained.

'In his political principles he was then a Jacobite : which was perhaps owing partly to this, that his father was originally from the estate of Lord Marischal. Indeed he did not appear to have thought much on such subjects, nor very consistently. He had a very strong sense of religion, and expressed deep regret at the levity with which he had heard it treated occasionally in some convivial meetings which he frequented. I speak of him as he was in the winter of 1786–7 ; for afterwards we met but seldom, and our conversations turned chiefly on his literary projects or his private affairs.

'I do not recollect whether it appears or not from any of your letters to me that you had ever seen Burns. If you have, it is superfluous for me to add, that the idea which his conversation conveyed of the powers of his mind, exceeded, if possible, that which is suggested by his writings. Among the poets whom I have happened to know, I have been struck, in more than one instance, with the unaccountable disparity between their general talents and the occasional inspirations of their more favoured moments. But all the faculties of Burns's mind were, as far as I could judge, equally vigorous ; and his predilection for poetry was rather the result of his own enthusiastic and impassioned temper, than of a genius exclusively adapted to that species of composition. From his conversation, I should have pronounced him to be fitted to excel in whatever walk of ambition he had chosen to exert his abilities.

'Among the subjects on which he was accustomed to dwell, the characters of the individuals with whom he happened to meet was plainly a favourite one. The remarks he made on them were always shrewd and pointed, though frequently inclining too much to sarcasm. His praise of those he loved was sometimes indiscriminate and extravagant ; but this, I suspect, proceeded rather from the caprice and humour of the moment, than from the effects of attachment in blinding his judgment. His wit was ready, and always impressed with the marks of a vigorous understanding ; but, to my taste, not often pleasing or happy.'

Mrs Alison Cockburn,* the authoress (1765) of one of the two exquisite versions of 'The Flowers of the Forest,' and for sixty years one of the acknowledged 'queens of Edinburgh society,' has thus told what she saw and heard of Burns : †

The town is at present (December 1786) agog with the ploughman poet, who receives adulation with native dignity, and is the very figure of his profession, strong and coarse, but has a most enthusiastic heart of love. He has seen Duchess Gordon and all the gay world : his favourite for looks and manners is Bess Burnet—no bad judge, indeed.

. . . .

Sorry I am my poems are not returned from niece Scott, though she promised them this week. I would have been glad to oblige Miss Douglas with them. The one I admire most is the 'Cottar's Saturday Night.' The man will be spoiled, if he can spoil ; but he keeps his simple manners, and is quite sober. No doubt he will be at the Hunters' Ball to-morrow, which has made all women and milliners mad. Not a gauze-cap under two guineas—many ten, twelve.

Andrew Dalzel, professor of Greek in Edinburgh University,‡ also recorded his impressions of Burns in a letter to Sir Robert Liston, January 25, 1787 :

. . . We have got a poet in town just now, whom everybody is taking notice of—a ploughman from Ayrshire—a man of unquestionable genius, who has produced admirable verses, mostly in the Scottish dialect, though some of them are nearly in English. He is a fellow of strong common sense, and by his own industry has read a good deal of English, both prose and verse. The first edition of his poems was published at Kilmarnock, and sold in that part of the country very soon, insomuch that they are now not to be got. I, among others, have seen them, and admire some of them exceedingly. A new edition of them is now in the

---

* Mrs Cockburn was the daughter of Robert Rutherford of Fairnilee, Selkirkshire, and born in 1713. In 1731 she married Patrick Cockburn, an advocate, who died in 1753. She herself died in 1795. Nine years before she met Burns, she had pronounced Walter Scott to be 'the most extraordinary genius of a boy.'

† From letters in *The Songstresses of Scotland*, by Sarah Tytler [Henrietta Keddie] and Jean L. Watson (2 vols., Edinburgh, 1871).

‡ *Memoirs of Andrew Dalzel, Professor of Greek in the University of Edinburgh.* By Cosmo Innes (Edinburgh, 1861). Andrew Dalzel, born in 1742 at Gateside of Newliston, Linlithgowshire, was professor of Greek in the University of Edinburgh for thirty-four years, 1772-1806. In 1785 he was appointed librarian to the University. This position offered special facilities to him in his compilation of a History of that University. The work, however, was never completed : the incomplete work was issued in 1862. Dalzel died in 1806.

press here, and he is encouraged by a most numerous subscription. It is thought he will get some hundred pounds by it, which will enable him to take a small farm. He runs the risk, however, of being spoiled by the excessive attention paid him just now by persons of all ranks. Those who know him best, say he has too much good sense to allow himself to be spoiled. Everybody is fond of showing him everything here that the place furnishes. I saw him at an assembly t'other night. The Duchess of Gordon and other ladies of rank took notice of him there. He behaves wonderfully well; very independent in his sentiments, and has none of the *mauvaise honte* about him, though he is not forward.

Walter Scott was in 1787 a boy of sixteen; but, while still condemned to task-work in his father's office, he was endowed by nature with the feelings which qualified him to appreciate the society of Burns. He had read the poetry, and he ardently desired to see the poet. An opportunity was at length furnished when Burns came to the house of Dr Adam Ferguson,* whose eldest son (afterwards Sir Adam Ferguson) was Scott's intimate friend and companion. He subsequently communicated an account of the meeting to Lockhart : ' Of course,' says he, ' we youngsters sat silent, looked, and listened. The only thing I remember which was remarkable in Burns's manner, was the effect produced upon him by a print of Bunbury's,† representing a soldier lying dead on the snow, his dog sitting in misery on one side—on the other his widow, with a child in her arms. These lines were written underneath :

> Cold on Canadian hills, or Minden's plain,
> Perhaps that parent wept her soldier slain—
> Bent o'er her babe, her eye dissolved in dew,
> The big drops mingling with the milk he drew,
> Gave the sad presage of his future years,
> The child of misery baptised in tears.

Burns seemed much affected by the print, or rather the ideas which it suggested to his mind. He actually shed tears. He asked whose the lines were, and it chanced that nobody but myself remembered that they occur in a half-forgotten poem of Lang-

---

* Adam Ferguson, born at Logierait, Perthshire, in 1724; appointed professor of Natural Philosophy in Edinburgh University in 1759; appointed professor of Moral Philosophy in 1764; published *Essay on Civil Society* in 1767, and *History of the Roman Republic* in 1783; died at St Andrews in 1816.

† This identical print is now in the Museum of the Chambers Institution, Peebles.

horne's, called by the unpromising title of the "Justice of Peace."*
I whispered my information to a friend present, who mentioned
it to Burns, who rewarded me with a look and a word which,
though in mere civility, I then received, and still recollect, with
great pleasure. His person was strong and robust; his manners
rustic, not clownish; a sort of dignified plainness and simplicity,
which received part of its effect perhaps from one's knowledge of
his extraordinary talents. His features are represented in Mr
Nasmyth's picture; but to me it conveys the idea that they are
diminished, as if seen in perspective. I think his countenance
was more massive than it looks in any of the portraits. I would
have taken the poet, had I not known what he was, for a very
sagacious country farmer of the old Scotch school; that is, none
of your modern agriculturists, who keep labourers for their
drudgery, but the *douce guidman* who held his own plough. There
was a strong expression of sense and shrewdness in all his linea-
ments: the eye alone, I think, indicated the poetical character

* Langhorne wrote 'The Country Justice,' a poem in three parts, at the request of
Richard Burn, author of a well-known work on the duties of a justice-of-peace. The
dedication to Burn is dated 1774. Here are some of the best lines in the poem:

'Be this, ye rural magistrates, your plan:
    Firm be your justice, but be friends to man. . . .
Frail in his genius, in his heart too frail,
Born but to err, and erring to bewail,
Shalt thou his faults with eye severe explore,
And give to life one human weakness more?

Still mark if vice or nature prompts the deed;
Still mark the strong temptation and the need;
On pressing want, on famine's powerful call,
At least more lenient let thy justice fall.

For him who, lost to every hope of life,
Has long with fortune held unequal strife,
Known to no human love, no human care,
The friendless, homeless object of despair;
For the poor vagrant feel, while he complains,
Nor from sad freedom send to sadder chains.
Alike if folly or misfortune brought
Those last of woes his evil days have wrought;
Believe with social misery and with me,
Folly's misfortune in the first degree.

Perhaps on some inhospitable shore
The houseless wretch a widowed parent bore;
Who, then no more by golden prospects led,
Of the poor Indian begged a leafy bed,
Cold on Canadian hills,' &c.

and temperament. It was large, and of a cast which glowed (I
say literally *glowed*) when he spoke with feeling or interest. I
never saw such another eye in a human head, though I have seen
the most distinguished men of my time. His conversation expressed perfect self-confidence, without the slightest presumption.
Among the men who were the most learned of their time and
country, he expressed himself with perfect firmness, but without
the least intrusive forwardness ; and when he differed in opinion,
he did not hesitate to express it firmly, yet at the same time with
modesty. * * * I have only to add, that his dress corresponded
with his manner. He was like a farmer dressed in his best to
dine with the laird. I do not speak *in malam partem*, when I
say I never saw a man in company with his superiors in station
and information, more perfectly free from either the reality or the
affectation of embarrassment. I was told, but did not observe it,
that his address to females was extremely deferential, and always
with a turn either to the pathetic or humorous, which engaged
their attention particularly. I have heard the Duchess of Gordon
remark this.'

Sir Adam Ferguson * also supplied some particulars of this visit
of Burns to his father's house. 'It was the custom of Dr Ferguson
to have a conversazione at his house in the Sheens (Sciennes Hill
House) once a week for his principal literary friends. Professor
Stewart on this occasion offered to bring Burns, and Dr Ferguson
readily assented. The poet found himself in the most brilliant
literary society which Edinburgh then contained. Black, Hutton,
and John Home were amongst those present. Adam had himself
brought his young friend Walter Scott, as yet unnoted by his
seniors. Burns seemed at first little inclined to mingle easily in
the company ; he went round the room, looking at the pictures on
the walls. The print described by Scott arrested his attention ;
he read aloud the lines underneath, but before he reached the
end his voice faltered, and his eye filled with tears. A little
after, he turned with much interest to the company, pointed to
the picture, and with some eagerness asked if any one could tell
him who had written those affecting lines. The philosophers were

* Eldest son of Professor Adam Ferguson ; born in 1771 ; entered the army in 1800 ;
served with Wellington in the Peninsula ; taken prisoner in 1812, and released in 1818 ; settled
at Huntly Burn, near Abbotsford ; appointed deputy-keeper of Scottish regalia ; knighted
by George IV. in 1822 ; died in Edinburgh, 1854.

silent; no one knew: but, after a decent interval, the pale lame boy near by said in a negligent manner: "They 're written by one Langhorne." An explanation of the place where they occur followed, and Burns fixed a look of half-serious interest on the youth, while he said: "You 'll be a man yet, sir." ' Scott may be said to have derived literary ordination from Burns.*

In this memorable spring Burns commenced a second Commonplace Book.†

EDINR., *April ninth*, 1787.

As I have seen a good deal of human life in Edinr., a great many characters which are new to one bred up in the shades of life as I have been, I am determined to take down my remarks on the spot. Gray observes in a letter of his to Mr Palgrave, that 'Half a word fixed upon or near the spot, is worth a cart-load of recollection.'‡ I don't know how it is with the world in general, but with me, making remarks is by no means a solitary pleasure. I want some one to laugh with me, some one to be grave with me; some one to please me and help my discrimination with his or her own remark, and at times, no doubt, to admire my acuteness and penetration. The World are so busied with selfish pursuits, ambition, vanity, interest or pleasure, that very few think it worth their while to make any observation on what passes around them;

---

* Scott relates elsewhere that the house of Dr Ferguson, 'while he continued to reside in Edinburgh, was a general point of reunion among his friends, particularly of a Sunday, where there generally met, at a hospitable dinner-party, the most distinguished literati of the old time who still remained, with such young persons as were thought worthy to approach their circle, and listen to their conversation. The place of his residence was an insulated house at some distance from the town, which its visitors (notwithstanding its internal comforts) chose to call for that reason Kamtschatka.'—*Quarterly Review*, xxxvi., 197. This house formed part of a street called *Sciennes*, or *the Sheens*, from its proximity to the remains of an ancient monastery dedicated to St Catherine of Sienna. It stood at the south end of the street, on the east side, with its gable facing along a lane. It was in a room upstairs, now used as a bedroom, that Burns met Scott.

Somewhat oddly, the name 'LANGHORNE' is quoted at the bottom of the lines in the copy of the print which affected Burns, but in so small a character that the poet must have failed to catch it.

† It is a post-folio manuscript book, 13¼ inches long by 8¼ broad, containing 240 pages of unglazed, rather strong writing-paper, bound in half-calf. It is marked on the paper board outside with a large A, as if intended to be the first of a series. The book is in almost perfect condition. Under the price-mark, 4s. 3d., which occurs in the left top corner of the cover, Burns has written,

'R. Burns was born 25th Jan. 1759.
See this Book, pa. 3, note.'

The volume, which was long in the possession of Mr Alexander Macmillan, publisher, London, is supposed to have been presented by Burns to Mrs Dunlop in the year 1788. It was first printed in its entirety by Professor Jack (of Glasgow University), in *Macmillan's Magazine* (vols. xxxix-xl., 1878–79).

‡ Letter from Thomas Gray to William Palgrave, dated [from Stoke] September 6, 1758.

except where that observation is a sucker or branch of the darling
plant they are rearing in their fancy.   Nor am I sure, notwithstanding
all the sentimental flights of Novel-writers and the sage philosophy of
Moralists, if we are capable of so intimate and cordial a coalition of
friendship as that one of us may pour out his bosom, his every thought
and floating fancy, his very inmost soul, with unreserved confidence, to
another, without hazard of losing part of that respect man demands from
man ; or, from the unavoidable imperfections attending human nature,
of one day repenting his confidence.

For these reasons, I am determined to make these pages my Con-
fidante.   I will sketch every character that anyway strikes me, to the
best of my observation, with unshrinking justice; I will insert anecdotes,
and take down remarks, in the old law phrase, without feud or favor :
where I hit on any thing clever, my own applause will, in some measure,
feast my vanity ; and (begging Patroclus' and Achates's pardon) I think
a lock and key a security at least equal to the bosom of any friend
whatever.

My own private story likewise, my amours, my rambles, the smiles
and frowns of Fortune on my Bardship, my Poems and fragments that
must never see the light, shall be occasionally inserted : in short, never
did four shillings * purchase so much friendship since Confidence went
first to market, or Honesty was set to Sale.

To these seemingly invidious, but too just ideas of human friendship,
I shall chearfully and truly make one exception—the connection between
two persons of different sex, when their interests are united or absorbed
by the sacred tie of Love—

> When thought meets thought ere from the lips it part,
> And each warm wish springs mutual from the heart.

There Confidence, confidence that exalts them the more in one another's
opinion, confidence that endears them the more to one another's heart,
unreservedly and luxuriantly 'reigns and revels.'   But this is not my
lot, and in my situation, if I am wise (which by the by I have no great
chance of being) my fate should be cast with the Psalmist's sparrow,
'To watch alone on the house-tops.'   Oh, the pity ! ! !

A FRAGMENT.

TUNE—*Daintie Davie.*

I.

There was a birkie born in Kyle,   lively fellow
But what na day, o' what na style,
I doubt it 's hardly worth the while
    To be sae nice wi' Davie.

---

* The Poet paid 4s. 3d. for the book.

Leeze me on thy curly pow,*
    Bonie Davie, daintie Davie ;
Leeze me on thy curly pow,
    Thou 'se ay my daintie Davie.†

II.

Our Monarch's hindmost year but ane ‡
Was five an' twenty days begun,
'Twas then a blast o' Janwar win'
    Blew hansel in on Davie.

III.

The Gossip keekit in his loof,	peeped—palm
Quo she, wha lives 'll see the proof,	Quoth
This walie boy will be nae coof,	goodly—fool
I think we 'll ca' him Davie.	call

IV.

He 'll hae misfortunes great an' sma',	
But ay a heart aboon them a' ;	above
He 'll gie his Daddie's name a blaw,	
We 'll a' be proud o' Davie.	

V.

But sure as three times three maks nine,	
I see by ilka score an' line	every
This chap will dearly like our kin',	fellow—kind, sex
So leeze me on thee, Davie.	

VI.

Guid faith, quo she, I doubt you, Sir,	
Ye 'll gar the lasses lie aspar ;	make
But twenty fauts ye may hae waur,	faults—worse
So blessins on thee, Davie.§	

---

* 'Leeze me :' an expression of affection = Dear to me is thy curly head.
† Thou 'se (idiom) = Thou is (art) or Thou shalt be.
‡ For explanations of the allusions in this poem, see Vol. I., p. 126.
§ Cf. this version, written two years after the immortal ' There was a Lad,' with the popular version in Vol. I., p. 136.

There are few of the sore evils under the sun give me more uneasiness and chagrin than the comparison how a man of genius, nay, avowed worth, is everywhere received, with the reception which a meer ordinary character, decorated with the trappings and futile distinctions of Fortune, meets. Imagine a man of abilities, his breast glowing with honest pride, conscious that men are born equal, still giving that 'honor to whom honor is due;' he meets at a Great man's table a Squire Something, or a Sir Somebody; he knows the noble landlord at heart gives the Bard or whatever he is a share of his good wishes beyond any at table perhaps, yet how will it mortify him to see a fellow whose abilities would scarcely have made an eight penny taylor, and whose heart is not worth three farthings, meet with attention and notice that are forgot to the Son of Genius and Poverty?

The noble Glencairn has wounded me to the soul here, because I dearly esteem, respect and love him. He showed so much attention, engrossing attention, one day, to the only blockhead, as there was none but his lordship, the Dunderpate and myself, that I was within half a point of throwing down my gage of contemptuous defiance, but he shook my hand and looked so benevolently good at parting—God bless him, though I should never see him more, I shall love him untill my dying day! I am pleased to think I am so capable of the throes of gratitude, as I am miserably defficient in some other virtues. With Dr Blair I am more at ease. I never respect him with humble veneration; but when he kindly interests himself in my welfare, or, still more, when he descends from his pinnacle and meets me on equal ground, my heart overflows with what is called *liking:* when he neglects me for the meer carcase of Greatness, or when his eye measures the difference of our points of elevation, I say to myself with scarcely an emotion, what do I care for him or his pomp either?

It is not easy forming an exact judging judgement of any one, but in my opinion Dr Blair is meerly an astonishing proof what industry and application can do.* Natural parts like his are frequently to be met with; his vanity is proverbially known among his acquaintances; but he is justly at the head of what may be called fine writing; and a Critic of the first, the very first rank in Prose; even in Poesy a good Bard of Nature's making can only take the pas of him. He has a heart, not of the finest water, but far from being an ordinary one. In short, he is [a] truly worthy and most respectable character.

Mr Greenfield is of a superiour order. The bleedings of humanity, the generous resolve, a manly disregard of the paltry subjects of vanity, virgin modesty, the truest taste, and a very sound judgement, char-

---

* Hugh Blair, born in Edinburgh in 1718; educated for the ministry of the Church of Scotland, and licensed to preach in 1741; held in succession the charges of Collessie in Fife, the Canongate, and Lady Yester's; became in 1758 one of the ministers of the High Church; appointed in 1762 to the new chair of Rhetoric in Edinburgh University; obtained a pension of £200 a year from George II.; published the first of a series of volumes of Sermons in 1777, and Lectures on Rhetoric in 1783; died December 27, 1800.

acterize him. His being the first Speaker I ever heard is perhaps half owing to industry. He certainly possesses no small share of poetic abilities; he is a steady, most disinterested friend, without the least affectation of seeming so; and as a companion, his good sense, his joyous hilarity, his sweetness of manners and modesty, are most engagingly charming.

The most perfect character I ever saw is Mr Stuart [Dugald Stewart]. An exalted judge of the human heart, and of composition. One of the very first public speakers; and equally capable of generosity as humanity. His principal discriminating feature is; from a mixture of benevolence, strength of mind and manly dignity, he not only at heart values, but in his deportment and address bears himself to all the Actors, high and low, in the drama of Life, simply as they merit in playing their parts. Wealth, honors, all that is extraneous of the man, have no more influence with him than they will have at the Last Day. His wit, in the hour of social hilarity, proceeds almost to good-natured waggishness; and in telling a story he particularly excels.

The next I shall mention, my worthy Bookseller, Mr C[reech] is a strange multiform character. His ruling passions of the left hand kind are extreme vanity, and something of the more harmless modifications of selfishness. The one, mixed, as it often is, with great goodness of heart, makes him rush into all public matters, and take every instance of unprotected merit by the hand, provided it is in his power to hand it into public notice; the other quality makes him, amid all the embarras in which his vanity entangles him, now and then to cast half a squint at his own interest. His parts as a man, his deportment as a gentleman, and his abilities as a scholar are much above mediocrity. Of all the Edinr. literati and wit he writes the most like a gentleman. He does not awe you with the profoundness of the philosopher, or strike your eye with the soarings of genius; but he pleases you with the handsome turn of his expression, and the polite ease of his paragraph. His social demeanour and powers, particularly at his own table, are the most engaging I have ever met with. On the whole he is, as I said before, a multiform, but an exceedingly respectable, worthy character.*

Amongst the men whom Burns had met and liked at the meetings of the Canongate Kilwinning Lodge was William Woods,† an actor so popular as to be termed 'the Scottish Roscius.' This explains a

---

* Compare the 'Epistle to William Creech,' written May 13th, 1787, *infra*.

† William Woods (*circa* 1751–1802) first appeared on the stage (the Haymarket, Edinburgh, according to one biographer, the Haymarket, London, according to another) in 1771. His career was almost entirely confined to the Scottish capital, he having been a member of the Edinburgh Company of Players for thirty-one years. He was an intimate friend of Robert Fergusson, and is said to have regularly taken him into the theatre and given him a free seat. He retired from the stage in April 1802, and set up as a teacher of elocution. He died in December following, and is buried in Calton Burying-ground.

PROLOGUE SPOKEN BY MR WOODS
ON HIS BENEFIT NIGHT,*

Monday, 16*th April* 1787.

When, by a generous Public's kind acclaim,
That dearest meed is granted—honest fame;
When *here* your favour is the *actor's* lot,
Nor even the *man* in *private life* forgot;
What breast so dead to heav'nly Virtue's glow
But heaves impassion'd with the grateful throe?

    Poor is the task to please a barb'rous throng,†
It needs no Siddons'‡ powers in Southern's song;
But here, an ancient nation fam'd afar,
For genius, learning high, as great in war—
Hail, CALEDONIA, name for ever dear!
Before whose sons I'm honour'd to appear!
Where every science—every noble art
That can inform the mind, or mend the heart,
Is known; as grateful nations oft have found
Far as the rude barbarian marks the bound.

---

* The play on this night was Shakespeare's *The Merry Wives of Windsor.*

† In the original draft of the poem there were given these two variations of the next few lines :

       'Small is the task to please a gaping throng,
       Unmeaning rant, extravagance of song :
       Heavy Stupidity all rueful views
       The Tyburn humours of the tragic Muse,
       Or roars at times the loud, rough laugh between,
       As horse-play nonsense shows her comic scene.
       But here,' &c.

and

       '. . . extravagance of song :
       The vacant, staring eye all rueful views,
       The Tyburn humours of the tragic Muse ;
       Or comic scenes the merry roar engage
       As horse-play nonsense thunders o'er the stage.
       But here,' &c.

‡ Mrs Siddons had made her debût in Edinburgh in 1784. She had returned again in the following year. On both occasions the town was thrown into an extraordinary state of excitement. Mrs Siddons revisited the Scottish capital in July 1788, the first piece in which she played being 'Douglas,' taking the character of Lady Randolph. Her representation of Isabella in 'The Fatal Marriage' of the dramatist 'Honest Tom Southerne' (1660-1746) was very celebrated.

Philosophy,* no idle pedant dream,
Here holds her search by heaven-taught Reason's beam ;
Here History † paints, with elegance and force,
The tide of Empire's fluctuating course ;
Here Douglas ‡ forms wild Shakespeare into plan,
And Harley § rouses all the God in man.
When well-form'd taste and sparkling wit unite
With manly lore, or female beauty bright
(Beauty, where faultless symmetry and grace
Can only charm us in the second place)—
Witness my heart, how oft with panting fear,
As on this night, I 've met these judges here !
But still the hope Experience taught to live,
Equal to judge--you 're candid to forgive.
No hundred-headed Riot here we meet
With decency and law beneath his feet ;
Nor Insolence assumes fair Freedom's name :
Like CALEDONIANS, you applaud or blame.

O Thou dread Power ! whose empire-giving hand
Has oft been stretch'd to shield the honour'd land !
Strong may she glow with all her ancient fire ;
May every son be worthy of his sire ;
Firm may she rise with generous disdain ‖
At Tyranny's, or direr Pleasure's, chain ;
Still self-dependent in her native shore,
Bold may she brave grim Danger's loudest roar,
Till Fate the curtain drop on worlds to be no more.

* In Professors Dugald Stewart of Edinburgh and Thomas Reid of Aberdeen.

† The allusion here is to David Hume and William Robertson.

‡ John Home's 'Douglas,' which was first performed in Edinburgh in 1757.   Here Burns
must be regarded as complimenting the friends of his friends, not as deliberately giving
Home a superior position among dramatists to Shakespeare.

§ Henry Mackenzie's *Man of Feeling.*

‖ In the original draft the closing five lines are as follows :

> 'May never sallow Want her bounty stint,
> Nor selfish maxim dare the sordid hint ;
> But may her virtues ever be her prop ;
> Thou her best stay, and Thou her surest hope,
> Till Fate on worlds the eternal curtain drop.'

CHAPTER II.

THE new edition of the *Poems* appeared on the 21st April, in a handsome octavo volume, price five shillings. Creech's advertisement contained the following note: 'As the book is published for the sole benefit of the author, it is requested that subscribers will send for their copies; and none will be delivered without money.' The Kilmarnock Preface was abandoned, and in its stead appeared a

DEDICATION

TO THE NOBLEMEN AND GENTLEMEN OF THE CALEDONIAN HUNT.

MY LORDS, AND GENTLEMEN—A Scottish Bard, proud of the name, and whose highest ambition is to sing in his Country's service, where shall he so properly look for patronage as to the illustrious Names of his native Land; those who bear the honours and inherit the virtues of their Ancestors? The Poetic Genius of my Country found me as the prophetic bard Elijah did Elisha—at the *plough;* and threw her inspiring mantle over me. She bade me sing the loves, the joys, the rural scenes and rural pleasures of my natal Soil, in my native tongue: I tuned my wild, artless notes, as she inspired. She whispered me to come to this ancient metropolis of Caledonia, and lay my Songs under your honoured protection: I now obey her dictates.

Though much indebted to your goodness, I do not approach you, my Lords and Gentlemen, in the usual style of dedication, to thank you for past favours; that path is so hackneyed by prostituted Learning, that honest Rusticity is ashamed of it. Nor do I present this Address with the venal soul of a servile Author, looking for a continuation of those favours: I was bred to the Plough, and am independent. I come to claim the common Scottish name with you, my illustrious Countrymen;

and to tell the world that I glory in the title. I come to congratulate my Country, that the blood of her ancient heroes still runs uncontaminated; and that from your courage, knowledge, and public spirit, she may expect protection, wealth, and liberty. In the last place, I come to proffer my warmest wishes to the Great Fountain of Honour, the Monarch of the Universe, for your welfare and happiness.

When you go forth to waken the Echoes, in the ancient and favourite amusement of your Forefathers, may Pleasure ever be of your party; and may Social-joy await your return! When harassed in courts or camps with the justlings of bad men and bad measures, may the honest consciousness of injured Worth attend your return to your native Seats; and may Domestic Happiness, with a smiling welcome, meet you at your gates! May Corruption shrink at your kindling indignant glance; and may tyranny in the Ruler and licentiousness in the People equally find you an inexorable foe!

I have the honour to be, With the sincerest gratitude and highest respect, My Lords and Gentlemen, Your most devoted humble servant,

ROBERT BURNS.

EDINBURGH, *April* 4, 1787.

The volume contained another most remarkable document—a list of subscribers extending over thirty-eight pages. Several of Burns's friends had been very active in promoting this subscription, and the terms of praise in which he had been spoken of in various publications had disposed the public to extend its patronage liberally. Fifteen hundred persons subscribed for two thousand eight hundred copies. The Caledonian Hunt headed the list for a hundred copies. Creech took five hundred. Very many of the nobility and gentry, and a great number of the most prominent members of Scottish society figure in the list; in many instances, two, four, or five copies were taken; in some even a larger number. The Earl of Glencairn subscribed for eight copies, the Countess for sixteen, and Lady Elizabeth Cunningham for four. The Duchess of Gordon took twenty-one, and the Earl of Eglintoun forty-two. Robert Muir of Kilmarnock, who had taken seventy-two copies of the earlier edition, was a subscriber for forty of the second; and Archibald Prentice, farmer at Covington-Mains, took twenty. Interspersed with the names of individuals occur those of corporations such as the Scots College at Valladolid, the Scots College at Douay, the Scots College at Paris, the Scots Benedictine Monastery at Ratisbon, and the Scots Benedictine Monastery at Maryborough.

Although Burns is not commonly spoken of as a good man of business, he had friends who looked after his interests, and insisted that Creech should pay him a lump sum for the property of his *Poems*. It is evident from the following document that Henry Mackenzie took a leading part in the negotiations on this point, which, though they began before the new edition was out, were not completed—much to Burns's annoyance, as will subsequently be seen—till near the end of October.

17*th April* 1787.—MEMORANDUM OF AGREEMENT betwixt Mr Creech and Mr Burns, respecting the property of Mr Burns's *Poems*.

By advice of friends, Mr Burns having resolved to dispose of the property of his *Poems*, and having consulted with Mr Henry M'Kenzie upon the subject, Mr Creech met with Mr Burns at Mr M'Kenzie's house upon Tuesday, the 17th April 1787, in the evening, and they three having retired and conversed upon the subject, Mr Burns and Mr Creech referred the sum, to be named by Mr M'Kenzie, as being well acquainted with matters of this kind, when Mr M'Kenzie said he thought Mr Burns should have a hundred guineas for the property of his *Poems*.

Mr Creech said that he agreed to the proposal, but as Scotland was now amply supplied with the very numerous edition now printed, he could write to Mr Caddell of London, to know if he would take a share of the Book, but at any rate Mr Burns should have the money named by Mr M'Kenzie, which Mr Burns most cordially agreed to, and to make over the property upon these terms, whenever Mr Creech required him.

Upon Monday the 23d of April 1787, Mr Creech informed Mr Burns that he had remained in Town expecting Mr Caddell's answer, for three days, as to his taking a share of the property of the *Poems*; but that he had received no answer; yet he would, as formerly proposed and agreed to, take the whole upon himself, that Mr Burns might be at no uncertainty in the matter.

Upon this, both parties considered the transaction as finished.

EDINBURGH, Oct. 23d, 1787.

On demand I promise to pay Mr Robert Burns, or Order, One Hundred Guineas, value received.   WILLIAM CREECH.

Received the contents—May 30, 1788.   ROBERT BURNS.

TO JOHN BALLANTINE, ESQ., AYR.

SIR—I have taken the liberty to send a hundred copies of my book to your care. I trouble you then, Sir, to find a proper person, of the mercantile folks I suppose will be best, that for a moderate consideration will retail the books to subscribers as they are called for. Several of the Subscription bills have been mislaid, so all who say they have subscribed must be served at subscription price; otherwise, those who have not subscribed must pay six shillings. Should more copies be needed, an order by post will be immediately answered.

My respectful Compliments to Mr Aiken. I wrote him by David Shaw, which I hope he received.

I have the honor to be, with the most grateful sincerity, Sir, your oblidged and very humble servt., ROBERT BURNS.

EDINR., 18th April 1787.

TO MR GEORGE REID, BARQUHARIE,
WITH A PARCEL,
CARE OF WM. RONALD, TOBACCONIST, MAUCHLINE.

MY DEAR SIR—The fewer words I can tell my story in, so much the better, as I am in an unco tirryfyke * of a hurry.

I have sent two copies of my book to you; one of them as a present to yourself, or rather, to your wife, the other present in my name to Miss Jenny. It goes to my heart that time does not allow me to make some very fine turned periods on the occasion, as I generally like pretty well to hear myself speak; at least, fully as well as anybody else.

Tell Miss Jenny that I had wrote her a long letter, wherein I had taken to pieces rt. Honorables, Honorables, and Reverends not a few; but it, with many more of my written things were stolen from my room, which terrified me from ' scanding my lips in ither folk's kail ' again. By good luck, the fellow † is gone to Gibraltar, and I trust in heaven he will go to the bottom for his pains. I will write you by post when I leave Auld Reekie, which will be in about ten days.

ROBT. BURNS.

EDINBURGH, 19th April 1787.

TO DR MOORE.

EDINBURGH, 23d April 1787.

I RECEIVED the books, and sent the one you mentioned to Mrs Dunlop. I am ill-skilled in beating the coverts of imagination for metaphors of gratitude. I thank you, sir, for the honor you have done me; and to my latest hour will warmly remember it. To be highly pleased with

---

* Passion or agony.

† The thief was not traced. According to tradition, he was a carpenter in Leith, a friend of Burns, and in the habit of calling upon him. He had enlisted, hence Burns's allusion to his having ' gone to Gibraltar.' Possibly also the story, as told by Burns, is one of the mystifications in which he occasionally indulged.

your book is what I have in common with the world; but to regard these volumes as a mark of the author's friendly esteem, is a still more supreme gratification.

I leave Edinburgh in the course of ten days or a fortnight, and, after a few pilgrimages over some of the classic ground of Caledonia, *Cowden Knowes, Banks of Yarrow, Tweed, &c.*, I shall return to my rural shades, in all likelihood never more to quit them. I have formed many intimacies and friendships here, but I am afraid they are all of too tender a construction to bear carriage a hundred and fifty miles. To the rich, the great, the fashionable, the polite, I have no equivalent to offer; and I am afraid my meteor appearance will by no means entitle me to a settled correspondence with any of you, who are the permanent lights of genius and literature.

My most respectful compliments to Miss Williams. If once this tangent flight of mine were over, and I were returned to my wonted leisurely motion in my old circle, I may probably endeavour to return her poetic compliment in kind.   ROBT. BURNS.

The answer of Dr Moore was as follows:

DEAR SIR—I had the pleasure of your letter by Mr Creech, and soon after he sent me the new edition of your *Poems*. You seem to think it incumbent on you to send to each subscriber a number of copies proportionate to his subscription money, but you may depend upon it, few subscribers expect more than one copy, whatever they subscribed; I must inform you, however, that I took twelve copies for those subscribers, for whose money you were so accurate as to send me a receipt, and Lord Eglintoun told me he had sent for six copies for himself, as he wished to give five of them in presents.

Some of the poems you have added in this last edition are very beautiful, particularly the 'Winter Night,' the 'Address to Edinburgh,' 'Green grow the Rashes,' and the two songs immediately following: the latter of which is exquisite.* By the way, I imagine you have a peculiar talent for such compositions, which you ought to indulge. No kind of poetry demands more delicacy or higher polishing. Horace is more admired on account of his Odes than all his other writings. But nothing now added is equal to your 'Vision' and 'Cotter's Saturday Night.' In these are united fine imagery, natural and pathetic description, with sublimity of language and thought. It is evident that you already possess a great variety of expression and command of the English language, you ought, therefore, to deal more sparingly, for the future, in the provincial dialect—why should you, by using *that*, limit the number of your admirers to those who understand the Scottish, when you can extend it to all persons of taste who understand the English

---

* 'The Gloomy Night is gath'ring fast.'

language? In my opinion, you should plan some larger work than any you have as yet attempted. I mean, reflect upon some proper subject, and arrange the plan in your mind, without beginning to execute any part of it till you have studied most of the best English poets, and read a little more of history. The Greek and Roman stories you can read in some abridgment, and soon become master of the most brilliant facts, which must highly delight a poetical mind. You *should* also, and very soon *may*, become master of the heathen mythology, to which there are everlasting allusions in all the poets, and which in itself is charmingly fanciful. What will require to be studied with more attention, is modern history: that is, the history of France and Great Britain, from the beginning of Henry the Seventh's reign. I know very well you have a mind capable of attaining knowledge by a shorter process than is commonly used, and I am certain you are capable of making a better use of it, when attained, than is generally done.

I beg you will not give yourself the trouble of writing to me when it is *inconvenient*, and make no apology when you do write for having postponed it—be assured of this, however, that I shall always be happy to hear from you. I think my friend, Mr ——, told me that you had some poems in manuscript by you, of a satirical and humorous nature (in which, by the way, I think you very strong), which your prudent friends prevailed on you to omit, particularly one called ‘Somebody's Confession;’* if you will intrust me with a sight of any of these, I will pawn my word to give no copies, and will be obliged to you for a perusal of them.

I understand you intend to take a farm, and make the useful and respectable business of husbandry your chief occupation: this, I hope, will not prevent your making occasional addresses to the nine ladies who have shewn you such favour, one of whom visited you in the ‘auld clay biggin.’ Virgil, before you, proved to the world that there is nothing in the business of husbandry inimical to poetry; and I sincerely hope that you may afford an example of a good poet being a successful farmer. I fear it will not be in my power to visit Scotland this season; when I do, I shall endeavour to find you out, for I heartily wish to see and converse with you. If ever your occasions call you to this place, I make no doubt of your paying me a visit, and you may depend on a very cordial welcome from this family. I am, Dear Sir, Your friend and obedient servant, J. MOORE.

The following letter reveals a strong feature in Burns's character. Mrs Dunlop had sent him a letter of comment on his volume, particularly dwelling with regret on the reprinting of ‘The Dream,’ which she conceived to be likely to damage the poet at court, if his fame should ever extend thither. His reply

* No doubt ‘Holy Willie's Prayer.’

shows that, while good-natured and complaisant up to a certain point with friendly critics, he could also stand firm to any position he had once taken up.

EXTRACT FROM A LETTER TO MRS DUNLOP.

EDINBURGH, 30th April 1787.

——Your criticisms, madam, I understand very well, and could have wished to have pleased you better. You are right in your guess that I am not very amenable to counsel. Poets, much my superiors, have so flattered those who possessed the adventitious qualities of wealth and power, that I am determined to flatter no created being, either in prose or verse.

I set as little by ***** [kings?], lords, clergy, critics, &c., as all these respective gentry do by my bardship. I know what I may expect from the world by and by; illiberal abuse, and perhaps contemptuous neglect.

I am happy, madam, that some of my own favorite pieces are distinguished by your particular approbation. For my 'Dream,' which has unfortunately incurred your loyal displeasure, I hope in four weeks, or less, to have the honor of appearing at Dunlop, in its defence, in person. ROBT. BURNS.

The next letters show that Burns thoroughly appreciated the 'meteor-like novelty of his appearance,' and was already prepared for neglect and unfavourable criticism.

TO MR WILLIAM DUNBAR, W.S.

LAWNMARKET, Monday morning.
[April 30th, 1787.]

DEAR SIR—In justice to Spenser, I must acknowledge that there is scarcely a Poet in the language could have been a more agreeable present to me; and in justice to you, allow me to say, Sir, that I have not met with a man in Edinburgh to whom I would so willingly have been indebted for the gift. The tattered rhymes I herewith present you, and the handsome volumes of Spenser for which I am so much indebted to your goodness, may perhaps be not in proportion to one another as do their late author, but be that as it may, my gift, though far less valuable, is as sincere a mark of esteem as yours.

The time is approaching when I shall return to my shades; and I am afraid my numerous Edinburgh friendships are of so tender a construction,

that they will not bear carriage with me.   Yours is one of the few that
I could wish of a more robust constitution.   It is indeed very probable
that when I leave this city, we part never more to meet in this sublunary
sphere ; but I have a strong fancy that in some future eccentric planet,
the comet of happier systems than any with which astronomy is yet
acquainted, you and I, among the harum-scarum sons of imagination
and whim, with a hearty shake of a hand, a metaphor and a laugh,
shall recognise old acquaintances :

> Where wit may sparkle all its rays,
>   Uncurst with caution's fears ;
> That pleasure, basking in the blaze,
>   Rejoice for endless years.

I have the honour to be, with the warmest sincerity, Dear Sir, &c.

R. B.

TO THE REV. DR HUGH BLAIR.

LAWNMARKET, EDINBURGH, 3d *May* 1787.

REVEREND AND MUCH RESPECTED SIR—I leave Edinburgh to-morrow
morning, but could not go without troubling you with half a line
sincerely to thank you for the kindness, patronage, and friendship you
have shewn me.   I often felt the embarrassment of my singular situation : drawn forth from the veriest shades of life to the glare of remark ;
and honored by the notice of those illustrious names of my country,
whose works, while they are applauded to the end of time, will ever
instruct and mend the heart.   However the meteor-like novelty of my
appearance in the world might attract notice, and honor me with the
acquaintance of the permanent lights of genius and literature, those who
are truly benefactors of the immortal nature of man, I knew very well
that my utmost merit was far unequal to the task of preserving that
character when once the novelty was over : I have made up my mind
that abuse, or almost even neglect, will not surprize me in my quarters.

I have sent you a proof-impression of Beugo's work for me, done on
India paper, as a trifling but sincere testimony with what heart-warm
gratitude I am, &c.   R. B.

Both the good sense and the self-complacency of Blair are
admirably illustrated by his kind but egotistical and stilted reply :

ARGYLE-SQUARE, EDINBURGH, 4th *May* 1787.

DEAR SIR—I was favored this forenoon with your very obliging
letter, together with an impression of your portrait, for which I return

you my best thanks. The success you have met with I do not think was beyond your merits; and if I have had any small hand in contributing to it, it gives me great pleasure. I know no way in which literary persons who are advanced in years can do more service to the world, than in forwarding the efforts of rising genius, or bringing forth unknown merit from obscurity. I was the first person who brought out to the notice of the world the poems of Ossian: first, by the *Fragments of ancient Poetry* which I published;* and afterwards, by my setting on foot the undertaking for collecting and publishing the *Works of Ossian;* and I have always considered this as a meritorious action of my life.

Your situation, as you say, was indeed very singular; and in being brought out all at once from the shades of deepest privacy to so great a share of public notice and observation, you had to stand a severe trial. I am happy that you have stood it so well; and, as far as I have known or heard, though in the midst of many temptations, without reproach to your character and behaviour.

You are now, I presume, to retire to a more private walk of life; and I trust will conduct yourself there with industry, prudence and honour. You have laid the foundation for just public esteem. In the midst of those employments which your situation will render proper, you will not,·I hope, neglect to promote that esteem, by cultivating your genius, and attending to such productions of it as may raise your character still higher. At the same time, be not in too great a haste to come forward. Take time and leisure to improve and mature your talents. For on any second production you give the world, your fate as a poet will very much depend. There is no doubt a gloss of novelty, which time wears off. As you very properly hint yourself, you are not to be surprized if in your rural retreat you do not find yourself surrounded with that glare of notice and applause which here shone upon you. No man can be a good poet without being somewhat of a philosopher. He must lay his account that any one, who exposes himself to public observation, will occasionally meet with the attacks of illiberal censure, which it is always best to overlook and despise. He will be inclined sometimes to court retreat, and to disappear from public view. He will not affect to shine always, that he may at proper seasons come forth with more advantage and energy. He will not think himself neglected if he be not always praised. I have taken the liberty, you see, of an old man, to give advice and make reflections, which your own good sense will, I dare say, render unnecessary.

As you mention your being just about to leave town, you are going, I should suppose, to Dumfries-shire, to look at some of Mr Miller's farms. I heartily wish the offers to be made you there may answer; as I am per-

---

* What Blair actually did was to furnish the preface to the *Fragments* published by James Macpherson, in which he committed himself to this opinion. The translation is extremely literal.

suaded you will not easily find a more generous and better-hearted proprietor to live under than Mr Miller. When you return, if you come this way, I will be happy to see you, and to know concerning your future plans of life. You will find me by the 22d of this month, not in my house in Argyle-square, but at a country house at Restalrig, about a mile east from Edinburgh, near the Musselburgh road. Wishing you all success and prosperity, I am, with real regard and esteem, Dear sir, Yours sincerely, HUGH BLAIR.

Burns had become acquainted during this spring with a young man who afterwards figures largely in his correspondence. This was Robert Ainslie, afterwards well known as a Writer to the Signet in Edinburgh, and, late in life, as a lay theologian. Ainslie was serving his apprenticeship in the office of Samuel Mitchelson in Carrubber's Close—a personage, by the way, who is otherwise connected with Scottish literature; for the haggis scene in *Humphrey Clinker* is understood to have been drawn from an actual occurrence in his house, when Smollett was one of his guests. Ainslie was as thoughtless and light-hearted as a writer's apprentice could well be, and only twenty-one years of age;* though he was clever and intelligent, it is probable that his good-nature and love of fun were his principal attractions in the eyes of the Poet.

Burns was now preparing for a tour of the south of Scotland, and had secured, for part of the time at least, the company of young Ainslie, who had obtained a fortnight's leave of absence to visit his relatives in Berwickshire. Before starting, the poet sent a letter to James Johnson, an engraver, who had commenced the preparation of a collection of all Scottish songs, arranged for the pianoforte. The Poet had entered into Johnson's design with the greatest cordiality, become a contributor of songs of his own composition, and obtained for the work old songs and airs hitherto inedited. When the first volume appeared, at the end of May, it was found to contain two acknowledged songs by 'Mr Burns'—'Green grow the Rashes' and 'Young Peggy blooms our bonniest lass'—besides two of inferior quality which have since been placed to his account, and which are preserved in a subordinate part of the present work.†

---

* Robert Ainslie was born at Berrywell, near Duns, on January 13, 1766.
† See Vol. IV., Supplement.

TO MR JAMES JOHNSON, EDITOR OF THE 'SCOTS MUSICAL MUSEUM.'*

LAWNMARKET, *Friday Noon*, 3d *May* 1787.

DEAR SIR—I have sent you a song never before known, for your collection; the air by Mr Gibbon, but I know not the author of the words, as I got it from Dr Blacklock.

Farewell, my dear Sir! I wished to have seen you, but I have been dreadfully throng [busy], as I march to-morrow. Had my acquaintance with you been a little older, I would have asked the favour of your correspondence, as I have met with few people whose company and conversation gave me so much pleasure, because I have met with few whose sentiments are so congenial to my own.

When Dunbar and you meet, tell him that I left Edinburgh with the idea of him hanging somewhere about my heart.

Keep the original of this song till we meet again, whenever that may be.　　　　　　　　　　　　　　　　　　　　　　　R. B.

The Poet seems to have been pleased with Beugo's engraving of his 'phiz,' which had been prepared for his second edition, for he had three dozen proof impressions of it printed on quarto India paper.† These copies he presented to his more particular friends, among them Blair ‡ and William Tytler of Woodhouselee. The copy to the latter was sent with a poetical address.

ADDRESS TO WILLIAM TYTLER, ESQ.

Reverèd defender of beauteous Stuart,§
　　Of Stuart, a name once respected ;
A name which to love was the mark of a true heart,
　　But now 'tis despised and neglected.

---

* There is some reason to suppose that Burns made a rapid excursion into Lanarkshire in the interval between the dates of the two last letters, as a journal kept by his friend Prentice of Covington Mains has the following entry :

[1787] 'May 1.　Cold.　Making bear
　　　　　　　　　　land.　Mr Burns here.'

Mr John Prentice, son of the farmer of Covington Mains, who preserved the journal, had no doubt that the poet paid his father a visit that day. If such an excursion took place, it was probably connected with some circumstances about which Burns desired to observe silence. He says of one of his songs, in which a Clydesdale heroine is celebrated, and which will be given in its proper place, that it 'alludes to a part of my private history, which it is of no consequence to the world to know.' The present might be a similar case, if not the same.

† The account to James Kirkwood, still in existence, shows that the thirty-six copies cost the Poet twelve shillings.

‡ See letter to Blair, 3d May 1787.

§ William Tytler (b. 1711, d. 1792) was the son of a Writer to the Signet in Edinburgh.

Tho' something like moisture conglobes in my eye,
    Let no one misdeem me disloyal :
A poor friendless wand'rer may well claim a sigh,
    Still more, if that wand'rer were royal.

My fathers that name have rever'd on a throne :
    My fathers have fallen to right it ;
Those fathers would spurn their degenerate son,
    That name should he scoffingly slight it.

Still in prayers for King George I most heartily join,
    The Queen, and the rest of the gentry :
Be they wise, be they foolish, is nothing of mine,
    Their title 's avow'd by my country.

But why of that epocha make such a fuss,
    That gave us th' Electoral* stem ?
If bringing them over was lucky for us,
    I 'm sure 'twas as lucky for them.†

But loyalty, truce ! we 're on dangerous ground :
    Who knows how the fashions may alter ?
The doctrine, to-day, that is loyalty sound,
    To-morrow may bring us a halter !

I send you a trifle, a head of a bard,
    A trifle scarce worthy your care ;
But accept it, good Sir, as a mark of regard,
    Sincere as a saint's dying prayer.

Now life's chilly evening dim shades on your eye,
    And ushers the long dreary night :
But you, like the star that athwart gilds the sky,
    Your course to the latest is bright.

He was himself trained to the legal profession, and practised as a Writer to the Signet from 1744 till his death. He had published, in 1759, *An Enquiry, Historical and Critical, into the Evidence against Mary Queen of Scots* (2 vols.), which was a defence against what its author believed to be the calumnies of Robertson and Hume. It was sufficiently popular to be translated into French in 1772. Alexander Fraser Tytler, Lord Woodhouselee, was a son of William Tytler ; Patrick Fraser Tytler, the historian, a grandson.

  * Variation—' the Hanover.'

  † In Currie's edition (1800), lines 2–4 of this verse are omitted. Their place is supplied by asterisks.

My muse [he adds] jilted me here, and turned a corner on me, and I have not got again into her good graces. . . . Do me the justice to believe me sincere in my grateful remembrance of the many civilities you have honored me with since I came to Edinburgh, and in assuring you that I have the honor to be, revered Sir, Your obliged and very humble servant,   ROBERT BURNS.

LAWNMARKET, *Friday noon* [4th *May* 1787].

TO THE EARL OF GLENCAIRN.

MY LORD—I go away to-morrow morning early, and allow me to vent the fulness of my heart in thanking your Lordship for all that patronage, that benevolence, and that friendship with which you have honored me. With brimful eyes, I pray that you may find, in that great Being whose image you so nobly bear, that Friend which I have found in you. My gratitude is not selfish design—that I disdain ; it is not dodging after the heel of greatness—that is an offering you disdain. It is a feeling of the same kind with my devotion.   R. B.

LAWNMARKET, *Friday noon.*

Burns and Ainslie set out on their tour on Saturday the 5th of May. They travelled on horseback—Burns mounted on a mare, the celebrated 'Jenny Geddes,' which he had bought in Edinburgh— and arrived on the first evening at Berrywell, near Duns, the residence of Mr Ainslie's father, who was land-steward on the Berwickshire estates of Lord Douglas. Burns kept a journal of the tour, entering not merely the events of the road, but observa- tions on the persons whom he met. This we shall now give, accompanied with explanatory memoranda :

Left Edinburgh [*May* 5, 1787]—Lammermuir Hills miserably dreary, but at times very picturesque. Langton-edge, a glorious view of the Merse—Reach Berrywell—old Mr Ainslie an uncommon character ; his hobbies, agriculture, natural philosophy, and politics. In the first he is unexceptionably the clearest-headed, best-informed man I ever met with ; in the other two, very intelligent :—As a man of business he has uncom- mon merit, and by fairly deserving it, has made a very decent independ- ence. Mrs Ainslie, an excellent, sensible, cheerful, amiable old woman. Miss Ainslie—her person a little *embonpoint*, but handsome ; her face, particularly her eyes, full of sweetness and good humour—she unites three qualities rarely to be found together—keen, solid penetration ; sly, witty observation and remark ; and the gentlest, most unaffected female modesty. Douglas, a clever, fine, promising young fellow.* The family-

---

* Douglas Ainslie was born 6th May 1771. He succeeded his father as writer and land- factor, made a considerable fortune, acquired the property of Cairnbank, in Berwickshire, and died at Eden Bank, near Banff, on 19th September 1850. A third son of Mr Ainslie, Whitelaw, an Indian medical officer, knighted by William IV., was maternal grandfather of Sir Mountstuart Grant Duff, statesman, born 1829.

meeting with their brother, my *compagnon de voyage*, very charming; particularly the sister. The whole family remarkably attached to their menials—Mrs A. full of stories of the sagacity and sense of the little girl in the kitchen. Mr A. high in the praises of an African, his house servant—all his people old in his service—Douglas's old nurse came to Berrywell yesterday, to remind them of its being his birth-day.

A Mr Dudgeon,* a poet at times, a worthy remarkable character—natural penetration, a great deal of information, some genius, and extreme modesty.

Sunday [*May* 6.]—Went to church at Dunse—Dr Bowmaker a man of strong lungs and pretty judicious remark; but ill-skilled in propriety, and altogether unconscious of his want of it.†

During the discourse, Burns produced a neat impromptu conveying a graceful compliment to Miss Ainslie. Dr Bowmaker had selected a text of Scripture that contained a severe denunciation of obstinate sinners. In the course of the sermon Burns observed his companion turning over the leaves of her Bible with much earnestness, in search of the text. He immediately wrote the following lines, and presented them to her :

> Fair maid, you need not take the hint,
>   Nor idle texts pursue :
> 'Twas *guilty sinners* that he meant,
>   Not *Angels* such as you ! ‡

Monday [*May* 7.]—Coldstream—went over to England—Cornhill—glorious river Tweed—clear and majestic—fine bridge.

An anecdote relating to this portion of Burns's tour was published by Robert Ainslie many years afterwards : 'The weather was charming, the travellers youthful and in good spirits, and the poet delighted with the fine scenery and the poetical associations connected with it. When they arrived at Coldstream, where the dividing line between England and Scotland is the Tweed, Mr Ainslie suggested going across to the other side of the river by the Coldstream Bridge, that Burns might be enabled to say he had been in England. They did so, and were pacing slowly along on English ground, enjoying their walk, when Mr Ainslie was surprised to see

---

* William Dudgeon, a Duns farmer as well as 'poet at times,' was the author of a popular Scottish song entitled 'The Maid that tends the Goats.' He died at Newmains, Whitekirk, in 1813, at the age of sixty.

† Dr Bowmaker, who was ordained to the parish of Dunse in 1769, died in 1797, at the age of sixty-six.

‡ On Burns leaving Berrywell, his host presented him with a copy of the *Letters of Junius*, 'in testimony of the most sincere friendship and esteem.'

the poet throw away his hat, and, thus uncovered, kneel down
with uplifted hands, and apparently rapt in a fit of enthusiasm.
Mr Ainslie kept silence, uncertain what was next to be done,
when Burns, with extreme emotion, and an expression of countenance which his companion could never forget, prayed for and
blessed Scotland most solemnly, by pronouncing aloud, in tones of
the deepest devotion, the two concluding stanzas of the "Cotter's
Saturday Night :"

> ' Oh Scotia ! my dear, my native soil !
>   For whom my warmest wish to Heaven is sent !
> Long may thy hardy sons of rustic toil
>   Be blest with health, and peace, and sweet content !
>   And oh ! may Heaven their simple lives prevent
> From luxury's contagion, weak and vile !
>   Then, howe'er crowns and coronets be rent,
>   A virtuous populace may rise the while,
> And stand a wall of fire around their much-loved isle.

> ' Oh Thou ! who poured the patriotic tide,
>   That streamed through Wallace's undaunted heart
> Who dared to nobly stem tyrannic pride,
>   Or nobly die, the second glorious part,
>   (The patriot's God, peculiarly Thou art,
> His friend, inspirer, guardian, and reward !)
>   Oh never, never, Scotia's realm desert ;
>   But still the patriot, and the patriot bard,
> In bright succession raise, her ornament and guard !'*

Dine at Coldstream with Mr Ainslie and Mr Foreman—beat Mr F. in
a dispute about Voltaire. Tea at Lennel House with Mr Brydone.† Mr
Brydone a most excellent heart, kind, joyous and benevolent; but a good
deal of the French indiscriminate complaisance—from his situation past
and present, an admirer of everything that bears a splendid title, or that
possesses a large estate.—Mrs Brydone [a daughter of Dr Robertson, the
historian] a most elegant woman in her person and manners ; the tones
of her voice remarkably sweet—my reception extremely flattering—sleep
at Coldstream.

Tuesday [*May* 8.]—Breakfast at Kelso—charming situation of Kelso—

---

* *Chambers's Edinburgh Journal*, April 28, 1832.

† Patrick Brydone, traveller and author, born about 1741. His chief tours were through
Switzerland and Sicily. His work (1773) on the second of these tours was most popular,
having gone through nine editions in his lifetime, besides being translated into French and
German. He latterly was Comptroller of the Stamp Office. Died at Lennel House,
Berwickshire, in 1818. See also Vol. I., p. 260.

fine bridge over the Tweed—enchanting views and prospects on both sides of the river, particularly the Scotch side ; introduced to Mr Scot of the Royal Bank—an excellent modest fellow—fine situation of it—ruins of Roxburgh Castle—a holly-bush growing where James II. of Scotland was accidentally killed by the bursting of a cannon. A small old religious ruin and a fine old garden planted by the religious, rooted out and destroyed by an English Hottentot—a *maitre d'hotel* of the Duke's, a Mr Cole—climate and soil of Berwickshire, and even Roxburghshire, superior to Ayrshire—bad roads. Turnip and sheep husbandry, their great improvements—Mr McDowal, at Caverton Mill, a friend of Mr Ainslie's, with whom I dined to-day, sold his sheep, ewe and lamb together, at two guineas a piece—wash their sheep before shearing—7 or 8 lbs. of washen wool in a fleece—low markets, consequently low rents— fine lands not above sixteen shillings a Scotch acre—magnificence of farmers and farm houses [Farms in Roxburgh and Berwickshire were then, as now, on a large scale in comparison with Ayrshire.]—come up Teviot and up Jed to Jedburgh to lie, and so wish myself a good night.

Wednesday [May 9.]—Breakfast with Mr —— in Jedburgh—a squabble between Mrs ——, a crazed, talkative slattern, and a sister of hers, an old maid, respecting a Relief minister—Miss gives Madam the lie ; and Madam, by way of revenge, upbraids her that she laid snares to entangle the said minister, then a widower, in the net of matrimony—go about two miles out of Jedburgh to a roup of parks [auction-sale of crops on some fields]—meet a polite, soldier-like gentleman, a Captain Rutherford, who had been many years through the wilds of America, a prisoner among the Indians—charming, romantic situation of Jedburgh, with gardens, orchards, &c., intermingled among the houses—fine old ruins—a once magnificent cathedral, and strong castle. All the towns here have the appearance of old, rude grandeur, but the people extremely idle— Jed a fine romantic little river.

Dine with Captain Rutherford—the Captain a polite fellow, fond of money in his farming way ; shewed a particular respect to my bardship —his lady exactly a proper matrimonial second part for him. Miss Rutherford a beautiful girl, but too far gone woman to expose so much of a fine swelling bosom—her face very fine.

Return to Jedburgh—walk up Jed with some ladies to be shewn Love-lane and Blackburn, two fairy scenes. Introduced to Mr Potts, writer, a very clever fellow ; and Mr Somerville, the clergyman of the place, a man, and a gentleman, but sadly addicted to punning.

Dr Thomas Somerville (1741-1830) was author of a *History of Great Britain during the Reign of Queen Anne*, which was published in 1798. He was uncle and father-in-law of Mrs Mary Somerville, an eminent mathematician and physicist. After the appearance of this passage in Dr Currie's memoir of the poet, he is said to have absolutely abandoned punning.

The walking-party of ladies, Mrs —— and Miss ——, her sister,
before mentioned.—*N.B.*—These two appear still more comfortably
ugly and stupid, and bore me most shockingly. Two Miss ——, tolerably agreeable. Miss Hope, a tolerably pretty girl, fond of laughing
and fun. Miss Lindsay, a good-humoured, amiable girl; rather short
et embonpoint, but handsome, and extremely graceful — beautiful
hazel eyes, full of spirit, and sparkling with delicious moisture—an
engaging face *un tout ensemble* that speaks her of the first order of
female minds—her sister, a bonnie, strappan, rosy, **sonsie** lass. Shake
myself loose, after several unsuccessful efforts, of Mrs —— and Miss ——,
and somehow or other get hold of Miss Lindsay's arm. My heart is
thawed into melting pleasure after being so long frozen up in the Greenland bay of indifference, amid the noise and nonsense of Edinburgh.
Miss seems very well pleased with my bardship's distinguishing her; and
after some slight qualms, which I could easily mark, she sets the titter
round at defiance, and kindly allows me to keep my hold; and when
parted by the ceremony of my introduction to Mr Somerville, she met
me half, to resume my situation. *Nota Bene*—The poet within a point
and a half of being d—mnably in love—I am afraid my bosom is still
nearly as much tinder as ever.

The old, cross-grained, whiggish [sour or pietistical], ugly, slanderous
Miss ——, with all the poisonous spleen of a disappointed, ancient
maid, stops me very unseasonably to ease her bursting breast, by falling
abusively foul on the Miss Lindsays, particularly on my Dulcinea;—I
hardly refrain from cursing her to her face for daring to mouth her
calumnious slander on one of the finest pieces of the workmanship of
Almighty Excellence! Sup at Mr ——'s; vexed that the Miss Lindsays
are not of the supper-party, as they only are wanting. Mrs —— and
Miss —— still improve infernally on my hands.

Set out next morning [*May* 10] for Wauchope, the seat of my correspondent, Mrs Scot—breakfast by the way with Dr Elliot, an agreeable,
good-hearted, climate-beaten, old veteran, in the medical line; now
retired to a romantic, but rather moorish place, on the banks of the
Roole [Rule]—he accompanies us almost to Wauchope—we traverse the
country to the top of Bochester [Bonchester], the scene of an old
encampment, and Woolee [Wolflee] Hill.

Wauchope.—Mr Scot exactly the figure and face commonly given to
Sancho Panza—very shrewd in his farming matters, and not unfrequently
stumbles on what may be called a strong thing rather than a good thing.
Mrs Scot all the sense, taste, intrepidity of face, and bold, critical
decision, which usually distinguish female authors. Sup with Mr Potts—
agreeable party. Breakfast next morning [*May* 11] with Mr Somerville
—the *bruit* of Miss Lindsay and my bardship, by means of the invention
and malice of Miss ——. Mr Somerville sends to Dr Lindsay, begging
him and family to breakfast if convenient, but at all events to send Miss
Lindsay; accordingly, Miss Lindsay only comes. I find Miss Lindsay
would soon play the devil with me—I met with some little flattering

attentions from her. Mrs Somerville an excellent, motherly, agreeable woman, and a fine family. Mr Ainslie and Mrs S——, junrs., with Mr ——, Miss Lindsay, and myself, go to see *Esther* [*Easton*], a very remarkable woman for reciting poetry of all kinds, and sometimes making Scotch doggerel herself—she can repeat by heart almost every thing she has ever read, particularly Pope's *Homer* from end to end—has studied *Euclid* by herself, and, in short, is a woman of very extraordinary abilities. On conversing with her, I find her fully equal to the character given of her. She is very much flattered that I send for her, and that she sees a poet who has *put out a book*, as she says. She is, among other things, a great florist, and is rather past the meridian of once celebrated beauty.

I walk in *Esther's* garden with Miss Lindsay, and after some little chit-chat of the tender kind, I presented her with a proofprint of my *Nob*, which she accepted with something more tender than gratitude. She told me many little stories which Miss —— had retailed concerning her and me, with prolonging pleasure—God bless her! Was waited on by the Magistrates, and presented with the freedom of the burgh.

Took farewell of Jedburgh, with some melancholy, disagreeable sensations. Jed, pure be thy crystal streams, and hallowed thy sylvan banks! Sweet Isabella Lindsay, may peace dwell in thy bosom, uninterrupted, except by the tumultuous throbbings of rapturous love! That love-kindling eye must beam on another, not on me: that graceful form must bless another's arms; not mine!*

Kelso. Dine with the Farmer's Club—all gentlemen, talking of high matters—each of them keeps a hunter from £30 to £50 value, and attends the fox-huntings in the county—go out with Mr Ker, one of the club, and a friend of Mr Anslie's to lie. [*May* 12]—Mr Ker, a most gentlemanly, clever, handsome fellow, a widower with some fine children —his mind and manner astonishingly like my dear old friend Robert Muir, in Kilmarnock—every thing in Mr Ker's most elegant—he offers to accompany me in my English tour. Dine with Sir Alexander Don—a pretty clever fellow, but far from being a match for his divine lady [Lady Harriet Don, sister of the Earl of Glencairn]. A very wet day. . . . Sleep at Stodrig again, and [*Sunday, May* 13] set out for Melrose—visit Dryburgh, a fine old ruined abbey—still bad weather—cross Leader, and come up Tweed to Melrose—dine there, and visit that far-famed, glorious ruin—come to Selkirk, up Ettrick—the whole country hereabout, both on Tweed and Ettrick, remarkably stony.†

---

* Isabella Lindsay and her sister lived with their brother, a young surgeon in Jedburgh. Isabella married Adam Armstrong, who held a situation under the Russian government. She died young, leaving four children; the youngest son rose to be a general, and director of the Imperial Mint at St Petersburg. Peggy, the youngest sister, died shortly after Burns's visit, at the age of twenty-two.

† 'I have often heard Dr Clarkson tell, with a heavy heart and a loss of all patience with himself, that when Mr Anslie and Burns arrived at Selkirk that evening, "they were just like twa drunkit craws." The doctor and other two gentlemen were sitting in Veitch's Inn, near the West Port, taking their glass (for Selkirk has a West Port as well as Edinburgh). When the travellers arrived, the two within viewed them out at the window as they alighted.

It is plain that Burns was disappointed of his intended visit to the Vale of Yarrow. Rain seems to have forced him to take refuge in the inn at Selkirk. The Ettrick, however, which was also to him classical, by virtue of a fine pastoral song, was now in his ken, for it runs by Selkirk.

The Poet seems to have spent part of the day in penning a letter, containing some verses, to his publisher, who had just gone to London.

TO WILLIAM CREECH, ESQ.

SELKIRK, 13th May 1787.

MY HONORED FRIEND—The inclosed I have just wrote, nearly extempore, in a solitary Inn in Selkirk, after a miserable wet day's riding. I have been over most of East Lothian, Berwick, Roxburgh, and Selkirk shires, and next week I begin a tour through the north of England. Yesterday, I dined with Lady Hariot, sister to my noble patron, *Quem Deus conservat!* I would write till I would tire you as much with dull prose as I dare say by this time you are with wretched verse; but I am jaded to death; so, with a grateful farewell, I have the honor to be, Good Sir, yours sincerely,   R. B.

The 'inclosed' was the following set of verses:

WILLIE'S AWA'.

Auld chuckie * Reekie's † sair distrest,	sore
Down droops her ance weel burnish'd crest,	once
Nae joy her bonie buskit nest	decorated
Can yield ava,	at all
Her darling bird that she lo'es best—	loves
Willie, 's awa.	

and certainly conceived no very high opinion of them. In a short time, however, they sent Mr Veitch to the doctor and his friends, requesting permission for two strangers to take a glass with them. The doctor objected, and asked Mr Veitch what the men were like? Mr Veitch said he could not well say: the one spoke *rather* like a gentleman, but the other was a drover-looking chap; so they refused to admit them, sending them word that they were sorry they were engaged elsewhere, and obliged to go away. The doctor saw them ride off next morning, and it was not till the third day that he knew it had been the celebrated Scottish poet whom they had refused to admit. That refusal hangs about the doctor's heart like a deadweight to this day, and will do till the day of his death, for the bard had not a more enthusiastic admirer.'—JAMES HOGG, in his edition of Burns.

* Literally, a hen; secondarily, a familiar term of address:

    'Gin ony sour-mou'd girning bucky
    Ca' me conceited keckling chucky.'—RAMSAY

† Literally, smoky; a familiar sobriquet for Edinburgh.

O' Willie was a witty wight,
And had o' things an unco' sleight,   *uncommon knowledge*
Auld Reekie ay he keepit tight,   *trig*
  And trig an' braw :   *neat—handsome*
But now they'll busk her like a **fright**—   *dress*
  Willie's awa !

The stiffest o' them a' he bow'd ;
The bauldest o' them a' he cow'd :   *boldest*
They durst nae mair than he allow'd,   *dared—more*
  That was a law :
We've lost a birkie weel worth gowd :   *fellow—gold*
  Willie's awa !

Now gawkies, tawpies, gowks * and fools,
Frae colleges and boarding schools,   *From*
May sprout like simmer puddock-stools   *summer toad-stools*
  In glen or shaw ;   *wood*
He wha could brush them down to mools—   *the dust*
  Willie's awa !

The brethren o' the Commerce-Chaumer †
May mourn their loss wi' doolfu' clamour ;   *doleful*
He was a dictionar and grammar
  Amang them a' ;
I fear they'll now make mony a stammer :
  Willie's awa !

Nae mair we see his levee door ‡   *No more*
Philosophers and Poets pour,

---

* 'Gawky,' a simpleton ; 'tawpy,' usually applied to an indolent, spiritless woman ; 'gowk,' literally, the cuckoo—secondarily, a fool.

† The Chamber of Commerce in Edinburgh, of which Creech was secretary.

‡ Creech lived on familiar terms with many of the literary Scotsmen of his day. His house, in one of the elevated floors of a tenement in the High Street, accessible from a wretched alley called Craig's Close, was frequented in the mornings by company of that kind, to such an extent that the meeting used to be called Creech's Levee. Burns here enumerates as attending it, Dr James Gregory (1753-1821), Alexander Fraser Tytler, afterwards Lord Woodhouselee (1747-1813), Rev. William Greenfield, Henry Mackenzie, and Dugald Stewart.

And toothy critics by the score,
   In bloody raw !   row
The adjutant o' a' the core—   corps
   Willie 's awa !

Now worthy Gregory's Latin face ;
Tytler's and Greenfield's modest grace ;
M'Kenzie, Stewart, such a brace
   As Rome ne'er saw ;
They a' maun meet some ither place,   must—other
   Willie 's awa !

Poor Burns ev'n 'Scotch drink ' canna quicken, cannot
He cheeps like some bewilder'd chicken   chirps
Scar'd frae its minnie and the cleckin mother—brood
   By hoodie-craw ;   carrion crow
Grief 's gien his heart an unco kickin,   given—sad
   Willie 's awa !

Now ev'ry sour-mou'd girnin' blellum, sour-mouthed,
            scowling chatterer
And Calvin's folk,* are fit to fell him ;†
Ilk self-conceited critic skellum ‡   Every
   His quill may draw :
He wha could brawlie ward their 'bellum'— bravely resist
            their violence
   Willie 's awa !

Up wimpling stately Tweed I 've sped,   winding
And Eden scenes on crystal Jed,
And Ettrick banks now roaring red
   While tempests blaw ;   blow
But every joy and pleasure 's fled—
   Willie 's awa !

May I be Slander's common speech ;
A text of Infamy to preach ;

---

* Here again Burns indulges in a hit at the evangelicals.
† Angry enough to knock him down.
‡ A term of contempt :
   'She tauld thee weel thou was a skellum.'—'Tam o' Shanter.'

And lastly, streekit out to bleach   *stretched*
      In winter snaw ;   *snow*
When I forget thee, WILLIE CREECH,
      Tho' far awa !

May never wicked Fortune touzle him !   *ruffle, toss*
May never wicked men bamboozle him !
Until a pow as auld 's Methusalem   *head—old*
         —Methuselah
      He, canty, claw !   *cheerful*
Then to the blessèd New Jerusalem
      Fleet wing awa !

Monday [*May* 14.]—Come to Inverleithen, a famous spa, and in the vicinity of the palace of Traquair, where, having dined, and drank some Galloway-whey, I here remain till to-morrow — saw Elibanks and Elibraes, on the other side of the Tweed.

Burns, so far as can be gathered, had no motive for making this digression of twenty miles up the Tweed, except a desire to see certain places referred to in Scottish song. At Innerleithen, where he spent the afternoon and night of Monday, he saw the *Bush aboon Traquair.*

He was similarly interested in Elibank, an old castle situated amongst hanging woods, mainly perhaps because of an old free-spoken song, the burden of which is 'Elibank and Elibraes.' Such were the fancies which led him into twenty-mile digressions on this tour.

Tuesday [*May* 15.]—Drank tea yesternight at Pirn, with Mr Horsburgh.—Breakfasted to-day with Mr Ballantyne of Hollowlie [Holylee]. —Proposal for a four-horse team, to consist of Mr Scot of Wauchope, Fittieland : Logan of Logan, Fittiefurr : Ballantyne of Hollowlie, Forewynd : Horsburgh of Horsburgh. Dine at a country inn, kept by a miller, in Earlston, the birth-place and residence of the celebrated Thomas a Rhymer—saw the ruins of his castle—come to Berrywell.

Though he takes no notice of the circumstance, his reason for a detour by Earlston was doubtless his desire to see the much-sung *Cowdenknowes.*

Wednesday [*May* 16.]—Dine at Dunse with the Farmers' Club company—impossible to do them justice—Rev. Mr Smith,[*] a famous punster,

---

[*] Andrew Smith, minister of Langton, Presbytery of Duns, from 1766 till his death in 1789.

and Mr Meikle, a celebrated mechanic, and inventor of the threshing-mill.[*]

Thursday [*May* 17.]—breakfast at Berrywell, and walk into Dunse to see a famous knife made by a cutler there, and to be presented to an Italian prince.—A pleasant ride with my friend Mr Robert Ainslie, and his sister, to Mr Thomson's, a man who has newly commenced farmer, and has married a Miss Patty Grieve, formerly a flame of Mr Robert Ainslie's. Company—Miss Jacky Grieve, an amiable sister of Mrs Thomson's, and Mr Hood, an honest, worthy, facetious farmer, in the neighbourhood.

A letter written at Berrywell gives some curious particulars regarding his volume : it is addressed to a Paisley manufacturer, whom the bard playfully styles 'bookseller,' in allusion to his success in disposing of a considerable number of copies of the recently published volume :

TO MR PATTISON, 'BOOKSELLER,' PAISLEY.

BERRYWELL, *near Dunse, May* 17th, 1787.

DEAR SIR—I am sorry I was out of Edinburgh, making a slight pilgrimage to the classic scenes of this country, when I was favoured with yours of the 11th instant, inclosing an order of the Paisley Banking Company on the Royal Bank, for twenty-two pounds, seven shillings sterling, payment in full, after carriage deducted, for ninety copies of my book I sent you. According to your motions, I see you will have left Scotland before this reaches you, otherwise I would send you 'Holy Willie' with all my heart. I was so hurried that I absolutely forgot several things I ought to have minded, among the rest, sending books to Mr Cowan, but any order of yours will be answered at Creech's shop. You will please remember that non-subscribers pay six shillings, this is Creech's profit ; but those who have subscribed, though their names have been neglected in the printed list, which is very incorrect, they are supplied at the subscription price. I was not at Glasgow, nor do I intend for London ; and I think Mrs Fame is very idle to tell so many lies on a poor Poet. When you or Mr Cowan write for copies, if you should want any, direct to Mr Hill at Mr Creech's shop, and I write to Mr Hill by this post, to answer either of your orders. Hill is Mr Creech's first clerk, and Creech himself is presently in London. I suppose I shall have the pleasure, against your return to Paisley, of assuring you how much I am, Dear Sir, Your obliged humble servant.   R. B.

---

[*] Andrew Meikle (1719-1811) was a millwright at Houston Mill, near Dunbar. He perfected his thrashing-machine in 1784, but did not take out a patent for it till the year after he met Burns.

As promised, he wrote

TO MR PETER HILL,*

CARE OF MR CREECH, BOOKSELLER, EDINBURGH.

Dr. Sir—If Mr Alexr. Pattison, or Mr Cowan from Paisley, or in general any other of those to whom I have sent copies on credit before [apply to you], you will give them what number they demand, when they require it; provided always that those who are non subscribers shall pay one shilling more than subscribers. This I write to you when I am miserably fou [full = drunk], consequently it must be the sentiments of my heart.　　　　　　　　　　　　　　ROBERT BURNS.

May 17th, 1787.

A young man living in Duns, named Symon Gray, had taken to verse-making, and hearing that Burns was at Berrywell, took the liberty of submitting a specimen of his work to the latter's judgment. The poet gave it a hasty perusal, and returned it with the remark:

Symon Gray,
You 're dull to-day.

Symon, not abashed, immediately sent a fresh packet, which the poet as quickly returned, with an inscription on the outside:

Dulness, with redoubled sway,
Has seized the wits of Symon Gray.

Two rebuffs were, however, insufficient to take the edge off Symon's vanity, and he sent a third packet containing several of his most elaborate performances. It came too late for Burns to pay it any immediate attention, as he was about to proceed on an excursion to the eastern parts of the country; but on his return a few days after to Berrywell, he took it up, and gave its author the *coup-de-grâce*, as follows:

DEAR SYMON GRAY,
The other day,
When you sent me some rhyme,
I could not then just ascertain
Its worth, for want of time.

* Peter Hill (1754–1837) was Creech's clerk when the poet met him. In 1788 he started on his own account as a bookseller, and the subsequent correspondence between the poet and the bookseller contains evidence that Burns must have had an extraordinary library. Hill became treasurer of Edinburgh city and also of Heriot's Hospital. He was appointed Collector of Cess in 1814.

But now to-day, good Mr Gray,
　　I've read it o'er and o'er,
Tried all my skill, but find I'm still
　　Just where I was before.
We, auld wives' minions, gie our opinions,
　　Solicited or no,
Then of its faults, my honest thoughts
　　I'll give—and here they go.
　　*　　　　*　　　　*　　　　*　　　　*

The opinion of Burns cannot be given in its entirety; but an idea of its general bearing may be gathered from one passage :

　　Such damned bombast no age that's past
　　Will shew, or time to come.

Friday [*May* 18.]—Ride to Berwick—An idle town, rudely picturesque—Meet Lord Errol in walking round the walls—His Lordship's flattering notice of me—Dine with Mr Clunzie, merchant—nothing particular in company or conversation—Come up a bold shore, and over a wild country to Eyemouth—sup and sleep at Mr Grieve's.

Saturday [*May* 19.]—Spent the day at Mr Grieve's—made a Royal-arch Mason of St Abb's Lodge. Mr Wm. Grieve, the oldest brother, a joyous, warm-hearted, jolly, clever fellow—takes a hearty glass, and sings a good song. Mr Robert, his brother, and partner in trade, a good fellow, but says little—take a sail after dinner—fishing of all kinds pays tithes at Eyemouth.

The entry made on this occasion in the lodge-books is as follows :

EYEMOUTH, 19*th May* 1787.

At a general encampment held this day, the following brethren were made Royal Arch Masons—namely, Robert Burns, from the Lodge of St James's, Tarbolton, Ayrshire, and Robert Ainslie, from the Lodge of St Luke's, Edinburgh, by James Carmichael, Wm. Grieve, Daniel Dow, John Clay, Robert Grieve, &c. &c. Robert Ainslie paid one guinea admission dues ; but on account of R. Burns's remarkable poetical genius, the encampment unanimously agreed to admit him gratis, and considered themselves honoured by having a man of such shining abilities for one of their companions.

Extracted from the Minute-book of the Lodge by Thomas Bowhill.

Burns makes no allusion in his journal to a country-gentleman of this neighbourhood, with whom, undoubtedly, he was at some period of his life acquainted—Mr Renton of Lamerton. At Mordington House, Mr Renton's residence near Berwick, he would have been certain of a cordial welcome. There is some reason to think that Mr Renton attempted, on this very occasion, to form an appointment with Burns for a meeting and a ride together, for a note in the poet's handwriting was subsequently found among Mr Renton's papers :

Your billet, sir, I grant receipt :
Wi' you I 'll canter ony gate,   *any direction*
Though 'twere a trip to yon blue warl'   *world*
Whare birkies march on burning marl :   *fellows*
Then, sir, God willing, I 'll attend ye,
And to his goodness I commend ye.—R. BURNS.

Sunday [*May* 20.]—A Mr Robinson, brewer at Ednam, sets out with us to Dunbar.

The Miss Grieves very good girls.—My bardship's heart got a brush from Miss Betsey.

Mr William Grieve's attachment to the family-circle so fond, that when he is out, which by the bye is often the case, he cannot go to bed till he sees if all his sisters are sleeping well—Pass the famous Abbey of Coldingham, and Pease-bridge—Call at Mr Sheriff's, where Mr A. and I dine—Mr S. talkative and conceited. I talk of love to Nancy the whole evening, while her brother escorts home some companions like himself—Sir James Hall of Dunglass, having heard of my being in the neighbourhood, comes to Mr Sheriff's to breakfast—[*May* 21]—takes me to see his fine scenery on the stream of Dunglass—Dunglass the most romantic, sweet place I ever saw—Sir James and his lady a pleasant happy couple. He points out a walk for which he has an uncommon respect, as it was made by an aunt of his, to whom he owes much.*

Miss —— will accompany me to Dunbar, by way of making a parade of me as a sweet heart of hers, among her relations. She mounts an old cart-horse, as huge and as lean as a house ; a rusty old side-saddle without girth or stirrup, but fastened on with an old pillion-girth—herself as fine as hands could make her, in cream-coloured riding-clothes, hat and feather, &c.—I, ashamed of my situation, ride like the devil, and almost shake her to pieces on old Jolly—get rid of her by refusing to call at her uncle's with her.

Past through the most glorious corn country I ever saw, till I reached Dunbar, a neat little town—dine with Provost Fall,† an eminent merchant, and most respectable character, but undescribable, as he exhibits no marked traits. Mrs Fall, a genius in painting ; fully more clever in the fine arts and sciences than my friend Lady Wauchope, without her con-

---

* Sir James Hall (1761-1832) was a well-known chemist and geologist. He wrote several papers to support and illustrate the Huttonian theory of the earth, and for a time was President of the Royal Society of Edinburgh. His second son was the well-known Captain Basil Hall, naval officer, traveller, and friend of Scott.

† Provost Fall was said to be of gipsy, or ' Fa,' origin. The family of Fall figure largely in the history of Dunbar. Their house was for more than a century one of the chief merchant houses in the country.

summate assurance of her own abilities.—Call with Mr Robinson (who, by the bye, I find to be a worthy, much respected man, very modest; warm, social heart, which with less good sense than his would be perhaps with the children of prim precision and pride, rather inimical to that respect which is man's due from man)—with him I call on Miss Clarke, a maiden, in the Scotch phrase, '*Guid enough, but no brent new:*' a clever woman, with tolerable pretensions to remark and wit; while time had blown the blushing bud of bashful modesty into the flower of easy confidence. She wanted to see what sort of *raree show* an author was; and to let him know, that though Dunbar was but a little town, yet it was not destitute of people of parts.

Breakfast next morning [*May* 22] at Skateraw, at Mr Lee's, a farmer of great note.—Mr Lee, an excellent, hospitable, social fellow, rather oldish; warm-hearted and chatty—a most judicious, sensible farmer. Mr Lee detains me till next morning—Company at dinner—My Rev. acquaintance Dr Bowmaker, a reverend, rattling old fellow. Two sea lieutenants; a cousin of the landlord's, a fellow whose looks are of that kind which deceived me in a gentleman at Kelso, and has often deceived me : a goodly handsome figure and face, which incline one to give them credit for parts which they have not. Mr Clarke, a much cleverer fellow, but whose looks a little cloudy, and his appearance rather ungainly, with an every day observer may prejudice the opinion against him. Dr Brown, a medical young gentleman from Dunbar, a fellow whose face and manners are open and engaging. Leave Skateraw for Dunse next day [*May* 23], along with Collector ——, a lad of slender abilities, and bashfully diffident to an extreme.

Found Miss Ainslie, the amiable, the sensible, the good-humoured, the sweet Miss Ainslie, all alone at Berrywell.—Heavenly powers, who know the weakness of human hearts, support mine ! What happiness must I see only to remind me that I cannot enjoy it !

Lammermuir Hills, from East Lothian to Dunse very wild.—Dine with the Farmers' Club at Kelso. Sir John Hume and Mr Lumsden there, but nothing worth remembrance when the following circumstance is considered—I walk into Dunse before dinner, and out to Berrywell in the evening with Miss Ainslie—how well-bred, how frank, how good she is ! Charming Rachel ! may thy bosom never be wrung by the evils of this life of sorrows, or by the villainy of this world's sons ! *

Burns here lost the company of Robert Ainslie, who returned to Edinburgh. The following letter was posted from Duns.

TO MR PETER HILL,
AT MR CREECH'S SHOP, EDINBURGH.

DEAR SIR—Any more letters for me that may come to your care, send them to Dumfries, directed to be detained till called for. I mean this

---

* Miss Ainslie, who was born 19th March 1768, died unmarried.

direction only for a week; afterwards direct to me at Mossgiel, near Mauchline. To-day I set out for a ride thro' Northumberlandshire. I beg you or Mr Creech will acquaint me whenever he returns. I am, Dear Sir, yours, ROBERT BURNS.

BERRYWELL, 24th May 1787.

P.S.—I recd. a bill from Mr Pattison, which he has wrote to you about. My letter granting receipt had miscarried, but I have wrote him again to-day. R. B.

Thursday [*May* 24.]—Mr Ker and I set out to dine at Mr Hood's on our way to England.

I am taken extremely ill with strong feverish symptoms, and take a servant of Mr Hood's to watch me all night—embittering remorse scares my fancy at the gloomy forebodings of death.—I am determined to live for the future in such a manner as not to be scared at the approach of death—I am sure I could meet him with indifference, but for 'The something beyond the grave.' Mr Hood agrees to accompany us to England if we will wait till Sunday.

Friday [*May* 25.]—I go with Mr Hood to see a roup of an unfortunate farmer's stock—rigid economy, and decent industry, do you preserve me from being the principal *dramatis persona* in such a scene of horror!

Meet my good old friend Mr Ainslie, who calls on Mr Hood in the evening to take farewell of my bardship. This day I feel myself warm with sentiments of gratitude to the Great Preserver of men, who has kindly restored me to health and strength once more.

A pleasant walk with my young friend Douglas Ainslie, a sweet, modest, clever young fellow.

Sunday, 27th *May.*—Cross Tweed, and traverse the moors through a wild country till I reach Alnwick—Alnwick Castle, a seat of the Duke of Northumberland, furnished in a most princely manner.—A Mr Wilkin, agent of His Grace's, shows us the house and policies. Mr Wilkin, a discreet, sensible, ingenious man.

Monday [*May* 28.]—Come, still through by-ways, to Warkworth, where we dine.—Hermitage and old castle. Warkworth situated very picturesque, with Coquet Island, a small rocky spot, the seat of an old monastery, facing it a little in the sea; and the small but romantic river Coquet running through it.—Sleep at Morpeth, a pleasant enough little town, and on next day [*May* 29) to Newcastle.—Meet with a very agreeable, sensible fellow, a Mr Chattox, who shows us a great many civilities, and who dines and sups with us.

Tuesday seems to have been a blank day. Burns wrote, however, a rollicking letter to his friend Ainslie, descriptive of some of his adventures after they had parted:

MON CHER COMPAGNON DE VOYAGE—Here am I, a woeful wight on the banks of Tyne. Old Mr Thos. Hood has been persuaded to join our *Partie*, and Mr Kerr and he do very well, but alas! I dare not talk nonsense lest I lose all the little dignity I have among the sober sons of wisdom and discretion, and I have not had one hearty mouthful of laughter since that merry melancholy moment we parted.

Mr Sherriff tired me to death ; but as my good star directed, Sir James Hall detained him on some business, as he is Sir James's tenant, till near eleven at night, which time I spent with Miss —— till I was, in the language of the royal Voluptuary Solomon, 'Sick of "Love."' Next morning, Sir James, who had been informed by the Sh—— of my Bardship's arrival, came to breakfast with us and carried me with him, and his charming Lady and he did me the honor to accompany me the whole forenoon through the glorious, romantic Deane of Dunglass. I would not stay dinner ; and when I returned to my horse, I found Miss —— ready equipp'd to escort me to Dunbar, with the view of making a parade of me as a Sweetheart among her relations by the way and at Dunbar. She was *bien poudre, bien frise* in her fine cream-colored riding clothes, mounted on an old, dun carthorse that had once been fat ; a broken, old side saddle, without crupper, stirrup or girth; a bridle that in former times had had buckles, and a crooked, meandring hazel stick which might have borne a place with credit in a scrubbing besom. In the words of the Highlandman when he saw the Deil on Shanter-hill in the shape of five swine—' My hair stood . . . and I swat and trembled.' Nothing could prevail with her, no distant insinuation, no broad hint would make her give over her purpose ; at last vexed, disgusted, enraged to a high degree, I pretended a fire-haste and rode so hard that she was almost shaken to pieces on old Jolly, and, to my great joy, found it convenient to stop at an uncle's house by the way ; I refused to call with her, and so we quarrelled and parted.—You shall hear from me at Dumfries.—Farewell !

Robt. Burns.

Newcastle, *29th May* 1787.

Wednesday [*May* 30.]—Left Newcastle early in the morning, and rode over a fine country to Hexham to breakfast—from Hexham to Wardrue [Wardrew], the celebrated Spa, where we slept.

Thursday [*May* 31.]—Reach Longtown to dine, and part there with my good friends Messrs Hood and Ker.—A hiring day in Longtown.—I am uncommonly happy to see so many young folks enjoying life.—I come to Carlisle. (Meet a strange enough romantic adventure by the way, in falling in with a girl and her married sister—the girl, after some overtures of gallantry on my side, sees me a little cut with the bottle, and offers to take me in for a Gretna-green affair. I, not being quite such a gull as she imagines, make an appointment with her, by way of *vive la bagatelle*, to hold a conference on it when we reach town.—I meet her in town and give her a brush of caressing and a bottle of cyder ; but finding herself *un peu trompée* in her man, she sheers off.) Next day [*June* 1] I meet my good friend, Mr Mitchell, and walk with him round the town and its environs, and through his printing-works, &c.—four or five hundred people employed, many of them women and children.—Dine

with Mr Mitchell, and leave Carlisle.—Come by the coast to Annan.—
Overtaken on the way by a curious old fish of a shoemaker, and miner
from Cumberland mines.

[Here the Manuscript abruptly terminates.]

In the following letter, written from Carlisle, we first encounter the name of Mr William Nicol,* one of the classical
masters of the High School of Edinburgh, though Burns must
have been for some time acquainted with him. Of considerable natural ability and eminently warm-hearted, Nicol
almost thrust his friendship upon the Poet, whom he sincerely
admired. Burns, on his part, found in Nicol a congenial
companion, who heartily denounced religious hypocrisy and
kindred vices. Ultimately, however, he became quite alive to
the violence of temper, vanity, and impracticability which
ruined his friend's professional career. Burns's letter is what he
himself called a 'Scots fragment'—written in a broad vernacular,
which he must have expected to be pleasing to Nicol.

TO MR WILLIAM NICOL.

CARLISLE, *June* 1, 1787.

KIND, HONEST-HEARTED WILLIE—I'm sitten doun here, after seven
and forty miles ridin, e'en as forjesket and forniaw'd as a forfoughten
cock, to gie you some notion o' my land-lowper-like stravaiguin sin the
sorrowfu' hour that I sheuk hands and parted wi' Auld Reekie.

My auld, ga'd gleyde o' a meere has huchyall'd up hill and down brae,
in Scotland and England, as teugh and birnie as a vera devil wi' me.
It's true, she's as poor's a sang-maker and as hard's a kirk, and tipper-
taipers when she taks the gate first, like a lady's gentlewoman in a
minuwae or a hen on a het girdle, but she's a yauld, poutherie Girran
for a' that, and has a stomach like Willie Stalker's meere that wad hae
disgeested tumbler-wheels, for she'll whip me aff her five stimparts o'
the best aits at a down-sittin and ne'er fash her thumb. When anee
her ringbanes and spavies, her crucks and cramps, are fairly soupl'd, she

---

* William Nicol was the son of a poor tradesman at Dumbretton, parish of Annan,
where he was born in 1744. His father died early, leaving his widow, with an only son,
unprovided for. The son's first education was received from an itinerant teacher named
John Orr. When but a lad he opened a school in his mother's house. He afterwards
attended Annan Academy, and passed through the University of Edinburgh, studying first
theology and then medicine. On a vacancy occurring in the High School of Edinburgh in
1774, he applied and was successful. He was one of the most popular of masters, and but
for an irascible temper would probably have outshone most of his compeers. In October
1795, having three months previously (in consequence of a quarrel with the Rector, Dr
Adam) resigned his mastership, he opened an academy in Jackson's Land, High Street.
This he carried on till his death in April 1797. He is interred in Calton Burying-ground.

beets to, beets to, and ay the hindmost hour the tightest. I could wager her price (and that, ye ken, was odds o' four pund sterling) to a thretty pennies that, for twa or three wooks ridin at fifty mile a day, the deil-sticket a five gallopers acqueesh Clyde and Whithorn could cast saut on her tail.

I hae dander'd owre a' the Kintra frae Dunbar to Seleraig, and hae forgather'd wi' mony a guid fallow, and monie a weel-far'd hizzie. I met wi' twa dink quines in particular, ane o' them a sonsie, fine, fodgel lass, baith braw and bonie; the tither was a clean-shankit, straught, tight, weel-far'd winch, as blythe 's a lintwhite on a floweric thorn, and as sweet and modest 's a new-blawn plumrose in a hazle shaw. They were baith bred to mainers by the beuk, and onie ane o' them had as muckle smeddum and rumblgumption as the half o' some presbytries that you and I baith ken. They play'd me sic a deevil o' a shavie that I daur say if my harigals were turn'd out, ye wad see twa nicks i' the heart o' me like the mark o' a kail-whittle in a castock.

I was gaun to write you a lang pystle, but, Guid forgie me, I gat my-sel sae notouriously bitchify'd the day, after kail-time, that I can hardly stoiter but and ben.

My best respecks to the guidwife and a' our common friens, especiall Mr and Mrs Cruikshank and the honest guidman o' Jock's Lodge.[*]

I 'll be in Dumfries the morn, gif the beast be to the fore and the branks bide hale. Gude be wi' you, Willie! Amen!   R. B.

This letter may be thus translated: —

KIND, HONEST-HEARTED WILLIE—I have sat down here, after forty-seven miles' hard riding, as jaded and fatigued as an overfought cock, to give you some notion of my vagabond-like wandering since the sorrow-ful hour that I shook hands and parted with Auld Reekie [Edinburgh].

My old galled mare has hobbled up and down hill in Scotland and England, as tough and lively as a very devil with me. It is true she is as poor as a song-maker, and as hard as a church, and totters when she takes the road, just like a lady's gentlewoman in a minuet or a hen on a hot oven; but she is an alert, spirited beast notwithstanding, and has a stomach like Willie Stalker's mare, that would have digested cart-wheels, for she 'll whip me off five-eighths of a Winchester bushel of the best oats at a time, with no difficulty. When once her ill-assorted joints and spavins, her lameness and cramps, are fairly suppled, she improves by little and little, and always the last hour is her best. I could wager her price (which, you know, was over £4 sterling) against twopence-halfpenny, that for two or three weeks' riding at fifty miles a day, the devil a galloper between Clyde and Whithorn could cast salt on her tail.

---

* Probably Louis Cauvin (circa 1754-1825), who gave Burns instruction in French.—Cauvin, whose father was also a teacher of French in Edinburgh, ultimately retired to a farm at Duddingston, to which parish he left his fortune to found and endow an hospital (Cauvin's Hospital). He has recorded that Burns made more progress in his three months' study than any of his ordinary pupils did in as many years.

I have sauntered over the whole country from Dunbar to Selkirk, and have met with many a good fellow and many a well-favoured maiden. I met with two fine girls, in particular, one of them a fine, plump, comfortable-looking lass, well dressed and pretty; the other a well-limbed, straight, tight, well-favoured wench, as blithe as a linnet on a flowering thorn, and as sweet and modest as a new-blown primrose in a hazel-wood. They had both acquired manners from the book, and any one of them had as much smartness and sense as the half of some of the presbyteries that you and I know. They played me such a devil of a prank, that if my inside were turned out, you would see two nicks on my heart like the mark of a knife on a cabbage-stalk.

I was going to write a long epistle; but, God forgive me, I got myself so dreadfully tipsy to-day, after dinner, that I can hardly crawl from one room to another.

My best respects to your lady and all our common friends, especially Mr and Mrs Cruikshanks, and the honest goodman of Jock's Lodge.

I shall be in Dumfries to-morrow, if the beast survive and the bridle keep whole. God be with you, Willie! Amen! R. B.

Burns remained a couple of days in Dumfries, and was presented with the freedom of the burgh. His burgess-ticket, which is dated 4th June, and was subsequently of use to him, bore this inscription: 'The said day, 4th June 1787, Mr Robert Burns, Ayrshire, was admitted burgess of this burgh, with liberty to exercise and enjoy the whole immunities and privileges thereof as freely as any other does, may, or can enjoy, who, being present, accepted the same, and gave his oath of burgess-ship to his Majesty and the burgh in common form.'* In Dumfries also he obtained the first intimation that the 'passions wild and strong,' to which he confessed, had again involved him in difficulty. He found a pitiful letter, dated May 26, awaiting him from a domestic servant in Edinburgh, named May Cameron, asking help, as she was 'in trouble.' The poor girl, who had to get a friend to write for her, did not reproach Burns, nor did she say directly that he was the cause of her 'trouble.' She described herself as his 'sincere well-wisher,' and apologised for writing: but 'out of quarters, without friends, my situation at present is really deplorable. I beg, for God sake, you will write and let me know how I am to do. You can write to any person you can trust to get me a place to stay in till such time as you come to town yourself.'

* William Clark was the name of the Provost of Dumfries at this time. No record appears to be discoverable of any public ceremony having taken place on the occasion.

Burns may have held what was then undoubtedly the popular 'young-man-about-town' view of an intrigue with a servant-girl. But he was incapable of behaving cruelly. He at once wrote to Ainslie: 'Please call for the wench; give her ten or twelve shillings, and advise her to some country friends.' How Ainslie, himself at the time in a similar predicament, discharged the commission entrusted to him has not been definitely ascertained.

From Dumfries Burns proceeded to Dalswinton, the estate of Patrick Miller, who, it will be remembered, had expressed a wish to see the poet settled on one of his farms. Burns must have admired the delightful scenery of this district, but the estate itself could scarcely have been inviting to a farmer's eye, for it was at this time, even by the confession of its owner, in exceedingly bad condition. He seems to have lingered about a week in the district. Turning homeward at length, he passed by Sanquhar, and arrived at Mauchline on the 9th of June. Mrs Begg used to recall the arrival of her brother. He came in unheralded, and was in the midst of them before they knew. It was a quiet meeting—for the Mossgiel family had the true Scottish reticence or reserve; but though their words were few, their feelings were strong.

Burns seems to have taken an early opportunity of calling at Mr Armour's, professedly to see his child; and his reception was more cordial than he expected, or even desired. This appears from a letter to Smith, who had now left Mauchline and was settled at Linlithgow:

TO MR JAMES SMITH, LINLITHGOW.

MAUCHLINE, 11th June 1787.

MY EVER DEAR SIR—I date this from Mauchline, where I arrived on Friday even last. I slept at John Dow's, and called for my daughter; Mr Hamilton and family; your mother, sister, and brother; my quondam Eliza,* &c., all, all well. If any thing had been wanting to disgust me completely at Armour's family, their mean, servile compliance would have done it.

Give me a spirit like my favourite hero, Milton's Satan:

Hail, horrors! hail,
Infernal world! and thou profoundest hell
Receive thy new possessor! one who brings
A mind not to be changed by *place* or *time!*

---

* Eliza Miller had probably by this time become Mrs Templeton.

I cannot settle to my mind. Farming, the only thing of which I know anything, and, heaven above knows, but little do I understand of that, I cannot, dare not, risk on farms as they are. If I do not fix, I will go for Jamaica. Should I stay in an unsettled state at home, I would only dissipate my little fortune, and ruin what I intend shall compensate my little ones for the stigma I have brought on their names.

I shall write you more at length soon; as this letter costs you no postage, if it be worth reading you cannot complain of your penny-worth. I am ever, my dear Sir, yours, R. B.

P.S.—The cloot* has unfortunately broke, but I have provided a fine buffalo-horn, on which I am going to affix the same cypher which you will remember was on the lid of the cloot.

TO MR WILLIAM NICOL.

MAUCHLINE, *June* 18, 1787.

MY DEAR FRIEND—I am now arrived safe in my native country, after a very agreeable jaunt, and have the pleasure to find all my friends well. I breakfasted with your gray-headed, reverend friend, Mr Smith; and was highly pleased both with the cordial welcome he gave me, and his most excellent appearance and sterling good sense.

I have been with Mr Miller at Dalswinton, and am to meet him again in August. From my view of the lands and his reception of my bard-ship, my hopes in that business are rather mended; but still they are but slender.

I am quite charmed with Dumfries folks—Mr Burnside,† the clergyman, in particular, is a man whom I shall ever gratefully remember; and his wife, Gude forgie me! I had almost broke the tenth commandment on her account. Simplicity, elegance, good sense, sweetness of disposition, good humor, kind hospitality, are the constituents of her manner and heart; in short—but if I say one word more about her, I shall be directly in love with her.

I never, my friend, thought mankind very capable of any thing generous; but the stateliness of the Patricians in Edinburgh, and the servility of my plebeian brethren (who perhaps formerly eyed me askance) since I returned home, have nearly put me out of conceit altogether with my species. I have bought a pocket Milton, which I carry perpetually about

---

* A snuff-box made of a sheep's hoof. It has been conjectured, with a fair show of reason, that this was the same snuff-box that he afterwards presented to Bacon, landlord of the Brownhill Inn, Dumfriesshire.

† Dr William Burnside was at this time minister of the New Church in Dumfries. He was translated to St Michael's parish, in the same town, in 1794. He died 6th January 1806, at the age of fifty-five. He wrote a history of Dumfries, a portion of which was embodied in Sir John Sinclair's *Statistical Account*, for which it was originally prepared. Dr Burnside's wife, Anne, eulogised by Burns, survived her husband thirty-two years, dying in 1838, at the age of seventy-nine.

with me, in order to study the sentiments—the dauntless magnanimity, the intrepid, unyielding independence, the desperate daring, and noble defiance of hardship, in that great personage, SATAN. 'Tis true, I have just now a little cash ; but I am afraid the star that hitherto has shed its malignant, purpose-blasting rays full in my zenith ; that noxious planet so baneful in its influences to the rhyming tribe, I much dread it is not yet beneath my horizon. Misfortune dodges the path of human life ; the poetic mind finds itself miserably deranged in, and unfit for, the walks of business ; add to all, that thoughtless follies and hare-brained whims, like so many *ignes fatui*, eternally diverging from the right line of sober discretion, sparkle with step-bewitching blaze in the idly-gazing eyes of the poor heedless Bard, till, pop, ' he falls like Lucifer, never to hope again.' God grant this may be an unreal picture with respect to me ! but should it not, I have very little dependence on man-kind. I will close my letter with this tribute my heart bids me pay you —the many ties of acquaintance and friendship which I have, or think I have, in life, I have felt along the lines, and, damn them ! they are almost all of them of such frail contexture, that I am sure they would not stand the breath of the least adverse breeze of fortune ; but from you, my ever dear sir, I look with confidence for the Apostolic love that shall wait on me ' through good report and bad report '—the love which Solomon emphatically says ' Is strong as death.' My compliments to Mrs Nicol, and all the circle of our common friends.   R. B.

P.S.—I shall be in Edinburgh about the latter end of July.

Though Burns had been, in his own opinion at all events, practically divorced from Jean Armour, and had been much incensed by her conduct and that of her relatives, he had never been able to detach her from his heart. He had conceived a passion for several women while resting in what he called ' the Greenland bay of indifference' in Edinburgh, and had, it may be inferred from a letter to Hamilton, asked at least one to be his wife. But, when on returning to Mauchline, he met Jean in her father's house, to which, in what appeared to be the hour of his prosperity, he was now welcomed, the two became as intimate as ever. ' On my *éclatant* return to Mauchline,' he subsequently wrote to Mrs Dunlop, ' I was made very welcome to visit my girl, and the usual circumstances began to betray her at the time I was laid up a cripple in Edinburgh.'

The later part of the month appears to have been devoted to a short Highland tour, of which we have only an imperfect and obscure account. Currie says that, having remained with his friends at Mauchline a few days, 'he proceeded again to Edinburgh, and immediately set out on a journey to the Highlands;' but 'no particulars of the tour have been found among his manuscripts.' It is nearly certain that Burns did not visit Edinburgh on this occasion. Mrs Begg's impression was 'that he went first to Glasgow, from which he sent home a present to his mother and three sisters; namely, a quantity of *mode silk*, sufficient to make a bonnet and cloak to each, and a gown to his mother and youngest sister, the whole being a recognition of their title to a share of his good-fortune.' Mrs Begg remembered going for rather more than a week to Ayr, to assist in the making-up of these dresses; and when she came back on a Saturday, he had returned, and she recollected being requested by him to put on her dress, that he might see how smart she looked in it. Almost the only other certain trace we have of Burns in this trip is in the West Highlands. To this district he might be drawn by his former feelings towards Mary Campbell. It is not impossible that he visited her relatives at Greenock. On this point, however, there are no facts to draw sentimental or other conclusions from.

It is possible that at this time he may have copied into one of his notebooks—it is almost incredible that he should have written—a long poem, the sentiments of which certainly harmonise with a visit to the grave of Mary in the West Kirkyard. He transcribed it in his second Common-place Book.

ELEGY ON 'STELLA.'

The following Poem is the work of some hapless, unknown Son of the Muses, who deserved a better fate. There is a great deal of 'The voice of Cona' in his solitary, mournful notes; and had the sentiments been clothed in Shenstone's language, they would have been no discredit even to that elegant Poet.—*R. B.*

Strait is the spot and green the sod
  From whence my sorrows flow:
And soundly rests the ever dear
  Inhabitant below.

Pardon my transport, gentle Shade,
  While o'er the turf I bow!
Thy earthly house is circumscrib'd
  And solitary now.

Not one poor stone to tell thy name
   Or make thy virtues known :
But what avails to me, to thee,
   The sculpture of a stone ?

I 'll sit me down upon this turf,
   And wipe away this tear :
The chill blast passes swiftly by,
   And flits around thy bier.

Dark is the dwelling of the Dead,
   And sad their house of rest :
Low lies the head by Death's cold arm
   In aweful fold embrac'd.

I saw the grim Avenger stand
   Incessant by thy side ;
Unseen by thee, his deadly breath
   Thy lingering frame destroy'd.

Pale grew the roses on thy cheek,
   And wither'd was thy bloom,
Till the slow poison brought thy youth
   Untimely to the tomb.

Thus wasted are the ranks of men,
   Youth, Health, and Beauty fall ;
The ruthless ruin spreads around,
   And overwhelms us all.

Behold where, round thy narrow house,
   The graves unnumber'd lie !
The multitudes that sleep below
   Existed but to die.

Some, with the tottering steps of Age,
   Trod down the darksome way :
And some, in youth's lamented prime,
   Like thee, were torn away.

Yet these, however hard their fate,
   Their native earth receives :
Amid their weeping friends they died,
   And fill their fathers' graves.

From thy lov'd friends, when first thy breath
  Was taught by Heaven to blow:
Far, far remov'd, the ruthless stroke
  Surpris'd and laid thee low.

At the last limits of our Isle,
  Wash'd by the western wave,
Touch'd by thy fate, a thoughtful bard
  Sits lonely on thy grave.

Pensive he eyes, before him spread,
  The deep outstretch'd and vast;
His mourning notes are borne away
  Along the rapid blast.

And while, amid the silent Dead
  Thy hapless fate he mourns,
His own long sorrows freshly bleed,
  And all his grief returns.

Like thee, cut off in early youth
  And flower of beauty's pride,
His friend, his first and only joy,
  His much lov'd Stella, died.

Him, too, the stern impulse of Fate
  Resistless bears along;
And the same rapid tide shall whelm
  The Poet and the Song.

The tear of pity which he shed,
  He asks not to receive;
Let but his poor remains be laid
  Obscurely in the grave.

His grief-worn heart, with truest joy,
  Shall meet the welcome shock;
His airy harp shall lie unstrung
  And silent on the rock.

O my dear maid, my Stella, when
  Shall this sick period close;
And lead the solitary Bard
  To his belov'd repose?

We light upon Burns first with certainty at Inveraray, where he
was unfortunate; for the Duke of Argyll had an overabundance

of guests in the castle, and the innkeeper was too much occupied
with those quartered upon him to have any attention to spare for
passing travellers. At the inn Burns penned an epigram, which
it is supposed he left inscribed on one of the windows:

ON INCIVILITY SHOWN HIM AT INVERARAY.

> Whoe'er he be that sojourns here,
>   I pity much his case—
> Unless he come to wait upon
>   The Lord *their* God, 'His Grace.'

> There's naething here but Highland pride,
>   And Highland scab and hunger;
> If Providence has sent me here,
>   'Twas surely in an anger.*

This seems on the surface a regrettable act of discourtesy towards
a highly respected nobleman,† whose name, with that of his
duchess, stood at the head of the list of subscribers for his
Poems. The next authentic account we have of Burns's journey
treats of the homeward route.

TO MR ROBERT AINSLIE, EDINBURGH.

ARROCHAR, NEAR CROCHARIBAS, BY LOCH LOANG, *June 25th*, 1787.

MY DEAR FRIEND AND BROTHER ARCH—I write you this on my tour
through a country where savage streams tumble over savage mountains,

---

* The late Dr Hately Waddell in his *Life and Works of Robert Burns* (1870), gives, from
Hints respecting Burns, the Ayrshire Poet, by G. Grierson, another version of the epigram:

> 'Whoe'er thou art that lodgest here,
>   Heaven help thy wofu' case;
> Unless thou com'st to visit Him,
>   That king of kings, his Grace.

> There's Highland greed, there's Highland pride;
>   There's Highland scab and hunger;
> If heaven it was that sent me here
>   It sent me in an anger.'

To this version is attached the note 'The above lines were written at the inn at Inveraray,
by R. Burns, in presence of George Grierson, in 1878.' The erroneous date given is
sufficient to make this version 'suspect.'

† John, fifth Duke of Argyll, was then in his sixty-fourth year. The duchess was the
celebrated beauty, Elizabeth Gunning, and was the widow of the Duke of Hamilton when
she married the Duke of Argyll.

thinly overspread with savage flocks, which starvingly support as savage inhabitants. My last stage was Inverary—to-morrow night's stage, Dumbarton. I ought sooner to have answered your kind letter, but you know I am a man of many sins. . . .*   R. B.

He appears to have gone home by Paisley. In a letter which appeared in the *Liverpool Mercury* on May 29, 1847, Mr John Taylor, cotton-broker, Liverpool, gave an account of some circumstances connected with the poet's brief stay at that place. 'It must have been,' he says, 'on Friday the 29th of June, about noon, that Dr John Taylor of Paisley, who had been charmed with the poems of the Ayrshire Ploughman, readily recognised him from his portrait, as he stood in the street with his friend Mr Alexander Pattison. Having induced both Burns and Pattison to go to his house, notwithstanding some hesitation on the part of the poet, who expressed himself as eager to proceed on his journey, Dr Taylor entered into conversation on what was with himself a favourite subject—poetry. Burns made the observation that perhaps people were ready to attach more merit to poetry than was its due, for that, after all, it was only natural ideas expressed in melodious words; to which his host assented, and, in illustration, remarked that nothing was more common than for children in a winter's night to say : " What will become of the puir birdies the nicht ?" But what says the poet ?

> Ilk happing bird, wee, helpless thing,   hopping—little
> That, in the merry months o' spring,
> Delighted me to hear thee sing,
>   What comes o' thee ?
> Whare wilt thou cower thy chittering wing,   shivering
>   An' close thy e'e ?   eye

The compliment pleased : Burns started on his feet, and bowing, expressed his thanks for the obliging quotation. After this, Burns seemed to forget the haste which he had before alleged ; the conversation became animated, and, as it appeared, interesting to both. Burns spoke of his reception at Edinburgh, and dwelt

---

* This fragment of a letter now forms part of the Watson collection in the National Portrait Gallery, Edinburgh. The reverse contains part of a sentence which suggests the possibility that in his 'kind letter,' Ainslie had, as requested by Burns, seen May Cameron, and given her money. It also appears to throw out a hint that while Burns admitted his intimacy with the girl, he did not believe himself to be the father of her expected child.

much on the kindness which he had experienced from the Earl of Glencairn, showing a ring that he wore, a gift from that nobleman. However fond Burns was of the produce of his Muse, the other was probably no less so of his young family, who were all summoned. One of the children, a fat chubby boy, the poet took on his knee, and said "he would make an excellent subject for a poem;" an idea which the father assured him he should be highly gratified to see carried into effect. An elder one was sent for, and desired to go in; but from the great talk he had heard about poets, and particularly about Poet Burns, this one did not feel well assured that it was safe for him to trust his person within the poet's clutches. He therefore watched his opportunity, and ventured merely to pass from one door to another through the room, taking the best look he could of the poet, as he stood up with a small black profile of Mrs Taylor's in his hand, which he was then examining. The small black profiles, called silhouettes, were then coming into fashion. From that time, although the observer was then hardly more than a child, the remembrance of the poet's figure, face, and general appearance, has never been lost; the recollection of him is distinct, and is that of a big, stout, athletic man, of a brown, ruddy complexion, broad-chested, erect, and standing firmly on his legs, which perhaps were rather clumsy, though hid in yellow topped-boots. His dress was a blue coat and buckskin breeches, and his *caste* seemed what we should now style that of a gentleman-farmer. The impression made by the poet on his host was highly favourable, but the lady was struck with a certain gloominess that seemed to have possession of his countenance and general bearing.'

A letter, written immediately after he reached home, to James Smith, gives some particulars of the later part of his Highland tour. He had stayed a night at Arrochar, at the head of Loch Long, had dined next day on Loch Lomond side, and spent a night at Dumbarton. There is but the faintest trace of the men he met on this occasion.* His friend Kennedy, formerly of Dumfries House in Ayrshire, but now settled in this district, is the person most likely to have been the means of introducing him in that

* No confirmation can be obtained of a tradition that Burns was publicly entertained at Dumbarton, and presented with the freedom of the burgh; and that the Rev. James Oliphant, celebrated in the 'Ordination,' and at this time minister of Dumbarton, denounced the magistrates for their action.

Highland circle. His chief entertainer, there is every reason to believe, was John M'Auley, at that time town-clerk of Dumbarton. M'Auley, who had helped to secure subscriptions for the Edinburgh edition, then resided in Levengrove House,* which he had built on a little property he had bought—known as the Ferrylands of Cardross, and separated from Dumbarton by the river Leven. It is highly probable that Burns remained over one night at Levengrove House. There is a tradition in Dumbarton that he paid a visit to the Freemasons' Lodge, and colour is given to it by the fact that Robert Lindsay, Master of the lodge, and a number of other active members, were subscribers to the Edinburgh edition.

TO MR JAMES SMITH, LINLITHGOW.

June 30th, 1787.

*　　　*　　　*　　　*　　　*

On our return, at a Highland gentleman's hospitable mansion, we fell in with a merry party, and danced till the ladies left us, at three in the morning. Our dancing was none of the French or English insipid formal movements; the ladies sang Scotch songs like angels, at intervals; then we flew at 'Bab at the Bowster,' 'Tullochgorum,' 'Loch Erroch-side,'† &c., like midges sporting in the mottie sun, or craws prognosticating a storm in a hairst-day. When the dear lasses left us, we ranged round the bowl till the good-fellow hour of six; except a few minutes that we went out to pay our devotions to the glorious lamp of day peering over the towering top of Ben-Lomond. We all kneeled; our worthy land-lord's son held the bowl; each man a full glass in his hand; and I as priest, repeated some rhyming nonsense, like 'Thomas-a-Rhymer's prophecies, I suppose. After a small refreshment of the gifts of Somnus, we proceeded to spend the day on Lochlomond, and reach Dumbarton in the evening. We dined at another good fellow's house, and consequently push'd the bottle: when we went out to mount our horses, we found ourselves 'No verra fou but gaylie yet.' My two friends and I rode soberly down the Loch side, till by came a Highlandman at the gallop, on a tolerably good horse, but which had never known the

---

* Levengrove House no longer exists. The site on which it stood forms part of Levengrove Park. One of the descendants of John M'Auley resided, within the memory of old folk still alive, in the 'Half-way House,' Dumbarton. The Half-way House has been demolished, and its site included in the shipbuilding yard of Messrs William Denny & Bros.

† Names of familiar Scots dancing-tunes.

ornaments of iron or leather. We scorned to be out-galloped by a Highlandman, so off we started, whip and spur. My companions, though
seemingly gayly mounted, fell sadly astern; but my old mare, Jenny
Geddes, one of the Rosinante family, she strained past the Highlandman
in spite of all his efforts with the hair halter: just as I was passing him,
Donald wheeled his horse as if to cross before me to mar my progress,
when down came his horse, and threw his rider's breekless a—e in a clipt
hedge; and down came Jenny Geddes over all, and my bardship between
her and the Highlandman's horse. Jenny Geddes trod over me with
such cautious reverence that matters were not so bad as might well
have been expected; so I came off with a few cuts and bruises, and a
thorough resolution to be a pattern of sobriety for the future.

I have yet fixed on nothing with respect to the serious business of life.
I am, just as usual, a rhyming, mason-making, rattling, aimless, idle
fellow. However, I shall somewhere have a farm soon. I was going to
say a wife too; but that must never be my blessed lot. I am but a
younger son of Parnassus, and, like other younger sons of great families,
I may intrigue, if I choose to run all risks, but must not marry.

I am afraid I have almost ruined one source, the principal one, indeed,
of my former happiness—that eternal propensity I always had to fall in
love. My heart no more glows with feverish raptures—I have no
paradisaical evening interviews, stolen from the restless cares and prying
inhabitants of this weary world. I have only * * * *. This last is one
of your distant acquaintances, has a fine figure, and elegant manners;
and, in the train of some great folks whom you know, has seen the
politest quarters in Europe. I do like her a good deal; but what piques
me is her conduct at the commencement of our acquaintance. I
frequently visited her when I was in —— ; and after passing regularly
the intermediate degrees between the distant formal bow and the
familiar grasp round the waist, I ventured, in my careless way, to talk
of friendship in rather ambiguous terms; and after her return to ——, I
wrote to her in the same style. Miss, construing my words farther than
even I intended, flew off in a tangent of female dignity and reserve,
like a mounting lark in an April morning; and wrote me an answer
which measured me out very completely, what an immense way I had to
travel before I could reach the climate of her favour. But I am an old
hawk at the sport, and wrote her such a cool, deliberate, prudent reply,
as brought my bird from her aërial towerings, pop, down at my foot,
like Corporal Trim's hat.

As for the rest of my acts, and my wars, and all my wise sayings, and
why my mare was called Jenny Geddes; they shall be recorded in a few
weeks hence at Linlithgow, in the chronicles of your memory, by

                                    ROBERT BURNS.

It might have been at M'Auley's house, and by way of *amende* for
the Inveraray epigram, that Burns penned this well-known quatrain,

although it falls in quite as appropriately with the later tour in the north :

COMPOSED ON LEAVING A PLACE IN THE HIGHLANDS WHERE HE HAD BEEN KINDLY ENTERTAINED.

When Death's dark stream I ferry o'er
(A time that surely shall come),
In Heav'n itself I 'll ask no more
Than just a Highland welcome.

Respecting the love affair alluded to, there is no further light, unless we connect with it a stray letter which has found its way into print without a superscription. No absolutely safe conjecture can be formed as to the identity of the Ayrshire girl (implied in the phrase 'countrywoman') who was 'a distant acquaintance' of Smith; although it has been suggested, not without plausibility, that she may have been Margaret Chalmers, daughter of Mr Chalmers of Fingland, Kirkcudbrightshire, some time a farmer in the neighbourhood of Mauchline, where probably the Poet had made her acquaintance. The mother of Margaret Chalmers, to whom we shall have occasion to refer at length further on, was a sister of Gavin Hamilton's stepmother.

TO MISS ——.

MY DEAR COUNTRYWOMAN—I am so impatient to show you that I am once more at peace with you, that I send you the book I mentioned, directly, rather than wait the uncertain time of my seeing you. I am afraid I have mislaid or lost Collins' *Poems*, which I promised to Miss Irvin. If I can find them, I will forward them by you ; if not, you must apologize for me.

I know you will laugh at it when I tell you that your piano and you together have played the deuce somehow about my heart. My breast has been widowed these many months, and I thought myself proof against the fascinating witchcraft ; but I am afraid you will 'feelingly convince me what I am.' I say, I am afraid, because I am not sure what is the matter with me. I have one miserable bad symptom : when you whisper, or look kindly, to another, it gives me a draught of damnation. I have a kind of wayward wish to be with you ten minutes by yourself, though what I would say, Heaven above knows, for I am sure I know not. I have no formed design in all this ; but just, in the nakedness of my heart, write you down a mere matter-of-fact story. You may perhaps give yourself airs of distance on this, and that will completely cure me ;

but I wish you would not : just let us meet, if you please, in the old beaten way of friendship.

I will not subscribe myself your humble servant, for that is a phrase, I think, at least fifty miles off from the heart; but I will conclude with sincerely wishing that the Great Protector of innocence may shield you from the barbed dart of calumny, and hand you by the covert snare of deceit.   R. B.

The following letter, here printed for the first time, is now in The Athenæum at Liverpool. It is in very fragmentary condition, even the name of the person to whom it was sent being mutilated. The poem mentioned is the copy of 'The Poet's Welcome to his Love-begotten Daughter,' noted in Vol. I., Appendix IX., p. 482, as having title 'A Poet's Welcome to his bastart wean.'

TO MR WILL............

MY DEAR SIR—The above is the Poem I promised you, and much [good may it do] . . . to my much esteem[ed] . . . a copy of it.

My brother, Rog . . . some time in Nov[ember] . . . minate himself . . . -tance cannot aid . . . best advice will . . . the . . . My dear Sir, Yours sincerely,   ROBT. BU[RNS.]

MOSSGIEL, 2d *July* 1787.

TO MR JOHN RICHMOND.

MOSSGIEL, 7th *July* 1787.

MY DEAR RICHMOND—I am all impatience to hear of your fate since the old confounder of right and wrong has turned you out of place, by his journey to answer his indictment at the bar of the other world.* He will find the practice of the court so different from the practice in which he has for so many years been thoroughly hackneyed, that his friends, if he had any connections truly of that kind, which I rather doubt, may well tremble for his sake. His chicane, his left-handed wisdom, which stood so firmly by him, to such good purpose, here, like other accomplices in robbery and plunder, will, now the piratical business is blown, in all probability turn king's evidence, and then the devil's bagpiper will touch him off ' Bundle and go !'

If he has left you any legacy, I beg your pardon for all this ; if not, I know you will swear to every word I said about him.

I have lately been rambling over by Dumbarton and Inveraray, and running a drunken race on the side of Loch Lomond with a wild High-landman ; his horse, which had never known the ornaments of iron or

---

* Alluding to the recent decease of Richmond's employer, William Wilson, W.S.

leather, zigzagged across before my old spavin'd hunter, whose name is
Jenny Geddes, and down came the Highlandman, horse and all, and
down came Jenny and my bardship; so I have got such a skinful of
bruises and wounds, that I shall be at least four weeks before I dare
venture on my journey to Edinburgh.

Not one new thing under the sun has happened in Mauchline since
you left it. I hope this will find you as comfortably situated as formerly,
or, if heaven pleases, more so; but, at all events, I trust you will let me
know of course how matters stand with you, well or ill. 'Tis but poor
consolation to tell the world when matters go wrong; but you know very
well your connection and mine stands on a different footing. I am ever,
my dear friend, yours, R. B.

TO MR PETER HILL, AT MR CREECH'S, EDINBURGH.

DR SIR—I have just got a letter from Scot the Bookbinder, where he
tells me he needs a little money at present. I have written him to call
on you; and I beg you will pay him his acct., or give him part payment,
as you see proper.

When Mr Creech returns, I beg you will let me know by first convenient Post,—I am, dear Sir, your very humble servt.,

ROBT. BURNS.

MAUCHLINE, 10th July 1787.

It is possible that the Mr Scot here mentioned is the 'Mr
Scott' mentioned in the following hitherto unpublished note,
which is now in the possession of Mr A. C. Lamb, Dundee.
It is also possible that he was Walter Scot, the husband of the
guidwife of Wauchope, who, according to Burns, was 'very
shrewd in his farming matters.' The letter runs thus:

Mr SCOTT—Give the gentleman who delivers you this, Mr Richmond,
my Small 'on Ploughs.' ROBT. BURNS.
Saturday morn.

Very singularly, the volume also has come into possession of the
owner of the letter. It is 'A Treatise on Ploughs and Wheel
Carriages, by James Small, plough and cart-wright, formerly at
Blackadder-Mount, now at Rosebank, near Foord, Mid-Lothian.'
The title-page, which carries the signature 'Robt. Burns, Poet,'
further contains this recommendation: 'I boldly recommend a
plough introduced into Scotland about twelve years ago, by James
Small at Blackadder-Mount, Berwickshire, which is now in great
request. The plough may be considered as a capital improvement.'
—Lord Kames' Gentleman Farmer. The book purports to have

been printed for the author in 1784. Possibly, therefore, it was one of the 'farming books' which Burns testifies, in his letter to Moore, to having read when he entered on the farm of Mossgiel, 'with a full resolution' to become 'a wise man.' The designation by Burns of himself as a 'poet' would seem to indicate that he placed his name upon the book after 1784, and it is not improbable that he asked the return of it from 'Mr Scott' when he had resolved to again turn farmer in Dumfriesshire. The book is in such admirable state of preservation as to suggest the probability that Burns's reading of 'farming books' had been neither profound nor sustained.

TO MR ROBERT AINSLIE.

MAUCHLINE, 23d July 1787.

MY DEAR AINSLIE—There is one thing for which I set great store by you as a friend, and it is this, that I have not a friend upon earth, besides yourself, to whom I can talk nonsense without forfeiting some degree of his esteem. Now, to one like me, who never cares for speaking any thing else but nonsense, such a friend as you is an invaluable treasure. I was never a rogue, but have been a fool all my life; and, in spite of all my endeavours, I see now plainly that I shall never be wise. Now it rejoices my heart to have met with such a fellow as you, who, though you are not just such a hopeless fool as I, yet I trust you will never listen so much to the temptations of the devil as to grow so very wise that you will in the least disrespect an honest fellow because he is a fool. In short, I have set you down as the staff of my old age, when the whole list of my friends will, after a decent share of pity, have forgot me.

> Though in the morn come sturt and strife,
>   Yet joy may come at noon;
> And I hope to live a merry, merry life
>   When a' thir days are done.   all these

Write me soon, were it but a few lines just to tell me how that good, sagacious man, your father, is—that kind, dainty body, your mother—that strapping chiel, your brother Douglas—and my friend Rachel, who is as far before Rachel of old, as she was before her blear-eyed sister Leah.   R. B.

While in Edinburgh, Burns had been introduced to M'Leod of Raasay, a Highland gentleman, one of whose daughters married James Mure Campbell of Rowallan, who in 1782 succeeded to the earldom of Loudoun. The countess died in 1780, and the earl

himself in **1786**. Their daughter, Flora Mure Campbell,* was
brought up by her aunts, the Misses M'Leod. Possibly **Burns**
was introduced to the family by Gavin Hamilton, who was factor
on the Loudoun estates. A Perthshire lady used to tell how she
met Burns at an evening-party in the house of an aunt of M'Leod
of Raasay in St John Street, where he seemed to be on easy terms.
'He had been on the previous night at a ball in Dunn's Rooms
(now the National Bank, St Andrew Square), and he spoke in high
terms of the beauty of the ladies, as well as of the witchery of the
music. His manner, however, was not prepossessing—scarcely
manly or natural. It seemed as if he affected a rusticity or
landertness, so that when he said the music was "bonie, bonie," he
spoke almost like a child.'

In opposition to this impression of Burns, that of another **Perth**-
shire lady may be given: 'A most estimable lady lately deceased,
in the immediate neighbourhood of **Perth**, who was more nearly
connected with the **poetry of** Burns than I feel at liberty to state
here, told me some years before her death that she dined with the
poet at Sir **James** Hunter **Blair's** in the beginning of **1787**, where
there was a large party **to meet him.** I shall endeavour to **repeat**
as nearly as I can her own words: "**I was** young at the time, and
I suppose rather handsome, **and** they made me sit on **the poet's**
right hand. During the evening, when he addressed **me** or said
anything for the general company, all **eyes were turned on** the
poet, no doubt; but, being so near, the general gaze **made me very**
unhappy, **and cost me** many blushes." **I asked her what she**
thought of **the poet's** appearance and **manners. She said she**
thought him "**manly** and free from affectation, and though it was
long ago, she had a vivid recollection of his appearance. That he
was stout, dark-complexioned, and had **fine** eyes; **and** did **not**
seem the least put about **by** the presence **of so many people of a**
much higher rank **than himself**, but appeared wishful to avoid the
perpetual reference made to him."'—Letter to the *Perthshire Journal*, **January** 17, 1865, **from** Mr P. **R.** Drummond.

The father of the countess—the **same** M'Leod who had entertained Johnson **in 1773**—died in Edinburgh in **1786. His son**

---

* **Flora, Countess of Loudoun,** married, in 1804, Francis Rawdon Hastings, Earl of
Moira, and commander-in-chief of the forces in Scotland, and subsequently Marquis of
Hastings. **She died in 1840.**

John died on 20th July of the following year. Burns, then at
Mossgiel, wrote the following sympathetic lines to the young
man's sister, Isabella:

ON READING IN A NEWSPAPER AN ACCOUNT OF
THE DEATH OF JOHN M'LEOD, ESQ.,
BROTHER TO A YOUNG LADY, A PARTICULAR FRIEND
OF THE AUTHOR'S.*

Sad thy tale, thou idle page,
  And rueful thy alarms:
Death tears the brother of her love
  From Isabella's arms.

Sweetly deckt with pearly dew
  The morning rose may blow;
But cold successive noontide blasts
  May lay its beauties low.

Fair on Isabella's morn
  The sun propitious smil'd,
But, long ere noon, succeeding clouds
  Succeeding hopes beguil'd.

Fate oft tears the bosom chords
  That Nature finest strung:
So Isabella's heart was form'd,
  And so that heart was wrung.

Dread Omnipotence alone
  Can heal the wound He gave;
Can point the brimful grief-worn eyes
  To scenes beyond the grave.

Virtue's blossoms there shall blow,
  And fear no withering blast;
There Isabella's spotless worth
  Shall happy be at last.

* This poem is entered in the Glenriddel volume of poetry, with note: 'This poetic compliment, what few poetic compliments are, was from the heart.'

It was probably to this same Isabella M'Leod that Burns had
sent the following verses, which have recently come to light.
They are dated :

The crimson blossom charms the bee,
The summer sun the swallow,
So dear this tuneful gift* to me
From lovely Isabella.

Her portrait [*strong*] fair upon my mind,
Revolving time shall mellow ;
And mem'ry's latest effort find
The lovely Isabella.

No bard nor lover's rapture this,
In fancies vain and shallow ;
She is, so come my soul to bliss,
The lovely Isabella.

ROBERT BURNS.

Burns never neglected his duties as a Mason.   He might be
'rhyming,' 'aimless,' and 'idle,' but he was also 'mason-making.'
The following entry in the books of St James's Lodge, Tarbolton,
dated 'Mauchline, 25th July 1787,' speaks for itself :

MAUCHLINE, 25*th July* 1787.

This night the Deputation of the Lodge met at Mauchline, and entered
Brother Alexander Allison of Barnmuir an apprentice.   Likewise ad-
mitted Brs. Professor Stuart of Cathrine, and Claude Alexander, Esq.,
of Ballochmyle ; Claude Neilson, Esq., Paisley ; John Farquhar Gray,
Esq., of Gilmiscroft ;† and Dr George Grierson, Glasgow, Honorary
Members of the Lodge.   ROBT. BURNS, *D.M.*

Of this meeting Stewart has given his recollections: 'In summer
1787, I passed some weeks in Ayrshire, and saw Burns occasionally.   I think he told me that he had made an excursion that
season to the West Highlands, and that he also visited what

---

* What the 'tuneful gift' was is not known.
† This was probably ' the Laird of Gilmilnscroft,' in the parish of Sorn, by whom, acting as
Justice of the Peace, Burns and Jean, according to one tradition, were finally married in a
Mauchline ale-house.

Beattie calls the Arcadian ground of Scotland, upon the banks of the Teviot and the Tweed. In the course of the same season, I was led by curiosity to attend for an hour or two a mason lodge in Mauchline, where Burns presided. He had occasion to make some short, unpremeditated compliments to different individuals, from whom he had no reason to expect a visit, and everything he said was happily conceived, and forcibly, as well as fluently, expressed. His manner of speaking in public had evidently the marks of some practice in extempore elocution.'

It was also during this brief stay at Mossgiel that Burns penned his autobiographical letter to Dr Moore, of which the introduction and termination are as follows:

SIR—For some time past I have been rambling over the country, partly on account of some little business I have to settle in various places; but of late I have been confined with some lingering complaints, originating, as I take it, in the stomach. To divert my spirits a little in this miserable fog of *ennui*, I have taken a whim to give you a history of myself.

My name has made a small noise in the country; you have done me the honor to interest yourself very warmly in my behalf; and I think a faithful account of what character of a man I am, and how I came by that character, may perhaps amuse you in an idle moment. I will give you an honest narrative, though I know it will be at the expence of frequently being laugh'd at; for I assure you, Sir, I have, like Solomon, whose character, excepting in the trifling affair of WISDOM, I sometimes think I resemble,—I have, I say, like him, 'turned my eyes to behold madness and folly,' and like him, too frequently shaken hands with their intoxicating friendship. In the very polite letter Miss Williams did me the honor to write me, she tells me you have got a complaint in your eyes. I pray God it may be removed; for, considering that lady and you are my common friends, you will probably employ her to read this letter; and then good-night to that esteem with which she was pleased to honor the Scotch Bard !

After you have perused these pages, should you think them trifling and impertinent, I only beg leave to tell you, that the poor author wrote them under some very twitching qualms of conscience, that, perhaps, he was doing what he ought not to do; a predicament he has more than once been in before.

*   *   *   *   *   *

[The Autobiography, which forms the first chapter of Volume I. of this work, follows.]

My most respectful compliments to Miss Williams. The very elegant and friendly letter she honored me with a few days ago, I cannot answer at present, as my presence is required at Edinburgh for a week or so, and I set off to-morrow.

I enclose you 'Holy Willie' for the sake of giving you a little further information of the affair than Mr Creech could do. An Elegy I composed the other day on Sir James H. Blair, if time allow, I will transcribe. The merit is just mediocre.

If you will oblige me so highly and do me so much honor as now and then to drop me a line, please direct to me at Mauchline, Ayrshire. With the most grateful respect, I have the honor to be, Sir, your very humble servant, ROBT. BURNS.

MAUCHLINE, 2nd August 1787.

Direct to me at Mauchline, Ayrshire.

EDINBURGH, 23d September.

SIR—The foregoing letter was unluckily forgot among other papers at Glasgow on my way to Edinburgh. Soon after I came to Edinburgh I went on a tour through the Highlands, and did not recover the letter till my return to town, which was the other day. My ideas, picked up in my pilgrimage, and some rhymes of my earlier years, I shall soon be at leisure to give you at large—so soon as I hear from you whether you are in London. I am, again, Sir, yours most gratefully, R. BURNS.

It was necessary that Burns should return to Edinburgh. He had to settle with his bookseller, Creech; and Edinburgh was the best starting-point for some excursions which he contemplated to what he regarded as 'the classic scenes of his native country.' He returned on the 7th August.*

* This date is assumed on the strength of a passage in a letter to Dr Moore, Jan. 4, 1789: 'He (Creech) kept me hanging about Edinburgh from the 7th August 1787 until the 13th April 1788.'

CHAPTER III.

THE only literary incident of note that preceded Burns's departure on his Highland tour was the composition of an elegy on the death of Sir James Hunter Blair. Sir James was an Ayrshire squire, and a member of the banking-house of Sir William Forbes and Company ; he had been member of parliament for Edinburgh from 1781 till 1786, and Lord Provost from 1784 to 1786 ; in the last year he had been made a baronet. He had been one of Burns's kindest friends, when the poet first came to town, taking, doubtless, a particular interest in his fortunes because he was from Ayrshire.* He died on the 1st of July, at the early age of forty-six. It cannot be said that Burns's verses are a happy example of his powers ; they are interesting chiefly from their local allusions.

ON THE DEATH OF SIR JAMES HUNTER BLAIR.

The Performance is but mediocre, but my grief was sincere. The last time I saw the worthy, public-spirited man—A MAN he was ! How few of the two-legged breed that pass for such, deserve the designation !—he pressed my hand, and asked me with the most friendly warmth if it was in his power to serve me ; and if so, that I would oblige him by telling him how. I had nothing to ask of him ; but if ever a child of his should be so unfortunate as to be under the necessity of asking any thing of so

---

* Sir David Hunter Blair, second son of Sir James, and who died in 1857, used to relate how he sat at his father's breakfast-table with Burns, in the family residence in the eastern division of Queen Street.

poor a man as I am, it may not be in my power to grant it, but, by G—,
I shall try ! ! !—*R. B., in Glenriddel MSS.*

The lamp of day, with ill-presaging glare,
  Dim, cloudy, sunk beyond the western wave ;
Th' inconstant blast howl'd through the darkening air,
  And hollow whistled in the rocky cave.

Lone as I wander'd by each cliff and dell,
  Once the lov'd haunts of Scotia's royal train ; *
Or mus'd where limpid streams, once hallow'd, well,†
  Or mould'ring ruins mark the sacred Fane. ‡

Th' increasing blast roar'd round the beetling rocks,
  The clouds, swift-wing'd, flew o'er the starry sky,
The groaning trees untimely shed their locks,
  And shooting meteors caught the startled eye.

The paly moon rose in the livid east,
  And 'mong the cliffs disclos'd a stately Form
In weeds of woe, that frantic beat her breast,
  And mix'd her wailings with the raving storm.

Wild to my heart the filial pulses glow,
  'Twas Caledonia's trophied shield I view'd :
Her form majestic droop'd in pensive woe,
  The lightning of her eye in tears imbued.

Revers'd that spear, redoubtable in war,
  Reclined that banner, erst in fields unfurl'd,
That like a deathful meteor gleam'd afar,
  And brav'd the mighty monarchs of the world.

' My patriot son fills an untimely grave ! '
  With accents wild and lifted arms she cried—
' Low lies the hand that oft was stretch'd to save,
  Low lies the heart that swell'd with honest pride !

---

* The Queen's Park, at Holyrood House.   † St Anthony's Well.
‡ St Anthony's Chapel.

'A weeping country joins a widow's tear,
    The helpless poor mix with the orphan's cry ;
The drooping arts surround their patron's bier,
    And grateful science heaves the heartfelt sigh.

'I saw my sons resume their ancient fire ;
    I saw fair freedom's blossoms richly blow :
But ah ! how hope is born but to expire !
    Relentless fate has laid their guardian low.

'My patriot falls, but shall he lie unsung,
    While empty greatness saves a worthless name ?
No ; every Muse shall join her tuneful tongue,
    And future ages hear his growing fame.

'And I will join a mother's tender cares,
    Thro' future times to make his virtues last :
That distant years may boast of other Blairs '—
    She said, and vanish'd with the sweeping blast.

TO ROBERT AIKEN, ESQ., AYR.
WITH COPY OF 'ELEGY FOR SIR JAMES HUNTER BLAIR.'

MAUCHLINE, [14th July 1787.]

MY HONORED FRIEND—The melancholy occasion of the foregoing
Poem affects not only individuals, but a Country. That I have lost a
Friend, is but repeating after Caledonia. This copy, rather an incorrect
one, I beg you will accept, till I have an opportunity in person, which I
expect to have on Tuesday first, of assuring you how sincerely I ever am,
honored Sir, your oft obliged,   ROBT. BURNS.

MR HAMILTON'S OFFICE, *Saturday Evening.*

Amongst the poet's Edinburgh friends was James Ferrier, Writer
to the Signet, principal clerk to the Court of Session, and father
of Miss Susan Edmonstone Ferrier (b. 1782, d. 1854), the author
of the popular Scottish novels *Marriage, The Inheritance,* and *Des-
tiny,* and the friend of Sir Walter Scott. Mr Ferrier had, in 1784,
built a house in George Street, a few doors west of St Andrew's
Church. It was the most westerly house in that part of the New
Town in its day, and was considered so far from the centres of
business, that Mr Ferrier's legal brethren were generally impressed

with the idea that his residence there would be seriously injurious
to his prospects in his profession.

TO MISS FERRIER.*

ENCLOSING THE 'ELEGY ON SIR J. H. BLAIR.'

Nae heathen name shall I prefix
   Frae Pindus or Parnassus :
Auld Reekie dings them a' to sticks,   knocks—shivers
   For rhyme-inspiring lasses.

Jove's tunefu' dochters three times three   daughters
   Made Homer deep their debtor :
But, gi'en the body half an e'e,   given—eye
   Nine Ferriers wad done better !   would

Last day my mind was in a bog,
   Down George's Street I stoited :   staggered
A creeping cauld prosaic fog   cold
   My very senses doited.   stupefied

Do what I dought to set her free,   could
   My saul lay in the mire :   soul
Ye turned a neuk—I saw your e'e—   corner
   She took the wing like fire !

The mournfu' sang I here enclose,   song
   In gratitude I send you ;
And [wish and] pray in rhyme sincere,
   A' gude things may attend you !   good

As has already been seen, a servant girl named May Cameron
was now—to use a phrase of Burns's own—under a cloud on his
account in Edinburgh. During this very month, while preparing
for a tour in the north, he was served on her behalf with a
legal instrument similar to that which had sent him into hiding
a twelvemonth before; the fact is placed beyond doubt by a
document dated the 15th of August, liberating him from the

* Eldest daughter of Mr Ferrier, and afterwards Mrs General Graham.

restraints of a writ *in meditatione fugæ.** The document he had himself preserved, and probably carried about for some time, using it for hastily jotting down memoranda. It contains, scribbled with a pencil in his own hand, a couple of verses of an old and broadly humorous song, which he had probably heard sung somewhere, and wished to preserve.

Burns, on this visit to the capital, seems to have returned to his old lodging in the Lawnmarket, only to quit it. His friend Richmond, with whom he is said to have quarrelled, had taken in another fellow-lodger. He is believed to have accepted temporary accommodation in the house of Nicol. At all events, he dates only one letter from the Lawnmarket.

TO WILLIAM TYTLER, ESQ., OF WOODHOUSELEE.

SIR—Inclosed I have sent you a sample of the old pieces that are still to be found among our peasantry in the West.† I had once a great many of such fragments; and some of these *more entire;* but as I had no idea that any body cared for them, I have forgotten them. I invariably hold it sacrilege to add any thing of my own to help out with the shattered wrecks of these venerable old compositions; but they have many various readings. If you have not seen these before, I know they will flatter your true old-style Caledonian feelings; at any rate, I am truly happy to have an opportunity of assuring you how sincerely I am, Revered Sir, your gratefully indebted humble servant,

ROBERT BURNS.

LAWNMARKET, *Aug.* 1787.

A letter of Burns, dated a week after his arrival in town, and apparently addressed to Archibald Lawrie, the son of his Loudon host, was probably written in Nicol's house.

TO [MR ARCHIBALD LAWRIE.]

EDINBURGH, *14th August* 1787.

MY DEAR SIR—Here am I—that is all I can tell you of that unaccountable being—myself. What I am doing, no mortal can tell; what I am thinking, I myself cannot tell; what I am usually saying, is not worth telling. The clock is just striking, one, two, three, four, —, —, —, —, —, —, —, twelve, forenoon; and here I sit, in the attic story,

---

* The terms of this writ must have been merely used formally, in order to force him to grant the required security.

† The pieces enclosed were 'The Braes o' Yarrow' (*Tune*—'Willie's Ewie'), 'Rob Roy the Younger' (*Tune*—A rude set of 'The Mill, Mill, O'), and 'Young Hynhorn' (to its own tune).

alias the garret, with a friend on the right hand of my standish—a friend whose kindness I shall largely experience at the close of this line—there —thank you—a friend, my dear Mr Lawrie, whose kindness often makes me blush ; a friend who has more of the milk of human kindness than all the human race put together, and what is highly to his honour, peculiarly a friend to the friendless as often as they come in his way ; in short, sir, he is, without the least alloy, a universal philanthropist ; and his much-beloved name is—a bottle of good old Port ! In a week, if whim and weather serve, I shall set out for the north—a tour to the Highlands.

I ate some Newhaven broth, in other words, boiled mussels, with Mr Farquhar's family, t' other day. Now I see you prick up your ears. They are all well, and Mademoiselle is particularly well. She begs her respects to you all ; along with which please present those of your humble servant. I can no more. I have so high a veneration, or rather idolatrisation, for the cleric character, that even a little *futurum esse vel fuisse Priestling* in his *Penna pennæ pennæ*, &c., throws an awe over my mind in his presence, and shortens my sentences into single ideas.

Farewell, and believe me to be ever, my dear sir, yours,

ROBERT BURNS.[*]

The next letter was

TO MR ROBERT AINSLIE, JUNIOR,

BERRYWELL, DUNSE.

| As I gaed up to Dunse, | went |
| To warp a pickle yarn, &c. | small quantity |

From henceforth, my dear Sir, I am determined to set off with my letters like the periodical Writers ; viz., prefix a kind of text quoted from some Classic of undoubted authority, such as the Author of the immortal piece of which my text is a part. What I have to say on my text is exhausted in a letter I wrote you the other day, before I had the pleasure of receiving yours from Inverleithen ; and sure never was anything more lucky, as I have but the time to write this, that Mr Nicol on the opposite side of the table takes to correct a proof-sheet of a thesis. They are gabbling Latin so loud that I cannot hear what my own soul is saying in my own scull, so must just give you a matter-of-fact sentence or two, and end, if time permit, with a verse *de rei generatione.*

To-morrow, I leave Edinr. in a chaise ; Nicol thinks it more comfortable than horseback, to which I say, Amen ; so Jenny Geddes goes home to Ayrshire, to use a phrase of my mother's, ' wi' her finger in her mouth. '

* First published in the *Glasgow Citizen* (newspaper), April 8, 1854.

Now for a modest verse of classical authority :

> The cats like kitchen ;*
>   The dogs like broo;   broth
>   The lasses like the lads weel,   well
>   And th' auld wives too.   old
>
> Chorus—An' we're a' noddin,
>   Nid, nid, noddin,   nodding in sleep
>   We're a' noddin fou at e'en.   drunk

If this does not please you, let me hear from you : if you write any time before the first of September, direct to Inverness, to be left at the post Office till call'd for; the next week at Aberdeen; the next at Edinr. The sheet is done, and I shall just conclude with assuring you that I am, and ever with pride shall be, My dear Sir,

ROBT. BURNS.

Call your boy what you think proper, only interject BURNS. What say you to a Scripture name ; for instance—

Zimri Burns Ainslie,
or
Achitophel, &c., &c. ?

look your bible for these two heroes. If you do this, I will repay the Compliment.

EDINR., 23rd Aug. 1787.

TO THE FREE MASONS OF ST JAMES'S LODGE, CARE OF H. MANSON, TARBOLTON.

EDINBURGH, 23d August 1787.

MEN AND BRETHREN—I am truly sorry it is not in my power to be at your quarterly meeting. If I must be absent in body, believe me I shall be present in spirit. I suppose those who owe us monies, by bill or otherwise, will appear—I mean those we summoned. If you please, I wish you would delay prosecuting defaulters till I come home. The court is up, and I will be home before it sits down. In the meantime, to take a note of who appear and who do not, of our faulty debtors, will be right in my humble opinion ; and those who confess debt and crave days, I think we should spare them. Farewell !

> Within your dear mansion may wayward Contention
>   And withered Envy ne'er enter ;
> May Secrecy round be the mystical bound,
>   And brotherly Love be the centre.

ROBT. BURNS.

* Any kind of better food taken as a relish is called *kitchen* in Scotland.

Of his Highland excursion Burns has left a diary similar to that which he kept during his southern tour. This we now give, with necessary explanations :

[*Saturday*] *25th August* 1787.—I set out for the north in company with my good friend Mr Nicol. From Corstorphine, by Kirkliston and Winchburgh, fine, improven, fertile country : near Linlithgow the lands worse, light and sandy. LINLITHGOW, the appearance of rude, decayed, idle grandeur, charmingly rural, retired situation. The old rough palace a tolerably fine but melancholy ruin—sweetly situated on a small elevation on the brink of a loch. Shown the room where the beautiful, injured Mary Queen of Scots was born—A pretty good old Gothic church—the infamous stool of repentance standing, in the old Romish way, in a lofty situation. What a poor, pimping business is a Presbyterian place of worship! dirty, narrow, squalid ; stuck in a corner of old popish grandeur such as Linlithgow, and much more Melrose. Ceremony and show, if judiciously thrown in, absolutely necessary for the bulk of mankind, both in religious and civil matters.

West Lothian.—The more elegance and luxury among the farmers, I always observe, in equal proportions, the rudeness and stupidity of the peasantry. This remark I have made all over the Lothians, Merse, Roxburgh, &c. ; and for this, among other reasons, I think that a man of romantic taste, a 'man of feeling,' will be better pleased with the poverty, but intelligent minds of the peasantry in Ayrshire (peasantry they are all below the Justice of Peace) than the opulence of a club of Merse farmers, when he at the same time considers the Vandalism of *their* plough-folks, &c. I carry this idea so far, that an uninclosed, half-improven country is to me actually more agreeable, and gives me more pleasure as a prospect, than a country cultivated like a garden.

Dine.—Go to my friend Mr Smith's at Avon Printfield *—find nobody but Mrs Miller, an agreeable, sensible, modest, good body ; as useful, but not so ornamental, as Fielding's Miss Western—not rigidly polite *à la Française*, but easy, hospitable, and housewifely.

An old lady from Paisley, a Mrs Dawson, whom I promise to call for in Paisley—like old Lady W[auchope],† and still more like Mrs C——, her conversation is pregnant with strong sense and just remark, but, like them, a certain air of self-importance and a *duresse* in the eye, seem to indicate, as the Ayrshire wife observed of her cow, that 'she had a mind o' her ain.'

Pleasant distant view of Dunfermline and the rest of the fertile coast of Fife, as we go down to that dirty, ugly place, Borrowstonness. See a horse-race, and call on a friend of Mr Nicol's, a Bailie Cowan, of whom

---

* Smith had, as has been already noticed, removed from Mauchline to this place.

† Lady W—— was Mrs Scot of Wauchope. It has been conjectured that Mrs C—— was Mrs Alison Cockburn.

I know too little to attempt his portrait. Come through the rich Carse of Falkirk to Falkirk to pass the night.

[*Sunday, 26th August*].—Falkirk nothing remarkable, except the tomb of Sir John the Graham, over which, in the succession of time, four [three] stones have been laid.

The travellers appear to have spent the night in the Cross Keys Inn at Falkirk. Burns had lately provided himself with a diamond pen ; and it is said that this verse was afterwards found on a window of the inn :

> Sound be his sleep and blithe his morn
>   That never did a lassie wrang ;
> Who poverty ne'er held in scorn—
>   For misery ever tholed a pang.*   endured

Camelon, the ancient metropolis of the Picts, now a small village, in the neighbourhood of Falkirk.† Cross the grand canal to Carron.—Breakfast—come past Larbert, and admire a fine monument of cast-iron erected by Mr Bruce, the African traveller, to his [second] wife.‡ *N.B.*—He used her very ill, and I suppose he meant it as much out of gratitude to Heaven as anything else.

It would seem that the travellers zigzagged a little on their route between Falkirk and Stirling. They went to Carron, in the hope of seeing the celebrated ironworks there, although, the day being Sunday, it is difficult to understand how they could have expected admission. The following epigram was the result of their disappointment :

VERSES

WRITTEN ON A WINDOW OF THE INN AT CARRON.

> We cam na here to view your warks,   came not—works
>   In hopes to be mair wise,   more
> But only, lest we gang to hell,   go
>   It may be nae surprise :

---

* This was given on the authority of Mr G. Boyack, St Andrews, in the *Fifeshire Journal*, Nov. 4, 1847. The last line is there printed : ' For misery *never* tholed a pang.'

† It will subsequently be seen that Burns utilised his knowledge of Camelon in his poem beginning—
    ' There was once a time, but old Time was then young.'

‡ James Bruce, the African traveller, born at Kinnaird House, Stirlingshire, in 1730 ; died 1794. Married, first, Adriana Allan, daughter of a wine-merchant in Portugal, who died 1754 ; second, Mary, eldest daughter of Thomas Dundas of Carronhall, in 1776. She died in 1784.

But when we tirl'd at your door,   knocked
    Your porter dought na hear us ;   could not
Sae may, shou'd we to hell's yetts come,   gates
    Your billy Satan sair us !   crony—serve

Lockhart tells a story which may be applicable to the preceding evening : 'I have heard that, riding one dark night near Carron, his companion teased him with noisy exclamations of delight and wonder whenever an opening in the wood permitted them to see the magnificent glare of the furnaces : "Look, Burns ! Good Heaven ! Look, look ! What a glorious sight !" "Sir," said Burns, "I would not *look, look* at your bidding, if it were the mouth of hell !"'

Pass Dunipace, a place laid out with fine taste—a charming amphitheatre bounded by Denny village, and pleasant seats of Herbertshire, Denovan, and down to Dunipace. The Carron running down the bosom of the whole makes it one of the most charming little prospects I have seen.

Dine at Auchenbowie—Mr Monro an excellent, worthy old man—Miss Monro an amiable, sensible, sweet young woman, much resembling Mrs Grierson.* Come to Bannockburn—shewn the old house† where James III. was murdered. The field of Bannockburn—the hole where glorious Bruce set his standard. Here no Scot can pass uninterested. I fancy to myself that I see my gallant, heroic countrymen coming o'er the hill, and down upon the plunderers of their country, the murderers of their fathers ; noble revenge and just hate glowing in every vein, striding more and more eagerly as they approach the oppressive, insulting, bloodthirsty foe. I see them meet in gloriously triumphant congratulation on the victorious field, exulting in their heroic royal leader, and rescued liberty and independence.--Come to Stirling.

TO MR ROBERT MUIR.‡

My dear Sir—I intended to have written you from Edinburgh, and now write you from Stirling to make an excuse. Here am I on my way to Inverness, with a truly original, but very worthy, man, a Mr Nicol,

---

* Wife of Burns's friend and brother-mason, Dr George Grierson of Glasgow.

† 'Beaton's mill,' at Milton, near Bannockburn, is still pointed out as the scene of the tragedy.

‡ This letter was first printed in *The Brougham* (a Glasgow weekly), No. 10, Saturday, May 5, 1832.

one of the Masters of the High-school in Edinburgh. I left Auld Reekie yesterday morning, and have passed, besides bye-excursions, Linlithgow, Borrowstouness, Falkirk, and here am I undoubtedly. This morning I kneeled at the tomb of Sir John the Graham, the gallant friend of the immortal Wallace; and two hours ago I said a fervent prayer for Old Caledonia over the hole of a blue whin stone, where Robert de Bruce fixed his royal standard on the banks of Bannockburn; and just now, from Stirling Castle, I have seen by the setting sun the glorious prospect of the windings of the Forth through the rich carse of Stirling,* and skirting the equally rich carse of Falkirk. The crops are very strong, but so very late, that there is no harvest, except a ridge or two perhaps in ten miles, all the way I have travelled from Edinburgh.

I left Andrew Bruce and family all well. I will be at least three weeks in making my tour, as I shall return by the coast, and have many people to call for.

My best compliments to Charles, our dear kinsman and fellow-saint; and Messrs W. and H. Parkers. I hope Hughoc† is going on and pros- pering with God and Miss M'Causlin.

If I could think on any thing sprightly, I should let you hear every other post; but a dull, matter-of-fact business like this scrawl, the less and seldomer one writes, the better.

Among other matters-of-fact, I shall add this, that I am and ever shall be, My dear Sir, your obliged ROBERT BURNS.

STIRLING, 26th Aug. 1787.

At Stirling, Burns left his companion for a day, to pay a visit to Harvieston, in the valley of the Devon, which flows from the Ochil Hills to the Forth. Among the acquaintance- ships Burns had made or renewed at Dr Blacklock's was, as has already been noticed, that of Margaret Chalmers, a connection of his friend Gavin Hamilton, and then about twenty-four years of age. Margaret Chalmers, although not a beauty, had a pleasant, intelligent face; without any preten- sions to literary talent or studious habits, she had strong sense, and was in every way capable of appreciating the society of men of letters. Blacklock adored her for her delightful voice, which was admirably suited for the singing of national ballads.

Mrs Barbara Hamilton, the stepmother of Gavin; Mrs Euphemia Chalmers, the mother of this Margaret; and the deceased Mrs Charlotte Tait of Harvieston, were sisters, being the children of

---

* Carse means an alluvial level beside a river.
† Hugh Parker; 'Charles' was Charles Samson, a brother of 'Tam.'

Thomas Murdoch of Cumloden, in Galloway, the representative of a peasant, who, according to tradition, had received lands for the help he gave to Bruce at a time of danger.* Margaret's father, Mr Chalmers of Fingland in Dalry, Kirkcudbrightshire, had been compelled, owing to financial embarrassments, to part with his estate, and had retired to a beautifully situated farm on the Ayr, in the neighbourhood of Mauchline. There the families of Mrs Chalmers and Mrs Hamilton had grown up in the greatest intimacy. At length, however, Mrs Chalmers, being left a widow, removed to Edinburgh. About the same time Mr Tait, a widower with a son and daughter, invited his sister-in-law, Mrs Hamilton, to take up her residence at Harvieston, that she might preside over his household until his daughter grew up. Mrs Hamilton, accordingly, lived there with her son and two daughters, Grace and Charlotte, the latter of whom had just come to womanhood, with the promise of uncommon beauty. Mrs Chalmers also occasionally lived there in summer with her two daughters—Margaret, and Cochrane, her senior by about twenty years, who, in 1777 had married her cousin, Sir Henry Mackenzie of Gairloch. When Burns visited Harvieston, Mrs Chalmers and Lady Mackenzie were there; but Miss Chalmers had remained in Edinburgh.

Burns's entry in his journal on the subject of his excursion to the Devon Valley is brief, consisting only of these words: '*Monday* [27th August].—Go to Harvieston.—Mrs Hamilton and family—Mrs Chalmers—Mrs Shields.--Go to see Cauldron linn, and Rumbling-brig, and the Deil's mill. Return in the evening to Stirling.' But he has left us a more satisfactory account of the day in a letter

* 'Through their mother, the three ladies were grand-nieces of Grizel Cochrane of Ochiltree, the heroine of a remarkable anecdote of the difficult times of James II. Her father, the Hon. John Cochrane, being condemned to die in Edinburgh for his share in Argyle's rebellion, the young lady disguised herself, attacked the post-messenger as he crossed the Border, and robbed him of the warrant for the execution. Thus she is said to have saved her father's life several times. Grizel Cochrane, who became Mrs Kerr of Morriston, in Berwickshire, is represented in her picture as a gentle girl of seventeen, with handsome features of sweet expression, leaning on a table, on which are pistols and the disguise she wore.'—*Letter from a relation of Mrs Chalmers.* This romantic story, which is still prevalent in the south and south-west of Scotland, is told at length in *Chambers's Miscellany*, vol. iii., No. 23, 'Scottish Traditionary Stories,' and is inwoven by Mr S. R. Crockett in the closing chapters of his romance, *The Men of the Moss Hags.* Sir John Cochrane of Ochiltree did undoubtedly take part in Argyll's rebellion, and suffered imprisonment. According to Fountainhall, he turned 'approver,' urged the indulgence on Presbyterians, and died a farmer of taxes, leaving two sons. Authentic history is silent on the subject of Grizel and the death-warrant.

TO MR GAVIN HAMILTON.

STIRLING, 28th Aug. 1787.

MY DEAR SIR—Here am I on my way to Inverness. I have rambled over the rich, fertile carses of Falkirk and Stirling, and am delighted with their appearance: richly waving crops of wheat, barley, &c., but no harvest at all yet, except, in one or two places, an old wife's ridge. Yesterday morning I rode from this town up the meandring Devon's banks to pay my respects to some Ayrshire folks at Harvieston. After breakfast, we made a party to go and see the famous Caudron-linn, a remarkable cascade in the Devon, about five miles above Harvieston; and after spending one of the most pleasant days I ever had in my life, I returned to Stirling in the evening. They are a family, Sir, though I had not had any prior tie; though they had not been the brother and sisters of a certain generous friend of mine, I would never forget them. I am told you have not seen them these several years, so you can have very little idea of what such young folks as they, are now. Your brother [step-brother] is as tall as you are, but slender rather than otherwise; and I have the satisfaction to inform you that he is getting the better of those consumptive symptoms which I suppose you know were threatening him. His make and particularly his manner resemble you, but he will still have a finer face. (I put in the word *still*, to please Mrs Hamilton.) Good-sense, modesty, and at the same time a just idea of that respect that man owes to man and has a right in his turn to exact, are striking features in his character; and, what with me is the Alpha and the Omega, he has a heart might adorn the breast of a Poet! Grace has a good figure and the look of health and cheerfulness, but nothing else remarkable in her person. I scarcely ever saw so striking a likeness as is between her and your little Beennie; the mouth and chin particularly. She is reserved at first; but as we grew better acquainted, I was delighted with the native frankness of her manner and the sterling sense of her observation. Of Charlotte, I cannot speak in common terms of admiration: she is not only beautiful, but lovely. Her form is elegant; her features not regular, but they have the smile of sweetness and the settled complacency of good nature in the highest degree; and her complexion, now that she has happily recovered her wonted health, is equal to Miss Burnet's. After the exercise of our ride to the falls, Charlotte was exactly Dr Donne's Mistress:

> ——— Her pure and eloquent blood
> Flow'd in her cheeks, and so distinctly wrought
> That one would almost say her body thought.*

Her eyes are fascinating; at once expressive of good-sense, tenderness, and a noble mind.

* From *Of the Progress of the Soul: the Second Anniversarie* (*Elegy on Mistress Elizabeth Drury*), by John Donne, D.D.

I do not give you all this account, my good Sir, to flatter you. I mean it to reproach you. Such relations, the first Peer in the realm might own with pride; then why but you keep up more correspondence with these so amiable young folks? I had a thousand questions to answer about you all: I had to describe the little ones with the minuteness of anatomy. They were highly delighted when I told them that John [*] was so good a boy and so fine a scholar, and that Willie was going on still very pretty; but I have it in commission to tell her from them that beauty is a poor, silly bauble, without she be good. Miss Chalmers I had left in Edinburgh, but I had the pleasure of meeting with Mrs Chalmers, only Lady M'Kenzie being rather a little alarmingly ill of a sore throat somewhat marr'd our enjoyment. I shall not be in Ayrshire for four weeks. My most respectful Compliments to Mrs Hamilton, Miss Kennedy, and Doctor M'Kenzie. I shall probably write him from some stage or other. I am ever, Sir, yours most gratefully,

Robt. Burns.

In the evening the travellers supped in a company which the poet sketches off in brief terms: 'Supper—Messrs Doig [†] (the Schoolmaster) and Bell; Captain Forrester of the Castle—Doig a queerish figure, and something of a pedant—Bell a joyous, vacant fellow who sings a good song—Forrester a merry, swearing kind of man, with a dash of the Sodger.'

At Stirling, on the Saturday night, the travellers had not been more charmed with the magnificent panorama of the Grampians, viewed from the battlements of the castle, than their patriotic and quasi-Jacobitical feelings had been outraged by the ruinous state of the ancient hall in which parliaments had occasionally been held

---

[*] 'May Health and Peace, with mutual rays,
 Shine on the ev'ning o' his days;
 Till his *wee, curlie John's* ier-oe,   great-grandchild
 When ebbing life nae mair shall flow,   no more
 The last, sad, mournful rites bestow!'
             —*Dedication to Gavin Hamilton.*

John Hamilton, the eldest son of his father, was then six years of age. He carried on his father's business in Mauchline along with his younger brother, Alexander. In 1806 he was appointed factor to the Earl of Moira, and took up his residence in Loudoun Castle. Twenty years after, he became factor to the Duke of Portland, and lived in Kilmarnock. Finally, he became the duke's private secretary, and removed to London, where he died in 1862. 'Willie' was Wilhelmina, second daughter of Gavin, and then about eight years of age. In 1806 she married the Rev. John Tod of Mauchline, 'Daddy Auld's' successor. Mrs Tod died in 1858. Her sister Jacobina, 'little Beenie,' died unmarried in 1822.

[†] David Doig, born in 1719; educated for the ministry of the Church of Scotland, but became a teacher; rector of Stirling Grammar-school at the time Burns met him; contributed on classical and oriental literature to the *Encyclopædia Britannica*, and had a protracted controversy with Lord Kames on the origin of civilisation; died in 1800.

under the Scottish kings. An inscription was afterwards found
on the window of their room :

> Here Stewarts once in glory reigned,
> And laws for Scotland's weal ordained ;
> But now unroofed their palace stands,
> Their sceptre 's swayed by other hands ;
> Fallen indeed, and to the earth
> Whence grovelling reptiles take their birth,
> The injured Stewart line is gone,
> A race outlandish fills their throne ;
> An idiot race, to honour lost ;
> Who know them best despise them most.

Allan Cunningham has given some particulars of this affair,
which may be given, although their accuracy cannot be vouched
for. 'The poet seems not to have been very sensible at
that time of his imprudence : for some one said : "Burns, this
will do you no good." "I shall reprove myself," he said, and
proceeded to aggravate his offence by adding these lines :

> " Rash mortal, and slanderous Poet, thy name
> Shall no longer appear in the records of fame ;
> Dost not know that old Mansfield, who writes like the Bible,
> Says the more 'tis a truth, Sir, the more 'tis a libel ? " '

It is stated that the Rev. Mr Hamilton of Gladsmuir,* in East
Lothian, soon after seeing the verses, added the following :

> Thus wretches rail whom sordid gain
> Drags in Faction's gilded chain ;
> But can a mind which Fame inspires,
> Where genius lights her brightest fires—
> Can BURNS, disdaining truth and law,
> Faction's venomed dagger draw ;
> And, skulking with a villain's aim,
> Basely stab his monarch's fame ?
> Yes, Burns, 'tis o'er, thy race is run,
> And shades receive thy setting sun :

* George Hamilton, minister of Gladsmuir from 1790 till his death in 1832. He was
Moderator of the General Assembly of 1805.

With pain thy wayward fate I see,
And mourn the lot that's doomed for thee :
These few rash lines will damn thy name,
And blast thy hopes of future fame.*

In the Glenriddel MSS. Burns, under the title of 'The Poet's
Reply to the Threat of a Censorious Critic,' alluded to this matter
thus : 'My imprudent lines were answered, very petulantly, by
somebody, I believe a Rev. Mr Hamilton.† In a MS. where I met
the answer, I wrote below :—

With Æsop's lion, Burns says, sore I feel
Each other blow, but d—n that ass's heel.'

Tuesday Morning [*28th August*].—Breakfast with Captain Forrester—
leave Stirling—Ochil Hills—Devon River—Forth and Teith—Allan River
—Strathallan, a fine country but little improven—Ardoch Camp—Cross
Earn to Crieff—Dine, and go to Arbruchil ; cold reception at Arbruchil—
A most romantically pleasant ride up Earn, by Auchtertyre and Comrie—
Sup at Crieff.

Wednesday Morning [*29th*].—Leave Crieff—Glen Almond—Almond
River—Ossian's grave—Loch Frioch—Glenquaich—Landlord and land-
lady remarkable characters—Taymouth—described in rhyme—Meet the
Hon. Charles Townshend.‡

VERSES

WRITTEN 'WITH MY PENCIL OVER THE CHIMNEY-PIECE IN THE PAR-
LOUR OF THE INN AT KENMORE, AT THE OUTLET OF LOCH TAY.'

Admiring Nature in her wildest grace,
These northern scenes with weary feet I trace ;
O'er many a winding dale and painful steep,
Th' abodes of covey'd grouse and timid sheep,
My savage journey, curious, I pursue,
Till fam'd Breadalbane opens to my view.—

* Cunningham states the fact as to Hamilton ; but his rejoinder is here given from a
manuscript source.
† Cunningham's rendering of the lines are :

'Like Esop's lion, Burns says, sore I feel
All others scorn—but damn that ass's heel.'

‡ This was in all probability the same Hon. Charles Townshend who, in 1797, was created
Baron Bayning—the title is now extinct—and died in 1810. He was the cousin of the more
celebrated Charles Townshend (d. 1767), Chancellor of the Exchequer in the Earl of Chatham's
administration, hero of the 'champagne speech,' and distinguished as one of the most
brilliant orators and unreliable politicians of his time.

The meeting cliffs each deep-sunk glen divides,
The woods, wild-scatter'd, clothe their ample sides ;
Th' outstretching lake, imbosomed 'mong the hills,
The eye with wonder and amazement fills ;
The Tay meand'ring sweet in infant pride ;
The palace rising on its verdant side ;
The lawns wood-fring'd in Nature's native taste ;
The hillocks dropt in Nature's careless haste ;
The arches striding o'er the new-born stream ;
The village glittering in the noontide beam—

    *   *   *   *

Poetic ardors in my bosom swell,
Lone-wand'ring by the hermit's mossy cell :
The sweeping theatre of hanging woods ;
Th' incessant roar of headlong tumbling floods—

    *   *   *   *

Here Poesy might wake her heav'n-taught lyre,
And look through Nature with creative fire ;
Here, to the wrongs of Fate half reconcil'd,
Misfortune's lighten'd steps might wander wild ;
And Disappointment, in these lonely bounds,
Find balm to sooth her bitter, rankling wounds :
Here heart-struck Grief might heav'nward stretch her scan,
And injur'd Worth forget and pardon man.

    *   *   *   *

Thursday [*30th August*].—Come down Tay to Dunkeld—Glenlyon House—Lyon River—Druid's Temple—three circles of stones, the outer-most sunk ; the second has thirteen stones remaining ; the innermost has eight ; two large detached ones like a gate, to the south-east—Say prayers in it—Pass Tay Bridge—Aberfeldy—described in rhyme—Castle Menzies, beyond Grandtully—Balleighan—Logierait—Inver—Dr Stewart—Sup.

Of his next poem Burns writes expressly in a note in the Glenriddel volume : 'I composed these stanzas standing under the Falls of Moness, near Aberfeldy.' He had in his mind at the time a popular song, 'The Birks of Abergeldie,' which celebrated the beauties of a well-known and richly wooded estate on Deeside, Aberdeenshire, which has been leased for many years by Her

R.B.Nisbet A.R.S.A.   F.Jenkins Heliog Paris

The Birks of Aberfeldy
(Falls of Moness)

Majesty Queen Victoria. It seems that he transferred the 'birks'
from Abergeldie to Aberfeldy. At all events, they were not in
evidence when Dorothy Wordsworth visited the Falls of Moness
in 1803.

THE BIRKS OF ABERFELDY.

Tune—The Birks of Abergeldie.

Chorus—Bonny lassie, will ye go,
    Will ye go, will ye go,
    Bonny lassie, will ye go
      To the Birks of Aberfeldy ?   birches

Now Simmer blinks on flowery braes,   Summer glances
And o'er the crystal streamlets plays,
Come, let us spend the lightsome days
    In the birks of Aberfeldy.

The little birdies blythely sing,
While o'er their heads the hazels hing,   hang
Or lightly flit on wanton wing
    In the birks of Aberfeldy.

The braes ascend like lofty wa's,   hills—walls
The foamy stream deep-roaring fa's,   falls
O'erhung wi' fragrant-spreading shaws,   foliage
    The birks of Aberfeldy.

The hoary cliffs are crown'd wi' flowers,
White o'er the linns the burnie pours,   cascades—stream
And rising, weets wi' misty showers   wets
    The birks of Aberfeldy.

Let Fortune's gifts at random flee,
They ne'er shall draw a wish frae me ;   from
Supremely blest wi' love and thee
    In the birks of Aberfeldy.

Friday [31st Aug.].—Walk with Mrs Stewart and Beard to Birnam top—fine prospect down Tay—Craigiebarns Hills—Hermitage on the Bran Water, with a picture of Ossian—Breakfast with Dr Stewart—Neil Gow * plays; a short, stout-built Highland figure, with his greyish hair shed on his honest social brow—an interesting face, marking strong sense, kind open-heartedness, mixed with unmistrusting simplicity—visit his house—Margaret Gow. Ride up Tummel River to Blair [the seat of the Duke of Athole†] Fascally, a beautiful, romantic nest—wild grandeur of the pass of Gilliecrankie—visit the gallant Lord Dundee's stone. Blair—Sup with the Duchess—easy and happy from the manners of that family—confirmed in my good opinion of my friend Walker.

Saturday [*Sept.* 1.]—Visit the scenes round Blair—fine, but spoilt with bad taste—Tilt and Garrie rivers—Falls on the Tilt—Heather seat—Ride in company with Sir William Murray and Mr Walker to Loch Tummel—meanderings of the Rannoch, which runs thro' *quondam* Struan Robertson's estate from Loch Rannoch to Loch Tummel—Dine at Blair—Company—General Murray, Orien. Capt. Murray, an honest Tar; Sir William Murray, an honest, worthy man, but tormented with the hypochondria; Mrs Graham, *belle et aimable;* Miss Cathcart; Mrs Murray, a painter; Mrs King; Duchess and fine family, the Marquis, Lords James, Edward, and Robert; Ladies Charlotte, Emelia, and children—Dance—Sup—Duke; Mr Graham of Fintray; Mr M'Laggan; Mr and Mrs Stewart.

Burns had at Edinburgh formed the acquaintance of Josiah Walker, the son of the Rev. Thomas Walker, minister of the Ayrshire parish of Dundonald, and two years his junior. They had often met at Dr Blacklock's, Professor Stewart's, and other houses. Coming now with a letter of introduction to Blair, the poet and Nicol were fortunate in finding young Walker residing there in the capacity of tutor to the Marquis of Tullibardine, eldest son of the Duke of Athole, and then a boy of nine. Of the visit, which Burns enjoyed exceedingly, Walker subsequently furnished the following account:

'On reaching Blair, he sent me notice of his arrival (as I had been previously acquainted with him), and I hastened to meet him at the inn. The Duke, to whom he brought a letter of introduction, was from home; but the Duchess, being informed of his

---

* Neil Gow, the famous Scottish violinist and composer, was then sixty years of age. He was born at Inver, near Dunkeld, in 1727, and died in 1807.

† John, fourth Duke of Athole, was born in 1755, succeeded his father in 1774, and died in 1830.

arrival, gave him an invitation to sup and sleep at Athole-house [Blair]. He accepted the invitation, but as the hour of supper was at some distance, begged I would in the interval be his guide through the grounds. It was already growing dark; yet the softened, though faint and uncertain, view of their beauties, which the moonlight afforded us, seemed exactly suited to the state of his feelings at the time. I had often, like others, experienced the pleasures which arise from the sublime or elegant landscape, but I never saw those feelings so intense as in Burns. When we reached a rustic hut on the river Tilt, where it is overhung by a woody precipice, from which there is a noble waterfall, he threw himself on the heathy seat, and gave himself up to a tender, abstracted, and voluptuous enthusiasm of imagination. I cannot help thinking it might have been here that he conceived the idea of the following lines, which he afterwards introduced into his poem on Bruar Water, when only fancying such a combination of objects as were now present to his eye.

> Or, by the reaper's nightly beam,
>   Mild-chequering thro' the trees,
> Rave to my darkly-dashing stream,
>   Hoarse-swelling on the breeze.

It was with much difficulty I prevailed on him to quit this spot, and to be introduced in proper time to supper.

'My curiosity was great to see how he would conduct himself in company so different from what he had been accustomed to. His manner was unembarrassed, plain, and firm. He appeared to have complete reliance on his own native good sense for directing his behaviour. He seemed at once to perceive and to appreciate what was due to the company and to himself, and never to forget a proper respect for the separate species of dignity belonging to each. He did not arrogate conversation, but when led into it, he spoke with ease, propriety, and manliness. He tried to exert his abilities, because he knew it was ability alone gave him a title to be there. The Duke's fine young family attracted much of his admiration; he drank their healths as *honest men and bonie lasses*, an idea which was much applauded by the company, and with which he has very felicitously closed his poem [alluded to].

'Next day I took a ride with him through some of the most romantic parts of that neighbourhood, and was highly gratified by his conversation. As a specimen of his happiness of conception and strength of expression, I will mention a remark which he made on his fellow-traveller, who was walking, at the time, a few paces before us. He was a man of a robust but clumsy person; and while Burns was expressing to me the value he entertained for him, on account of his vigorous talents, although they were clouded at times by coarseness of manners; "in short," he added, "his mind is like his body, he has a confounded strong in-knee'd sort of a soul."

'Much attention was paid to Burns both before and after the Duke's return, of which he was perfectly sensible, without being vain; and at his departure I recommended to him, as the most appropriate return he could make, to write some descriptive verses on any of the scenes with which he had been so much delighted. After leaving Blair, he, by the Duke's advice, visited the Falls of Bruar, and in a few days I received a letter from Inverness with the verses enclosed [" Bruar Water "].'

The Friday and Saturday which Burns spent at Blair (31st August and 1st September) he afterwards declared to have been among the happiest days of his life. The Athole family were as much pleased with the poet as he was with them; they entreated him to prolong his stay; and he would have complied, but for the eagerness of Nicol to get away. Walker relates that 'the ladies, in their anxiety to have a little more of Burns's company, sent a servant to the inn, to bribe his driver to loosen or pull off a horse's shoe. But the ambush failed. *Proh mirum!* The driver was *incorruptible*.' * It was the more to be regretted that Burns did not wait a little longer, as Henry Dundas † was daily expected as a guest. Had he met that great dispenser of patronage —the ' uncrowned king of Scotland '—who knows what favourable influence might not have been exerted on his future fortunes? As it was, he was fortunate in meeting Mr Graham of Fintray, who afterwards proved a good friend.

The verses and letter to which Walker alludes at the close of his account of Burns's visit to Blair Castle were as follow :

* Letter from Walker to Dr Currie. *Burns's Works* (Liverpool, 1800), vol. ii., pp. 99-103.
† Henry Dundas was at this time president of the Board of Control.

THE HUMBLE PETITION OF BRUAR WATER*
TO THE NOBLE DUKE OF ATHOLE.

My Lord, I know your noble ear
    Woe ne'er assails in vain;
Embolden'd thus, I beg you 'll hear
    Your humble slave complain
How saucy Phœbus' scorching beams,
    In flaming summer-pride,
Dry-withering, waste my foamy streams,
    And drink my crystal tide.

The lightly-jumping, glowrin' trouts   *staring*
    That thro' my waters play,
If, in their random, wanton spouts,
    They near the margin stray;
If, hapless chance! they linger lang,   *long*
    I 'm scorching up so shallow
They 're left the whitening stanes amang
    In gasping death to wallow.

Last day I grat wi' spite and teen,   *wept—vexation*
    As Poet Burns came by,
That, to a Bard, I should be seen
    Wi' half my channel dry:
A panegyric rhyme, I ween,
    Even as I was, he shor'd me;   *threatened*
But had I in my glory been,
    He, kneeling, wad ador'd me.   *would*

* 'The first object of interest that occurs upon the public road after leaving Blair, is a chasm in the hill on the right hand, through which the little river Bruar falls over a series of beautiful cascades. Formerly, the Falls of the Bruar were unadorned by wood; but the poet Burns, being conducted to see them (September 1787) after visiting the Duke of Athole, recommended that they should be invested with that necessary decoration. Accordingly, trees have been thickly planted along the chasm, and are now far advanced to maturity. Throughout this young forest a walk has been cut, and a number of fantastic little grottoes erected for the conveniency of those who visit the spot. The river not only makes several distinct falls, but rushes on through a channel, whose roughness and haggard sublimity adds greatly to the merits of the scene, as an object of interest among tourists.' —R. Chambers's *Picture of Scotland.* Most of the 'fragrant birks' planted in answer to Burns's 'humble petition' have been blown down by gales.

Here, foaming down the skelvy rocks,   shelvy
    In twisting strength I rin ;   rin
There, high my boiling torrent smokes,
    Wild-roaring o'er a linn :   face of a precipice
Enjoying large each spring and well
    As Nature gave them me,
I am, altho' I say 't mysel,   myself
    Worth gaun a mile to see.   going

Would, then, my noble master please
    To grant my highest wishes ?
He 'll shade my banks wi' tow'ring trees,
    And bonie spreading bushes.
Delighted doubly then, my Lord,
    You 'll wander on my banks,
And listen mony a grateful bird   many
    Return you tuneful thanks.

The sober laverock, warbling wild,   lark
    Shall to the skies aspire ;
The gowdspink, Music's gayest child,   goldfinch
    Shall sweetly join the choir ;
The blackbird strong, the lintwhite clear,   linnet
    The mavis mild and mellow ;   thrush
The robin pensive Autumn cheer
    In all her locks of yellow.

This, too, a covert shall ensure
    To shield them from the storm ;
And coward maukin sleep secure,   hare
    Low in her grassy form :
Here shall the shepherd make his seat,
    To weave his crown of flow'rs ;
Or find a shelt'ring, safe retreat,
    From prone-descending show'rs.

And here, by sweet, endearing stealth,
    Shall meet the loving pair,
Despising worlds, with all their wealth,
    As empty, idle care :

The flow'rs shall vie in all their charms
   The hour of heav'n to grace,
And birks extend their fragrant arms   birches
   To screen the dear embrace.

Here haply, too, at vernal dawn
   Some musing bard may stray,
And eye the smoking, dewy lawn,
   And misty mountain grey ;
Or, by the reaper's nightly beam,
   Mild-chequering thro' the trees,
Rave to my darkly dashing stream,
   Hoarse-swelling on the breeze.

Let lofty firs, and ashes cool,
   My lowly banks o'erspread,
And view, deep-bending in the pool,
   Their shadows' wat'ry-bed :
Let fragrant birks, in woodbines drest,
   My craggy cliffs adorn ;
And, for the little songster's nest,
   The close embow'ring thorn.

So may, Old Scotia's darling hope,
   Your little angel band
Spring, like their fathers, up to prop
   Their honour'd native land !
So may, thro' Albion's farthest ken,
   To social-flowing glasses
The grace be—'Athole's honest men,
   And Athole's bonie lasses !'

TO MR JOSIAH WALKER, BLAIR OF ATHOLE.*

INVERNESS, 5th September 1787.

MY DEAR SIR—I have just time to write the foregoing, and to tell you
that it was (at least most part of it) the effusion of an half-hour I spent
at Bruar. I do not mean it was *extempore*, for I have endeavoured to
brush it up as well as Mr Nicol's chat and the jogging of the chaise

* Josiah Walker (1761–1831) graduated at the University of Edinburgh. Early in 1787
he was appointed tutor to the Marquis of Tullibardine, eldest son of the Duke of Athole.
This position he held until the death of his pupil in 1796. Thereafter he edited *The Perthshire Courier*, and contributed to the *Encyclopædia Perthensis* and Brewster's *Edinburgh*

would allow. It eases my heart a good deal, as rhyme is the coin with which a poet pays his debts of honour or gratitude. What I owe to the noble family of Athole, of the first kind, I shall ever proudly boast; what I owe of the last, so help me God in my hour of need! I shall never forget.

The 'little angel-band!' I declare I prayed for them very sincerely to-day at the Fall of Fyars [Foyers]. I shall never forget the fine family piece I saw at Blair: the amiable, the truly noble Duchess,* with her smiling little seraph in her lap, at the head of the table; the lovely 'olive-plants,' as the Hebrew bard finely says, round the happy mother; the beautiful Mrs Graham; the lovely, sweet Miss Cathcart, &c. I wish I had the powers of Guido to do them justice! My Lord Duke's kind hospitality—markedly kind indeed. Mr Graham of Fintray's charms of conversation—Sir W. Murray's friendship. In short, the recollection of all that polite, agreeable company raises an honest glow in my bosom.

                                                                R. B.

The Mrs Graham and Miss Cathcart whom Burns eulogises in this letter, were daughters of Lord Cathcart, and sisters of the Duchess of Athole. The husband of the elder was at this time a quiet country gentleman, Thomas Graham of Balgowan. The war with France broke out, and Thomas Graham, though in middle life, volunteered as a soldier. He commanded the British troops at the battle of Barossa in 1811, and was raised to a peerage with the title of Lord Lynedoch. He died in 1843, at the advanced age of ninety-four. The younger sister, who had been born in Russia while her father was ambassador there, was now seventeen years of age, and noted equally for beauty and amiability. Unfortunately she died of consumption at four-and-twenty. All three sisters predeceased Burns.

Sunday [*Sept.* 2.]—Come up the Garrie—Falls of Bruar—Allecairoch—Dalwhinnie—Dine—Snow on the hills, 17 feet deep; no corn from Loch Gairic to Dalwhinnie—cross the Spey, and come down the stream to Pitnim—Straths rich; *les environs* picturesque—Craigow hill—Ruthven of Badenoch—Barrack—wild and magnificent. Rothemurche on the other side, and Glenmore—Grant of Rothemurche's poetry—told me by the Duke of Gordon; Strathspeys rich and romantic.

Encyclopædia. From 1815 till his death he was professor of Humanity in the University of Glasgow. His chief works are *The Defence of Order:* a poem (1802), and a *Life of Burns* prefixed to Morison's edition (1811).

* Jane, daughter of Charles, ninth Lord Cathcart, and the duke's first wife. She died in 1790. The 'little angel band' consisted of Lady Charlotte Murray, aged twelve, afterwards the wife of Sir John Menzies of Castle-Menzies; Lady Amelia, aged seven, afterwards Viscountess Strathallan; and Lady Elizabeth, an infant of five months, afterwards Lady Macgregor Murray of Laurick.

Monday [*Sept.* 3.]—Breakfast at Aviemore, a wild romantic spot—Snows in patches on the hills 18 feet deep—Enter Strathspey—come to Sir James Grant's—dine—company—Lady Grant a sweet pleasant body—Mr and Miss Bailie; Mrs Bailie; Dr and Mrs Grant—Clergymen—Mr Hepburn—come through mist and darkness to Dulsie to lie [sleep].

Tuesday.—Findhorn River—rocky banks—come on to Castle Cawdor, where Macbeth murdered King Duncan—saw the bed in which King Duncan was stabbed [a fable]—dine at Kilraik [Kilravock]—Mrs Rose, senr., a true chieftain's wife, a daughter of Clephane—Mrs Rose, junr.—Fort George—Inverness.

Burns had written to his Montrose cousin from Edinburgh, intimating his intention of being in the north. He now wrote more precisely:

TO MR JAMES BURNESS, MONTROSE.

DR COUSIN—I wrote you from Edinr. that I intended being north. I shall be in Stonhive [Stonehaven] sometime on Monday the 10th Inst., and I beg the favor of you to meet me there. I understand there is but one Inn at Stonhive, so you cannot miss me. As I am in the country, I certainly shall see any of my father's relations that are any way near my road; but I do not even know their names, or where one of them lives, so I hope you will meet me and be my guide. Farewell, till I have the pleasure of meeting you. I am ever, Dr Sir, Yours,

ROBT. BURNS.

INVERNESS, *4th Sept.* 1787.

TO WILLIAM INGLIS, ESQ., INVERNESS.

Mr Burns presents his most respectful compliments to Mr Inglis—would have waited on him with the inclosed [letter of introduction from William Dunbar], but is jaded to death with the fatigue of to-day's journey—won't leave Inverness till Thursday morning.

ETTLES HOTEL, *Tuesday Evening.*

Wednesday.—Loch Ness—Braes of Ness—General's Hut—Fall of Fyers—Urquhart Castle and Strath—Dine at ———, Sup at Mr Inglis's—Mr Inglis and Mrs Inglis: three young ladies.

VERSES

WRITTEN WITH A PENCIL, STANDING BY THE FALL OF FYERS, NEAR LOCH-NESS.

Among the heathy hills and ragged woods
The foaming Fyers pours his mossy floods;

Till full he dashes on the rocky mounds,
Where, thro' a shapeless breach, his stream resounds
As high in air the bursting torrents flow,
As deep recoiling surges foam below,
Prone down the rock the whitening sheet descends,
And viewless Echo's ear, astonished, rends.
Dim seen, through rising mists and ceaseless show'rs,
The hoary cavern, wide-surrounding, low'rs.
Still thro' the gap the struggling river toils,
And still, below, the horrid caldron boils.—

*   *   *   *

In the evening, after returning from his drive to the Falls of Foyers,* Burns (accompanied, presumably, by Nicol) dined by appointment with Mr Inglis, the provost, to whom, as has been seen, he had brought a letter of introduction from his friend William Dunbar, who belonged to this district. He was enraptured with the Highland scenery, but thoughtful and silent during the evening.

Thursday. — Come over Culloden muir — reflections on the field of battle — breakfast at Kilraick [Kilravock] — [He probably was introduced here by Mr Mackenzie, author of the *Man of Feeling*, who was a cousin of Mrs Rose, jun.]—old Mrs Rose, sterling sense, warm heart, strong passion, honest pride, all in an uncommon degree—Mrs Rose, jun., a little milder than the mother; this perhaps owing to her being younger †—Mr Grant,‡ minister at Calder, resembles Mr Scott at Inverleithen—Mrs Rose and Mr Grant accompany us to Kildrummie—two young ladies, Miss Rose, who sang two Gaelic songs, beautiful and lovely; Miss Sophie Brodie, not very beautiful, but most agreeable and amiable—both of them the gentlest, mildest, sweetest creatures on earth, and happiness be with them!

In a letter written in the following February to Mrs Rose, junior, the poet shows a lively and grateful recollection of this happy day. It appears that here, again, he would have prolonged his stay but for the impatience of Nicol.

---

* Acquired in 1895 by a company which proposes to utilise the water-power (without interfering with the amenity) for aluminium works.

† Mrs Elizabeth Rose was a widow at this time: her husband (Dr Hugh Rose) had died in 1780, after two years of married life. By a strange vicissitude of fortune the estate of Kilravock reverted to her, and in 1783, with her mother and her infant son, she returned to Kilravock Castle, where she ruled as mistress till her death in 1813.

‡ Alexander Grant, minister of Calder or Cawdor, 1780-1828.

Dine at Nairn—fall in with a pleasant enough gentleman, Dr Stewart, who had been long abroad with his father in [consequence of] the *Forty-five;* and Mr Falconer, a spare, irascible, warm-hearted Norland, and a non-juror—wastes of sand. Brodie House to lie. Mr Brodie* truly polite, but not just the Highland cordiality.

Friday [*Sept.* 7.]—Cross the Findhorn to Forres—Mr Brodie tells me that the muir where Shakespeare lays Macbeth's witch-meeting is still so haunted that the country-folks won't pass it by night. Elgin to breakfast; meet with Mr ——, Mr Dunbar's friend, a pleasant sort of a man; can come no nearer. Venerable ruins of Elgin Abbey [Cathedral] —A grander effect at first glance than Melrose, but nothing near so beautiful.

Cross Spey to Fochabers—fine palace [Gordon Castle,† the seat of the Duke of Gordon], worthy of the generous proprietor—dine—company— Duke and Duchess, Ladies Charlotte and Madeline; ‡ Colonel Abercrombie and Lady; Mr Gordon, and Mr ——, a clergyman, a venerable, aged figure, and Mr Hoy, a clergyman, I suppose, a pleasant open manner. The Duke makes me happier than ever great man did—noble, princely; yet mild, condescending and affable, gay, and kind. The Duchess charming, witty, and sensible—God bless them !

Currie obtained some particulars of Burns's too brief visit to Gordon Castle, from Dr Couper of Fochabers. 'In the course of the preceding winter,' he says, 'Burns had been introduced to the Duchess of Gordon at Edinburgh; and, presuming on this acquaintance, he proceeded to Gordon Castle, leaving Mr Nicol at the inn of the village. At the castle, our poet was received with the utmost hospitality and kindness; and the family being about to sit down to dinner, he was invited to take his place at table as a matter of course. This invitation he accepted, and after drinking a few glasses of wine, he rose up, and proposed to withdraw. On being pressed to stay, he mentioned, for the first time, his engagement with his fellow-traveller; and his noble host offering to send a servant to conduct Mr Nicol to the castle, Burns insisted on undertaking that office himself. He was, however, accompanied

---

* James Brodie of Brodie (1744–1824), the representative of an old Scottish family, was well-known as botanist and naturalist. Only the year previous to Burns's visit, his wife, youngest daughter of the first Earl of Fife (with whom he had eloped), had been accidentally burned to death in Brodie House.

† 'Though still in character of a castle, it is at once an elegant and majestic edifice: it extends upwards of five hundred and fifty feet in front; and the higher parts of the building, towering amidst the lofty trees in the park, present an image of magnificence to all the country round.'—From *Antiquities and Scenery of the North of Scotland,* by the Rev. Chas. Cordiner, minister of St Andrew's Chapel, Banff. (London, 1780.)

‡ Lady Charlotte, who was now nineteen years of age, afterwards became Duchess of Richmond; Lady Madelina married Sir Robert Sinclair of Murkle.

by a gentleman, a particular acquaintance of the Duke, by whom the invitation was delivered in all the forms of politeness. The invitation came too late; the pride of Nicol was inflamed into a high degree of passion by the neglect to which he thought he was being subjected. He had ordered the horses to be put to the carriage, being determined to proceed on his journey alone; and they found him parading the streets of Fochabers, before the door of the inn, venting his anger on the postillion for the slowness with which he obeyed his commands. As no explanation nor entreaty could change the purpose of his fellow-traveller, our poet was reduced to the necessity of separating from him entirely, or of instantly proceeding with him on their journey. He chose the latter of these alternatives; and seating himself beside Nicol in the post-chaise, with mortification and regret he turned his back on Gordon Castle, where he had promised himself some happy days.' Sensible, however, of the great kindness of the noble family, he made the best return in his power by a poem

ON CASTLE GORDON.

Streams that glide in orient plains,
Never bound by winter's chains;
  Glowing here on golden sands,
There commix'd with foulest stains
  From tyranny's empurpled hands:
These, their richly gleaming waves,
I leave to tyrants and their slaves;
Give me the stream that sweetly laves
    The banks by Castle Gordon.

Spicy forests, ever gay,
Shading from the burning ray
  Hapless wretches sold to toil,
Or the ruthless native's way,
  Bent on slaughter, blood and spoil:
Woods that ever verdant wave,
I leave the tyrant and the slave,
Give me the groves that lofty brave
    The storms, by Castle Gordon.

Wildly here, without controul,
Nature reigns and rules the whole ;
   In that sober pensive mood,
Dearest to the feeling soul,
   She plants the forest, pours the flood ;
Life's poor day I 'll musing rave,
And find at night a sheltering cave,
Where waters flow and wild woods wave,
     By bonie Castle Gordon.*

Allan Cunningham states that the Duchess of Gordon, knowing that Henry Addington (afterwards Lord Sidmouth) was a warm admirer of Burns's poetry, planned a meeting between them, with Dr Beattie, at Gordon Castle. 'The future premier,' says Cunningham, 'was unable to accept the invitation ; but wrote and forwarded, it is said, these memorable lines—memorable as the first indication of that deep love which England now entertains for the genius of Burns :

Yes ! pride of Scotia's favoured plains, 'tis thine
   The warmest feelings of the heart to move ;
To bid it throb with sympathy divine,
   To glow with friendship or to melt with love.

What though each morning sees thee rise to toil,
   Though Plenty on thy cot no blessing showers,
Yet Independence cheers thee with her smile,
   And Fancy strews thy moorland with her flowers !

And dost thou blame the impartial will of Heaven,
   Untaught of life the good and ill to scan ?
To thee the Muse's choicest wreath is given—
   To thee the genuine dignity of man !

Then, to the want of worldly gear resigned,
Be grateful for the wealth of thy exhaustless mind.'

[*Friday night, Sept. 7.*]—Sleep at Cullen. Hitherto the country is sadly poor and unimproven ; the houses, crops, horses, cattle, &c., all in unison with their cart-wheels ; and these are of low, coarse, unshod, clumsy work, with an axle-tree which had been made with other design than to be a resting shaft between the wheels.

* Designed to be sung to 'Morag,' a Highland tune of which Burns was extremely fond.—CURRIE.

[*Saturday, Sept.* 8.]—Breakfasted at Banff—Improvements over this part of the country—Portsoy Bay—pleasant ride along the shore—country almost wild again between Banff and Newbyth ; quite wild as we come through Buchan to Old Deer ; but near the village both lands and crops rich—lie.

It was with Dr Chapman, head-master of the Grammar-school of Banff, that Burns and Nicol breakfasted. Nicol had been a junior master under Chapman when the latter was head-master of Dumfries Academy.

A boy of thirteen, who was then attending the Greek class, and was asked by Chapman to join the party, related many years afterwards his recollections of what passed :*

'During breakfast, Burns played off some sportive jests at his touchy *compagnon de voyage*, about some misunderstanding which took place between them at Fochabers, in consequence of Burns having visited the castle without him ; and the good old doctor seemed much amused with the way the poet chose to smoothe down the yet lurking ire of the dominie. After breakfast, Dr Chapman sent me to the bookseller's shop for a new copy of the *Antiquities and Scenery of the North of Scotland*, by the Reverend Charles Cordiner, minister of the English Chapel in Banff, which he presented as a mark of his regard to Mr Nicol, and for a useful guide-book to the travellers in their progress. As they were to visit Duff House, the splendid mansion of the Earl of Fife, and drive through the park on their way south, after delivering the book to Mr Nicol I accompanied the two gentlemen from the town to the house, carrying a note to the steward there from my father, that they might see the interior of the house, the paintings, and valuable library. In driving through the park, Mr Nicol, while engaged in looking at the plates of the book, asked me whether I was aware that the gentleman who was speaking to me about the park was the author of the poems I had no doubt heard of. " Yes," I replied ; " Dr Chapman told me so when he asked me to breakfast." " Then, have you read the poems?" " Oh, yes ! I was glad to do that," was my reply. " Then, which of them did you like best?" Nicol asked. I said : " I was much entertained with the 'Twa Dogs,' and 'Death and Dr Hornbook ;' but I like best by far the 'Cotter's Saturday Night,' although

* This story appeared in *Chambers's Edinburgh Journal*, vol. viii., p. 405.

it made me *greet* when my father had me to read it to my mother."

' Burns, with a sort of sudden start, looked in my face intently, and patting my shoulder, said : " Well, my callant, I don't wonder at your *greeting* at reading the poem ; it made me *greet* more than once when I was writing it at *my* father's fireside."

' I recollect very well that while Mr Nicol loitered in the library, looking at the fine collection of old classics there, Burns, taking me with him for a guide, went a second time through some of the rooms to look at the old paintings, with the catalogue in his hand, and remarked particularly those of the Stuart family in the great drawing-room, on which he seemed to look with intense interest, making some remarks on them to his boy-guide, which the *man* fails to recollect. But the face and look of Robert Burns were such as, either boy or man, he never could forget.'

[*Sunday, Sept.* 9.]—Set out for Peterhead. Near Peterhead come along the shore by the famous Bullars of Buchan, and Blain's Castle.* The soil rich ; crops of wheat, turnips, &c. ; but no inclosing : soil rather light. Come to Ellon and dine—Lord Aberdeen's seat : entrance denied to everybody owing to the jealousy of threescore over a kept country-wench. Soil and improvements as before, till [*Sunday night*] we come to Aberdeen to lie.

[*Monday, Sept.* 10.]—Meet with Mr Chalmers, printer, a facetious fellow—Mr Ross, a fine fellow, like Professor Tytler—Mr Marshall, one of the *poetæ minores*—Mr Sheriffs, author of ' Jamie and Bess,' a little decrepid body, with some abilities †—Bishop Skinner, a non-juror, son of the author of ' Tullochgorum :' a man whose mild, venerable manner is the most marked of any in so young a man—Professor Gordon, a good-natured, jolly-looking professor ‡—Aberdeen, a lazy town.

It was at the printing-office of Mr Chalmers that Burns met

* Burns here means Slains Castle, residence of the Earls of Erroll, and a mile and a half from the Bullers of Buchan.

† Andrew Shirrefs, A.M., published, in 1790, a volume of *Poems chiefly in the Scottish Dialect*, one of many such brought forth by the success of the Ayrshire poet, but brought forth in vain. James Chalmers (1742-1810) was son of the founder of the *Aberdeen Journal*. He had passed through Marischal College, studied printing at London and Cambridge, and on his father's death in 1764, took up the position of editor, as well as printer, of the *Aberdeen Journal*. This he held for forty-six years. Marshall may have been William Marshall (1748-1833), factor to the Duke of Gordon, author of 'Scottish Airs, Melodies, &c., for piano, violin, and violoncello' (Edinburgh, 1828).

‡ Thomas Gordon (*circa* 1714-1797), an eminent professor in King's College. He held in succession the professorships of Humanity and Philosophy for sixty-one years, and is said to have been a particularly able teacher. He was author of MS. collections illustrative of the history of King's College, which are still preserved.

Bishop Skinner.   To the poet he was an interesting personality, not so much on account of the office he bore in the cavalier Episcopal Church of Scotland, as because he was the son of a man who had written popular songs in the vernacular language.*   Burns talked with him about his father ; and on learning that the latter lived at Linshart, near Lonmay, a village to the west of Peterhead, expressed great regret that he had not learned the fact before leaving Banff, as he would have gladly gone twenty miles out of his way to have seen the author of 'Tullochgorum.'   He would have found the old parson living in a cottage—what is called in Scotland *a but and a ben*—with earthen floors and grateless fireplaces, with less than the income of a foreman mechanic, yet happy, cheerful, and the centre of a cultured and accomplished family circle.

From Aberdeen, Burns proceeded southward into Kincardine-shire, the native county of his father, and then the dwelling-place of most of his paternal kindred.   As he was a firm believer in the proverb which declares blood to be thicker than water, he entered this district with special interest, expecting to meet many relatives.

Near Stonehive (the diary continues) the coast a good deal romantic.   Meet my relations.   Robert Burnes, Writer in Stonehive,† one of those who love fun, a gill, a punning joke, and have not a bad heart—his wife a sweet, hospitable body, without any affectation of what is called town-breeding.

Tuesday.—Breakfast with Mr Burnes—lie at Laurencekirk—Album —Library—Mrs ——, a jolly, frank, sensible, love-inspiring widow—Howe of the Mearns, a rich, cultivated, but still uninclosed, country.

* John Skinner, born in 1721 in the parish of Birse, Aberdeenshire, where his father was schoolmaster ; graduated at the age of seventeen ; left the Presbyterian for the Episcopalian Church, and ordained deacon at Longside, where he ministered for sixty-four years ; in 1753 imprisoned for six months for evading the Toleration Act ; published in 1780 an *Ecclesiastical History of Scotland*, in two volumes ; appointed dean of the diocese of Aberdeen ; died in 1807 ; his *Poems*, including 'The Ewie wi' the Crookit Horn' and 'Tullochgorum,' collected and published in 1809. His son, John Skinner, primus of Scotland, born at Longside in 1744 ; imprisoned with his father in 1753 ; graduated at the age of sixteen ; appointed to the charge of Ellon in 1763 ; called to Aberdeen in 1774 ; appointed bishop of diocese in 1787, and primus in 1788 ; died in 1816.

† This Robert Burnes was the son of William Burnes, the elder brother of James of Bralinmuir ; he died in 1816. 'By his wife, Anne Paul,' writes Mr J. Crabb Watt, in an interesting article on 'The Land of the Burnesses,' which appeared in the *Scots Magazine* for February 1890, ' he had a son William, who established a weaving business in Allardyce Street, Stonehaven, and his son, who is proud to wear the name Robert Burness, lives in Stonehaven still.' John, a younger brother of this Robert Burnes, is known as the author of 'Thrummy Cap,' and a few other poems. He visited his kinsman in Dumfries in 1796. He perished in a snowstorm in 1826.

Wednesday.—Cross North Esk River and a rich country to Craigow.

*   *   *   *

He then says, with provoking brevity, 'Go to Montrose, that finely situated, handsome town.' He here found his cousin, Mr James Burness, a writer or law-agent of good standing. A second James Burnes, father of Sir Alexander Burnes of Cabul memory, was then a little boy, and could afterwards remember sitting upon the poet's knee. Here Burns had to bid farewell to his Montrose cousin in writing :

TO MR JAMES BURNESS, MONTROSE.

TOWNFIELD, six o'clock morning.

MY DEAR COUSIN—Mr Nicol and Mr Carnegie have taken some freak in their head and have wakened me just now with the rattling of the chaise, to carry me to meet them at Craigie to go on our journey some other road and breakfast by the way. I must go, which makes me very sorry. I beg my kindest, best Compliments to your wife and all the good friends I saw yesternight.

Write me to Edinr. in this week, with a direction for your nephew in Glasgow. Direct to me, care of Mr Creech, Edinr. I am ever, my dear Cousin, Yours truly,   ROBT. BURNS.*

[*Sept.* 1787.]

The journal proceeds :

Leave Montrose [*Sept.* 13], breakfast at Auchmuthie, and sail along that wild, rocky coast, and see the famous caverns, particularly the Garie-pot.—Land and dine at Arbroath—stately ruins of Arbroath Abbey—come to Dundee through a fertile country. Dundee a low-lying but pleasant town—old steeple—Tay frith—Broughty Castle, a finely situated ruin, jutting into the Tay.

Friday.—Breakfast with the Miss Scotts—Mr Mitchell,† an honest clergyman—Mr Bruce ‡ another, but pleasant, agreeable, and engaging—the first from Aberlemno, the second from Forfar. Dine with Mr Anderson, a brother-in-law of Miss Scotts. Miss Bess Scott like Mrs Greenfield—my bardship almost in love with her—come through the rich harvests and fine hedgerows of the Carse of Gowrie, along the romantic

---

* The original of this note, with date at bottom in the handwriting of James Burness, is now in the museum attached to the City Chambers, Edinburgh.

† Andrew Mitchel was minister of Aberlemno, presbytery of Forfar, 1750-1794. His father had been minister of the church before him ; and his own son succeeded him.

‡ John Bruce was minister of Forfar parish from 1782-1817. He had been assistant in the same parish, 1780-1782.

margin of the Grampian Hills, to Perth—Castle Huntley *—Sir Stewart Thriepland. †

The little that remains of the journal again shows how keen was Burns's interest in the localities of Scottish songs. He seems to have taken measures to be introduced to the Belshes family at Invermay, near Perth, in order that he might see the pretty little valley celebrated in 'The Birks of Invermay.' ‡ He took pains also to learn the whereabouts of the spot consecrated by the ballad history of 'Bessie Bell and Mary Gray.'

Saturday.—Perth—Scoon—picture of the Chevalier and his sister; Queen Mary's bed, the hangings wrought with her own hands.—Fine, fruitful, hilly, woody country round Perth. Taybridge. Mr and Mrs Hastings—Major Scott—Castle Gowrie. Leave Perth—come to Strathearn to Endermay to dine. Fine, fruitful, cultivated Strath—the scene of 'Bessy Bell and Mary Gray,' near Perth—fine scenery on the banks of the May—Mrs Belches, gawcie, frank, affable, fond of rural sports, hunting, &c.—Mrs Stirling, her sister, *en verité.*—Come to Kinross to lie—reflections in a fit of the colic.

Sunday [Sept. 16.]—Pass through a cold, barren country to Queensferry—dine—cross the ferry, and on to Edinburgh.

TO MR GILBERT BURNS, MOSSGIEL.

EDINBURGH, 17*th Sept.* 1787.

MY DEAR SIR §—I arrived here safe yesterday evening, after a tour of twenty-two days, and travelling near 600 miles, windings included. My farthest stretch was about ten miles beyond Inverness. I went thro' the heart of the Highlands by Crieff, Taymouth, the famous seat of Lord Breadalbane, down the Tay, among cascades and Druidical circles of stones, to Dunkeld, a seat of the Duke of Athole; thence across Tay, and up one of his tributary streams to Blair of Athole, another of the Duke's seats, where I had the honor of spending nearly two days with

---

* Castle Huntly was at this time the property of George Paterson, a son-in-law of the twelfth Lord Gray, who had had it 'renovated without and modernised within, enlarged with wings, battlements, round tower and corner turrets, and altogether rendered it one of the most remarkable combinations of old and modern masonry in the kingdom.'

† Sir Stuart Thriepland (1716–1805) had joined the '45, escaped to France, was attainted and forfeited by Act of Parliament, returned to Scotland on the passing of the Act of Indemnity, and re-purchased his paternal estates (1782).

‡ Invermay was for centuries the property of the Belshes. It now belongs to Lord Clinton.

§ It was no doubt by an oversight that Burns addressed his brother as 'Sir.'

his Grace and family ; thence many miles through a wild country, among cliffs grey with eternal snows, and gloomy savage glens, till I cross Spey, and went down the stream through Strathspey, so famous in Scottish music ;* Badenoch, &c., till I reached Grant Castle, where I spent half a day with Sir James Grant and family; and then crossed the country for Fort-George, but called by the way at Cawdor, the ancient seat of Macbeth ; there I saw the identical bed in which tradition says King Duncan was murdered ; lastly, from Fort-George to Inverness.

I returned by the coast, through Nairn, Forres, and so on to Aberdeen, thence to Stonehive [Stonehaven], where James Burness, from Montrose, met me by appointment. I spent two days among our relations,† and found our aunts, Jean and Isabel, still alive, and hale old women. John Caird, though born the same year with our father, walks as vigorously as I can : they have had several letters from his son in New York. William Brand is likewise a stout old fellow ; but further particulars I delay till I see you, which will be in two or three weeks. The rest of my stages are not worth rehearsing ; warm as I was from Ossian's country, where I had seen his very grave, what cared I for fishing-towns or fertile carses? I slept at the famous Brodie of Brodie's one night, and dined at Gordon Castle next day, with the Duke, Duchess, and family. I am thinking to cause my old mare to meet me, by means of John Ronald,‡ at Glasgow ; but you shall hear further from me before I leave Edinburgh. My duty and many compliments from the north to my mother ; and my brotherly compliments to the rest. I have been trying for a berth for William,§ but am not likely to be successful. Farewell.

R. B.

Two days later he again writes to his cousin :

TO MR JAMES BURNESS, WRITER, MONTROSE.

MY DEAR COUSIN—I send you along with this nine Copies [of the second edition of his *Poems*] which you will transmit as marked on the blank leaves. The one to Lord Gardenstone you will transmit as soon as

---

* A quick kind of dancing-tunes are called Strathspeys, after the valley in which they originated.

† Robert Burnes of Clochnahill had by his wife, Isabella Keith, nine children. The lives of three of these—James, born in 1717; Robert, born in 1719 ; and William, born in 1721—have already been partially traced. A fourth son, George, born in 1729, died in early life. Margaret Burnes, the eldest of Robert's daughters, was born in 1723, married Archibald Walker, farmer, Crawton, Dunnottar ; Elspet, the second daughter, born in 1725, married John Caird, farmer at Denside, in Dunnottar, who subsequently retired to Stonehaven ; Jean, born in 1727, married her relative, John Burnes, sub-tenant in Bogjorgan ; Isabel, born in 1730, married William Brand, dyer, Auchenblae ; Mary, born in 1732, died young and unmarried. Robert Burnes has many descendants alive.

‡ A carrier between Mauchline and Glasgow ; uncle to William Ronald, ploughman at Mossgiel.

§ Younger brother of Robert and Gilbert, and then twenty years of age. He had been brought up as a saddler.

possible. Your hints about young Hudson I shall carefully remember when I call for him.

Any thing you send me, direct to the care of Mr Andrew Bruce, Merchant, Bridge street, Edinburgh, but I am afraid that your kind offer of the dry fish will cost more than they are worth, to Carriers. My Compliments to your wife and all friends ; and excuse this brevity in,—Yours ever, ROBT. BURNS.

EDINR., 19th Sept. 1787.

Journeying through the Highlands with a Jacobite companion, Burns could not but feel a little more enthusiastic than usual over the memory of the Stuarts. His visit to the home of those ancestors whom he believed to have followed the Cavalier standard would probably give a fillip to his feelings of romantic loyalty. It was possibly, therefore, about this time that he composed the following poem on Charlotte Stuart, commonly styled the Duchess of Albany. She was the child of Prince Charles Edward by his mistress, Clementina Walkinshaw, daughter of John Walkinshaw of Barrowfield, a Lanarkshire laird, who had fought on the side of the Pretender at Sheriffmuir, and acted as his secret agent in some of the capitals of Europe. Charles's mother had acted as godmother to Clementina in Rome, and there the two children were playmates. They met again at Bannockburn during the '45, after the battle of Falkirk. Clementina followed her lover to the Continent, bore him a daughter in 1753, and lived with him till 1760, when she left him on account of ill-usage. The Jacobites, who had long deplored his being without offspring by his wife Louise, Princess of Stolberg, best known as the Countess of Albany and for her intimacy with the poet Alfieri, heard with a sort of melancholy satisfaction that his one child, whatever were the circumstances of her birth, was legitimated under the title of Duchess of Albany, by a deed registered (September 6, 1784) by the Parliament of Paris.*

----

* 'At the beginning of July 1784, he recognised Lady Charlotte Stuart, his natural daughter by Miss Clementina Walkinshaw, by a legal document, in virtue of the right he possessed ; and, inclosing the document, wrote to the Duke of Vergennes requesting him to secure the royal sanction, and then have the deed registered by the Parliament of Paris ; and this was duly done on the 6th September of the same year. At the same time he wrote to his *chère fille*, telling her what had been done, and inviting her to come to him at Florence.'—ALFRED VON REUMONT, in *Die Gräfin von Albany*, vol. i., p. 265.

THE BONIE LASS OF ALBANIE.

TUNE—*Mary, weep no more for me.*

My heart is wae, and unco wae,   sad
   To think upon the raging sea,
That roars between her gardens green
   And th' bonie lass of Albanie.*

This lovely maid's of noble † blood
   That ruled Albion's kingdoms three;
But Oh, Alas, for her bonie face!
   They hae wrang'd the lass of Albanie.

In the rolling tide of spreading Clyde
   There sits an isle of high degree; ‡
And a town of fame whose princely name
   Should grace the lass of Albanie. §

* It has been conjectured in some quarters that it was the death of the young Pretender, on the 31st January 1788, that induced Burns to write 'The Bonie lass of Albanie,' and Mr R. B. Drummond of Perth has thus ingeniously attempted to fix the actual date and circumstances of its conception: 'On the 18th February 1788, Burns left Edinburgh for Mossgiel. On his way he spent a night at Glasgow with his friend Brown, and one at Paisley with Mr Patterson; and on the morning of the 20th he left Paisley on foot, and walked over the Gleniffer Braes to Dunlop House, the seat of his constant and attached friend Mrs Dunlop, where he remained two days. From Dunlop House he walked to Kilmarnock, where he arrived on the afternoon of the 22d. The road from Dunlop to Kilmarnock passes over the ridge of Cunningham, from whence, in a clear day in February, the view is extensive and interesting. The poet saw to the north-west the little Island of Bute, nestling on the bosom of the silver-grey firth, and sheltered by the mountains of Arran and the mainland. Away to the south, as far as the eye could reach, he could see long ranges of the Ayr and the Nith, bounded by the mountains of Galloway, the scene of "Mary's Dream." The situation, coupled with the poet's newly-excited grief for the exiled Stuarts, found utterance in the following song.' This view may be correct. In a volume of manuscripts which was long in the possession of Mr Benjamin Nightingale, London, however, the song follows the lines written on the inn window at Stirling. It was first printed from the Nightingale manuscripts, in vol. vi. (1843) of *Bentley's Miscellany.* It is believed to have been submitted to Allan Cunningham, when he was preparing his edition of Burns for the press, and that he declined to insert it on the ground that 'George IV. and the Duke of York were too recently deceased, and their brother William IV. then occupied the throne.'

† Variation—'Royal.'

‡ Bute.

§ Rothesay, the county town of Bute, gave a title to the eldest son of the king of Scotland (Duke of Rothesay).

But there is a youth, a witless youth
 That fills the place where she should be ;*
We 'll send him o'er to his native shore,
 And bring our ain sweet Albanie.   own

Alas the day, and woe the day,
 A false Usurper wan the gree, won—superiority, victory
That now commands the towers and lands,
 The royal right of Albanie.

We 'll daily pray, we 'll nightly pray,
 On bended knees most ferventlie,
That the time may come, with pipe and drum
 We 'll welcome home fair Albanie.†

On the 28th of September, Burns was still in Edinburgh. At his meeting with Mr Miller of Dalswinton in June, he had promised to return in August, and more carefully inspect the farms he had seen. He had been unable to fulfil this engagement, and he could not even now contemplate an immediate visit to Dumfriesshire. This letter explains his intended movements.

TO PATRICK MILLER, ESQ., DALSWINTON.

EDINBURGH, 28th September 1787.

SIR—I have been on a tour through the Highlands, and arrived in town but the other day, so could not wait on you at Dalswinton about the latter end of August, as I had promised and intended.

Independent of any views of future connections, what I owe you for the past, as a friend and benefactor, when friends I had few, and benefactors I had none, strongly in my bosom prohibits the most distant

---

* The 'witless youth' was the then Prince of Wales, afterwards George IV., who was born in 1762, and had, in the first three years after attaining his majority, accumulated debts to the amount of half-a-million. 'It was in 1787,' Professor Jack has pertinently pointed out in *Macmillan's Magazine* (May 1879), 'that Parliament granted him £160,000 to pay them. In the same year he repudiated Mrs Fitzherbert under the advice of his friend, Charles James Fox. She afterwards received a pension of £8000 a year from the royal family. The position of the Prince of Wales was discussed in the debates on the regency (December 1787—March 1788) which arose on the apparently permanent disablement of King George III.'

† The Duchess of Albany went to live with her father immediately after her legitimation. He left her his heiress, but she survived him less than two years, dying on the 14th November 1789. Her story is told very fully in Alfred von Reumont's monograph *Die Gräfin von Albany*, to which allusion has already been made, and by Professor Jack in *Macmillan's Magazine* for May 1879.

instance of ungrateful disrespect. I am informed you do not come to town for a month still, and within that time I shall certainly wait on you, as by this time I suppose you will have settled your scheme with respect to your farms.

My journey through the Highlands was perfectly inspiring, and I hope I have laid in a good stock of new poetical ideas from it. I shall make no apology for sending you the enclosed : it is a small but grateful tribute to the memory of our common countryman.* I have the honour to be, with the most grateful sincerity, sir, your obliged humble servant,

ROBT. BURNS.

P.S.—I have added another poem,† partly as it alludes to some folks nearly and dearly connected with Ayrshire, and partly as rhymes are the only coin in which the poor poet can pay his debts of gratitude. The lady alluded to is Miss Isabella M'Leod, aunt to the young Countess of London.

As I am determined not to leave Edinburgh till I wind up my matters with Mr Creech, which I am afraid will be a tedious business, should I unfortunately miss you at Dalswinton, perhaps your factor will be able to inform me of your intentions with respect to Elesland farm [*so in MS.*], which will save me a jaunt to Edinburgh again.

There is something so suspicious in the professions of attachment from a little man to a great man, that I know not how to do justice to the grateful warmth of my heart when I would say how truly I am interested in the welfare of your little troop of angels,‡ and how much I have the honour to be again, sir, your obliged humble servant,

ROBT. BURNS.

When John Skinner learned from his son, the bishop, that Burns had passed near his residence and missed seeing him, he felt as much regret as his brother poet had expressed. He resolved to open a correspondence with Burns in the style of certain versified epistles which Allan Ramsay and Hamilton of Gilbertfield had exchanged. His own first address to Burns, dated the 25th of September 1787, opens with an expression of his pleasure at his son having met Burns, and a regret at his own absence :

Oh happy hour for evermair,	evermore
That led my chill up Chalmers' stair,§	
And ga'e him, what he values sair,	gave—much
Sae braw a skance	so goodly—sight

* Evidently, from the expression 'our common countryman,' this refers to the elegy on Sir James Hunter Blair—Miller also being a native of Ayrshire.
† The verses on the death of John M'Leod, Esq.
‡ Patrick Miller had five 'angels.'
§ The stair of Mr Chalmers's printing-office in Aberdeen, where Burns and Bishop Skinner met. 'Chill' is 'chield,' or son.

Of Ayrshire's dainty poet there,   *good-humoured—genial*
    By lucky chance.

Waes my auld heart, I was na wi' you,   *Alas for—not*
Though worth-your-while I couldna gi'e you,
But sin' I hadna hap to see you,   *since—did not chance*
    When ye was north,
I 'm bauld to send my service to you,   *bold*
    Hence o'er the Forth.

After some verses expressing admiration of Burns and his several poems, the old man urges further labours in the field of poetry, and concludes by proposing a correspondence :

—— thanks to Praise, you 're in your prime,
And may chant on this lang, lang time ;   *long*
For, let me tell you, 'twere a crime
    To haud your tongue,   *hold*
Wi' sic a knack ye hae at rhyme,   *such*
    And you sae young.

Ye ken it 's no for ane like me   *know—one*
To be sae droll as ye can be ;
But ony help that I can gie,   *any*
    Though 't be but sma',   *small*
Your least command, I 'll let you see,
    Shall gar me draw.   *make*

An hour or twa, by hook or crook,
And maybe three, some orra ouk,   *odd week*
That I can spare frae haly beuk   *from holy book (Bible)*
    (For that 's my hobby),
I 'll steal awa' to some bye-neuk,   *corner*
    And crack wi' Robie.   *converse*
    *   *   *   *

Sae, canty Ploughman, fare ye weel ;   *lively*
Lord bless ye lang wi' ha'e and heal,   *property (wealth)—health*
And keep ye aye the honest chiel   *fellow*
    That ye hae been,
Syne lift ye to a better biel   *Then—shelter*
    Whan this is dune.   *When—done*

Burns was heartily pleased with this cordial recognition by a poet who, like Skinner, had been one of the gods of his youthful idolatry. He did not, however, reply immediately; and when he did, it was not in 'rhyming ware.'

TO REV. JOHN SKINNER.

EDINBURGH, *October* 25, 1787.

REVEREND AND VENERABLE SIR—Accept, in plain dull prose, my most sincere thanks for the best poetical compliment I ever received. I assure you, Sir, as a poet, you have conjured up an airy demon of vanity in my fancy, which the best abilities in your other capacity would be ill able to lay. I regret, and while I live I shall regret, that when I was in the north, I had not the pleasure of paying a younger brother's dutiful respect to the author of the best Scotch song ever Scotland saw—'Tulloch-gorum's my delight!' The world may think slightingly of the craft of song-making, if they please, but, as Job says, 'O! that mine adversary had written a book!'—let them try. There is a certain something in the old Scotch songs, a wild happiness of thought and expression, which peculiarly marks them not only from English songs, but also from the modern efforts of song-wrights, in our native manner and language. The only remains of this enchantment, these spells of the imagination, rests with you. Our true brother, Ross of Lochlee,* was likewise 'owre cannie'—a 'wild warlock'—but now he sings among the 'sons of the morning.'

I have often wished, and will certainly endeavour, to form a kind of common acquaintance among all the genuine sons of Caledonian song. The world, busy in low prosaic pursuits, may overlook most of us; but 'reverence thyself.' The world is not our *peers*, so we challenge the jury. We can lash that world, and find ourselves a very great source of amusement and happiness independent of that world.

There is a work going on in Edinburgh, just now, which claims your best assistance. An engraver in this town has set about collecting and publishing all the Scotch songs, with the music, that can be found. Songs in the English language, if by Scotchmen, are admitted, but the music must all be Scotch. Drs Beattie and Blacklock are lending a hand, and the first musician in town† presides over that department. I have been absolutely crazed about it, collecting old stanzas, and every information remaining respecting their origin, authors, &c., &c. This last is but a very fragment-business; but at the end of his second number—the first is already published—a small account will be given of the authors, particularly to preserve those of latter times. Your three songs, 'Tullochgorum,' 'John of Badenyon,' and 'Ewie wi' the crookit Horn,' go in this second number. I was determined, before I got your

---

* Allusion is here again made to Alexander Ross, the author of 'Woo'd and Married an' a'.' See note, Vol. I., p. 262.

† Stephen Clarke was at this time organist of the Episcopal Chapel of Edinburgh, in which city he also gave lessons in music. He harmonised the airs for the *Museum*, a work which, on his death in 1797, was continued by his son William.

letter, to write you, begging that you would let me know where the editions
of these pieces may be found, as you would wish them to continue in future
times ; and if you would be so kind to this undertaking as send any
songs, of your own or others, that you would think proper to publish,
your name will be inserted among the other authors—'Nill ye, will ye.'
One half of Scotland already give your songs to other authors. Paper is
done. I beg to hear from you ; the sooner the better, as I leave Edinburgh in a fortnight or three weeks. I am, With the warmest
sincerity, Sir, Your obliged humble servant,   R. B.

To this letter Mr Skinner sent the following reply :

LINSHART, 14th November 1787.

SIR—Your kind return without date, but of post-mark October 25th,
came to my hand only this day ; and to testify my punctuality to my
poetic engagement, I sit down immediately to answer it in kind. Your
acknowledgment of my poor but just encomiums on your surprising genius,
and your opinion of my rhyming excursions, are both, I think, by far too
high. The difference between our two tracks of education and ways of
life is entirely in your favour, and gives you the preference every manner
of way. I know a classical education will not create a versifying taste,
but it mightily improves and assists it ; and though, where both these
meet, there may sometimes be ground for approbation, yet where taste
appears single, as it were, and neither cramped nor supported by acquisi-
tion, I will always sustain the justice of its prior claim to applause. A
small portion of taste, this way, I have had almost from childhood,
especially in the old Scottish dialect: and it is as old a thing as I
remember, my fondness for 'Christ-kirk o' the Green,' which I had by
heart ere I was twelve years of age, and which, some years ago, I
attempted to turn into Latin verse. While I was young, I dabbled a
good deal in these things ; but on getting the black gown, I gave it
pretty much over, till my daughters grew up, who, being all good singers,
plagued me for words to some of their favourite tunes, and so extorted
these effusions, which have made a public appearance beyond my expectations, and contrary to my intentions, at the same time that I hope
there is nothing to be found in them uncharacteristic or unbecoming the
cloth, which I would always wish to see respected.

As to the assistance you propose from me in the undertaking you are
engaged in,* I am sorry I cannot give it so far as I could wish and you
perhaps expect. My daughters, who were my only intelligencers, are all
foris-familiate,† and the old woman their mother has lost that taste.
There are two from my own pen, which I might give you, if worth the
while. One to the old Scotch tune of 'Dumbarton's Drums.' The other,
perhaps, you have met with, as your noble friend the duchess has, I am

---

* Johnson's *Museum*.

† Skinner here uses a legal term to indicate that his daughters were ' separated from the
family '—*i.e.* married.

told, heard of it. It was squeezed out of me by a brother parson in her neighbourhood, to accommodate a new Highland reel for the marquis's birthday,* to the stanza of

> Tune your fiddles, tune them sweetly, &c.

If this last answer your purpose, you may have it from a brother of mine, Mr James Skinner, writer in Edinburgh, who, I believe, can give the music too.

There is another humorous thing I have heard, said to be done by the Catholic priest Geddes,† and which hit my taste much :—

There was a wee wifeikie was coming frae the fair,	from
Had gotten a little drapikie ‡ which bred her meikle care ;	much
It took upo' the wifie's heart, and she began to spew,	
And quo' the wee wifeikie, I wish I binna fou.	be (were) not drunk
I wish, &c., &c.	

I have heard of another new composition, by a young ploughman of my acquaintance, that I am vastly pleased with, to the tune of 'The Humours of Glen,' which I fear won't do, as the music, I am told, is of Irish original. I have mentioned these, such as they are, to shew my readiness to oblige you, and to contribute my mite, if I could, to the patriotic work you have in hand, and which I wish all success to. You have only to notify your mind, and what you want of the above shall be sent you.

Meantime, while you are thus publicly, I may say, employed, do not sheathe your own proper and piercing weapon. From what I have seen of yours already, I am inclined to hope for much good. One lesson of virtue and morality, delivered in your amusing style, and from such as you, will operate more than dozens would do from such as me, who shall be told it is our employment, and be never more minded : whereas, from a pen like yours, as being one of the many, what comes will be admired. Admiration will produce regard, and regard will leave an impression, especially when example goes along.

Now binna saying I 'm ill-bred,	be not
Else, by my troth, I 'll no be glad ;	
For cadgers, ye have heard it said,	hucksters
And sic-like fry,	such-like
Maun aye be harland in their trade,	must—jogging on
And sae maun I.	

Wishing you, from my poet pen, all success, and, in my other character, all happiness and heavenly direction, I remain, with esteem, your sincere friend, JOHN SKINNER.

---

* The Marquis of Huntly, eldest son of the Duke of Gordon.

† Geddes, who appears later on as a correspondent of Burns, is now believed *not* to have been the author of this poem.

‡ Diminutive of drap (drop) = a little drop (drink).

Before Burns had been many days in Edinburgh after his return from the north, he had to fulfil a promise to Charlotte Hamilton, and thus wrote to her friend at Harvieston :

TO MISS CHALMERS.

Sept. 26, 1787.*

I send Charlotte the first number of the songs ;† I would not wait for the second number ; I hate delays in little marks of friendship, as I hate dissimulation in the language of the heart. I am determined to pay Charlotte a poetic compliment, if I could hit on some glorious old Scotch air, in number second. You will see a small attempt on a shred of paper in the book ; but though Dr Blacklock commended it very highly, I am not just satisfied with it myself. I intend to make it *description* of some kind : the whining cant of love, except in real passion, and by a masterly hand, is to me as insufferable as the preaching cant of old Father Smeaton, Whig-minister at Kilmaurs.‡ Darts, flames, cupids, loves, graces, and all that farrago, are just a Mauchline sacrament—a senseless rabble.

I got an excellent poetic epistle yesternight from the old, venerable author of 'Tullochgorum,' 'John of Badenyon,' &c. I suppose you know he is a clergyman. It is by far the finest poetic compliment I ever got. I will send you a copy of it.

I go on Thursday or Friday to Dumfries, to wait on Mr Miller about his farms. Do tell that to Lady M'Kenzie, that she may give me credit for a little wisdom. 'I wisdom dwell with prudence.' What a blessed fire-side ! How happy should I be to pass a winter evening under their venerable roof ! and smoke a pipe of tobacco, or drink water-gruel with them ! What solemn, lengthened, laughter-quashing gravity of phiz ! What sage remarks on the good-for-nothing sons and daughters of indiscretion and folly ! And what frugal lessons, as we straitened the fire-side circle, on the uses of the poker and tongs !

Miss N[immo]§ is very well, and begs to be remembered in the old way to you. I used all my eloquence, all the persuasive flourishes of the hand, and heart-melting modulation of periods in my power, to urge her out to Harvieston, but all in vain. My rhetoric seems quite to have lost its effect on the lovely half of mankind. I have seen the day—but that is a 'tale of other years.'‖ In my conscience I believe that my heart has

---

* Internal evidence shows that either Skinner's poetical epistle of 25th September 1787 is *post*-dated, or this is *ante*-dated.

† The first volume of the *Scots Musical Museum*.

‡ Burns here alludes to the Rev. D. Smytane, or Smeaton, who, originally an itinerant Dissenting (Whig or Cameronian) minister in Ayrshire, was ordained to the Burgher pastorate of Kilmaurs in 1740. It is uncertain when he died, but his successor was ordained in 1789.

§ Miss Erskine Nimmo, a friend of Miss Chalmers, residing in Edinburgh.

‖ Burns seems to have anticipated by a century Mr Rudyard Kipling's 'But that is another story.'

been so oft on fire that it is absolutely vitrified. I look on the sex with something like the admiration with which I regard the starry sky in a frosty December night. I admire the beauty of the Creator's workmanship; I am charmed with the wild but graceful eccentricity of their motions; and—wish them good-night. I mean this with respect to a certain passion *dont j'ai eu l'honneur d'être un misérable esclave :* as for friendship, you and Charlotte have given me pleasure, permanent pleasure, 'which the world cannot give, nor take away,' I hope; and which will outlast the heavens and the earth.   R. B.

The wish of Burns for an immediate sight of Miller's farms does not appear to have been gratified. Before October was far advanced, he had undoubtedly left Edinburgh on an excursion of a different character, and in a different direction. He had various objects to accomplish. He wished to see more of the family at Harvieston. He desired to take advantage of the invitation which Sir William Murray of Ochtertyre had given him at Blair. He also carried a letter of introduction from Dr Blacklock for Mr Ramsay of Ochtertyre (another Ochtertyre, near Stirling), a man thoroughly qualified to appreciate his genius, and to assist in his literary schemes. Burns started in company with Dr James M'Kittrick Adair, the son of a physician in Ayr, and a relative of Mrs Dunlop, to whom he had been introduced in 1787 by the Rev. Mr Lawrie, minister of Loudoun. Dr Adair gave Dr Currie an account of the tour, which may be received as faithful in most particulars, but inaccurate as regards dates.

'Burns and I,' he says, 'left Edinburgh in August 1787.' It will be seen from a note below,* that the circumstances alluded to by Dr Adair himself require a later date. He continues: 'We rode by Linlithgow and Carron, to Stirling. We visited the iron-works at Carron, with which the poet was forcibly struck. The resemblance between that place and its inhabitants to the cave of the Cyclops, which must have occurred to every

---

* 'Burns and I,' says Dr Adair, 'left Edinburgh in August 1787.' Clearly, the memory of Dr Adair, who wrote of his excursion with Burns twelve years after it took place, played him false. As has been seen, Burns had to make a personal appearance in Edinburgh on the 15th August, on account of certain legal proceedings against him. As he arrived in Edinburgh from Mossgiel on the 7th, attended to these matters on, or perhaps before, the 14th, wrote to Robert Ainslie from Nicol's house on the 23d, and set out on his post-chaise journey with the latter on the 25th, there is no time for a ten days' tour with Dr Adair during this month. The early and middle part of October is the first clear space of time to which such a tour can be assigned. This view seems to be confirmed by Burns's letter to Patrick Miller of the 23d October.

classical reader, presented itself to Burns. At Stirling the prospects from the castle strongly interested him; in a former visit to
which, his national feelings had been powerfully excited by the
ruinous and roofless state of the hall in which the Scottish
parliaments had frequently been held. His indignation had vented
itself in some imprudent, but not unpoetical lines, which had
given much offence, and which he took this opportunity of erasing,
by breaking the pane of the window at the inn on which they
were written. At Stirling we met with a company of travellers
from Edinburgh, among whom was a character in many respects
congenial with that of Burns. This was Nicol, one of the teachers
of the High-Grammar-school at Edinburgh—the same wit and
power of conversation; the same fondness for convivial society,
and thoughtlessness of to-morrow, characterized both. Jacobitical
principles in politics were common to both of them; and these have
been suspected, since the revolution of France, to have given place
in each, to opinions apparently opposite. I regret that I have preserved no *memorabilia* of their conversation, either on this or on
other occasions, when I happened to meet them together. Many
songs were sung; which I mention for the sake of observing, that
when Burns was called on in his turn, he was accustomed, instead
of singing, to recite one or other of his own shorter poems, with a
tone and emphasis which, though not correct or harmonious, were
impressive and pathetic. This he did on the present occasion.

'From Stirling we went next morning through the romantic and
fertile vale of Devon to Harvieston, in Clackmannan-shire, then
inhabited by Mrs Hamilton, with the younger part of whose family
Burns had been previously acquainted. He introduced me to the
family, and there was formed my first acquaintance with Mrs
Hamilton's eldest daughter, to whom I have been married for nine
years.* Thus was I indebted to Burns for a connexion from
which I have derived, and expect further to derive, much
happiness.'

Burns appears to have intended to stay for a very short time at

---

* 'Nov. 16, 1789. At Harvieston, Dr James M'Kittrick Adair to Miss Charlotte Hamilton.'
—*Scots Magazine.* Dr Adair, who, after his marriage, took a medical practice at the
Pleasance, Edinburgh, subsequently removed to Harrogate, where he died in 1802, at the
age of thirty-seven. His widow survived him four years, dying at Edinburgh at the age of
forty-three. His only sister, Anne, married the Rev. Archibald Lawrie, who succeeded his
father as minister of Loudoun. She died at Glasgow in 1822.

Harvieston. He was, however, detained by a violent storm, accompanied by heavy floods, which took place on the 10th of October.

'During a residence of about ten days at Harvieston, we made excursions to visit various parts of the surrounding scenery, inferior to none in Scotland in beauty, sublimity, and romantic interest; particularly Castle Campbell, the ancient seat of the family of Argyle; the famous cataract of the Devon, called the Caldron Linn; and the Rumbling Bridge, a single broad arch, thrown by the Devil, if tradition is to be believed, across the river, at about the height of a hundred feet above its bed. I am surprised that none of these scenes should have called forth an exertion of Burns's muse. But I doubt if he had much taste for the picturesque. I well remember, that the ladies at Harvieston, who accompanied us on this jaunt, expressed their disappointment at his not expressing in more glowing and fervid language, his impressions of the Caldron Linn scene, certainly highly sublime, and somewhat horrible.'

Among these excursions, though Dr Adair makes no allusion to it, we must include one which the poet made by himself to the two Ochtertyres. A forenoon's ride would bring him to the 'Tusculum' of Mr Ramsay on the Teith, where his reception was so cordial that he promised, if possible, to see his host a second time on his return. Mr Ramsay* was an admirable specimen of the scholarly country gentleman, living in Horatian ease and unpretentious simplicity on his own property. He had a great love for Scottish literature and history, and thus was particularly disposed to admire and sympathise with Burns. Before many years passed, he received into the same house Sir Walter Scott, also destined to world-wide fame, and then engaged in visiting the romantic scenery of Scotland, and storing his mind with Scots lore. After an informal call, Burns appears to have proceeded to Ochtertyre in Strathearn, to visit Sir William Murray.

* John Ramsay was born in Edinburgh on 20th August 1736. His father, who was proprietor of the estate of Ochtertyre (also spelt Auchtertyre) in the parish of Kincardine, in Menteith, near Stirling, practised as a Writer to the Signet in Edinburgh. He himself was trained as an advocate, but never practised. His father died while he was still under age, and he gave himself up to the life of a country gentleman. Fond of letters and literary society, he spent his winters in Edinburgh, where he was very friendly with, among others, Dr Gleig, editor of the *Encyclopædia Britannica*, and Lord Kames. An expert in Latin, he conducted correspondence, and even conversation, with some of his friends in that language. He was a keen antiquary, and Scott reproduced some of his characteristics in 'Jonathan Oldbuck' (*The Antiquary*). Ramsay, who never married, died at Ochtertyre on 2d March 1814.

He greatly enjoyed the few days he spent at Ochtertyre. Sir William was an amiable and intelligent man, who had already, at Blair, shown a friendly disposition towards him. His wife, Lady Augusta Mackenzie, was interesting to Burns from associations connected with her parentage; for she was youngest daughter of the Jacobite (third) Earl of Cromartie, who so narrowly escaped accompanying Kilmarnock and Balmerino to the scaffold on Tower Hill in 1746. 'Born in the Tower, not long after that harassing time, during which her mother was anxiously engaged in pleading for the earl's life, she bore what all her friends believed to be the image of an axe upon her neck.'* The Jacobitical feelings of Burns must have been pleasingly stimulated in such society. That he was in other respects comfortably situated, appears from two short letters addressed to friends in Edinburgh:

TO WILLIAM NICOL, ESQ.

AUCHTERTYRE, *Monday [Oct.* 15, 1787].

MY DEAR SIR—I find myself very comfortable here, neither oppressed by ceremony nor mortified by neglect. Lady Augusta is a most engaging woman, and very happy in her family, which makes one's outgoings and incomings very agreeable. I called at Mr Ramsay's of Auchtertyre as I came up the country, and am so delighted with him that I shall certainly accept of his invitation to spend a day or two with him as I return. I leave this place on Wednesday or Thursday.

Make my kind compliments to Mr and Mrs Cruikshank and Mrs Nicol, if she is returned. I am ever, dear Sir, Your deeply indebted

R. B.

---

* It is commonly supposed that the countess was pregnant at the time her husband was under condemnation. But this does not appear to have been the case, the child having been born in July 1747. In the *Gentleman's Magazine* for November that year occur lines 'Occasioned by a reflection lately published on the new-born daughter of Mr Mackenzie, late Earl of Cromertie:

"Ill flows the verse that brands an infant's name,
   And loads a babe yet innocent with shame;
   Heir to misfortune, let its fate suffice.
   Nor for the father's crimes the child despise;
   The generous heart laments the guiltless moan,
   The future sighs, for follies not its own;
   E'en there perhaps we err—succeeding days
   May see this child our warmest wishes raise,
   Retrieve the honours that her father lost,
   And match some Briton, Britain's future boast,
   Who, fired, celestial Liberty, by thee,
   From hell-born faction shall his country free."—C. B.'

[TO MR WILLIAM CRUIKSHANK.]*

I have nothing, my dear Sir, to write you but that I feel myself exceedingly comfortably situated in this good family; just notice enough to make me easy but not to embarrass me.   I was storm-steaded two days at the foot of the Ochel Hills, with Mr Tait of Harvieston and Mr Johnson of Alva, but was so well pleased that I shall certainly spend a day on the banks of Devon as I return. I leave this place, I suppose, on Wednesday, and shall devote a day to Mr Ramsay at Ochtertyre, near Stirling; a man to whose worth I cannot do justice. My most respectful kind compliments to Mrs Cruikshank and my dear little Jeany; and if you see Mr Masterton,† please remember me to him.   I am ever, my dear Sir, yours most gratefully,   ROBT. BURNS.

AUCHTERTYRE, *Monday Morn [Oct.* 15, 1787].

It is probable, from an expression which Walker uses in a letter printed by Currie, that the poet on this occasion visited also Mr Graham of Balgowan, already mentioned, who, with his wife, had offered to conduct him to Dronach-haugh, hallowed in Scottish song as the grave of Bessie Bell and Mary Gray.‡

Among the hills behind Ochtertyre are a wildly picturesque valley, and a lake (Loch Turit or Turrit), which is a great attraction to visitors.

ON SCARING SOME WATER-FOWL IN LOCH-TURIT.

This was the production of a solitary forenoon's walk from Oughtertyre-house.   I lived there, Sir William's guest, for two or three weeks, and was much flattered by my hospitable reception.   What a pity that the mere emotions of gratitude are so impotent in this world ! 'Tis lucky that, as we are told, they will be of some avail in the world to come.— *R. B., Glenriddel MSS.*

Why, ye tenants of the lake,
For me your wat'ry haunt forsake ?

' This letter was printed in the *Gentleman's Magazine,* August 1832, without address. That it was meant for Mr Cruikshank, notwithstanding that Burns in the preceding letter implies the reverse of an intention of writing to him, is evident from the expressions at the close.

† Of Allan Masterton little information is to be found.   In 1795 he was appointed joint writing-master (with Dugald Masterton and Dugald Masterton, jun.) in the High School of Edinburgh.   He died in 1799.   He is the 'Allan' of 'Willie brew'd a peck o' maut,' to which he composed the music which appears in Johnson's *Museum.*

‡ The subjects of a romantic ballad of that name.   To escape the plague, they retired to a bower erected near Burnbraes (west of Lynedoch House), where they were visited by a young man who was in love with them.   He communicated the infection to the ladies, who both succumbed to it.

Tell me, fellow-creatures, why
At my presence thus you fly ?
Why disturb your social joys,
Parent, filial, kindred ties?—
Common friend to you and me,
Nature's gifts to all are free :
Peaceful keep your dimpling wave,
Busy feed, or wanton lave ;
Or, beneath the sheltering rock,
Bide the surging billow's shock.

Conscious, blushing for our race,
Soon, too soon, your fears I trace.
Man, your proud usurping foe,
Would be lord of all below:
Plumes himself in Freedom's pride,
Tyrant stern to all beside.

The eagle, from the cliffy brow,
Marking you his prey below,
In his breast no pity dwells,
Strong Necessity compels.
But Man, to whom alone is giv'n
A ray direct from pitying Heav'n,
Glories in his heart humane—
And creatures for his pleasure slain.

In these savage, liquid plains,
Only known to wand'ring swains,
Where the mossy riv'let strays,
Far from human haunts and ways ;
All on Nature you depend,
And life's poor season peaceful spend.

Or, if man's superior might
Dare invade your native right,
On the lofty ether borne,
Man with all his pow'rs you scorn ;

Swiftly seek, on clanging wings,
Other lakes and other springs ;
And the foe you cannot brave,
Scorn at least to be his slave.

Among the inmates of Ochtertyre House was a young cousin of
Sir William, Euphemia, daughter of Mr Mungo Murray of Lintrose,
a beautiful girl of eighteen, known in the district as ' The Flower of
Strathmore.'*		Burns made her the subject of a pastoral song :

BLYTHE WAS SHE.

TUNE—*Andro and his Cutty Gun.*

Chorus—Blythe, blythe and merry was she,
			Blythe was she but and ben ; †
			Blythe by the banks of Earn,
			And blythe in Glenturit glen.

By Oughtertyre grows the aik,	oak
On Yarrow banks, the birken shaw ;	birch-woods
But Phemie was a bonier lass	
Than braes o' Yarrow ever saw.	

Her looks were like a flow'r in May,	
Her smile was like a simmer morn ;	summer
She trippèd by the banks o' Earn	
As light 's a bird upon a thorn.	

Her bonny face it was as meek	
As ony lamb upon a lee ;	any—lea
The evening sun was ne'er sae sweet	so
As was the blink o' Phemie's e'e.	eye

The Highland hills I 've wander'd wide,	
And o'er the Lawlands I hae been ;	Lowlands
But Phemie was the blythest lass	
That ever trode the dewy green.	

* In 1794 Miss Murray married Mr Smythe of Methven, one of the senators of the
College of Justice (Lord Methven).   ' Mrs Smythe always manifested a disinclination to
speak on the subject of her meeting with Burns.   But she once told me that she remembered his reciting the poem " On Scaring the Wild-fowl" one evening after supper,
and that he gave the concluding lines with the greatest possible vigour.'—*Letter of a relation of Mrs Smythe.*

† Literally, in both rooms of the house ; here, throughout the house.

A letter of Mr Ramsay to Dr Currie, and one which he addressed to Burns (22d October 1787), and which Currie published, give some idea of what passed at the Menteith Ochtertyre, on Burns's way back to Harvieston : 'I have been in the company of many men of genius,' says Mr Ramsay, 'some of them poets, but never witnessed such flashes of intellectual brightness as from him, the impulse of the moment, sparks of celestial fire ! I never was more delighted, therefore, than with his company for two days, *tête-à-tête.* In a mixed company I should have made little of him, for, in the gamester's phrase, he did not always know when to play off and when to play on. . . . I not only proposed to him the writing of a play similar to the 'Gentle Shepherd,' *qualem decet esse sororem,* but Scottish Georgics, a subject which Thomson has by no means exhausted in his *Seasons.* What beautiful landscapes of rural life and manners might not have been expected from a pencil so faithful and forcible as his, which could have exhibited scenes as familiar and interesting as those in the 'Gentle Shepherd,' which every one who knows our swains in their unadulterated state instantly recognises as true to nature ! But to have executed either of these plans, steadiness and abstraction from company were wanting, not talents. When I asked him whether the Edinburgh Literati had mended his poems by their criticisms, "Sir," said he, " these gentlemen remind me of some spinsters in my country, who spin their thread so fine, that it is neither fit for weft nor woof." He said he had not changed a word except one, to please Dr Blair.'

Mr Ramsay had put up a Latin inscription over his door, expressing his wish to live in peace and die in joyful hope in the small but pleasant inheritance of his fathers. With another he graced a *Salictum,* or plantation of willows—

> Salubritatis voluptatisque causa,
> Hoc salictum,
> Paludem olim infidam,
> Mihi meisque desicco et exorno.
> Hic, procul negotiis strepituque,
> Innocuis deliciis
> Silvulas inter nascentes reptandi,
> Apiumque labores suspiciendi,
> Fruiscor.

Hic, si faxit Deus Opt. Max.,
Prope hunc fontem pellucidum
Cum quodam juventutis amico superstite
Sæpe conquiescam senex,
Contentus modicis, meoque lactus.
Sin aliter,
Ævique paululum supersit,
Vos, silvulæ et amici cæteraque amata,
Valete diuque lactamini.

Burns admired the general meaning of these inscriptions, the Latinity of which is not beyond reproach, and asked for copies of them, which Mr Ramsay sent him. The poet made his host aware of his having lately heard some Highland airs, with which he was much charmed, and for which he was writing verses. He mentioned also his desire to collect airs for Johnson's *Museum*. Mr Ramsay accordingly furnished him with a letter of introduction to the Rev. Walter Young,* minister of Erskine, on the Clyde, as a person qualified to give him full information about Highland music. He added a transcript of a Highland tradition which had made an impression on the poet's mind when he was told it. 'Its hero was a Highlander named Omeron Cameron, who received the Earl of Mar in his humble cottage, when the earl had to skulk from his enemies. Being himself forced into exile on this account by his own clan, he went to Kildrummy Castle with his wife and children, to claim a requital from the earl, who had bidden him do so if ever misfortune should befall him. Upon hearing who it was, the earl started from his seat with a joyful exclamation, and caused Omeron to be conducted with all possible respect into the hall. He afterwards conferred on him a four-merk land near the castle.' Out of these elements Mr Ramsay thought that Burns might compose a play. 'I approve of your plan,' also wrote Mr Ramsay, 'of retiring from din and dissipation to a farm of very moderate size, sufficient to find exercise for mind and body, but not so great as to absorb better things. And if some intellectual pursuit be well chosen and steadily pursued, it will be more lucrative than most farms in this age of rapid improvement. Upon this subject, as your well-wisher and admirer, permit me to go a step further. Let those

* Walter Young, minister of Erskine parish, 1771–1814, is said to have been the most accomplished private musician of his day.

bright talents which the Almighty has bestowed on you, be henceforth employed to the noble purpose of supporting the cause of truth and virtue. An imagination so varied and forcible as yours may do this in many different modes; nor is it necessary to be always serious, which you have been to good purpose; good morals may be recommended in a comedy, or even in a song.'

Burns and Mr Ramsay had talked about a Jacobite old lady, a relic of a former generation, who lived at Harvieston. Mrs Bruce of Clackmannan, or (to use the Scotch title of courtesy) Lady Clackmannan, lived in the ancient and now ruined tower of that name, overlooking the Firth of Forth at Alloa. Allied in blood to Robert Bruce, and in sentiments to the Stuart family, tall and dignified, though she was on the verge of ninety, with a lively imagination, balanced by strong common-sense—the old lady, with her tartan scarf and a white rose in her breast, as she is represented in her portrait, must have been an interesting study for Burns. Dr Adair, adverting to the faint impression which the Glendevon scenery seemed to make on Burns, says: 'A visit to Mrs Bruce of Clackmannan, a lady above ninety, the lineal descendant of that race which gave the Scottish throne its brightest ornament, interested his feelings more powerfully. This venerable dame, with characteristical dignity, informed me, on my observing that I believed she was descended from the family of Robert Bruce, that Robert Bruce was sprung from her family. Though almost deprived of speech by a paralytic affection, she preserved her hospitality and urbanity. She was in possession of the hero's helmet and two-handed sword, with which she conferred on Burns and myself the honour of knighthood, remarking that she had a better right to confer that title than *some people*. . . . You will, of course, conclude that the old lady's political tenets were as Jacobitical as the poet's, a conformity which contributed not a little to the cordiality of our reception and entertainment. She gave, as her first toast after dinner, *Awa' Uncos*, or Away with the Strangers—Who these strangers were, you will readily understand. Mrs Adair corrects me by saying it should be *Hooi*, or *Hoohi uncos*, a sound used by shepherds to direct their dogs to drive away the sheep.'*

* It is barely necessary to remark that Lady Clackmannan had no historical ground for her statement that Robert Bruce was sprung from *her* family; for all that the Bruces of

Dr Adair states that he and Burns returned to Edinburgh by Kinross and Queensferry. The reason for their making a circuit by Kinross was probably Burns's wish to see the island-fortress of Lochleven, in which Queen Mary, under compulsion, signed a surrender of the kingdom to her son. 'At Dunfermline,' says Dr Adair, 'we visited the ruined Abbey, and the Abbey Church, now consecrated to Presbyterian worship. Here I mounted the *culty stool*, or stool of repentance, assuming the character of a penitent for fornication; while Burns from the pulpit addressed to me a ludicrous reproof and exhortation, parodied from that which had been delivered to himself in Ayr-shire, where he had, as he assured me, once been one of seven * who mounted the "*seat of shame*" together.

'In the church-yard, two broad flag-stones mark the grave of Robert Bruce, for whose memory Burns had more than common veneration. He knelt and kissed the stone with sacred fervour, and heartily (*suus ut mos erat*) execrated the worse than Gothic neglect of the first of Scottish heroes.'

Burns returned to Edinburgh on the 20th October, but was confined to his lodging for some time by a cold. He had now to bethink himself of his long-promised visit to Dumfriesshire, so immediately communicated with Mr Miller.

TO PATRICK MILLER, ESQ., DALSWINTON.

EDINBURGH, *20th October* 1787.

SIR—I was spending a few days at Sir William Murray's, Oughtertyre, and did not get your obliging letter till to-day I came to town. I was still more unlucky in catching a miserable cold, for which the medical gentlemen have ordered me into close confinement, 'under pain of death' —the severest of penalties. In two or three days, if I get better, and if I hear at your lodgings that you are still at Dalswinton, I will take a ride to Dumfries directly. From something in your last, I would wish to explain my idea of being your tenant. I want to be a farmer in a small farm, about a plough-gang, in a pleasant country under the

---

Stirling and Clackmannan shires know of their earliest recorded ancestor is that David II., the son of Bruce, addresses him in a charter as 'our relative.' The old lady probably founded upon some family legend. She died in 1791, when the sword and helmet of the hero of Bannockburn fell into the hands of her kinsman, the Earl of Elgin, in whose family they still remain.

* The session-book of Mauchline says *five*.

auspices of a good landlord. I have no foolish notion of being a tenant on easier terms than another. To find a farm where one can live at all is not easy—I only mean living soberly, like an old-style farmer, and joining personal industry. The banks of the Nith are as sweet, poetic ground as any I ever saw; and besides, sir, 'tis but justice to the feelings of my own heart, and the opinion of my best friends, to say that I would wish to call you landlord sooner than any landed gentleman I know. These are my views and wishes; and in whatever way you think best to lay out your farms, I shall be happy to rent one of them. I shall certainly be able to ride to Dalswinton about the middle of next week, if I hear you are not gone. I have the honour to be, sir, your obliged, humble servant,   ROBT. BURNS.

Burns appears now to have taken up his quarters with William Cruikshank,* a colleague of Nicol in the High School. The house consisted of the two upper floors of a lofty building, in an airy situation in the New Town—then marked No. 2 (now 30) St James's Square. The poet's room had a window overlooking the green behind the Register House, as well as the street entering the Square. It was by far the most comfortable place in which he had ever had more than the most temporary lodging. Mr Cruikshank had a daughter, Janet, who was a pretty young girl and a promising pianist. Burns spent many a pleasant hour listening to her playing his favourite Scottish airs. He also took advantage of her voice and instrument in the work of adapting new verses to old airs for the *Scots Musical Museum*. Walker says: 'About the end of October, I called for him at the house of a friend [Mr Cruikshank], whose daughter, though not more than twelve, was a considerable proficient in music. I found him seated by the harpsichord of this young lady, listening with the keenest interest to his own verses, which she sung and accompanied, and adjusting them to the music by repeated trials of the effect. In this occupation he was so totally absorbed, that it was difficult to draw his attention from it for a moment.'† This gives us some idea of the care and study

---

* William Cruikshank, M.A., had been trained under his uncle (his namesake), the famous schoolmaster of Duns; he had afterwards studied at the University of Edinburgh. In 1770 he was appointed Rector of the High School of the Canongate; and two years later received a classical mastership in the High School of Edinburgh. He was described by Lord Brougham as a 'very able and successful teacher, as well as a worthy man.' He died in 1795.

† Walker's *Life of Burns*, p. lxxxi.

bestowed by Burns upon his songs, which resulted in their almost perfect adaptation to their respective airs. He gratefully celebrated his favourite, Jenny Cruikshank, in

A ROSE BUD BY MY EARLY WALK.

TUNE—*The Shepherd's Wife.*

A rose bud by my early walk
Adown a corn-inclosèd bawk,*
Sae gently bent its thorny stalk,
    All on a dewy morning.
Ere twice the shades o' dawn are fled,
In a' its crimson glory spread,
And drooping rich the dewy head,
    It scents the early morning.

Within the bush her covert nest
A little linnet fondly prest,
The dew sat chilly on her breast
    Sae early in the morning.
She soon shall see her tender brood,
The pride, the pleasure o' the wood,
Amang the fresh green leaves bedew'd,
    Awauk the early morning.   Awake

So thou, dear bird, young Jeany fair,
On trembling string or vocal air
Shall sweetly pay the tender care
    That tents thy early morning.   guards
So thou, sweet Rose bud, young and gay,
Shalt beauteous blaze upon the day,
And bless the Parent's evening ray
    That watch'd thy early morning.

Nor was this the only proof of the esteem in which Burns held his 'Rosebud:'

* An open space in a cornfield.

TO MISS CRUIKSHANK, A VERY YOUNG LADY.*

WRITTEN ON THE BLANK LEAF OF A BOOK PRESENTED
TO HER BY THE AUTHOR.

Beauteous rose-bud, young and gay,
Blooming on thy early May,
Never may'st thou, lovely Flow'r,
Chilly shrink in sleety show'r !
Never Boreas' hoary path,
Never Eurus' pois'nous breath,
Never baleful stellar lights,
Taint thee with untimely blights !
Never, never reptile thief
Riot on thy virgin leaf !
Nor even Sol too fiercely view
Thy bosom blushing still with dew !†

May'st thou long, sweet crimson gem,
Richly deck thy native stem ;
Till some ev'ning, sober, calm,
Dropping dews, and breathing balm,
While all around the woodland rings,
And ev'ry bird thy requiem sings ;
Thou, amid the dirgeful sound,
Shed thy dying honours round,
And resign to Parent Earth
The loveliest form she e'er gave birth.

The zeal of Burns for the collection, illustration, and enlargement of Scottish song, was at this period—and indeed at all
times—very warm. He entered into the views of Johnson with
an energy and enthusiasm which money could not have purchased. His sentiments on this subject were characteristic.
Burns regarded poetry as too sacred to be associated with mercenary
considerations. He wrote in numbers, 'for the numbers came.'

---

* The 'Rosebud' became, in 1804, wife of James Henderson, a legal practitioner at
Jedburgh. There she died in 1835. Her husband survived her four years.
  † Variation—
                    'Nor Phebus drink with scorching ray
                    The freshness of thine early day.'

Though he had published a volume, and consented to realise a profit by it, he could not have composed either poems or songs with the deliberate purpose of selling them.

At Gordon Castle, Burns had formed an acquaintance with James Hoy, the duke's librarian, companion, and friend, a well-read man, who lived in the castle for forty-six years (he died in 1828) without ever losing the Dominie-Sampson-like purity of heart and simplicity of manners by which he was distinguished. Burns now wrote to him on behalf of the *Museum*. The duke, a plain, unpretentious laird, was a song-writer of some ability, and had produced at least one popular ditty, bearing the title 'Cauld Kail in Aberdeen.' This Burns wished to secure.

TO JAMES HOY, ESQ., GORDON CASTLE.

EDINBURGH, *20th October* 1787.

SIR—I will defend my conduct in giving you this trouble, on the best of Christian principles—'Whatsoever ye would that men should do unto you, do ye even so unto them.' I shall certainly, among my legacies, leave my latest curse to that unlucky predicament which hurried—tore me away from Castle-Gordon. May that obstinate son of Latin prose [Nicol] be curst to Scotch-mile periods, and damned to seven-league paragraphs; while Declension and Conjugation, Gender, Number, and Time,* under the ragged banners of Dissonance and Disarrangement, eternally rank against him in hostile array !

Allow me, sir, to strengthen the small claim I have to your acquaintance by the following request. An engraver, James Johnson, in Edinburgh, has, not from mercenary views, but from an honest Scotch enthusiasm, set about collecting all our native songs, and setting them to music, particularly those that have never been set before. Clarke, the well-known musician, presides over the musical arrangement, and Drs Beattie and Blacklock, Mr Tytler of Woodhouselee, and your humble servant to the utmost of his small power, assist in collecting the old poetry, or sometimes, for a fine air, make a stanza when it has no words. The enclosed is one which, like some other misbegotten brats, 'too tedious to mention,' claims a parental pang from my bardship, I suppose will appear in Johnson's second number—the first was published before my acquaintance with him. My request is—'Cauld Kail in Aberdeen' is one intended for this number, and I beg a copy of his Grace of Gordon's words to it, which you were so kind as to repeat to me. You may be sure we won't prefix the author's name, except you like, though I look on it as no small merit to this work, that the names of so many of the authors of our old Scotch songs, names almost forgotten, will be inserted. I do not well know

---

* 'Tense' appears in most printed versions of the letter.

where to write to you—I rather write at you; but if you will be so obliging, immediately on receipt of this, as to write me a few lines, I shall perhaps pay you in kind, though not in quality. Johnson's terms are :—each number a handsome pocket volume, to consist of a hundred Scotch songs, with basses for the harpsichord, &c. The price to subscribers, 5s. : to non-subscribers, 6s. He will have three numbers, I conjecture.

My direction, for two or three weeks, will be at Mr William Cruikshank's, St James's Square, New-town, Edinburgh. I am, Sir, Yours to command,   R. B.

Hoy answered :

GORDON CASTLE, 31st *October* 1787.

SIR—If you were not sensible of your fault as well as of your loss, in leaving this place so suddenly, I should condemn you to starve upon *cauld kail for ae towmont** at least ; and as for *Dick Latine*,† your travelling companion, without banning him wi' a' the curses contained in your letter (which he'll no value a bawbee [a halfpenny]), I should give him nought but *Stra'bogie castocks*‡ to chew for *sax ouks*,§ or ay until he was as sensible of his error as you seem to be of yours. . . .

Your song I shewed without producing the author ; and it was judged by the Duchess to be the production of Dr Beattie. I sent a copy of it, by her Grace's desire, to a Mrs M'Pherson, in Badenoch, who sings 'Morag,' and all other Gaelic songs, in great perfection. I have recorded it likewise, by Lady Charlotte's desire, in a book belonging to her ladyship, where it is in company with a great many other poems and verses, some of the writers of which are no less eminent for their political than for their poetical abilities. When the Duchess was informed that you were the author, she wished you had written the verses in Scotch.

Any letter directed to me here will come to hand safely, and if sent under the Duke's cover, it will likewise come free ; that is, as long as the Duke is in this country. I am, Sir, yours sincerely,

JAMES HOY.

A week later Burns again wrote :

EDINBURGH, 6th *November* 1787.

DEAR SIR—I would have wrote you immediately on receipt of your kind letter ; but a mixed impulse of gratitude and esteem whispered to me that I ought to send you something by way of return. When a poet owes anything, particularly when he is indebted for good offices, the payment that usually recurs to him—the only coin, indeed, in which he is probably conversant—is rhyme. Johnson sends the books by the fly,

---

* Cold broth for a twelvemonth.   † William Nicol.
‡ The song speaks of *castocks* (cabbage-stalks) *in Strathbogie.*   § Six weeks.

as directed, and begs me to enclose his most grateful thanks ; my return I intended should have been one or two poetic bagatelles which the world have not seen, or perhaps, for obvious reasons, cannot see. These I shall send you before I leave Edinburgh. They may make you laugh a little, which, on the whole, is no bad way of spending one's precious hours and still more precious breath : at anyrate, they will be, though a small, yet a very sincere mark of my respectful esteem for a gentleman whose farther acquaintance I should look upon as a peculiar obligation.

The Duke's song, independent totally of his dukeship, charms me. There is I know not what of wild happiness of thought and expression peculiarly beautiful in the old Scottish song style, of which his Grace, old venerable Skinner, the author of 'Tullochgorum,' &c., and the late Ross, at Lochlee, of true Scottish poetic memory, are the only modern instances that I recollect, since Ramsay, with his contemporaries, and poor Bob Fergusson, went to the world of deathless existence and truly immortal song. The mob of mankind, that many-headed beast, would laugh at so serious a speech about an old song ; but as Job says, 'Oh that mine adversary had written a book !' Those who think that composing a Scotch song is a trifling business, let them try.

I wish my Lord Duke would pay a proper attention to the Christian admonition—'Hide not your candle under a bushel,' but 'let your light shine before men.' I could name half-a-dozen dukes that I guess are a devilish deal worse employed ; nay, I question if there are half-a-dozen better : perhaps there are not half that scanty number whom Heaven has favored with the tuneful, happy, and I will say glorious, gift. I am, dear sir, your obliged humble servant, R. B.

Burns at this time received a letter from his old teacher Murdoch, who was now in London. It was the first he had had for several years :

LONDON, 28th October 1787.

MY DEAR SIR—As my friend, Mr Brown, is going from this place to your neighbourhood, I embrace the opportunity of telling you that I am yet alive, tolerably well, and always in expectation of being better. By the much-valued letters before me, I see that it was my duty to have given you this intelligence about three years and nine months ago ; and have nothing to allege as an excuse, but that we poor, busy, bustling bodies in London are so much taken up with the various pursuits in which we are here engaged, that we seldom think of any person, creature, place, or thing, that is absent. But this is not altogether the case with me ; for I often think of you, and *Hornie*, and *Russel*, and an *unfathomed depth*, and *lowan brunstane*, all in the same minute, although you and they are (as I suppose) at a considerable distance. I flatter myself, however, with the pleasing thought that you and I shall meet some time or

other, either in Scotland or England.   If ever you come hither, you will
have the satisfaction of seeing your poems relished by the Caledonians in
London full as much as they can be by those of Edinburgh.   We frequently repeat some of your verses in our Caledonian Society ; and you
may believe that I am not a little vain that I have had some share in
cultivating such a genius.   I was not absolutely certain that you were
the author till a few days ago, when I made a visit to Mrs Hill, Dr
M'Comb's eldest daughter, who lives in town, and who told me that she
was informed of it by a letter from her sister in Edinburgh, with whom
you had been in company when in that capital.

Pray let me know if you have any intention of visiting this huge, over-
grown metropolis.   It would afford matter for a large poem.   Here you
would have an opportunity of indulging your vein in the study of mankind, perhaps to a greater degree than in any city upon the face of the
globe ; for the inhabitants of London, as you know, are a collection of
all nations, kindreds, and tongues, who make it, as it were, the centre
of their commerce. . . .

Present my respectful compliments to Mrs Burns, to my dear friend
Gilbert, and all the rest of her amiable children.   May the Father of the
Universe bless you all with those principles and dispositions that the best
of parents took such uncommon pains to instil into your minds from
your earliest infancy.   May you live as he did : if you do, you can
never be unhappy.   I feel myself grown serious all at once, and affected
in a manner I cannot describe.   I shall only add, that it is one of the
greatest pleasures I promise myself before I die, that of seeing the family
of a man whose memory I revere more than that of any person that ever
I was acquainted with.   I am, my dear Friend, Yours sincerely,

JOHN MURDOCH.

TO MRS DUNLOP.

MADAM—I will bear the reproaches of my conscience respecting this
letter no longer.   I was indebted to you some time ago for a kind, long
letter (your letters the longer the better), and again the other day I heard
from you, enclosing a very friendly letter from Dr Moore.   I thought
with myself, in the height of my gratitude and pride, of my remark that
I would sit down some hour of inspiration, and write you a letter at
least worth twa groats ; consequently you would have been a great
gainer, as you are so benevolent as to bestow your epistolary correspondence on me (I am sure) without the least idea of being paid in
kind.

When you talk of correspondence and friendship to me, Madam, you
do me too much honor ; but, as I shall soon be at my wonted leisure and
rural occupation, if any remark on what I have read or seen, or any new
rhyme I may twist, that is worth while—if such a letter, Madam, can

give a person of your rank, information, and abilities any entertainment, you shall have it with all my heart and soul.

It requires no common exertion of good sense and philosophy in persons of elevated rank, to keep a friendship properly alive with one much their inferior. Externals, things totally extraneous of the man, steal upon the hearts and judgments of almost, if not altogether, all mankind ; nor do I know more than one instance of a man who fully and truly regards ' all the world as a stage, and all the men and women merely players,' and who (the dancing-school bow excepted) only values these players— the *dramatis personæ*, who build cities, and who rear hedges ; who govern provinces, or superintend flocks, merely as they *act their parts.* For the honor of Ayrshire, this man is Professor Dugald Stewart of Catrine. To him I might perhaps add another instance, a Popish Bishop, Geddes ; but I have outraged that gloomy, fiery Presbyterianism enough already, though I don't spit in her lugubrious face by telling her that the first [*i.e.* the best] Cleric character I ever saw was a Roman Catholic.

I ever could ill endure those surly cubs of ' chaos and old night '—those ghostly beasts of prey who foul the hallowed ground of Religion with their nocturnal prowlings ; but if the prosecution which I hear the Erebean fanatics are projecting against my learned and truly worthy friend, Dr M'Gill, goes on, I shall keep no measure with the savages, but fly at them with the *faucons* of Ridicule, or run them down with the bloodhounds of Satire, as lawful game, wherever I start them.

I expect to leave Edinr. in eight or ten days, and shall certainly do myself the honor of calling at Dunlop House as I return to Ayrshire. I have the honor to be, Madam, your obliged humble servant,

ROBT. BURNS.

EDINR., 4*th Nov.* 1787.

This letter proves Burns to have retained a lively interest in the theologico-ecclesiastical disputes of Ayrshire. The prosecution of Dr M'Gill for heresy is subsequently alluded to in ' The Kirk's Alarm.' We have here also the first mention of Dr John Geddes,* coadjutor-bishop in the Roman Catholic Church in Scotland, to whom Burns had been introduced by Lord Monboddo. Geddes, who must not be confounded with his younger brother, Alexander (1737–1802), the minor poet, and pronouncedly liberal Roman Catholic Biblical critic, had been instrumental in procuring sub-

---

* John Geddes was born at the Mains of Curridoun, in the Enzie of Banffshire, in 1735. He entered the Scots College at Rome in 1750. In 1779 he was appointed coadjutor to Bishop Hay, vicar-apostolic of the lowland district of Scotland. The following year he was consecrated Bishop of Morocco, *in partibus infidelium*, at Madrid. After this he lived in Edinburgh. He resigned his coadjutorship, on account of an attack of paralysis, in 1797, and died at Aberdeen in 1799.

scriptions for Burns's Edinburgh edition from the Scots College at Valladolid, of which he had been for many years rector, as well as from other Roman Catholic seminaries.

As evidence that Burns still stood well with his countrymen generally at this time, it may be noted that on the 10th November he was presented with the freedom of the burgh of Linlithgow. The burgess-ticket, which has been preserved, runs thus : ' At Linlithgow, the sixteenth day of November, one thousand seven hundred and eighty-seven years, the which day, in the presence of James Andrew, Esquire, Provost of the Burgh of Linlithgow ; William Napier, James Walton, Stephen Mitchell, John Gibson, bailies ; and Robert Speedie, Dean-of-Guild ; compeared Mr Robert Burns, Mossgiel, Ayrshire, who was made and created Burgess and Guild Brother of the said Burgh, having given his oath of fidelity according to the form used thereanent.'

Having received an answer from Charlotte Hamilton or Margaret Chalmers to one of his letters, he replied as follows :

TO MISS CHALMERS.

Edinburgh, Nov. 21, 1787.

I have one vexatious fault to the kindly-welcome, well-filled sheet which I owe to your and Charlotte's goodness—it contains too much sense, sentiment, and good-spelling. It is impossible that even you two, whom I declare to my God I will give credit for any degree of excellence the sex are capable of attaining, it is impossible you can go on to correspond at that rate; so, like those who, Shenstone says, retire because they have made a good speech, I shall after a few letters hear no more of you. I insist that you shall write whatever comes first : what you see, what you read, what you hear, what you admire, what you dislike, trifles, bagatelles, nonsense ; or to fill up a corner, e'en put down a laugh at full length. Now, none of your polite hints about flattery I leave that to your lovers, if you have or shall have any ; though thank Heaven I have found at last two girls who can be luxuriantly happy in their own minds and with one another, without that commonly necessary appendage to female bliss, A LOVER.

Charlotte and you are just two favourite resting-places for my soul in her wanderings through the weary, thorny wilderness of this world—God knows I am ill-fitted for the struggle : I glory in being a Poet, and I want to be thought a wise man—I would fondly be generous, and I wish to be rich. After all, I am afraid I am a lost subject. ' Some folk hae a bantle o' fauts [many faults], an' I 'm but a ne'er-do-weel.'

Afternoon.—To close the melancholy reflections at the end of last sheet,

I shall just add a piece of devotion commonly known in Carrick by the title of the 'Wabster's grace:'

> Some say we're thieves, and e'en sae are we,
> Some say we lie, and e'en sae do we,
> Gude forgie us, and I hope sae will he!
> ——Up and to your looms, lads!
>
> R. B.

Burns was now in close friendship with Margaret Chalmers and Charlotte Hamilton. Of the two, Charlotte had the greater personal attractions. Margaret was, however, a woman of culture and *esprit*, and had a genuine love for letters.* Burns, in consequence, celebrated her in two songs, couched, of course, in the language of a lover:

WHERE, BRAVING ANGRY WINTER'S STORMS.

TUNE—*Neil Gow's Lamentation for Abercairny.*

> Where, braving angry winter's storms,
>   The lofty Ochils rise,
> Far in their shade my Peggy's charms
>   First blest my wondering eyes;
> As one who by some savage stream
>   A lonely gem surveys,
> Astonish'd, doubly marks it beam
>   With art's most polish'd blaze.
>
> Blest be the wild, sequester'd shade,
>   And blest the day and hour,
> Where Peggy's charms I first survey'd,
>   When first I felt their pow'r!
> The tyrant death with grim controul,
>   May seize my fleeting breath,
> But tearing Peggy from my soul
>   Must be a stronger death.

---

* A relative of Margaret Chalmers wrote of her to Dr Robert Chambers: 'In early life, when her hazel eyes were large and bright, and her teeth white and regular, her face must have had a charm not always the result or the accompaniment of fine features. She was little, but her figure was perfect. . . . She rarely talked of books, but greatly liked reading. She spoke readily and well, but preferred listening to others. . . . Her heart was warm, her temper even, and her conversation lively. I have often been told that her gentleness and vivacity had a favourable influence on the manner of Burns.'

MY PEGGY'S FACE, MY PEGGY'S FORM.

My Peggy's face, my Peggy's form,
The frost of Hermit age might warm ;
My Peggy's worth, my Peggy's mind,
Might charm the first of human kind.
I love my Peggy's angel air,
Her face so truly, heavenly fair,
Her native grace so void of art,
But I adore my Peggy's heart.

The lily's hue, the rose's dye,
The kindling lustre of an eye ;
Who but owns their magic sway !
Who but knows they all decay !
The tender thrill, the pitying tear,
The generous purpose, nobly dear,
The gentle look that rage disarms,
These are all immortal charms.

TO MISS CHALMERS.

EDINBURGH, *Dec.* 1787.

MY DEAR MADAM—I just now have read yours. The poetic compliments I pay cannot be misunderstood. They are neither of them so particular as to point *you* out to the world at large ; and the circle of your acquaintances will allow all I have said. Besides, I have complimented you chiefly, almost solely, on your mental charms. Shall I be plain with you ? I will ; so look to it. Personal attractions, madam, you have much above par ; wit, understanding, and worth, you possess in the first class. This is a cursed flat way of telling you these truths, but let me hear no more of your sheepish timidity. I know the world a little. I know what they will say of my poems ; by second-sight, I suppose, for I am seldom out in my conjectures ; and you may believe me, my dear madam, I would not run any risk of hurting you by any ill-judged compliment. I wish to show to the world the odds between a poet's friends and those of simple prosemen. More for your information, *both* the pieces go in. One of them, ' Where braving all the winter's harms,' is already set—the tune is Neil Gow's ' Lamentation for Abercairny ;' the other is to be set to an old Highland air in Daniel Dow's ' Collection of ancient Scots music ;' the name is ' Ha a Chaillich air mo

Dheidh.' My treacherous memory has forgot every circumstance about 'Les Incas,' only I think you mentioned them as being in Creech's possession. I shall ask him about it. I am afraid the song of 'Somebody' will come too late—as I shall, for certain, leave town in a week for Ayrshire, and from that to Dumfries ; but there my hopes are slender. I leave my direction in town, so any thing, wherever I am, will reach me.

I saw your's to ——, it is not too severe, nor did he take it amiss. On the contrary, like a whipt spaniel, he talks of being with you in the Christmas days. Mr Tait has given him the invitation, and he is determined to accept of it. O selfishness ! he owns in his sober moments, that from his own volatility of inclination, the circumstances in which he is situated, and his knowledge of his father's disposition,—the whole affair is chimerical—yet he *will* gratify an idle *penchant* at the enormous, cruel expense of perhaps ruining the peace of the very woman for whom he professes the generous passion of love ! He is a gentleman in his mind and manners—*tant pis !* He is a volatile school-boy : The heir of a man's fortune who well knows the value of two times two !

Perdition seize them and their fortunes, before they should make the amiable, the lovely —— the derided object of their purse-proud contempt.

I am doubly happy to hear of Mrs ——'s recovery, because I really thought all was over with her. There are days of pleasure yet awaiting her :

> As I came in by Glenap
> I met with an aged woman ;
> She bad me chear up my heart,
> For the best o' my days was comin.*

This day will decide my affairs with Creech. Things are, like myself, not what they ought to be ; yet better than what they appear to be.

> Heaven's Sovereign saves all beings but Himself
> That hideous sight—a naked human heart.†

Farewell ! remember me to Charlotte. R. B.

This letter indicates very clearly the footing on which Burns stood with Margaret Chalmers. They were in the habit of exchanging confidences. There is good reason to believe, apart altogether from the possibility, to which allusion has already been made, of Burns having made advances to her in Ayrshire, that when in Edinburgh he asked her to marry him. He may well have believed that with her accomplishments, her literary tastes, and her strong sense, she would have made the wife he was in

---

* This is an old rhyme. Glenapp is a picturesque glen and estate in Ballantrae parish, SW. Ayrshire.

† Young's *Night Thoughts*, iii., 226.

search of. When, subsequently, he was in the full tide of his correspondence with Clarinda, he wrote her (10th January 1788), 'The name I register in my heart's core is *Peggy Chalmers*,' and she three weeks later asked him, ' Why did not such a woman secure your heart?' It is quite certain that Margaret Chalmers informed Thomas Campbell, the poet, that Burns had asked her in marriage, and that she declined. She was then engaged to Lewis Hay,* who had long been a clerk in the Edinburgh banking house of Sir William Forbes. He became a partner in the house in 1788, and on the 9th December of that year married Margaret Chalmers.

TO MR ROBT. AINSLIE.

Sunday Morning, Nov. 25, 1787.

I beg, my dear Sir, you will not make any appointment to take us to Mr Ainslie's† to-night. On looking over my engagements, constitution, present state of my health, some little vexatious soul concerns, &c., I find I can't sup abroad to-night. I shall be in to-day till one o'clock, if you have a leisure hour.

You will think it romantic when I tell you, that I find the idea of your friendship almost necessary to my existence. You assume a proper length of face in my bitter hours of blue-devilism, and you laugh fully up to my highest wishes at my good things. I don't know, upon the whole, if you are one of the first fellows in God's world, but you are so to me. I tell you this just now, in the conviction that some inequalities in my temper and manner may perhaps sometimes make you suspect that I am not so warmly as I ought to be your friend,   R. B.

Robert Ainslie was living on the north side of St James's Square, so that at this time the two friends were at one another's call. The young lawyer used to tell a story to prove that Burns was, in his later years, no Bacchanalian. Though but an apprentice, Ainslie had a wine-cellar—not indeed an extensive one, as it consisted simply of the recess under a *bunker-seat* in one of the windows of his apartment; an arrangement long ago common in Scotland, but now seen only in old-fashioned houses. ' His

---

* Lewis Hay, who is described in one biography as ' son of Captain John Hay, of the *Princess Anne* yacht,' was no relation of Sir John Hay, another partner in Forbes's bank. He was indebted for his original connection with it to Sir James Hunter Blair, whose school-fellow he had been in Ayr. He died in Edinburgh on 28th February 1800. His widow survived him three years.

† A bookseller, and a relative of Robert Ainslie.

stock of wine consisted of five bottles of port, all that remained of a dozen of good quality which had been presented to him by a friend, a wine-merchant. On Burns calling for him one day, Ainslie proposed that they should spend the afternoon over a bottle; but Burns said: 'No, my friend, we 'll have no wine to-day—to sit dozing in the house on such a fine afternoon as this would be insufferable. Besides, you know that you and I don't require wine to sharpen our wit, nor its adventitious aid to make us happy. No; we 'll take a ramble over Arthur's Seat to admire the beauties of nature, and come in to a late tea.' They did so; and Ainslie used to declare, that he had never known the poet's conversation so amusing, so instructive, and altogether so delightful, as during the cheerful stroll they had over the hill, and during the sober tea-drinking which followed.'

At this time, an artist named Miers or Myers was practising in Edinburgh as a taker of silhouette portraits, which he professed to execute at a two minutes' sitting.* Their cheapness as well as their felicity as likenesses brought him many sitters, and among the rest Burns, who presented silhouettes to several of his friends.

There is some obscurity about the date of Burns's second visit to Dalswinton, and it is doubtful if he visited Ayrshire on that occasion, though it is probable that he did so. The excursion to Dumfriesshire, and the considerations connected with it, are alluded to in an undated letter

TO MISS CHALMERS.

I have been at Dumfries, and at one visit more shall be decided about a farm in that country. I am rather hopeless in it; but as my brother is an excellent farmer, and is, besides, an exceedingly prudent, sober man (qualities which are only a younger brother's fortune in our family), I am determined, if my Dumfries business fail me, to return into partnership with him, and at our leisure take another farm in the neighbourhood. I assure you I look for high compliments from you and Charlotte on this very sage instance of my unfathomable, incomprehensible wisdom. Talking of Charlotte, I must tell her that I have, to the best of my power, paid her a poetic compliment, now compleated. The air is admirable: true old Highland. It was the tune of a Gaelic song which an Inverness lady sang me when I was there; and I was so charmed with it that I begged her to write me a set of it from her singing;

---

* They cost, in frames, from 6s. to 10s. 6d.—*Newspaper advertisement.*

for it had never been set before.   I am fixed that it shall go in Johnson's
next number; so Charlotte and you need not spend your precious time
in contradicting me.   I won't say the poetry is first-rate; though I am
convinced it is very well: and, what is not always the case with compliments to ladies, it is not only *sincere* but *just*.   R. B.

The air here alluded to is a beautiful Highland one, well known
in connection with a song of Allaster Macdonald's, entitled
' Bhanarach dhonn a chruidh,' or 'The Pretty Milkmaid.'

THE BANKS OF THE DEVON.

How pleasant the banks of the clear winding Devon,
    With green-spreading bushes, and flow'rs blooming fair !
But the bonniest flow'r on the banks of the Devon
    Was once a sweet bud on the braes of the Ayr.*
Mild be the sun on this sweet blushing Flower
    In the gay, rosy morn, as it bathes in the dew ;
And gentle the fall of the soft vernal shower
    That steals on the evening each leaf to renew !

O spare the dear blossom, ye orient breezes
    With chill, hoary wing as ye usher the dawn !
And far be thou distant, thou reptile that seizest
    The verdure and pride of the garden or lawn !
Let Bourbon exult in his gay, gilded Lilies,
    And England triumphant display her proud Rose ;
A fairer than either adorns the green vallies
    Where Devon, sweet Devon, meandering flows.

TO GAVIN HAMILTON, ESQ.

EDINBURGH, *Dec.* 1787.

DEAR SIR—It is indeed with the highest pleasure that I congratulate
you on the return of days of ease and nights of pleasure, after the horrid
hours of misery in which I saw you suffering existence when last in Ayrshire.   I seldom pray for anybody, but most fervently do I beseech the
Holy Trinity, or the Holy Something that directs this world, that you may
live long and be happy, but live no longer than you are happy.   It is

---

* Miss Hamilton was born on the banks of the Ayr.   She was now living at Harvieston,
on the banks of the Devon.

needless for me to advise you to have a reverend care of your health. I know you will make it a point never at one time to drink more than a pint of wine (I mean an English pint), and that you will never be witness to more than one bowl of punch at a time, and that after drinking perhaps boiling punch, you will never mount your horse and gallop home in a chill late hour. Above all things, as I understand you are now in habits of intimacy with that Boanerges of Gospel power, Father Auld, be earnest with him that he will wrestle in prayer for you, that you may see the vanity of vanities in trusting to, or even practising, the carnal moral works of charity, humanity, generosity, and forgiveness, things which you practised so flagrantly, that it was evident you delighted in them, neglecting, or, perhaps, profanely despising, the wholesome doctrine of *faith without works*, the only anchor of salvation. A hymn of thanksgiving would, in my opinion, be highly becoming from you at present; and in my zeal for your well-being, I earnestly press on you to be diligent in chaunting over the two enclosed pieces of sacred poesy. My best compliments to Mrs Hamilton and Miss Kennedy. Yours in the Lord,

ROBT. BURNS.

TO MISS MABANE, EDINBURGH.*

*Saturday, Noon [Dec. 1, 1787], No. 2 St James's Square,
New Town, Edinburgh.*

Here have I sat, my dear madam, in the stony attitude of perplexed study for fifteen vexatious minutes, my head askew, bending over the intended card; my fixed eye insensible to the very light of day poured around; my pendulous goose feather, loaded with ink, hanging over the future letter, all for the important purpose of writing a complimentary card to accompany your trinket.

Compliment is such a miserable Greenland expression, and lies at such a chilly polar distance from the torrid zone of my constitution, that I cannot, for the very soul of me, use it to any person for whom I have the twentieth part of the esteem every one must have for you who knows you.

As I leave town in three or four days, I can give myself the pleasure of calling on you only for a minute. Tuesday evening, sometime about seven or after, I shall wait on you for your farewell commands.

The hinge of your box I put into the hands of the proper connoisseur. The broken glass likewise went under review; but deliberative wisdom thought it would too much endanger the whole fabric [to replace it]. I am, dear Madam, with all sincerity of enthusiasm,—Your very obedient servant, ROBT. BURNS.

Burns had returned to Edinburgh after his summer visit to Ayrshire mainly to obtain a settlement of accounts with Creech.

* Miss Mabane became Mrs Colonel Wright, and died in Edinburgh.

The autumn had worn into winter, and still the end of the
transaction appeared as remote as ever. There is, indeed, a
want of clear light as to the commercial relations of the poet
with his publisher. One thing is notorious—Creech never settled
an account till it became impossible to put off his creditor any
longer. This might seem enough to explain the delay of settlement with Burns; but, on the other hand, the time which had
elapsed since the publication of the volume would not seem
very long in 'the trade'—the ordinary practice of a publisher
who issues a book for an author being to render accounts
annually, at June 30 or December 31, always upwards of six
months from the date of publication, and to pay only six months
thereafter. If Creech had acted as publisher for Burns on this
footing, there would have been nothing unusual in his still
delaying payment; the money, indeed, for sales previous to June,
would not have been due till the middle of the ensuing year.
But we know that Burns's poems were published by subscription,
Creech taking five hundred copies at the same rate as the other
subscribers, with the view of selling them at one shilling more by
way of profit. The publisher must have received the money due
from a large proportion of the subscribers; and for this, as well as
for his own copies (the full price of which was £125), it might be
alleged that he was bound to pay immediately. He, on the other
hand, would probably have to show that much was still unpaid to
him by the public; and, if there were even a doubt on this point
in his favour, he would be sure to take advantage of it. However
matters actually stood, it is clear that Burns was much irritated
at the delay in coming to a settlement.

CHAPTER IV.

BURNS had, however, at the beginning of December, resolved to leave Edinburgh, when an accident, caused by the carelessness of a drunken coachman, confined him to the house for several weeks. This delay led, among other consequences, to what was in many respects the most remarkable of Burns's love attachments. On the 4th December he was at a tea-party given by Miss Nimmo, an acquaintance of Margaret Chalmers, at her house in Alison Square.* Among the guests was Mrs Agnes Craig M'Lehose, an intimate friend of the hostess, and then living with her children in the first floor of a house at the back of General's Entry, Potterrow. Agnes Craig was the daughter of Andrew Craig, a surgeon in Glasgow, and was born in April 1759. She was 'well connected.' Lord Craig, one of the Senators of the College of Justice, and one of the founders of the *Mirror* and the *Lounger*, was her cousin-german, and in her days of misfortune, her kindest friend. On the maternal side she was the grandniece of Colin M'Laurin, professor of Mathematics in the University of Edinburgh, friend and correspondent of Sir Isaac Newton, whose son was a distinguished advocate, and raised to the bench with the title of Lord Dreghorn. Owing partly to an extreme delicacy of constitution, and partly to the death of her mother, she seems to have received a somewhat imperfect education. As she grew into womanhood, however, she was recognised

---

* 'He became a frequent visitor at the house of Mr Nimmo, excise officer, Alison Square.' —From *Burns, Excise officer and Poet*, by John Sinton, Supervisor of Inland Revenue, Carlisle (1896). It appears uncertain whether Miss Nimmo was a sister or a daughter of this officer.

as a beauty, and was known in her own circle as 'pretty Miss Nancie.' Among her admirers was James M'Lehose, a young solicitor in Glasgow, who, disappointed in procuring an introduction to her, fell upon a stratagem to form her acquaintance. 'Learning that she was to be sent to Edinburgh to a boarding-school,' the story goes, 'he ascertained the time of her departure, and engaged all the seats in the interior of the stage-coach, excepting the one which had been secured to her. The journey occupied a whole day, and Mr M'Lehose, who possessed a handsome person and a most insinuating address, improved the opportunity which he had purchased. Fascinated by his demeanour, Miss Craig allowed him to understand that his attentions were not disagreeable to her. On her return from Edinburgh, six months afterwards, Mr M'Lehose followed up his suit. Remarking her predilection, Miss Craig's relatives entreated that she would not rashly form an engagement, but to their counsels she preferred her own judgment. She accepted Mr M'Lehose's offer of marriage, and at the early age of seventeen became his wife.'*

Four children were the result of this somewhat hasty union : one of them died in infancy. The marriage, however, was an unhappy one. According to Mrs M'Lehose's own statement, 'our disagreements rose to such a height, and my husband's treatment was so harsh, that it was thought advisable by my friends a separation should take place, which accordingly followed in December 1780.' Deprived of her children, who were boarded with her husband's relatives, she returned to her father, and lived with him till his death in 1782. Her husband, having now resolved to go abroad, left their three children in her hands. 'The goodness of some worthy gentlemen in Glasgow procuring me a small annuity from the Writers (£10), and one from the Surgeons (£8), I set out for Edinburgh with them in August 1782 ; and by the strictest economy made my little income go as far as possible.' Of one of her kinsmen in Edinburgh, Lord Dreghorn, Mrs M'Lehose has recorded : 'He used me in a manner unfeelingly harsh beyond description, at one of the darkest periods of my chequered life.' Lord Craig, however, acted very differently. He

* The marriage is thus recorded in the Glasgow parish register—'1776, July—James M'Elhose, writer in Glasgow, and Agnes Craig, residing there, regularly married the 1st inst.' Burns almost invariably spells the name 'M'Ilhose.'

befriended her from the first, introduced her to the literary society she specially affected, and when, owing to the prospering of her husband in Jamaica—he did not proceed thither till 1784—she was deprived of her annuities, made good the loss she sustained. Mrs M'Lehose devoted much of her time to the education of her children, but she also, according to one of her biographers, 'studied the best authors.' At length she acquired what then was known as 'a correct style,' and composed in prose and verse with power and elegance. She had heard of Burns from some of her friends, and, as she expressly stated in the first of her letters to him, it was at her special request that Miss Nimmo arranged a meeting between them. They were at once attracted to each other. 'Of a somewhat voluptuous style of beauty, of lively and easy manners, of a poetical cast of mind, with some wit, and not too high a degree of refinement or delicacy, Mrs M'Lehose was exactly the kind of woman to fascinate Burns.'* On her side, she was ready to be impressed by him. A correspondence between them commenced immediately after their meeting:

TO MRS M'LEHOSE.

MADAM—I had set no small store by my tea-drinking to-night, and have not often been so disappointed. Saturday evening I shall embrace the opportunity with the greatest pleasure. I leave this town this day se'ennight, and probably I shall not return for a couple of twelvemonths; but I must ever regret that I so lately got an acquaintance I shall ever highly esteem, and in whose welfare I shall ever be warmly interested. Our worthy common friend, Miss Nimmo, in her usual pleasant way, rallied me a good deal on my new acquaintance, and, in the humour of her ideas, I wrote some lines, which I enclose you,† as I think they have a good deal of poetic merit; and Miss Nimmo tells me that you are not only a critic but a poetess. Fiction, you know, is the native region of poetry; and I hope you will pardon my vanity in sending you the bagatelle as a tolerable off-hand *jeu d'esprit*. I have several poetic trifles, which I shall gladly leave with Miss Nimmo or you, if they were worth house-room; as there are scarcely two people on earth by whom it would mortify me more to

---

* Mrs M'Lehose's charms have been thus more minutely described : ' Short in stature, her form was graceful, her hands and feet small and delicate. Her features were regular and pleasing, her eyes lustrous, her complexion fair, her cheeks ruddy, and a well-formed mouth displayed teeth beautifully white.'

† It is not known what the lines were. The same has to be said of Clarinda's lines in reply (see her letter of December 8th).

be forgotten, though at the distance of nine score miles. I am, Madam,
With the highest respect, Your very humble servant,

ROBERT BURNS.

Thursday Even. [*December 6, 1787.*]

On Saturday the 8th, as implied in this letter, he was to have
taken tea at Mrs M'Lehose's house ; but the night before—or
more probably (see p. 222) early the same morning—a fall from a
coach confined him to his lodging with a severely bruised knee.
The feelings with which Miss Nimmo's friend had inspired him
at the first interview, and the interest with which he had looked
forward to a second meeting, are expressed in his note of apology
for non-appearance at her table :

TO MRS M'LEHOSE.

I can say with truth, Madam, that I never met with a person in my
life whom I more anxiously wished to meet again than yourself. To-
night I was to have had that very great pleasure,—I was intoxicated with
the idea ; but an unlucky fall from a coach has so bruised one of my
knees that I can't stir my leg off the cushion. So, if I don't see you
again, I shall not rest in my grave for chagrin. I was vexed to the soul
I had not seen you sooner. I determined to cultivate your friendship
with the enthusiasm of religion ; but thus has Fortune ever served me.
I cannot bear the idea of leaving Edinburgh without seeing you. I
know not how to account for it—I am strangely taken with some people,
nor am I often mistaken. You are a stranger to me ;—but I am an odd
being ; some yet unnamed feelings—things, not principles, but better
than whims — carry me farther than boasted reason ever did a
philosopher.

Farewell ! every happiness be yours.   ROBERT BURNS.

Saturday Even. [*December 8, 1787.*]
ST. JAMES' SQR., NO. 2.

Mrs M'Lehose answered post-haste :

TO MR ROBERT BURNS, MR CRUIKSHANK'S, JAMES' SQUARE.

Saturday Ev. [*December 8th, 1787.*]

Enured as I have been to disappointments, I never felt more, nay, nor
half so severely, for one of the same nature ! The cruel cause, too,
augments my uneasiness. I trust you 'll soon recover it ; meantime, if
my sympathy, my friendship, can alleviate your pain, be assured you
possess them. I am much flattered at being a favourite of yours. Miss
Nimmo can tell you how earnestly I had long pressed her to make us
acquainted. I had a presentiment that we should derive pleasure from
the society of each other. To-night I had thought of fifty things to say

to you; how unfortunate this prevention! Do not accuse Fortune; had I not known she was *blind* before, her ill-usuage of *you* had marked it sufficiently. However, she is a fickle, old, envious beldame, and I'd much rather be indebted to *Nature*. You shall *not* leave town without seeing me, if I should come along with good Miss Nimmo and call for you. I am determined to see you; and am ready to exclaim with Yorick, 'Tut! are we not all relations?' We are, indeed, *strangers* in one sense; but of near kin in many respects: these 'nameless feelings' I perfectly comprehend, tho' the pen of a Locke could not define them. Perhaps *instinct* comes nearer their description than either 'Principles or Whims.' Think ye they have any connection with that 'heavenly light which leads astray?' One thing I know, that they have a powerful effect upon me; and are delightful when under the check of *reason* and *religion*.

Miss Nimmo was a favourite of mine from the first hour I met her. There is a softness, a nameless something about her that, was I a man, old as she is, I should have chosen her before most women that I know. I fear, however, this liking is not *mutual*. I'll tell you why I think so, at meeting. She was in mere jest when she told you I was a *Poetess*. I have often composed rhyme, (if not *reason*), but never one line of *poetry*. The distinction is obvious to every one of the least discernment. Your lines are truly poetical; give me all you can spare. Not one living has a higher relish for poetry than I have; and my reading everything of the kind makes me a tolerable judge. Ten years ago, such lines from such a hand would have half-turned my head. Perhaps you thought it might have done so even *yet*, and wisely premised that '*Fiction* was the native region of poetry.' Read the enclosed, which I scrawled just after reading yours. Be sincere, and own that, whatever merit it has, it has not a line resembling poetry. Pardon any little freedoms I take with you; if they entertain a heavy hour, they have all the merit I intended. Will you let me know, now and then, how your leg is? If I was your *sister*, I would call and see you; but 'tis a censorious world this; and (in this sense) 'you and I are not of this world.' Adieu. Keep up your heart, you will soon get well, and we shall *meet*. Farewell. God bless you!
A. M.

TO MRS M'LEHOSE.

[*December* 12.]

I stretch a point, indeed, my dearest Madam, when I answer your card on the rack of my present agony. Your friendship, Madam! By heavens, I was never proud before. Your lines, I maintain it, are poetry, and good poetry; mine were, indeed, partly fiction, and partly a friendship which, had I been so blest as to have met with you *in time*, might have led me—God of love only knows where. Time is too short for ceremonies.

I swear solemnly, (in all the tenor of my former oath,) to remember you in all the pride and warmth of friendship until—I cease to be!

To-morrow, and every day, till I see you, you shall hear from me.

Farewell ! May you enjoy a better night's repose than I am likely to have.   R. B.

TO MR ROBERT BURNS.

Sunday, Noon [December 16].

Miss Nimmo and I had a long conversation last night. Little did I suspect that she was of the party. Gentle, sweet soul ! She is accusing herself as the cause of your misfortune. It was in vain I rallied her upon such an excess of sensibility, (as I termed it). She is lineally descended from ' My Uncle Toby ;' has hopes of the Devil, and would not hurt a fly. How could you tell me that you were in 'agony?' I hope you would swallow laudanum, and procure some ease from sleep. I am glad to hear Mr Wood attends you. He is a good soul, and a safe surgeon. I know him a little. Do as he bids, and I trust your leg will soon be quite well. When I meet you, I must chide you for writing in your romantic style. Do you remember that she whom you address is a married woman ? or, Jacob-like, would you wait seven years, and even then, perhaps, be disappointed, as he was ? No ; I know you better : you have too much of that impetuosity which generally accompanies noble minds. To be serious, most people would think, by your style, that you were writing to some vain, silly woman to make a fool of her—or worse. I have too much vanity to ascribe it to the former motive, and too much charity to harbour an idea of the latter ; and viewing it as the effusion of a bene-volent heart upon meeting one somewhat similar to itself, I have promised you my friendship : it will be your own fault if I ever withdraw it. Would to God I had it in my power to give you some solid proofs of it ! Were I the Duchess of Gordon, you should be possessed of that independ-ence which every generous mind pants after ; but I fear she is 'no Duchess at the heart.' Obscure as I am (comparatively,) I enjoy all the necessaries of life as fully as I desire, and wish for wealth only to procure the ' luxury of doing good.'

My chief design in writing you to-day was to beg you would not write me often, lest the exertion should hurt you. Meantime, if my scrawls can amuse you in your confinement, you shall have them occasionally. I shall hear of you every day from my beloved Miss Nimmo. Do you know, the very first time I was in her house, most of our conversation was about a certain (lame) poet? I read her soul in her expressive countenance, and have been attached to her ever since. Adieu ! Be patient. Take care of yourself. My best wishes attend you.   A. M.

TO MRS M'LEHOSE.

[December 20.]

Your last, my dear Madam, had the effect on me that Job's situation had on his friends, when ' they sat down seven days and seven nights astonied, and spake not a word.'—' Pay my addresses to a married woman !' I started as if I had seen the ghost of him I had injured : I recollected my expressions ; some of them indeed were, in the law phrase, ' habit and repute,' which is being half guilty. I cannot positively say, Madam, whether my heart might not have gone astray a little ; but I can declare, upon the honour of a poet, that the vagrant has wandered unknown to me. I have a pretty handsome troop of follies of my own ; and like some other people's retinue, they are but undisciplined black-guards : but the luckless rascals have something of honor in them ; they would not do a dishonest thing.

To meet with an unfortunate woman, amiable and young, deserted and widowed by those who were bound by every tie of duty, nature, and gratitude, to protect, comfort, and cherish her ; add to all, when she is perhaps one of the first of lovely forms and noble minds, the mind, too, that hits one's taste as the joys of Heaven do a saint—should a vague infant-idea, the natural child of imagination, thoughtlessly peep over the fence—were you, my friend, to sit in judgment, and the poor, airy straggler brought before you, trembling, self-condemned, with artless eyes, brimful of contrition, looking wistfully on its judge,—you could not, my dear Madam, condemn the hapless wretch to ' death without benefit of clergy ?'

I won't tell you what reply my heart made to your raillery of ' seven years ; ' but I will give you what a brother of my trade says on the same allusion :—

> The Patriarch to gain a wife,
> Chaste, beautiful, and young,
> Served fourteen years a painful life,
> And never thought it long.
>
> Oh were you to reward such cares,
> And life so long would stay,
> Not fourteen but four hundred years
> Would seem as but one day ! *

I have written you this scrawl because I have nothing else to do, and you may sit down and find fault with it, if you have no better way of consuming your time ; but finding fault with the vagaries of a poet's fancy is much such another business as Xerxes chastising the waves of Hellespont.

My limb now allows me to sit in some peace ; to walk I have yet no prospect of, as I can't mark it to the ground.

I have just now looked over what I have written, and it is such a chaos of nonsense that I daresay you will throw it into the fire, and call me an idle, stupid fellow ; but whatever you think of my brains, believe me to be, with the most sacred respect and heartfelt esteem, My dear Madam, Your humble servant,   ROBERT BURNS.

---

* These eight lines form the concluding verse of ' The Perfection, A New Song,' in Tom D'Urfey's *Wit and Mirth* (vol. ii., 1719).

Burns presents another view of the state of his mind to a female correspondent of a different type from Mrs M'Lehose :

TO MISS CHALMERS.

EDINBURGH, *Dec.* 12, 1787.

I am here under the care of a surgeon, with a bruised limb extended on a cushion ; and the tints of my mind vying with the livid horror preceding a midnight thunder-storm. A drunken coachman was the cause of the first, and incomparably the lightest, evil ; misfortune, bodily constitution, hell and myself, have formed a ' Quadruple Alliance ' to guarantee the other. I got my fall on Saturday [*Dec.* 8], and am getting slowly better.

I have taken tooth and nail to the Bible, and am got through the five books of Moses, and half way in Joshua. It is really a glorious book. I sent for my book-binder to-day, and ordered him to get me an octavo Bible in sheets, the best paper and print in town ; and bind it with all the elegance of his craft.

I would give my best song to my worst enemy, I mean the merit of making it, to have you and Charlotte by me. You are angelic creatures, and would pour oil and wine into my wounded spirit.

I enclose you a proof copy of the ' Banks of the Devon,' which present with my best wishes to Charlotte. The ' Ochil-hills '* you shall probably have next week for yourself. None of your fine speeches !

R. B.

The Lord President of the Court of Session (Dundas) died on the 13th December, and it seems to have been suggested to Burns by his friend, Mr Alexander Wood,† surgeon, backed up by Charles Hay,‡ an advocate and brother-Crochallan, that he should celebrate the event in verse. He gave effect to the suggestion, with reluctance, and, as he himself admitted, with but indifferent success :

ON THE DEATH OF LORD PRESIDENT DUNDAS.§

Lone on the bleaky hills, the straying flocks
Shun the fierce storms among the sheltering rocks ;

* The song in honour of Miss Chalmers, beginning ' Where, braving angry winter's storms.'
† Alexander Wood, who belonged to a well-known Edinburgh family, the Woods of Warriston, was born in 1725, and died in 1807.
‡ Lord Newton, the son of James Hay of Cocklaw, W.S., was born about 1740 ; was called to the bar in 1768 ; succeeded Smythe of Methven on the bench ; and died in 1811.
§ Robert Dundas of Arniston, elder brother of Viscount Melville, was born 1713, appointed Lord President of the Court of Session in 1760, and died December 13, 1787, after a short illness.

Down foam the rivulets, red with dashing rains,
The gathering floods burst o'er the distant plains ;
Beneath the blast the leafless forests groan,
The hollow caves return a sullen moan.

Ye hills, ye plains, ye forests and ye caves,
Ye howling winds, and wintry-swelling waves,
Unheard, unseen, by human ear or eye,
Sad to your sympathetic scenes I fly ;
Where to the whistling blast and waters' roar
Pale Scotia's recent wound I may deplore.

O heavy loss thy Country ill could bear !
A loss these evil days can ne'er repair !
Justice, the high vicegerent of her God,
Her doubtful balance ey'd and sway'd her rod ;
Hearing the tidings of the fatal blow
She sank abandon'd to the wildest woe.

Wrongs, Injuries, from many a darksome den,
Now gay in hope explore the paths of men.
See from his cavern grim Oppression rise,
And throw on Poverty his cruel eyes ;
Keen on the helpless victim see him fly,
And stifle, dark, the feebly-bursting cry.
Mark ruffian Violence, distain'd with crimes,
Rousing elate in these degenerate times ;
View unsuspecting Innocence a prey,
As guileful Fraud points out the erring way :
While subtle Litigation's pliant tongue
The life-blood equal sucks of Right and Wrong.
Hark, injur'd Want recounts th' unlisten'd tale,
And much-wrong'd Mis'ry pours th' unpitied wail !

Ye dark, waste hills, ye brown, unsightly plains,
Congenial scenes ! ye soothe my mournful strains :
Ye tempests, rage ; ye turbid torrents, roll ;
Ye suit the joyless tenor of my soul :

Life's social haunts and pleasures I resign,
Be nameless wilds and lonely wanderings mine,
To mourn the woes my Country must endure,
That wound degenerate ages cannot cure.

TO CHARLES HAY, ESQ., ADVOCATE.

(ENCLOSING VERSES ON THE DEATH OF THE LORD PRESIDENT.)

SIR—The enclosed poem was written in consequence of your suggestion last time I had the pleasure of seeing you. It cost me an hour or two of next morning's sleep, but did not please me; so it lay by, an ill-digested effort, till the other day that I gave it a critic brush. These kind of subjects are much hackneyed; and, besides, the wailings of the rhyming tribe over the ashes of the great are cursedly suspicious, and out of all character for sincerity. These ideas damped my muse's fire; however, I have done the best I could, and, at all events, it gives me an opportunity of declaring that I have the honour to be, sir, your obliged humble servant, R. B.

Burns sent a copy of the poem also to Dundas's son, afterwards Lord Advocate and Lord Chief-Baron, but received no answer to it. An extract from a letter (of date 11th March 1791) to his friend Cunningham betrays his feelings.

'I have two or three times in my life composed from the wish, rather than from the impulse, but I never succeeded to any purpose. One of these times I shall ever remember with gnashing of teeth. 'Twas on the death of the late Lord President Dundas. My very worthy and most respected friend, Mr Alex. Wood, Surgeon, urged me to pay a compliment in the way of my trade to his Lordship's memory. Well, to work I went, and produced a copy of Elegaic verses, some of them I own rather common-place, and others rather hide-bound, but on the whole, though they were far from being in my best manner, they were tolerable, and might have been thought very clever. I wrote a letter, which, however, *was* in my very best manner; and inclosing my poem, Mr Wood carried all together to Mr Solicitor Dundas that then was, and not finding him at home, left the parcel for him. His Solicitorship never took the smallest notice of the letter, the Poem, or the Poet. From that time, highly as I respect the talents of the family, I never see the name of Dundas in the column of a newspaper, but my heart seems straitened for room in my bosom; and if I am obliged to read aloud a paragraph relating to one of them, I feel my forehead flush, and my nether lip quiver. Had I been an obscure scribbler, as I was then in the hey-day of my fame ; or had I been a dependent hanger-on for favour or pay ; or had the bearer of the letter been any other than a gentleman who has done honor to the city in which he lives, to the country that produced him, and to the God that created him, Mr Solicitor might have had some apology—but enough of this ungracious subject.'

TO MR FRANCIS HOWDEN,
JEWELLER, PARLIAMENT SQUARE.*

The bearer of this will deliver you a small shade† to set; which, my dear sir, if you would highly oblige a poor cripple devil as I am at present, you will finish at farthest against to-morrow evening. It goes a hundred miles into the country; and if it is at me by five o'clock to-morrow evening, I have an opportunity of a private hand to convey it; if not, I don't know how to get it sent. Set it just as you did the others you did for me, 'in the neatest and cheapest manner;' both to answer as a breast-pin, and with a ring to answer as a locket. Do despatch it; as it is, I believe, the pledge of love, and perhaps the prelude to ma-tri-mo-ny. Everybody knows the auld wife's observation when she saw a poor dog going to be hanged—'God help us! it's the gate we ha'e a' to gang!' [We all have to go the same road.]

The parties, one of them at least, is a very particular acquaintance of mine—the honest lover. He only needs a little of an advice which my grandmother, rest her soul, often gave me, and I as often neglected—

Leuk twice or ye loup ance. ‡

Let me conjure you, my friend, by the bended bow of Cupid—by the unloosed cestus of Venus—by the lighted torch of Hymen—that you will have the locket finished by the time mentioned! And if your worship would have as much Christian charity as call with it yourself, and comfort a poor wretch, not wounded indeed by Cupid's arrow, but bruised by a good, serious, agonizing, damned, hard knock on the knee, you will gain the earnest prayers, when he does pray, of, dear sir, your humble servant,   ROBT. BURNS.

ST JAMES'S SQUARE, *No.* 2, *Attic Storey.*

TO MISS CHALMERS.

EDINBURGH, *Dec.* 19, 1787.

I begin this letter in answer to yours of the 17th current, which is not yet cold since I read it. The atmosphere of my soul is vastly clearer than when I wrote you last. For the first time, yesterday I crossed the room on crutches. It would do your heart good to see my bardship, not on my *poetic*, but on my *oaken* stilts; throwing my best leg with an air! and

---

* Francis Howden died at an advanced age in 1848.
† A silhouette portrait.
‡ Look twice before you jump once.

with as much hilarity in my gait and countenance, as a May frog leaping across the newly harrowed ridge, enjoying the fragrance of the refreshed earth after the long-expected shower ! . . .

I can't say I am altogether at my ease when I see any where in my path, that meagre, squalid, famine-faced spectre, poverty; attended as he always is by iron-fisted oppression and leering contempt; but I have sturdily withstood his buffetings many a hard-labored day already, and still my motto is—I DARE ! My worst enemy is *Moimême*. I lie so miserably open to the inroads and incursions of a mischievous, light-armed, well-mounted banditti, under the banners of imagination, whim, caprice, and passion : and the heavy-armed veteran regulars of wisdom, prudence, and fore-thought move so very, very slow, that I am almost in a state of perpetual warfare, and, alas ! frequent defeat.   There are just two creatures that I would envy, a horse in his wild state traversing the forests of Asia, or an oyster on some of the desert shores of Europe. The one has not a wish without enjoyment, the other has neither wish nor fear.   R. B.

There is a gap in the M'Lehose correspondence after the letter of about December 20.   In some one of the missing letters, it had been arranged that they should for the future sign their epistles respectively ' Sylvander ' and ' Clarinda.'

ON MR BURNS SAYING THAT HE HAD ' NOTHING ELSE TO DO.'

> When first you saw *Clarinda's* charms
>   What raptures in your bosom grew !
> Her heart was shut to love's alarms,
>   But then—you 'd nothing else to do.
>
> Apollo oft had lent his harp,
>   But now 'twas strung from Cupid's bow ;
> You sung, it reach'd Clarinda's heart,
>   She wish'd—you 'd nothing else to do.
>
> Fair Venus smil'd, Minerva frown'd,
>   Cupid observ'd, the arrow flew :
> Indifference (ere a week went round)
>   Shew'd—you 'd nothing else to do.*

CLARINDA.

Christmas Eve, 1787.

* There were originally six stanzas : these three only are entered in the Glenriddel volume of poems.

SYLVANDER TO CLARINDA.

ANSWER TO THE FOREGOING—EXTEMPORE.

When dear Clarinda, matchless fair,
  First struck Sylvander's raptur'd view,
He gaz'd, he listen'd, to despair
  Alas! 'twas all he dar'd to do.

Love, from Clarinda's heavenly eyes,
  Translix'd his bosom thro' and thro';
But still in Friendship's guarded guise,
  For more the demon fear'd to do.

That heart, already more than lost,
  The imp beleaguer'd all *perdue;*
For frowning Honor kept his post,
  To meet that frown he shrunk to do.

His pangs the Bard refus'd to own,
  Tho' half he wish'd Clarinda knew:
But Anguish wrung th' unweeting groan—
  Who blames what frantic Pain must do?

That heart, where motley follies blend,
  Was sternly still to Honor true:
To prove Clarinda's fondest friend,
  Was what a Lover sure might do.

The Muse his ready quill employ'd,
  No nearer bliss he could pursue;
That bliss Clarinda cold deny'd—
  'Send word by Charles how you do!'

The chill behest disarm'd his muse,
  Till Passion all impatient grew:
He wrote, and hinted for excuse
  '"Twas 'cause he 'd nothing else to do.'

But by those hopes I have above!
    And by those faults I dearly rue!
The deed, the boldest mark of love,
    For thee that deed I dare to do!

O, could the Fates but name the price
    Would bless me with your charms and you!
With frantic joy I 'd pay it thrice,
    If human art or power could do!

Then take, Clarinda, friendship's hand,
    (Friendship, at least, I may avow;)
And lay no more your chill command,
    I 'll write, whatever I 've to do.

SYLVANDER.

SYLVANDER TO CLARINDA.

I beg your pardon, my dear 'Clarinda,' for the fragment scrawl I sent you yesterday. I really don't know what I wrote. A gentleman for whose character, abilities, and critical knowledge I have the highest veneration, called in just as I had begun the second sentence, and I would not make the porter wait. I read to my much-respected friend several of my own bagatelles, and, among others, your lines, which I had copied out. He began some criticisms on them as on the other pieces, when I informed him they were the work of a young lady in this town, which, I assure you, made him stare. My learned friend seriously protested, that he did not believe any young woman in Edinburgh was capable of such lines; and, if you know anything of Professor Gregory,* you will neither doubt of his abilities nor his sincerity. I do love you, if possible, still better for having so fine a taste and turn for poesy. I have again gone wrong in my usual unguarded way; but you may erase the word, and put esteem, respect, or any other tame Dutch expression you please, in its place. I believe there is no holding converse, or carrying on correspondence, with an amiable woman, much less a *gloriously-amiable fine woman*, without some mixture of that delicious passion whose most devoted slave I have, more than once, had the honour of being. But why be hurt, or offended on that account? Can no honest man have a pre-

---

* James Gregory, born in Aberdeen in 1753; educated at Aberdeen, Edinburgh, and Leyden; appointed professor of the Theory of Physick in Edinburgh University in 1776, and in 1790 professor of the Practice of Medicine; published *Conspectus Medicinæ Theoreticæ* in 1780; died in 1821. Burns had a very high respect for Gregory. On the flyleaf of a copy of an English translation of Cicero (London, 1756), which the physician had presented to him, he wrote: 'EDIN., *April* 23d 1787.—This book, a present from the truly worthy and learned Dr GREGORY, I shall preserve to my latest hour, as a mark of the gratitude, esteem, and veneration I bear the Donor. So help me God! ROBERT BURNS.

possession for a fine woman, but he must run his head against an intrigue? Take a little of the tender witchcraft of love, and add it to the generous, the honourable sentiments of manly friendship, and I know but one more delightful morsel, which few, few in any rank, ever taste. Such a composition is like adding cream to strawberries: it not only gives the fruit a more elegant richness, but has a peculiar deliciousness of its own.

I enclose you a few lines I composed on a late melancholy occasion.* I will not give above five or six copies of it at all, and I would be hurt if any friend should give any copies without my consent.

You cannot imagine, Clarinda, (I like the idea of Arcadian names in a commerce of this kind,) how much store I have set by the hopes of your future friendship. I don't know if you have a just idea of my character, but I wish you to see me *as I am*. I am, as most people of my trade are, a strange Will-o'-wisp being; the victim, too frequently, of much imprudence and many follies. My great constituent elements are pride and passion: the first I have endeavoured to humanize into integrity and honour; the last makes me a devotee, to the warmest degree of enthusiasm, in love, religion, or friendship: either of them, or all together, as I happen to be inspired. 'Tis true, I never saw you but once; but how much acquaintance did I form with you at that once! Do not think I flatter you, or have a design upon you, Clarinda: I have too much pride for the one, and too little cold contrivance for the other; but of all God's creatures I ever could approach in the beaten way of acquaintance, you struck me with the deepest, the strongest, the most permanent impression. I say the most permanent, because I know myself well, and how far I can promise either on my prepossessions or powers. Why are you unhappy?—and why are so many of our fellow-creatures, unworthy to belong to the same species with you, blest with all they can wish? You have a hand all-benevolent to give,—why were you denied the pleasure? You have a heart formed, gloriously formed, for all the most refined luxuries of love,—why was that heart ever wrung? O Clarinda! shall we not meet in a state, some yet unknown state of being, where the lavish hand of Plenty shall minister to the highest wish of Benevolence, and where the chill north-wind of Prudence shall never blow over the flowery fields of enjoyment? If we do not, man was made in vain! I deserved most of the unhappy hours that have lingered over my head; they were the wages of my labour. But what unprovoked demon, malignant as hell, stole upon the confidence of unmistrusting, busy fate, and dashed your cup of life with undeserved sorrow?

Let me know how long your stay will be out of town; I shall count the hours till you inform me of your return. Cursed etiquette forbids your seeing me just now; and so soon as I can walk I must bid Edinburgh adieu. Lord, why was I born to see misery which I cannot relieve, and to meet with friends whom I can't enjoy? I look back with the pang of unavailing avarice on my loss in not knowing you

---

* Probably the verses on the death of the Lord President.

sooner. All last winter—these three months past—what luxury of intercourse have I not lost! Perhaps, though, 'twas better for my peace.
You see I am either above, or incapable of, dissimulation. I believe it
is want of that particular genius. I despise design, because I want
either coolness or wisdom to be capable of it. I am interrupted. Adieu!
my dear Clarinda!   SYLVANDER.

Friday Evening, [*December 28th.*]

CLARINDA TO SYLVANDER.

Friday Evening [*Dec.* 28.]

I go to the country early to-morrow morning, but will be home by
Tuesday—sooner than I expected. I have not time to answer yours as
it deserves; nor, had I the age of Methusalem, could I answer it in kind.
I shall grow *vain.* Your praises were enough,—but those of a Dr
Gregory superadded! Take care: many a 'glorious' woman has been
undone by having her head turned. 'Know you!' I know you far
better than you do me. Like yourself, I am a bit of an enthusiast. In
religion and friendship quite a bigot—perhaps I could be so in love too;
but everything dear to me in heaven and earth forbids! This is my fixed
principle; and the person who would dare to endeavour to remove it I
would hold as my chief enemy. Like you, I am incapable of dissimulation; nor am I, as you suppose, unhappy. I have been unfortunate;
but guilt alone could make me unhappy. Possessed of fine children,—
competence,—fame,—friends, kind and attentive,—what a monster of ingratitude should I be in the eye of Heaven were I to style myself unhappy!
True, I have met with scenes horrible to recollection—even at six years'
distance; but adversity, my friend, is allowed to be the school of virtue.
It oft confers that chastened softness which is unknown among the
favourites of Fortune! Even a mind possessed of natural sensibility,
without this, never feels that exquisite pleasure which nature has
annexed to our sympathetic sorrows. Religion, the only refuge of the
unfortunate, has been my balm in every woe. O! could I make her
appear to you as she has done to me! Instead of ridiculing her tenets,
you would fall down and worship her very semblance wherever you
found it!

I will write you again at more leisure, and notice other parts of yours.
I send you a simile upon a character I don't know if you are acquainted
with. I am confounded at your admiring my lines. I shall begin to
question your taste,—but Dr G.! When I am low-spirited (which I am
at times) I shall think of this as a *restorative.*

Now for the simile :—

> The morning sun shines glorious and bright,
> And fills the heart with wonder and delight!
> He dazzles in meridian splendour seen,
> Without a blackening cloud to intervene.

So, at a distance viewed, your genius bright,
Your wit, your flowing numbers give delight.
But, ah! when error's dark'ning clouds arise,
When passion's thunder, folly's lightning flies,
More safe we gaze, but admiration dies.
And as the tempting brightness snares the moth,
Sure ruin marks too near approach to both.

Good night; for Clarinda's 'heavenly eyes' need the earthly aid of sleep. Adieu. CLARINDA.

P.S.—I entreat you not to mention our corresponding to one on earth. Though I've conscious innocence, my situation is a delicate one.

CLARINDA TO SYLVANDER.

January 1, 1788.

Many happy returns of this day to you, my dear, pleasant friend! May each revolving year find you *wiser and happier!* I embrace the first spare hour to fulfil my promise; and begin with thanking you for the enclosed lines—they are very pretty: I like the idea of personifying the vices rising in the absence of *Justice.* It is a constant source of refined pleasure, giving 'to airy nothings a local habitation and a name,' which people of a luxuriant imagination only can enjoy. Yet, to a mind of a benevolent turn, it is delightful to observe how equal the distribution of happiness is among all ranks! If stupid people are rendered incapable of tasting the refined pleasures of the intelligent and feeling mind, they are likewise exempted from the thousand distractions and disquietudes peculiar to sensibility.

I have been staying with a dear female friend,* who has long been an admirer of yours, and was once on the brink of meeting with you in the house of a Mrs Bruce. She would have been a much better *Clarinda.* She is comely, without being beautiful,—and has a large share of sense, taste, and sensibility; added to all, a violent penchant for poetry. If I ever have an opportunity, I shall make you and her acquainted. No wonder Dr Gregory criticised my lines. I saw several defects in them myself; but had neither time nor patience (nor ability, perhaps,) to correct them. The three last verses were longer than the former; and in the conclusion, I saw a vile tautology which I could not get rid of. But you will not wonder when I tell you, that I am not only ignorant of every language except my own, but never so much as knew a syllable of the English grammar. If I ever write grammatically, 'tis through mere habit. I rejoice to hear of Dr Gregory being your particular friend. Though unacquainted, I am no stranger to his character: where worth unites with abilities, it commands our love as well as admiration. Alas!

---

* Miss Mary Peacock, afterwards second wife of James Gray, master in the High School, Edinburgh. She died in India.

they are too seldom found in one character! Those possessed of great talents would do well to remember, that all depends upon the use made of them. Shining abilities improperly applied only serve to accelerate our destruction in both worlds. I loved you, for your fine taste in poetry, long before I saw you; so shall not trouble myself erasing the same word applied in the same way to me. You say, 'there is no corresponding with an agreeable woman without a mixture of the tender passion.' I believe there is no friendship between people of sentiment and of different sexes, without a *little* softness; but when kept within proper bounds, it only serves to give a higher relish to such intercourse. Love and Friendship are names in every one's mouth; but few, extremely few, understand their meaning. Love (or affection) cannot be genuine if it hesitate a moment to sacrifice every selfish gratification to the happiness of its object. On the contrary, when it would purchase that at the expense of this, it deserves to be styled, not love, but by a name too gross to mention. Therefore, I contend, that an honest man *may* have a friendly prepossession for a woman whose soul would abhor the idea of an intrigue with her. These are my sentiments upon this subject: I hope they correspond with yours. 'Tis honest in you to wish me to see you 'just as you are.' I believe I have a tolerably just idea of your character. No wonder; for had I been a man, I should have been you. I am not vain enough to think myself equal in abilities; but I am formed with a liveliness of fancy, and a strength of passion little inferior. Situation and circumstances have, however, had the effects upon each of us which might be expected. Misfortune has wonderfully contributed to subdue the keenness of my passions, while success and adulation have served to nourish and inflame yours. Both of us are incapable of deceit, because we want coolness and command of our feelings. Art is what I never could attain to, even in situations where a little would have been prudent. Now and then, I am favoured with a salutary blast of 'the north wind of Prudence.' The southern zephyrs of Kindness, too, often send up their sultry fogs, and cloud the atmosphere of my understanding. I have thought that 'Nature' threw me off in the same mould, just after you. We were born, I believe, in one year. Madam Nature has some merit by her work that year. Don't you think so? I suppose the carline has had a flying visit of Venus and the Graces; and Minerva has been jealous of her attention, and sent Apollo with his harp to charm them away.

But why do you accuse Fate for my misfortunes? There is a noble independence of mind which I do admire; but, when not checked by Religion, it is apt to degenerate into a criminal arraignment of Providence. No 'malignant demon,' as you suppose, was 'permitted to dash my cup of life with sorrow:' it was the kindness of a wise and tender Father, who foresaw that I needed chastisement ere I could be brought to himself. Ah, my friend, Religion converts our heaviest misfortunes into blessings! I feel it to be so. These passions, naturally too violent for my peace, have been broken and moderated by adversity; and if even

that has been unable to conquer my vivacity, what lengths might I not
have gone, had I been permitted to glide along in the sunshine of prosperity? I should have forgot my future destination, and fixed my
happiness on the fleeting shadows below! My hand was denied the
bliss of giving, but Heaven accepts of the wish. My heart was formed
for love, and I desire to devote it to Him who is the source of love! Yes:
we shall surely meet in an 'unknown state of being,' where there will be
full scope for every kind, heartfelt affection—love without alloy, and
without end. Your paragraph upon this made the tears flow down my
face! I will not tell you the reflections which it raised in my mind; but
I wish that a heart susceptible of such a sentiment took more pains
about its accomplishment. I fancy you will not wish me to write again;
you'll think me too serious and grave. I know not how I have been led
to be so; but I make no excuse, because I must be allowed to write to
you as I feel, or not at all. You say you have humanized pride into
'honour and integrity.' 'Tis a good endeavour; and could you command
your too-impetuous passions, it would be a more glorious achievement
than his who conquered the world, and wept because he had no more
worlds to subdue. Forgive my freedom with you: I never trouble
myself with the faults of those I don't esteem, and only notice those of
friends to themselves. I am pleased with friends when they tell me
mine, and look upon it as a test of real friendship.

I have your poems in loan just now. I've read them many times, and
with new pleasure. Sometime I shall give you my opinion upon them
severally. Let me have a sight of some of your 'Bagatelles,' as you
style them. If ever I write any more, you shall have them; and I'll
thank you to correct their errors. I wrote lines on Bishop G., by way of
blank verse; but they were what Pope describes—'Ten low words do
creep in one dull line.' I believe you (being a genius) have inspired me;
for I never wrote so well before. Pray, is Dr Gregory pious? I have
heard so. I wish I knew him. Adieu! You have quantity enough!
whatever be the quality. Good night. Believe me your sincere friend,
                                                    CLARINDA.

A communication from Sylvander is evidently wanting here.
He seems to have sent Clarinda some 'lines,' which are lost.

CLARINDA TO SYLVANDER.

Thursday, Jan. [3d,] 1788.

I got your lines: they are 'in *kind!*' I can't but laugh at my presumption in pretending to send my poor ones to *you!* but it was to
amuse myself. At this season, when others are joyous, I am the reverse.
I have no *near* relations; and while others are with theirs, I sit alone,
musing upon several of mine with whom I used to be—now gone to the
land of forgetfulness.

You have put me in a rhyming humour. The moment I read yours, I wrote the following lines—

> Talk not of Love! it gives me pain—
>   For Love has been my foe:
> He bound me in an iron chain!
>   And plunged me deep in woe!
>
> But Friendship's pure and lasting joys
>   My heart was form'd to prove—
> The worthy object be of those,
>   But never talk of Love.
>
> The 'Hand of Friendship' I accept—
>   May Honour be our guard!
> *Virtue* our intercourse direct,
>   Her smiles our dear reward!

But I wish to know (in sober prose) how your leg is? I would have inquired sooner had I known it would have been acceptable. Miss N. informs me now and then; but I have not seen her dear face for some time. Do you think you could venture this length in a coach, without hurting yourself? I go out of town the beginning of the week, for a few days. I wish you could come to-morrow or Saturday. I long for a conversation with you, and lameness of body won't hinder that. 'Tis really curious—so much *fun* passing between two persons who saw one another only *once!* Say if you think you dare venture;—only let the coachman be 'adorned with sobriety.'

Adieu! Believe me, (on my simple word), Your real friend and well-wisher,   A. M.

SYLVANDER TO CLARINDA.

[*January* 3*d.*]

MY DEAR CLARINDA—Your last verses have so delighted me, that I have copied them in among some of my own most valued pieces, which I keep sacred for my own use. Do let me have a few now and then.

Did you, Madam, know what I feel when you talk of your sorrows!

Good God! that one who has so much worth in the sight of heaven, and is so amiable to her fellow-creatures, should be so unhappy! I can't venture out for cold. My limb is vastly better; but I have not any use of it without my crutches. Monday, for the first time, I dine in a neighbour's, next door. As soon as I can go so far, *even in a coach*, my first visit shall be to you. Write me when you leave town, and immediately when you return; and I earnestly pray your stay may be short. You can't imagine how miserable you made me when you hinted to me not to write. Farewell.   SYLVANDER.

Some further light is thrown on Burns's feelings at this time by a letter to his old Irvine friend, Richard Brown, who was now at home, while his vessel, the *Mary and Jean*, lay at Greenock waiting cargo for Grenada.

TO MR RICHARD BROWN, IRVINE.

EDINBURGH, *30th Dec.* 1787.

MY DEAR SIR—I have met with few things in life which have given me more pleasure than Fortune's kindness to you since those days in which we met in the vale of misery; as I can honestly say that I never knew a man who more truly deserved it, or to whom my heart more truly wished it. I have been much indebted since that time to your story and sentiments for steeling my mind against evils, of which I have had a pretty decent share. My Will-o'-wisp fate you know: do you recollect a Sunday we spent together in Eglinton Woods? You told me, on my repeating some verses to you, that you wondered I could resist the temptation of sending verses of such merit to a magazine. It was from this remark I derived that idea of my own pieces which encouraged me to endeavour at the character of a poet. I am happy to hear that you will be two or three months at home. As soon as a bruised limb will permit me, I shall return to Ayrshire, and we shall meet; 'and faith, I hope we'll not sit dumb, nor yet cast out!'

I have much to tell you 'of men, their manners, and their ways;' perhaps a little of the other sex. *Apropos*, I beg to be remembered to Mrs Brown. There, I doubt not, my dear friend, but you have found substantial happiness. I expect to find you something of an altered, but not a different man; the wild, bold, generous young fellow, composed into the steady affectionate husband, and the fond, careful parent. For me, I am just the same will-o'-wisp being I used to be. About the first and fourth quarters of the moon, I generally set in for the trade-wind of Wisdom; but about the full and change, I am the luckless victim of mad tornadoes, which blow me into Chaos. Almighty Love still reigns and revels in my bosom; and I am at this moment ready to hang myself for a young Edinburgh widow, who has wit and wisdom more murderously fatal than the assassinating stiletto of the Sicilian bandit, or the poisoned arrow of the savage African. My Highland dirk, that used to hang beside my crutches, I have removed into a neighbouring closet, the key of which I cannot command, in case of spring-tide paroxysms. You may guess of her wit by the following verses * which she sent me the other day. * * *

My best compliment to my friend, Allan. Adieu!　　　　R. B.

Letters such as this, written in the height of his reputation to

---

* Probably the verses sent were those beginning 'When first you saw *Clarinda's* charms.' —See page 226.

an old friend of his obscure days, gives us a most favourable impression of Burns's character. A well-authenticated anecdote relating to this period speaks to the same effect: 'One day, walking from Edinburgh to Leith with a modish city friend, he met on Leith Walk a rustic in very plain attire, whom he instantly hailed as an old Ayrshire acquaintance. After a short, but friendly conversation with this person, he rejoined his city friend, who expressed some surprise at his condescending to speak to any such shabby clown. "What!" said the manly bard, "do you think it was the man's clothes I was speaking to—his hat, his coat, and his waistcoat? No! It was the man within the coat and waistcoat I was speaking to; and that man, let me tell you, has more sense and worth than nine out of ten of my fine Edinburgh friends!"'

Burns received an invitation to attend a symposium of a few Jacobites to celebrate the birthday of Prince Charles Edward, held in the house of Mr James Steuart, 'Cleland's Gardens,' an alehouse that stood at the east end of North St James Street.

TO JAMES STEUART, ESQ., CLELAND'S GARDENS.

SIR—Monday next is a day of the year with me hallowed as the ceremonies of Religion and sacred to the memory of the sufferings of my King and my Forefathers. The honour you do me by your invitation I most cordially accept.

> Tho' something like moisture conglobes in my eye,
>   Let no one misdeem me disloyal;
> A poor friendless wand'rer may well claim a sigh,
>   Still more, if that wand'rer were royal.
>
> My Fathers that name have rever'd on a throne;
>   My Fathers have died to right it;
> Those Fathers would spurn their degenerate son,
>   That name if he scoffingly slight it.

I am, Sir, Your obliged humble Sert.,   ROBT. BURNS.

ST JAMES SQR., *Weden. even.*

It would appear to be doubtful whether he was able to attend this meeting, for, writing to Clarinda on 3d January following, he says, 'Monday, for the first time, I dine in a neighbour's house.' It is impossible to say, therefore, whether he actually recited or merely composed his

BIRTHDAY ODE FOR 31st DECEMBER, 1787.

Afar the illustrious Exile roams
   Whom kingdoms on this day should hail ;
An inmate in the casual shed,
On transient pity's bounty fed,
   Haunted by busy memory's bitter tale !
Beasts of the forest have their savage homes,
   But He who should imperial purple wear
Owns not the lap of earth where rests his royal head !
   His wretched refuge, dark despair,
While ravening wrongs and woes pursue,
And distant far the faithful few
   Who would his sorrows share.

False flatterer, Hope, away !
   Nor think to lure us as in days of yore :
We solemnize this sorrowing natal day
   To prove our loyal truth—we can no more,
And owning Heaven's mysterious sway,
   Submissive, low adore.
Ye honored, mighty Dead,
   Who nobly perished in the glorious cause,
   Your KING, your Country, and her laws,
From great DUNDEE, who smiling Victory led,
And fell a Martyr in her arms,
(What breast of northern ice but warms !)
To bold BALMERINO's undying name,
Whose soul of fire, lighted at Heaven's high flame,
Deserves the proudest wreath departed heroes claim :
Not unrevenged your fate shall lie,
   It only lags, the fatal hour,
Your blood shall, with incessant cry,
   Awake at last th' unsparing Power ;
As from the cliff, with thundering course
   The snowy ruin smokes along
With doubling speed and gathering force,

Till deep it, crushing, whelms the cottage in the vale !
   So Vengeance' arm, ensanguin'd, strong,
Shall with resistless might assail,
Usurping Brunswick's pride shall lay,
And STEWART's wrongs and yours, with tenfold weight,
    repay.

PERDITION, baleful child of night !
Rise and revenge the injured right
   Of STEWART's royal race :
Lead on the unmuzzled hounds of hell,
Till all the frighted echoes tell
   The blood-notes of the chase !
Full on the quarry point their view,
Full on the base usurping crew,
The tools of faction, and the nation's curse !
   Hark how the cry grows on the wind ;
   They leave the lagging gale behind,
   Their savage fury, pityless, they pour ;
With murdering eyes already they devour ;
See Brunswick spent, a wretched prey,
His life one poor despairing day,
Where each avenging hour still ushers in a worse !
   Such havock, howling all abroad,
    Their utter ruin bring ;
The base apostates to their GOD,
   Or rebels to their KING.

SYLVANDER TO CLARINDA.

[*January 4th.*]

  You are right, my dear Clarinda ; a friendly correspondence goes for nothing, except one write their undisguised sentiments. Yours please me for their intrinsic merit, as well as because they are yours, which, I assure you, is to me a high recommendation. Your religious sentiments, Madam, I revere. If you have, on some suspicious evidence, from some lying oracle, learned that I despise or ridicule so sacredly-important a matter as real religion, you have, my Clarinda, much misconstrued your friend. 'I am not mad, most noble Festus !' Have you ever met a perfect character? Do we not sometimes rather exchange faults than

get rid of them? For instance, I am perhaps tired with and shocked at
a life too much the prey of giddy inconsistences and thoughtless follies.
By degrees I grow sober, prudent, and statedly pious. I say statedly;
because the most unaffected devotion is not at all inconsistent with my
first character. I join the world in congratulating myself on the happy
change. But let me pry more narrowly into this affair. Have I at
bottom anything of a secret pride in these endowments and emenda-
tions? Have I nothing of a Presbyterian sourness, a hypercritical
severity, when I survey my less regular neighbours? In a word, have I
missed all those nameless and numberless modifications of indistinct selfishness which are so near our own eyes that we can scarce bring them
within our sphere of vision, and which the known spotless cambric of our
character hides from the ordinary observer?

My definition of worth is short: truth and humanity respecting our
fellow-creatures; reverence and humility in the presence of that Being,
my Creator and Preserver, and who, I have every reason to believe, will
one day be my Judge. The first part of my definition is the creature of
unbiassed instinct; the last is the child of after-reflection. Where I
found these two essentials, I would gently note and slightly mention
any attendant flaws—flaws, the marks, the consequences of human
nature.

I can easily enter into the sublime pleasures that your strong imagination and keen sensibility must derive from religion, particularly if a little
in the shade of misfortune; but I own I cannot, without a marked
grudge, see Heaven totally engross so amiable, so charming a woman, as
my friend Clarinda; and should be very well pleased at *a circumstance*
that would put it in the power of somebody, happy somebody! to divide
her attention, with all the delicacy and tenderness of an earthly attachment.

You will not easily persuade me that you have not a grammatical
knowledge of the English language. So far from being inaccurate, you
are elegant beyond any woman of my acquaintance, except one, whom I
wish you knew.*

Your last verses to me have so delighted me, that I have got an excellent old Scots air that suits the measure, and you shall see them in
print in the *Scots Musical Museum*—a work publishing by a friend of mine
in this town. I want four stanzas; you gave me but three, and one of
them alluded to an expression in my former letter: so I have taken your
two first verses, with a slight alteration in the second, and have added a
third; but you must help me to a fourth. Here they are: the latter
half of the first stanza would have been worthy of Sappho. I am in raptures with it.

> Talk not of Love! it gives me pain—
>   For Love has been my foe:
> He bound me with an iron chain,
>   And sunk me deep in woe.

* Probably Miss Chalmers.

> But Friendship's pure and lasting joys
> 　My heart was form'd to prove :
> There, welcome win and wear the prize,
> 　But never talk of Love.

> Your friendship much can make me blest,
> 　O, why that bliss destroy !
> 　　　　[only]
> Why urge the odious one request,
> 　　　[will]
> 　You know I must deny.

The alteration in the second four lines is no improvement, but there was a slight inaccuracy in your rhyme. The third I only offer to your choice, and have left two words for your determination. The air is ' The Banks of Spey,' and is most beautiful.

To-morrow evening I intend taking a chair, and paying a visit at Park Place, to a much-valued old friend.* If I could be sure of finding you at home (and I will send one of the chairmen to call), I would spend from five to six o'clock with you, as I go past. I cannot do more at this time, as I have something on my hand that hurries me much. I propose giving you the first call, my old friend the second, and Miss Nimmo as I return home. Do not break any engagement for me, as I will spend another evening with you at any rate before I leave town.

Do not tell me that you are pleased when your friends inform you of your faults. I am ignorant what they are ; but I am sure they must be such evanescent trifles, compared with your personal and mental accomplishments, that I would despise the ungenerous, narrow soul, who would notice any shadow of imperfections you may seem to have, any other way than in the most delicate agreeable raillery. Coarse minds are not aware how much they injure the keenly feeling tie of bosom-friendship, when in their foolish officiousness they mention what nobody cares for recollecting. People of nice sensibility and generous minds have a certain intrinsic dignity, that fires at being trifled with, or lowered, or even too nearly approached.

You need make no apology for long letters : I am even with you. Many happy New Years to you, charming Clarinda ! I can't dissemble, were it to shun perdition. He who sees you as I have done, and does not love you, deserves to be damned for his stupidity ! He who loves you and would injure you, deserves to be doubly damned for his villainy ! Adieu.　　　　　　　　　　　　　　　SYLVANDER.

P.S.—What would you think of this for a fourth stanza?

> Your thought, if Love must harbour there,
> 　Conceal it in that thought ;
> Nor cause me from my bosom tear
> 　The very friend I sought.

----

* Probably William Nicol.

The visit promised by the poet in his last letter took place, and seems to have afforded him an opportunity for giving Clarinda some account of his past life and present circumstances. He had, among other things, spoken of his infant son, now the only survivor of the twins born in September of 1786.

SYLVANDER TO CLARINDA.

Some days, some nights, nay, some *hours*, like the 'ten righteous persons in Sodom,' save the rest of the vapid, tiresome, miserable months and years of life. One of these *hours* my dear Clarinda blest me with yesternight.

> ——One well-spent hour,
> In such a tender circumstance for friends,
> Is better than an age of common time !—THOMSON.

My favourite feature in Milton's Satan is his manly fortitude in supporting what cannot be remedied,—in short, the wild broken fragments of a noble exalted mind in ruins. I meant no more by saying he was a favourite hero of mine.

I mentioned to you my letter to Dr Moore, giving an account of my life : it is truth, every word of it; and will give you the just idea of a man whom you have honoured with your friendship. I am afraid you will hardly be able to make sense of so torn a piece. Your verses I shall muse on—deliciously—as I gaze on your image, in my mind's eye, in my heart's core: they will be in time enough for a week to come. I am truly happy your headache is better. Oh, how can pain or evil be so daringly, unfeelingly, cruelly savage, as to wound so noble a mind, so lovely a form !

My little fellow is all my namesake. Write me soon. My every, strongest good wish attend you, Clarinda !   SYLVANDER.

Saturday, Noon [January 5th.]

I know not what I have written. I am pestered with people around me.

In this letter his autobiography was enclosed, apparently in fulfilment of a promise.

CLARINDA TO SYLVANDER.

Monday Night [January 7th.]

I cannot delay thanking you for the packet of Saturday ; twice have I read it with close attention. Some parts of it did beguile me of my tears. With Desdemona, I felt—''twas pitiful, 'twas wond'rous pitiful.' When I reached the paragraph where Lord Glencairn is mentioned, I burst out into tears. 'Twas that delightful swell of the heart which arises from a combination of the most pleasurable feelings. Nothing is so binding to a generous mind as placing confidence in it. I have ever felt it so. You seem to have known this feature in my character intuitively; and, therefore, intrusted me with all your faults and follies. The description of your first love-scene delighted me. It recalled the idea of some tender circumstances which happened to myself, at the same period of life—only mine did not go so far. Perhaps, in return, I'll tell you the particulars when we meet. Ah, my friend! our early love emotions are surely the most exquisite. In riper years we may acquire more knowledge, sentiment, &c.; but none of these can yield such rapture as the dear delusions of heart-throbbing youth! Like yours, mine was a rural scene, too, which adds much to the tender meeting. But no more of these recollections.

One thing alone hurt me, though I regretted many—your avowal of being an enemy to Calvinism. I guessed it was so by some of your pieces; but the confirmation of it gave me a shock I could only have felt for one I was interested in. You will not wonder at this, when I inform you that I am a strict Calvinist, *one or two* dark tenets excepted, which I never meddle with. Like many others, you are so, either from never having examined it with candour and impartiality, or from having unfortunately met with weak professors, who did not understand it; and hypocritical ones, who make it a cloak for their knavery. Both of these, I am aware, abound in country life; nor am I surprised at their having had this effect upon your more enlightened understanding. I fear your friend, the captain of the ship, was of no advantage to you in this and many other respects.

My dear Sylvander, I flatter myself you have some opinion of Clarinda's understanding. Her belief in Calvinism is not (as you will be apt to suppose) the prejudice of education. I was bred by my father in the Arminian principles. My mother, who was an angel, died when I was in my tenth year. She was a Calvinist,—was adored in her life,—and died triumphing in the prospect of immortality. I was too young, at that period, to know the difference; but her pious precepts and example often recurred to my mind amidst the giddiness and adulation of Miss in her teens. 'Twas since I came to this town, five years ago, that I imbibed my present principles. They were those of a dear, valued friend, in whose judgment and integrity I had entire confidence. I listened often to him, with delight, upon the subject. My mind was docile and open to conviction. I resolved to investigate, with deep attention, that scheme of doctrine which had such happy effects upon him. Conviction of understanding, and peace of mind, were the happy consequences. Thus have I given you a true account of my faith. I trust my practice will ever correspond. Were I to narrate my past life as honestly as you have done, you would soon be convinced that neither of us could hope to be justified by our good works.

If you have time and inclination, I should wish to hear your chief objections to Calvinism. They have been often confuted by men of great minds and exemplary lives,—but perhaps you never inquired into these. Ah, Sylvander! Heaven has not endowed you with such uncommon powers of mind to employ them in the manner you have done. This long, serious subject will, I know, have one of *three* effects: either to make you laugh in derision—yawn in supine indifference—or set about examining the hitherto-despised subject. Judge of the interest Clarinda takes in you when she affirms that there are but few events could take place that would afford her the heartfelt pleasure of the latter.

Read this letter attentively, and answer me at leisure. Do not be frightened at its gravity—believe me, I can be as lively as you please. Though I wish Madam Minerva for my guide, I shall not be hindered from rambling sometimes in the fields of Fancy. I must tell you that I admire your narrative, in point of composition, beyond all your other productions. One thing I am afraid of; there is not a trace of friendship towards a female: now, in the case of Clarinda, this is the only 'consummation devoutly to be wished.'

You told me you never had met with a woman who could love as ardently as yourself. I believe it; and would advise you never to tie yourself, till you meet with such a one. Alas! you'll find many who *canna* [can not], and some who *manna* [must not]; but to be joined to one of the former description would make you miserable. I think you had almost best resolve against wedlock: for unless a woman were qualified for the companion, the friend, and the mistress, she would not do for you. The last may gain Sylvander, but the others alone can keep him. Sleep, and want of room, prevent my explaining myself upon 'infidelity in a husband,' which made you stare at me. This, and other things, shall be matter for another letter, if you are not wishing this to be the last. If agreeable to you, I'll keep the narrative till we meet. Adieu! 'Charming Clarinda' must e'en resign herself to the arms of Morpheus. Your true friend,   CLARINDA.

P.S. —Don't detain the porter. Write when convenient.

I am probably to be in your Square this afternoon, near two o'clock. If your room be to the street, I shall have the pleasure of giving you a nod. I have paid the porter, and you may do so when you write. I'm sure they sometimes have made us pay double. Adieu!

Tuesday Morning.

SYLVANDER TO CLARINDA.

I am delighted, charming Clarinda, with your honest enthusiasm for religion. Those of either sex, but particularly the female, who are lukewarm in that most important of all things, 'O my soul, come not thou into their secrets!'

I feel myself deeply interested in your good opinion, and will lay before you the outlines of my belief:—He who is our Author and Preserver, and will one day be our Judge, must be,—not for His sake, in the way of duty, but from the native impulse of our hearts,—the object of our reverential awe and grateful adoration. He is almighty and all-bounteous; we are weak and dependent: hence prayer and every other sort of devotion. 'He is not willing that any should perish, but that all should come to everlasting life;' consequently, it must be in every one's power to embrace His offer of 'everlasting life;' otherwise He could not in justice condemn those who did not. A mind pervaded, actuated, and governed by purity, truth, and charity, though it does not *merit* heaven, yet is an absolutely necessary pre-requisite, without which heaven can neither be obtained nor enjoyed; and, by Divine promise, such a mind shall never fail of attaining 'everlasting life:' hence the impure, the deceiving, and the uncharitable exclude themselves from eternal bliss, by their unfitness for enjoying it. The Supreme Being has put the immediate administration of all this—for wise and good ends known to Himself—into the hands of Jesus Christ, a great Personage, whose relation to Him we cannot comprehend, but whose relation to us is [that of] a Guide and Saviour; and who, except for our own obstinacy and misconduct, will bring us all, through various ways and by various means, to bliss at last.

These are my tenets, my lovely friend; and which, I think, cannot be well disputed. My creed is pretty nearly expressed in the last clause of Jamie Dean's grace, an honest weaver in Ayrshire:—'Lord, grant that we may lead a gude life! for a gude life maks a gude end: at least it helps weel!'

I am flattered by the entertainment you tell me you have found in my packet. You see me as I have been, you know me as I am, and may guess at what I am likely to be. I, too, may say, 'Talk not of Love,' &c.; for, indeed, he has 'plunged me deep in woe!' Not that I ever saw a woman who pleased unexceptionably, as my Clarinda elegantly says, 'in the companion, the friend, and the mistress.' *One*, indeed, I could except; one, before passion threw its mists over my discernment, I knew,—the first of women! Her name is indelibly written in my heart's core; but I dare not look in on it,—a degree of agony would be the consequence. Oh, thou perfidious, cruel, mischief-making demon, who presidest o'er that frantic passion,—thou mayest, thou dost poison my peace, but thou shalt not taint my honour! I would not for a single moment give an asylum to the most distant imagination that would shadow the faintest outline of a selfish gratification at the expense of *her* whose happiness is twisted with the threads of my existence. May she be as happy, as she deserves! And if my tenderest, faithfulest friendship can add to her bliss, I shall, at least, have one solid mine of enjoyment in my bosom! *Don't guess at these ravings!*

I watched at our front window to-day, but was disappointed. It has been a day of disappointments. I am just risen from a two-hours' bout after supper, with silly or sordid souls who could relish nothing in common with me but the Port.——'*One*.'——'Tis now the 'witching time of night,' and whatever is out of joint in the foregoing scrawl, impute it to enchantments and spells; for I can't look over it, but will seal it up directly, as I don't care for to-morrow's criticisms on it.

You are by this time fast asleep, Clarinda; may good angels attend and guard you as constantly and faithfully as my good wishes do !

> Beauty which, whether waking or asleep,
> Shot forth peculiar graces. *

John Milton, I wish thy soul better rest than I expect on my pillow to-night ! O for a little of the cart-horse part of human nature ! Good night, my dearest Clarinda ! SYLVANDER.

Tuesday Night [January 8th.]

CLARINDA TO SYLVANDER.

Wednesday, 10 P.M. [January 9th.]

This moment your letter was delivered to me. My boys are asleep. The youngest has been for some time in a crazy state of health, but has been worse these two days past. Partly this and the badness of the day prevented my exchanging a heartfelt How d' ye, yesterday. Friday, if nothing prevents, I shall have that pleasure, about two o'clock, or a little before it.

I wonder how you could write so distinctly after two or three hours over a bottle; but they were not congenial whom you sat with, and therefore your spirits remained unexhausted; and when quit of them, you fled to a friend who can relish most things in common with you (except Port). 'Tis dreadful what a variety of these 'silly, sordid' souls one meets with in life ! but in scenes of mere sociability these pass. In reading the account you give of your inveterate turn for social pleasure, I smiled at its resemblance to my own. It is so great, that I often think I had been a man but for some mistake of Nature. If you saw me in a merry party, you would suppose me only an enthusiast in *fun;* but I now avoid such parties. My spirits are sunk for days after; and, what is worse, there are sometimes dull or malicious souls who censure me loudly for what their sluggish natures cannot comprehend. Were I possessed of an independent fortune, I would scorn their pitiful remarks; but everything in my situation renders prudence necessary.

I have slept little these two nights. My child was uneasy, and that kept me awake watching him ! Sylvander, if I have merit in anything, 'tis in an unremitting attention to my two children; but it cannot be denominated merit, since 'tis as much inclination as duty. A prudent woman (as the world goes) told me she was surprised I loved them, 'considering what a father they had.' I replied with acrimony, I could not but love my children in any case; but my having given them the

* From *Paradise Lost*, Book V., lines 14-15.

misfortune of such a father, endears them doubly to my heart: they are innocent—they depend upon me—and I feel this the most tender of all claims. While I live, my fondest attention shall be theirs !

All my life I loved the unfortunate, and ever will. Did you ever read Fielding's *Amelia?* If you have not, I beg you would. There are scenes in it, tender, domestic scenes, which I have read over and over, with feelings too delightful to describe ! I meant a 'Booth,' as such a one infinitely to be preferred to a brutal, though perhaps constant, husband. I can conceive a man fond of his wife, yet, (Sylvander-like), hurried into a momentary deviation, while his heart remained faithful. If he concealed it, it could not hurt me ; but if, unable to bear the anguish of self-reproach, he unbosomed it to me, I would not only forgive him, but comfort and speak kindly, and in secret only weep. Reconciliation, in such a case, would be exquisite beyond almost anything I can conceive ! Do you now understand me on this subject? I was uneasy till it was explained ; for all I have said, I know not if I had been an 'Amelia,' even with a 'Booth.' My resentments are keen, like all my other feelings : I am exquisitely alive to kindness and to unkindness. The first binds me for ever ! But I have none of the spaniel in my nature. The last would soon cure me, though I loved to distraction. But all this is not, perhaps, interesting to Sylvander. I have seen nobody to-day ; and, like a true egotist, talk away to please myself. I am not in a humour to answer your creed to-night.

I have been puzzling my brain about the fair one you bid me 'not guess at.' I first thought it your Jean ; but I don't know if she now possesses your 'tenderest, faithfulest friendship.' I can't understand that bonny lassie : her refusal, after such proofs of love, proves her to be either an angel or a dolt. I beg pardon ; I know not all the circumstances, and am no judge therefore. I love you for your continued fondness, even after enjoyment : few of your sex have souls in such cases. But I take this to be the test of true love—mere desire is all the bulk of people are susceptible of ; and that is soon satiated. 'Your good wishes.' You had mine, Sylvander, before I saw you. You will have them while I live. With you, I wish I had a little of the cart-horse in me. You and I have some horse properties ; but more of the eagle, and too much of the turtle dove ! Good night ! Your friend,   CLARINDA.

Thursday Morning.

This day is so good that I 'll make out my call to your Square. I am laughing to myself at announcing this for the third time. Were she who 'poisons your peace' to intend you a Pisgah view, she could do no more than I have done on this trivial occasion. Keep a good heart, Sylvander ; the eternity of your love-sufferings will be ended before six weeks. Such perjuries the 'Laughing gods allow.' But remember, there is no such toleration in friendship, and——I am yours,

CLARINDA.

SYLVANDER TO CLARINDA.

I am certain I saw you, Clarinda; but you don't look to the proper story for a poet's lodging,

Where Speculation roosted near the sky.

I could almost have thrown myself over, for very vexation. Why didn't you look higher? It has spoilt my peace for this day. To be so near my charming Clarinda; to miss her look while it was searching for me. I am sure the soul is capable of disease; for mine has convulsed itself into an inflammatory fever. I am sorry for your little boy: do let me know to-morrow how he is.

You have converted me, Clarinda, (I shall love that name while I live: there is heavenly music in it). Booth and Amelia I know well. Your sentiments on that subject, as they are on every subject, are just and noble. 'To be feelingly alive to kindness and to unkindness' is a charming female character.

What I said in my last letter, the powers of fuddling sociality only know for me. By yours, I understand my good star has been partly in my horizon, when I got wild in my reveries. Had that evil planet, which has almost all my life shed its baleful rays on my devoted head, been as usual in its zenith, I had certainly blabbed something that would have pointed out to you the dear object of my tenderest friendship, and, in spite of me, something more. Had that fatal information escaped me, and it was merely chance or kind stars that it did not, I had been undone! You would never have written me, except, perhaps, *once* more! O, I could curse circumstances! and the coarse tie of human laws which keeps fast what common sense would loose, and which bars that, happiness itself cannot give—happiness which otherwise love and honour would warrant! But hold—I shall make no more 'hairbreadth 'scapes.'

My friendship, Clarinda, is a liferent business. My likings are both strong and eternal. I told you I had but one male friend: I have but two female. I should have a third, but she is surrounded by the blandishments of flattery and courtship. Her I register in my heart's core by Peggy Chalmers: Miss Nimmo can tell you how divine she is. She is worthy of a place in the same bosom with my Clarinda! That is the highest compliment I can pay her. Farewell, Clarinda! Remember   SYLVANDER.

Thursday, Noon [January 10th.]

CLARINDA TO SYLVANDER.

Thursday Eve [January 10.]

I could not see you, Sylvander, though I had twice traversed the Square. I'm persuaded you saw not me either. I met the young lady I meant to call for first; and returned to seek another acquaintance, but found her moved. All the time, my eye soared to poetic heights, *alias* garrets, but not a glimpse of you could I obtain! You surely was within the glass, at least. I returned, finding my intrinsic dignity a good deal hurt, as I missed my friend. Perhaps I shall see you again next week: say how high you are. Thanks for your inquiry about my child; his complaints are of a tedious kind, and require patience and resignation. Religion has taught me both. By nature I inherit as little of them as a certain harum-scarum friend of mine. In what respects has Clarinda 'converted you?' Tell me. It were an arduous task indeed!

Your 'ravings' last night, and your ambiguous remarks upon them, I cannot, perhaps ought not, to comprehend. I am your friend, Sylvander: take care lest virtue demand even friendship as a sacrifice. You need not curse the tie of human laws; since what is the happiness Clarinda would derive from being loosed? At present, she enjoys the hope of having her children provided for. In the other case, she is left, indeed, at liberty, but half dependent on the bounty of a friend,—kind in substantials, but having no feelings of romance: and who are the generous, the disinterested, who would risk the world's 'dread laugh' to protect her and her little ones? Perhaps a Sylvander-like son of 'whim and fancy' might, in a sudden fit of romance: but would not ruin be the consequence? Perhaps one of the former . . . yet if he was not dearer to her than all the world—such are still her romantic ideas—she could not be his.

You see, Sylvander, you have no cause to regret my bondage. The above is a true picture. Have I not reason to rejoice that I have it not in my power to dispose of myself? 'I commit myself into thy hands, thou Supreme Disposer of all events! do with me as seemeth to thee good.' Who is this one male friend? I know your third female. Ah, Sylvander! many 'that are first shall be last,' and *vice versa!* I am proud of being compared to Miss Chalmers: I have heard how amiable she is. She cannot be more so than Miss Nimmo: why do ye not register her also? She is warmly your friend;—surely you are incapable of ingratitude. She has almost wept to me at mentioning your intimacy with a certain famous, or infamous, man in town.* Do you think Clarinda could anger you just now? I composed lines addressed to you, some time ago, containing a hint upon the occasion. I had not courage to send them then: if you say you'll not be angry, I will yet.

I know not how 'tis, but I felt an irresistible impulse to write you the moment I read yours. I have a design in it. Part of your interest in me is owing to mere novelty. You'll be tired of my correspondence ere you leave town, and will never fash [trouble] to write me from the country. I forgive you in a 'state of celibacy.' Sylvander, I wish I saw you happily married: you are so formed, you cannot be happy without a tender attachment. Heaven direct you!

When you see Bishop Geddes, ask him if he remembers a lady at Mrs

---

* Probably William Nicol.

Kemp's,' on a Sunday night, who listened to every word he uttered with the gaze of attention. I saw he observed me, and returned that glance of cordial warmth which assured me he was pleased with my delicate flattery. I wished that night he had been my father, that I might shelter me in his bosom.

You shall have this, as you desired, to-morrow ; and, if possible, none for four or five days. I say, if possible : for I really can't but write, as if I had nothing else to do. I admire your Epitaph ; but while I read it, my heart swells at the sad idea of its realization. Did you ever read Sancho's Letters ?† they would hit your taste. My next will be on my favourite theme—religion.

Farewell, Sylvander ! Be wise, be prudent, and be happy.

CLARINDA.

Let your next be sent in the morning.

If you were well, I would ask you to meet me to-morrow at twelve o'clock. I go down in the Leith Fly, with poor Willie : what a pleasant chat we might have ! But I fancy 'tis impossible. Adieu !

Friday, One o'clock.

SYLVANDER TO CLARINDA.

Saturday Morning [*January* 12.]

Your thoughts on religion, Clarinda, shall be welcome. You may perhaps distrust me when I say 'tis also *my* favourite topic ; but mine is the religion of the bosom. I hate the very idea of a controversial divinity ; as I firmly believe that every honest, upright man, of whatever sect, will be accepted of the Deity. If your verses, as you seem to hint, contain censure, except you want an occasion to break with me, don't send them. I have a little infirmity in my disposition, that where I fondly love or highly esteem, I cannot bear reproach.

' Reverence thyself,' is a sacred maxim ; and I wish to cherish it. I think I told you Lord Bolingbroke's saying to Swift,—' Adieu, dear Swift ! with all thy faults I love thee entirely : make an effort to love me with all mine.' A glorious sentiment, and without which there can be no friendship ! I do highly, very highly, esteem you indeed, Clarinda : you merit it all ! Perhaps, too—I scorn dissimulation—I could fondly love you : judge, then, what a maddening sting your reproach would be. ' Oh ! I have sins to Heaven, but none to you.' With what pleasure would I meet you to-day, but I cannot walk to meet the Fly. I hope to be able to see you, *on foot*, about the middle of next week. I am interrupted—perhaps you are not sorry for it. You will tell me : but I won't

---

* Probably (first) wife of Clarinda's minister. She was daughter of a merchant named Andrew Simpson, of Edinburgh. She was married in 1780 and died in 1796.

† *Letters of the late Ignatius Sancho, an African* (London, 1782, 2 vols.). Sancho was a negro of extraordinary character. His letters ' possess great originality and display strong powers of intellect.'

anticipate blame. O, Clarinda! did you know how dear to me is your look of kindness, your smile of approbation, you would not, either in prose or verse, risk a censorious remark.

> Curst be the verse, how well soe'er it flow,
> That tends to make one worthy man my foe ! *

SYLVANDER.

The letter to which the following is reply is wanting.

SYLVANDER TO CLARINDA.

[January 12.]

You talk of weeping, Clarinda : some involuntary drops wet your lines as I read them. Offend me, my dearest angel ! You cannot offend me,—you never offended me. If you had ever given me the least shadow of offence, so pardon me my God as I forgive Clarinda. I have read yours again ; it has blotted my paper. Though I find your letter has agitated me into a violent headache, I shall take a chair and be with you about eight. A friend is to be with us at tea, on my account, which hinders me from coming sooner. Forgive, my dearest Clarinda, my unguarded expressions ! For Heaven's sake, forgive me, or I shall never be able to bear my own mind. Your unhappy   SYLVANDER.

On a Saturday night, after eight o'clock, Burns and Mrs M'Lehose had their *third* meeting—the second which had taken place in her house.

CLARINDA TO SYLVANDER.

Sunday Evening [January 13.]

I will not deny it, Sylvander, last night was one of the most exquisite I ever experienced. Few such fall to the lot of mortals ! Few, extremely few, are formed to relish such refined enjoyment. That it should be so, vindicates the wisdom of Heaven. But, though our enjoyment did not lead beyond the limits of virtue, yet to-day's reflections have not been altogether unmixed with regret. The idea of the pain it would have given, were it known to a friend to whom I am bound by the sacred ties of gratitude,† (no more,) the opinion Sylvander may have formed from my unreservedness ; and, above all, some secret misgivings that Heaven may not approve, situated as I am—these procured me a sleepless night ; and, though at church, I am not at all well.

Sylvander, you saw Clarinda last night, behind the scenes ! Now, you'll be convinced she has faults. If she knows herself, her intention is always good ; but she is too often the victim of sensibility, and, hence,

---

is seldom pleased with herself. A rencontre to-day I will relate to you, because it will show you I have my own share of pride. I met with a sister of Lord Napier, at the house of a friend with whom I sat between sermons: I knew who she was; but paid her no other marks of respect than I do to any gentlewoman. She eyed me with minute, supercilious attention, never looking at me, when I spoke, but even half interrupted me, before I had done addressing the lady of the house. I felt my face glow with resentment, and consoled myself with the idea of being her superior in every respect but the accidental, trifling one of birth! I was disgusted at the fawning deference the lady showed her; and when she told me at the door that it was my Lord Napier's sister, I replied, 'Is it, indeed? by her ill-breeding I should have taken her for the daughter of some upstart tradesman!'

Sylvander, my sentiments as to birth and fortune are truly unfashionable: I despise the persons who pique themselves on either,—the former especially. Something may be allowed to bright talents, or even external beauty—these belong to us essentially; but birth in no respect can confer merit, because it is not our own. A person of a vulgar, uncultivated mind I would not take to my bosom, in any station; but one possessed of natural genius, improved by education and diligence, such an one I'd take for my friend, be her extraction ever so mean. These, alone, constitute any real distinction between man and man. Are we not all the offspring of Adam? have we not one God? one Saviour? one Immortality? I have found but one among all my acquaintance who agreed with me—my Mary,* whom I mentioned to you. I am to spend to-morrow with her, if I am better. I like her the more that she likes me.

I intended to resume a little upon your favourite topic, the 'Religion of the Bosom.' Did you ever imagine that I meant any other? Poor were that religion and unprofitable whose seat was merely in the brain. In most points we seem to agree: only I found all my hopes of pardon and acceptance with Heaven upon the merit of Christ's atonement,—whereas you do upon a good life. You think 'it helps weel, at least.' If anything we could do had been able to atone for the violation of God's Law, where was the need (I speak it with reverence) of such an astonishing Sacrifice? Job was an 'upright man.' In the dark season of adversity, when other sins were brought to his remembrance, he boasted of his integrity; but no sooner did God reveal Himself to him, than he exclaims: 'Behold I am vile, and abhor myself in dust and ashes.' Ah! my friend, 'tis pride that hinders us from embracing Jesus! we would be our own Saviour, and scorn to be indebted even to the 'Son of the Most High.' But this is the only sure foundation of our hopes. It is said by God Himself, ''tis to some a stumbling-block, to others foolishness;' but they who believe, feel it to be the 'Wisdom of God, and the Power of God.'

---

* Mary Peacock—already mentioned.

If my head did not ache, I would continue the subject. I, too, hate controversial religion; but this is the 'Religion of the Bosom.' My God! Sylvander, why am I so anxious to make you embrace the Gospel? I dare not probe too deep for an answer—let your heart answer: in a word—Benevolence. When I return, I'll finish this. Meantime, adieu! Sylvander, I intended doing you good: if it prove the reverse, I shall never forgive myself. Good night.

Tuesday, Noon.

Just returned from the Dean, where I dined and supped with fourteen of both sexes: all stupid. My Mary and I alone understood each other. However, we were joyous, and I sang in spite of my cold; but no wit. 'Twould have been pearls before swine literalized. I recollect promising to write you. Sylvander, you 'll never find me worse than my word. If you have written me, (which I hope), send it to me when convenient, either at nine in the morning or evening. I fear your limb may be worse from staying so late. I have other fears too: guess them! Oh! my friend, I wish ardently to maintain your esteem: rather than forfeit one iota of it, I 'd be content never to be wiser than now. Our last interview has raised you very high in mine. I have met with few, indeed, of your sex who understood delicacy in such circumstances; yet 'tis that only which gives a relish to such delightful intercourse. Do you wish to preserve my esteem, Sylvander? do not be proud to Clarinda! She deserves it not. I subscribe to Lord B.'s sentiment to Swift; yet some faults I shall still sigh over, though you style it reproach even to hint them. Adieu! You have it much in your power to add to the happiness or unhappiness of   CLARINDA.

SYLVANDER TO CLARINDA.

Monday Evening, 11 o'clock [Jan. 14th.]

Why have I not heard from you, Clarinda? To-day I well expected it; and before supper when a letter to me was announced, my heart danced with rapture; but behold, 'twas some fool who had taken it into his head to turn poet, and made me an offer of the first fruits of his nonsense. 'It is not poetry, but prose run mad.'

Did I ever repeat to you an epigram I made on a Mr Elphinstone,[*] who has given a translation of *Martial*, a famous Latin poet? The poetry of Elphinstone can only equal his prose notes. I was sitting in a merchant's[†] shop of my acquaintance, waiting somebody; he put *Elphin-*

---

[*] James Elphinston, born at Edinburgh 1721, kept a boarding-school at Kensington, London, and died 1809. Samuel Johnson was his friend.

[†] Supposed to have been Creech. This volume (*The epigrams of M. Val. Martial, in twelve books; with a comment; by James Elphinston.* London: Printed by Baker and Galabin. MDCCLXXXII. 4to.), containing the quatrain, is now the property of Mr Robert Munro, Ibrox, Glasgow. The 'Table of Subscribers' is followed by lines 'To the Subscribers' signed 'James Elphinston;' underneath these lines (page 37) is the epigram. The Poet had evidently commenced to write in pencil, but had stopped and begun anew in ink. A description of the volume is given by Mr William Young, R.S.W., in the *Burns Chronicle*, 1894.

stone into my hand, and asked my opinion of it : I begged leave to write it on a blank leaf, which I did, as you shall see on a new page :

TO MR ELPHINSTONE.

O thou whom Poesy abhors,
  Whom Prose has turned out of doors !
Heard'st thou yon groan? proceed no further ;
  'Twas laurell'd Martial calling Murther !

I am determined to see you, if at all possible, on Saturday evening. Next week I must sing—

The night is my departing night,
  The morn 's the day I maun awa :   must away
There 's neither friend nor foe o' mine
  But wishes that I were awa !
What I hae done for lack o' wit,
  I never, never can reca' ;
I hope ye 're a' my friends as yet,
  Gude night, and joy be wi' you a' ! *

If I could see you sooner, I would be so much the happier ; but I would not purchase the dearest gratification on earth, if it must be at your expense in wordly censure, far less, inward peace.

I shall certainly be ashamed of thus scrawling whole sheets of in-coherence. The only unity (a sad word with poets and critics !) in my ideas, is CLARINDA.—There my heart 'reigns and revels.'

What art thou, Love? whence are those charms,
  That thus thou bear'st an universal rule ?
For thee the soldier quits his arms,
  The king turns slave, the wise man fool.
In vain we chase thee from the field,
  And with cool thoughts resist thy yoke ;
Next tide of blood, alas ! we yield,
  And all those high resolves are broke !

I like to have quotations for every occasion. They give one's ideas so pat, and save one the trouble of finding expression adequate to one's feelings. I think it is one of the greatest pleasures attending a poetic genius, that we can give our woes, cares, joys, loves, &c., an embodied form in verse, which, to me, is ever immediate ease. Goldsmith says finely of his muse :

Thou source of all my bliss and all my woe ;
Who found'st me poor at first, and keep'st me so.†

My limb has been so well to-day, that I have gone up and down stairs

---

* ' Guid night, and joy be wi' you a' '—an old Scots song.
† *The Deserted Village*, lines 413-4.

often without my staff. To-morrow I hope to walk once again on my own legs to dinner. It is only next street. Adieu !

SYLVANDER.

The last letter from Clarinda having been received soon after the above epistle had been despatched, Sylvander writes again :

SYLVANDER TO CLARINDA.

Tuesday Evening [January 15.]

That you have faults, my Clarinda, I never doubted ; but I knew not where they existed ; and Saturday night made me more in the dark than ever. O, Clarinda ! why would you wound my soul by hinting that last night must have lessened my opinion of you ? True, I was behind the scenes with you ; but what did I see ? A bosom glowing with honour and benevolence ; a mind ennobled by genius, informed and refined by education and reflection, and exalted by native religion, genuine as in the climes of Heaven ; a heart formed for all the glorious meltings of friendship, love, and pity. These I saw. I saw the noblest immortal soul creation ever showed me.

I looked long, my dear Clarinda, for your letter ; and am vexed that you are complaining. I have not caught you so far wrong as in your idea—that the commerce you have with one friend hurts you, if you cannot tell every tittle of it to another. Why have so injurious a suspicion of a good God, Clarinda, as to think that Friendship and Love, on the sacred, inviolate principles of Truth, Honour and Religion, can be anything else than an object of His divine approbation ?

I have mentioned, in some of my former scrawls, Saturday evening next. Do allow me to wait on you that evening. Oh, my angel ! how soon must we part !—and when can we meet again ? I look forward on the horrid interval with tearful eyes. What have not I lost by not knowing you sooner ! I fear, I fear, my acquaintance with you is too short to make that lasting impression on your heart I could wish.

SYLVANDER.

CLARINDA TO SYLVANDER.

Wed. Morn [January 16th.]

Your mother's wish was fully realized. I slept sounder to-night than for weeks past, and I had ' a blythe waukening ;' for your letter was the first object my eyes opened on. Sylvander, I fancy you and 'Vulcan' are intimates : he had lent you a key which opens Clarinda's heart at pleasure—shews you what is there, and enables you to adapt yourself to its every feeling ! I believe I shall give over writing you. Your letters are too much ! my way is, alas ! ' hedged in ;' but had I, like Sylvander, ' the world before me,' I should bid him, ' if he had a friend that loved me,' tell him to WRITE as he does, and ' that would woo me.' Seriously, you are the first letter-writer I ever knew, and I only

wonder how you can be *fashed* [troubled] with my scrawls. I impute it
to partiality.

Either *to-morrow*, or *Friday*, I shall be happy to see you. On *Saturday*, I am not *sure* of being alone, or at home. Say which you'll come?
Come to tea if you please; but eight will be an hour less liable to intru-
sions. I hope you'll *come afoot*, even tho' you take a chair home. A
chair is so uncommon a thing in our neighbourhood, it is apt to raise
speculation; but they are all asleep by ten. I'm happy to hear of your
being able to '*walk*'—even to the next street. You are a consummate
flatterer; really my cheeks glow while I read your flights of fancy. I
fancy you see I like it, when you peep into the *Repository*. I know none
insensible to that 'delightful essence.' If I grow *affected* or *conceited*,
you are alone to blame. Ah! my friend, these are disgusting qualities!
but I'm not afraid. I know any merit I have perfectly; but I know
many sad *counterbalances*.

Your lines on Elphinstone were CLEVER, beyond anything I ever saw of
the kind; I know the character—the figure is enough to make one cry
Murder! He is a complete pedant in language; but are not you and I
pedants in something else? Yes, but in far superior things—Love, Friendship, Poesy, Religion! Ah, Sylvander! you have murdered Humility,
and I can say thou didst it.

You carry your warmth too far as to Miss Napier (not Nairn); yet I
am pleased at it. She is sensible, lively, and well-liked, they say. She
was not to know Clarinda was 'divine,' and therefore kept her distance. She is comely, but a thick bad figure, waddles in her pace,
and has rosy cheeks.

> Wha is that clumsy damsel there?   Who
> 'Whisht! it's the daughter of a Peer,
>   Right Honorably Great!'
>
> The daughter of a Peer, I cried,
>   It doth not *yet* appear
> What we *shall* be (in t'other world),
>   God keep us frae this here!   from
> That she has *Blude*, I'se no dispute,   I shall
>   I see it in her face;
> Her honor's in her *name*, I fear,
>   And in nae other place.   no

I hate myself for being satirical—hate me for it too. I'll certainly go
to Miers to please you, either with Mary or Miss Nimmo. Sylvander,
some most interesting parts of yours I cannot enter upon at present. I
dare not think upon parting—upon the *interval;* but I'm sure both are
wisely order'd for our good. A line in return to tell me which night
you'll be with me—'*lasting impression!*' Your key might have shewn
you me better. Say

> ——my lover, poet, and my friend,
> What day next month th' Eternity will end?

When you use your key, don't rummage too much, lest you find I am half as great a fool in the *tender* as yourself. Farewell, Sylvander! I may sign, for I am already sealed, your friend.   CLARINDA.

SYLVANDER TO CLARINDA.

Saturday Morning [January 19.]

There is no time, my Clarinda, when the conscious thrilling chords of Love and Friendship give such delight, as in the pensive hours of what our favourite Thomson calls 'philosophic melancholy.' The sportive insects who bask in the sunshine of Prosperity, or the worms that luxuriant crawl amid their ample wealth of earth ; they need no Clarinda —they would despise Sylvander, if they dared. The family of Misfortune, a numerous group of brothers and sisters !—they need a resting-place to their souls. Unnoticed, often condemned by the world—in some degree, perhaps, condemned by themselves—they feel the full enjoyment of ardent love, delicate tender endearments, mutual esteem, and mutual reliance.

In this light I have often admired religion. In proportion as we are wrung with grief, or distracted with anxiety, the ideas of a compassionate Deity, an Almighty Protector, are doubly dear.

> 'Tis this, my friend, that streaks our morning bright ;
> 'Tis this that gilds the horrors of our night.*

I have been this morning taking a peep through, as Young finely says, ' the dark postern of time long elapsed ;' and you will easily guess 'twas a rueful prospect : what a tissue of thoughtlessness, weakness, and folly ! My life reminded me of a ruined temple : what strength, what proportion in some parts !—what unsightly gaps, what prostrate ruins in others ! I kneeled down before the Father of Mercies, and said, ' Father, I have sinned against Heaven, and in Thy sight, and am no more worthy to be called Thy son !' I rose eased and strengthened. I despise the superstition of a fanatic ; but I love the religion of a man. 'The future,' said I to myself, ' is still before me : there let me

> On reason build resolve—
> That column of true majesty in man !†

I have difficulties many to encounter,' said I, ' but they are not absolutely insuperable :—and where is firmness of mind shown, but in exertion?

---

* These lines on religion are from ' Verses to Mr James Hervey, on his *Meditations*,' by a physician. The verses are usually prefixed, with others, to the *Meditations and Contemplations*.

† From *Night Thoughts*, by Edward Young.

Mere declamation is bombast rant. Besides, wherever I am or in whatever situation I may be,

> ———— 'Tis nought to me,
> Since God is ever present, ever felt,
> In the void waste as in the city full ;
> And where he vital breathes, there must be joy.

Saturday Night, Half after Ten.

What luxury of bliss I was enjoying this time yesternight ! My ever
dearest Clarinda, you have stolen away my soul : but you have refined,
you have exalted it ; you have given it a stronger sense of virtue, and a
stronger relish for piety. Clarinda, first of your sex ! if ever I am the
veriest wretch on earth to forget you ; if ever your lovely image is
effaced from my soul,

> May I be lost, no eye to weep my end,
> And find no earth that 's base enough to bury me !

What trifling silliness is the childish fondness of the every-day children
of the world ! 'Tis the unmeaning toying of the younglings of the fields
and forests ; but, where Sentiment and Fancy unite their sweets, where
Taste and Delicacy refine, where Wit adds the flavour, and Good sense
gives strength and spirit to all ; what a delicious draught is the hour of
tender endearment ! Beauty and Grace in the arms of Truth and
Honour, in all the luxury of mutual love.

Clarinda, have you ever seen the picture realized ? not in all its very
richest colouring, but

> Hope, thou nurse of young Desire,
> Fair promiser of Joy.—

Last night, Clarinda, but for one slight shade, was the glorious
picture—

> ———Innocence
> Look'd gaily smiling on ; while rosy Pleasure
> Hid young Desire amid her flowery wreath,
> And poured her cup luxuriant, mantling high,
> The sparkling, Heavenly vintage—Love and Bliss !

Clarinda, when a poet and poetess of Nature's making—two of
Nature's noblest productions !—when they drink together of the same
cup of Love and Bliss, attempt not, ye coarser stuff of human nature !
profanely to measure enjoyment ye never can know.

Good night, my dear Clarinda !   SYLVANDER.

CLARINDA TO SYLVANDER.

Saturday Evening [19th January.]

I am wishing, Sylvander, for the power of looking into your heart. It
would be but fair—for you have the key of mine. You are possessed of

acute discernment. I am not deficient either in that respect. Last night must have shown you Clarinda not ' divine '—but as she really is. I can't recollect some things I said without a degree of pain. Nature has been kind to me in several respects; but one essential she has denied me entirely : it is that instantaneous preception of fit and unfit, which is so useful in the conduct of life. No one can discriminate more accurately afterwards than Clarinda. But when her heart is expanded by the influence of kindness, she loses all command of it, and often suffers severely in the recollection of her unguardedness. You must have perceived this ; but, at any rate, I wish you to know me, as ' I really am.' I would have given much for society to-day ; for I can't bear my own : but no human being has come near me. Well as I like you, Sylvander, I would rather lose your love, than your esteem : the first I ought not to wish ; the other I shall ever endeavour to maintain. But no more of this : you prohibit it, and I obey.

For many years, have I sought for a male friend, endowed with sentiments like yours; one who could love me with tenderness, yet unmixed with selfishness: who could be my friend, companion, protector, and who would die sooner than injure me. I sought—but I sought in vain ! Heaven has, I hope, sent me this blessing in my Sylvander ! Whatever weaknesses may cleave to Clarinda, her heart is not to blame: whatever it may have been by nature, it is unsullied by art. If she dare dispose of it—last night can leave you at no loss to guess the man :

Then, dear Sylvander, use it weel,	well
An' row it in your bosom's biel ;	wrap—shelter
Ye 'll find it aye baith kind and leal,	both—loyal
And fou o' glee ;	full
It wad na wrang the vera deil,—	wrong the very devil
Ah, far less thee !	

How do you like this parody on a passage of my favourite poet?—it is extempore—from the heart ; and let it be to the heart. I am to enclose the first fruits of my muse, ' To a Blackbird.' It has no poetic merit ; but it bespeaks a sweet feminine mind—such a one as I wish mine to be ; but my vivacity deprives me of that softness which is, in my opinion, the first female ornament. It was written to soothe an aching heart. I then laboured under a cruel anguish of soul, which I cannot tell you of. If I ever take a walk to the Temple of H[ymen], I 'll disclose it ; but you and I (were it even possible) would ' fall out by the way.' The lines on the Soldier were occasioned by reading a book entitled the *Sorrows of the Heart*. Miss Nimmo was pleased with them, and sent them to the gentleman. They are not poetry, but they speak what I felt at a survey of so much filial tenderness.

I agree with you in liking quotations. If they are apt, they often give one's ideas more pleasantly than our own language can at all times. I am stupid to-night. I have a soreness at my heart. I conclude, therefore, with a verse of Goldsmith, which, of late, has become an immense favourite of mine :—

> In Nature's simplest habit clad,
>   No wealth nor power had he ;
> Genius and worth were all he had,
>   But these were all to me.

Good night, 'my dear Sylvander ;' say this (like Werter *) to yourself. Your   CLARINDA.

Sunday Evening.

I would have given much, Sylvander, that you had heard Mr Kemp†
this afternoon. You would have heard my principles, and the foundation of all my immortal hopes, elegantly delivered. 'Let me live the
life of the righteous, and my latter end be like his' was the text. Who
are the righteous? 'Those,' says Sylvander, 'whose minds are actuated
and governed by purity, truth, and charity.' But where does such a
mind exist? It must be where the 'soul is made perfect,' for I know
none such on earth. 'The righteous,' then, must mean those who believe
in Christ, and rely on his perfect righteous for their salvation. 'Everlasting' life, as you observe, it is in the power of all to embrace ; and
this is eternal life, to 'believe in Him whom God hath sent.' Purity,
truth, and charity will flow from this belief, as naturally as the stream
from the fountain. These are, indeed, the only evidences we can have of
the reality of our faith ; and they must be produced in a degree ere we
can be fit for the enjoyment of Heaven. But where is the man who dare
plead these before 'Infinite Holiness?' Will Inflexible Justice pardon
our thousand violations of his laws? Will our imperfect repentance and
amendments atone for past guilt? or will we presume to present our
best services (spotted as they are) as worthy of acceptance before
Unerring Rectitude? I am astonished how any intelligent mind, blessed
with a divine revelation, can pause a moment on the subject. 'Enter
not into judgment with me, O Lord ! in thy sight no flesh can be justified !' This must be the result of every candid mind, upon surveying
its own deserts. If God had not been pleased to reveal His own Son, as
our all-sufficient Saviour, what could we have done but cried for mercy,
without any sure hope of obtaining it? But when we have Him clearly
announced as our surety, our guide, our blessed advocate with the
Father, who, in their senses, ought to hesitate, in putting their souls
into the hands of this glorious 'Prince of Peace?' Without this, we

---

* Allusion is here made to Goethe's *Die Leiden des Jungen Werther*, which was finished in
1774, and which, giving in its fascinating form the sentimental movement of the eighteenth
century, doubtless appealed to the heart and imagination of Clarinda.

† John Kemp (born *circa* 1744) had been translated from Trinity Gask to the Tolbooth
(Edinburgh) in 1779. This he held till his death in 1805. He was three times married, the
second and third times to titled ladies.

may admire the Creator in his works, but we can never approach him with the confidential tenderness of children. 'I will arise, and go to my father.' This is the blessed language of every one who believes and trusts in Jesus. Oh, Sylvander, who would go on fighting with themselves, resolving and resolving, while they can thus fly to their Father's house? But, alas! it is not till we tire of these husks of our own, that we recollect that *there* there is bread enough, and to spare. Whenever the wish is sincerely formed in our hearts, our Heavenly Father will have compassion upon us—'though a great way off.' This is the 'religion of the bosom.' I BELIEVE that there will be many of every sect, nation, and people, who will 'stand before the throne;' but I believe that it will be the effect of Christ's atonement, conveyed to them by ways too complicated for our finite minds to comprehend. But why should we, who know 'the way, the truth, and the life,' deprive ourselves of the comfort it is fitted to yield? Let my earnest wish for your eternal, as well as temporal happiness, excuse the warmth with which I have unfolded what has been my own fixed point of rest. I want no controversy —I hate it; let our only strivings be, who shall be the most constant and attached friend, — which of us shall render our conduct most approved to the other. I am well aware how vain it were (vain in every sense of the expression) to hope to sway a mind so intelligent as yours, by any arguments I could devise. May that God, who spoke worlds into existence, open your eyes to see 'the truth, as it is in Jesus!' Forgive me, Sylvander, if I've been tedious upon my favourite theme. You know who it was who could not stop when his divinity came across him. Even there you see we are congenial.

I'll tell you a pretty apt quotation I made to-day, warm from my heart. I met the Judges in the morning, as I went into the Parliament Square, among whom was Lord Dreghorn, in his new robes of purple. He is my mother's cousin-german, the greatest real honour he could ever claim; but used me in a manner unfeeling, harsh beyond description, at one of the darkest periods of my chequered life. I looked steadfastly in his sour face; his eye met mine. I was a female, and therefore he stared; but, when he knew who it was, he averted his eyes suddenly. Instantaneously these lines darted into my mind:

> Would you the purple should your limbs adorn,
> Go wash the conscious blemish with a tear.

The man who enjoys more pleasure in the mercenary embrace of a courtezan than in relieving the unfortunate, is a detestable character, whatever his bright talents may be.

I pity him! Sylvander, all his fortune could not purchase half the luxury of Friday night! Let us be grateful to Heaven, though it has denied us wealth and power, for being endued with feelings fitted to yield the most exquisite enjoyments here and hereafter! May I hope you'll read what I have urged on religion with attention, Sylvander! when Reason resumes her reign? I've none of these future delusive hopes, which you too vainly express as having towards Clarinda. Do not indulge them; my wishes extend to your immortal welfare. Let your first care be to please God: for that which He delights in must be happiness. I must conclude, or I'll relapse. I have not a grain of humour to-night in my composition; so, lest 'charming Clarinda' should make you yawn, she'll decently say good night! I laugh to myself at the recollection of your earnest asservations as to your being anti-Platonic! Want of passions is not merit: strong ones, under the control of reason and religion—let these be our glory. Once more good night.   CLARINDA.

The 'first fruits of my muse' which Clarinda sent with her letter were, besides (lost) *Lines on the Soldier* referred to, verses

TO A BLACKBIRD SINGING ON A TREE.*

Go on, sweet bird, and soothe my care,
Thy cheerful notes will hush despair;
Thy tuneful warblings, void of art,
Thrill sweetly through my aching heart.
Now choose thy mate and fondly love,
And all the charming transport prove;
Those sweet emotions all enjoy,
Let Love and Song thy hours employ;
Whilst I, a love-lorn exile, live,
And rapture nor receive nor give.
Go on, sweet bird, and soothe my care,
Thy cheerful notes will hush despair.

SYLVANDER TO CLARINDA.

Sunday Night [January 20th].

The impertinence of fools has joined with a return of an old indisposition to make me good for nothing to-day. The paper has lain before me all this evening to write to my dear Clarinda; but

Fools rush'd on fools, as waves succeed to waves.

I cursed them in my soul: they sacrilegiously disturb my meditations on her who holds my heart. What a creature is man! A little alarm last night and to-day that I am mortal, has made such a revolution in my spirits! There is no philosophy, no divinity, comes half so home to the mind. I have no idea of courage that braves Heaven. 'Tis the wild ravings of an imaginary hero in Bedlam. I can no more, Clarinda; I can scarce hold up my head; but I am happy you don't know it, you would be so uneasy.   SYLVANDER.

* 'To a Blackbird;' by a Lady—is Song 190 in the *Scots Musical Museum* (vol. ii.). Its insertion was due to Burns, who had improved it.

I am, my lovely friend, much better this morning, on the whole; but I have a horrid languor on my spirits.

> Sick of the world and all its joy,
> My soul in pining sadness mourns;
> Dark scenes of woe my mind employ,
> The past and present in their turns.

Have you ever met with a saying of the great and likewise good Mr Locke, author of the famous *Essay on the Human Understanding?* He wrote a letter to a friend, directing it 'Not to be delivered till after my decease.' It ended thus,—'I know you loved me when living, and will preserve my memory now I am dead. All the use to be made of it is, that this life affords no solid satisfaction, but in the consciousness of having done well, and the hopes of another life. Adieu! I leave my best wishes with you.—J. LOCKE.'*

Clarinda, may I reckon on your friendship for life? I think I may. Thou Almighty Preserver of men! Thy friendship, which hitherto I have too much neglected, to secure it shall, all the future days and nights of my life, be my steady care. The idea of my Clarinda follows:—

> Hide it, my heart, within that close disguise,
> Where, mix'd with God's, her loved idea lies.

But I fear inconstancy, the consequent imperfection of human weakness. Shall I meet with a friendship that defies years of absence and the chances and changes of fortune? Perhaps 'such things are.' *One* honest man I have great hopes from, that way; but who, except a romance writer, would think on a *love* that could promise for life, in spite of distance, absence, chance, and change, and that, too, with slender hopes of fruition?

For my own part, I can say to myself in both requisitions—'Thou art the man!' I dare, in cool resolve, I dare declare myself that friend and that lover. If womankind is capable of such things, Clarinda is. I trust that she is; and feel I shall be miserable if she is not. There is not one virtue which gives worth, or one sentiment which does honour to the sex, that she does not possess superior to any woman I ever saw: her exalted mind, aided a little, perhaps, by her situation, is, I think, capable of that nobly-romantic love-enthusiasm. May I see you on Wednesday evening, my dear angel? The next Wednesday again, will, I conjecture, be a hated day to us both. I tremble for censorious remarks, for your sake; but in extraordinary cases, may not usual and useful precautions be a little dispensed with? Three evenings, three swift-winged evenings, with pinions of down, are all the past—I dare not calculate the future. I shall call at Miss Nimmo's to-morrow evening; 'twill be a farewell call.

---

* Almost verbatim from Locke's last letter to his friend and executor, Antony Collins the Deist. See Fox Bourne's *Life of John Locke*, vol. ii., p. 550.

I have written out my last sheet of paper, so I am reduced to my last half sheet. What a strange, mysterious faculty is that thing called imagination! We have no ideas almost at all, of another world; but I have often amused myself with visionary schemes of what happiness might be enjoyed by small alterations, alterations that we can fully enter to in this present state of existence. For instance: suppose you and I just as we are at present; the same reasoning powers, sentiments, and even desires; the same fond curiosity for knowledge and remarking observation in our minds; and imagine our bodies free from pain, and the necessary supplies for the wants of nature at all times and easily within our reach. Imagine further, that we were set free from the laws of gravitation, which bind us to this globe, and could at pleasure fly, without inconvenience, through all the yet unconjectured bounds of creation; what a life of bliss should we lead in our mutual pursuit of virtue and knowledge, and our mutual enjoyment of friendship and love!

I see you laughing at my fairy fancies, and calling me a voluptuous Mahometan; but I am certain I should be a happy creature, beyond anything we call bliss here below; nay, it would be a paradise congenial to you too. Don't you see us hand in hand, or rather my arm about your lovely waist, making our remarks on Sirius, the nearest of the fixed stars; or surveying a comet flaming innoxious by us, as we just now would mark the passing pomp of a travelling monarch; or, in a shady bower of Mercury or Venus, dedicating the hour to love, in mutual converse, relying honour, and revelling endearment, while the most exalted strains of poesy and harmony would be the ready, spontaneous language of our souls! Devotion is the favourite employment of your heart; so is it of mine: what incentives then to, and powers for, reverence, gratitude, faith, and hope, in all the fervour of adoration and praise to that Being whose unsearchable wisdom, power, and goodness, so pervaded, so inspired, every sense and feeling! By this time, I daresay, you will be blessing the neglect of the maid that leaves me destitute of paper.

SYLVANDER.

SYLVANDER TO CLARINDA.

[Monday, 21st Jany.]

*   *   *   I am a discontented ghost, a perturbed spirit. Clarinda, if ever you forget Sylvander, may you be happy, but he will be miserable.

O, what a fool I am in love!—what an extravagant prodigal of affection! Why are your sex called the tender sex, when I never have met with one who can repay me in passion? They are either not so rich in love as I am, or they are niggards where I am lavish.

O Thou whose I am and whose are all my ways! Thou see'st me here, the hapless wreck of tides and tempests in my own bosom: do Thou direct to thyself that ardent love, for which I have so often sought a return, in vain, from my fellow-creatures! If Thy goodness has yet such a gift in store for me, as an equal return of affection from her who, Thou knowest, is dearer to me than life, do Thou bless and hallow our band of love and friendship ; watch over us, in all our outgoings and incomings, for good ; and may the tie that unites our hearts be strong and indissoluble as the thread of man's immortal life !

I am just going to take your Blackbird,* the sweetest, I am sure, that ever sung, and prune its wings a little. SYLVANDER.

During this month he was endeavouring to bring his publisher, Creech, to a settlement of accounts. His sufferings under the uncertainty as to his prospects, his painful accident, and a return of his nervous ailment brought him once more to the lowest depth of depression. In that depression he wrote

TO MISS CHALMERS.

[*Tuesday, 22d Jan.* 1788.]

. . . Now for that wayward, unfortunate thing, myself. I have broke measures with Creech, and last week I wrote him a frosty, keen letter. He replied in terms of chastisement, and promised me upon his honor that I should have the account on Monday ; but this is Tuesday, and yet I have not heard a word from him. God have mercy on me ! a poor, damned, incautious, duped, unfortunate fool ! The sport, the miserable victim, of rebellious pride, hypochondriac imagination, agonizing sensibility, and bedlam passions !

'*I wish that I were dead, but I'm no like to die!*' I had lately 'a hairbreadth 'scape, in th' imminent deadly breach' of love too. Thank my stars I got off heart-whole, 'waur-fley'd [worse frightened] than hurt.'—*Interruption.*

I have this moment got a hint. . . . I fear I am something like—undone—but I hope for the best. Come, stubborn pride and unshrinking resolution ! accompany me through this, to me, miserable world ! You must not desert me ! Your friendship I think I can count on, though I should date my letters from a marching regiment. Early in life, and all my life, I reckoned on a recruiting drum as my forlorn hope. Seriously though, life at present presents me with but a melancholy path : but —my limb will soon be sound, and I shall struggle on. R. B.

TO THE EARL OF GLENCAIRN, BARNTOWN.

[EDIN., *Jan.* 1788.]

MY LORD—I know your Lordship will disapprove of my ideas in a request I am going to make to you ; but I have weighed my situation, my hopes, and turn of mind, and am fully fixed to my scheme, if I can possibly effectuate it. I wish to get into the Excise. I am told that your

* Clarinda's song, 'To a Blackbird.'

Lordship's interest will easily procure me the grant from the Commissioners ; and your Lordship's patronage and goodness, which have already rescued me from obscurity, wretchedness and exile, embolden me to ask that interest. You have put it in my power to save the little home that sheltered an aged mother, two brothers, and three sisters, from destruction.

My brother's lease is but a wretched one, though I think he will probably weather out the remaining seven years of it. After what I have given and will give him as a small farming capital to keep the family together, I guess my remaining all will be about two hundred pounds. Instead of beggaring myself with a small, dear farm, I will lodge my little stock, a sacred deposit, in a banking-house. Extraordinary distress, or helpless old age, have often harrowed my soul with fear ; and I have one or two claims on me in the name of father. I will stoop to anything that honesty warrants to have it in my power to leave them some better remembrance of me than the odium of illegitimacy.

These, my Lord, are my views. I have resolved on the maturest deliberation ; and, now I am fixed, I shall leave no stone unturned to carry my resolve into execution. Your Lordship's patronage is by far the strength of my hopes ; nor have I yet applied to anybody else. Indeed, I know not how to apply to anybody else. I am ill qualified to dog the heels of greatness with the impertinence of solicitation, and tremble nearly as much at the idea of the cold promise as the cold denial ; but to your Lordship I have not only the honor and the happiness, but the pleasure, of being, my Lord, your Lordship's much obliged and deeply indebted humble servant, ROBT. BURNS.

P.S.—I have enclosed your Lordship ' Holy Willie,' and will wait on you the beginning of next week, as against then I hope to have settled my business with Mr Creech.

TO MRS DUNLOP.

EDINBURGH, 21*st January* 1788.

After six weeks' confinement, I am beginning to walk across the room. They have been six horrible weeks ; anguish and low spirits made me unfit to read, write, or think.

I have a hundred times wished that one could resign life as an officer resigns a commission : for I would not *take in* any poor, ignorant wretch, by *selling out*. Lately I was a sixpenny private ; and, God knows, a miserable soldier enough ; now I march to the campaign, a starving cadet : a little more conspicuously wretched.

I am ashamed of all this ; for though I do want bravery for the warfare of life, I could wish, like some other soldiers, to have as much fortitude or cunning as to dissemble or conceal my cowardice.

As soon as I can bear the journey, which will be, I suppose, about the middle of next week, I leave Edinburgh, and soon after I shall pay my grateful duty at Dunlop-house. R. B.

The allusions in the letter to Margaret Chalmers are said by Allan Cunningham to refer to whispers which had reached his ear about the solvency of Creech. As far as can be now ascertained, such rumours had no foundation.* But it may well be supposed that, having no exact knowledge of the facts, and tantalised by the apparently unreasonable delay of a settlement, Burns would receive the 'hint' as something like the knell of doom. Another vexation of this period arose from circumstances of a different nature. The consequences of his renewed intimacy with Jean Armour could not be concealed any longer. Her father became aware of her condition, and would not allow her to remain under his roof. In Burns's phrase: 'she was turned, literally turned, out of doors.' Such were the extraordinary circumstances under which he conducted his correspondence with Clarinda.

If Burns had had reason to believe himself married to Jean, to have regarded any of the women whom he speaks of as possible objects of his addresses during his residence in Edinburgh, would of course have been sheer blackguardism. There would have been scarcely less guilt in allowing Mrs M'Lehose to entertain even her faint hopes, dependent as they were upon a remote contingency. But Burns had every reason to believe himself at this time free from what he termed 'nuptial bonds.' He had gone through a humiliating process at Mauchline to ensure for Jean that liberation which she and her friends desired. Ecclesiastical authority had assured him of his bachelorhood. Jean would, to all appearance, have been the last to think that, even after her second pregnancy, she had the claims of a wife upon Burns. It is possible that all concerned were under a mistake as to the effect of the proceedings of April 1786, by which it was supposed that the private marriage of Burns and Jean was

* An Edinburgh bookseller, who for a time was in Creech's employment, supplied Dr Robert Chambers with these memoranda as to his habits: 'My friend, Mr Creech, was rather a tardy man of business, and paid little attention to it. Previous to my becoming his clerk, he had my friend, Mr Robert Miller, and several other respectable young men, to take care of his business. Being so much occupied with literary people, he seldom handled his own money. His clerk balanced the cash every night, and carried on that to next day. He had a levée in his house till twelve every day, attended by literary men and printers. Between twelve and one he came to the shop, where the same flow of company lasted till four, and then he left us, and we saw no more of him till next day. He was a very good-natured man, and was never known to prosecute any one for a debt. Mr Robert Miller, here mentioned, was the publisher of the first work of Scott—his translation of Bürger's Ballads. He sang several of Burns's songs with a felicity only to be equalled by that with which he recited some of Mr Creech's stories.'

annulled. But the present question is as to the *bona fides* of Burns in the view he took of his separation from his mistress. The whole series of facts shows him absolved from his marriage tie, not merely with the consent, but at the express and urgent instance, of the persons most concerned. It would appear, indeed, that before the 3d of March 1788 Burns had found reason to fear that he might after all be liable, in the event of a second marriage, to trouble on account of Jean Armour, if she or any other person should feel interested in bringing evidence against him for the establishment of previous nuptials. But we are not yet come to that period. We are considering Burns's presumable belief during 1787; and it is enough that no evidence exists to show that he had then any reason for apprehension on the subject, or for regarding himself otherwise than as a man free to give his hand to whomsoever he chose.

The pressing question for Burns at this time, however, was not so much how he was to live righteously, as how he was to live at all. He himself thought of a return to his original profession; but the period immediately following the close of the colonial war was a bad time for farming in Britain. Nor could he expect much at the hands of the dominant party of the day, or of Henry Dundas, who in reality governed Scotland. On the contrary, he had, with characteristic fearlessness, ranged himself on the side of Fox. He had given offence to the more frantic partisans of the Hanoverian monarchy by his unpublished but not unknown lines on the Stirling window. Could Burns hope without any preliminary training to succeed in any kind of commercial career? Need the question be answered? Could he, at nine-and-twenty, commence a course of education for any of the learned professions? Scarcely, with a reasonable prospect of success. Was it possible for him to make a livelihood as a man of letters? Such a feat was not a common one in those days, and probably the idea of attempting it never once occurred to him or to any of his friends. It was most desirable that some kind of official position should be procured for Burns; but what appointment of that nature could be at once obtained? It may be doubted if any post was readily available, except that of an exciseman.

After all, it is creditable to Burns that he took no high-flown views of his situation and pretensions, and was willing, with a

view to preserving his independence, to subdue himself to uncongenial drudgery, since it appeared that no better course was
open to him. The idea was not new to his mind. It had been
suggested in the autumn of 1786, when he contemplated exile to
the West Indies. It was at this time, at all events, that Burns's
wishes regarding the Excise were gratified to the extent of his being
assured of an appointment, or enrolled on the list of expectant
officers. According to tradition, he was immediately indebted for
this favour to the surgeon who attended him when confined to his
room with a bruised limb. Alexander Wood, usually called, on
account of his lanky figure, Lang Sandy Wood, was a man greatly
to Burns's liking—warm-hearted and generous. Wood no sooner
became aware of the wishes of his patient, whose genius he greatly
admired, than he exerted himself in recommending him to the
Commissioners of Excise, and the enrolment followed.

TO ROBERT GRAHAM, ESQ. OF FINTRY.

[EDINBURGH, *January* 1788.]

SIR—When I had the honour of being introduced to you at Athole-
house, I did not think so soon of asking a favour of you. When Lear, in
Shakespear, asks old Kent why he wished to be in his service, he
answers, ‘Because you have that in your face which I could like to call
master.’ For some such reason, Sir, do I now solicit your patronage.
You know, I dare say, of an application I lately made to your Board
to be admitted an officer of excise. I have according to form been
examined by a supervisor, and to-day I gave in his certificate with a
request for an order for instructions. In this affair, if I succeed, I am
afraid I shall but too much need a patronizing friend. Propriety of
conduct as a man, and fidelity and attention as an officer, I dare engage
for; but with any thing like business, except manual labor, I am totally
unacquainted. . . .

I had intended to have closed my late appearance on the stage of life,
in the character of a country farmer; but after discharging some filial
and fraternal claims, I find I could only fight for existence in that miserable manner which I have lived to see throw a venerable parent into the
jaws of a jail; whence death, the poor man's last and often best friend,
rescued him.

I know, Sir, that to need your goodness, is to have a claim on it: may
I therefore beg your patronage to forward me in this affair, 'till I be
appointed to a division, where, by the help of rigid economy, I will try
to support that independence so dear to my soul, but which has been too
often so distant from my situation.   R. B.

The letter says *nothing* about an interview. Another interview (the fourth) between Sylvander and Clarinda had taken place on the night which we set down conjecturally as that of Wednesday, the 23d January, being the second last Wednesday which he expected to spend in Edinburgh on the present occasion. At this meeting, it would appear, the communications of the pair had been of a more unreserved kind than heretofore. Each wrote a letter to the other next day.

SYLVANDER TO CLARINDA.

Thursday Morning [*Jan.* 24.]

Unlavish Wisdom never works in vain.

I have been tasking my reason, Clarinda, why a woman, who, for native genius, poignant wit, strength of mind, generous sincerity of soul, and the sweetest female tenderness, is without a peer; and whose personal charms have few, very few, parallels among her sex; why, or how, she should fall to the blessed lot of a poor harum-scarum poet, whom Fortune had kept for her particular use to wreak her temper on, whenever she was in ill-humour.

One time I conjectured that, as Fortune is the most capricious jade ever known, she may have taken, not a fit of remorse, but a paroxysm of whim, to raise the poor devil out of the mire where he had so often, and so conveniently, served her as a stepping-stone, and given him the most glorious boon she ever had in her gift, merely for the maggot's sake, to see how his fool head and his fool heart will bear it.

At other times, I was vain enough to think that Nature, who has a great deal to say with Fortune, had given the coquettish goddess some such hint as—'Here is a paragon of female excellence, whose equal, in all my former compositions, I never was lucky enough to hit on, and despair of ever doing so again : you have cast her rather in the shades of life. There is a certain poet of my making : among your frolics, it would not be amiss to attach him to this masterpiece of my hand, to give her that immortality among mankind, which no woman of any age ever more deserved, and which few rhymesters of this age are better able to confer.

Evening, Nine o'clock.

I am here—absolutely unfit to finish my letter—pretty hearty, after a bowl which has been constantly plied since dinner till this moment. I have been with Mr Schetki,* the musician, and he has set the song finely.

---

* Johann George Christoff Schetky was born at Darmstadt in 1740. He was intended for the law, but became devoted to music, studied under Filtz, and became violoncellist at the court of Hesse. In 1773, having been engaged for the St Cecilia concerts in Edinburgh, he settled as a teacher of music there. He died in 1824. One of his sons, John Christian Schetky, attained eminence as a painter.

I have no distinct ideas of anything but that I have drunk your health twice to-night, and that you are all my soul holds dear in this world.

SYLVANDER.

The song referred to was

A FAREWELL TO CLARINDA

ON LEAVING EDINBURGH.

Clarinda, mistress of my soul,
   The measured time is run!
The wretch beneath the dreary pole
   So marks his latest sun.

To what dark cave of frozen night
   Shall poor Sylvander hie,
Deprived of thee, his life and light—
   The sun of all his joy?

We part—but by those precious drops
   That fill thy lovely eyes!
No other light shall guide my steps
   Till thy bright beams arise.

She, the fair sun of all her sex,
   Has blest my glorious day;
And shall a glimmering planet fix
   My worship to its ray?

CLARINDA TO SYLVANDER.

Thursday Forenoon [*January* 24th.]

Sylvander, the moment I waked this morning, I received a summons from Conscience to appear at the Bar of Reason. While I trembled before this sacred throne, I beheld a succession of figures pass before me in awful brightness! Religion, clad in a robe of light, stalked majestically along, her hair dishevelled, and in her hand the Scriptures of Truth held open at these words—'If you love me, keep my commandments.' Reputation followed: her eyes darted indignation, while she waved a beautiful wreath of laurel, intermixed with flowers, gathered by Modesty in the Bower of Peace. Consideration held her bright mirror close to my

eyes, and made me start at my own image! Love alone appeared as counsel in my behalf. She was adorned with a veil, borrowed from Friendship, which hid her defects, and set off her beauties to advantage. She had no plea to offer but that of being the sister of Friendship and the offspring of Charity. But Reason refused to listen to her defence, because she brought no certificate from the Temple of Hymen! While I trembled before her, Reason addressed me in the following manner:—
'Return to my paths, which alone are peace; shut your heart against the fascinating intrusion of the passions; take Consideration for your guide, and you will soon arrive at the Bower of Tranquillity.'

Sylvander, to drop my metaphor, I am neither well nor happy to-day: my heart reproaches me for last night. If you wish Clarinda to regain her peace, determine against everything but what the strictest delicacy warrants.

I do not blame you, but myself. I must not see you on Saturday, unless I find I can depend on myself acting otherwise. Delicacy, you know, it was which won me to you at once: take care you do not loosen the dearest, most sacred tie that unites us? Remember Clarinda's present and eternal happiness depends upon her adherence to Virtue. Happy Sylvander! that can be attached to Heaven and Clarinda together. Alas! I feel I cannot serve two masters. God pity me!!

Thursday Night.

Why have I not heard from you, Sylvander? Everything in nature seems tinged with gloom to-day. Ah! Sylvander—

> The heart's ay the part ay
> That makes us right or wrang!

How forcibly have these lines recurred to my thoughts! Did I not tell you what a wretch love rendered me? Affection to the strongest height, I am capable of, to a man of my Sylvander's merit—if it did not lead me into weaknesses and follies my heart utterly condemns. I am convinced, without the approbation of Heaven and my own mind, existence would be to me a heavy curse. Sylvander, why do not your Clarinda's repeated levities cure the too passionate fondness you express for her? Perhaps it has a little removed esteem. But I dare not touch this string—it would fill up the cup of my present misery. Oh, Sylvander, may the friendship of that God you and I have too much neglected to secure, be henceforth our chief study and delight. I cannot live deprived of the consciousness of His favour. I feel something of this awful state all this day. Nay, while I approached God with my lips, my heart was not fully there.

Mr Locke's posthumous letter ought to be written in letters of gold. What heartfelt joy does the consciousness of having done well in any one instance confer; and what agony the reverse! Do not be displeased when I tell you I wish our parting was over. At a distance we shall retain the same heartfelt affection and interestedness in each other's

concerns ;—but absence will mellow and restrain those violent heart-
agitations which, if continued much longer, would unhinge my very soul,
and render me unfit for the duties of life. You and I are capable of that
ardency of love, for which the wide creation cannot afford an adequate
object. Let us seek to repose it in the bosom of our God. Let us next
give a place to those dearest on earth—the tender charities of parent,
sister, child! I bid you good night with this short prayer of Thomson's :—

> Father of Light and Life, thou good Supreme!
> Oh teach us what is good—teach us Thyself!
> Save us from Folly, Vanity, and Vice, &c.

Your letter—I should have liked had it contained a little of the last
one's seriousness. Bless me! You must not flatter so; but it's in a
'merry mood,' and I make allowances. Part of some of your encomiums
I know I deserve; but you are far out when you enumerate 'strength of
mind' among them. I have not even an ordinary share of it—every
passion does what it will with me; and all my life, I have been guided
by the impulse of the moment—unsteady, and weak! I thank you for
the letter, though it sticket my prayer. Why did you tell me you drank
away Reason, 'that Heaven-lighted lamp in man?' When Sylvander
utters a calm, sober sentiment, he is never half so charming.* I have
read several of these in your last letter with vast pleasure. Good night!

Friday Morning.

My servant (who is a good soul) will deliver you this. She is going
down to Leith, and will return about two or three o'clock. I have
ordered her to call then, in case you have ought to say to Clarinda to-day.
I am better of that sickness at my heart I had yesterday; but there's a
sting remains which will not be removed till I am at peace with Heaven
and myself. Another interview, spent as we ought, will help to procure
this. A day when the sun shines gloriously always makes me devout!
I hope 'tis an earnest (to-day) of being soon restored to the 'light of His
countenance' who is the source of love and standard of perfection. Adieu!
                                                                CLARINDA.

SYLVANDER TO CLARINDA.†

[*January* 25.]

Clarinda, my life, you have wounded my soul. Can I think of your
being unhappy, even tho' it be not described in your pathetic elegance
of language, without being miserable? Clarinda, can I bear to be told
from you, that 'you will not see me tomorrow night—that you wish
the hour of parting were come?' Do not let us impose on ourselves by

---

* Clarinda's agitation here proved fatal to her 'correct style.' She says exactly the
opposite of what she meant.

† The original of this letter is now in the Watson collection in the National Portrait
Gallery, Edinburgh.

sounds: if in the moment of fond endearment and tender dalliance, I perhaps trespassed against the *letter* of Decorum's law, I appeal, even to you, whether I ever sinned in the very least degree against the *spirit* of her strictest statute. But why, My Love, talk to me in such strong terms; every word of which cuts me to the very soul? You know, a hint, the slightest signification of your wish, is to me a sacred command. Be reconciled, My Angel, to your God, your self, and me; and I pledge you *Sylvander's honor*, an oath, I dare say, you will trust without reserve, that you shall never more have reason to complain of his conduct. Now, my Love, do not wound our next meeting with any averted looks or restrained caresses: I have marked the line of conduct, a line, I know exactly to your taste, and which I will inviolably keep; but do not *you* show the least inclination to make boundaries: seeming distrust, where you know you may confide, is a cruel sin against sensibility.

'Delicacy, you know it, was what won me to you at once—*take care* you do not loosen the dearest, most sacred tie that unites us.' Clarinda, I would not have stung *your* soul—I would not have bruised *your* spirit, as that harsh crucifying 'Take care' did *mine;* no, not to have gained heaven! Let me again appeal to your dear Self, if Sylvander, even when he seemingly half-transgressed the laws of Decorum, if he did not shew more chastened trembling, faltering delicacy, than the Many of the world do in keeping these laws.

O Love and Sensibility, ye have conspired against My Peace! I love to madness, and I feel to torture! Clarinda, how can I forgive myself, that I ever have touched a single chord in your bosom with pain! would I do it willingly? Would any consideration, any gratification, make me do so? O, did you love like me, you would not, you could not, deny or put off a meeting with the Man who adores you; who would die a thousand deaths before he would injure you; and who must soon bid you a long farewell!

I had proposed bringing my bosom friend, Mr Ainslie, tomorrow evening, at his strong request, to see you; as he only has time to stay with us about ten minutes, for an engagement; but—I shall hear from you: this afternoon, for mercy's sake! for till I hear from you, I am wretched. O Clarinda, the tie that binds me to thee is entwisted, incorporated, with my dearest threads of life! SYLVANDER.

Another interview took place on January 25th, and yet another, Ainslie being present, on the following day.

SYLVANDER TO CLARINDA.

[*January 26th.*]

I was on the way, my *Love,* to meet you, (I never do things by halves,) when I got your card. Mr Ainslie goes out of town to-morrow morning, to see a brother of his who is newly arrived from France. I am determined that he and I shall call on you together. So, look you, lest I should never see to-morrow, we will call on you to-night. Mary * and you may put off tea till about seven, at which time, in the Galloway phrase, 'an' the beast be to the fore, and the branks bide hale,'† expect the humblest of your humble servants, and his dearest friend. We only propose staying half an hour—'for ought we ken.' I could suffer the lash of misery eleven months in the year, were the twelfth to be composed of hours like yesternight. You are the soul of my enjoyment; all else is of the stuff of stocks and stones.   SYLVANDER.

SYLVANDER TO CLARINDA.

Sunday, Noon [Jan. 27th.]

I have almost given up the Excise idea. I have been just now to wait on a great person, Miss ——'s friend, ——. Why will great people not only deafen us with the din of their equipage, and dazzle us with their fastidious pomp, but they must also be so very dictatorially wise? I have been questioned like a child about my matters, and blamed and schooled for my Inscription on Stirling window. Come, Clarinda!—'Come, curse me, Jacob; come, defy me, Israel!'

Sunday Night.

I have been with Miss Nimmo. She is, indeed, 'a good soul,' as my Clarinda finely says. She has reconciled me, in a good measure, to the world with her friendly prattle.

Schetki has sent me the song, set to a fine air of his composing. I have called the song 'Clarinda;'‡ I have carried it about in my pocket and thumbed§ it over all day. I trust you have spent a pleasant day, and that no idea or recollection of me gives you pain.

Monday Morning.

If my prayers have any weight in heaven, this morning looks in on you and finds you in the arms of peace, except where it is charmingly interrupted by the ardours of devotion. I find so much serenity of mind, so much positive pleasure, so much fearless daring toward the world, when I warm in devotion, or feel the glorious sensation—a consciousness of Almighty friendship—that I am sure I shall soon be an honest enthusiast.

> How are thy servants blest, O Lord!
> How sure is their defence!
> Eternal wisdom is their guide,
> Their help Omnipotence.

I am, my dear Madam, yours,   [SYLVANDER.]

---

* Mary Peacock.

† That is, if the horse is still in life, and the bridle bears the strain.

‡ The song given on p. 270. It appeared in vol. ii. of the *Scots Musical Museum*, under the title 'Clarinda.'

§ So in MS.: 'hummed' is usually given.

CLARINDA TO SYLVANDER.

Sunday 8 Ev. [27th Jan.]

Sylvander, when I think of you as my *dearest* and most attached *friend*, I am highly pleased; but when you come across my mind as my *lover*, something within gives a *sting* resembling that of guilt! Tell me why is this? It must be from the idea that I am another's. What! another's wife! O cruel Fate! I am indeed bound in an 'iron chain!' Forgive me, if this should give you pain. You know I must (I told you I *must*) tell you my genuine feelings, or be silent. Last night we were happy! beyond what the bulk of mankind can conceive! Perhaps the 'line' you had mark'd was a *little* infringed—it was really; but, tho' I *disapprove*, I have not been *unhappy* about it. I am convinced no less of your *discernment* than of your *wish* to make your Clarinda happy. I know you *sincere*, when you profess horror at the idea of what would render her miserable forever. But we must *guard* against going to the *verge* of danger. Ah! my friend, much need had we to 'watch and pray!' May these benevolent spirits whose office it is to 'save the fall of Virtue struggling on the brink of vice' be ever present to protect and guide us in right paths!

I had an hour's conversation to-day with my worthy friend Mr Kemp. You'll attribute, perhaps, to *this*, the above sentiments. 'Tis true, there's not one on earth has so much influence on me, except Sylvander; *partly* it has forced me 'to feel along the mental intelligence.' However, I've broke the ice. I confessed I had conceived a tender impression of late—that it was mutual, and that I had wish'd to unbosom myself to him (as I did), particularly to ask if he thought I should, or not, mention it to my *friend?* * I saw he felt for me (for I was in tears); but he bewail'd that I had given my *heart*, while in my present state of bondage—wish'd I had made it friendship *only*—in short, talk'd to me in the style of a tender Parent, *anxious* for my happiness. He disapproves altogether of my saying a syllable of the matter to my friend; says it could only make him uneasy; and that I'm in no way bound to do it by any one tie. This has eased me of a *load* which has lain upon my mind ever since our intimacy. Sylvander, I wish you and Mr Kemp were acquainted—such worth and sensibility! If you had his piety and sobriety of manners, united to the shining abilities you possess! you'd be 'a faultless monster which the world ne'er saw.' He too has great talents. His imagination is rich, his feelings delicate, his discernment acute; yet there are *shades* in his, as in all characters: but these it would ill become Clarinda to point out. Alas! I know too many blots in my own!

Sylvander, I believe nothing were a more impracticable task than to make you feel a little of genuine Gospel *humility!* Believe me, I wish not

* Lord Craig, her cousin.

to see you deprived of that noble fire of an exalted mind which you eminently possess. Yet a sense of your faults—a *feeling* sense of them! —were devoutly to be wish'd. Tell me, did you ever, or how oft, have you smote on your breast, and cried ' God be merciful to me a sinner?' I fancy, once or twice when suffering from the effects of your errors. Pardon me if I be hurting your 'intrinsic dignity;' it need not—even ' divine Clarinda ' has been in this *mortal* predicament.

Pray, what does Mr Ainslie think of her! was he not astonished to find her merely human? Three weeks ago, I suppose you would have walked into her presence *unshod ;* but one must *bury* even divinities when they discover symptoms of mortality! (Let *these* be interred in Sylvander's bosom!)

My dearest friend, there are two wishes uppermost in my heart ; to see you think alike with Clarinda on religion ; and to see you settled in some creditable line of business. The warm interest I take in both these is perhaps the best proof of the sincerity of my friendship, as well as the earnest of its duration. As to the first, I devolve it over into the hands of the Omniscient! May He raise up friends who will effectuate the other! While I breathe these fervent wishes, think not that any-thing but pure *disinterested* regard prompts them. They 're fond, but chimerical ideas. They are never indulged but in the hour of tender endearment, when

> ———— Innocence
> Looks gaily smiling on; while rosy Pleasure
> Hides young Desire amid her flowery wreath,
> And pours her cup luxuriant, mantling high
> The sparkling heavenly vintage—Love and Bliss!

'Tis past ten ; and I please myself with thinking Sylvander will be about to retire, and write to Clarinda. I fancy you 'll find this *stupid* enough ; but I can't be always bright ; the *sun* will be *sometimes* under a cloud. Sylvander, I wish our kind feelings were more moderate ; why set one's heart upon *impossibilities?* Try me merely as your friend (alas! all I ought to be) ; believe me, you 'll find me most rational. If you'd caress the ' mental intelligence ' as you do the corporeal frame, indeed, Sylvander, you'd make me a philosopher. I see you fidgetting at this *violently* blasting rationality. I have a headache which brings home those things to the mind. To-morrow I 'll hear from you, I hope! This is Sunday, and not a word on our favorite subject. O fy! ' divine Clarinda.' I intend giving you *my* idea of Heaven in opposition to your heathenish description (which, by the by, was elegantly drawn). Mine shall be founded on Reason and supported by Scripture ; but it 's too late, my head aches, but my heart is affectionately yours.

Monday Morning.

I am not sorry almost at the Excise affair misgiving. You will be better out of Edin.; it is full of temptation to one of your social turn. Providence (if you be wise in future) will order something better for you. I'm half-glad you were school'd about the Inscription; 'twill be a lesson, I hope, in future. Clarinda would have lectured you on it before, 'if she durst.' Miss Nimmo is a woman after my own heart. You are reconciled to the world by her 'friendly prattle!' How can you talk so diminutively of the conversation of a woman of solid sense? what will you say of Clarinda's chit chat? I suppose you will give it a still more insignificant term, if you durst; but it is mixed with *something* that makes it more bearable, were it even weaker than it is. Miss Nimmo is right in both her conjectures. Ah, Sylvander! my peace *must* suffer; yours cannot. *You* think, in loving Clarinda, you are doing right; all Sylvander's eloquence cannot convince me that it is so! If I were but at liberty—O how I would indulge in all the luxury of *innocent* love! It is, I fear, I fear, too late to talk in this strain after indulging you and myself so much; but would Sylvander shelter his Love in Friendship's *allowed* garb, Clarinda would be much happier!

'To-morrow,' did'st thou say? The time is short *now;* is it not *too* frequent? Do not sweetest dainties cloy soonest? Take your chance— come half-past eight. If anything particular occur to render it improper *to-morrow,* I'll send you word, and name another evening. Mr Kemp is to call to-night, I believe. *He,* too, 'trembles for my peace.' Two such worthies to be interested about my foolish ladyship! The Apostle Paul, with all his rhetoric, could not reconcile me to the *great* (little souls) when I think of them and Sylvander together; but I *pity* them.

> If e'er ambition did my fancy cheat,
> With any wish so *mean,* as to be great,
> Continue, Heav'n, far from me to remove
> The humble blessings of that life I'd love.*

Till we meet, my dear Sylvander, adieu !   CLARINDA.

SYLVANDER TO CLARINDA.

Tuesday Morn [29th January].

I cannot go out to-day, my dearest Love, without sending you half a line by way of a sin offering; but, believe me, 'twas the sin of ignorance. Could you think that I intended to hurt you by anything I said yester-night? Nature has been too kind to you for your happiness, your delicacy, your sensibility. O why should such glorious qualifications be the fruitful source of wo! You have 'murdered sleep' to me last night. I went to bed impressed with an idea that you were unhappy; and every start I closed my eyes, busy Fancy painted you in such scenes of

---

* Quoted from a poem by Abraham Cowley.

romantic misery, that I would almost be persuaded you are not well this morning.

> ——If I unwitting have offended,
> Impute it not,
> ——But while we live,
> But one short hour, perhaps, between us two
> Let there be peace.*

If Mary is not gone by the time this reaches you, give her my best compliments. She is a charming girl, and highly worthy of the noblest love.

I send you a poem to read till I call on you this night, which will be about nine. I wish I could procure some potent spell, some fairy charm, that would protect from injury, or restore to rest, that bosom chord, 'tremblingly alive all o'er,' on which hangs your peace of mind. I thought, vainly, I fear, thought, that the devotion of love, love strong as even you can feel, love guarded, invulnerably guarded by all the purity of virtue, and all the pride of honour,—I thought such a love might make you happy. Shall I be mistaken? I can no more, for hurry.

SYLVANDER.

CLARINDA TO SYLVANDER.

Thursday, Twelve [31st January].

I have been giving Mary a convoy; the day is a genial one. Mary is a happy woman to-day. Mrs Cockburn† has seen her 'Henry,' and admired it vastly. She talked of you, told her she saw you, and that her lines even met your applause. Sylvander, I share in the joy of every one; and am ready to 'weep with those who weep,' as well as 'rejoice with those who rejoice.' I wish all the human race well,—my heart throbs with the large ambitious wish to see them blest; yet I seem sometimes as if born to inflict misery. What a cordial evening we had last night! I only tremble at the ardent manner Mary talks of Sylvander! She knows where his affections lie, and is quite unconscious of the eagerness of her expressions. All night I could get no sleep for her admiration. I like her for it, and am proud of it; but I know how much violent admiration is akin to love.

I go out to dinner, and mean to leave this, in case of one from you to-day. Miss Chalmers's letters are charming. Why did not such a woman secure your heart? O the caprice of human nature, to fix on impossibilities.

I am, however, happy you have such valuable friends. What a pity that those who will be most apt to feel your merit, will be probably among the number who have not the power of serving you! Sylvander,

---

* Cf. Shakespeare's *King Richard the Third*, Act II., scene i., lines 56–60.

† Mrs Alison Cockburn, the poetess. ' Henry ' was evidently the title of a poem by Miss Peacock.

I never was ambitious; but of late I have wished for wealth, with an ardour unfelt before, to be able to say 'Be independent, thou dear friend of my heart!' What exquisite joy! Then 'your head would be lifted up above your enemies.' Oh, then, what little shuffling, sneaking attentions!—shame upon the world! Wealth and power command its adulation, while real genius and worth, without these, are neglected and contemned.

> In nature's simplest habit clad,
>   No wealth nor power had he;
> Genius and worth were all he had,
>   But these were all to me.

Forgive my quoting my most favourite lines. You spoke of being here to-morrow evening. I believe you would be the first to tire of our society; but I tremble for censorious remarks: however, we must be sober in our hours. I am flat to-day—so adieu! I was not so cheerful last night as I wished. Forgive me. I am yours,   CLARINDA.

SYLVANDER TO CLARINDA.

Friday Morning, 7 o'clock [*February* 1].

Your fears for Mary are truly laughable. I suppose, my love, you and I showed her a scene which, perhaps, made her wish that she had a swain, and one who could love like me; and 'tis a thousand pities that so good a heart as hers should want an aim, an object. I am miserably stupid this morning. Yesterday I dined with a Baronet, and sat pretty late over the bottle. And 'who hath wo—who hath sorrow? they that tarry long at the wine; they that go to seek mixed wine.'* Forgive me, likewise, a quotation from my favourite author. Solomon's knowledge of the world is very great. He may be looked on as the 'Spectator' or 'Adventurer' of his day: and it is, indeed, surprising what a sameness has ever been in human nature. The broken, but strongly characterizing, hints that the royal author gives us of the manners of the court of Jerusalem and country of Israel are, in their great outlines, the same pictures that London and England, Versailles and France exhibit some three thousand years later. The loves in the 'Song of songs' are all in the spirit of Lady M. W. Montague, or Madam Ninon de l'Enclos; † though, for my part, I dislike both the ancient and modern voluptuaries; and will dare to affirm, that such an attachment as mine to Clarinda, and such evenings as she and I have spent, are what these greatly respectable and deeply experienced Judges of Life and Love never dreamed of.

* Proverbs xxiii., 29, 30.

† It does not appear quite clear why Burns should have classed Lady Mary Wortley Montagu (1690–1762) and Ninon de l'Enclos (1616–1706) as 'modern voluptuaries.' They were both noted for *esprit* and beauty, but their characters were widely different. Yet Lady Mary inspired Pope's *Epistle of Eloisa to Abelard*, and to her Pope addressed letters of the most stilted and fine-spun gallantry; nor are her own letters always too delicate.

I shall be with you this evening between eight and nine, and shall keep as sober hours as you could wish. I am ever, my dear Madam, yours,   SYLVANDER.

SYLVANDER TO CLARINDA.

Sunday Morning [February 3].

I have just been before the throne of my God, Clarinda. According to my association of ideas, my sentiments of love and friendship, I next devote myself to you. Yesternight I was happy — happiness 'that the world cannot give.' I kindle at the recollection; but it is a flame where Innocence looks smiling on, and Honour stands by, a sacred guard. Your heart, your fondest wishes, your dearest thoughts, these are yours to bestow: your person is unapproachable, by the laws of your country; and he loves not as I do who would make you miserable.

You are an angel, Clarinda: you are surely no mortal that 'the earth owns.' To kiss your hand, to live on your smile, is to me far more exquisite bliss than any the dearest favours that the fairest of the sex, yourself excepted, can bestow.

Sunday Evening.

You are the constant companion of my thoughts. How wretched is the condition of one who is haunted with conscious guilt, and trembling under the idea of dreaded vengeance! And what a placid calm, what a charming secret enjoyment is given to one's bosom by the kind feelings of friendship, and the fond throes of love! Out upon the tempest of Anger, the acrimonious gall of fretful Impatience, the sullen frost of lowering Resentment, or the corroding poison of withered Envy! They eat up the immortal part of man! If they spent their fury only on the unfortunate objects of them, it would be something in their favour; but these miserable passions, like traitor Iscariot, betray their Lord and Master.

Thou Almighty Author of peace, and goodness, and love! do Thou give me the social heart that kindly tastes of every man's cup! Is it a draught of joy?—warm and open my heart to share it with cordial, unenvying rejoicing! Is it the bitter potion of sorrow?—melt my heart with sincerely sympathetic woe! Above all, do Thou give me the manly mind that resolutely exemplifies in life and manners those sentiments which I would wish to be thought to possess! The friend of my soul— there may I never deviate from the firmest fidelity and most active kindness! Clarinda, the dear object of my fondest love; there, may the most sacred, inviolate honour, the most faithful, kindling constancy, ever watch and animate my every thought and imagination!

Did you ever meet with the following lines spoken of Religion, your darling topic?—

'Tis *this*, my friend, that streaks our morning bright!
'Tis *this* that gilds the horror of our night!
When wealth forsakes us, and when friends are few;
When friends are faithless, or when foes pursue;
'Tis this that wards the blow or stills the smart,
Disarms affliction or repels its dart:
Within the breast bids purest rapture rise,
Bids smiling Conscience spread her cloudless skies. *

I met with these verses very early in life, and was so delighted with them that I have them by me, copied at school.

Good night and sound rest, My dearest Clarinda.　　SYLVANDER.

CLARINDA TO SYLVANDER.

Wednesday Evening, Nine [February 6.]

There is not a sentiment in your last dear letter but must meet the approbation of every worthy discerning mind: except one—'that my heart, my fondest wishes' are mine to bestow. True, they are not, they cannot be, placed upon him who ought to have had them, but whose conduct (I dare not say more against him) has justly forfeited them. But is it not too near an infringement of the sacred obligations of marriage to bestow one's heart, wishes, and thoughts upon another? Something in my soul whispers that it approaches criminality. I obey the voice. Let me cast every kind feeling into the allowed bond of Friendship. If 'tis accompanied with a shadow of a softer feeling, it shall be poured into the bosom of a merciful God! If a confession of my warmest, tenderest friendship does not satisfy you, duty forbids Clarinda should do more! Sylvander, I never expect to be happy here below! Why was I formed so susceptible of emotions I dare not indulge? Never were there two hearts formed so exactly alike, as ours! No wonder our friendship is heightened by the 'sympathetic glow.' In reading your Life,† I find the very first poems that hit your fancy were those that first engaged mine. While almost a child, the hymn you mentioned, and another of Addison's, 'When all thy mercies,' &c., were my chief favourites. They are much so to this hour; and I make my boys repeat them every Sabbath day. When about fifteen, I took a great fondness for Pope's 'Messiah,' which I still reckon one of the sublimest pieces I ever met with.

Sylvander, I believe our friendship will be lasting; its basis has been virtue, similarity of tastes, feelings, and sentiments. Alas! I shudder at the idea of an hundred miles distance. You'll hardly write me once a month, and other objects will weaken your affection for Clarinda. Yet I cannot believe so. Oh, let the scenes of Nature remind you of Clarinda! In winter, remember the dark shades of her fate; in summer, the warmth, the cordial warmth, of her friendship; in autumn, her glowing wishes to bestow plenty on all; and let spring animate you with hopes that your friend may yet live to surmount the wintry blasts of life and revive to

* See note on p. 256.　　　　† Burns had lent her a copy of his letter to Moore.

taste a spring-time of happiness! At all events, Sylvander, the storms of life will quickly pass, and 'one unbounded spring encircle all.'* There, Sylvander, I trust we'll meet. Love, there, is not a crime. I charge you to meet me there—Oh, God!—I must lay down my pen.——I repent, almost, flattering your writing talents so much : I can see you know all the merit you possess. The allusion of the key † is true—therefore I won't recant it ; but I rather was too humble about my own letters. I have met with several who wrote worse than myself, and few, of my own sex, better ; so I don't give you great credit for being fashed with them.

Sylvander, I have things with different friends I can't tell to another, yet am not hurt ; but I told you of that particular friend : he was, for near four years, the one I confided in. He is very worthy, and answers your description in the 'Epistle to J. S.' exactly. When I had hardly a friend to care for me in Edinburgh, he befriended me. I saw, too soon, 'twas with him a warmer feeling : perhaps a little infection was the natural effect. I told you the circumstances which helped to eradicate the tender impression in me ; but I perceive (though he never tells me so)—I see it in every instance—*his* prepossession still remains. I esteem him as a faithful friend ; but I can never feel more for him. I fear he's not convinced of that. He sees no man with me half so often as himself ; and thinks I surely am at least partial to no other. I cannot bear to deceive one in so tender a point, and am hurt at his harbouring an attachment I never can return. I have thoughts of owning my intimacy with Sylvander ; but a thousand things forbid it. I should be tortured with Jealousy, that 'green-eyed monster ;' and, besides, I fear 'twould wound his peace. 'Tis a delicate affair. I wish your judgment on it. O Sylvander, I cannot bear to give pain to any creature, far less to one who pays me the attention of a brother !

I never met with a man congenial, perfectly congenial, to myself but *one*—ask no questions. Is Friday to be the last night ? I wish, Sylvander, you'd steal away—I cannot bear farewell ! I can hardly relish the idea of meeting—for the idea ! but we will meet again, at least in Heaven, I hope. Sylvander, when I survey myself, my returning weaknesses, I am consoled that my hopes, my immortal hopes, are founded in the complete righteousness of a compassionate Saviour. 'In all our afflictions, He is afflicted, and the angel of His presence guards us.'

I am charmed with the Lines on Religion, and with you for relishing them. I only wish the world saw you as you appear in your letters to me. Why did you send forth to them the 'Holy Fair,' &c. ? Had Clarinda known you, she would have held you in her arms till she had your promise to suppress them. Do not publish the 'Moor Hen.' Do not, for your sake, and for mine. I wish you vastly to hear my valued friend, Mr Kemp. Come to hear him on Sunday afternoon. 'Tis the first favour I have asked you : I expect you'll not refuse me. You'll

---

* 'The storms of Wintry time will quickly pass,
    And one unbounded Spring encircle all.'—THOMSON's *Winter*.

† 'The key.'—See Clarinda's letters of January 16th and 19th, *ante*.

easily get a seat. Your favourite, Mr Gould,* I admired much. His composition is elegant indeed !—but 'tis like beholding a beautiful superstructure built on a sandy foundation : 'tis fine to look upon ; but one dares not abide in it with safety. Mr Kemp's language is very good,—perhaps not such studied periods as Mr G.'s ; but he is far more animated. He is pathetic in a degree that touches one's soul ! and then, 'tis all built upon a rock.

I could chide you for the Parting Song. † It wrings my heart. ' You may reca' '—by being wise in future—' your friend as yet.' I will be your friend for ever ! Good night ! God bless you ! prays

CLARINDA.

Thursday, Noon.

I shall go to-morrow forenoon to Miers alone : 'tis quite a usual thing, I hear. Mary is not in town ; and I don't care to ask Miss Nimmo, or anybody else. What size do you want it about? O Sylvander, if you wish my peace, let Friendship be the word between us : I tremble at more. ' Talk not of Love,' &c. To-morrow I'll expect you. Adieu !

CLARINDA.

Mrs M'Lehose expressed, at the age of seventy-five, the same hope to meet in another sphere the one heart that she had ever found herself able entirely to sympathise with.

SYLVANDER TO CLARINDA.

Thursday Night [February 7].

I cannot be easy, my Clarinda, while any sentiment respecting me in your bosom gives you pain. If there is no man on earth to whom your heart and affections are justly due, it may savour of imprudence, but never of criminality, to bestow that heart and those affections where you please. The God of love meant and made those delicious attachments to be bestowed on somebody ; and even all the imprudence lies in bestowing them on an unworthy object. If this reasoning is conclusive, as it certainly is, I must be allowed to ' talk of Love.'

It is, perhaps, rather wrong to speak highly to a friend of his letter : it is apt to lay one under a little restraint in their future letters, and restraint is the death of a friendly epistle ; but there is one passage in your last charming letter, Thomson nor Shenstone never exceeded it, nor often came up to it. I shall certainly steal it, and set it in some future poetic production, and get immortal fame by it. 'Tis when you bid the scenes of nature remind me of Clarinda. Can I forget you, Clarinda ? I would detest myself as a tasteless, unfeeling, insipid, infamous blockhead ! I have loved women of ordinary merit, whom I could have loved

---

* ' Greenfield ' evidently is meant.
† ' Clarinda '—the song set to music by Schetky. See p. 270.

for ever.   You are the first, the only unexceptionable individual of the beauteous sex that I ever met with ; and never woman more entirely possessed my soul !   I know myself, and how far I can depend on passions, well.   It has been my peculiar study.

I thank you for going to Miers.*   Urge him, for necessity calls, to have it done by the middle of next week : Wednesday the latest day.   I want it for a breast-pin, to wear next my heart.   I propose to keep sacred set times, to wander in the woods and wilds for meditation on you.   Then, and only then, your lovely image shall be produced to the day, with a reverence akin to devotion.

    *   *   *   *   *

To-morrow night shall not be the last.   Good night !   I am perfectly stupid, as I supped late yesternight.   SYLVANDER.

In anticipation of his visit to Dumfriesshire, he now wrote

TO MR JOHN TENNANT, GLENCONNER.

MY DEAR FRIEND—I shall see you in eight or ten days, so shall merely make this a business letter.   I go on my return home to take the decisive look of a farm near Dumfries ; where, if you will do me the favour to accompany me, your judgment shall determine me.   I met with an ugly accident about ten weeks ago, by the drunkenness of a coachman ; I fell and dislocated the cap of my knee, which laid me up a cripple, that I have but just lately laid aside my crutches.   I shall not have the use of my limb as formerly, for some months, perhaps years, to come.

My best compliments to all your family, and Mr Reid.   I am at present crazed with thought and anxiety, but particulars I refer till meeting.—I am ever, my dearest sir, yours,   ROBT. BURNS.†

EDINR., 7th Feb. 1788.

Meanwhile Burns was not neglectful of Johnson's collection of Scottish songs.   The second volume, proceeding rapidly to completion, was indebted to him for both music and poetry.   Of the songs which he contributed to it, some were given with his name ; a few others that were wholly, and some that were

---

* The poet had, presumably, requested Clarinda to sit to Miers that he might have her silhouette.

† This letter, now published for the first time, is in the possession of Sir Charles Tennant.   Glenconner is a small farm in an undulating upland two miles to the south-west of the village of Ochiltree.   The humble range of farm steadings, partially sheltered by a clump of wood, stands near the edge of the deep glen of the Burnock Water.   Till recently Glenconner was farmed by members of the Tennant family.   The Mr Reid mentioned was doubtless Burns's friend George Reid, Barquharie.

partially, his, appeared anonymously. We find, in the second volume, besides some already given here, the following acknowledged contributions:

WHISTLE, AN' I'LL COME TO YOU, MY LAD.

O whistle, an' I'll come to you, my lad,
O whistle, an' I'll come to you, my lad,
Though father and mither should baith gae mad,   mother
                                              —both go
O whistle, an' I'll come to you, my lad.

Come down the back stairs when ye come to court me,
Come down the back stairs when ye come to court me,
Come down the back stairs, and let naebody see,
And come as ye were na coming to me.*   not

M'PHERSON'S FAREWELL.

TUNE—*M'Pherson's Rant.*

[The freebooter James M'Pherson was a bastard of the Invereshie family by a Gypsy mother. Of great personal strength, and an excellent violinist, he had held the counties of Aberdeen, Banff, and Moray in fear for some years, when, with his Gypsy followers, he was seized by Duff of Braco, ancestor of the Duke of Fife, and tried before the sheriff of Banff (November 7, 1700). In the prison, while he lay under the sentence of death, he composed a song and an appropriate air, the former commencing thus:

I've spent my time in rioting,
   Debauched my health and strength;
I squandered fast as pillage came,
   And fell to shame at length.
      But dantonly, and wantonly,   defiantly
       And rantingly I'll gae;   go
    I'll play a tune, and dance it roun'   round
      Beneath the gallows-tree.

When brought to the place of execution, at the cross of Banff (Nov. 16), he played the tune on his violin, and then asked if any friend was present who would accept the instrument as a gift at his hands. No one coming forward, he snapped the fiddle across his knee, and threw away

* Burns afterwards altered and extended this song. See Vol. IV.

the fragments; after which he submitted to the executioner.* Burns's
verses were designed as an improvement on those ascribed to the freebooter, and were set to the same air.

> Farewell, ye † dungeons dark and strong,
>   The wretch's destinie!
> M'Pherson's time will not be long
>   On yonder gallows-tree.
> *Chorus*—Sae rantingly, sae wantonly,
>   Sae dauntingly gaed he;   *defiantly went*
>   He play'd a spring, and danc'd it round   *tune*
>   Below the gallows-tree.

> O what is death but parting breath?
>   On many a bloody plain
> I've dar'd his face, and in this place
>   I scorn him yet again!

> Untie these bands from off my hands
>   And bring to me my sword;
> And there's no a man in all Scotland
>   But I'll brave him at a word.

> I've liv'd a life of sturt and strife;   *violence*
>   I die by treacherie:
> It burns my heart I must depart
>   And not avengèd be.

> Now farewell, light, thou sunshine bright,
>   And all beneath the sky!
> May coward shame distain his name,   *stain*
>   The wretch that dares not die! ‡

---

* Cramond's *Annals of Banff.* New Spalding Club, 1892.

† Variation—'you.'

‡ It is interesting to know that M'Pherson's Rant was played once at Chelsea to Tenny-
son. 'I never hear it,' Carlyle wrote afterwards (1844) to Edward FitzGerald, 'without
something of emotion—poor Macpherson; though the artist hates to play it. Alfred's
dark face grew darker, and I saw his lip slightly quivering.'

STAY, MY CHARMER, CAN YOU LEAVE ME?

TUNE—*An Gille dubh ciar dhubh.*

Stay, my charmer, can you leave me?
Cruel, cruel to deceive me!
Well you know how much you grieve me:
   Cruel charmer, can you go!

By my love so ill-requited,
By the faith you fondly plighted,
By the pangs of lovers slighted,
   Do not, do not leave me so!

STRATHALLAN'S LAMENT.*

Thickest night surround my dwelling!
   Howling tempests o'er me rave!
Turbid torrents, wintry swelling,
   Roaring by my lonely cave.
Crystal streamlets gently flowing,
   Busy haunts of base mankind,
Western breezes softly blowing,
   Suit not my distracted mind.

In the cause of Right engagèd
   Wrongs injurious to redress,
Honor's war we strongly wagèd,
   But the heavens deny'd success:
Ruin's wheel has driven o'er us,
   Not a hope that dare attend,
The wide world is all before us—
   But a world without a friend!

* William Drummond, fourth Viscount Strathallan, was killed at Culloden, 1746. His name, with that of his eldest son James, was included in a Bill of Attainder passed in the same year. James became fifth Viscount, and died in 1765. It was most probably into the mouth of the latter that the poet put the 'Lament.'

THE YOUNG HIGHLAND ROVER.

TUNE—*Morag.*

Loud blaw the frosty breezes,   blow
    The snaws the mountains cover,   snows
Like winter on me seizes,
    Since my young Highland Rover *
Far wanders nations over.

Chorus—Where'er he go, where'er he stray,
      May Heaven be his warden :
      Return him safe to fair Strathspey
      And bonie Castle-Gordon !

The trees now naked groaning,
    Shall soon wi' leaves be hinging,   hanging
The birdies dowie moaning,   dolefully
    Shall a' be blythely singing,
And every flower be springing.

Chorus—Sae I 'll rejoice the lee-lang day,   livelong
      When by his mighty Warden
      My youth 's return'd to fair Strathspey
      And bonie Castle-Gordon.

RAVING WINDS AROUND HER BLOWING.

TUNE—*M'Grigor of Ruara's Lament.*

I composed these verses on Miss Isabella M'Leod of Raasay, alluding to her feelings on the death of her sister, and the still more melancholy death (1786) of her sister's husband, the late Earl of Loudon, who shot himself out of sheer heart-break at some mortifications he suffered, owing to the deranged state of his finances.—*B.*

Raving winds around her blowing,
Yellow leaves the woodlands strowing,
By a river hoarsely roaring
Isabella stray'd deploring.

* Prince Charles Stuart.

Farewell, hours that late did measure
Sunshine days of joy and pleasure ;
Hail, thou gloomy night of sorrow,
Cheerless night that knows no morrow.

O'er the Past too fondly wandering,
On the hopeless Future pondering,
Chilly Grief my life-blood freezes,
Fell Despair my fancy seizes.
Life, thou soul of every blessing,
Load to Misery most distressing,
Gladly how would I resign thee,
And to dark Oblivion join thee !

MUSING ON THE ROARING OCEAN.

TUNE—*Druimion Dubh.*

I composed these verses out of compliment to a Mrs M'Lauchlan, whose
husband is an officer in the East Indies.—*B.*

Musing on the roaring ocean
  Which divides my love and me ;
Wearying Heav'n in warm devotion
  For his weal where'er he be.

Hope and Fear's alternate billow
  Yielding late to Nature's law,
Whisp'ring spirits round my pillow
  Talk of him that's far awa.

Ye whom Sorrow never wounded,
  Ye who never shed a tear,
Care-untroubled, joy-surrounded,
  Gaudy Day to you is dear.

Gentle Night, do thou befriend me ;
  Downy Sleep, the curtain draw ;
Spirits kind, again attend me,
  Talk of him that's far awa !

The volume contained also Clarinda's song 'Talk not of love, it gives me pain,' with the improvements effected by Burns, and set to the tune 'Banks of Spey.' The initial 'M' appears at the end of the song. Over the same initial appeared a canzonet, 'To a Blackbird,' with 'its wings pruned by Burns.'

> Go on, sweet bird, and soothe my care,
> Thy tuneful notes will hush despair ;
> Thy plaintive warblings, void of art,
> Thrill sweetly thro' my aching heart.
> Now chuse thy mate, and fondly love,
> And all the charming transport prove ;
> While I, a love-lorn exile, live,
> Nor transport or receive or give.　　　　　either
>
> For thee is laughing nature gay,
> For thee she pours the vernal day ;
> For me in vain is nature drest,
> While joy 's a stranger to my breast !
> These sweet emotions all enjoy ;
> Let love and song thy hours employ !
> Go on, sweet bird, and soothe my care,
> Thy tuneful notes will hush despair.

The volume, which was published on the 14th of February,[*] contained a preface, which, if not the composition of Burns, at any rate bears evidence of his hand : 'In the first Volume of this work, two or three Airs not of Scots composition have been inadvertently inserted ; which, whatever excellence they may have, was improper, as the Collection is meant to be solely the music of our own Country. The Songs contained in this Volume, both music and poetry, are all of them the work of Scotsmen. Wherever the old words could be recovered, they have been preserved ; both as generally suiting better the genius of the tunes, and to preserve the productions of those earlier Sons of the Scottish Muses, some of whose names deserved a better fate than has befallen them—"Buried 'mong the wreck of things which were." Of our more modern Songs, the Editor has inserted

---

* Burns says so in a letter to Mr Skinner of that date. The volume is advertised on the 20th of February as 'published this day,' but the preface is dated 'March 1, 1788.'

the Authors' names as far as he could ascertain them; and as that was neglected in the first Volume, it is annexed here. If he have made any mistakes in this affair, which he possibly may, he shall be very grateful at being set right.

'Ignorance and Prejudice may perhaps affect to sneer at the simplicity of the poetry or music of some of these pieces; but their having been for ages the favorites of Nature's Judges—the Common People, was to the Editor a sufficient test of their merit. . . .'

—————— ——————

Five letters of Burns to Clarinda follow. The answers have been lost. It appears that the apprehensions about the remarks of friends and neighbours *had* been realised.

SYLVANDER TO CLARINDA.

Wednesday, [*February* 13*th*].

MY EVER DEAREST CLARINDA—I make a numerous dinner-party wait me while I read yours and write this. Do not require that I should cease to love you, to adore you in my soul; 'tis to me impossible: your peace and happiness are to me dearer than my soul. Name the terms on which you wish to see me, to correspond with me, and you have them. I must love, pine, mourn, and adore in secret: this you must not deny me. You will ever be to me

> Dear as the light that visits those sad eyes,
> Dear as the ruddy drops that warm my heart.*

I have not patience to read the Puritanic scrawl. Damned sophistry. Ye heavens, thou God of nature, thou Redeemer of mankind! ye look down with approving eyes on a passion inspired by the purest flame, and guarded by truth, delicacy, and honour; but the half-inch soul of an unfeeling, cold-blooded, pitiful Presbyterian bigot cannot forgive anything above his dungeon-bosom and foggy head.

Farewell! I'll be with you to-morrow evening; and be at rest in your mind. I will be yours in the way you think most to your happiness. I dare not proceed. I love, and will love you; and will, with joyous confidence, approach the throne of the Almighty Judge of men with your dear idea; and will despise the scum of sentiment, and the mist of sophistry.   SYLVANDER.

* From *The Bard, a Pindaric Ode* (Stanza 3), by Thomas Gray. Cf. Brutus's words to Portia (Shakespeare's *Julius Cæsar*, Act II., scene i.), beginning 'You are my true and honourable wife.'

SYLVANDER TO CLARINDA.

Wednesday, Midnight [February 13th].

MADAM—After a wretched day, I am preparing for a sleepless night. I am going to address myself to the Almighty Witness of my actions—some time, perhaps very soon, my Almighty Judge. I am not going to be the advocate of Passion : be Thou my inspirer and testimony, O God, as I plead the cause of truth !

I have read over your friend's haughty dictatorial letter : you are only answerable to your God in such a matter. Who gave any fellow-creature of yours (a fellow-creature incapable of being your judge, because not your peer) a right to catechise, scold, undervalue, abuse, and insult, wantonly and unhumanly to insult, you thus ? I don't wish, not even wish, to deceive you, Madam. The Searcher of hearts is my witness how dear you are to me ; but though it were possible you could be still dearer to me, I would not even kiss your hand, at the expense of your conscience. Away with declamation ! let us appeal to the bar of common sense. It is not mouthing everything sacred ; it is not vague ranting assertions ; it is not assuming, haughtily and insultingly assuming, the dictatorial language of a Roman Pontiff, that must dissolve a union like ours. Tell me, Madam, are you under the least shadow of an obligation to bestow your love, tenderness, caresses, affections, heart and soul, on Mr M'Lehose—the man who has repeatedly, habitually, and barbarously broken through every tie of duty, nature, or gratitude to you ? The laws of your country, indeed, for the most useful reasons of policy and sound government, have made your person inviolate ; but are your heart and affections bound to one who gives not the least return of either to you ? You cannot do it ; it is not in the nature of things that you are bound to do it ; the common feelings of humanity forbid it. Have you, then, a heart and affections which are no man's right ? You have. It would be highly, ridiculously absurd to suppose the contrary. Tell me then, in the name of common sense, can it be wrong, is such a supposition compatible with the plainest ideas of right and wrong, that it is improper to bestow the heart and these affections on another—while that bestowing is not in the smallest degree hurtful to your duty to God, to your children, to yourself, or to society at large ?

This is the great test ; the consequences : let us see them. In a widowed, forlorn, lonely situation, with a bosom glowing with love and tenderness, yet so delicately situated that you cannot indulge these nobler feelings except you meet with a man who has a soul capable . . .

SYLVANDER TO CLARINDA.

[Thursday, February 14th.]

'I am distressed for thee, my brother Jonathan.' I have suffered, Clarinda, from your letter. My Soul was in arms at the sad perusal I

dreaded that I had acted wrong. If I have robbed you of a friend, God
forgive me! But, Clarinda, be comforted: let us raise the tone of our
feelings a little higher and bolder. A fellow-creature who leaves us, who
spurns us without just cause, tho' once our bosom friend—up with a little
honest pride—let them go! How shall I comfort you who am the cause
of the injury? Can I wish that I had never seen you? that we had
never met? No: I never will! But have I thrown you friendless?
there is almost distraction in that thought. Father of mercies! against
Thee often have I sinned: through Thy grace I will endeavor to do so
no more! She who, Thou knowest, is dearer to me than myself; Pour
Thou the balm of peace into her past wounds, and hedge her about with
Thy peculiar care, all her future days and nights! Strengthen her
tender, noble mind firmly to suffer and magnanimously to bear! Make
me worthy of that friendship, that love she honors me with. May my
attachment to her be pure as Devotion, and lasting as immortal
life! O Almighty Goodness, hear me! Be to her, at all times, particularly in the hour of distress or trial, a Friend and Comforter, a Guide
and Guard.

> How are Thy servants blest, O Lord,
> How sure is their defence!
> Eternal Wisdom is their guide,
> Their help, Omnipotence!

Forgive me, Clarinda, the injury I have done you! To-night I shall
be with you, as indeed I shall be ill at ease till I see you.

[SYLVANDER.]

SYLVANDER TO CLARINDA.

Two o'clock [February 14th].

I just now received your first letter of yesterday, by the careless negligence of the penny post. Clarinda, matters are grown very serious
with us: then seriously hear me, and hear me Heaven!

I met you, my dear Clarinda, by far the first of womankind, at least
to me. I esteemed, I loved, you at first sight, both of which attachments
you have done me the honour to return. The longer I am acquainted
with you, the more innate amiableness and worth I discover in you.
You have suffered a loss, I confess, for my sake; but if the firmest,
steadiest, warmest friendship; if every endeavour to be worthy of your
friendship; if a love strong as the ties of nature and holy as the duties
of religion; if all these can make anything like a compensation for the
evil I have occasioned you; if they be worth your acceptance, or can in
the least add to your enjoyments,—so help Sylvander, ye Powers above,
in his hour of need, as he freely gives these all to Clarinda!

I esteem you, I love you, as a friend; I admire you, I love you, as a
woman, beyond any one in all the circle of creation. I know I shall
continue to esteem you, to love you, to pray for you, nay, to pray for
myself for your sake.

Expect me at eight; and believe me to be ever, my dearest Madam, yours most entirely,   SYLVANDER.

SYLVANDER TO CLARINDA.

[*Friday, February 15th.*]

When matters, my love, are desperate, we must put on a desperate face—

On reason build resolve,
That column of true majesty in man—

or, as the same author * finely says in another place,

Let thy soul spring up,
And lay strong hold for help on him that made thee.

I am yours, Clarinda, for life. Never be discouraged at all this. Look forward : in a few weeks I shall be somewhere or other, out of the possibility of seeing you : till then, I shall write you often, but visit you seldom. Your fame, your welfare, your happiness, are dearer to me than any gratification whatever. Be comforted, my love ! the present moment is the worst ; the lenient hand of time is daily and hourly either lightening the burden, or making us insensible to the weight. None of these friends—I mean Mr —— and the other gentleman—can hurt your worldly support : and of their friendship, in a little time you will learn to be easy, and by and by to be happy without it. A decent means of livelihood in the world, an approving God, a peaceful conscience, and one firm trusty friend—can anybody that has these be said to be unhappy ? These are yours.

To-morrow evening I shall be with you about eight, probably for the last time till I return to Edinburgh. In the meantime, should any of these two unlucky friends question you respecting me, whether I am *the man*, I do not think they are entitled to any information. As to their jealousy and spying, I despise them.

Adieu, my dearest Madam !   SYLVANDER.

While the time was thus drawing near for leaving Edinburgh, he found time to write a few letters to other friends.

TO MR JAMES CANDLISH, GLASGOW.

[EDINBURGH, *February* 1788.]

MY DEAR FRIEND—If once I were gone from this scene of hurry and dissipation, I promise myself the pleasure of that correspondence being renewed which has been so long broken. At present I have time for

* Young—*Night Thoughts.*

nothing. Dissipation and business engross every moment. I am engaged in assisting an honest Scots enthusiast,* a friend of mine, who is an engraver, and has taken it into his head to publish a collection of all our songs set to music, of which the words and music are done by Scotsmen. This, you will easily guess, is an undertaking exactly to my taste. I have collected, begged, borrowed, and stolen all the songs I could meet with. 'Pompey's Ghost,'† words and music, I beg from you immediately, to go into his second number: the first is already published. I shall shew you the first number when I see you in Glasgow, which will be in a fortnight or less. Do be so kind as send me the song in a day or two: you cannot imagine how much it will oblige me.

Direct to me at Mr W. Cruikshank's, St James's Square, New Town, Edinburgh. R. B.

Candlish replied:

Your kind letter came to hand, and I would have answered it sooner, had I not delayed in expectation of finding some person who could enable me to comply with your request. Being myself unskilled in music as a science, I made an attempt to get the song you mentioned set by some other hand; but, as I could not accomplish this, I must send you the words without the music. Some of Edina's fair nymphs may perhaps be able to do you the piece of service which I would have done with greatest pleasure had it been in my power. It is with the greatest sincerity I applaud your attempt to give the world a more correct and more elegant collection of Scottish songs than has hitherto appeared. They have been long and much admired; and yet, perhaps, no poetical compositions ever met with approbation more disproportioned to their merit. Many, from an affectation, perhaps, of a more than usual knowledge of ancient literature, extol with the most extravagant praises the pastoral productions of the Greek and Roman poets, and attempt to persuade us that in them alone is to be found that natural simplicity, and the tenderness of sentiment, which constitute the true excellence of that species of writing. For my own part, though I cannot altogether divest myself of partiality to the ancients, whose merit will cease only to be admired with the universal wreck of men and letters, yet I am persuaded that in many of the songs of our own nation there are beauties which it would be vain to look for in the most admired poetical compositions of antiquity. They are the offspring of nature; they are expressed in the language of simplicity: and the love songs, breathing sentiments that are inspired by the most tender and exquisite feelings, are in unison with the human heart. There is no one in whose veins the smallest drop of Scottish blood circulates but must feel the most heartfelt pleasure when he reflects that those songs which do such honour to both the genius and feelings of his countrymen, which, in simplicity of

---

* James Johnson, publisher of the *Scots Musical Museum*.
† 'Pompey's Ghost' appeared in *The Blackbird* (Edinburgh, 1764).

language, and in the sensibility that pervades them, have never been
equalled by those of any nation, and which have been so much admired
by foreigners, will continue to be sung with delight by both sexes while
Scotsmen and the Scots language remain. If the collection is to be
published by subscription put down my name for a copy. My time this
winter is very much employed—no less than ten hours a day.

TO MRS DUNLOP.

EDINBURGH, 12th February 1788.

Some things in your late letters hurt me: not that *you say them*, but
that *you mistake me*. Religion, my honored madam, has not only been
all my life my chief dependence, but my dearest enjoyment. I have
indeed been the luckless victim of wayward follies; but, alas! I have
ever been 'more fool than knave.' A mathematician without religion is
a probable character; an irreligious poet is a monster. . . .

R. B.

TO THE REV. JOHN SKINNER.

EDINBURGH, 14th February 1788.

REVEREND AND DEAR SIR—I have been a cripple now near three
months, though I am getting vastly better, and have been very much
hurried besides, or else I would have wrote you sooner. I must beg
your pardon for the epistle you sent me appearing in the Magazine. I
had given a copy or two to some of my intimate friends, but did not
know of the printing of it till the publication of the Magazine. However, as it does great honour to us both, you will forgive it.

The second volume of the songs I mentioned to you in my last is published to-day. I send you a copy, which I beg you will accept as a mark
of the veneration I have long had, and shall ever have, for your character,
and of the claim I make to your continued acquaintance. Your songs
appear in the third volume, with your name in the index; as I assure
you, Sir, I have heard your 'Tullochgorum,' particularly among our west-
country folks, given to many different names, and most commonly to the
immortal author of 'The Minstrel,' who, indeed, never wrote any thing
superior to 'Gie's a sang, Montgomery cried.' Your brother * has promised me your verses to the Marquis of Huntly's reel, which certainly
deserve a place in the collection. My kind host, Mr Cruikshank, of the
high school here, and said to be one of the best Latins in this age, begs
me to make you his grateful acknowledgments for the entertainment he

---

* Mr James Skinner, a legal practitioner in Edinburgh. He was half-brother of the poet-
clergyman, and thirty years his junior.

has got in a Latin publication of yours that I borrowed for him from your acquaintance and much respected friend in this place, the Reverend Dr Webster.* Mr Cruikshank maintains that you write the best Latin since [George] Buchanan. I leave Edinburgh to-morrow, but shall return in three weeks. Your song you mentioned in your last, to the tune of 'Dumbarton Drums,' and the other, which you say was done by a brother by trade of mine, a ploughman, I shall thank you for a copy of each. I am ever, Reverend Sir, with the most respectful esteem and sincere veneration, yours,

R. B.

TO MR RICHARD BROWN, GREENOCK.

EDINBURGH, 15th February 1788.

MY DEAR FRIEND—I received yours with the greatest pleasure. I shall arrive at Glasgow on Monday evening; and beg, if possible, you will meet me on Tuesday, I shall wait you Tuesday all day. I shall be found at Durie's, Black Bull Inn. I am hurried, as if hunted by fifty devils, else I should go to Greenock; but if you cannot possibly come, write me, if possible, to Glasgow, on Monday; or direct to me at Mossgiel by Mauchline; and name a day and place in Ayrshire, within a fortnight from this date, where I may meet you. I only stay a fortnight in Ayrshire, and return to Edinburgh. I am ever, my dearest friend, yours,

ROBERT BURNS.

TO MISS CHALMERS.

EDINBURGH, Sunday [February 17].

To-morrow, my dear madam, I leave Edinburgh. . . . I have altered all my plans of future life. A farm that I could live in, I could not find; and indeed, after the necessary support my brother and the rest of the family required, I could not venture on farming in that style suitable to my feelings. You will condemn me for the next step I have taken. I have entered into the excise. I stay in the west about three weeks, and then return to Edinburgh for six weeks' instructions; afterwards, for I get employ instantly, I go *où il plait à Dieu—et mon Roi.* I have chosen this, my dear friend, after mature deliberation. The question is not at what door of fortune's palace shall we enter in; but what doors does she open to us? I was not likely to get any thing to do. I wanted *un but,* which is a dangerous, an unhappy situation. I got this without any hanging on or mortifying solicitation; it is immediate bread, and though poor in comparison of the last eighteen months of my existence, 'tis luxury in comparison of all my preceding life: besides, the commissioners are some of them my acquaintances, and all of them my firm friends.

R. B.

* A clergyman of the Scottish Episcopal Church in Edinburgh.

Mrs Rose of Kilravock had, on Burns's visit there, under-
taken to obtain for him copies of two Highland airs which
he had heard sung by her sister-in-law, Miss Rose, at Kildrummie. On the 30th November she sent him the airs he had
desired. In an accompanying letter she says they are already
'clothed with thoughts that breathe and words that burn;' but
'these being in an unknown tongue to you, you must again have
recourse to that same fertile imagination of yours to interpret
them, and suppose a lover's description of the beauties of an
adored mistress—why did I say unknown? The language of love
is an universal one, that seems to have escaped the confusion of
Babel, and to be understood by all nations.' She adds, with reference to a letter of his: 'Allow me to believe that " friendship will
maintain the ground she has occupied " in both our hearts in spite
of absence, and that when we do meet, it will be as acquaintance
of a score of years' standing. . . . Farewell, sir; I can only contribute the *widow's mite* to the esteem and admiration excited by your
merits and genius; but this I give as she did—with all my heart.'*

TO MRS ROSE, OF KILRAVOCK.

EDINBURGH, *February 17th,* 1788.

MADAM—You are much indebted to some indispensable business I
have had on my hands, otherwise my gratitude threatened such a return
for your obliging favour as would have tired your patience. It but
poorly expresses my feelings to say that I am sensible of your kindness:
it may be said of hearts such as yours is, and such, I hope, mine is, much
more justly than Addison applies it—

Some souls by instinct to each other turn.

---

* Mrs Elizabeth Rose, of Kilravock, who was born in 1747, was a remarkable woman.
In a *Genealogical Deduction of the Family of Rose of Kilravock,* edited from old documents by Cosmo Innes (1848), she is described as ' the choice companion, the leader of
all cheerful amusements, the humorous story-teller, the clever mimic, the very soul of
society.' She was very fond of reading, and had a great admiration for literary men. ' In
conversation, she was always animated and natural, full of genuine humour, and keen and
quick perception of the ludicrous. . . . She sung the airs of her own country, and she had
learned to take a part in catches and glees, to make up the party with her father and
brother. The same motive led her to study the violin, which she played like male artists—
supported against her shoulder. . . . She was enthusiastic and yet steady in her friendships;
benevolent, hospitable, kind, and generous beyond her means.' Lady Kilravock, as she was
called, had married a gentleman of her own family name, then dead, and was the mother of
Hugh, twentieth laird of Kilravock, who is spoken of as a boy in Burns's letter. Hugh
died in 1827.

There was something in my reception at Kilravock so different from the cold, obsequious, dancing-school bow of politeness, that it almost got into my head that friendship had occupied her ground without the intermediate march of acquaintance. I wish I could transcribe, or rather transfuse into language, the glow of my heart when I read your letter. My ready fancy, with colours more mellow than life itself, painted the beautifully wild scenery of Kilravock—the venerable grandeur of the castle—the spreading woods—the winding river, gladly leaving his unsightly, heathy source, and lingering with apparent delight as he passes the fairy walk at the bottom of the garden ;—your late distressful anxieties *—your present enjoyments—your dear little angel, the pride of your hopes ;—my aged friend, venerable in worth and years, whose loyalty and other virtues will strongly entitle her to the support of the Almighty Spirit here, and his peculiar favour in a happier state of existence. You cannot imagine, Madam, how much such feelings delight me ; they are my dearest proofs of my own immortality. Should I never revisit the north, as probably I never will, nor again see your hospitable mansion, were I, some twenty years hence, to see your little fellow's name making a proper figure in a newspaper paragraph, my heart would bound with pleasure.

I am assisting a friend in a collection of Scottish songs, set to their proper tunes ; every air worth preserving is to be included : among others I have given ' Morag,' and some few Highland airs which pleased me most, a dress which will be more generally known, though far, far inferior in real merit. As a small mark of my grateful esteem, I beg leave to present you with a copy of the work, as far as it is printed ; the Man of Feeling, that first of men,† has promised to transmit it by the first opportunity.

I beg to be remembered most respectfully to my venerable friend and to your little Highland chieftain.‡ When you see the ' two fair spirits of the hill ' at Kildrummie,§ tell them that I have done myself the honour of setting myself down as one of their admirers for at least twenty years to come, consequently they must look upon me as an acquaintance for the same period ; but, as the Apostle Paul says, ' this I ask of grace, not of debt.' I have the honour to be, Madam, &c.   R. B.

Burns left Edinburgh on Monday the 18th of February. He took Glasgow on his way, chiefly to have a meeting with Richard Brown, whose vessel, the *Mary and Jean*, was now advertised as to be ready at Greenock on the 1st of March, to receive goods for

---

* A litigation for the protection and establishment of Mrs Rose's ancestral rights had just ended.
† Mr Henry Mackenzie was cousin to Mrs Rose, jun.
‡ Mrs Rose's mother, and her son, Hugh.
§ Miss Sophia Brodie of Lethin and Miss Rose of Kilravock.

Grenada.* Arrived at the Black Bull † Inn there, he lost little time in penning a letter to Clarinda.

SYLVANDER TO CLARINDA.

GLASGOW, *Monday Evening, Nine o'clock* [*February* 18*th*].

The attraction of Love, I find, is in an inverse proportion to the attraction of the Newtonian philosophy. In the system of Sir Isaac, the nearer objects were to one another, the stronger was the attractive force. In my system, every milestone that marked my progress from Clarinda, awakened a keener pang of attachment to her. How do you feel, my love? Is your heart ill at ease? I fear it. God forbid that these persecutors should harass that peace which is more precious to me than my own. Be assured I shall ever think on you, muse on you, and, in my moments of devotion, pray for you. The hour that you are not in my thoughts, ' be that hour darkness ; let the shadows of death cover it ; let it not be numbered in the hours of the day !'

> When I forget the darling theme,
> Be my tongue mute ! my fancy paint no more !
> And, dead to joy, forget my heart to beat !

I have just met with my old friend the ship Captain‡—guess my pleasure : to meet you could alone have given me more. My brother William, too, the young saddler,§ has come to Glasgow to meet me ; and here are we three spending the evening.

I arrived here too late to write by post ; but I 'll wrap half-a-dozen sheets of blank paper together, and send it by the Fly, under the name of a parcel. You shall hear from me next post town. I would write you a longer letter, but for the present circumstances of my friend.

Adieu, my Clarinda ! I am just going to propose your health by way of grace-drink.   SYLVANDER.

CLARINDA TO SYLVANDER.

EDINBURGH, *Tuesday Evening, Nine o'clock*
[19*th February* 1788].

Mr —— has just left me, after half an hour's most pathetic conversation. I told him of the usage I had met with on Sunday night, which he condemned much, as unmanly and ungenerous. I expressed my thanks for his call ; but he told me it ' was merely to hide the change in his

---

* ' For Grenada.—The new ship *Mary and Jean*, Richard Brown, master, will be ready to receive goods at Greenock by the 1st of next month, and clear to sail the 10th of March. She has the best accommodation for passengers, and will land them at any time at any of the islands to windward . . .'—*Glasgow Mercury*, January 30 to February 6, 1788. From the same paper we find that Brown's ship did not sail till March 20th—ten days late.

† The Black Bull, Argyle Street, was for near eighty years one of the leading inns of the city. The proprietor at this time was George Durie. The site is now occupied by the warehouse of Mann, Byars & Co.

‡ Richard Brown.

§ William Burns was then about twenty-one years old.

friendship from the world.' Think how I was mortified : I was, indeed ; and affected so, as hardly to restrain tears. He did not name you ; but spoke in terms that showed plainly he knew. Would to God he knew my Sylvander as I do ! then might I hope to retain his friendship still ; but I have made my choice, and you alone can ever make me repent it. Yet, while I live, I must regret the loss of such a man's friendship. My dear, generous friend of my soul does so too. I love him for it ! Yesterday I thought of you, and went over to Miss Nimmo, to have the luxury of talking of you. She was most kind ; and praised you more than ever, as a man of worth, honour, genius. Oh, how I could have listened to her for ever ! She says she is afraid our attachment will be lasting. I stayed tea, was asked kindly, and did not choose to refuse, as I stayed last time, when you were of the party. I wish you were here to-night to comfort me. I feel hurt and depressed ; but to-morrow I hope for a cordial from your dear hand ! I must bid you good night. Remember your Clarinda. Every blessing be yours !

Your letter this moment. Why did you write before to-day ? Thank you for it. I figure your heartfelt enjoyment last night. Oh, to have been of the party ! Where was it ? I'd like to know the very spot. My head aches so I can't write more ; but I have kissed your dear lines over and over. Adieu ! I'll finish this to-morrow. Your CLARINDA.

Wednesday, Eleven.

Mary was at my bedside by eight this morning. We had much chat about you. She is an affectionate, faithful soul. She tells me her defence of you was so warm, in a large company where you were blamed for some trivial affair, that she left them impressed with the idea of her being in love. She laughs and says ''tis pity to have the skaith [blame], and nothing for her pains.'

My spirits are greatly better to-day. I am a little anxious about Willie : his leg is to be lanced this day, and I shall be fluttered till the operation is fairly over. Mr Wood thinks he will soon get well, when the matter lodged in it is discussed. God grant it ! Oh, how can I ever be ungrateful to that good Providence who has blest me with so many undeserved mercies, and saved me often from the ruin I courted ! The heart that feels its continual dependence on the Almighty is bound to keep His laws by a tie stronger and tenderer than any human obligation. The feeling of Honour is a noble and powerful one ; but can we be honourable to a fellow-creature, and basely unmindful of our Bountiful Benefactor, to whom we are indebted for life and all its blessings ; and even for those very distinguishing qualities, Honour, Genius, and Benevolence ?

I am sure you enter into these ideas ; did you think with me in all points I should be too happy ; but I'll be silent. I may wish and pray, but you shall never again accuse me of presumption. My dear, I write you this to Mauchline, to be waiting you. I hope, nay I am sure, 'twill be welcome.

You are an extravagant prodigal in more essential things than affection. To-day's post would have brought me yours and saved you sixpence. However, it pleased me to know that, though absent in body, 'you were present with me in spirit.'

Do you know a Miss Nelly Hamilton in Ayr, daughter to a Captain John H. of the Excise cutter? I staid with her at Kailzie [Peeblesshire], and love her. She is a dear, amiable, romantic girl. I wish much to write to her, and will enclose it for you to deliver, personally, if agreeable. She raved about your poems in summer, and wished to be acquainted. Let me know if you have any objections. She is an intimate of Miss Nimmo, too. I think the streets look deserted-like since Monday; and there's a certain insipidity in good kind of folks I once enjoyed not a little. You, who are a casuist, explain these deep enigmas. Miss Wardrobe supped here on Monday. She once named you, which kept me from falling asleep. I drank your health in a glass of ale—as the lasses do at Hallowe'en,—'in to mysel.' *

Happy Sylvander! to meet with the dear charities of brother, sister, parent! whilst I have none of these, and belong to nobody. Yes, I have my children, and my heart's friend, Sylvander—the only one I have ever found capable of that nameless, delicate attachment, which none but noble, romantic minds can comprehend. I envy you the Captain's society. Don't tell him of the 'Iron Chain,' lest he call us both fools. I saw the happy trio in my mind's eye. So absence increases your fondness: 'tis ever so in great souls. Let the poor worldlings enjoy (possess, I mean, for they can't enjoy) their golden dish; we have each of us an estate, derived from the Father of the Universe, into whose hands I trust we'll return it, cultivated, so as to prove an inexhaustible treasure through the endless ages of eternity!

Afternoon.

Mr Wood has not come, so the affair is not over. I hesitate about sending this till I hear further; but I think you said you'd be at M[auchline] on Thursday: at any rate you'll get this on your arrival.

Farewell! may you ever abide under the shadow of the Almighty. Yours,   CLARINDA.

Burns proceeded on the 19th to Paisley, and thence to Dunlop House, where he stayed two days. From Kilmarnock he gave Clarinda an account of his progress.

SYLVANDER TO CLARINDA.

KILMARNOCK, *Friday* [22d February].

I wrote you, my dear Madam, the moment I alighted in Glasgow.

---

* *i.e.* silently.

Since then I have not had opportunity: for in Paisley, where I arrived next day, my worthy, wise friend, Mr Pattison,* did not allow me a moment's respite. I was there ten hours; during which time I was introduced to nine men worth six thousands; five men worth ten thousands; his brother, richly worth twenty thousands; and a young weaver, who will have thirty thousands good when his father, who has no more children than the said weaver, and a Whig-kirk,† dies. Mr P. was bred a zealous Antiburgher; but, during his widowerhood, he has found their strictness incompatible with certain compromises he is often obliged to make with those Powers of darkness—the devil, the world, and the flesh: so he, good, merciful man! talked privately to me of the absurdity of eternal torments; the liberality of sentiment in indulging the honest instincts of nature; the mysteries of concubinage, &c. He has a son, however, that, at sixteen, has repeatedly insisted on certain privileges, only proper for sober, staid men who can use the *good things* of this life without abusing them; but the father's parental vigilance has hitherto hedged him in, amid a corrupt and evil world.

His only daughter, who, 'if the beast be to the fore, and the branks bide hale,' will have seven thousand pounds when her old father steps into the dark Factory-office of Eternity with his well-thummed web of life, has put him again and again in a commendable fit of indignation, by requesting a harpsichord. 'O! these boarding-schools!' exclaims my prudent friend. 'She was a good spinner and sewer, till I was advised by her foes and mine to give her a year of Edinburgh!'

After two bottles more, my much-respected friend opened up to me a project, a legitimate child of Wisdom and Good Sense; 'twas no less than a long-thought-on and deeply-matured design to marry a girl, fully as elegant in her form as the famous priestess‡ whom Saul consulted in his last hours, and who had been second maid of honour to his deceased wife. This, you may be sure, I highly applauded, so I hope for a pair of gloves by and by. I spent the two bypast days at Dunlop House with that worthy family to whom I was deeply indebted early in my poetic career; and in about two hours I shall present your 'twa wee sarkies' [shirts] to the little fellow. My dearest Clarinda, you are ever present with me; and these hours that drawl by among the fools and rascals of this world are only supportable in the idea that they are the forerunners of that happy hour that ushers me to 'the mistress of my soul.' Next week I shall visit Dumfries, and next again return to Edinburgh. My letters, in these hurrying dissipated hours, will be heavy trash; but you know the writer. God bless you.   SYLVANDER.

---

* Mr Alexander Pattison, 'bookseller.' See p. 112.

† This probably means that the Whig (Cameronian) Kirk expected the equivalent of a son's share in the fortune.

‡ The witch of Endor.

CLARINDA TO SYLVANDER.

EDINBURGH, *Friday Evening* [22d *Feb.* 1788].

I wish you had given me a hint, my dear Sylvander, that you were to write me only once in a week. Yesterday I looked for a letter; to-day, never doubted it; but both days have terminated in disappointment. A thousand conjectures have conspired to make me most unhappy. Often have I suffered much disquiet from forming the idea of such an attention, on such and such an occasion, and experienced quite the reverse. But in you, and you alone, I have ever found my highest demands of kindness accomplished; nay, even my fondest wishes, not gratified only, but anticipated! To what, then, can I attribute your not writing me one line since Monday?

God forbid that your nervous ailment has incapacitated you for that office, from which you derived pleasure singly; as well as that most delicate of all enjoyments, pleasure reflected. To-morrow I shall hope to hear from you. Hope, blessed hope, thou balm of every wo, possess and fill my bosom with thy benign influence.

I have been solitary since the tender farewell till to-night. I was solicited to go to Dr Moyes's lecture with Miss Craig and a gallant of hers, a student; one of the many stupid animals, knowing only in the Science of Puppyism, 'or the nice conduct of a clouded cane.'* With that sovereign contempt did I compare his trite, insipid frivolity with the intelligent, manly observation which ever marks the conversation of Sylvander. He is a glorious piece of Divine workmanship, Dr Moyes. The subject to-night was the origin of minerals, springs, lakes, and the ocean. Many parts were far beyond my weak comprehension, and indeed that of most women. What I understood delighted me, and altogether raised my thoughts to the infinite wisdom and boundless goodness of the Deity. The man himself marks both. Presented with a universal blank of Nature's works,† his mind appears to be illuminated with Celestial light. He concluded with some lines of the Essay on Man: 'All are but parts of one stupendous whole,' &c.; a passage I have often read with sublime pleasure.

Miss Burnet sat just behind me. What an angelic girl! I stared at her, having never seen her so near. I remembered you talking of her, &c. What felicity to witness her 'Softly speak and sweetly smile!' How could you celebrate any other Clarinda! Oh, I would have adored you, as Pope of exquisite taste and refinement, had you loved, sighed, and written upon her for ever! breathing your passion only to the woods and streams. But Poets, I find, are not quite incorporeal, more than others. My dear Sylvander, to be serious, I really wonder you ever admired Clarinda, after beholding Miss Burnet's superior charms. If I don't

---

* From Pope's *Rape of the Lock*, iv., 124.

† Dr Moyes, lecturer on natural philosophy, was totally blind.

hear to-morrow, I shall form dreadful reasons. God forbid ! Bishop
Geddes was within a foot of me, too. What field of contemplation—
both !

Good-night, God bless you, prays   CLARINDA.

Next day Burns arrived at Mossgiel.

TO MR RICHARD BROWN, GREENOCK.

MOSSGIEL, 24th February 1788.

MY DEAR SIR—I cannot get the proper direction for my friend in
Jamaica ; but the following will do : To Mr Jo. Hutchinson,* at Jo.
Brownrigg's, Esq., care of Mr Benjamin Henriquez, merchant, Orange
Street, Kingston. I arrived here, at my brother's, only yesterday, after
fighting my way through Paisley and Kilmarnock, against those old
powerful foes of mine, the devil, the world, and the flesh ; so terrible in
the fields of dissipation. I have met with few incidents in my life which
gave me so much pleasure as meeting you in Glasgow. There is a time
of life beyond which we cannot form a tie worth the name of friendship.
'O youth ! enchanting stage, profusely blest !'† Life is a fairy scene :
Almost all that deserves the name of enjoyment or pleasure is only a
charming delusion : and in comes repining Age, in all the gravity of
hoary wisdom, and wretchedly chases away the bewitching phantom.
When I think of life, I resolve to keep a strict look-out, in the course of
economy, for the sake of worldly convenience and independence of mind ;
to cultivate intimacy with a few of the companions of youth, that they
may be the friends of age ; never to refuse my liquorish humour a hand-
ful of the sweetmeats of life, when they come not too dear ; and, for
Futurity,—

> The present moment is our ain,
> The niest [next] we never saw !

How like you my philosophy ? Give my best compliments to Mrs B. ;
and believe me to be, my dear Sir, yours most truly   R. B.

SYLVANDER TO CLARINDA.‡

[MOSSGIEL, Sat., 23 Feb. 1788.]

I have just now, my ever dear Madam, delivered your kind present to
my sweet little Bobbie, whom I find a very fine fellow. Your letter was
waiting me. Your interview with Mr Kemp opens a wound, ill-closed,

---

* Doubtless the correspondent of Burns who congratulated him on being saved from
going to Jamaica. See Vol. I., p. 394.
† This was to the last a favourite quotation of Clarinda.
‡ First printed in the Banffshire Journal, from a 'mutilated' original.

in my breast; not that I think his friendship is of so much consequence to you, but because you set such a value on it.

Now for a little news that will please you. I, this morning, as I came home, called for a certain woman [Jean Armour]. I am disgusted with her—I cannot endure her! I, while my heart smote me for the profanity, tried to compare her with my Clarinda: 'twas setting the expiring glimmer of a farthing taper beside the cloudless glory of the meridian sun. *Here* was tasteless insipidity, vulgarity of soul, and mercenary fawning; *there* polished good sense, Heaven-born genius, and the most generous, the most delicate, the most tender, passion. I have done with her, and she with me.

I set off to-morrow for Dumfries-shire. 'Tis merely out of compliment to Mr Miller; for I know the Indies must be my lot.* I will write you from Dumfries, if these horrid postages don't frighten me.

> Whatever place, whatever land I see,
> My heart, untravell'd, fondly turns to thee;
> Still to 'Clarinda' turns with ceaseless pain,
> And drags at each remove a lengthen'd chain.

I just stay to write you a few lines, before I go to call on my friend, Mr Gavin Hamilton. I hate myself as an unworthy sinner because these interviews of old dear friends make me, for half a moment, almost forget Clarinda.

Remember to-morrow evening, at eight o'clock, I shall be with the Father of Mercies, at that hour on your own account. Farewell! If the post goes not to-night, I'll finish the other page to-morrow morning.

SYLVANDER.

P.S.—Remember.

It was probably on Monday the 25th that he proceeded to Dumfriesshire, with his friend John Tennant, to view and judge of Mr Miller's farms on the banks of the Nith. He was not at all confident of being able to find one which it would be prudent to lease.

SYLVANDER TO CLARINDA.

CUMNOCK, 2d March 1788.

I hope, and am certain, that my generous Clarinda will not think my silence, for now a long week, has been in any degree owing to my forgetfulness. I have been tossed about through the country ever since I wrote you; and am here, returning from Dumfries-shire, at an inn, the post-office of the place, with just so long time as my horse eats his corn, to write you. I have been hurried with business and dissipation, almost

---

* If this letter is authentic, Burns must still have had some thoughts of Jamaica as a last resort.

equal to the insidious decree of the Persian monarch's mandate, when he forbade asking petition of God or man for forty days.* Had the venerable prophet been as throng [busy] as I, he had not broken the decree ; at least not thrice a day.

I am thinking my farming scheme will yet hold. A worthy intelligent farmer, my father's friend and my own, has been with me on the spot : he thinks the bargain practicable. I am myself, on a more serious review of the lands, much better pleased with them. I won't mention this in writing to anybody but you and Mr Ainslie. Don't accuse me of being fickle ; I have the two plans of life before me, and I wish to adopt the one most likely to procure me independence.

I shall be in Edinburgh next week. I long to see you ; your image is omnipresent to me ; nay, I am convinced I would soon idolatrize it most seriously ; so much do absence and memory improve the medium through which one sees the much-loved object. To-night, at the sacred hour of eight, I expect to meet you, at the Throne of Grace. I hope, as I go home to-night, to find a letter from you at the post-office in Mauchline ; I have just once seen that dear hand since I left Edinburgh ; a letter, indeed, which much affected me. Tell me, first of womankind, will my warmest attachment, my sincerest friendship, my correspondence—will they be any compensation for the sacrifices you make for my sake ? If they will, they are yours. If I settle on the farm I propose, I am just a day and a half's ride from Edinburgh.† We shall meet : don't you say ' Perhaps, too often !'

Farewell, my fair, my charming Poetess ! May all good things ever attend you.

I am ever, my dearest Madam, Yours,   SYLVANDER.

TO MR WILLIAM CRUIKSHANK.

MY DEAR SIR—Apologies for not writing are frequently like apologies for not singing, the apology better than the song. I have fought my way severely through the savage hospitality of this country—[the object of all hosts being] to send every guest drunk to bed if they can.

I executed your commission in Glasgow, and I hope the cocoa came safe. 'Twas the same price and the very same kind as your former parcel ; for the gentleman recollected your buying there perfectly well.

I should return my thanks for your —— hospitality (I leave a blank for the epithet, as I know none can do it justice) to a poor way-faring Bard, who was spent and almost overpowered fighting with Prosaic wickedness in high places ; but I am afraid lest you should burn the letter whenever you come to the passage, so I pass over it in silence.

I am just returned from visiting Mr Miller's farm. The friend whom I

* Daniel vi. 7. The number of the days is thirty, not forty.

† The distance is a little over seventy miles. At this time there was no public coach on even so important a line of communication as the road between Edinburgh and Dumfries. A mail-coach commenced running upon it on the 1st of September 1790.

told you I would take with me was highly pleased with the farm ; and
as he is, without exception, the most intelligent farmer in the country,
he has staggered me a good deal ; I have the two plans of life before me :
I shall balance them to the best of my judgment, and fix on the most
eligible.   I have written Mr Miller, and shall wait on him when I come to
town, which shall be the beginning or middle of next week.   I would be
in sooner, but my unlucky knee is rather worse, and I fear for some time
will scarcely stand the fatigue of my excise instructions.   I only mention
these ideas to you ; and indeed, except Mr Ainslie, whom I intend
writing to to-morrow, I will not write at all to Edinburgh till I return to
it.   I would send my compliments to Mr Nicol, but he would be hurt
if he knew I wrote to any body and not to him, so I shall only beg my
best, kindest compliments to my worthy hostess and the sweet little rose-
bud.   So soon as I am settled in the routine of life, either as an excise
officer or as a farmer, I propose myself great pleasure from a regular correspondence with the only man almost I ever knew, who joined the most
attentive prudence with the warmest generosity.

I am much interested for that best of men, Mr Wood.   I hope he is in
better health and spirits than when I saw him last.   I am ever, my
dearest friend, your obliged, humble servant,   ROBT. BURNS.

MAUCHLINE, 3 *March* 1788.

TO MR ROBERT AINSLIE,

AT MR SAML. MITCHELSON'S, W.S., CARRUBBER'S CLOSE, EDINBURGH.

MAUCHLINE, 3d *March* 1788.*

MY DEAR FRIEND—I am just returned from Mr Miller's farm.   My
old friend whom I took with me was highly pleased with the bargain,
and advised me to accept of it.   He is the most intelligent, sensible farmer
in the county, and his advice has staggered me a good deal.   I have the
two plans before me : I shall endeavour to balance them to the best of
my judgment, and fix on the most eligible.   On the whole, if I find Mr
Miller in the same favourable disposition as when I saw him last, I shall
in all probability turn farmer.

I have been through sore tribulation, and under much buffeting of the
wicked one, since I came to this country.   JEAN I found banished, like
a martyr—forlorn, destitute, and friendless ; all for the good old cause :
I have reconciled her to her fate : I have reconciled her to her mother. . . .

I shall be in Edinburgh the middle of next week.   My farming ideas I
shall keep private till I see.   I got a letter from Clarinda yesterday, and
she tells me she has got no letter of mine but one.   Tell her that I wrote
to her from Glasgow, from Kilmarnock, from Mauchline, and yesterday
from Cumnock as I returned from Dumfries.   Indeed, she is the only
person in Edinburgh I have written to till this day.   How are your soul
and body putting up?—a little like man and wife, I suppose.   Your
faithful friend,   ROBT. BURNS.

* This letter is undated, but has been so endorsed by Ainslie.

[T O ———— ?]*

MAUCHLINE [*March* 1788].

MY DEAR SIR:—My life, since I saw you last, has been one continued hurry; that savage hospitality which knocks a man down with strong liquors is the devil. I have a sore warfare in this world: the devil, the world, and the flesh are three formidable foes. The first I generally try to fly from; the second, alas! generally flies from me; but the third is my plague, worse than the ten plagues of Egypt.

I have been looking over several farms in this country; one, in particular, in Nithsdale, pleased me so well, that if my offer to the proprietor is accepted, I shall commence farmer at Whit-Sunday. If farming do not appear eligible, I shall have recourse to my other shift: † but this to a friend.

I set out for Edinburgh on Monday morning; how long I stay there is uncertain, but you will know so soon as I can inform you myself. However I determine, poesy must be laid aside for some time; my mind has been vitiated with idleness, and it will take a good deal of effort to habituate it to the routine of business. I am, my dear Sir, yours sincerely,

R. B.

Jean Armour was, for the second time, about to become a mother. From his letter of 3d March to Robert Ainslie it fully appears that Burns had no design at that time of renewing his offer of marriage to Jean. On the contrary, anxious perhaps to keep himself free to secure Clarinda, and not perhaps without some apprehension that the marriage certificate of March 1786, though destroyed, might prove an impediment to that consummation, he tells that he had taken a solemn promise from Jean—'never to attempt any claim upon me as a husband, even though any one should persuade her she had such a claim, which she had not, neither during my life nor after my death.' Jean he regarded as one, in short, to whom he was not bound by any moral tie, though he held himself under an obligation of humanity to protect her in her present circumstances.

When Jean was expelled, in the middle of winter, from her father's house, she was sheltered by the wife of the Poet's friend, William Muir, the miller of Tarbolton. He now secured for

---

* Allan Cunningham published this letter as addressed to Robert Ainslie, Esq., and under date July 1787. The letter must have been written at this period of Burns's life, seeing that it alludes to his offer for Miller's farm. Since we have already an undoubted letter of this time to Ainslie, it may not be incorrect to surmise that the superscription of 'honest Allan,' like the date, has been given upon conjecture, and is equally erroneous.

† The Excise.

her a room in Mauchline.* There she was visited by her mother, who attended her during her confinement.

No allusion is made by Burns in any of his letters to the second accouchement. It is recorded in his family-Bible thus—'March 3, 1788, were born to them twins again, two daughters, who died within a few days after their birth.' †

CLARINDA TO SYLVANDER.

EDINBURGH, *March* 5, 1788.

I received yours from Cumnock about an hour ago ; and to show you my good-nature, sit down to write to you immediately. I fear, Sylvander, you overvalue my generosity ; for, believe me, it will be some time ere I can cordially forgive you the pain your silence has caused me ! Did you ever feel that sickness of heart which arises from ' hope deferred ?' That, the cruelest of pains, you have inflicted on me for eight days by-past. I hope I can make every reasonable allowance for the hurry of business and dissipation. Yet, had I been ever so engrossed, I should have found one hour out of the twenty-four to write you. No more of it : I accept of your apologies ; but am hurt that any should have been necessary betwixt us on such a tender occasion.

* Previously to this time, death had relieved Jean of the charge of her daughter, born in September 1786, and named after herself. The infant lived only fourteen months. The other child, Robert, still remained under the care of his grandmother and uncle at Mossgiel. Jean's own account of this portion of the story (*Memoranda by Mr M'Diarmid, from Mrs Burns's Dictation*, in Dr Hately Waddell's Critical Edition of *The Works of Robert Burns*) is : ' The father was no doubt angry that his daughter continued to correspond with the Bard—after he had written to her—but he had no opportunity of turning her out of doors. Her mother had warned her that her father was angry, and that she had better remain from home a little. She was then on a visit to William Muir, miller, Tarbolton Mill.' The house, opposite Nance Tannock's hostelry, in which Burns took a room, is still pointed out. At present the house has two apartments, kitchen and room.

' I am informed that the Poet only rented the kitchen. It is in its original form, but nothing else remains of interest. This house Burns rented for Jean in the month of February 1788, and it was in this house she gave birth to the second twins, on the 3rd of March, previous to the month of August, when, according to the Kirk Session records, she and the Poet were publicly rebuked and possibly re-married (but there is no proof of the fact) according to the ecclesiastical law. This statement may surprise many who hold that these twins were born at Willie's Mill, where Burns had procured an asylum for Jean with his friend, William Muir ; but from a poem by Alexander Tait, in a collection of poems and songs printed and sold by the author only, of date 1790, I quote the following lines, which point in the same direction :

> " Mackenzie he does her deliver
> In Mauchline ' Toun.' "

Mackenzie was then a doctor in the village, and is identified with the "Common Sense" of the "Holy Fair," and the correspondence of the Poet.'—JOHN TAYLOR GIBB, in *Burns Chronicle* for 1896.

† The birth of these infants is not recorded in the parish register of Mauchline—probably because they did not live to be baptised.

I am happy that the farming scheme promises so well. There's no fickleness, my dear Sir, in changing for the better. I never liked the Excise for you; and feel a sensible pleasure in the hope of your becoming a sober, industrious farmer. My prayers, in this affair, are heard, I hope, so far: may they be answered completely! The distance is the only thing I regret; but whatever tends to your welfare overweighs all other considerations. I hope ere then to grow wiser, and to lie easy under weeks' silence. I had begun to think that you had fully experienced the truth of Sir Isaac's philosophy.

I have been under unspeakable obligations to your friend, Mr Ainslie. I had not a mortal to whom I could speak of your name but him. He has called often; and, by sympathy, not a little alleviated my anxiety. I tremble lest you should have devolved, what you used to term your 'folly,' upon Clarinda: more's the pity. 'Tis never graceful but on the male side; but I shall learn more wisdom in future. Example has often good effects.

I got both your letters from Kilmarnock and Mauchline, and would, perhaps, have written to you unbidden, had I known anything of the geography of the country; but I knew not whether you would return by Mauchline or not, nor could Mr Ainslie inform me. I have met with several little rubs, that hurt me the more that I had not a bosom to pour them into—

On some fond breast the feeling soul relies.

Mary I have not once set eyes on since I wrote to you. Oh, that I should be formed susceptible of kindness, never, never to be fully, or, at least, habitually returned! 'Trim,' (said my Uncle Toby,) 'I wish, Trim, I were dead.'

Mr Ainslie called just now to tell me he had heard from you. You would see, by my last, how anxious I was, even then, to hear from you. 'Tis the first time I ever had reason to be so: I hope 'twill be the last. My thoughts were yours both Sunday nights at eight. Why should my letter have affected you? You know I count all things (Heaven excepted) but loss, that I may win and keep you. I supped at Mr Kemp's on Friday. Had you been an invisible spectator with what perfect ease I acquitted myself, you would have been pleased, highly pleased, with me.

Interrupted by a visit from Miss R——. She was inquiring kindly for you. I delivered your compliments to her. She means (as you once said) all the kindness in the world, but she wants that 'finer chord.' Ah! Sylvander, happy, in my mind, are they who are void of it. Alas! it too often thrills with anguish.

I hope you have not forgotten to kiss the little cherub for me. Give him fifty, and think Clarinda blessing him all the while. I pity his mother sincerely, and wish a certain affair happily over. My Willie is in good health, except his leg, which confines him close since it was opened; and Mr Wood says it will be a very tedious affair. He has prescribed sea-bathing as soon as the season admits. I never see Miss Nimmo. Her indifference wounds me; but all these things make me fly to the Father of Mercies, who is the inexhaustible Fountain of all kindness. How could you ever mention 'postages?' I counted on a crown at least; and have only spent one poor shilling. If I had but a shilling in the world you should have sixpence; nay, eightpence, if I could contrive to live on a groat. I am avaricious only in your letters; you are so, indeed. Farewell. Yours,   CLARINDA.

SYLVANDER TO CLARINDA.

[MAUCHLINE, *6th March* 1788.]

I own myself guilty, Clarinda: I should have written you last week. But when you recollect, my dearest Madam, that yours of this night's post is only the third I have from you, and that this is the fifth or sixth I have sent to you, you will not reproach me, with a good grace, for unkindness. I have always some kind of idea not to sit down to write a letter except I have time and possession of my faculties, so as to do some justice to my letter; which at present is rarely my situation. For instance, yesterday I dined at a friend's at some distance: the savage hospitality of this country spent me the most part of the night over the nauseous potion in the bowl. This day—sick—headache—low spirits—miserable—fasting, except for a draught of water or small beer. Now eight o'clock at night; only able to crawl ten minutes' walk into Mauchline, to wait the post, in the pleasurable hope of hearing from the mistress of my soul.

But truce with all this. When I sit down to write to you, all is happiness and peace. A hundred times a-day do I figure you before your taper—your book or work laid aside as I get within the room. How happy have I been! and how little of that scantling portion of time, called the life of man, is sacred to happiness, much less transport.

I could moralize to-night, like a death's-head.

> O what is life, that thoughtless wish of all!
> A drop of honey in a draught of gall.

Nothing astonishes me more, when a little sickness clogs the wheels of life, than the thoughtless career we run in the hour of health. 'None saith, where is God, my Maker, that giveth songs in the night: who teacheth us more knowledge than the beasts of the field, and more understanding than the fowls of the air?'

Give me, my Maker, to remember thee! Give me to act up to the dignity of my nature! Give me to feel 'another's wo;' and continue with me that dear-loved friend that feels with mine!

The dignifying and dignified consciousness of an honest man, and the well-grounded trust in approving Heaven, are two most substantial foundations of happiness. * * * *

I could not have written a page to any mortal except yourself. I'll write you by Sunday's post. Adieu. Good night.

SYLVANDER.

SYLVANDER TO CLARINDA.

MOSSGIEL, *7th March* 1788.

Clarinda, I have been so stung with your reproach for unkindness—a sin so unlike me, a sin I detest more than a breach of the whole Decalogue, fifth, sixth, seventh and ninth articles excepted—that I believe I shall not rest in my grave about it, if I die before I see you. You have often allowed me the head to judge, and the heart to feel, the influence of female excellence : was it not blasphemy, then, against your own charms, and against my feelings, to suppose that a short fortnight could abate my passion?

You, my love, may have your cares and anxieties to disturb you ; but they are the usual occurrences of life. Your future views are fixed, and your mind in a settled routine. Could not you, my ever dearest Madam, make a little allowance for a man, after long absence, paying a short visit to a country full of friends, relations, and early intimates? Cannot you guess, my Clarinda, what thoughts, what cares, what anxious forebodings, hopes and fears, must crowd the breast of the man of keen sensibility, when no less is on the tapis than his aim, his employment, his very existence through future life?

To be overtopped in anything else, I can bear; but in the tests of generous love, I defy all mankind ! not even to the tender, the fond, the loving, Clarinda—she whose strength of attachment, whose melting soul, may vie with Eloisa and Sappho, not even she can overpay the affection she owes me !

Now that, not my apology, but my defence is made, I feel my soul respire more easily. I know you will go along with me in my justification: would to Heaven you could in my adoption, too ! I mean an adoption beneath the stars—an adoption where I might revel in the immediate beams of

She the bright sun of all her sex.

I would not have you, my dear Madam, so much hurt at Miss N[immo]'s coldness. 'Tis placing yourself below her, an honour she by no means deserves. We ought, when we wish to be economists in happiness,—we ought, in the first place, to fix the standard of our own character ; and when, on full examination, we know where we stand, and how much ground we occupy, let us contend for it as property ; and those who seem to doubt, or deny us, what is justly ours, let us either pity their prejudices or despise their judgment. I know, my dear, you will say this is self-conceit ; but I call it self-knowledge : the one is the overweening opinion of a fool, who fancies himself to be what he wishes himself to be thought ; the other is the honest justice that a man of sense, who has thoroughly examined the subject, owes to himself. Without this standard, this column in our own mind, we are perpetually at the mercy of the petulance, the mistakes, the prejudices, nay, the very weakness and wickedness, of our fellow-creatures.

I urge this, my dear, both to confirm myself in the doctrine, which, I assure you, I sometimes need, and because I know, that this causes you often much disquiet. To return to Miss N[immo]. She is, most certainly, a worthy soul; and equalled by very, very few in goodness of heart. But can she boast more goodness of heart than Clarinda? Not even prejudice will dare to say so: for penetration and discernment, Clarinda sees far beyond her. To wit, Miss N[immo] dare make no pretence: to Clarinda's wit, scarce any of her sex dare make pretence. Personal charms, it would be ridiculous to run the parallel: and for conduct in life, Miss N[immo] was never called out, either much to do, or to suffer. Clarinda has been both; and has performed her part where Miss N[immo] would have sunk at the bare idea.

Away, then, with these disquietudes! Let us pray with the honest weaver of Kilbarchan, 'Lord, send us a gude conceit o' oursel'!' or in the words of the auld sang,

> Who does me disdain, I can scorn them again,
> And I'll never mind any such foes.

There is an error in the commerce of intimacy [on brief acquaintance-ship] which has led me far astray. [We are apt to be taken in by] those who, by way of exchange, have not an equivalent to give us; and what is still worse, have no idea of the value of our goods. Happy is our lot, indeed, when we meet with an honest merchant who is qualified to deal with us on our own terms; but this is a rarity. With almost everybody, we must pocket our pearls, less or more; and learn, is the old Scots phrase, 'to gie sic like as we get.' For this reason, we should try to erect a kind of bank or storehouse in our own minds; or, as the Psalmist recommends, 'commune with our own hearts, and be still.' This is exactly the [course to adopt with those who interfere with our choice of friends; for] if the friend be so peculiarly favored of Heaven as to have a soul as noble and exalted as yours, sooner or later your bosom will ache with disappointment.*

I wrote you yesternight, which will reach you long before this can. I may write Mr Ainslie before I see him, but I am not sure.

Farewell! and remember   SYLVANDER.

CLARINDA TO SYLVANDER.

EDINBURGH, *8th March* 1788.

I was agreeably surprised by your answer to mine of Wednesday coming this morning. I thought it alway took two days, a letter from this to Mauchline, and did not expect yours sooner than Monday. This

---

* 'The latter portion of the MS. of this letter is in a dilapidated condition, and the passages within square brackets are supplied by conjecture.'—W. SCOTT DOUGLAS's Edition of *Burns*, VOL. V., p. 103.

is the fifth from you, and the fourth time I am now writing you. I hate
calculating them : like some things, they don't do to be numbered. I
wish you had written from Dumfries, as you promised ; but I do not
impute it to any cause but hurry of business, &c. I hope I shall never
live to reproach you with unkindness. You never ought to put off till
you 'have time to do justice to your letters.' I have sufficient memorials
of your abilities in that way ; and last week, two lines, to have said
'How do ye, my Clarinda,' would have saved me days and nights of
cruel disquietude. 'A word to the wise' you know. I know human
nature better than to expect always fine flights of fancy, or exertions of
genius, and feel in myself the effects of this 'crazy mortal coil' upon its
glorious inhabitant. To-day, I have a clogging headache ; but, however
stupid, I know (at least I hope) a letter from your heart's friend will be
acceptable. It will reach you to-morrow, I hope. Shocking custom !
one can't entertain with hospitality, without taxing their guests with the
consequences you mention.

Your reflections upon the effects which sickness has on our retrospect
of ourselves, are noble. I see my Sylvander will be all I wish him,
before he leaves this world. Do you remember what simple eulogium I
pronounced on you, when Miss Nimmo asked what I thought of you :—
'He is ane of God's ain ; but his time's no come yet.' It was like a
speech from your worthy mother,—whom I revere. She would have
joined me with a heartfelt sigh, which none but mothers know. It is
rather a bad picture of us, that we are most prone to call upon God in
trouble. Ought not the daily blessings of health, peace, competence,
friends,—ought not these to awaken our constant gratitude to the Giver
of all? I imagine that the heart which does not occasionally glow with
filial love in the hours of prosperity can hardly hope to feel much
comfort in flying to God in the time of distress. O my dear Sylvander !
that we may be enabled to set Him before us as our witness, benefactor
and judge, at all times, and on all occasions !

In the name of wonder how could you spend ten hours with such a
—— as Mr Pattison? What a despicable character ! Religion ! he
knows only the name ; none of her real votaries ever wished to make
any such shameful compromises. But 'tis Scripture verified — the
demon of avarice, his original devil, finding him empty, called other
seven more impure spirits, and so completely infernalized him. Destitute of discernment to perceive your merit, or taste to relish it,
my astonishment at his fondness of you, is only surpassed by your
more than Puritanic patience in listening to his shocking nonsense !
I hope you renewed his certificate. I was told it was in a tattered
condition some months ago, and that then he proposed putting it on
parchment, by way of preserving it. Don't call me severe : I hate all
who would turn the 'Grace of God into licentiousness ;' 'tis commonly the weaker part of mankind who attempt it.

Religion, Thou the soul of happiness.

Yesterday morning in bed I happened to think of you. I said to myself 'My bonnie Lizzie Baillie,' &c., and laughed; but I felt a delicious swell of heart, and my eyes swam in tears. I know not if your sex ever feel this burst of affection; 'tis an emotion indescribable. You see I'm grown a fool since you left me. You know I was rational, when you first knew me, but I always grow more foolish the farther I am from those I love; by and by I suppose I shall be insane altogether.

I am happy your little lamb is doing so well. Did you execute my commission?* You had a great stock in hand; and, if any agreeable customers came in the way, you would dispose of some of them, I fancy, hoping soon to be supplied with a fresh assortment. For my part, I can truly say I have had no demand. I really believe you have taught me dignity, which, partly through good nature and partly by misfortune, had been too much laid aside; which now I never will part with. Why should I not keep it up? Admired, esteemed, beloved, by one of the first of mankind! Not all the wealth of Peru could have purchased these. Oh, Sylvander, I am great in my own eyes, when I think how high I am in your esteem! You have shown me the merit I possess; I knew it not before. Even Joseph † trembled t'other day in my presence. 'Husbands looked mild, and savages grew tame!' Love and cherish your friend Mr Ainslie. He is your friend indeed. I long for next week; happy days, I hope, yet await us. When you meet young Beauties, think of Clarinda's affection—of her situation—of how much her happiness depends on you.

Farewell, till we meet. God be with you.　　　　CLARINDA.

P.S.—Will you take the trouble to send for a small parcel left at Dunlop and Wilson's, Booksellers, Trongate, Glasgow, for me, and bring it with you in the Fly?

TO MR RICHARD BROWN.

MAUCHLINE, *7th March* 1788.

I have been out of the country, my dear friend, and have not had an opportunity of writing till now, when I am afraid you will be gone out of the country too. I have been looking at farms, and, after all, perhaps I may settle in the character of a farmer. I have got so vicious a bent to idleness, and have ever been so little a man of business, that it will take no ordinary effort to bring my mind properly into the routine: But you will say a 'great effort is worthy of you.' I say so myself; and butter up my vanity with all the stimulating compliments I can think of. Men of grave, geometrical minds, the sons of 'which was to be demonstrated,'‡ may cry up Reason as much as they please; but I have always found an honest passion, or native instinct, the truest auxiliary in the

---

* The 'kisses' referred to in Clarinda's previous letter (March 5).
† 'Joseph' was probably the porter who carried the lovers' letters.
‡ Q.E.D. = *Quod erat demonstrandum* (Which was to be demonstrated) is the formal conclusion of theorems in Euclid.

warfare of this world. Reason almost always comes to me like an unlucky wife to a poor devil of a husband, just in sufficient time to add her reproaches to his other grievances. . . . I am gratified with your kind inquiries after her [Jean], as, after all, I may say with Othello—

———— Excellent wretch,
Perdition catch my soul, but I do love thee !

I go for Edinburgh on Monday. &c.,   R. B.

TO MR ROBERT MUIR.

MOSSGIEL, *7th March* 1788.

DEAR SIR—I have partly changed my ideas, my dear Friend, since I saw you. I took old Glenconner with me to Mr Miller's farm, and he was so pleased with it, that I have wrote an offer to Mr Miller, which, if he accepts, I shall sit down a plain farmer, the happiest of lives when a man can live by it. In this case I shall not stay in Edinburgh above a week. I set out on Monday, and would have come by Kilmarnock, but there are several small sums owing me for my first edition, about Galston and Newmills; and I shall set off so early as to dispatch my business and reach Glasgow by night. When I return, I shall devote a forenoon or two to make some kind of acknowledgment for all the kindness I owe your friendship. Now that I hope to settle with some credit and comfort at home, there was not any friendship or friendly correspondence that promised me more pleasure than yours; I hope I will not be disappointed. I trust the Spring will renew your shattered frame, and make your friends happy.* You and I have often agreed that life is no great blessing on the whole. The close of life, indeed, to a reasoning eye, is

> Dark as was chaos, ere the infant sun
> Was roll'd together, or had try'd his beams
> Athwart the gloom profound—

But an honest man has nothing to fear. If we lie down in the grave, the whole man a piece of broke machinery, to moulder with the clods of the valley,—be it so; at least there is an end of pain, care, woes and wants : if that part of us called Mind does survive the apparent destruction of the man—away with the old-wife prejudices and tales ! Every age and every nation has had a different set of stories; and as the many are always weak, of consequence they have often, perhaps always, been deceived : a man, conscious of having acted an honest part among his fellow-creatures; even granting that he may have been the sport, at times, of passions and instincts; he goes to a great unknown Being, who could have no other end in giving him existence but to make him happy; who gave him those passions and instincts, and well knows their force.

* The wish was not fulfilled : Robert Muir died on 22d April following.

These, my worthy friend, are my ideas; and I know they are not far different from yours. It becomes a man of sense to think for himself; particularly in a case where all men are equally interested, and where, indeed, all men are equally in the dark. . . .

Adieu, my dear Sir! God send us a chearful meeting!

ROBT. BURNS.

TO MRS DUNLOP.*

MOSSGIEL, *7th March* 1788.

MADAM—The last paragraph in yours of the 30th February affected me most, so I shall begin my answer where you ended your letter. That I am often a sinner with any little wit I have, I do confess: but I have taxed my recollection to no purpose, to find out when it was employed against you. I hate an ungenerous sarcasm, a great deal worse than I do the devil; at least as Milton describes him; and though I may be rascally enough to be sometimes guilty of it myself, I cannot endure it in others. You, my honored friend, who cannot appear in any light but you are sure of being respectable—you can afford to pass by an occasion to display your wit, because you may depend for fame, on your sense; or if you chuse to be silent, you know you can rely on the gratitude of many and the esteem of all; but God help us who are wits or witlings by profession, if we stand not for fame there, we sink unsupported!

I am highly flattered by the news you tell me of Coila.† I may say to the fair painter who does me so much honor, as Dr Beattie says to Ross the poet, of his muse Scota, from which, by the bye, I took the idea of Coila: ('Tis a poem of Beattie's in the Scots dialect,‡ which perhaps you have never seen.)

Ye shak your head, but, o' my fegs,	shake—by my faith
Ye've set auld Scota on her legs:	old Scotland
Lang had she lien wi' buffs and flegs,	Long—slept with = submitted to—blows—kicks
Bombaz'd and dizzie,	stupefied
Her fiddle wanted strings and pegs,	
Waes me, poor hizzie!	Woe's me—hussy

R. B.

Burns, if he abode by his intention, left Mauchline on the 10th of March, on his return to Edinburgh. A letter to Miss Chalmers announces a notable event in his life:

---

* This letter is indexed in Currie's second vol. (1800 edition): 'To a lady. 7th March, 1788. *Who had heard that he had ridiculed her.*'

† A daughter of Mrs Dunlop was painting a sketch of Coila.

‡ 'To Mr Alexander Ross, at Lochlee, Author of "The Fortunate Shepherdess," and other Poems in the broad Scotch Dialect.'

TO MISS CHALMERS.

EDINBURGH, *March* 14, 1788.

I know, my ever dear friend, that you will be pleased with the news, when I tell you I have at last taken a lease of a farm. Yesternight I compleated a bargain with Mr Miller, of Dalswinton, for the farm of Ellisland, on the banks of the Nith, between five and six miles above Dumfries. I begin at Whitsunday to build a house, drive lime, &c., and heaven be my help! for it will take a strong effort to bring my mind into the routine of business. I have discharged all the army of my former pursuits, fancies, and pleasures; a motley host! and have literally and strictly retained only the ideas of a few friends, which I have incorporated into a life-guard. I trust in Dr Johnson's observation, 'Where much is attempted, something is done.' Firmness both in sufferance and exertion, is a character I would wish to be thought to possess: and have always despised the whining yelp of complaint, and the cowardly, feeble resolve. . . .

Poor Miss Kennedy* is ailing a good deal this winter, and begged me to remember her to you the first time I wrote you. Surely woman, amiable woman, is often made in vain. Too delicately formed for the rougher pursuits of ambition; too noble for the dirt of avarice, and even too gentle for the rage of pleasure; formed indeed for, and highly susceptible of, enjoyment and rapture; but that enjoyment, alas! almost wholly at the mercy of the caprice, malevolence, stupidity or wickedness of an animal at all times comparatively unfeeling, and often brutal.

R. B.

As has already been noticed, Patrick Miller was proprietor of the estate of Dalswinton, situated in the lower portion of the valley of the Nith. The lands and castle had once been the property of the family of Comyn, the ruin of which is dated from their opposition to Robert Bruce, by whom the then chief was slain in the Greyfriars' Church, Dumfries. The estate consists partly of some fine holm-land adjacent to the river, and partly of a series of well-wooded terraces ascending towards the neighbouring hills. Miller, we have seen, had actively befriended Burns in Edinburgh. Besides sending him a present, he had expressed

---

* Miss Kennedy, sister of Mrs Gavin Hamilton. This lady, who is so frequently alluded to by Burns, survived him about forty years. She was noted in her own circle for her cheerful disposition. The story goes, that 'when she was several years above ninety, she broke her arm by a fall down stairs. Her nephew, a medical man, immediately went to her in great solicitude. But the good old lady was quite placid and happy. "Isn't it," said she, "such a great mercy that it is not my leg. For in that case I might have been lame for life!"'

a strong wish to have him for a tenant. Burns, with some
reluctance, had gone at the end of autumn to see the lands
Mr Miller had to offer; he had returned to see them again in
March, when, contrary to his expectation, he found reason to hope
that a living might be made out of one of the Dalswinton farms.
Three were offered to him—Foregirth, a fine piece of the haugh,
bearing heavy crops of wheat; Bankhead, only a little less rich;
and Ellisland, close to the river, on its right bank, opposite the
mansion-house. The factor, father of Allan Cunningham, showed
Burns over them, and pointed out their various merits. There
seems to be little room for doubt that the poet ought to have
pitched upon Foregirth—of which it is related that it yielded
£40 an acre in the famine year of 1800, and that the tenant of
that period left it a gainer by £3000. Burns, however, was
captivated by the fine situation of Ellisland, with its views up
and down the river, and of the pleasure-grounds of Dalswinton;
and made what the factor called a poet's, not a farmer's, choice.

There is no reason to suppose that Mr Miller* drove a hard
bargain with Burns. He granted a lease for seventy-six years, at
an annual rent of £50 for the first three years, and £70 for the
remainder; agreeing further to give his tenant £300 to build a
new farm-steading and enclose the fields.† The only reservation
he made was one which the poet must himself have been pleased
with—a right to plant a belt of about two acres to screen the
farm on the north-west. Mr Miller was himself one of the
attractions of the place. His mind was active, cultivated, and
inventive. He had made three boats with paddles, driven by
manual labour, before 1788: and on the 14th November of that
year a small pleasure-boat, fitted with a steam-engine made by
William Symington, an ingenious mechanic at the Wanlockhead

---

* Mr Miller gives an account of his estate at the time of his purchase, in the *General View
of the Agriculture, &c., of Dumfriesshire*; 8vo, Edin. 1812. His letter is dated 24th
September 1810. 'When I purchased this estate, about five-and-twenty years ago, I had
not seen it. *It was in the most miserable state of exhaustion*, and all the tenants in poverty.
Judge of the first when I inform you, that oats ready to be cut were sold at 25s. per acre
upon the holm-grounds. *When I went to view my purchase, I was so much disgusted for eight
or ten days, that I then meant never to return to this county.*'

† The account which Gilbert Burns gave Dr Currie as to his brother's lease of Ellisland
differs slightly from the foregoing. 'I never understood,' he says, 'that Mr Miller gave my
brother the choice of any farm but Ellisland, on which Mr Miller fixed the rent himself,
but allowed my brother fifty-seven years of a lease, and to point out what restrictions he
should be under in the management.'

mines, was tried with perfect success on a small loch in the grounds of Dalswinton House. James Nasmyth, in his auto-biography, says that Burns and Lord Brougham (then a boy) were present on the occasion. Lord Brougham certainly did not visit Dalswinton until the year afterwards; and there is no positive evidence that Burns was there, though it is not impossible. Miller made further experiments with a larger boat, also engined by Symington, on the Forth and Clyde Canal, in 1789, but withdrew soon after from his costly experimenting. 'He spent his life and fortune in that adventure,' says Carlyle, 'and is heard no more of in those parts, having had to sell Dalswinton, and die quasi-bankrupt, and I should think broken-hearted.' This is obviously exaggerated: the *Dictionary of National Biography*, from materials supplied by his descendants, shows that Miller carried on agri-cultural experiments with success long after, and died at Dalswinton House in 1815. Symington resumed the scheme of steam-naviga-tion, and in 1801–2 designed, constructed, and engined, for Lord Dundas, a large steamboat for the Forth and Clyde Canal, which worked successfully, but was disapproved of by the Commissioners, as it would, they said, destroy the banks by the wash. This boat, the *Charlotte Dundas*, was examined both by Robert Fulton and by Henry Bell, who successfully established steam-navigation on the waters of America and Britain respectively.

While in Edinburgh on this occasion, Burns concluded two other transactions of no small importance to him: he obtained an order from the Board of Excise for tuition in the duties of a gauger, and settled accounts with Creech, his publisher. In the following four letters to Clarinda, undated, but undoubtedly belonging to this period, allusion is made to these matters:

SYLVANDER TO CLARINDA.

I will meet you to-morrow, Clarinda, as you appoint. My Excise affair is just concluded, and I have got my orders for instructions: so far good. Wednesday night I am engaged to sup among some of the principals of the Excise: so can only make a call for you that evening; but next day, I stay to dine with one of the Commissioners, so cannot go till Friday morning.

Your hopes, your fears, your cares, my love, are mine; so don't mind them. I will take you in my hand through the dreary wilds of this world, and scare away the ravening bird or beast that would annoy you.

I saw Mary in town to-day, and asked her if she had seen you. I shall
certainly bespeak Mr Ainslie as you desire.

Excuse me, my dearest angel, this hurried scrawl and miserable paper;
circumstances make both.   Farewell till to-morrow.

SYLVANDER.

Monday Noon [17th March.] *

SYLVANDER TO CLARINDA.

I am just hurrying away to wait on the Great Man, Clarinda ; but I
have more respect to my own peace and happiness, than to set out without
waiting on you ; for my imagination, like a child's favourite bird, will
fondly flutter along with this scrawl, till it perch on your bosom. I
thank you for all the happiness bestowed on me yesterday. The walk—
delightful ; the evening—rapture. Do not be uneasy to-day, Clarinda ;
forgive me. I am in rather better spirits to-day, though I had but an
indifferent night. Care, anxiety, sat on my spirits ; and all the cheerfulness of this morning is the fruit of some serious, important ideas that
lie, in their realities, beyond 'the dark and the narrow house,' as Ossian,
prince of poets, says. The Father of Mercies be with you, Clarinda !
and every good thing attend you !   SYLVANDER.

Tuesday Morning [18th March].

SYLVANDER TO CLARINDA.

Wednesday Morning [19th March.]

Clarinda, will that envious night-cap hinder you from appearing at
the window as I pass ? † 'Who is she that looketh forth as the morning ;
fair as the sun, clear as the moon, terrible as an army with banners ?'

Do not accuse me of fond folly for this line ; you know I am a cool
lover. I mean by these presents greeting, to let you to wit, that arch-
rascal, Creech, has not done my business yesternight, which has put off
my leaving town till Monday morning. To-morrow, at eleven, I meet
with him for the last time ; just the hour I should have met far more
agreeable company.

You will tell me this evening, whether you cannot make our hour of

---

* In the authorised edition of the Clarinda correspondence (1843), a date *two* weeks later
is conjecturally assigned to this letter ; while the three following are assigned dates
three weeks later.

† Probably the poet at this time was lodging with Nicol, whose house was in Buccleuch
Street ; in which case the Potterrow, where Mrs M'Lehose lived, would be on the line of his
walk into town. The residence of Mrs M'Lehose, at the time when Burns visited her, was,
as has already been observed, a small *flat*, or floor of a house, situated over an alley, part
of which still remains, and which bears the name of General's Entry, in consequence, it is
said, of General Monk having lived there when in command in Scotland. Alison's Square,
where Miss Nimmo lived, being right opposite, it is easy to understand why Clarinda
thought it necessary to be cautious about the number of Burns's visits. Through this
entry Walter Scott daily limped in the winter of 1787-8 to attend the civil law classes in
the University.

meeting to-morrow, one o'clock. I have just now written Creech such a
letter, that the very goose-feather in my hand shrunk back from the line,
and seemed to say 'I exceedingly fear and quake!' I am forming ideal
schemes of vengeance. O for a little of my will on him! I just wished
he loved as I do—as glorious an object as Clarinda—and that he were
doomed. Adieu, and think on   SYLVANDER.

SYLVANDER TO CLARINDA.

Friday, Nine o'clock, Night [21st March].

I am just now come in, and have read your letter. The first thing I
did was to thank the Divine Disposer of events, that he has had such
happiness in store for me as the connexion I have with you. Life, my
Clarinda, is a weary, barren path; and wo be to him or her that
ventures on it alone! For me, I have my dearest partner of my soul:
Clarinda and I will make out our pilgrimage together. Wherever I am,
I shall constantly let her know how I go on, what I observe in the
world around me, and what adventures I meet with. Will it please you,
my love, to get, every week, or, at least, every fortnight, a packet, two or
three sheets, full of remarks, nonsense, news, rhymes, and old songs?

Will you open, with satisfaction and delight, a letter from a man who
loves you, who has loved you, and who will love you to death, through
death, and for ever? Oh Clarinda! what do I owe to Heaven for blessing
me with such a piece of exalted excellence as you! I call over your idea
as a miser counts over his treasure! Tell me, were you studious to
please me last night? I am sure you did it to transport. How rich am
I who have such a treasure as you! You know me; you know how to
make me happy, and you do it most effectually. God bless you with

Long life, long youth, long pleasure, and a friend!

To-morrow night, according to your own direction, I shall watch the
window: 'tis the star that guides me to paradise. The great relish to all
is, that Honour, that Innocence, that Religion, are the witnesses and
guarantees of our happiness. 'The Lord God knoweth,' and, perhaps,
'Israel he shall know,' my love and your merit. Adieu, Clarinda! I am
going to remember you in my prayers.   SYLVANDER.

The poet, on leaving Edinburgh, sent Clarinda a pair of small
drinking-glasses, along with the following verses:

TO CLARINDA.

Fair Empress of the Poet's soul,
   And Queen of Poetesses,
Clarinda, take this little boon,
   This humble pair of glasses;

And fill them up with generous juice,
    As generous as your mind,
And pledge me in the generous toast
    'The whole of humankind!'

'To those who love us!' second fill,
    But not to those whom we love:
Lest we love those who love not us.
A third, 'To thee and me, love!'*

Burns would appear to have come to a reckoning with Creech on the 20th, and thus, after spending the evening of the 22d (Saturday) with Clarinda, to have been enabled to leave Edinburgh on the 24th. The amount of his profits from the *Poems* has been variously stated, but cannot now be ascertained. The most authoritative statement we have on the subject is contained in a letter from the poet himself, dated January 1789, to Dr Moore, where he says: 'I believe I shall, in whole, £100 copyright included, clear about £400, some little odds; and even part of this depends on what the gentleman [Creech] has yet to settle with me.' William Nicol wrote to John Lewars of Dumfries, after Burns's death: 'He certainly received £600 for the sale of the first [Edinburgh] edition of his poems, and £100 more for the copyright.' This report from so intimate a friend as Nicol would be entitled to weight, if it did not differ so widely from the poet's own statement. Dr Currie, who derived his information from Gilbert Burns, sets down the poet's profits at £500. Mrs Begg named the same figure. It may, then, fairly be surmised that, when Burns spoke to Dr Moore of £400 and some little odds, he mentally discounted the expense he incurred in Edinburgh while seeing the work through the press. A rough calculation of the receipts and expenses gives the author a surplus of about £420; if £100 for copyright be added to that, the total is only above the sum stated by Currie.†

---

* Charles Kirkpatrick Sharpe obtained, as a gift from Clarinda, a copy of Young's *Night Thoughts*, bearing inscription:

'To Mrs M'Lehose, this Poem, the sentiments of the heirs of Immortality, told in the numbers of Paradise, is respectfully presented by   ROBT. BURNS.'

† Heron, in his *Life of Burns*, says: 'Mr Creech has obligingly informed me that the whole sum paid to the poet for the copyright, and for the subscription copies of his book, amounted to nearly £1100. Out of this sum, indeed, the expences of printing the edition for the subscribers were to be deducted.'

Probably Burns had not more than £400 when he re-started farming. His tours, his accident, and the time he spent in Edinburgh, must have caused a drain on his little capital.

TO MR RICHARD BROWN.

GLASGOW, 26th March 1788.

I am monstrously to blame, my dear Sir, in not writing to you, and sending you the Directory. I have been getting my Tack extended, as I have taken a farm, and I have been racking shop accounts with Mr Creech; both of which, together with watching, fatigue, and a load of care almost too heavy for my shoulders, have in some degree actually fevered me. I really forgot the Directory yesterday, which vexed me; but I was convulsed with rage a great part of the day. I have to thank you for the ingenious, friendly, and elegant epistle from your friend, Mr Crawford. I shall certainly write to him, but not now. This is merely a card to you, as I am posting to Dumfriesshire, where many perplexing arrangements await me. I am vexed about the Directory; but, my dear Sir, forgive me: these eight days I have been positively crazed. My compliments to Mrs B. I shall write to you at Grenada. I am ever, my dearest friend, yours,   ROBT. BURNS.

Mr Crawford * here alluded to was the laird of Cartsburn, near Greenock, an open-hearted, worthy man, who, having read the Poems of Burns, and heard of him from Richard Brown, sent him this letter:

FROM THOMAS CRAWFORD, OF CARTSBURN, ESQ., TO ROBERT BURNS.

CARTSBURN, 16th March 1788.

MY DEAR SIR—For congeniality of mind entitles me to the freedom of this appellation, and never did I use it with more cordial sincerity. Through the medium of our mutual friend Brown, I hazard inviting you to the participation of an agreeable rural retirement, at a convenient distance from a town where there are many of your admirers (but indeed it is not distinguished by that from any town in Great Britain): a library I hope not ill chosen; a cellar not ill stored; a hearty cock of a landlord, whom his perhaps too partial friends regard as destitute neither of taste nor letters. He has reached his eighth lustre untrammelled by the matrimonial chain; and having neither wife nor ostensible child to disturb his tranquillity or divide his affection, he can offer you a whole heart. Halt!—this is going too far; for he is not so forlorn a wretch as

---

* Thomas Crawford (1741-1791) had succeeded to the estate of Cartsburn in 1783. He had spent much of his time on the continent, and was a more than ordinarily accomplished country gentleman.

to be without both a *friend* and a *mistress*—a *Davie* and a *Jean ;* but this does not hinder his having a very warm place in that same heart (for though the fellow's person be little, his heart is *large*) most cordially at your service ! How do you like the bill of fare? Not amiss, provided it be not a vapouring sign to a wretched ale-house—' Good wine needs no " bush." ' *Well-come* try (I must pun), and *welcome*, and I hope you will find it deficient neither in spirit nor flavour ; but this sage reflection of yours prevents my proceeding to raise your expectations too high. This much I will, however, in justice to myself, add—namely, that if you should be disappointed, I shall be much more so. Shall I, then, be blest with your society ? Answer me, my dear boy !

But I forget myself : you are no classic—no Latin one, I mean—though certainly to be *classed* (allow me a jingle) among the first Caledonian *classics.* Tell me where you are. God knows I would gladly come for you in person ; but as this is not in my power, will you allow me to send a servant and a horse for you ? Do, my dear Burns, and bless me with your assent. Your hearty friend,   T. CRAWFORD.

This letter shows the kind of feeling with which Burns was hailed on his appearance as a poet by men of warm heart and unsuspicious temper. At an ordinary time, nothing could have given him greater pleasure than to cultivate the friendship of so frank and generous a man as his correspondent, but now he was hardly in the mood for making new friends. Between Wednesday, 26th March, and the end of the week, he had travelled from Glasgow into Dumfriesshire, and attended to business there. During his recent absence in Edinburgh, he must have received a succession of letters from home, telling him, first, that Jean had again given birth to twins ; and next, that they were dead. A letter of the Sunday after his return from Dumfriesshire reveals the depressed state of his mind :

TO MR ROBERT CLEGHORN.

MAUCHLINE, 31*st March* 1788.

Yesterday, my dear Sir, as I was riding thro' a track of melancholy, joyless muirs, between Galloway and Ayrshire, it being Sunday, I turned my thoughts to psalms, and hymns, and spiritual songs ; and your favorite air, ' Captain O'Kean,' coming at length into my head, I tried these words to it. You will see that the first part of the tune must be repeated.

> The small birds rejoice in the green leaves returning,
> The murmuring streamlet winds clear thro' the vale,
> The hawthorn trees blow in the dews of the morning,
> And wild scattered cowslips bedeck the green dale :

But what can give pleasure, or what can seem fair,
   While the lingering moments are numbered wi' care?
No flowers gayly springing, nor birds sweetly singing,
   Can soothe the sad bosom of joyless despair.

I am tolerably pleased with these verses, but as I have only a sketch of the tune, I leave it with you to try if they suit the measure of the music.

I am so harassed with care and anxiety about this farming project of mine, that my muse has degenerated into the veriest prose-wench that ever picked cinders or followed a tinker. When I am fairly got into the routine of business I shall trouble you with a longer epistle ; perhaps with some queries respecting farming : at present, the world sits such a load on my mind, that it has effaced almost every trace of the poet in me.

My very best compliments and good wishes to Mrs Cleghorn.

R. B.

Cleghorn replied on the 27th April, offering his assistance in farming and expressing much gratification with the verses. He added : ' I wish you would send me a verse or two more ; and, if you have no objection, I would have it in the Jacobite style. Suppose it should be sung after the fatal field of Culloden by the unfortunate Charles.' Burns consequently added two verses, and called the whole

THE CHEVALIER'S LAMENT.

The small birds rejoice in the green leaves returning,
   The murmuring streamlet winds clear thro' the vale,
The hawthorn trees blow in the dews of the morning,
   And wild scattered cowslips bedeck the green dale :

But what can give pleasure, or what can seem fair,
   While the lingering moments are numbered wi' care?
No flowers gayly springing, nor birds sweetly singing,
   Can soothe the sad bosom of joyless despair.

The deed that I dared, could it merit their malice?
   A king and a father to place on his throne :
His right are these hills, and his right are these vallies
   Where the wild beasts find shelter, but I can find none.

But 'tis not my sufferings, thus wretched, forlorn,
　My brave gallant friends, 'tis your ruin I mourn ;
Your deeds proved so loyal in hot bloody trial,
　Alas ! can I make you no sweeter return !

On the same day that he wrote Cleghorn he also gave the
dilatory Creech a hint of the desirability of his obtaining the
money that was his due.

TO WILLIAM CREECH, ESQ.

MAUCHLINE, 31st *March* 1788.

As I am seriously set in for my farming operations, I shall need that
sum your kindness procured me for my copyright.　I have sent the line
to Mr John Somerville, a particular friend of mine, who will call on you ;
but as I do not need the sum, at least I can make a shift without it till
then.　Any time between now and the first of May, as it may suit your
convenience to pay it, will do for me.

Burns was now settled in Ayrshire for tuition in the duties
of an exciseman, the order for which was issued to an officer at
Tarbolton on the 31st March.*　It was his object to have this
business finished before Whitsunday term (25th May), when he
had to take possession of his farm in Dumfriesshire.　He had,
however, a duty to perform towards the household at Mossgiel.
Gilbert had been struggling alone in the farm, only to sink year

---

* The letter of instruction by the Board of Excise to the officer who trained Burns runs
thus :

'MR JAMES FINDLAY, OFFICER, TARBOLTON.

' The Commissioners order, that you instruct the bearer, Mr Robert Burns, in the art of
gauging, and practical dry gauging casks and utensils ; and that you fit him for surveying
victuallers, rectifiers, chandlers, tanners, tawers, maltsters, &c. ; and when he has kept
books regularly for six weeks at least, and drawn true vouchers and abstracts therefrom
(which books, vouchers, and abstracts must be signed by your supervisor and yourself, as
well as the said Mr Robert Burns), and sent to the Commissioners at his expense ; and when
he is furnished with proper instruments, and well instructed and qualified for an officer
(then and not before, at your perils), you and your supervisor are to certify the same to the
Board, expressing particularly therein the date of this letter ; and that the above Mr
Robert Burns hath cleared his quarters both for lodging and diet ; that he has actually paid
each of you for his instructions and examination ; and that he has sufficient at the time to
purchase a horse for his business.　I am, your humble servant,　　　'A. PEARSON.
　'EXCISE OFFICE,
'*Edinburgh*, 31st *March* 1788.'

This officer was, through Burns's means, introduced to Miss Markland, one of the six
Mauchline belles, and married her in the following September.　Mrs Findlay died in August
1851, at the age of eighty-six.

after year deeper into debt. The following undated letter was probably addressed to Gavin Hamilton, on a proposal being made to relieve Gilbert, by his brother becoming his guarantee to a considerable amount. The Poet, at no time imprudent in the management of money, declined the proposal.

TO [MR GAVIN HAMILTON?]

SIR—the language of refusal is to me the most difficult language on earth, and you are the man of the world, excepting One of Rt. Honble. designation,* to whom it gives me the greatest pain to hold such language. My brother has already got money, and shall want nothing in my power to enable him to fulfil his engagement with you ; but to be security on so large a scale, even for a brother, is what I dare not do, except I were in such circumstances of life as that the worst that might happen could not greatly injure me. I never wrote a letter which gave me so much pain in my life, as I know the unhappy consequences ; I shall incur the displeasure of a Gentleman for whom I have the highest respect, and to whom I am deeply obliged. I am, ever, Sir, your obliged and very humble servt.,   ROBT. BURNS.†

MOSSGIEL, *Friday Morn.*

When, however, he realised the proceeds of his *Poems*, Robert advanced to Gilbert the sum of £180. In his letter of the ensuing January to Dr Moore, he says : 'I give myself no airs on this, for it was mere selfishness on my part : I am conscious that the wrong scale of the balance was pretty heavily charged, and I thought that throwing a little filial piety and fraternal affection into the scale in my favour might help to smooth matters at the grand reckoning.' According to Mrs Begg, the family understood the transaction to mean that the money was lent to Gilbert without interest, and was to be considered as Robert's contribution for the future support of his mother, on the occasion of his marriage, and consequent departure from the household. It will be found that this loan had a somewhat curious and protracted history.

---

* Probably the Earl of Glencairn.

† This letter has been published in *fac-simile.* Appended to it is this note : 'This spirited reply, so characteristic of the independent mind of Caledonia's favorite Bard, was found about ten days ago covering a small purchase made at a Butter Shop in London. It is to be regretted that the address had been used for a similar purpose to another customer, and that no trace of it can be found.'

TO ALEX. BLAIR, ESQ., CATRINE HOUSE, CATRINE.

MAUCHLINE, 3d April 1788.

SIR—I returned here yesterday, and received your letter, for which I return you my heartiest and warmest thanks. I am afraid I cannot at this moment accede to your request, as I am much harrassed with the care and anxiety of farming business, which at present is not propitious to poetry ; but if I have an opportunity you shall learn of my progress in a few weeks.

I cannot but feel gratitude to you for the kindly manner by which you have shewn your interest in my endeavours ; and I remain, your obedient servant, ROBERT BURNS.

TO MR WILLIAM DUNBAR, EDINBURGH.

MAUCHLINE, 7th April 1788.

I have not delayed so long to write you, my much respected friend, because I thought no farther of my promise. I have long since given up that kind of formal correspondence where one sits down irksomely to write a letter, because we are in duty bound to do so.

I have been roving over the country, as the farm I have taken is forty miles from this place, hiring servants and preparing matters ; but most of all, I am earnestly busy to bring about a revolution in my own mind. As, till within these eighteen months, I never was the wealthy master of ten guineas, my knowledge of business is to learn ; add to this, my late scenes of idleness and dissipation have enervated my mind to an alarming degree. Skill in the sober science of life is my most serious and hourly study. I have dropt all conversation and all reading (prose reading) but what tends in some way or other to my serious aim. Except one worthy young fellow,* I have not one single correspondent in Edinburgh. You have indeed kindly made me an offer of that kind. The world of wits, and *gens comme il faut* which I lately left, and with whom I never again will intimately mix—from that port, Sir, I expect your Gazette : what *les beaux esprits* are saying, what they are doing, and what they are singing. Any sober intelligence from my sequestered walks of life ; any droll original ; any passing remark, important, forsooth, because it is mine ; any little poetic effort, however embryoth ; these, my dear Sir, are all you have to expect from me. When I talk of poetic efforts, I must have it always understood that I appeal from your wit and taste to your friendship and good nature. The first would be my favourite tribunal, where I defied censure ; but the last, where I declined justice.

* Probably Ainslie.

I have scarcely made a single distich since I saw you. When I meet with an old Scots air that has any facetious idea in its name, I have a peculiar pleasure in following out that idea for a verse or two.

I trust that this will find you in better health than I did last time I called for you. A few lines from you, directed to me, at Mauchline, were it but to let me know how you are, will set my mind a good deal [at rest]. Now, never shun the idea of writing me because, perhaps, you may be out of humour or spirits. I could give you a hundred good consequences attending a dull letter; one, for example, and the remaining ninety nine some other time; it will always serve to keep in countenance, my much respected Sir, Your obliged friend, and humble servant,

R. B.

TO MISS CHALMERS.

MAUCHLINE, 7th April 1788.

I am indebted to you and Miss Nimmo for letting me know Miss Kennedy. Strange! how apt we are to indulge prejudices in our judgments of one another! Even I who pique myself on my skill in marking characters; because I am too proud of my character as a man, to be dazzled in my judgment *for* glaring wealth; and too proud of my situation as a poor man to be biassed *against* squalid poverty; I was unacquainted with Miss K.'s very uncommon worth.

I am going on a good deal progressive in *mon grand but*, the sober science of life. I have lately made some sacrifices, for which, were I *virâ voce* with you to paint the situation and recount the circumstances, you would applaud me. R. B.

The allusion in the last sentence is probably to his change of intention towards Jean Armour. A crisis had, indeed, now arrived in the life of Burns. How and when he faced it can never be accurately ascertained. But when he did face it, he took the only course that could meet with the approval of his conscience, which sometimes slumbered, but invariably awoke to the punitive duty of inflicting 'stabs of remorse.' Burns's views of the relations between the sexes are among the things he kept to himself. It is, to say the least, not improbable that, considering how eagerly he read the literature which heralded and accompanied that great social as well as political cataclysm, the French Revolution, he had imbibed,

although possibly in a modified form, certain of Rousseau's
views on these relations.   In Edinburgh, as in Mauchline,
he appears to have regarded an intrigue with a servant girl, an
Elizabeth Paton or a May Cameron, as a 'thoughtless folly,' a
mere 'sowing of wild oats,' and in this view he was sustained by
the practice not only of many of the men he was in the habit
of meeting, such as James Smith and Robert Ainslie, but by the
'lax views' which undoubtedly prevailed in that period of transi-
tion and revolt.   For the acceptance of such views, his own nature,
with its extraordinary endowment of passion, undoubtedly prepared
him.   At the same time, while he looked with no austere eye
on 'the sowing of wild oats,' he had always recommended marriage
to others, and had contemplated it for himself.   When he was
deserted by Jean Armour, and considered himself a bachelor, he
turned—such, at least, is the all but universal belief—to Mary
Campbell.   During his first winter in Edinburgh he had wished
to make Margaret Chalmers his wife.   We have his own word for
it that he almost persuaded the daughter of an East Lothian farmer
to accompany him to Ayrshire.   During the winter of 1787 Clarinda
had driven every other image from his thoughts.   Whether he ever
really reached the Sapphic stage of 'crazing the faculties of his soul'
about her may be doubted, in spite of his own assertions to that
effect.   But there can be no question whatever that the attachment
of Mrs M'Lehose for Burns had, before he left Edinburgh, become
an absorbing passion.   There is no means of deciding what she
contemplated as the outcome of this entanglement, although
it is not improbable that she entertained the idea of obtaining
a divorce from her husband and marrying Burns.   He, on his side,
had been perfectly frank with her as to his relations with Jean
Armour.   If she married him, or entered into any sort of connection with him, she did so with her eyes open, and aware of the
fact that he was already burdened with a mistress and two illegiti-
mate children.   It may seem strange that Mrs M'Lehose, whose
religious convictions were strong enough to control her affections
for a time, should have been willing to sacrifice another woman.
From the standpoint of the higher morality, her conduct was inde-
fensible.   Something, however, must be allowed for the power of
the strongest passion known to humanity.   The excuse of *autres
temps autres mœurs* is also not without some force.   Burns and

Clarinda lived, as has been seen, in a century of 'unsettled' views upon the relations between the sexes. It may, at least, be said of him that, even from the seventh commandment standpoint he was a 'better man' than Charles James Fox, while she may be favourably compared with Rousseau's Madame de Warens, and even with Voltaire's 'divine Emily.' Nor should it be forgotten that Mrs M'Lehose cherished for Jean Armour the contempt that is often entertained by a woman of superficial culture for a woman who can lay no claim to culture at all. She maintained to the day of her death that Burns's marriage was a fatal mistake.

Burns, on his part, was, while living in Mauchline, brought face to face with the fact that, on his account, a poor girl—Jean was only twenty-three years of age at this time, though he believed her to be but twenty-one—had been boycotted by her father and family. No impartial evidence has ever been adduced in support of the story that, while he was in Edinburgh, she had taken another lover; on this point the testimony of Burns's relatives, who, at first, at all events, disapproved of his connection with her, cannot in fairness be accepted. Even if she wavered in her loyalty during his absence, her old love returned in full force when he appeared once more on the scene. It may be regarded, too, as probable, if not morally certain, that although, while fresh from Edinburgh and the undoubted fascinations of Mrs M'Lehose,* he could not help—at all events, when writing to her—contrasting her accomplishments and the sweet, reluctant, amorous delay of her finished coquetry with the simplicity and 'meek surrender' of her rival, he could not fail to notice the solid sense, which, when allowed scope for development in the management of a household, secured for Jean Burns the respect of all who knew her either as his wife or his widow. Possibly Margaret Chalmers or Clarinda—who certainly had studied his nature more closely and would, to judge from her letters, have scanned his 'follies' more gently than any other woman he came across—would have come nearer to the

---

* 'On returning from Edinburgh [in spring '88], Burns wore a breast-pin with a miniature of Clarinda, which she had presented to him. After his marriage, he sent his brother William to Glasgow, with bonny Jean on a horse behind him, where an artist took a miniature of her, which was placed in the pin, with the motto: "To err is human, to forgive, divine."'—*Recollections of Mrs Begg.* The miniature of Clarinda is now (1896) in the possession of Mr James Barbour, Dumfries.

ideal wife for a poet. But would either the one or the other have made the ideal wife for a farmer or an exciseman? In any case, it is idle to conjecture. It is beyond all question that Burns, when he married Jean Armour,* took the only course that was open to him as a man of honour.†

TO MR JAMES SMITH, LINLITHGOW.

MAUCHLINE, *April 28th*, 1788.

Beware of your Strasburgh, my good Sir! Look on this as the opening of a correspondence, like the opening of a twenty-four gun battery!

There is no understanding a man properly without knowing sometimes of his previous ideas (that is to say, if the man has any ideas; for I know many who, in the animal-muster, pass for men, that are the scanty masters of only one idea on any given subject, and by far the greatest part of your acquaintances and mine can barely boast of ideas, 1·25—1·5—1·75, or some such fractional matter); so to let you a little into the secrets of my pericranium, there is, you must know, a certain clean-limbed, handsome, bewitching young hussy of your acquaintance, to whom I have lately and privately given a matrimonial title to my corpus.

| Bode a robe and wear it, | bid for |
| Bode a pock and bear it,‡ | poke, beggar's wallet |

says the wise old Scots adage! I hate to presage ill-luck; and as my girl has been *doubly* kinder to me than even the best of women usually are to their partners of our sex, in similar circumstances, I reckon on twelve times a brace of children against I celebrate my twelfth wedding day. * * *

'Light's heartsome' quo' the wife when she was stealing sheep. You see what a lamp I have hung up to lighten your paths, when you are idle

---

* 'Had Burns deserted Jean, he had merely been a heartless villain. In making her his lawful wedded wife, he did no more than any other man, in the same circumstances, would have done; and had he not, he would have walked in shame before men, and in fear and trembling before God.'—JOHN (PROFESSOR) WILSON in 1840.

† It is not unworthy of note, that in the same year, 1788, in which Burns broke off his connection with Clarinda and married Jean Armour, Goethe, the greatest of his contemporaries, his senior by ten years, and his elder brother, not certainly in misfortune, but in the muses and in erotic passion, broke off his intimacy with the Countess von Stein, and took Christiane Vulpius to live with him as his wife, although he did not go through the ceremony of marriage with her till 1806.

‡ 'Speak heartily and expect good, and it will fall out accordingly.'—KELLY'S *Scottish Proverbs*.

enough to explore the combinations and relations of my ideas. 'Tis now as plain as a pike staff, why a twenty-four gun battery was a metaphor I could readily employ.

Now for business. I intend to present Mrs Burns with a printed shawl, an article of which I daresay you have variety: 'tis my first present to her since I have irrevocably called her mine; and I have a kind of whimsical wish to get the first said present from an old and valued friend of hers and mine—a trusty Trojan whose friendship I count myself possessed of as a liferent lease.

Look on this letter as a 'beginning of sorrows;' I will write you till your eyes ache reading nonsense.

Mrs Burns ('tis only her private designation) begs her best compliments to you.   R. B.

This letter contains the first known reference to Burns's marriage. It does not imply a ceremonial marriage, but perhaps that verbal acknowledgment of marriage which in Scotland binds man to woman for all legal purposes. The eldest daughter of Gavin Hamilton affirmed that Burns made the first intimation of the fact at her father's breakfast-table, when Robert Aiken was present. 'Mrs Hamilton having to express regret for not being able to give Mr Aiken his customary egg, the poet said that if she would send over the way to "Mrs Burns," she might have some.' According to local tradition, Burns and Jean met in Gavin Hamilton's house,* and acknowledged each other as man and wife, and Hamilton, as a Justice of the Peace, gave them a marriage certificate. According to another story, the marriage took place in one of the hostelries of Mauchline, kept by one Hugh Morton, and the officiating Justice of the Peace was Farquhar Gray, laird of Gilmilnscroft, an estate in the parish of Sorn, which was formerly part of Mauchline, but had been disjoined before Burns's time.†

---

* This house is at present occupied by Mr William Wilson, inspector of poor for Mauchline parish.

† 'Returning to Mauchline, we entered the house of auld Nance Tannock. . . . Proceeding up-stairs, and opening a door at the top, you step into the graveyard. . . . Farther along the same street or lane, in the direction of the churchyard, stood a public-house, which has been demolished, on the site included within the churchyard walls. Our guide told us that a great deal of money was made in it of yore by penny reels. At that time the churchyard was imperfectly enclosed, if enclosed at all. At fair times, the lasses stood ranged along the street like so many cattle; and there being a right-of-way through the churchyard to the hostelry aforesaid, they were conducted over the graves of the rude forefathers of the hamlet by their rustic admirers, to tread a measure . . . to the strains of the village fiddler. The scandal was put an end to by enclosing the graveyard,

TO MRS DUNLOP.

MAUCHLINE, 28*th April* 1788.

MADAM—Your powers of reprehension must be great indeed, as I assure you they made my heart ache with penitential pangs, even though I was really not guilty. As I commence farmer at Whitsunday, you will easily guess I must be pretty busy; but that is not all. As I got the offer of the excise business without solicitation; and as it costs me only six weeks' * attendance for instruction, to entitle me to a commission, which commission lies by me, and at any future period, on my simple petition, can be resumed; I thought five and thirty pounds a-year was no bad *dernier ressort* for a poor poet, if fortune in her jade tricks should kick him down from the little eminence to which she has lately helped him up.

For this reason, I am at present attending these instructions, to have them completed before Whitsunday. Still, madam, I prepared with the sincerest pleasure to meet you at the Mount, and came to my brother's on Saturday night, to set out on Sunday; but for some nights preceding I had slept in an apartment where the force of the winds and rains was only mitigated by being sifted through numberless apertures in the windows, walls, &c. In consequence I was on Sunday, Monday, and part of Tuesday unable to stir out of bed, with all the miserable effects of a violent cold.

You see, madam, the truth of the French maxim *Le vrai n'est pas toujours le vrai-semblable*; your last was so full of expostulation, and was something so like the language of an offended friend, that I began to tremble for a correspondence, which I had with grateful pleasure set down as one of the greatest enjoyments of my future life. . . .

and demolishing the hostelry. It was in this hostelry that Burns was married by a Justice of the Peace. He never had the ceremony performed by a priest. . . . There used to be a thoroughfare between the churchyard and the Priory, the residence of Gavin Hamilton, now occupied by an addition to that mansion, by which one could, in a step or two, pop out of the Priory into the public-house before mentioned, or into the church. By this way Burns went and came when he took the famous notes of the sermon preached by "The Calf," and by this way stepped Gavin Hamilton when he acted *as a witness* to Burns's irregular marriage by the J. P., the Laird of Gilmilnscroft.'—W, GUNNYON, in *Kilmarnock Standard*, Sept. 28, 1867. A third local tradition may be given : ' Miss Caldwell, a lady now dead, but who, for many years, lived in the house opposite Nance Tannock's, used to say that Mrs Alexander, John Richmond's daughter, with whom she was personally acquainted from childhood, often told her that Burns and Jean Armour were married in John Ronald's, who, it will be remembered, was the carrier between Glasgow and Mauchline. There was a man of that name who kept a public-house in Loudoun Street, on the site now occupied by Thomas Learmont's house and baker's shop. But I have been unable to get any corroboration of Miss Caldwell's statement. All the same, it is a very probable one, coming, as it does, almost at first hand, from the tongue of the daughter of him who must have known more of the private life of the Poet than any of his contemporaries.'— JOHN TAYLOR GIBB, in *Burns Chronicle* for 1896.

* Currie quotes 'months.'

Your books have delighted me: Virgil, Dryden, and Tasso were all equally strangers to me; but of this more at large in my next.

R. B.

TO PROFESSOR DUGALD STEWART.

MAUCHLINE, 3d May 1788.

SIR—I enclose you one or two more of my bagatelles. If the fervent wishes of honest gratitude have any influence with that great unknown Being who frames the chain of causes and events, prosperity and happiness will attend your visit to the Continent, and return you safe to your native shore.

Wherever I am, allow me, Sir, to claim it as my privilege to acquaint you with my progress in my trade of rhymes; as I am sure I could say it with truth, that, next to my little fame, and the having it in my power to make life more comfortable to those whom nature has made dear to me, I shall ever regard your countenance, your patronage, your friendly good offices, as the most valued consequence of my late success in life.

R. B.

TO MRS DUNLOP.

MAUCHLINE, 4th May 1788.

MADAM—Dryden's *Virgil* has delighted me. I do not know whether the critics will agree with me, but the *Georgics* are to me by far the best of Virgil. It is indeed a species of writing entirely new to me, and has filled my head with a thousand fancies of emulation: but alas! when I read the *Georgics*, and then survey my own powers, 'tis like the idea of a Shetland pony drawn up by the side of a thorough-bred hunter, to start for the plate. I own I am disappointed in the *Æneid*. Faultless correctness may please, and does highly please, the lettered critic; but to that aweful character I have not the most distant pretensions. I do not know whether I do not hazard my pretensions to be a critic of any kind, when I say that I think Virgil, in many instances, a *servile* copier of Homer. If I had the *Odyssey* by me, I could parallel many passages where Virgil has evidently copied, but by no means improved, Homer. Nor can I think there is any thing of this owing to the translators; for, from every thing I have seen of Dryden, I think him in genius and fluency of language, Pope's master. I have not perused Tasso enough to form an opinion: in some future letter you shall have my ideas of him; though I am conscious my criticisms must be very inaccurate and imperfect, as there I have ever felt and lamented my want of learning most.

R. B.

TO MR SAMUEL BROWN, KIRKOSWALD.

MOSSGIEL, *4th May* 1788.

DEAR UNCLE—This, I hope, will find you and your conjugal yoke-fellow in your good old way. I am impatient to know if the Ailsa *
fowling be commenced for this season yet, as I want three or four
stones of feathers, and I hope you will bespeak them for me. It would
be a vain attempt for me to enumerate the various transactions I have
been engaged in since I saw you last; but this know—I engaged in a
smuggling trade, and God knows if ever any poor man experienced
better returns—two for one: but as freight and delivery have turned out
so dear, I am thinking of taking out a licence, and beginning in fair
trade.

I have taken a farm on the borders of the Nith, and in imitation of
the old patriarchs, get men-servants and maid-servants, and flocks and
herds, and beget sons and daughters. Your obedient nephew

ROBT. BURNS.

TO MR JAMES JOHNSON.

MAUCHLINE, *25th May* 1788.

MY DEAR SIR—I am really uneasy about that money which Mr
Creech owes me per note in your hand, and I want it much at present, as
I am engaging in business pretty deeply both for myself and my
brother. A hundred guineas can be but a trifling affair to him, and 'tis
a matter of most serious importance to me. To-morrow I begin my
operations as a farmer, and God speed the plough!

I am so enamoured of a certain girl's prolific, twin-bearing merit, that
I have given her a legal title to the best blood in my body, and so farewell rakery! To be serious, I found I had a long and much-loved
fellow-creature's happiness or misery in my hands; and though Pride
and seeming Justice were murderous King's Advocates on the one side,
yet Humanity, Generosity, and Forgiveness, were such powerful, such
irresistible, council on the other side, that a jury of all Endearments and
new attachments brought in a unanimous verdict *Not Guilty!* And the
Panel, be it known unto all whom it concerns, is installed and instated
into all the rights, privileges, immunities, franchises, services, and
paraphernalia that at present do, or at any time coming may, belong
to the name, title and designation [MS. torn away.]

Present my best Compliments to . . .

* It is worth noting that Burns, although living almost in sight of ' Paddy's Milestone.'
mentions it but twice : here, and in one of his poems.

TO MR ROBERT AINSLIE.

MAUCHLINE, *May* 26, 1788.

MY DEAR FRIEND—I am two kind letters in your debt, but I have been from home, and horridly busy buying and preparing for my farming business, over and above the plague of my Excise instructions, which this week will finish.

As I flatter my wishes that I forsee many future years' correspondence between us, 'tis foolish to talk of excusing dull epistles ; a dull letter may be a very kind one. I have the pleasure to tell you that I have been extremely fortunate in all my buyings and bargainings hitherto ; Mrs Burns not excepted ; which title I now avow to the world. I am truly pleased with this last affair : it has indeed added to my anxieties for futurity, but it has given a stability to my mind and my resolutions, unknown before ; and the poor girl has the most sacred enthusiasm of attachment to me, and has not a wish but to gratify my every idea of her deportment. I am interrupted, Farewel ! my dear Sir.

R. B.

TO MRS DUNLOP.

[MAUCHLINE,] 27*th May* 1788.

MADAM—I have been torturing my philosophy to no purpose, to account for that kind partiality of yours, which unlike . . . has followed me in my return to the shade of life, with assiduous benevolence. Often did I regret, in the fleeting hours of my late will-o'-wisp appearance, that 'here I had no continuing city ;' and, but for the consolation of a few solid guineas, could almost lament the time that a momentary acquaintance with wealth and splendor put me so much out of conceit with the sworn companions of my road through life, insignificance and poverty. . . .

There are few circumstances relating to the unequal distribution of the good things of this life, that give me more vexation (I mean in what I see around me) than the importance the opulent bestow on their trifling family affairs, compared with the very same things on the contracted scale of a cottage. Last afternoon, I had the honor to spend an hour or two at a good woman's fire side, where the planks that composed the floor were decorated with a splendid carpet, and the gay table sparkled with silver and china. 'Tis now about term day, and there has been a revolution among those creatures who, though in appearance partakers, and equally noble partakers, of the same nature with Madame, are, from time to time—their nerves, their sinews, their health, strength, wisdom, experience, genius, time, nay a good part of their very thoughts—sold for months and years, . . . not only to the necessities, the conveniences, but the caprices, of the important few.*

* In Scotland, servants are usually engaged by the half-year, the terms being Whitsunday (May 25) and Martinmas (November 22).

We talked of the insignificant creatures; nay, notwithstanding their general stupidity and rascality, did some of the poor devils the honour to commend them. But light be the turf upon his breast who taught 'Reverence thyself!' We looked down on the unpolished wretches, their impertinent wives and clouterly brats, as the lordly bull does on the little dirty ant-hill, whose puny inhabitants he crushes in the carelessness of his ramble, or tosses in air in the wantonness of his pride.   R. B.

With these letters, indicating increasing satisfaction on Burns's part with the step which he had taken, the Edinburgh period of his life comes to a close. That he bore himself all through it at once with manliness and with modesty has never been disputed. It was admitted by all who came in contact with him during the winter of 1786 and the spring of 1787 that 'in this prodigy will had dung [defeated] fate.'* But he never lost his head. He saw from the first that his reputation, so far as society in Edinburgh was concerned, must be evanescent, and he acted accordingly. His second Common-place Book proves that he measured himself deliberately against the men he met. He perceived his own superiority to them in natural force; he did not repine at their better fortune. It is morally certain that had Burns visited Edinburgh in the days of the literary supremacy of Scott and Jeffrey,† a vigorous and successful effort would have been made to secure for him a position which would have permitted free exercise for his extraordinary faculty. It is beyond all question that Scott, the least jealous of all the sons of letters, who welcomed genius in others as cordially as Goethe himself, who held out the right hand of brotherhood to James Hogg, would have bestirred himself in his usual effective manner to secure adequate

---

* 'Sir Gilbert Elliot, first Earl of Minto, in a letter written from London in 1787.'—*Life and Letters of Sir Gilbert Elliot, edited by his grand-niece*, 1874.

† 'Oh, my dear Empson, there must be something *terribly* wrong in the present arrangements of the Universe, when these things can happen, and be thought natural. I could lie down in the dirt and cry and grovel there, I think, for a century to save such a soul as Burns's from the suffering, and the contamination, and the degradation which these same arrangements imposed upon him; and fancy that if I could but have known him (in my present state of wealth and influence) I might have saved and reclaimed and preserved him even to the present day. . . . When I think on *his* position, I have no feeling for the ideal poverty of your Wordsworths or Coleridges; comfortable, flattered, very spoiled, idle beings, fantastically discontented because they can not make an easy tour to Italy, and buy casts and cameos—and what poor peddling, whining dwellers in comparison with him.'—From a letter of Jeffrey (who, it will be remembered, actually advanced money to Carlyle) to Empson, dated Nov. 11, 1837 (*Life of Lord Jeffrey*, by Lord Cockburn, 1852).

recognition for the genius of Robert Burns. Burns, however, asked nothing from his Edinburgh friends; when they helped him to a farm and a position in the Excise, believing, as they apparently did, that they were thereby gratifying his own wishes, he made no complaint, but cheerfully prepared himself for the necessarily uncongenial career which alone appeared open to him.

Burns was but twenty-seven years of age when he came to Edinburgh from Ayrshire. Of few men of warm temperament and exceptionally endowed by nature with those strong passions which are the sources at once of selfishness and of unselfishness can it be said with truth that 'the battle between the flesh and the spirit' which ends in the ruin or the consolidation of character has been fought out so early in life. His sociable temperament, his eager willingness to observe all sorts and conditions of men, inevitably led him into 'scenes of life,' the survey of which meant the enlargement of experience, but not—at least immediately—the enrichment of motive. But it is as certain that he never lost command of himself, amidst the Crochallan festivities, as that he acquitted himself with modesty and manliness at the tables of professors and senators of the College of Justice. There was an undoubted risk that, with his extraordinary susceptibility to female influence, he might have suffered moral shipwreck on the rock either of libertinage or of calculating selfishness. His nature might have been coarsened by a succession of essentially vulgar intrigues, such as that with May Cameron. He might have yielded to the growing passion of Mrs M'Lehose, and—perhaps only half-heartedly—have entered into a dubious connection with her. He might have contracted a marriage of prudence with Margaret Chalmers. But his better instincts guided him to the only right course. By marrying Jean Armour he deliberately cast libertinage behind him. He entered upon his farm at Ellisland by no means free from the moral embarrassments entailed by his past, and knowing well that, with his responsibilities as a married man, he could only trust to circumstances to fulfil the high mission which he had clearly perceived to be his when he wrote 'The Vision.' But he had taken the one step which made for—if it could not at once ensure—mental peace. He had a character to lose or to strengthen, as well as a reputation to sustain and increase—at intervals, and as opportunity offered.

CHAPTER V

URNS appears to have come to reside at his farm on the 13th of June. As the *steading* had to be rebuilt, he could not yet commence housekeeping with his wife and child. It was, therefore, arranged that, until the new house was ready, Jean and her son should remain at Mauchline, and that Burns should live alone at Ellisland. As a matter of fact he seems to have lived, not at Ellisland, but in a hut, with the outgoing tenant,* about half a mile below the farm, under the shadow of the ivy-covered tower of the Isle—a keep which dates from the days of the Red Comyn. Obliged to settle, in cheerless circumstances, and in a place where he was an entire stranger, he seems to have been at first far from happy.

TO MRS DUNLOP,

AT MR DUNLOP'S, HADDINGTON.

ELLISLAND, 13*th* [14*th*] *June* 1788.

Where'er I roam, whatever realms I see,
My heart, untravell'd, fondly turns to thee;
Still to my friend it turns with ceaseless pain,
And drags at each remove a lengthening chain.—GOLDSMITH.

This is the second day, my honored friend, that I have been on my farm. A solitary inmate of an old, smoky *Spence* (apartment); far from

* ' This was one David Cullie, or Kelly, who was a devoted member of the Anti-burgher congregation in Dumfries, that had for its minister the late Mr Inglis. . . . Before this time Burns had written the "Holy Fair," and an impression had gone abroad that he was

every object I love, or by whom I am beloved; nor any acquaintance older than yesterday, except *Jenny Geddes*, the old mare I ride on; while uncouth cares and novel plans hourly insult my awkward ignorance and bashful inexperience. There is a foggy atmosphere native to my soul in the hour of care, consequently the dreary objects seem larger than the life. Extreme sensibility, irritated and prejudiced on the gloomy side by a series of misfortunes and disappointments, at that period of my existence when the soul is laying in her cargo of ideas for the voyage of life, is, I believe, the principal cause of this unhappy frame of mind.

> The valiant, in himself what can he suffer?
> Or what need he regard his *single* woes? &c.

Your surmise, madam, is just: I am, indeed, a husband. . . .

I found a once much-loved and still much-loved female literally and truly cast out to the mercy of the naked elements, but as I enabled her to *purchase* a shelter, and there is no sporting with a fellow-creature's happiness or misery. . . .

The most placid good-nature and sweetness of disposition; a warm heart, gratefully devoted with all its powers to love me; vigorous health and sprightly cheerfulness, set off to the best advantage by a more than common handsome figure; these, I think, in a woman, may make a good wife, though she should never have read a page but 'The Scriptures of the Old and New Testament,' nor have danced in a brighter assembly than a penny-pay wedding.*

R. B.

TO MR ROBERT AINSLIE.

ELLISLAND, *June* 14 [15], 1788.

This is now the third day, my dearest Sir, that I have sojourned in these regions; and during these three days you have occupied more of my thoughts than in three weeks preceding: In Ayrshire I have several *variations* of friendship's compass, here it points invariably to the pole.

rather a scoffer or a free-thinker. David Cullie and his wife were aware of this; and although they treated him civilly as the incoming tenant, during the five months he resided under their roof, still they felt for him as one who was by no means on the right path. On one occasion Nance (Mrs Cullie) and the bard were sitting in the spence, when the former turned the conversation on her favourite topic, religion. Burns, from whatever motive, sympathised with the matron, and quoted so much scripture that she was fairly astonished. When she went ben she said to her husband—"Oh, David Cullie, how they have wranged that man, for I think he has mair o' the Bible off his tongue than Mr Inglis himsel'." The bard enjoyed the compliment, and about the first thing he communicated to his wife on her arrival was " the lift he had got from 'Old Nance.'"—*Mrs Burns's Memoranda.*

* A wedding of the humblest kind, where the guests pay a small sum towards the expenses of the entertainment.

My farm gives me a good many uncouth cares and anxieties, but I hate the language of complaint. Job, or some one of his friends, says well— 'Why should a living man complain?'

I have lately been much mortified with contemplating an unlucky imperfection in the very framing and construction of my soul; namely, a blundering inaccuracy of her olfactory organs in hitting the scent of craft or design in my fellow-creatures. I do not mean any compliment to my ingenuousness, or to hint that the defect is in consequence of the unsuspicious simplicity of conscious truth and honor: I take it to be, in some way or other, an imperfection in the mental sight; or, metaphor apart, some modification of dulness. In two or three small instances, lately, I have been most shamefully out.

I have all along, hitherto, in the warfare of life, been bred to arms among the light-horse—the piquet-guards of fancy; a kind of Hussars and Highlanders of the *Brain;* but I am firmly resolved to *sell out* of these giddy battalions, who have no ideas of a battle but fighting the foe, or of a siege but storming the town. Cost what it will, I am determined to *buy in* among the grave squadrons of heavy-armed thought or the artillery corps of plodding contrivance.

What books are you reading, or what is the subject of your thoughts, besides the great studies of your profession? You said something about Religion in your last. I don't exactly remember what it was, as the letter is in Ayrshire; but I thought it not only prettily said, but nobly thought. You will make a noble fellow, if once you were married. I make no reservation of your being *well*-married: You have so much sense, and knowledge of human nature, that though you may not realize perhaps the ideas of romance, yet you will never be *ill married.**

Were it not for the terrors of my ticklish situation respecting provision for a family of children, I am decidedly of opinion that the step I have taken is vastly for my happiness. As it is, I look to the excise scheme as a certainty of maintenance; a maintenance, luxury to what either Mrs Burns or I was born to. Adieu!   R. B.

The thoughts of Burns are further revealed by an entry in his second Common-place Book.

ELLISLAND, 14*th June* 1788. *Sunday.*

This is now the third day I have been in this country. Lord, what is man! what a bustling little bundle of passions, appetites, ideas and fancies! and what a capricious kind of existence he has here! If legendary stories be true, there is indeed an Elsewhere, where, as Thomson says, 'Virtue sole survives.'

---

* Ainslie remained a bachelor till ten years later: in 1798 he married Jean, daughter of Lieut.-Col. James Cunningham of the Scots Brigade.

> ————Tell us ye Dead;
> Will none of you in pity disclose the secret,
> What 'tis you are, and we must shortly be?
> ———————————a little time
> Will make us learned as you are and as close.*

I am such a coward in Life, so tired of the Service, that I would almost at any time with Milton's *Adam*—

> ——gladly lay me in my Mother's lap,
> And be at peace.

but a wife and children, in poetics, 'The fair Partner of my soul, and the little dear Pledges of our mutual love,' these bind me to struggle with the stream; till some chopping squall overset the silly vessel, or, in the listless return of years, its own craziness drive it to a wreck. Farewel, now, to those giddy Follies, those varnished Vices, which, though half sanctified by the bewitching levity of Wit and Humour, are at best but thriftless idling with the precious current of Existence; nay, often poisoning the whole, that, like the Plains of Jericho, 'The water is naught, and the ground barren,' and nothing short of a supernaturally gifted Elisha can ever after heal the evils.

Wedlock, the circumstance that buckles me hardest to Care, if Virtue and Religion were to be anything with me but mere names, was what in a few seasons I must have resolved on; in the present case it was unavoidably necessary. Humanity, Generosity, honest vanity of character, Justice to my own happiness for after-life, so far as it could depend, which it surely will a great deal, on internal peace, all these joined their warmest suffrages, their most powerful solicitations, with a rooted Attachment, to urge the step I have taken. Nor have I any reason on her part to rue it. I can fancy *how*, but have never seen *where*, I could have made it better. Come then, let me return to my favourite Motto, that glorious passage in Young—

> On REASON build RESOLVE,
> That column of true majesty in man.

In a different strain Burns addressed an early Kilmarnock friend on the circumstances of his life:

---

* As this was a favourite quotation (or misquotation from memory) of Burns, the correct reading, from Blair's *Grave* may here be given:

> Tell us, ye dead: will none of you in pity
> To these you left behind, disclose the secret?
> Oh! that some courteous ghost would blab it out,
> What 'tis you are and we must shortly be.
> ——————————well—'tis no matter:
> A very little time will clear up all,
> And make us learn'd as you are and as close.

EPISTLE TO HUGH PARKER.

In this strange land, this uncouth clime,	
A land unknown to prose or rhyme :	
Where words ne'er crost the muse's heckles,*	
Nor limpet in poetic shackles ;	limped
A land that prose did never view it,	
Except when drunk he stacher't thro' it ;	staggered
Here, ambush'd by the chimla cheek,	chimney = fireside
Hid in an atmosphere of reek,	smoke
I hear a wheel thrum † i' the neuk,	corner
I hear it—for in vain I leuk.	look
The red peat gleams, a fiery kernel,	
Enhuskèd by a fog infernal :	
Here, for my wonted rhyming raptures,	
I sit and count my sins by chapters ;	
For life and spunk like ither Christians,	spirit—other
I'm dwindled down to mere existence,	
Wi' nae converse but Gallowa' bodies,‡	no—folk
Wi' nae kend face but Jenny Geddes.§	known
Jenny, my Pegasean pride !	
Dowie she saunters down Nithside,	Sadly
And ay a westlin leuk she throws,	look westwards
While tears hap o'er her auld brown nose !	drop
Was it for this, wi' canny care	gentle
Thou bure the Bard through many a shire ?	bore
At howes or hillocks never stumbled,	hollows
And late or early never grumbled ?	
O, had I power like inclination,	
I'd heeze thee up a constellation,	raise
To canter with the Sagitarre,	Sagittarius
Or loup th' ecliptic like a bar,	leap over
Or turn the pole like any arrow,	
Or, when auld Phebus bids good-morrow,	

---

* Hackles—an instrument for dressing flax.
† 'Thrum' = sound of a spinning-wheel in motion.
‡ Ellisland, although in Dumfriesshire, is situated near the borders of the Stewartry of Kirkcudbright, which, with Wigtownshire, forms the district known as Galloway.
§ His mare.

Down the zodiac urge the race,
And cast dirt on his godship's face :
For I could lay my bread and kail   broth
He 'd ne'er cast saut upo' thy tail.   salt
Wi' a' this care and a' this grief,
And sma', sma' prospect of relief,   small
And nought but peat reek i' my head,   smoke
How can I write what ye can read ?
Tarbolton, twenty-fourth o' June,
Ye 'll find me in a better tune ;
But till we meet and weet our whistle,*   wet
Tak this excuse for nae epistle.   Take—nae epistle =
                                            what is not an epistle

June 1788.   ROBERT BURNS.

In his lonely wanderings by the Nith, his heart reverted to the
girl whom he had lately made his wife.   We have a memorial
of the feeling of such a moment in his popular song—

I LOVE MY JEAN.

TUNE—*Miss Admiral Gordon's Strathspey.*

Of a' the airts the wind can blaw,   directions—blow
    I dearly like the west,
For there the bonie Lassie lives,
    The Lassie I lo'e best :   love
There 's wild-woods grow, and rivers row,   roll
    And mony a hill between ;†
But day and night my fancy's flight
    Is ever wi' my Jean.

I see her in the dewy flowers,
    I see her sweet and fair ;
I hear her in the tunefu' birds,
    I hear her charm the air :

---

* ' Weet our whistle' means 'have a friendly drink.'

† The commencement of this stanza is usually given—' There wild woods grow,' &c., as
implying the nature of the scenery in the west. In Wood's *Songs of Scotland* the reading
is—

        ' Though wild woods grow and rivers row,
            Wi' mony a hill between,
        Baith day and night,' &c.,—

evidently an alteration designed to improve the reasoning of the verse. It appears that both
readings are wrong, for in the original manuscript (Burns's contribution to Johnson), now

> There's not a bonie flower that springs
> By fountain, shaw, or green ;   wood
> There's not a bonie bird that sings,
> But minds me o' my Jean.*

The same period produced, in honour of Jean, one of the most
fervid of his lyrics.   To understand it, the poet, living in solitude
at the Isle, must be supposed to be gazing towards the hill of Corsincon, at the head of Nithsdale, beyond which, some ten miles
distant, was the valley in which Jean lived.

O, WERE I ON PARNASSUS HILL.

TUNE—*My love is lost to me.*

> O, were I on Parnassus hill,
> Or had o' Helicon† my fill,
> That I might catch poetic skill
> To sing how dear I love thee.

in the British Museum, the line is written : 'There's wild woods grow,' &c., as in the text.
The idea is not new in verse :

$$\text{————'}\ \text{ἴτιή μάλα πολλὰ μεταξὺ}$$
$$\text{Οὐριά τι σκιόιντα, θάλασσά τι ἐχέεσσα.'}$$
                                        Iliad i., 156–7.

* These stanzas appeared in the third volume of Johnson's *Museum*.   Burns's note upon
it afterwards was : 'This song I composed out of compliment to Mrs Burns.   N.B.—It
was in the honeymoon.'   Two additional stanzas were some years afterwards produced
by a John Hamilton, music-seller in Edinburgh.   They are generally sung by way of
lengthening the song, but their inferiority to Burns's lines is painfully obvious :

> O blaw, ye westlin winds, blaw saft,   blow—west—softly
>   Amang the leafy trees ;   Among
> Wi' gentle gale, frae muir and dale,   from
>   Bring hame the laden bees ;   home
> And bring the lassie back to me,
>   That's ay sae neat and clean :   so—handsome
> Ae blink o' her wad banish care,   One—would
>   Sae charming is my Jean.

> What sighs and vows, among the knowes,   hillocks
>   Hae pass'd atween us twa !   two
> How fain to meet, how wae to part,   sorry
>   That day she gaed awa !   went away
> The Powers aboon can only ken,   above—know
>   (To whom the heart is seen)
> That nane can be sae dear to me   none
>   As my sweet, lovely Jean.

† British poets have from a very early period been unwilling to content themselves
with *Mount* Helicon as the haunt of the Muses, and its fountains Aganippe and Hippocrene.
Montgomerie, in *The Cherry and the Slae*, has 'at fontaine Helicon ;' and the song, 'Declare
ye banks of Helicon' (probably Montgomerie's ; see Cranstoun's edition for the Scottish Text

On the Nith. Elliotland

But Nith maun be my Muses' well,   *must*
My Muse maun be thy bonie sel',*   *self*
On Corsincon I 'll glow'r and spell,   *gaze*
    And write how dear I love thee !

Then come, sweet Muse, inspire my lay !
For a' the lee-lang simmer's day   *live-long summer's day*
I couldna sing, I couldna say,   *could not*
How much, how dear, I love thee.
I see thee dancing o'er the green,
Thy waist sae jimp, thy limbs sae clean,†   *neat*
Thy tempting lips, thy roguish een—   *eyes*
    By Heaven and Earth I love thee !

By night, by day, a-field, at hame,
The thoughts o' thee my breast inflame ;
And ay I muse and sing thy name,
I only live to love thee.
Tho' I were doom'd to wander on
Beyond the sea, beyond the sun,
Till my last weary sand was run,
    Till then—and then I love thee !

TO ROBERT AINSLIE, ESQ.

MAUCHLINE, 23rd June 1788.

This letter, my dear Sir, is only a business scrap. Mr Miers, profile painter in your town, has executed a profile of Dr Blacklock for me : do me the favour to call for it, and sit to him yourself for me, which put in the same size as the doctor's. The account of both profiles will be fifteen shillings, which I have given to James Connel, our Mauchline

Society, 1887 ; see also the Appendix to Vol. I. of this work, pp. 465-6) points the same way. Spenser has 'Parnasse . . . whence floweth Helicon the learned well,' a usage expressly defended in a gloss. Nor was he the only English poet to write thus. It has been pointed out that Pausanias describes a small stream called Helicon north of Mount Olympus, which, however, seems to have had no special connection with the Muses. See *Notes and Queries*, 4th series, ii., 243–475.

* A writer in *Notes and Queries* has pointed out a similar idea to this in Propertius :

    'Non hæc Calliope, non hæc mihi cantat Apollo,
    Ingenium nobis ipsa puella facit.'

† 'Clean,' in this relation, means 'well-shaped, handsome.'

carrier, to pay you when you give him the parcel. You must not, my friend, refuse to sit. The time is short; when I sat to Mr Miers, I am sure he did not exceed two minutes. I propose hanging Lord Glencairn, the Doctor, and you, in trio, over my new chimney-piece that is to be. Adieu !   R. B.

At the Isle, Burns was fortunate in having for his nearest neighbour, less than a mile distant along the bank of the Nith, Captain Robert Riddel of Glenriddel, a man of literary and antiquarian tastes, and of a warmly sociable temperament. Riddel possessed a beautiful small estate, with a mansion romantically situated on a rocky promontory at a bend in the river, which was formerly the site of a small monastic establishment that recalled the days when the monks of Melrose owned this fertile portion of Nithsdale : a long carse (alluvial plain) extends to the eastward, bounded by beautiful shrubberies, which reach nearly to Ellisland. The proprietor of Friars' Carse* gave Burns a key admitting him to the grounds, and it seems to have been one of the poet's chief pleasures to wander in these grounds, and meditate in a little cot or Hermitage which Captain Riddel had built. On the 28th of June he composed, assuming the character of a bedesman, or mendicant recluse, lines

WRITTEN IN FRIARS' CARSE HERMITAGE.

(FIRST VERSION.)

Thou whom Chance may hither lead,
Be thou clad in russet weed,
Be thou deckt in silken stole,
Grave these maxims on thy soul.

* Friars' Carse passed in the early part of the present century into the hands of Dr Crichton, whose name is commemorated in the large institution founded by his trustees at Dumfries for the treatment of the insane. At the death of his widow the estate was bought by Mr Thomas Nelson of Carlisle, who rebuilt the mansion-house and restored the Hermitage, placing on its windows inscriptions in *fac-simile* of the verses Burns composed within it. He bought the original window of the Hermitage in an old curiosity shop in London ; it is now preserved in the museum of Dumfries Observatory. In 1895 the mansion-house, which contains the rooms in which Robert Riddel conversed with his neighbour, including the dining-room which was the scene of the contest for the Whistle, passed with the estate into the hands of the Crichton trustees, and is to be used as a supplementary asylum to the institution in Dumfries. The old castle of Glenriddel, from which Captain Riddel took his 'style,' and the site of which is now marked by a circle of yew-trees, was in Glencairn parish, and stood on an eminence overlooking the Cairn, a tributary of the Nith, having the Maxwelton braes, celebrated in 'Annie Laurie,' full in view.

Life is but a Day at most ;
Sprung from Night—in Darkness lost : *
Hope not Sunshine every hour,
Fear not Clouds will ever lour.
Happiness is but a name,
Make Content and Ease thy aim.
Ambition is a meteor-gleam ;
Fame, a restless idle dream ;
Pleasures, insects on the wing
Round Peace, the tenderest flower of Spring ;
Those that sip the dew alone,
Make the Butterflies thy own ;
Those that would the bloom devour,
Crush the Locusts, save the Flower.
For the Future be prepar'd,
Guard, wherever thou can'st guard ;
But thy Utmost duly done,
Welcome what thou canst not shun.
Follies past, give thou to air ;
Make their Consequence thy care.
Keep the name of Man in mind,
And dishonour not thy kind.
Reverence, with lowly heart,
Him whose wondrous Work thou art ;
Keep His Goodness still in view,
Thy trust, and thy example too.
Stranger, go ! Heaven be thy guide !
Quod, the Beads-mane of Nithe-side.

This is a reproduction of the text entered by Burns in the Edinburgh Common-place Book. A second version is entered later in the volume, with the heading 'Alteration of the lines wrote in Carse Hermitage.' In this version the couplet

Day, how rapid in its flight !
Day, how few must see the night !

is inserted between lines 6 and 7 of the original, and after line 8 the text, down to the concluding couplet, is entirely new. The poem as given in the 1793 edition is as follows :

* Compare Epicurus's ἀταραξία καὶ ἀτοτία.

WRITTEN IN FRIARS-CARSE HERMITAGE, ON NITH-SIDE.

Thou whom chance may hither lead,
Be thou clad in russet weed,
Be thou deckt in silken stole,
Grave these counsels on thy soul.

Life is but a day at most,
Sprung from night—in darkness lost :
Hope not sunshine ev'ry hour,
Fear not clouds will always lour.

As Youth and Love with sprightly dance
Beneath thy morning star advance,
Pleasure with her siren air
May delude the thoughtless pair :
Let Prudence bless Enjoyment's cup,
Then raptur'd sip, and sip it up.

As thy day grows warm and high,
Life's meridian flaming nigh,
Dost thou spurn the humble vale?
Life's proud summits would'st thou scale?
Check thy climbing step, elate,
Evils lurk in felon-wait :   hiding with felonious intent
Dangers, eagle-pinioned, bold,
Soar around each cliffy hold,
While cheerful peace, with linnet song,
Chants the lowly dells among.

As thy shades of ev'ning close,
Beck'ning thee to long repose ;
As life itself becomes disease,
Seek the chimney-nook of ease.
There ruminate with sober thought
On all thou 'st seen, and heard, and wrought ;
And teach the sportive younkers round,
Saws of experience, sage and sound.
Say, man's true, genuine estimate,
The grand criterion of his fate,

Is not, art thou high or low?
Did thy fortune ebb or flow?
Did many talents gild thy span?
Or frugal Nature grudge thee one?
Tell them, and press it on their mind,
As thou thyself must shortly find,
The smile or frown of aweful Heav'n,
To Virtue or to Vice is giv'n.
Say, to be just, and kind, and wise—
There, solid self-enjoyment lies;
That foolish, selfish, faithless ways
Lead to be wretched, vile and base.

    Thus resign'd and quiet, creep
To thy bed of lasting sleep:
Sleep, whence thou shalt ne'er awake,
Night, where dawn shall never break,
Till Future Life, future no more,
To light and joy the good restore,
To light and joy unknown before.

Stranger, go! Heav'n be thy guide!
Quod the Beadsman of Nith-side.*
                                            Quoth

TO MR ROBERT AINSLIE.

ELLISLAND, 30th June 1788.

MY DEAR SIR—I just now received your brief Epistle; and to take vengeance on your laziness, I have, you see, taken a long sheet of writing paper, and begun at the top of the page, intending to scribble on to the very last corner.

I am vexed at that affair of the girl, but dare not enlarge on the subject until you send me your direction, as I suppose that will be altered on your late Master and Friend's death.† I am concerned for the old fellow's exit, only as I fear it may be to your disadvantage in any respect—for an old man's dying, except he have been a very benevolent character, or in some particular situation of life, that the welfare of the Poor or the Helpless depended on him, I think it an event of the most trifling moment to the world. Man is naturally a kind, benevolent

* 'Quod Dunbar' is printed at the end of many of Dunbar's poems. So also with many of the poems of other 'makkars.'
† Samuel Mitchelson, W.S., had been Ainslie's employer: he died June 21, 1788.

animal, but he is dropt into such a damn'd needy situation here in this
vexatious world, and has such a whoreson, hungry, growling, multiplying
pack of Necessities, Appetites, Passions, and Desires about him, ready to
devour him for want of other food; that in fact he must lay aside his
cares for others that he may look properly to himself.   Every One, more
or less, in the words of the old Scots Proverb, ' Has his cods in a cloven
stick,* and maun wyse [must draw out] them out the best way he can.'
You have been imposed upon in paying Mr Miers for the profile of a Mr
Hamilton.   I did not mention it in my letter to you, nor did I ever give
Mr Miers any such order.   I went once, indeed, with young Hamilton
of B——, to shew him some profiles I was getting done for Mrs Blacklock, and he sat to Miers of his own accord to send it, as he said, to a
sweetheart; but for my own part, I would as soon think of ordering a
Profile of Tibby Nairn or Julie Rutherford as of such a contemptible
puppy as H[amilton].   I beg you will take the trouble to return the profile to Mr Miers : I have no objection to lose the money, but I won't have
any such Profile in my possession.   I desired the Carrier to pay you, but
as I mentioned only fifteen shillings to him, I will rather inclose you a
guinea note.   I have it not indeed to spare here, as I am only a sojourner
in a strange land in this place ; but in a day or two I return to Mauchline, and there I have the Bank-notes through the house like salt
permits.†

There is a great degree of folly in talking unnecessarily of one's private
affairs.   I have just now been interrupted by one of my new neighbours,
who has made himself absolutely contemptible in my eyes, by his silly,
garrulous pruriency.   I know it has been a fault of my own too ; but
from this moment I abjure it as I would the service of Hell !   Your Poets,
spendthrifts, and other fools of that kidney, pretend forsooth to crack
their jokes on Prudence ; but 'tis a squalid Vagabond glorying in his
rags.   Still, Imprudence respecting money-matters is much more pardon-
able than imprudence respecting character.   I have no objection to prefer
prodigality to avarice, in some few instances ; but I appeal to your observation, if you have not met, and often met, with the same disingenuous-
ness, the same hollow-hearted insincerity, and disintegritive depravity of
principle, in the hackneyed victims of Profusion, as in the unfeeling
children of Parsimony.   I have every possible reverence for the much-
talked-of world beyond the Grave, and I wish that which Piety believes,
and Virtue deserves, may be all matter of fact ; but in things belonging
to, and terminating in, this present scene of Existence, man has serious
and interesting business on hand.   Whether a man shall shake hands
with Welcome in the distinguished elevation of Respect, or shrink from
Contempt in the abject corner of Insignificance.   Whether he shall wanton
under the Tropic of Plenty, at least, enjoy himself in the comfortable

---

* ' I have his cods in a cleft stick ' is said by one when he has another at an advantage.
† There was an Excise duty on salt selling in those days. [The salt duty was first
exacted in 1702, and not remitted till 1825.] It was as high as 15s. per bushel during the
war with France.

latitudes of easy Convenience, or starve in the Arctic circle of dreary Poverty. Whether he shall rise in the manly consciousness of a self-approving mind, or sink beneath a galling load of Regret and Remorse—these are alternatives of the last moment.

You see how I preach. You used occasionally to sermonize too; I wish you would, in charity, favor me with a sheet full in your own way. At any rate write me with your convenience, to let me know your direction. I admire the close of a letter Lord Bolingbroke writes to Dean Swift: 'Adieu, dear Swift! with all thy faults I love thee entirely; make an effort to love me with all mine!' Humble servant, and all that trumpery, is now such a perversion, such a Sodomy of Language, that Honest Friendship, in her sincere way, must have recourse to her primitive, simple—Farewell!   R. B.

P.S.—I am a subscriber to Ainslie's large map of Scotland; if you are in the shop, please ask after the progress; and when published, secure me one of the earliest Impressions of the Plate. Forgive me for all this trouble. I seldom see a Newspaper, so do not know the state of Publications, the Stage, &c.   R. B.

Peter Hill, who had been Creech's chief assistant, had now set up in business for himself, with the afterwards notable Archibald Constable as his apprentice. Burns liked Hill for his lively conversation and kindly disposition, and had already become intimate with him. Considering his relations with Creech, it was natural that he should send to Hill for any books he might require.

TO MR PETER HILL.

MAUCHLINE, 18th July 1788.

You injured me, my dear Sir, in your construction of the cause of my silence. From Ellisland in Nithsdale to Mauchline in Kyle is forty and five miles. *There*, a house a-building and farm enclosures and improvements to tend; *here*, a new—not so much indeed a *new* as a *young* wife: good God, Sir, could my dearest brother expect a regular correspondence from me! . . . I am certain that you, my liberal-minded and much-respected friend, would have acquitted me, though I had obeyed to the very letter that famous statute among the irrevocable decrees of the Medes and Persians, 'not to ask petition for forty days of either God or man, save thee, O Queen, only!'

I am highly obliged to you, my dearest Sir, for your kind, your elegant, compliments on my becoming one of that most respectable, that most truly venerable, corps, they who are, without a metaphor, the fathers of posterity, the benefactors of all coming generations; the editors of Spiritual Nature, and the authors of Immortal Being. Now that I am 'one of you,' I shall humbly but fervently endeavour to be a conspicuous member. Now it is 'called to-day' with my powers and me, and the time fast approacheth when, beholding the debilitated victim of all-subduing Time, they shall exclaim 'How are the mighty fallen, and the weapons of war perished!'

Your book came safe, and I am going to trouble you with further commissions. I call it troubling you—because I want only BOOKS; the cheapest way, the best; so you may have to hunt for them in the evening auctions. I want Smollett's works, for the sake of his incomparable humour. I have already 'Roderick Random' and 'Humphry Clinker.' 'Peregrine Pickle,' 'Launcelot Greaves,' and 'Ferdinand Count Fathom' I still want; but, as I said, the veriest ordinary copies will serve me. I am nice only in the appearance of my poets. I forget the price of Cowper's 'Poems,' but I believe I must have them. I saw, the other day, proposals for a publication entitled, 'Banks's New and Complete Christian's Family Bible,' printed for C. Cooke, Paternoster-row, London. He promises at least to give in the work, I think it is, three hundred and odd engravings, to which he has put the names of the first artists in London.* You will know the character of the performance, as some numbers of it are published; and if it is really what it pretends to be, set me down as a subscriber, and send me the published numbers.

Let me hear from you your first leisure minute, and trust me, you shall in future have no reason to complain of my silence. The dazzling perplexity of novelty will dissipate, and leave me to pursue my course in the quiet path of methodical routine.†

I might go on to fill up the page, but I dare say you are already sufficiently tired of, my dear Sir, yours sincerely

ROBT. BURNS.

* 'Perhaps no set of men more effectually avail themselves of the easy credulity of the public than a certain description of Paternoster Row booksellers. Three hundred and odd engravings!—and by the first artists in London, too! No wonder that Burns was dazzled by the splendour of the promise. It is no unusual thing for this class of impostors to illustrate the Holy Scriptures by plates originally engraved for the *History of England*; and I have actually seen subjects designed by our celebrated artist Stothard, from *Clarissa Harlowe* and the *Novelist's Magazine*, converted, with incredible dexterity, by these bookselling Breslaws, into Scriptural embellishments! One of these vendors of "Family Bibles" lately called on me, to consult me professionally about a folio engraving he brought with him. It represented Mons. Buffon seated, contemplating various groups of animals that surrounded him: He merely wished, he said, to be informed whether, by unclothing the naturalist, and giving him a rather more resolute look, the plate could not, at a trifling expense, be made to pass for "Daniel in the Lions' Den!"'—CROMEK. Breslaw, a conjurer of Bartholomew Fair, is the original of the personage vituperated by Cromek. Having advertised a performance 'for the benefit of the poor,' he took the proceeds for himself, explaining that he and his comrades were the poorest people in the parish. 'Sir,' said the churchwardens, 'this is a trick.' 'I know it,' said the conjurer; 'I live by my tricks.' See *Notes and Queries*, 2d series, viii., 162.

† Cromek printed only the part of this letter from 'Your book came safe,' and he has unaccountably placed it in connection with a letter of Burns to Peter Hill dated February 2, 1790,

TO MR GEORGE LOCKHART,*

MERCHANT, AT MISS GRAY'S, GLASGOW.

MY DR. SIR—I am just going for Nithsdale, else I would certainly have transcribed some of my rhyming things for you. The Miss Bailies I have seen in Edinr. 'Fair and lovely are Thy Works, Lord God Almighty! who would not praise Thee for these Thy Gifts in Thy Goodness to the Sons of men!!!' It needed not your fine taste to admire them. I declare, one day I had the honor of dining at Mr Bailie's, I was almost in the predicament of the Children of Israel, when they could not look on Moses' face for the glory that shone in it when he descended from Mount Horeb.

I did once write a poetic Address from the Falls of Bruar to his Grace of Athole, when I was in the Highlands. When you return to Scotland let me know, and I will send such of my pieces as please myself best.

I return to Mauchline in about ten days. My Compliments to Mr Purden. I am in truth, but, at present, in haste, Yours sincerely,

ROBT. BURNS.

MAUCHLINE, *July 18th,* 1788.

Burns had never fully appreciated the beauty of his poems till he heard Mr Aiken read them. Mr Lockhart, of Glasgow, did him a similar service in respect of his songs. On hearing Lockhart for the first time sing some of his pieces, he exclaimed, with great *naïveté,* 'I'll be hanged if I ever knew half their merit till now!'

TO MR ALEXANDER CUNNINGHAM,†

WRITER, ST JAMES' SQUARE, EDINBURGH.

ELLISLAND, NITHSDALE, July 27th, 1788.

MY GODLIKE FRIEND—

Nay, do not stare,
You think the phrase is odd-like;
But 'God is Love' the saints declare,
Then surely thou art God-like.

* The name, 'George Lockhart, merchant and manufacturer,' appears in the first Glasgow Directory (1787). In the succeeding issue of the Directory it is noted that 'Miss Hanna Gray letts lodgings above the post-office, Princes-street.' Probably Lockhart lodged there.

† Cunningham became a W.S. in 1798; but later joined an uncle as jeweller. He died in 1812. 'Anna' was Miss Anne Stewart, daughter of John Stewart of East Craigs. Shortly after the date of writing this, she became wife of Mr Forrest Dewar, surgeon in Edinburgh, Cunningham's rival. Although Cunningham married four years later, it is said that he never completely recovered from the shock occasioned by this disappointment.

And is thy ardour still the same ?
   And kindled still at ANNA?
Others may boast a partial flame
   But thou art a volcano !

Ev'n Wedlock asks not love beyond
   Death's tie-dissolving portal ;
But thou, omnipotently fond,
   May'st promise love immortal !

Thy wounds such healing powers defy,
   Such symptoms dire attend them,
That last great antihectic try—
   MARRIAGE perhaps may mend them.

Sweet Anna has an air—a grace
   Divine, magnetic, touching ;
She talks, she charms—but who can trace
   The process of bewitching?

My spur-galled, spavened Pegasus makes so hobbling a progress over the course of Extempore, that I must here alight and try the foot-path of plain prose. I have not met with anything this long while, my dear Sir, that has given my inward man such a fillip as your kind epistle.

For my own Biographical story, I can only say with the venerable Hebrew Patriarch—'Here I am with the children God has given me!' I have been a farmer since Whitsunday, and am just now building a house—not a Palace to attract the train-attended steps of pride-swollen Greatness, but a plain, simple domicile for Humility and Contentment. I am, too, a married man. This was a step of which I had no idea when you and I were together. On my return to Ayrshire, I found a much-loved female's positive happiness or absolute misery among my hands, and I could not trifle with such a sacred deposit. I am, since, doubly pleased with my conduct. I have the consciousness of acting up to that generosity of principle which I would be thought to possess, and I am really more and more pleased with my choice. When I tell you that Mrs Burns was once 'my Jean,' you will know the rest. Of four children she bore me in seventeen months, my eldest boy is only living. By the bye, I intend breeding him up for the Church ; and from an innate dexterity in secret mischief which he possesses, and a certain hypo-critical gravity as he looks on the consequences, I have no small hopes of him in the sacerdotal line.

Mrs Burns does not come from Ayrshire till my said new house be ready, so I am eight or ten days at Mauchline and this place alternately.

Hitherto my direction was only 'at Mauchline,' but 'at Ellisland, near Dumfries' will now likewise find me; though I prefer the former. I need not tell you that I shall expect to hear from you soon. Adieu!

ROBT. BURNS.

Lowe's * poem I shall transcribe in my first leisure hour.

R. B.

TO MRS DUNLOP.

MAUCHLINE, 2d August 1788.

HONORED MADAM—Your kind letter welcomed me yesternight to Ayrshire. I am, indeed, seriously angry with you at the *quantum* of your *luckpenny;* but vexed and hurt as I was, I could not help laughing very heartily at the noble lord's apology for the missed napkin.

I would write you from Nithsdale, and give you my direction there, but I have scarce an opportunity of calling at a post office once in a fortnight. I am six miles from Dumfries, am scarcely ever in it myself, and, as yet, have little acquaintance in the neighbourhood. Besides, I am now very busy on my farm, building a dwelling-house; as at present I am almost an evangelical man in Nithsdale, for I have scarce ' where to lay my head.'

There are some passages in your last that brought tears in my eyes. 'The heart knoweth its own sorrows, and a stranger intermeddleth not therewith.' The repository of these 'sorrows of the heart' is a kind of *sanctum sanctorum ;* and 'tis only a chosen friend, and that too at particular, sacred times, who dares enter into them.

> Heav'n oft tears the bosom-chords
> That nature finest strung.†

You will excuse this quotation for the sake of the author. Instead of entering on this subject farther, I shall transcribe you a few lines I wrote in a hermitage belonging to a gentleman in my Nithsdale neighbourhood. They are almost the only favors the muses have conferred on me in that country.

[Here the poet transcribed the verses written in Friars' Carse Hermitage. (First version.) *See ante.*]

Since I am in the way of transcribing, the following were the production of yesterday, as I jogged through the wild hills of New Cumnock. I intend inserting them, or something like them, in an epistle I am going to write to the gentleman on whose friendship my

---

* John Lowe (1750-1798), author of 'Mary's Dream,' was the son of a gardener at Kenmore Castle, and ultimately became an Episcopal clergyman in the United States, where he died.

† 'Fate oft tears the bosom chords
    That Nature finest strung.'
—From the Poet's lines 'On the death of John M'Leod, Esq.,' verse 4 (see p. 138).

excise hopes depend, Mr Graham of Fintry; one of the worthiest and
most accomplished gentlemen, not only of this country, but I will dare
to say it, of this age. The following are just the first crude thoughts
'unhousel'd, unanointed, unaneal'd.' *

> Pity the tuneful muses' helpless train ;
> Weak, timid landsmen on life's stormy main :
> The world were blest, did bliss on them depend ;
> Ah, that 'the friendly e'er should want a friend ! '
> The little fate bestows they share as soon ;
> Unlike sage, proverb'd wisdom's hard-wrung boon.
> Let prudence number o'er each sturdy son
> Who life and wisdom at one race begun;
> Who feel by reason, and who give by rule ;
> Instinct 's a brute and sentiment a fool !
> Who make poor 'will do' wait upon 'I should ;'
> We own they 're prudent, but who owns they 're good ?
>
> Ye wise ones, hence ! ye hurt the social eye ;
> God's image rudely etch'd on base alloy !
> But come †   *   *   *   *

Here the muse left me. I am astonished at what you tell me of
Anthony's writing me. I never received it. Poor fellow ! you vex me
much by telling me that he is unfortunate. I shall be in Ayrshire
ten days from this date. I have just room for an old Roman farewell !

R. B.

TO MR ROBERT M'INDOE, MERCHANT, GLASGOW.

MAUCHLINE, 5th Aug. 1788.

MY DEAR SIR—I am vexed for nothing more, that I have not been
at Glasgow, than not meeting with you. I have seldom found my
friend Andrew M'Culloch wrong in his ideas of mankind ; but respecting your worship he was as true as Holy Writ. This is the night of
our Fair, and I, as you see, cannot keep well *in a line:* but if you
will send me by the bearer, John Ronald, carrier between Glasgow
and Mauchline, fifteen yards of black silk, the same kind as that of
which I bought a gown and petticoat from you formerly—lutestring,
I think, is its name—I shall send you the money and a more coherent
letter, when he goes again to your good town. To be brief, send me

---

* Shakespeare (*Hamlet*, I. v. 77).
† This was incorporated in the Poet's 'First Epistle to Robert Graham, Esq.' (pp. 369-372).

fifteen yards black lutestring silk, such as they used to make gowns and petticoats of, and I shall choose, some sober morning before breakfast, and write you a sober answer, with the sober sum* which will then be due from, dear Sir, fu' [full, especially of liquor] or fasting, yours sincerely, ROBT. BURNS.

Burns was very busy at Ellisland, taking an active part in farm work, and at the same time superintending the construction of his new *steading*. According to Allan Cunningham, he had to 'perform the duty of superintendent of the works; to dig the foundations, collect the stones, seek the sand, cart the lime, and see that all was performed according to the specifications : these were the uncouth cares of which he complained.' He even helped the masons at their work. The dwelling-house was a neat cottage, about fifty feet long, placed near the edge of the *scaur*, or broken bank, overhanging the Nith. The sitting-room in the east end had a window looking down the valley, and commanding beautiful glimpses of the stream. At the west end was the *spence*, or room reserved for 'company' occasions. A small kitchen and a bedroom lay between, while in the garret was accommodation for domestics. On the bank below was a spring of pure water. Assisted by his brother-in-law, Adam Armour, who helped to build the house, Burns made the spring into a well for the supply of his household. Running back from the house in two parallel lines were a barn, terminating in a stackyard, and a byre and stable.

It was not till now that the union of Burns with Jean was ratified by the Church. The communion was administered at Mauchline on the second Sunday of August, and, as usual, it was preceded by a 'purgation of the characters' of those who, until they had atoned for their transgressions to the satisfaction of the kirk-session, were debarred from partaking of the sacrament. Burns took this opportunity of making his peace with the Church. The entry in the kirk-session record regarding his case is as follows :

1788, *August* 5.—Compeared Robert Burns, with Jean Armour, his alledged Spouse. They both acknowledged their irregular marriage, and their sorrow for that irregularity, and desiring that the Session will take such steps as may seem to them proper, in order to the Solemn Confirmation of the said marriage.

---

* A memorandum on the MS. of the letter states that the price of the silk was 5s. 6d. or 5s. 9d. per yard.

The Session, taking this affair under their consideration, agree that they both be rebuked for this acknowledged irregularity, and that they be taken solemnly engaged to adhere faithfully to one another as husband and wife all the days of their life.

In regard the Session have a title in Law to some fine for behoof of the Poor, they agree to refer to Mr Burns his own generosity.

The above Sentence was accordingly executed, and the Session absolved the said parties from any scandal on this account.

WILLIAM AULD, *Moderator*.   ROBT. BURNS.
       JEAN ARMOUR.

(Mr Burns gave a guinea-note for behoof of the poor.)

TO MRS DUNLOP.

MAUCHLINE, 10th *August* 1788.

MY MUCH HONORED FRIEND—Yours of the 24th June is before me. I found it, as well as another valued friend — my wife, waiting to welcome me to Ayrshire : I met both with the sincerest pleasure.

When I write you, madam, I do not sit down to answer every paragraph of yours, by echoing every sentiment, like the faithful Commons of Great Britain in parliament assembled, answering a speech from the best of kings ! I express myself in the fulness of my heart, and may perhaps be guilty of neglecting some of your kind inquiries ; but not from your very odd reason that I do not read your letters. All your epistles for several months have cost me nothing except a swelling throb of gratitude, or a deep-felt sentiment of veneration.

Mrs Burns, madam, is the identical woman * * * . When she first found herself 'as women wish to be who love their lords,' as I loved her nearly to distraction, we took steps for a private marriage. Her parents got the hint ; and not only forbade me her company and their house, but on my rumoured West Indian voyage, got a warrant to put me in jail 'till I should find security in my about-to-be paternal relation. You know my lucky reverse of fortune. On my éclatant return to Mauchline, I was made very welcome to visit my girl. The usual consequences began to betray her ; and as I was at that time laid up a cripple in Edinburgh, she was turned, literally turned, out of doors, and I wrote to a friend to shelter her 'till my return, when our marriage was declared. Her happiness or misery were in my hands, and who could trifle with such a deposit?

To jealousy or infidelity I am an equal stranger : My preservative from the first is the most thorough consciousness of her sentiments of honor, and her attachment to me ; my antidote against the last is my long and deep-rooted affection for her. I can easily *fancy* a more agreeable companion for my journey of life, but, upon my honor, I have never *seen* the individual instance. In housewife matters, of aptness to learn and activity to execute, she is eminently mistress; and during my absence in Nithsdale, she is regularly and constantly apprentice to my mother and sisters in their dairy and other rural business. The Muses must not be offended when I tell them, the concerns of my wife and family will, in my mind, always take the *pas;* but I assure them their ladyships will ever come next in place. Circumstanced as I am, I could never have got a female partner, for life, who could have entered into my favourite studies, relished my favourite authors, &c., without probably entailing on me, at the same time, expensive living, fantastic caprice, perhaps apish affectation, with all the other blessed boarding-school acquirements, which (*pardonnez moi, Madame*) are sometimes to be found among females of the upper ranks, but almost universally pervade the misses of the would-be-gentry. You are right, that a bachelor state would have insured me more friends; but, from a cause you will easily guess, conscious peace in the enjoyment of my own mind, and unmistrusting confidence in approaching my God, would seldom have been of the number.

I like your way in your church-yard lucubrations. Thoughts that are the spontaneous result of accidental situations, either respecting health, place, or company, have often a strength, and always an originality, that would in vain be looked for in fancied circumstances and studied paragraphs. For me, I have often thought of keeping a letter, *in progression*, by me, to send you when the sheet was written out. Now I talk of sheets, I must tell you my reason for writing to you on paper of this kind, is my pruriency * of writing to you at large. A page of post is on such a dis-social, narrow-minded scale, that I cannot abide it; and double letters, at least in my miscellaneous reverie manner, are a monstrous tax in a close correspondence. R. B.

TO MRS DUNLOP.

ELLISLAND, 16*th August* 1788.

I am in a fine disposition, my honored friend, to send you an elegaic epistle; and want only genius to make it quite Shenstonian.

> Why droops my heart with fancied woes forlorn?
> Why sinks my soul beneath each wintry sky?†
>
> *   *   *   *   *   *

My increasing cares in this, as yet, strange country—gloomy conjectures in the dark vista of futurity—consciousness of my own inability

---

* This is quite a classical usage of the word 'pruriency,' which Burns had already used in a letter to Ainslie. Sterne has 'pruriency for new adventures;' Macaulay 'pruriency for renown.'

† This is the commencement of Shenstone's 20th Elegy, and is slightly varied by Burns.

for the struggle of the world—my broadened mark to misfortune in a wife and children :—I could indulge these reflections, 'till my humour should ferment into the most acid chagrin that would corrode the very thread of life.

To counterwork these baneful feelings, I have sat down to write to you ; as I declare upon my soul I always find *that* the most sovereign balm for my wounded spirit.

I was yesterday at Mr Miller's to dinner,* for the first time. My reception was quite to my mind : from the lady of the house quite flattering. She sometimes hits on a couplet or two, *impromptu*. She repeated one or two to the admiration of all present. My suffrage, as a professional man, was expected : I for once went agonizing over the belly of my conscience. Pardon me, ye, my adored household gods, Independence of spirit and Integrity of soul ! In the course of conversation, Johnson's *Musical Museum*, a collection of Scottish songs with the music, was talked of. We got a song on the harpsichord, beginning

Raving winds around her blowing.†

The air was much admired : the lady of the house asked me whose were the words : 'mine, madam—they are indeed my very best verses :' she took not the smallest notice of them ! The old Scottish proverb says well, 'king's caff is better than ither folks' corn.'‡ I was going to make a New Testament quotation about 'casting pearls,' but that would be too virulent, for the lady is actually a woman of sense and taste. . . .

After all that has been said on the other side of the question, man is by no means a happy creature. I do not speak of the selected few, favored by partial heaven, whose souls are tuned to gladness amid riches and honours, and prudence and wisdom. I speak of the neglected many, whose nerves, whose sinews, whose days, are sold to the minions of fortune.

If I thought you had never seen it, I would transcribe for you a stanza of an old Scottish ballad called *The life and age of man*, beginning thus,

'Twas in the sixteenth hunder year
    Of God and fifty-three,
Frae Christ was born, that bought us dear,
    As writings testifie. §

I had an old grand-uncle, with whom my mother lived a while in her girlish years ; the good old man, for such he was, was long blind ere he died, during which time his highest enjoyment was to sit down and cry, while my mother would sing the simple old song of *The life and age of man*.

---

* At Dalswinton House.
† See *ante*, pp. 288-9.
‡ 'King's chaff is worth other men's corn' = The perquisites that attend king's service is better than the wages of other persons.—KELLY's *Scottish Proverbs*.
§ Quoted also at Vol. I., p. 216. *The Life and Age of Man* was a popular chap-book.

It is this way of thinking, it is these melancholy truths, that make religion so precious to the poor, miserable children of men. If it is a mere phantom, existing only in the heated imagination of enthusiasm,

What truth on earth so precious as the lie?

My idle reasonings sometimes make me a little sceptical, but the necessities of my heart always give the cold philosophisings the lie. Who looks for the heart weaned from earth; the soul allianced to her God, the correspondence fixed with Heaven; the pious supplication and devout thanksgiving, constant as the vicissitudes of even and morn; who thinks to meet with these in the court, the palace, in the glare of public life? No: to find them in their precious importance and divine efficacy, we must search among the obscure recesses of disappointment, affliction, poverty and distress.

I am sure, dear madam, you are now *more* than pleased with the *length* of my letters. I return to Ayrshire, middle of next week; and it quickens my pace to think that there will be a letter from you waiting me there. I must be here again very soon for my harvest.

R. B.

TO MR ROBT. AINSLIE.

MAUCHLINE, 23d *Aug.* 1788.

I received your last, my dear friend, but I write you just now on a vexatious business.

I don't know if ever I told you some very bad reports that Mrs M'Lehose once told me of Mr Nicol. I had mentioned the affair to Mr Cruikshank, in the course of conversation about our common friend, that a lady had said so and so, which I suspected had originated from some malevolence of Dr. Adam. He had mentioned this story to Mr Nicol cursorily, and there it rested; till now, a prosecution has commenced between Dr Adam and Mr Nicol, and Mr Nicol has press'd me over and over to give up the lady's name. I have refused this; and last post Mr Nicol acquaints me, but in very good natured terms, that if I persist in my refusal, I am to be served with a summons to compear and declare the fact.

Heaven knows how I should proceed! I have this moment wrote Mrs M'Lehose, telling her that I have informed you of the affair; and I shall write Mr Nicol by Tuesday's post that I will not give up my female friend till farther consideration; but that I have acquainted you with the business and the name; and that I have desired you to wait on him, which I entreat, my dear Sir, you will do; and give up the name or not, as your and Mrs M'Lehose's prudence shall suggest.

I am vexed to the heart that Mr Ainslie has disappointed my brother: I grasp at your kind offer, and wish you to enquire for a place among the Saddlers' shops.　If I get him into a first rate shop, I will bind him a year or two, I almost do not care on what terms.　He is about eighteen; really very clever; and in what work he has seen, not a despicable tradesman; but I will have him a first rate hand if possible.

Why trouble yourself about Hamilton? let me pay the expence, for I don't know where he is now to be found.　Dr Blacklock, where he lodged, which caused me to meet with him; and Signior Dasti, Junr., one of his greatest cronies, are the only intelligencers to whom I can refer you.*　Adieu! I am ever most cordially yours,　ROBT. BURNS.

TO MR JOHN BEUGO, ENGRAVER.

ELLISLAND, *Sept.* 9, 1788.

My DEAR SIR—There is not in Edinburgh above the number of the graces whose letters would have given me so much pleasure as yours of the 3d instant, which only reached me yesternight.

I am here on my farm, busy with my harvest; but for all that most pleasurable part of life called SOCIAL COMMUNICATION, I am here at the very elbow of existence.　The only things that are to be found in this country, in any degree of perfection, are stupidity and canting.　Prose, they only know in graces, prayers, &c., and the value of these they estimate as they do their plaiding webs †—by the ell!　As for the muses, they have as much an idea of a rhinoceros as of a poet.　For my old capricious but good-natured hussy of a muse—

> By banks of Nith I sat and wept ‡
> 　When Coila I thought on,
> In midst thereof I hung my harp
> 　The willow trees upon.

I am generally about half my time in Ayrshire with my 'darling Jean,' and then I, at *lucid intervals*, throw my horny fist across my be-cob-webbed lyre, much in the same manner as an old wife throws her hand across the spokes of her spinning-wheel.

I will send you 'The Fortunate Shepherdess §' as soon as I return to Ayrshire, for there I keep it with other precious treasure.　I shall send it by a careful hand, as I would not for any thing it should be mislaid or lost.　I do not wish to serve you from any benevolence, or other grave

---

* This refers to the Miers silhouette of a Mr Hamilton, already spoken of in letter to Ainslie.　See p. 354.

† Webs of home-made cloth.

‡ An adaptation of the current Scottish version of Psalm cxxxvii.—

> 'By *Babel's* streams I sat and wept
> 　As *Zion* I thought on.'

§ *Helenore, or the Fortunate Shepherdess*, by Alexander Ross of Lochlee.　The author is frequently alluded to by Burns.

Christian virtue; 'tis purely a selfish gratification of my own feelings whenever I think of you.

You do not tell me if you are going to be married. Depend upon it, if you do not make some foolish choice, it will be a very great improvement upon the dish of life. I can speak from experience, though, God knows, my choice was as random as blind-man's buff. . . .

If your better functions would give you leisure to write to me, I should be extremely happy; that is to say, if you neither keep nor look for a regular correspondence. I hate the idea of being *obliged* to write a letter. I sometimes write a friend twice a week, at other times once a quarter.

I am exceedingly pleased with your fancy in making the author you mention place a map of Iceland instead of his portrait before his works: 'Twas a glorious idea.*

Could you conveniently do me one thing? Whenever you finish any head, I could like to have a proof copy of it. I might tell you a long story about your fine genius; but as what every body knows cannot have escaped you, I shall not say one syllable about it.

If you see Mr Nasmyth, remember me to him most respectfully, as he both loves and deserves respect; though if he would pay less respect to the mere carcase of greatness, I should think him much nearer perfection.

R. B.

TO ROBERT GRAHAM, ESQ., OF FINTRY.†

ELLISLAND, 10th Sep. 1788.

SIR—The scrapes and premunires‡ into which our indiscretions and follies, in the ordinary constitution of things, often bring us, are bad enough; but it is peculiarly hard that a man's virtues should involve him in disquiet, and the very goodness of his heart cause the persecution of his peace. You, sir, have patronised and befriended me—not by barren compliments, which merely fed my vanity, or little marks of notice, which perhaps only encumbered me more in the awkwardness of my native rusticity, but by being my persevering friend in real life; and now, as if your continued benevolence had given me a prescriptive right, I am going again to trouble you with my importunities.

Your Honourable Board sometime ago gave me my Excise commission, which I regard as my sheet-anchor in life. My farm, now that I have tried it a little, though I think it will in time be a saving bargain, yet does by no means promise to be such a pennyworth as I was taught to

---

* This has been sometimes said to be a hit at Creech and his cold temperament, he being about to publish his 'Fugitive Pieces.' But the 'Edinburgh Fugitive Pieces' did not actually appear until 1791.

† Robert Graham (1749–1815) was twelfth Laird of Fintry. He had been appointed a Commissioner of the Scottish Board of Excise in 1787.

‡ 'Premunires' is here used in the sense of 'penalties.'

expect. It is in the last stage of worn-out poverty, and it will take some time before it pay the rent. I might have had cash to supply the deficiencies of these hungry years; but I have a younger brother and three sisters on a farm in Ayrshire, and it took all my surplus, over what I thought necessary for my farming capital, to save not only the comfort, but the very existence, of that fireside family circle from impending destruction. This was done before I took the farm; and rather than abstract my money from my brother—a circumstance which would ruin him—I will resign the farm, and enter immediately into the service of your Honours. But I am embarked now in the farm; I have commenced married man; and I am determined to stand by my lease till resistless necessity compel me to quit my ground.

There is one way by which I might be enabled to extricate myself from this embarrassment—a scheme which I hope and am certain is in your power to effectuate. I live here, sir, in the very centre of a country Excise division; the present officer lately lived on a farm which he rented, in my nearest neighbourhood; and as the gentleman, owing to some legacies, is quite opulent, a removal could do him no manner of injury; and on a month's warning to give me a little time to look again over my instructions, I would not be afraid to enter on business. I do not know the name of his division, as I have not yet got acquainted with any of the Dumfries Excise people; but his own name is Leonard Smith. It would suit me to enter on it beginning of next summer; but I shall be in Edinburgh to wait upon you about the affair, sometime in the ensuing winter.

When I think how and on what I have written to you, sir, I shudder at my own *hardiesse*. Forgive me, sir, I have told you my situation. If asking anything less could possibly have done, I would not have asked so much.

If I were in the service, it would likewise favour my poetical schemes. I am thinking of something in the rural way, of the drama kind. Originality of character is, I think, the most striking beauty in that species of composition, and my wanderings in the way of my business would be vastly favourable to my picking up original traits of human nature.

I again, sir, earnestly beg your forgivness for this letter. I have done violence to my own feelings in writing it.

> If I in aught have done amiss,
> Impute it not!

My thoughts on this business, as usual with me when my mind is burdened, vented themselves in the enclosed verses, which I have taken the liberty to inscribe to you.

You, sir, have the power to bless; but the only claim I have to your friendly offices is my having already been the object of your goodness, which [indeed looks like] producing my debt instead of my discharge.

I am sure I go on Scripture grounds in this affair, for I 'ask in faith,

nothing doubting;' and for the true Scripture reason too, because I have
the fullest conviction that 'my benefactor is good.'

I have the honour to be, sir, your deeply indebted humble servant,

ROBT. BURNS.

About this time Burns fell in with the suggestion of some of his
literary friends, who warned him that if he wrote persistently in
Scots he would cut himself off from the appreciation of the larger
public in England. He therefore made a serious attempt to compose in English, but it was at least a comparative failure. It is
not the 'strength' but the weakness of his 'Muse's pinion' that is
illustrated in the poem which he enclosed with the letter to
Graham of Fintry:

FIRST EPISTLE TO ROBERT GRAHAM, ESQ., OF FINTRY,

REQUESTING A FAVOR.*

When Nature her great Masterpiece designed,
And framed her last, best work, the Human-mind,
Her eye intent on all the various plan,
She formed of various parts the various man.

Then first she calls the USEFUL MANY forth—
Plain, plodding Industry, and sober Worth:
Thence Peasants, Farmers, native sons of earth,
And Merchandise' whole genus take their birth,
Each prudent Cit a warm existence finds,
And all Mechanics' many-aproned kinds.
Some other rarer Sorts are wanted yet,
The lead and buoy are needful to the net:
The *Caput mortuum* of strong Desires
Makes a material for mere Knights and Squires;
The Martial Phosphorus is taught to flow;
She kneads the lumpish Philosophic Dough,
Then marks th' unyielding mass with grave Designs,
Law, Physics, Politics, and deep Divines:
Last, she sublimes th' Aurora of the Poles,
The flashing Elements of Female Souls.

* The favour requested was received almost a year later.

The ordered System fair before her stood,
Nature, well pleased, pronounced it very good ;
But ere she gave creating labour o'er,
Half-jest, she tried one curious labour more.
Some spumy, fiery, *ignis fatuus* matter,
Such as the slightest breath of air might scatter,
With arch-alacrity and conscious glee
(Nature may have her whim as well as we ;
Her Hogarth-art, perhaps she meant to show it)
She forms the thing, and christens it—a Poet.

Creature, tho' oft the prey of Care and Sorrow,
When blest today, unmindful of tomorrow ;
A being form'd t' amuse his graver friends,
Admir'd and prais'd—and there the wages ends ;
A mortal quite unfit for Fortune's strife,
Yet oft the sport of all the ills of life ;
Prone to enjoy each pleasure riches give,
Yet haply wanting wherewithal to live ;
Longing to wipe each tear, to heal each groan,
Yet frequent all-unheeded in his own.

But honest Nature is not quit a Turk,
She laugh'd at first, then felt for her poor work :
Pitying the propless Climber of mankind,
She cast about a Standard-tree to find ;
And to support his helpless woodbine state,
Attach'd him to the generous, truly great :
A title, and the only one I claim,
To lay strong hold for help on bounteous GRAHAM.

Pity the tuneful Muses' hapless train,
Weak, timid Landsmen on life's stormy main !
Their hearts no selfish stern absorbent stuff
That never gives—tho' humbly takes enough ;
The little Fate allows, they share as soon,
Unlike sage, proverb'd Wisdom's hard-wrung boon :
The world were blest did bliss on them depend,
Ah, that the Friendly e'er should want a friend !

Let Prudence number o'er each sturdy son
Who life and wisdom at one race begun,
Who feel by reason, and who give by rule,
(Instinct's a brute, and Sentiment a fool!)
Who make poor 'will do' wait upon 'I should:'
We own they 're prudent, but who owns they 're good?
Ye Wise-Ones, hence! ye hurt the social eye!
God's image rudely etch'd on base alloy!
But come ye who the godlike pleasure know,
Heaven's attribute distinguish'd—to bestow;
Whose arms of love would grasp the human race:
Come *thou* who giv'st with all a courtier's grace,
(*Friend of my life*, true Patron of my rhymes!)
Prop of my dearest hopes for future times.

Why shrinks my soul, half-blushing, half-afraid,
Backward, abash'd, to ask thy friendly aid?
I know my need, I know thy giving hand,
I tax thy friendship at thy kind command;
But there are such who court the tuneful Nine—
Heavens! should the branded character be mine!
Whose *verse* in manhood's pride sublimely flows,
Yet vilest reptiles in their begging *prose*.
Mark, how their lofty independent spirit
Soars on the spurning wing of injur'd Merit!
Seek you the proofs in *private life* to find?
Pity the best of words should be but wind!
So, to heaven's gates the lark's shrill song ascends,
But grovelling on the earth the carol ends.
In all the clamorous cry of starving want,
They dun Benevolence with shameless front;
Oblige them, patronise their tinsel lays,
They persecute you all your future days!
Ere my poor soul such deep damnation stain,
My horny fist assume the plough again,
The pie-bald jacket let me patch once more,
On eighteen pence a week I 've liv'd before.
Tho', thanks to Heaven! I dare even that last shift,
I trust, meantime, my boon is in thy gift;

That plac'd by thee upon the wish'd-for height,
Where Man and Nature fairer in her sight,
My Muse may imp * her wing for some sublimer flight.

TO MRS ROBERT BURNS, MAUCHLINE.

ELLISLAND, *Friday, 12th Sep.* 1788.

MY DEAR LOVE—I received your kind letter with a pleasure which
no letter but one from you could have given me. I dreamed of you the
whole night last; but alas! I fear it will be three weeks yet ere I can
hope for the happiness of seeing you. My harvest is going on. I have
some to cut down still, but I put in two stacks to-day, so I'm as tired
as a dog.

You might get one of Gilbert's sweet milk cheeses, and send it to . . .
On second thoughts, I believe you had best get the half of Gilbert's web
of table linen, and make it up; tho' I think it damnable dear, but it is
no outlaid money to us, you know. I have just now consulted my old
landlady about table linen, and she thinks I may have the best for two
shillings per yard; so after all, let it alone until I return; and some day
next week I will be in Dumfries, and will ask the price there. I expect
your new gowns will be very forward, or ready to make, against I be
home to get the baiveridge.† I have written my long-thought-on letter
to Mr Graham, the Commissioner of Excise; and have sent a sheetful of
Poetry besides. Now I talk of poetry, I had [a fine] strathspey among
my hands to make verses to, for Johnson's Collection, which I [intend as
my honey-moon song.]   [R. B.]

One of the products of the 'lucid intervals' in Ayrshire was a
ballad, now usually printed under the title 'The Fête Champêtre.'
According to Gilbert Burns, 'When Mr [William] Cunninghame, of
Enterkin,‡ came to his estate, two mansion-houses on it, Enterkin
and Annbank, were both in a ruinous state. Wishing to introduce
himself with some *éclat* to the county, he got temporary erections
made on the banks of Ayr, tastefully decorated with shrubs and
flowers, for a supper and ball, to which most of the respectable
families in the county were invited. It was a novelty, and
attracted much notice. A dissolution of parliament was soon

---

* Both Spenser and Shakespeare speak of 'imping' one's wings in the sense of strength-
ening them, fitting them for flight.

† Baiveridge : 'The *beverage* of a new piece of dress is a salute given by the person who
appears in it for the first time, more commonly by a male to a favourite female.'—JAMIESON'S
Scottish Dictionary.

‡ The Enterkin here alluded to is close to Ayr, and must not be confounded with the
famous Enterkin Pass between the counties of Lanark and Dumfries.

expected, and this festivity was thought to be an introduction to a canvass for representing the county. Several other candidates were spoken of, particularly Sir John Whitefoord, then residing at Cloncaird, commonly pronounced Glencaird, and James Boswell, the biographer of Dr Johnson. The political views of this festive assemblage, which are alluded to in the ballad, if they ever existed, were, however, laid aside, as Mr Cunninghame did not canvass the county.' The fête took place in the summer of 1788.

THE FÊTE CHAMPÊTRE.

Tune—*Killiecrankie.*

O wha will to Saint Stephen's House,   who
   To do our errands there, man?
O wha will to Saint Stephen's House
   O' th' merry lads of Ayr, man?
Or will we send a man o' law?
   Or will we send a sodger?   soldier
Or him wha led o'er Scotland a'   all
   The meikle Ursa-Major?*   great

Come, will ye court a noble lord,
   Or buy a score o' lairds, man?   landholders
For worth and honour pawn their word,
   Their vote shall be Glencaird's, man.
Ane gies them coin, ane gies them wine,   One gives
   Anither gies them clatter;   Another—glib talk
Annbank, wha guess'd the ladies' taste,
   He gies a Fête Champêtre.

When Love and Beauty heard the news,
   The gay green-woods amang, man;
Where, gathering flowers, and busking bowers,   decking
   They heard the blackbird's sang, man: song
A vow, they seal'd it with a kiss,
   Sir Politics to fetter;
As theirs alone, the patent bliss,
   To hold a Fête Champêtre.

* That is, James Boswell. The allusion is to the well-known joke of the elder Boswell, who, hearing his son speak of Johnson as a great luminary, quite a constellation, said: 'Yes, *Ursa Major.*'

Then mounted Mirth on gleesome wing,
　　O'er hill and dale she flew, man ;
Ilk wimpling burn, ilk crystal spring,　　　　　Each winding
　　Ilk glen and shaw she knew, man :　　　　　wood
She summon'd every social sprite
　　That sports by wood or water,
On th' bonie banks o' Ayr to meet,
　　And keep this Fête Champêtre.

Cauld Boreas wi' his boisterous crew　　　　　Cold
　　Were bound to stakes like kye, man ;　　　cattle
And Cynthia's car, o' silver fu',　　　　　　　full
　　Clamb up the starry sky, man :　　　　　　Climbed
Reflected beams dwell in the streams,
　　Or down the current shatter ;
The western breeze steals thro' the trees
　　To view this Fête Champêtre.

How many a robe sae gaily floats !　　　　　　so
　　What sparkling jewels glance, man,
To Harmony's enchanting notes,
　　As moves the mazy dance, man :
The echoing wood, the winding flood,
　　Like Paradise did glitter
When angels met, at Adam's yett,　　　　　　gate
　　To hold their Fête Champêtre.

When Politics came there, to mix
　　And make his ether-stane, man ! *
He circled round the magic ground,
　　But entrance found he nane, man :　　　　none
He blush'd for shame, he quat his name,　　　quitted
　　Forswore it, every letter,
Wi' humble prayer to join and share
　　This festive Fête Champêtre.

* This is an allusion to a very ancient superstition, referred to the Druids, which represents adders as forming annually from their slough certain little annular stones of streaked colouring, which are occasionally found, but which are in reality beads fashioned and used by our early ancestors. They were believed to act as charms.

TO MISS CHALMERS.*

ELLISLAND, NEAR DUMFRIES, *Sept.* 16, 1788.

Where are you? and how are you? and is Lady M'Kenzie recovering her health? for I have had but one solitary letter from you. I will not think you have forgot me, Madam; and for my part—

> When thee, Jerusalem, I forget,
> Skill part from my right hand!

'My heart is not of that rock, nor my soul careless as that sea.' I do not make my progress among mankind as a bowl does among its fellows—rolling through the crowd without bearing away any mark or impression, except where they hit in hostile collision.

I am here, driven in with my harvest-folks by bad weather; and as you and your sister once did me the honour of interesting yourselves much *à l'égard de moi,* I sit down to beg the continuation of your goodness. I can truly say that, all the exterior of life apart, I never saw two whose esteem flattered the nobler feelings of my soul—I will not say, more, but, so much, as Lady M'Kenzie and Miss Chalmers. When I think of you —hearts the best, minds the noblest, of human kind—unfortunate, even in the shades of life—when I think I have met with you, and have lived more of real life with you in eight days than I can do with almost any body I meet with in eight years—when I think on the improbability of meeting you in this world again—I could sit down and cry like a child! If ever you honored me with a place in your esteem, I trust I can now plead more desert. I am secure against that crushing grip of iron poverty, which, alas! is less or more fatal to the native worth and purity of, I fear, the noblest souls; and a late important step in my life has kindly taken me out of the way of those ungrateful iniquities, which, however overlooked in fashionable license, or varnished in fashionable phrase, are indeed but lighter and deeper shades of VILLAINY.

Shortly after my last return to Ayrshire, I married 'my Jean.' This was not in consequence of the attachment of romance, perhaps; but I had a long and much-loved fellow-creature's happiness or misery in my determination, and I durst not trifle with so important a deposit. Nor have I any cause to repent it. If I have not got polite tattle, modish manners, and fashionable dress, I am not sickened and disgusted with the multiform curse of boarding-school affectation; and I have got the handsomest figure, the sweetest temper, the soundest constitution, and the kindest heart in the county. Mrs Burns believes, as firmly as her creed, that I am *le plus bel esprit, et le plus honnête homme* in the universe; although she scarcely ever in her life, except the Scriptures of the Old and New Testament, and the Psalms of David in metre, spent five minutes together in either prose or verse. I must except, also, from this last, a certain late publication of Scots poems, which she has

---

* This is the last of the eleven letters addressed by Burns to Margaret Chalmers.

perused very devoutly; and all the ballads in the country, as she has (O the partial lover! you will cry) the finest 'wood note wild' I ever heard.* I am the more particular in this lady's character, as I know she will henceforth have the honor of a share in your best wishes. She is still at Mauchline, as I am building my house; for this hovel that I shelter in, while occasionally here, is pervious to every blast that blows and every shower that falls; and I am only preserved from being chilled to death, by being suffocated with smoke. I do not find my farm that pennyworth I was taught to expect, but I believe, in time, it may be a saving bargain. You will be pleased to hear that I have laid aside *éclat*, and bind [*i.e.* sheaves] every day after my reapers.

To save me from that horrid situation of at any time going down in a losing bargain of a farm, to misery, I have taken my excise instructions, and have my commission in my pocket for any emergency of fortune. If I could set *all* before your view, whatever disrespect you, in common with the world, have for this business, I know you would approve of my idea.

I will make no apology, dear Madam, for this egotistic detail: I know you and your sister will be interested in every circumstance of it. What signify the silly, idle gewgaws of wealth, or the ideal trumpery of greatness! When fellow-partakers of the same nature fear the same God, have the same benevolence of heart, the same nobleness of soul, the same detestation at every thing dishonest, and the same scorn at every thing unworthy—if they are not in the dependence of absolute beggary, in the name of common sense are they not EQUALS? And if the bias, the instinctive bias, of their souls run the same way, why may they not be FRIENDS?

When I may have an opportunity of sending you this, Heaven only knows. Shenstone says 'When one is confined idle within doors by bad weather, the best antidote against *ennui* is to read the letters of, or write to, one's friends;' in that case, then, if the weather continues thus, I may scrawl you half a quire.

I very lately, to wit, since harvest began, wrote a poem, not in imitation, but in the manner, of Pope's *Moral Epistles*. It is only a short essay, just to try the strength of my Muse's pinion in that way. I will send you a copy of it, when once I have heard from you. I have likewise been laying the foundation of some pretty large Poetic works: how the superstructure will come on, I leave to that great maker and marrer of projects—TIME. Johnson's collection of Scots songs is going on in the third volume; and, of consequence, finds me a consumpt for a great deal of idle metre. One of the most tolerable things I have done in that way is two stanzas that I made to an air a musical gentleman of my acquaintance [Captain Riddel of Glenriddel] composed for the anniversary of his wedding-day, which happens on the seventh of November.† Take it as follows:

---

* Mrs Burns is understood to have been a good singer, 'her voice rising with ease to B natural.'

† The song, with Riddel's music, appeared in the third volume of Johnson's *Museum*.

THE DAY RETURNS, MY BOSOM BURNS.

Tune—*Seventh of November.*

The day returns, my bosom burns,
  The blissful day we twa did meet:
Tho' winter wild in tempest toil'd,
  Ne'er summer-sun was half sae sweet.
Than a' the pride that loads the tide,
  And crosses o'er the sultry line;
Than kingly robes, than crowns and globes,
  Heav'n gave me more—it made thee mine!

While day and night can bring delight,
  Or nature aught of pleasure give;
While joys above my mind can move,
  For thee, and thee alone, I live!
When that grim foe of life below
  Comes in between, to make us part,
The iron hand that breaks our band,
  It breaks my bliss—it breaks my heart!

I shall give over this letter for shame. If I should be seized with a scribbling fit before this goes away, I shall make it another letter; and then you may allow your patience a week's respite between the two. I have not room for more than the old, kind, hearty, FAREWELL!

To make some amends, *mes chères Mesdames,* for dragging you on to this second sheet; and to relieve a little the tiresomeness of my unstudied and uncorrectable prose, I shall transcribe you some of my late poetic bagatelles; though I have, these eight or ten months, done very little that way. One day, in an Hermitage on the Banks of Nith belonging to a gentleman in my neighbourhood, who is so good as give me a key at pleasure, I wrote as follows; supposing myself the sequestered, venerable inhabitant of the lonely mansion.

Thou whom chance may hither lead, &c.*

R. B.

* See *ante,* 'Verses composed in Friars' Carse Hermitage.'

TO ROBERT GRAHAM, ESQ.

ELLISLAND, 23d *Sept.* 1788.

SIR—Though I am scarce able to hold up my head with this fashionable influenza, which is just now the rage hereabouts, yet, with half a spark of life, I would thank you for your most generous favour of the 14th, which, owing to my infrequent calls at the post-office, in the hurry of harvest, came only to hand yesternight. I assure you, my ever-honoured sir, I read it with eyes brimful of other drops than those of anguish. Oh, what means of happiness the Author of goodness has put in their hands to whom he has given the power to bless!—and what real happiness has he given to those on whom he has likewise bestowed kind, generous, benevolent dispositions! Did you know, sir, from how many fears and forebodings the friendly assurance of your patronage and protection has freed me, it would be some reward for your goodness.

I am cursed with a melancholy prescience, which makes me the veriest coward in life. There is not any exertion which I would not attempt, rather than be in that horrid situation—to be ready to call on the mountains to fall on me, and the hills to cover me from the presence of a haughty landlord, or his still more haughty underling, to whom I owed—what I could not pay. My muse, too, the circumstance that, after my domestic comfort, is by far the dearest to my soul, to have it in my power to cultivate her acquaintance to advantage—in short, sir, you have, like the great Being whose image you so richly bear, made a creature happy, who had no other claim to your goodness than his necessity, and who can make you no other return than his grateful acknowledgment.

My farm, I think I am certain, will in the long-run be an object for me; and as I rent it the first three years something under [its value], I will be able to weather by a twelvemonth, or perhaps more; though it would make me set fortune more at defiance, if it can be in your power to grant my request, as I mentioned, in the beginning of next summer. I was thinking that, as I am only a little more than five miles from Dumfries, I might perhaps officiate there, if any of these officers could be removed with more propriety than Mr Smith; but besides the monstrous inconvenience of it to me, I could not bear to injure a poor fellow by outing him to make way for myself; to a wealthy son of good-fortune like Smith, the injury is imaginary where the propriety of your rules admits.

Had I been well, I intended to have troubled you further with a description of my soil and plan of farming; but business will call me to town about February next. I hope then to have the honour of assuring you *in propriâ personâ*, how much and how truly I am, sir, your deeply indebted and ever-grateful, humble servant,

ROBT. BURNS.

TO MRS DUNLOP.

MAUCHLINE, 27th Sept. 1788.

I have received twins, Dear Madam, more than once, but scarcely ever with more pleasure than when I received yours of the 12th Inst. To make myself understood: I had wrote to Mr Graham, inclosing my Poem addressed to him, and the same Post which favoured me with yours, brought me an answer from him. It was dated the very day he had received mine; and I am quite at a loss to say whether it was most polite or kind.

Your Criticisms, my honored Benefactress, are truly the work of a Friend. They are not the blasting depredations of a canker-toothed caterpillar-critic; nor are they the fair statement of cold Impartiality, balancing with unfeeling exactitude, the *pro* and *con* of an Author's merits; they are the judicious observations of animated Friendship, selecting the beauties of the Piece.

I have just arrived from Nithsdale, and will be here a fortnight. I was on horseback this morning (for between my Wife and my farm is just 46 miles) by three o'clock. As I jogged on in the dark, I was taken with a Poetic-fit, as follows—

MRS FERGUSSON OF CRAIGDARROCH'S LAMENTATION FOR THE DEATH OF HER SON,

AN UNCOMMONLY PROMISING YOUTH OF EIGHTEEN OR NINETEEN YEARS OF AGE.*

'Fate gave the word, the arrow sped,'
 And pierced my Darling's heart;
And with him all the joys are fled
 Life can to me impart!

By cruel hands the Sapling drops,
 In dust dishonored laid:
So fell the pride of all my hopes,
 My age's future shade.

* ' Died here on Monday last [Nov. 19, 1787], James Fergusson, Esq., younger of Craigdarroch. The worth of this truly amiable and much-lamented youth can best be estimated by a sketch given of him on his leaving Glasgow college in May last: "Of all the young men of this age I have ever known, he is by much the most promising. His abilities are equal to anything he chooses to undertake. His understanding is clear and penetrating, and readily comprehends the most abstract subjects. His memory is retentive. He speaks with fluency and perspicuity; he writes with neatness and accuracy. No one can exceed him in the assiduity of his application, and he persists in it with the utmost steadiness, in spite of every allurement. United with all these shining qualifications, he discovers the most gentle temper, simple manners, and the amiable modesty of youth."'—*Newspaper Obituary.*

>   The mother-linnet in the brake
>   Bewails her ravished young;
>   So I, for my lost Darling's sake,
>   Lament the liveday long.
>
>   Death, oft I 've fear'd thy fatal blow;
>   Now, fond, I bare my breast;
>   O, do thou kindly lay me low
>   With him I love, at rest!

You will not send me your Poetic-rambles, but, you see, I am no niggard of mine. I am sure your Impromptus give me double pleasure: what falls from your Pen can neither be unentertaining in itself, nor indifferent to me.

The *one* fault you found, is just; but I cannot please myself in an emendation.

What a life of solicitude is the life of a Parent! You interested me much in your young Couple. I suppose it is not any of the ladies I have seen.

I would not take my folio [paper] for this epistle, and now I repent it. I am so jaded with my dirty long journey that I was afraid to drawl into the essence of dulness with any thing larger than a quarto, and so I must leave out another Rhyme of this morning's manufacture.

I 'll pay the sapientipotent George most chearfully, to hear from you ere I leave Ayrshire.

I have the honor to be, Dear Madam, your much obliged, and most respectful, humble servant,   ROBT. BURNS.

There is good reason to believe that the 'Lament' conveyed in this letter was made to do double duty. The family of Mr Allason Cunninghame of Logan House, Ayrshire, who possessed a copy of it, understood that it was sent to his grandmother, Burns's early patron, Mrs General Alexander Stewart of Afton, as an elegy on the death of her only son, Alexander Gordon Stewart, who died, aged sixteen, at a military academy at Strasburg, 5th December 1787. Allan Cunningham speaks of a copy of the poem in his possession bearing a note by the author, which shows that he really had endeavoured to turn this piece to account twice: 'The Mother's Lament' (he quotes from the MS.) 'was composed partly with a view to Mrs Fergusson of Craigdarroch, and partly to the worthy patroness of my early unknown muse, Mrs Stewart of Afton.' In like manner we shall find that the verses beginning

'Sensibility, how charming,' were first written on certain experiences of Mrs M'Lehose, and sent to her, but were afterwards addressed, with some alterations, to 'my dear and much-honoured friend, Mrs Dunlop.'

TO MR PETER HILL.

MAUCHLINE, 1st October 1788.

I have been here in this country about three days, and all that time my chief reading has been the 'Address to Loch Lomond' you were so obliging as to send to me.* Were I impanelled one of the author's jury, to determine his criminality respecting the sin of poesy, my verdict should be 'guilty! A poet of nature's making!' It is an excellent method for improvement, and what I believe every poet does: to place some favourite classic author in his own walks of study and composition before him, as a model. Though your author had not mentioned the name, I could have, at half a glance, guessed his model to be Thomson. Will my brother-poet forgive me, if I venture to hint that his imitation of that immortal bard is in two or three places rather more servile than such a genius as his required.—*e.g.*

> To soothe the madding passions all to peace.
>
> *Address.*

> To soothe the throbbing passions into peace.
>
> THOMSON.

I think the *Address* is, in simplicity, harmony and elegance of versification, fully equal to the *Seasons*. Like Thomson, too, he has looked into nature for himself: you meet with no copied description. One particular criticism I made at first reading; in no one instance has he said too much. He never flags in his progress, but, like a true poet of nature's making, kindles in his course. His beginning is simple and modest, as if distrustful of the strength of his pinion; only, I do not altogether like

> —————— truth,
> The soul of every song that's nobly great.

Fiction is the soul of many a song that is nobly great. Perhaps I am wrong: this may be but a prose-criticism. Is not the phrase in line 7, page 6, 'Great lake,' too much vulgarized by every-day language, for so sublime a poem?

> Great mass of waters, theme for nobler song,

----

* The author was James Cririe (1752-1835), then Rector of the High School at Leith. In 1795 he was appointed master in the High School of Edinburgh, in succession to Burns's friend, Cruikshank, who died in that year. In 1801 he was presented to the parish of Dalton, Dumfriesshire, where he remained until his death. The 'Address to Loch Lomond' was incorporated in a subsequent volume which he wrote, *Scottish Scenery; or, Sketches in Verse* (London, 1803).

is perhaps no amendation. His enumeration of a comparison with other lakes is at once harmonious and poetic. Every reader's ideas must sweep the

> winding margin of an hundred miles.

The perspective that follows : mountains blue—the imprisoned billows beating in vain—the wooded isles—the digression on the yew tree—'Ben-lomond's lofty, cloud-enveloped head,' &c., are beautiful. A thunder-storm is a subject which has been often tried, yet our poet, in his grand picture, has interjected a circumstance, so far as I know, entirely original.

> —————— the gloom
> Deep-seamed with frequent streaks of moving fire.

In his preface to the storm, 'the glens how dark between' is noble high-land landscape ! The 'rain ploughing the red mould,' too, is beautifully fancied. 'Ben-lomond's lofty, pathless top' is a good expression ; and the surrounding view from it is truly great : the

> —————— silver mist,
> Beneath the beaming sun,

is well described ; and here he has contrived to enliven his poem with a little of that passion which bids fair, I think, to usurp the modern muses altogether. I know not how far this episode is a beauty upon the whole, but the swain's wish to carry 'some faint idea of the vision bright,' to entertain her 'partial, listening ear,' is a pretty thought. But in my opinion the most beautiful passages in the whole poem are the fowls crowding, in wintry frosts, to Loch-lomond's 'hospitable flood ;' their wheeling round, their lighting, mixing, diving, &c. ; and the glorious description of the sportsman. This last is equal to any thing in the *Seasons*. The idea of 'the floating tribes far distant seen, all glistering to the moon,' provoking his eye as he is obliged to leave them, is a noble ray of poetic genius. 'The howling winds,' 'the hideous roar' of 'the white cascades,' are all in the same style.

I forget that while I am thus holding forth with the heedless warmth of an enthusiast, I am perhaps tiring you with nonsense. I must, how-ever, mention that the last verse of the sixteenth page is one of the most elegant compliments* I have ever seen. I must likewise notice that

---

* Numerous inquiries have failed to find a copy of the original edition of the *Address.* The compliment referred to is probably that part of the poem where the author says :

> 'Nor is thy boast to arms alone confin'd ;
> Fair Science, too, upon thy banks hath bloom'd,
> And sweetest fruits, of flavour rich, produc'd.'

> 'Thy banks are grac'd with names of highest note,
> Immortal names from age to age rever'd.'

> 'Napier, of judgment deep and thought profound . . .'

> 'Buchanan, elegant and pure . . .'

> 'And Smollet, full of humour . . .'

beautiful paragraph beginning, 'The gleaming lake,' &c. I dare not go into the particular beauties of the last two paragraphs, but they are admirably fine, and truly Ossianic.

I must beg your pardon for this lengthened scrawl. I had no idea of it when I began—I should like to know who the author is; but, whoever he be, please present him with my grateful thanks for the entertainment he has afforded me.

A friend of mine desired me to commission for him two books—*Letters on the Religion essential to man,* a book you sent me before; and *The World unmasked, or the Philosopher the greatest cheat.** Send me them by the first opportunity. The Bible you sent me is truly elegant; I only wish it had been in two volumes.   R. B.

The approach of the centenary of the landing of William of Orange at Torbay was now exciting some sensation in the country. The General Assembly of the Church of Scotland appointed Wednesday, the 5th of November, to be observed as 'a day of solemn thanksgiving for that most glorious event—the Revolution;' and it was so observed. In Burns's parish, Dunscore, the clergyman, the Rev. Joseph Kirkpatrick,† was a zealous Whig, approving strongly, on religious grounds, of the doings of 1688–89. The poet, whose leanings were altogether in the opposite direction, disliked the Calvinism of Mr Kirkpatrick, and was particularly displeased with the discourse which he delivered on this occasion. His deep feelings on the subject moved him to send a letter

TO THE EDITOR OF 'THE STAR[?].'

Nov. 8, 1788.

SIR—Notwithstanding the opprobrious epithets with which some of our philosophers and gloomy sectaries have branded our nature—the principle of universal selfishness, the proneness to all evil, they have

---

* It has been ascertained that *Lettres sur la Religion essentielle à l'homme, distinguée de ce qui n'en est que l'accessoire,* which, as stated on p. 31 of this volume, was published anonymously at Amsterdam in 1738, was written by Marie Huber, a celebrated Swiss mystic. She was born at Geneva about 1694, retired into solitude about 1712, afterwards returned to Geneva, joined the Church of Rome, and died at Lyons in 1759. She wrote several theological works, of which the *Lettres sur la Religion* is the most important. She was author also of the other work here mentioned by Burns. The title-page of the London edition (1738) of the *Letters on Religion* says that it is 'By the author of *The World Unmask'd.*' The latter appeared at Amsterdam in 1731 (2 vols.); a translation was published at London in 1736. The title is 'The World Unmask'd; or, the philosopher the greatest cheat; in twenty-four dialogues between Crito a philosopher, Philo a lawyer and Erastus a merchant. . . .'

† Rev. Joseph Kirkpatrick, minister of Dunscore, 1777–1806; transferred to Wamphray, where he died in 1824 (aged 75). He wrote the description of his parish for the old *Statistical Account of Scotland* (vol. iii., 1792).

given us; still, the detestation in which inhumanity to the distressed
or insolence to the fallen are held by all mankind, shews that they are
not natives of the human heart. Even the unhappy partner of our kind
who is undone, the bitter consequence of his follies or his crimes, who
but sympathizes with the miseries of this ruined profligate brother? we
forget the injuries, and feel for the man.

I went, last Wednesday, to my parish church, most cordially to join in
grateful acknowledgments to the AUTHOR OF ALL GOOD, for the consequent blessings of the glorious Revolution. To that auspicious event
we owe no less than our liberties, civil and religious; to it we are likewise indebted for the present Royal Family, the ruling features of whose
administration have ever been mildness to the subject and tenderness of
his rights.

Bred and educated in revolution principles, the principles of reason
and common sense, it could not be any silly political prejudice which
made my heart revolt at the harsh, abusive manner in which the
reverend gentleman mentioned the House of Stewart, and which, I
am afraid, was too much the language of the day. We may rejoice
sufficiently in our deliverance from past evils, without cruelly raking
up the ashes of those whose misfortune it was, perhaps as much as
their crime, to be the authors of those evils; and we may bless GOD
for all his goodness to us as a nation, without at the same time
cursing a few ruined, powerless exiles, who only harboured ideas and
made attempts that most of us would have done, had we been in
their situation.

'The bloody and tyrannical House of Stewart' may be said with
propriety and justice, when compared with the present royal family,
and the sentiments of our days; but is there no allowance to be made
for the manners of the times? Were the royal contemporaries of the
Stewarts more attentive to their subjects' rights? Might not the
epithets of 'bloody and tyrannical' be, with at least equal justice,
applied to the House of Tudor, of York, or any other of their
predecessors?

The simple state of the case, sir, seems to be this—At that period,
the science of government, the knowledge of the true relation
between king and subject, was, like other sciences and other knowledge, just in its infancy, emerging from dark ages of ignorance and
barbarity.

The Stewarts only contended for prerogatives which they knew their
predecessors enjoyed, and which they saw their contemporaries enjoying;
but these prerogatives were inimical to the happiness of a nation and the
rights of subjects.

In this contest between prince and people, the consequence of that
light of science which had lately dawned over Europe, the monarch of
France, for example, was victorious over the struggling liberties of his
people; with us, luckily, the monarch failed, and his unwarrantable
pretensions fell a sacrifice to our rights and happiness. Whether it

was owing to the wisdom of leading individuals or to the justling of parties, I cannot pretend to determine; but, likewise happily for us, the kingly power was shifted into another branch of the family, who, as they owed the throne solely to the call of a free people, could claim nothing inconsistent with the covenanted terms which placed them there.

The Stewarts have been condemned and laughed at for the folly and impracticability of their attempts in 1715 and 1745. That they failed, I bless GOD; but cannot join in the ridicule against them. Who does not know that the abilities or defects of leaders and commanders are often hidden until put to the touchstone of exigency; and that there is a caprice of fortune, an omnipotence in particular accidents and conjunctures of circumstances, which exalt us as heroes or brand us as madmen, just as they are for or against us?

Man, Mr Publisher, is a strange, weak, inconsistent being: Who would believe, sir, that in this our Augustan age of liberality and refinement, while we seem so justly sensible and jealous of our rights and liberties, and animated with such indignation against the very memory of those who would have subverted them—that a certain people under our national protection should complain, not against our monarch and a few favourite advisers, but against our WHOLE LEGISLATIVE BODY, for similar oppression, and almost in the very same terms, as our forefathers did of the House of Stewart! I will not, I cannot, enter into the merits of the case; but I dare say the American Congress in [of] 1776 will be allowed to be as able and as enlightened as the English convention was in 1688, and that their posterity will celebrate the centenary of their deliverance from us, as duly and sincerely as we do ours from the oppressive measures of the wrong-headed House of Stewart.

To conclude, sir: let every man who has a tear for the many miseries incident to humanity feel for a family illustrious as any in Europe and unfortunate beyond historic precedent; and let every Briton (and particularly every Scotsman) who ever looked with reverential pity on the dotage of a parent cast a veil over the fatal mistakes of the kings of his forefathers.   R. B.

TO MRS DUNLOP,

CARE OF WILLIAM KERR, ESQ., POST OFFICE, EDINBURGH.

MAUCHLINE, 13th Nov. 1788.

MADAM—I had the very great pleasure of dining at Dunlop yesterday. Men are said to flatter women because they are weak; if it is so, Poets must be weaker still; for Misses Rachel and Keith, and Miss Georgina M'Kay, with their flattering attentions and artful compliments, absolutely turned my head. I own they did not lard me over as many a Poet

does his Patron or still more his Patroness, nor did they sugar me up as
a Cameronian Preacher does Jesus Christ; but they so intoxicated me
with their sly insinuations and delicate innuendoes of Compliment that if
it had not been for a lucky recollection how much additional weight and
lustre your good opinion and friendship must give me in that circle, I
had certainly looked on myself as a person of no small consequence. I
dare not say one word how much I was charmed with the Major's friendly
welcome, elegant manner and acute remark, lest I should be thought to
balance my orientalisms of applause over against the finest Quey * in
Ayrshire, which he made me a present of to help and adorn my farm-
stock. As it was on Hallowday,† I am determined, annually as that
day returns, to decorate her horns with an Ode of gratitude to the family
of Dunlop.

The Songs in the second Vol. of the *Museum* marked D., are Dr Blacklock's; but, as I am sorry to say they are far short of his other works,
I, who only know the cyphers of them all, shall never let it be known.
Those marked T. are the works of an obscure, tippling, but extraordinary
body of the name of Tytler; a mortal who, though he drudges about
Edinburgh as a common Printer, with leaky shoes, a sky-lighted hat,
and knee-buckles as unlike as George-by-the-grace-of-God and Solomon-
the-son-of-David, yet that same unknown, drunken Mortal is Author
and compiler of three-fourth's of Elliot's pompous *Encyclopedia Britannica.*‡ Those marked Z. I have given to the world as old verses to their
respective tunes; but in fact, of a good many of them, little more than
the Chorus is ancient; tho' there is no reason for telling every body this
piece of intelligence. Next letter I write you, I shall send one or two
sets of verses I intend for Johnson's third Volume.

What you mention of the thanksgiving day is inspiration from above.
Is it not remarkable, odiously remarkable, that tho' manners are more
civilized, and the rights of mankind better understood, by an Augustan
Century's improvement, yet in this very reign of heavenly Hanoverian-
ism, and almost in this very year, an empire beyond the Atlantic has its
REVOLUTION too, and for the very same maladministration and legis-

---

* A young heifer.

† All Saints' Day, old style.

‡ James Tytler, M.A., a son of the manse, born 1747. Began life as a chemist, but ill-
luck, added to an inclination towards literary work, obliged him to give it up. He was
practically editor of the second edition of the *Encyclopædia Britannica* (1777-1784). His
extraordinary versatility is shown by the number of his works, many of which he printed
himself, having constructed a press from old material. His works include a *History
of Edinburgh* and a *System of Geography*; besides which he translated Virgil's *Eclogues*, wrote
poetry, commented on the origin and antiquity of the Scottish Nation, and was a volu-
minous contributor to the current periodical literature. He also experimented with a fire-
balloon with partial success, but want of means obliged him to discontinue. From this he
was nicknamed 'Balloon' Tytler. His political views brought him into trouble as one of
the Friends of the People; he fled to Ireland, and in 1793 was outlawed by the High
Court of Justiciary. He died in 1804 at Salem, Mass. Andrew Bell was chief proprietor
and publisher of the *Encyclopædia Britannica*; C. Elliot was an Edinburgh publisher who
had a share in the work.

lative misdemeanours in the illustrious and sapientipotent Family of Hanover as was complained of in the 'tyrannical and bloody house of Stuart.'

So soon as I know of your arrival at Dunlop, I shall take the first conveniency to dedicate a day or, perhaps, two, to you and Friendship, under the guarantee of the Major's hospitality. There will soon be threescore and ten miles of permanent distance between us; and now that your friendship and friendly correspondence is entwisted with the heart-strings of my enjoyment of life, I must indulge myself in a festive day of 'The feast of reason and the flow of soul.' I have the honor to be, Madam, your grateful humble servant, ROBT. BURNS.

TO DR BLACKLOCK.

MAUCHLINE, *Nov.* 15, 1788.

REV. AND DEAR SIR—As I hear nothing of your motions but that you are, or were, out of town, I do not know where this may find you, or whether it will find you at all. I wrote you a long letter, dated from the land of matrimony, in June; but either it had not found you, or, what I dread more, it found you or Mrs Blacklock in too precarious a state of health and spirits to take notice of an idle packet.

I have done many little things for Johnson since I had the pleasure of seeing you, and I have finished one piece, in the way of Pope's *Moral Epistles;* * but from your silence, I have every thing to fear, so I have only sent you two melancholy things, which I tremble lest they should too well suit the tone of your present feelings.

In a fortnight I move, bag and baggage, to Nithsdale; till then, my direction is at this place; after that period, it will be at Ellisland, near Dumfries. It would extremely oblige me, were it but half a line, to let me know how you are, and where you are. Can I be indifferent to the fate of a man to whom I owe so much? A man whom I not only esteem, but venerate.

My warmest good wishes and most respectful compliments to Mrs Blacklock and Miss Johnson, if she is with you.

I cannot conclude without telling you that I am more and more pleased with the step I took respecting 'my Jean.' Two things, from my happy experience, I set down as apophthegms in life. A wife's head is immaterial, compared with her heart—and—'Virtue's (for wisdom, what poet pretends to it?) ways are ways of pleasantness, and all her paths are peace.' Adieu! R. B.

One of the pieces enclosed was 'The Mother's Lament for the Death of her Son.' The other was

---

* The 'First Epistle to Robert Graham, Esq., of Fintry' (see pp. 369-372).

THE LAZY MIST HANGS FROM THE BROW OF THE HILL.

The lazy mist hangs from the brow of the hill,
Concealing the course of the dark winding rill;
How languid the scenes, late so sprightly, appear
As Autumn to Winter resigns the pale year.
The forests are leafless, the meadows are brown,
And all the gay foppery of summer is flown:
Apart let me wander, apart let me muse
How quick Time is flying, how keen Fate pursues.

How long I have liv'd—but how much liv'd in vain;
How little of life's scanty span may remain;
What aspects Old Time, in his progress, has worn;
What ties cruel Fate in my bosom has torn;
How foolish, or worse, till our summit is gain'd!
And downward, how weaken'd, how darken'd, how pain'd!
Life is not worth having with all it can give,
For something beyond it poor man sure must live.

TO MR JAMES JOHNSON.

MAUCHLINE, *Nov.* 15, 1788.

MY DEAR SIR—I have sent you two more songs. If you have got any tunes, or any thing to correct, please send them by return of the carrier.

I can easily see, my dear friend, that you will very probably have four volumes. Perhaps you may not find your account *lucratively* in this business; but you are a patriot for the music of your country; and I am certain posterity will look on themselves as highly indebted to your public spirit. Be not in a hurry; let us go on correctly; and your name shall be immortal.

I am preparing a flaming preface for your third volume.* I see, every day, new musical publications advertised: but what are they? Gaudy, hunted butterflies of a day, and then vanish for ever; but your work will

---

* The 'flaming preface' will appear, under date February 2d, 1790, in the third volume of this work.

outlive the momentary neglects of idle fashion, and defy the teeth of time.

Have you never a fair goddess that leads you a wild-goose chase of amorous devotion? Let me know a few of her qualities, such as whether she be rather black or fair, plump or thin, short or tall, &c.; and chuse your air, and I shall task my Muse to celebrate her. R. B.

The next letter shows that Burns remained on friendly terms with the Lawrie family:

TO MONSR. ARCHIBALD LAWRIE,
COLLINE DE ST MARGARETE.

MAUCHLINE, 15*th November* 1788.*

DEAR SIR—If convenient, please return me by Connel, the bearer, the two volumes of songs I left last time I was at St Margaret's Hill.

My best compliments to all the good family.

A Dieu je vous commende. ROBT. BURNS.

Even already, before he had settled down in Dumfriesshire, the Poet had made acquaintances. One of these was John M'Murdo.

TO JOHN M'MURDO, ESQ., DRUMLANRIG.

SANQUHAR, 26*th Nov.* 1788.

SIR—I write you this and the enclosed [a song†], literally *en passant*, for I am just baiting on my way to Ayrshire. I have philosophy or pride enough to support me with unwounded indifference against the neglect of my more dull superiors, the merely rank and file of noblesse and gentry—nay, even to keep my vanity quite sober under the larding of their compliments; but from those who are equally distinguished by their rank and character—those who bear the true elegant impressions of the Great Creator on the richest materials—their little notices and attentions are to me amongst the first of earthly enjoyments. The honor thou didst my fugitive pieces in requesting copies of them is so highly flattering to my feelings and poetic ambition, that I could not resist even this half opportunity of scrawling off for you the enclosed, as a small but honest testimony how truly and gratefully I have the honor to be, Sir, Your deeply obliged humble servant, ROBT. BURNS.

---

* The date of this note has hitherto been given as 1786, but in the original, now in the possession of Mr George Dunlop, Kilmarnock, the date is as given in the text.

† 'The song enclosed was, in all probability, the fine compliment to his wife, beginning "O, were I on Parnassus hill" [see pp. 348-9], perhaps composed on this very journey.'—W. SCOTT DOUGLAS's *Works of Burns*, vol. v.

The bachelor life of Burns was now drawing to a close. As his new house was not ready for the reception of his wife, he obtained temporary accommodation for her at a neighbouring farm. In the first week of December he brought Mrs Burns * to the Banks of the Nith. During the preceding week, two servant-lads and a servant-girl had come from Mauchline, with some cart-loads of the plenishing made by Morison, the Mauchline wright, besides, doubtless, a handsome four-posted bed, which was Mrs Dunlop's marriage gift. This girl stated that Mrs Burns was anxious, on going into a district where she was wholly a stranger, to obtain the services of a young woman whom she knew. She was engaged accordingly; but her father, in his anxiety for her moral welfare, exacted a formal promise from Burns to keep a strict watch over her conduct, and, in particular, to 'exercise her duly in the Catechism'—a promise which, she admitted, he kept most faithfully. We may well believe that this was a time of great happiness for Burns. According to Currie, 'animated sentiments of any kind almost always give rise in our poet to some production of his muse. His sentiments on this occasion were in part expressed by the following vigorous and characteristic, though not very delicate verses; they are in imitation of an old ballad.'

I HAE A WIFE O' MY AIN.

I hae a wife o' my ain,	have—own
I'll partake wi' naebody;	nobody
I'll tak cuckold frae nane,	take—from none
I'll gie cuckold to naebody.	

I hae a penny to spend,
   There—thanks to naebody;
I hae naething to lend,
   I'll borrow frae naebody.

I am naebody's lord,	
I'll be slave to naebody;	
I hae a gude braid sword,	good broad
I'll tak dunts frae naebody.	blows

---

* Mrs Burns only: her child Robert remained at Mossgiel.

I 'll be merry and free,
. I 'll be sad for naebody ;
If naebody care for me,
I 'll care for naebody.*

TO MRS DUNLOP.

ELLISLAND, 17th *December* 1788.

MY DEAR HONORED FRIEND—Yours, dated Edinburgh, which I have just read, makes me very unhappy. 'Almost blind and wholly deaf' are melancholy news of human-nature ; but when told of a much-loved and honored friend, they carry misery in the sound. Goodness on your part and gratitude on mine began a tie which has gradually and strongly entwisted itself among the dearest chords of my bosom ; and I tremble at the omens of your late and present ailing habit and shattered health. You miscalculate matters widely when you forbid my waiting on you, lest it should hurt my worldly concerns. My small scale of farming is exceedingly more simple and easy than what you have lately seen at Morcham Mains.† But be that as it may, the heart of the man and the fancy of the poet are the two grand considerations for which I live : if miry ridges and dirty dunghills are to engross the best part of the functions of my soul immortal, I had better been a rook or a magpie all at once, and then I should not have been plagued with any ideas superior to breaking of clods and picking up grubs, not to mention barn - door cocks or mallards, creatures with which I could almost exchange lives at any time. If you continue so deaf, I am afraid a visit will be no great pleasure to either of us ; but if I hear you are got so well again as to be able to relish conversation, look you to it, madam, for I will make my threatenings good. I am to be at the New-year-day fair of Ayr, and by all that is sacred in the world, friend ! I *will* come and see you. . . .

Your meeting, which you so well describe, with your old schoolfellow

---

* On the 28th of November 1788 the *Edinburgh Advertiser* noted that 'Burns, *the Ayrshire Bard*, is now enjoying the sweets of retirement at his farm. Burns, in thus retiring, has acted wisely. Stephen Duck, the *Poetical Thresher*, by his ill-advised patrons, was made a parson. The poor man, hurried out of his proper element, found himself quite unhappy ; became insane ; and with his own hands, it is said, ended his life. Burns, with propriety, has resumed the *flail*—but we hope he has not thrown away the *quill*.'

† Morham Mains, in the parish of Morham, Haddingtonshire, and three miles SE. of Haddington, had been purchased by John Dunlop of Dunlop (husband of Burns's correspondent), who had built a house, and occasionally lived, there. After his death (1785) Mrs Dunlop continued to visit the farm. It was because of the friendly relations between Burns and Mrs Dunlop that Captain Dunlop offered the management of this farm to Gilbert Burns. He was steward from 1799 till 1803, when the farm changed hands.

and friend was truly interesting.   Out upon the ways of the world!
They spoil these 'social offsprings of the heart.'   Two veterans of
the ' men of the world' would have met with little more heart-work-
ings than two old hacks worn out on the road.   Apropos, is not the
Scotch phrase 'Auld lang syne' exceedingly expressive?   There is an
old song and tune which has often thrilled through my soul.   You
know I am an enthusiast in old Scotch songs.   I shall give you the
verses on the other sheet, as I suppose Mr Ker* will save you the
postage.

AULD LANG SYNE.†

> Should auld acquaintance be forgot,   old
>   And never brought to mind?
> Should auld acquaintance be forgot,
>   And auld lang syne!   days of long ago

> *Chorus.*—For auld lang syne, my dear,
>   For auld lang syne,
>   We 'll tak a cup ‡ o' kindness yet
>   For auld lang syne.

> And surely ye 'll be your pint stowp!   tankard
>   And surely I 'll be mine!
> And we 'll tak a cup o' kindness yet,
>   For auld lang syne.

> We twa hae run about the braes,
>   And pou'd the gowans fine: pulled
> But we 've wander'd mony a weary fitt,   many—foot
>   Sin' auld lang syne.   Since

> We twa hae paidl'd in the burn   waded
>   Frae morning sun till dine: dinner-time
> But seas between us braid hae roar'd   broad
>   Sin' auld lang syne.

---

* Mr Ker was the postmaster of Edinburgh.   He was always ready to frank a letter for
a friend.   Strange stories are told of weighty packets—one, it is said, containing a pair of
buckskin-breeches for a sportsman in the Highlands—passing free through the post-office
in his day.

† The melody to which the song is now sung was composed by William Shield, and forms
part of the overture to his opera *Rosina* (1783).

‡ ' Some sing *kiss* in place of *cup.*'—Note in Johnson's *Museum.*

C. M. Hardie R.S.A.

F. Jenkins Heliog. Paris

We twa hae paidl't in the burn
Frae morning sun till dine.

And there 's a hand, my trusty fiere !   friend
  And gie 's a hand o' thine !   give
And we 'll tak a right gude-willie* waught   draught
  For auld lang syne.

Light be the turf on the breast of the Heaven-inspired poet who composed this glorious fragment !† There is more of the fire of native genius in it than in half-a-dozen of modern English Bacchanalians. Now I am on my hobby-horse, I cannot help inserting two other old stanzas which please me mightily.

MY BONIE MARY.‡

Go, fetch to me a pint o' wine,
  And fill it in a silver tassie,   cup
That I may drink, before I go,
  A service to my bonie lassie :
The boat rocks at the Pier o' Leith,
  Fu' loud the wind blaws frae the Ferry,   blows from
The ship rides by the Berwick-Law,§
  And I maun leave my bonie Mary.   must

The trumpets sound, the banners fly,
  The glittering spears are rankèd ready,
The shouts o' war are heard afar,
  The battle closes deep and bloody :
It 's not the roar o' sea or shore
  Wad make me langer wish to tarry ;   Would—longer
Nor shouts o' war that 's heard afar,
  It 's leaving thee, my bonie Mary !

ROBT. BURNS.

In this letter Burns deliberately threw Mrs Dunlop off the scent of his own authorship. He spoke of 'Auld Lang Syne' as an old fragment. In like manner, when he sent it to George Thomson, he congratulated himself on having been so fortunate as

* Gude-willie = with good-will.
† See Appendix IV.
‡ This song may be effectively sung to one of the numerous settings of the 'Highland Laddie,' to be found in Johnson's *Musical Museum.*
§ North Berwick Law, a conical hill near the shore of the Firth of Forth, very conspicuous at Edinburgh, from which it is distant about twenty miles. The Ferry is Queensferry.

to recover it from an old man's singing. Yet the third and fourth verses—those expressing the recollections of youth, and certainly the finest of the set—are by himself. So also of 'Go, fetch to me a pint o' wine:' he afterwards acknowledged that only the first verse (four lines) was old, and that the rest was his own. The old verse was probably the one that occurs near the close of a homely ballad (printed in Hogg and Motherwell's edition of Burns) as preserved by Peter Buchan, who states that the ballad was composed in 1636, by Alexander Lesly of Edin, on Dovern side, grandfather to the celebrated Archbishop Sharp :

> Ye'll bring me here a pint of wine,
> A server and a silver tassie,
> That I may drink, before I gang,
> A health to my ain bonny lassie.   own

The fact of Burns pitching upon this one fine stanza of an old ballad as a foundation for a new song shows the quick sense he had of all that was truly beautiful in poetry, and how ready his imagination was to take wing upon the slightest command.

TO MR JOHN TENNANT, AUCHENBAY.[*]
CARE OF MR JOHN ROBB, INNKEEPER, AYR.

December 22nd, 1788.

MY DEAR SIR—I yesterday tried my cask of whisky for the first time, and I assure you it does you great credit. It will bear five waters, strong, or six, ordinary, toddy. The whisky of this country is a most rascally liquor ; and, by consequence, only drunk by the most rascally part of the inhabitants. I am persuaded, if you once get a footing here, you might do a great deal of business, in the way of consumpt ; and should you commence Distiller again, this is the native barley country. I am ignorant if, in your present way of dealing, you would think it worth while to extend your business so far as this country side. I write you this on the account of an accident, which I must take the merit of having partly designed too. A neighbour of mine, a John Currie, miller in Carse-mill—a man who is, in a word, a good man, a 'very' good man, even for a £500 bargain—he and his wife were in my house the time I broke open the cask. They keep a country public-house and sell a great deal of foreign spirits, but all along thought that whisky would

---

* John Tennant (1760-1853) was second son of John Tennant of Glenconner, by his second wife. He is said to have started business as a distiller, but abandoning it, leased the farms of Auchenbay and Steelepark. The former is midway between Mauchline and Ochiltree, and about three miles from Glenconner.

have degraded their house. They were perfectly astonished at my whisky, both for its taste and strength; and, by their desire, I write you to know if you could supply them with liquor of an equal quality, and at what price. Please write me by first post, and direct to me at Ellisland, near Dumfries. If you could take a jaunt this way yourself, I have a spare spoon, knife and fork, very much at your service. My compliments to Mrs Tennant, and all the good folks in Glenconner and Barquharie.* I am, most truly, my dear Sir, yours, ROBT. BURNS.

TO MR WILLIAM CRUIKSHANK.

ELLISLAND [December], 1788.

I have not room, my ever-dear friend, to answer all the particulars of your last kind letter. I shall be in Edinburgh on some business very soon, and as I shall be two days, or perhaps three, in town, we shall discuss matters *vivâ voce*. My knee, I believe, never will be entirely well; and an unlucky fall this winter has made it still worse. I well remember the circumstance you allude to respecting Mr Creech's opinion of Mr Nicol, but as the first gentleman owes me still about fifty pounds, I dare not meddle in the affair.

It gave me a very heavy heart to read such accounts of the consequence of your quarrel with that puritanic, rotten-hearted, hell-commissioned scoundrel, Adam.† If, notwithstanding your unprecedented industry in public, and your irreproachable conduct in private, life, he still has you so much in his power, what ruin may he not bring on some others I could name?

Many and happy returns of seasons to you, with your dearest and worthiest friend, and the lovely little pledge of your happy union. May the Great Author of life, and of every enjoyment that can render life delightful, make her that comfort and blessing to you both which you so ardently wish for, and which, allow me to say, you so well deserve. Glance over the foregoing verses ['Lines written in Friars' Carse Hermitage,' *both versions*], and let me have your blots. Adieu!

ROBT. BURNS.

* The allusion here is to the family of George Reid of Barquharie, the next farm to Glenconner, who is understood to have been a nephew of the minister of Ochiltree, and who, as has been seen, lent a pony to the poet for his first journey to Edinburgh.

† Alexander Adam, LL.D., youngest son of a farmer, was born in 1741. He was headmaster of George Watson's Hospital from 1760 till 1768, when he was appointed rector of the High School, a post he held for over forty years. He died suddenly while engaged teaching his class (1809). He had a high reputation as a successful teacher, and was author of several works, chiefly philological. Sir Walter Scott wrote that 'It was from this respectable man that I first learned the value of the knowledge I had hitherto considered only as a burdensome task.' Lord Brougham said that 'Dr Adam was one of the very best teachers he ever heard of, and by far the best he ever knew. Dr Adam had the talent of making his pupils delight in learning, and he opened their minds to the knowledge both of the classics and the love of all other important studies.' Finally, Lord Cockburn maintained that 'he was born to teach Latin, some Greek, and all virtue.'

APPENDICES.

No. I.—BURNS AND THE CANONGATE KILWINNING LODGE.

THE principal documents in the case of Burns's poet-laureate-ship of Canongate Kilwinning Lodge, No. 2, are : (1) A collection of letters to *The Freemason*, entitled 'Burns—poet-laureate of Canongate Kilwinning Lodge—a Myth,' printed for private circulation by Mr William Officer, Edinburgh ; and (2) 'Robert Burns, Poet-Laureate of Lodge Canongate Kilwinning, Edinr. Facts substantiating his election and inauguration on 1st March 1787. By Hugh C. Peacock and Allan Mackenzie ; preface by R. W. Macleod Fullarton, Q.C. Christie & Son, Edinr., 1894.' It may be stated at once that there is no contemporary record of the election or installation of Burns as laureate of the lodge. The minute of 1st March 1787 does not so much as mention the poet. The first allusion to his laureateship—and it is an indirect allusion—occurs in a minute of 24th June 1802, on which date the lodge 'approved of four prints which were got for the lodge,' one of which is an engraving by Paton Thomson of the Skirving head, bearing inscription, 'Robert Burns, the Scottish Bard, Poet Laureat Lodge No. 2 Canongate Kilwinning.' There is not, however, till the year 1815, any evidence in the minute-book that the lodge claimed Burns as its laureate. On June 8th of that year a subscription was authorised for the mausoleum of ' Robert Burns, who had been Poet Laureat to the Lodge.' The resolution to this effect was seconded by Charles More, who, as depute-master, signed the minute of the meeting of 1st February 1787, at which the poet was affiliated, and who had since remained in unbroken connection with the lodge. There were, moreover, in the membership in 1815, about a hundred persons who had been members before and during 1787. Some of these must have been present when Burns's laureateship was formally asserted ; yet nobody appears to have dissented. Again, a number of these gentle-men must have been alive in 1835, when James Hogg was elected to succeed Burns as poet-laureate, on which occasion Hogg expressly acknowledged the compliment of being asked to succeed Burns, and the lodge toasted Burns as ' the last Poet Laureate of the Lodge.' The only other circumstance worth mentioning in support of the tradition is a statement, made in 1845 by a Brother William Petrie, that he had been present at the inauguration of the poet on 1st March 1787. This state-ment was made to Mr Stewart Watson, painter of the picture, ' The Inauguration of Robert Burns as Poet-Laureate of Lodge Canongate

Kilwinning, 1st March 1787,' which hangs on the wall of the Grand Lodge, Edinburgh. Mr Watson (born Edinburgh 1800, nephew of George Watson, first P.R.S.A.) was entered in Canongate Kilwinning, No. 2, in 1828, and must have known many other members who could recall the events of 1787. The chief grounds on which the tradition has been assailed are the absence of any record in the minutes, and the absence of any mention of the fact by Burns. The defence is that the minutes were very carelessly kept at the time, and that the secretary took more pains to record formalities than exceptional occurrences ; and that, as Burns did not mention even his affiliation to the lodge, it is not surprising that there is no allusion to the laureateship in any of his letters that are extant.

No. II.—PORTRAITS OF BURNS.

There are in the National Gallery at Edinburgh, two portraits of Burns painted by Alexander Nasmyth : the original done at sittings in Edinburgh, and the full-length from memory ; in the Scottish National Portrait Gallery are three others—an oil-painting, a miniature on ivory, and a silhouette. Besides these, there has not, as yet at least, been discovered any portrait of the poet which can be proved, by external or internal evidence, to have been done from life.

The most celebrated and best-authenticated of the paintings is that by Nasmyth showing the head and bust on a canvas fifteen inches by twelve. It was presented to Mrs Burns by the painter, and bequeathed to the Scottish nation by Colonel William Nicol Burns. This presentment of the poet has been familiarised by numerous reproductions, of which the best known is the engraving by Beugo done for the first Edinburgh edition of the *Poems.* Sir Walter Scott thought the painting represented the poet as if seen in perspective. Beugo, in retouching his plate after his interviews with Burns, tried to correct this over-refinement—he shortened the face, as Mr W. Craibe Angus has, in one of a series of articles which he contributed to the *Glasgow Herald* in 1890, pointed out, by rounding the chin—and, though Gilbert Burns thought the engraving showed more character and expression than the picture itself, in the opinion of Mr George Aikman, A.R.S.A., Beugo really vulgarised the face, the scale on which he worked being, moreover, too small to enable him to grasp the details of the face. The reproduction which pleased Nasmyth most—and, indeed, pleases nearly every one— was an engraving, published in 1830, stippled by William Walker and mezzotinted by Samuel Cousins. Nearly all the engravings that have been put in the market since are attempts to reproduce the Nasmyth portrait. Nasmyth made two replicas, one of which (probably touched by Raeburn) is in the National Portrait Gallery, London, the other in the possession of the Misses Cathcart, Auchendrane, near Ayr. The latter is different from the others in shape, being circular, 11½ inches in diameter. Nasmyth's full-length sketch of the poet, painted from memory for reproduction in Lockhart's *Life of Burns*, is also in the Scottish National Gallery.

The authenticity of the largest of the oil-paintings preserved in the Scottish National Portrait Gallery is very doubtful. It shows the head with a broad-brimmed hat, and the whole trunk. It was painted by Peter Taylor, said by Mrs M'Lehose in 1828 to have been an ' early friend ' of the poet, described by Lockhart as ' an artist of considerable celebrity at the time of Burns's visit to Edinburgh in 1786,' but declared by Nasmyth never to have ' pretended to be otherwise than a coach-painter.' He was, in fact, as the late J. M. Gray put it, a decorative artist who occasionally executed likenesses. He received a premium of £100 for introducing the manufacture of painted waxcloth into Scotland. Though Mr W. Craibe Angus holds that Taylor merely ' generalised Nasmyth's facts,' others think that this portrait of Burns bears some evidence of having been painted from life, but there is no proof that the poet sat to Taylor, except the statement of the latter's widow ; it is a very significant fact that Burns never mentions either Taylor or the fact of his having sat to any painter but Nasmyth and Reid. Gilbert Burns, who saw it for the first time in 1812, said it was ' particularly like Robert in the form and air.' Hogg, who saw it at the same time, discovered in it ' a family likeness.' Scott, in 1829, ' could not hesitate to recognise this portrait as a striking resemblance of the Poet, though it had been presented to me amid a whole exhibition.' And Mrs M'Lehose, in 1828, testified : ' In my opinion, it is the most striking likeness of the Poet I have ever seen.' On the other hand, the late William Hall, of Liverpool, who had met Burns several times, when he was appealed to, in 1829, to authenticate the Taylor portrait, saw in it not the slightest resemblance to Burns, and left it on record that he was confirmed in his scepticism by Dr M'Kenzie, formerly of Mauchline, Mr Nasmyth, Robert Ainslie, and William Tennant, son-in-law of Dr Dalrymple, of Ayr. Isabella Burns Begg said it was at first thought to be a portrait of Robert, but that the family afterwards agreed it was meant for Gilbert. An engraving of this painting, by J. Horsburgh, was published in 1829.

The Miers silhouette is declared by Mr D. W. Stevenson, R.S.A., to be ' in perfect harmony with Nasmyth's portrait.' It was bequeathed by Mr W. F. Watson to the Scottish National Portrait Gallery.

So also was the miniature on ivory, which, there is good reason to believe, is the portrait alluded to by Burns (January 29th, 1796) in a letter to Mrs Riddel : ' *Apropos* to pictures, I am sitting to Reid in this town for a miniature, and I think he has hit by far the best likeness of me ever taken.' The face is in profile, the left side being shown, while the Nasmyth and the Taylor show the right. The years that have passed have left their mark on the brow ; the features are harder, the eye more sunk. A small black whisker comes down to the lobe of the ear.

The favourite portrait of the poet is that by Archibald Skirving, done in crayon on grayish-toned paper, and now in the possession of Sir Theodore Martin. There is no record of the poet's sitting to Skirving, who might, however, have met him in Edinburgh. The portrait is a well-drawn copy of the Nasmyth painting, with variations in several features ; the eyes are smaller, the frontal ridge more developed, the hair thicker, the jaw squarer, and the head more compactly built.

No. III.—BURNS'S AUTOBIOGRAPHY.

(*From the Original in the British Museum.*)

' Know all whom it may concern, that I, the Author, am not answerable for the false spelling and injudicious punctuation in the foregoing transcript of my letter to Dr Moore. I have something generous in my temper that cannot bear to see or hear the Absent wronged, and I am very much hurt to observe that in several instances the transcriber has injured and mangled the proper name and principal title of a Personage of the very first distinction in all that is valuable among men, Antiquity, abilities and power (Virtue, every body knows, is an obsolete business) : I mean the Devil. Considering that the Transcriber was one of the Clergy, an order that owe the very bread they eat to the said Personage's exertions, the affair was absolutely unpardonable.—R. B.'

The foregoing note by Burns is appended to the transcript of his famous Letter to Moore, which stands as No. 12 of the Glenriddel MSS. now in The Athenæum at Liverpool. The transcript, which was made, as the note playfully indicates, by a licentiate of the Church of Scotland, having been revised by Burns, may fairly be regarded as the final and authoritative edition of what he undoubtedly regarded as his autobiography. As such it has been published as the first chapter of Vol. I. of the present work. The original letter was, however, written during the period which is embraced in our Vol. II., and we now give a transcript of the autobiographical portion of it. The manuscripts are by no means identical, although even so laborious a student of Burns as Mr William Scott Douglas has stated (Library Edition of *The Works of Robert Burns*, vol. iv., p. 1) that he found the Glenriddel transcript 'to correspond with the original in the British Museum.' The more important points of variation in the Glenriddel MS. from the original are given in foot-notes.

' I have not the most distant pretensions to what the pye-coated guardians of escutcheons call, A Gentleman.—When at Edinr. last winter, I got acquainted in the Herald's Office, and looking through that granary of Honors, I there found almost every name in the kingdom ; but for me,

> ——My ancient but ignoble blood
> Has crept thro' Scoundrels ever* since,the flood. †

---

* ' Ever' omitted in Glenriddel MS.

†   ' Go ! if your ancient but ignoble blood
         Has crept through Scoundrels since the flood,

Gules, Purpure, Argent, &c. quite disowned me.—My Fathers rented
land of the noble Keiths of Marshal, and had the honor to share their
fate.—I do not use the word, Honor, with any reference to political principles : loyal and disloyal I take to be merely relative terms in that
ancient and formidable court known in this Country by the name of Club-
law.—Those who dare welcome Ruin and shake hands with Infamy for
what they sincerely believe to be the cause of their God or their King—
" Brutus and Cassius are honorable men." *—I mention this circumstance
because it threw my father on the world at large ; where after many
years' wanderings and sojournings, he pickt up a pretty large quantity
of Observation and Experience, to which I am indebted for most of my
little † pretensions to wisdom.—I have met with few who understood
" Men, their manners and their ways " equal to him ; but stubborn, ungainly Integrity, and headlong, ungovernable Irrascibillity are disqualify-
ing circumstances : consequently I was born a very poor man's son.—For
the first six or seven years of my life, my father was gardiner to a worthy
gentleman of small estate in the neighbourhood of Ayr.—Had my father
continued in that situation, I must have marched off to be one of the
little underlings about a farm-house ; but it was his dearest wish and
prayer to have it in his power to keep his children under his own eye till
they could discern between good and evil ; so with the assistance of his
generous Master my father ventured on a small farm in his estate.—At
these years I was by no means a favorite with any body. I was a good
deal noted for a retentive memory, a stubborn, sturdy something in my
disposition, and an enthusiastic idiot-piety.—I say idiot-piety, because I
was then but a child. Though I cost the schoolmaster some thrashings,
I made an excellent English scholar ; and against the years of ten or
eleven, I was absolutely a Critic in substantives, verbs, and particles.—
In my infant and boyish days too, I owed much to an old Maid of my
Mother's, remarkable for her ignorance, credulity and superstition.—She
had, I suppose, the largest collection in the county of tales and songs
concerning devils, ghosts, fairies, brownies, witches, warlocks, spunkies,
kelpies, elf-candles, dead-lights, wraiths, apparitions, cantraips, giants,
inchanted towers, dragons and other trumpery.—This cultivated the
latent seeds of Poesy ; but had so strong an effect on my imagination,
that to this hour, in my nocturnal rambles, I sometimes keep a sharp
look-out in suspicious places ; and though nobody can be more sceptical
in these matters than I, yet it often takes an effort of Philosophy to
shake off these idle terrors.—The earliest thing of Composition that I
recollect taking pleasure in was The Vision of Mirza and a hymn of

Go and pretend your family is young,
Nor own your fathers have been fools so long.
What can ennoble sots, or slaves, or cowards?
Alas ! not all the blood of all the Howards.'
                                        —Pope's *Essay on Man*, iv., 211-216.
* ' 'Are—as Mark Antony in Shakespear says of Brutus and Cassius—" honorable men." '
† ' Little ' omitted in Glenriddel MS.

Addison's beginning—" How are Thy servants blest, O Lord !" I particularly remember one half-stanza which was music to my boyish ear :

> For though in dreadful whirls we hung,
> "High on the broken wave."——

I met with these pieces in Mason's English Collection, one of my school-
books. The two first books I ever read in private, and which gave me
more pleasure than any two books I ever read again, were, the life of
Hannibal and the history of Sir William Wallace.—Hannibal gave my
young ideas such a turn that I used to strut in raptures up and down
after the recruiting drum and bagpipe, and wish myself tall enough to be
a soldier ; while the story of Wallace poured a Scotish prejudice in my
veins, which will boil along there till the flood-gates of life shut in
eternal rest.—Polemical divinity about this time was putting the country
half-mad ; and I, ambitious of shining in conversation parties on sundays
between sermons, funerals, &c.* used in a few years more to puzzle
Calvinism with so much heat and indiscretion that I raised a hue and cry
of heresy against me which has not ceased to this hour.——

'My vicinity to Ayr was of great advantage to me.—My social disposition, when not checked by some modification of spited pride, like our
catechism['s] definition of Infinitude, was "without bounds or limits."—
I formed many connections with other younkers who possessed superiour
advantages ; the youngling Actors who were busy with the rehearsal of
Parts in which they were shortly to appear on that Stage where, Alas ! I
was destined to drudge behind the scenes.—It is not commonly at these
green years that the young Noblesse and Gentry have a just sense of the
immense distance between them and their ragged Playfellows.—It takes
a few dashes into the world to give the young Great man that proper,
decent, unnoticing disregard for the poor, insignificant, stupid devils, the
mechanics and peasantry around him ; who perhaps were born in the
same village.—My young Superiours never insulted the clouterly appearance of my ploughboy carcase, the two extremes of which were often
exposed to all the inclemencies of all the seasons.—They would give me
stray volumes of books ; among them, even then, I could pick up some
observations ; and One, whose heart I am sure not even the "MUNNY
BEGUMS'" scenes have tainted, helped me to a little French.—Parting
with these, my young friends and benefactors, as they dropped off for
the east or west Indies, was often to me a sore affliction ; but I was soon
called to more serious evils.—My father's generous Master died ; the farm
proved a ruinous bargain ; and, to clench the curse, we fell into the
hands of a Factor who sat for the picture I have drawn of one in my Tale
of two dogs.—My father was advanced in life when he married ; I was
the eldest of seven children ; and he, worn out by early hardship, was
unfit for labour.—My father's spirit was soon irritated, but not easily
broken.—There was a freedom in his lease in two years more, and to

---

* 'Ambitious of shining on Sundays, between sermons, in conversation parties, at
funerals, &c., in a few years more, used to puzzle Calvinism.'

weather these two years * we retrenched expences.—We lived very poorly; I was a dextrous Ploughman for my years; and the next eldest to me was a brother, who could drive the plough very well and help me to thrash.—A Novel-Writer might perhaps have viewed these scenes with some satisfaction, but so did not I: my indignation yet boils at the recollection of the scoundrel tyrant's insolent, threatening epistles, which used to set us all in tears.

'This kind of life, the cheerless gloom of a hermit with the unceasing moil of a galley-slave, brought me to my sixteenth year; a little before which period I first committed the sin of RHYME.—You know our country custom of coupling a man and woman together as partners in the labors of Harvest.—In my fifteenth autumn, my Partner was a bewitching creature who just counted an autumn less.—My scarcity of English denies me the power of doing her justice in that language; but you know the Scotch idiom, she was a bonie, sweet, sonsie lass.—In short, she altogether unwittingly to herself, initiated me in a certain delicious Passion, which in spite of acid Disappointment, gin-horse Prudence, and bookworm Philosophy, I hold to be the first of human joys, our dearest † pleasure here below.—How she caught the contagion I can't say; you medical folks talk much of infection by breathing the same air, the touch, &c. but I never expresly told her that I loved her.—Indeed I did not well know myself, why I liked so much to loiter behind with her, when returning in the evening from our labors; why the tones of her voice made my heartstrings thrill like an Eolian harp; and particularly, why my pulse beat such a furious ratann when I looked and fingered over her hand, to pick out the nettle-stings and thistles.—Among her other love-inspiring qualifications, she sung sweetly; and 'twas her favorite reel to which I attempted giving an embodied vehicle in rhyme.‡—I was not so presumtive as to imagine that I could make verses like printed ones, composed by men who had Greek and Latin; but my girl sung a song which was said to be composed by a small country laird's son, on one of his father's maids, with whom he was in love; and I saw no reason why I might not rhyme as well as he, for excepting shearing sheep and casting peats, his father living in the moors, he had no more scholarcraft than I had.

'Thus with me began Love and Poesy; which at times have been my only and till within this last twelvemonth have been my highest enjoyment.—My father struggled on till he reached the freedom in his lease, when he entered on a larger farm about ten miles farther in the country.—The nature of the bargain was such as to throw a little ready money in his hand at the commencement, otherwise the affair would have been impracticable.—For four years we lived comfortably here; but a lawsuit between him and his Landlord commencing, after three years tossing and

---

* 'Two years' omitted in Glenriddel MS.

† 'Chiefest.'

‡ 'And 'twas her favourite Scotch reel that I attempted to give an embodied vehicle to in rhyme.'

whirling in the vortex of Litigation, my father was just saved from absorption in a jail by phthisical consumption, which after two years promises, kindly stept in and snatch'd him away—"To where the wicked cease from troubling, and where the weary be at rest."

'It is during this climacterick that my little story is most eventful. I was, at the beginning of this period, perhaps the most ungainly, awkward being in the parish. No Solitaire was less acquainted with the ways of the world.—My knowledge of ancient story was gathered from Salmon's and Guthrie's geographical grammars; my knowledge of modern manners, and of literature and criticism, I got from the Spectator. These, with Pope's works, some plays of Shakespear, Tull and Dickson on Agriculture, The Pantheon, Locke's Essay on the human understanding, Stackhouse's history of the bible, Justice's British Gardiner's directory, Boyle's lectures, Allan Ramsay's works, Taylor's scripture doctrine of original sin, a select Collection of English songs, and Hervey's meditations had been the extent of my reading.—The Collection of Songs was my *vade mecum*. I pored over them, driving my cart or walking to labor, song by song, verse by verse; carefully noting the true tender or sublime from affectation and fustian.—I am convinced I owe much to this for my critic-craft, such as it is.

'In my seventeenth year, to give my manners a brush, I went to a country dancing school.—My father had an unaccountable antipathy against these meetings; and my going was, what to this hour I repent, in absolute defiance of his commands.—My father, as I said before, was the sport of strong passions: from that instance of rebellion he took a kind of dislike to me, which, I believe was one cause of that dissipation which marked my future years.—I only say, Dissipation comparative with the strictness and sobriety of Presbyterian country life; for though the will-o'-wisp meteors of thoughtless whim were almost the sole lights of my path, yet early ingrained Piety and Virtue never failed to point me out the line of Innocence.—The great misfortune of my life was, never to have AN AIM.—I had felt early some stirrings of Ambition, but they were the blind gropings of Homer's Cyclops round the walls of his cave: I saw my father's situation entailed on me perpetual labor.— The only two doors by which I could enter the fields of fortune were the most niggardly economy, or the little chicaning art of bargainmaking: the first is so contracted an aperture, I never could squeeze myself into it; the last, I always hated the contamination of the threshold. —Thus, abandoned of aim or view in life; with a strong appetite for sociability, as well from native hilarity as from a pride of observation and remark; a constitutional hypochondriac taint which made me fly solitude; add to all these incentives to social life, my reputation for bookish knowledge, a certain wild, logical talent, and a strength of thought something like the rudiments of good sense, made me generally a welcome guest; so 'tis no great wonder that always "where two or three met together, there was I in the midst of them."—But far beyond all the other impulses of my heart was, *un penchant à l'adorable moitié* *du genre humain.*—My heart was compleatly tinder, and was eternally lighted up by some Goddess or other; and like every other warfare in this world, I was sometimes crowned with success, and sometimes morti- fied with defeat.—At the plough, scythe or reap-hook I feared no com- petitor, and set Want at defiance : and as I never cared farther for my [*] labors than while I was in actual exercise, I spent the evening in the way after my own heart.—A country lad rarely [†] carries on an amour without an assisting confident. —I possessed a curiosity, zeal and intrepid dexterity in these matters which recommended me a proper Second in duels of that kind ; and I dare say, I felt as much pleasure at being in the secret of half the amours in the parish, as ever did Premier at knowing the intrigues of half the courts of Europe.

  ‘The very goose feather in my hand seems instinctively to know the well-worn path of my imagination, the favorite theme of my song ; and is with difficulty restrained from giving you a couple of paragraphs on the amours of my Compeers, the humble Inmates of the farm-house and cottage ; but the grave sons of Science, Ambition or Avarice baptize these things by the name of Follies.—To the sons and daughters of labor and poverty they are matters of the most serious nature ; to them, the ardent hope, the stolen interview, the tender farewell, are the greatest and most delicious part of their enjoyments.

  ‘Another circumstance in my life which made very considerable alter- ations on my mind and manners was, I spent my seventeenth [‡] summer on a smuggling [coast] a good distance from home at a noted school, to learn Mensuration,[§] Surveying, Dialling, &c. in which I made a pretty good progress.—But I made greater progress in the knowledge of man- kind.—The contraband trade was at that time very successful ; scenes of swaggering riot and roaring dissipation were as yet new to me, and I was no enemy to social life.—Here, though I learned to look unconcern- edly on a large tavern-bill, and mix without fear in a drunken squabble, yet I went on with a high hand in my Geometry ; till the sun entered Virgo, a month which is always a carnival in my bosom, a charming Fillette, who lived next door to the school overset my Trigonometry, and set me off in a tangent from the spheres of my studies.—I struggled on with my Sines and Co-sines for a few days more ; but stepping out to the garden one charming noon, to take the sun's altitude, I met with my Angel——

——Like Proserpine gathering flowers,
Herself a fairer flower——

It was vain to think of doing any more good at school.—The remaining week I staid, I did nothing but craze the faculties of my soul about her,

<hr/>

* ‘Any.’
† ‘Seldom.’
‡ Some hand has scored this word through and inserted ‘nineteenth or twentieth.’
§ ‘I spent my seventeenth summer a good distance from home, at a noted school on a smuggling coast, to learn mensuration.’

or steal out to meet with her ; and the two last nights of my stay in the country, had sleep been a mortal sin, I was innocent.

'I returned home very considerably improved. — My reading was enlarged with the very important addition of Thomson's and Shenstone's works ; I had seen mankind in a new phasis ; and I engaged several of my schoolfellows to keep up a literary correspondence with me.—This last helped me much on in composition.*—I had met with a collection of letters by the Wits of Queen Ann's reign, and I pored over them most devoutly.—I kept copies of any of my own letters that pleased me, and a comparison between them and the composition of most of my correspondents flattered my vanity.—I carried this whim so far that though I had not three farthings worth of business in the world, yet every post brought me as many letters as if I had been a broad, plodding son of Day-book & Ledger.——

'My life flowed on much in the same tenor till my twenty third year. —*Vive l'amour et vive la bagatelle*, were my sole principles of action.— The addition of two more Authors to my library gave me great pleasure ; Sterne and M'kenzie.—Tristram Shandy and the Man of Feeling were my bosom favorites. — Poesy was still a darling walk for my mind, but 'twas only the humour of the hour.—I had usually half a dozen or more pieces on hand ; I took up one or other as it suited the momentary tone of the mind, and dismissed it as it bordered on fatigue.—My passions when once they were lighted up, raged like so many devils, till they got vent in rhyme ; and then conning over my verses, like a spell, soothed all into quiet.—None of the rhymes of those days are in print, except, Winter, a dirge, the eldest of my printed pieces ; The death of Poor Mailie, John Barleycorn, And songs first, second and third : song second was the ebullition of that passion which ended the forementioned school-business.

'My twenty third year was to me an important era. Partly thro' whim, and partly that I wished to set about doing something in life, I joined with a flax-dresser in a neighbouring town,† to learn his trade and carry on the business of manufacturing and retailing flax.—This turned out a sadly unlucky affair.—My Partner was a scoundrel of the first water who made money by the mystery of thieving ; and to finish the whole, while we were giving a welcoming carousal to the New year, our shop, by the drunken carelessness of my Partner's wife, took fire and was burnt to ashes ; and left me ‡ like a true Poet, not worth six-pence.—I was obliged to give up business ; the clouds of misfortune were gathering thick round my father's head, the darkest of which was, he was visibly far gone in a consumption ; and to crown all, a *belle fille* whom I adored and who had pledged her soul to meet me in the field of matrimony, jilted me with peculiar circumstances of mortification.—The finishing evil that brought up the rear of this infernal file was my hypochondriac complaint being irritated to such a degree, that for three months I was in diseased state of body and mind, scarcely to be envied

---

* This sentence omitted in Glenriddel MS.   † 'Neighbouring country town.'
‡ 'I was left.'

by the hopeless wretches who have just got their mittimus,* "Depart from me, ye Cursed &c."

'From this adventure I learned something of a town-life. But the principal thing which gave my mind a turn was, I formed a bosom-friendship with a young fellow, the first created being I had ever seen, but a hapless son of misfortune.—He was the son of a plain mechanic; but a great Man in the neighbourhood taking him under his patronage gave him a genteel education with a view to bettering his situation in life.—The Patron dieing just as he was ready to launch forth † into the world, the poor fellow in despair went to sea; where after a variety of good and bad fortune, a little before I was acquainted with him, he had been set ashore by an American Privateer on the wild coast of Connaught, stript of every thing.—I cannot quit this poor fellow's story without adding that he is at this moment Captain of a large westindiaman belonging to the Thames.

'This gentleman's mind was fraught with courage, independence, Magnanimity, and every noble, manly virtue.—I loved him, I admired him, to a degree of enthusiasm; and I strove to imitate him.—In some measure I succeeded: I had the pride before, but he taught it to flow in proper channels.—His knowledge of the world was vastly superiour to mine, and I was all attention to learn.—He was the only man I ever saw who was a greater fool than myself when WOMAN was the presiding star; but he spoke of a certain fashionable failing with levity, which hitherto I had regarded with horror.—Here his friendship did me a mischief, and the consequence was, that soon after I resumed the plough I wrote the WELCOME ‡ inclosed.—My reading was only encreased by two stray volumes of Pamela, and one of Ferdinand Count Fathom, which gave me some idea of Novels.—Rhyme, except some religious pieces which are in print, I had given up; but meeting with Fergusson's Scotch Poems, I strung anew my wildly-sounding, rustic lyre with emulating vigour.—When my father died, his all went among the rapacious hell-hounds that growl in the kennel of justice; but we made a shift to scrape a little money in the family amongst us, with which, to keep us together, my brother and I took a neighbouring farm.—My brother wanted my hare-brained imagination as well as my social and amorous madness, but in good sense and every sober qualification he was far my superiour.——

'I entered on this farm with a full resolution, "Come, go to, I will be wise!"—I read farming books; I calculated crops; I attended markets; and in short, in spite of "The devil, the world and the flesh," I believe I would have been a wise man; but the first year from unfortunately buying in bad seed, the second from a late harvest, we lost half of both our crops: this overset all my wisdom, and I returned "Like the dog to his vomit, and the sow that was washed to her wallowing in the mire."—

---

* 'Sentence.'

† 'The patron dying, and leaving my friend unprovided for, just as he was ready to launch forth.'

‡ 'A Poet's Welcome to his Love-begotten Daughter.' See Vol I., pp. 124-126.

'I now began to be known in the neighbourhood as a maker of rhymes.—The first of my poetic offspring that saw the light was a burlesque lamentation on a quarrel between two revd. Calvinists, both of them *dramatis personæ* in my Holy Fair.—I had an idea myself that the piece had some merit; but to prevent the worst, I gave a copy of it to a friend who was very fond of these things, and told him I could not guess who was the Author of it, but that I thought it pretty clever.—With a certain side of both clergy and laity it met with a roar of applause. Holy Willie's Prayer next made its appearance, and alarmed the kirk-Session so much, that they held three several meetings to look over their holy artillery, if any of it was pointed against profane Rhymers.—Unluckily for me, my idle wanderings led me, on another side, point blank, within the reach of their heaviest metal.—This is the unfortunate story alluded to in my printed poem, The Lament.—'Twas a shocking affair, which I cannot yet bear to recollect; and had very nearly given [me] one or two of the principal qualifications for a place among those who have lost the chart and mistake the reckoning of Rationality.—I gave up my part of the farm to my brother, as in truth it was only nominally mine; and made what little preparation was in my power for Jamaica.—Before leaving my native country for ever,* I resolved to publish my Poems.—I weighed my productions as impartially as in my power; I thought they had merit; and 'twas a delicious idea that I would be called a clever fellow, even though it should never reach my ears, a poor Negro-driver, or perhaps a victim to that inhospitable clime gone to the world of Spirits.†—I can truly say, that *pauvre Inconnu* as I then was, I had pretty nearly as high an idea of myself and my works as I have at this moment.—It [was] ever my opinion that the great, unhappy mistakes and blunders, both in a rational and religious point of view, of which we see thousands daily guilty, are owing to their ignorance, or mistaken notions of themselves.—To know myself had been all along my constant study.—I weighed myself alone; I balanced myself with others; I watched every means of information how much ground I occupied both as a Man and as a Poet; I studied assiduously Nature's DESIGN, where she seem'd to have intended the various LIGHTS and SHADES in my character.—I was pretty sure my Poems would meet with some applause; but at the worst, the roar of the Atlantic would deafen the voice of Censure, and the novelty of west-Indian scenes make me forget Neglect. I threw off six hundred copies, of which I had got subscriptions for about three hundred and fifty.—My vanity was highly gratified by the reception I met with from the Public; besides pocketing, all expences deducted, near twenty pounds.—This last came very seasonable, as I was about to indent myself for want of money to pay my freight.—So soon as I was master of nine guineas, the price of wafting me to the torrid zone, I bespoke a passage in the very first ship that was to sail, for

* 'However.'
† 'Or perhaps gone to the world of spirits, a victim to that inhospitable clime.'

Hungry ruin* had me in the wind.——

'I had for some time been seulking from covert to covert under all the terrors of a Jail ; as some ill-advised, ungrateful people had uncoupled the merciless legal Pack at my heels.—I had taken the last farewel of my few friends ; my chest was on the road to Greenock ; I had composed my last song I should ever measure in Caledonia, "The gloomy night is gathering fast,"† when a letter from Dr Blacklock to a friend of mine overthrew all my schemes by rousing my poetic ambition.—The Doctor belonged to a class of Critics for whose applause I had not even dared to hope.—His idea that I would meet with every encouragement for a second edition fired me so much that away I posted to Edinburgh without a single acquaintance in town, or a single letter of introduction‡ in my pocket.—The baneful Star that had so long shed its blasting influence§ in my Zenith, for once made a revolution to the Nadir ; and the providential care of a good God placed me under the patronage of one of his noblest creatures, the Earl of Glencairn : "*Oublie moi, Grand Dieu, si jamais je l'oublie !*"

'I need relate no farther. At Edinr. I was in a new world : I mingled among many classes of men, but all of them new to me ; and I was all attention "to catch the manners living as they rise."

'You can now, Sir, form a pretty near guess what sort of Wight he is whom for some time you have honored with your correspondence. That Fancy, Whim, keen Sensibility and riotous Passions may still make him zig-zag in his future path of life, is far from being improbable ;‖ but come what will, I shall answer for him the most determinate integrity and honor ; and though his evil star should again blaze in his meridian with tenfold more direful influence, he may reluctantly tax Friendship with Pity but no more.'

No. IV.—AULD LANG SYNE.

'Is not the Scotch phrase "Auld lang syne" exceedingly expressive ? There is an old song and tune which has often thrilled through my soul. You know I am an enthusiast in old Scotch songs. I shall give you the verses.' (Letter to Mrs Dunlop, 17th December 1788.) In these words we have Burns's first mention of the song, and, like not a few of his remarks on his own productions, they must be accepted *cum grano salis*. The earliest version of the song has been traced in broadsides prior to the close of the seventeenth century. It also appeared in Watson's *Collection of Comic and Serious Scots Poems* (Part III., Edinburgh, 1711). At least two claims to its authorship have been made,

---

* Burns had written 'wind :' some hand has corrected it.

† 'I had composed a song, "The gloomy night is gathering fast," which was to be the last effort of my muse in Caledonia.'

‡ 'Recommendation.'

§ 'The baneful star that had so long presided in my zenith.'

‖ 'Is very probable.'

the one on behalf of Sir Robert Aytoun, the other for Francis Sempill of Beltrees :

(1) Rev. Charles Rogers, editor of *The Poems of Sir Robert Aytoun* (London, 1871), gives both parts of the song, and this note : 'Parts I. and II. of this song have been ascribed to Aytoun, chiefly on the ground of the sentiments and manner bearing such marked resemblance to his own. Neither "Parts" are included in our MSS.'

(2) James Paterson, editor of *The Poems of the Sempills of Beltrees* (Edinburgh, 1849), had access to some MSS. of 'pieces attributed to Francis Sempill, in different hands of write—*none of them holograph of the author himself.*' These MSS. included two headed 'A song called Old Longsyne, made by Francis Sempill of Beltrees.' This seemed proof sufficient to enable Paterson to 'entertain no doubt of their accuracy in attributing the verses in question to F. S.'

OLD·LONG·SYNE.

(FIRST PART.)

Should old Acquaintance be forgot,
    And never thought upon,
The Flames of Love extinguished,
    And freely past and gone?
Is thy kind Heart now grown so cold
    In that Loving Breast of thine
That thou canst never once reflect
    On Old-long-syne?

Where are thy Protestations,
    Thy Vows and Oaths, my Dear,
Thou made to me, and I to thee,
    In Register yet clear?
Is Faith and Truth so violate
    To the Immortal Gods Divine,
That thou canst never once reflect
    On Old-long-syne?

Is't Cupid's Fears, or frosty Cares,
    That makes thy Sp'rits decay?
Or is't some Object of more Worth
    That's stol'n thy Heart away?
Or some Desert makes thee neglect
    Him, so much once was thine,
That thou canst never once reflect
    On Old-long-syne?

Is't Worldly Cares so desperate,
    That makes thee to despair?

Is 't that makes thee exasperate,
   And makes thee to forbear?
If thou of that were free as I,
   Thou surely would be Mine;
If this were true, we should renew
   Kind Old-long-syne.

But since that nothing can prevail,
   And all Hope is in vain,
From these Dejected Eyes of mine
   Still Showers of Tears shall rain:
And though thou hast me now forgot,
   Yet I 'll continue Thine,
And ne'er forget for to reflect
   On Old-long-syne.

If e'er I have a House, my Dear,
   That truly is call'd mine,
And can afford but Country Cheer,
   Or ought that 's good therein;
Tho' thou were Rebel to the King,
   And beat with Wind and Rain,
Assure thy self of Welcome, Love,
   For Old-long-syne.

(SECOND PART.)

My Soul is ravish'd with Delight,
   When you I think upon;
All Griefs and Sorrows take the Flight
   And hastily are gone;
The fair Resemblance of your Face
   So fills this Breast of mine,
No Fate nor Force can it displace,
   For Old-long-syne.

Since Thoughts of you do banish Grief,
   When I 'm from you removed;
And if in them I find Relief,
   When with sad Cares I 'm moved,
How doth your Presence me affect
   With Ecstacies Divine,
Especially when I reflect
   On Old-long-syne.

Since thou has rob'd me of my Heart,
   By those resistless Powers

Which Madame Nature doth impart
  To those fair Eyes of yours ;
With Honour it doth not consist
  To hold a Slave in Pyne ;
Pray let your Rigour, then, desist
  For Old-long-syne.

'Tis not my Freedom I do crave
  By deprecating Pains ;
Sure, Liberty he would not have
  Who glories in his Chains :
But this I wish, the Gods would move
  That Noble Soul of thine
To Pity, if thou cannot love
  For Old-long-syne.

The second version, which follows, was written by Allan Ramsay, and included in his *Tea-Table Miscellany* (vol. i., Edinburgh, 1724).

AULD LANG SYNE.

Should auld acquaintance be forgot,
  Tho' they return with scars ?
These are the noble hero's lot,
  Obtain'd in glorious wars :
Welcome, my Varo, to my breast,
  Thy arms about me twine,
And make me once again as blest
  As I was lang syne.

Methinks around us on each bough
  A thousand cupids play,
Whilst thro' the groves I walk with you,
  Each object makes me gay :
Since your return the sun and moon
  With brighter beams do shine ;
Streams murmur soft notes while they run,
  As they did lang syne.

Despise the court and din of state ;
  Let that to their share fall
Who can esteem such slav'ry great,
  While bounded like a ball :
But sunk in love, upon my arms
  Let your brave head recline ;
We 'll please ourselves with mutual charms,
  As we did lang syne.

O'er moor and dale, with your gay friend,
   You may pursue the chace,
And, after a blyth bottle, end
   All cares in my embrace :
And in a vacant, rainy day,
   You shall be wholly mine ;
We 'll make the hours run smooth away,
   And laugh at lang syne.

The hero, pleas'd with the sweet air,
   And signs of gen'rous love,
Which had been utter'd by the fair,
   Bow'd to the powers above :
Next day, with consent and glad haste,
   Th' approach'd the sacred shrine ;
Where the good priest the couple blest,
   And put them out of pine.

No. V.—VARIATIONS IN TEXT OF POEMS.

Pages 25, 26.—'ADDRESS TO EDINBURGH.'

Verse 1, line 5—marking = gathering. }   (*These are repeated in last*
      "   "   8—thy = your.   }   *verse.*)
      "   2,   "   1—still swells = slow-swells.
      "   3,   "   4—rural = rustic.
      "   "   5—Sorrow's = Pity's.
      "   "   6—Or = And.
      "   5,   "   7—*read*, Oft has it stood assailing war.
      "   6,   "   8—Law = Truth.
      "   7,   "   1—*read*, My heart beats wild to trace your steps.
      "   "   5—in = with.

Pages 27, 28.—'TO A HAGGIS.'

Verse 8, line 3—skinking = stinking [*misprint*].

The misprinting of this word (with other differences) in *some* impressions of the second edition of the *Poems* has caused much speculation as to whether or not there were two *editions* published at Edinburgh in 1787. The question has been well thrashed out of late, particularly in a 'note' on 'The Second Edition of Burns,' by Mr J. Barclay Murdoch. Mr Murdoch is probably correct in his conclusion that there was but *one edition*, and *various impressions* of that edition. 'Stinking edition' is applied to one which has the misprint. It may be noted that all copies of the third edition (London, 1787) have the same misprint.

Pages 49-51.—'EPISTLE TO MRS SCOT, GUIDWIFE OF WAUKHOPE-
HOUSE, ROXBURGHSHIRE.'

Verse 1, line 4—at = o'.
"   " 14—time = day.
"   2,   " 9—weeding heuk = weeder-clips.
"   3,   " 9—*read*, Her witching smile, her pauky e'en.
"   " 11–14—*read*, I fir'd, inspir'd,
                              At every kindling keek,
                           But bashing and dashing,
                              I fear'd ay to speak.

Pages 63-66.—'BALLAD ON THE AMERICAN WAR.'

Verse 5, lines 3, 4—These originally read :
                 An' bauld G——ne * whom Minden's plain
                 To fame will ever blaw, man.

Burns, however, deleted the lines and substituted those in the text.
The MS. with the lines deleted is at present in the hands of Mr S. J.
Davey, Bloomsbury, to whom we are obliged for permission to collate.

Pages 100, 101.—'ADDRESS TO WILLIAM TYTLER, ESQ.'

Verse 1, line 3—the = once.
"   3,   " 2—fallen = died.

The omission (indicated by . . .) on page 102, is because of the
obliteration of three lines of the MS., 'most likely,' says Scott
Douglas, 'containing some ultra-Jacobite sally.'

Page 138.—'ON THE DEATH OF JOHN M'LEOD, ESQ.'

Verse 4, line 1—*read*, Heaven oft tears the bosom chords.
"   " 4—that = her.
"   5,   " 3—*read*, Can point those tearful, griefworn eyes ; *or*
                           Can point those griefworn, brimful eyes.

Between verses 4 and 5, Allan Cunningham inserted in his edition
(1834) the following four lines 'restored from the Poet's manuscripts.'
It will be observed they are incomplete. They had probably been
taken from a scroll MS.
                 Were it in the poet's power,
                    Strong as he shares the grief
                 That pierces Isabella's heart,
                    To give that heart relief.

Pages 142-144.—'ON THE DEATH OF SIR JAMES HUNTER BLAIR.'

Verse 1, line 2—beyond = beneath.
"   2,   " 3—*read*, Or mus'd where erst rever'd waters well ; *or*
                           Or mus'd where erst the Saint's rever'd waters
                           well.

* Germain (Lord George Sackville).

Verse 3, line 2—*read*, The wingèd clouds flew o'er the starry sky.
" 7, " 4—honest = honor's.
" 9, " 1—ancient = wonted.

Pages 157, 158.—'VERSES WRITTEN . . . AT KENMORE.'
Page 157, line 6—to = on.
" 158, " 1—cliffs = hills.
" " " 2—ample = towering.
" " " 4—wonder = pleasure.
" " " 7-10—*transposed:* thus—

The *striding arches* o'er the new-born stream,
The village glittering in the noontide beam,
The lawns wood-fringed in Nature's native taste,
Nor with a single Goth-conceit disgraced.

Pages 163-165.—'THE HUMBLE PETITION OF BRUAR WATER.'
Verse 2, line 3—random, wanton = wanton random.
" 3, " 2—As = When.
" 4, " 1—skelvy = shelvy.
" 6, " 3—*read*, The Bardie, Music's youngest child.
" " " 8—In = With.
" 7, " 3, 4—*read*, And coward maukins sleep secure,
Low in their grassy forms.
" 8, " 1—here = there.
" 9, " 1—Here haply, too = And haply here.
" 10, " 5—fragrant = spreading.

Pages 170, 171.—'ON CASTLE GORDON.'
Verse 1, line 4—commix'd = immixed.
" " " 5—hands = bands.
" " " 7—to = the.
" 2, " 1—Spicy = Torrid.

Pages 191-193.—'ON SCARING SOME WATER-FOWL IN LOCH TURIT.'
Page 192, line 17—the = his.
" 193, " 3—the = that.

Page 207.—'WHERE, BRAVING ANGRY WINTER'S STORMS.'
Verse 1, line 1—*read*, Where, braving all the Winter's harms.
" 2, " 1—shade = glade.
" " " 4—When = Where.

Page 222-224.—'ON THE DEATH OF LORD PRESIDENT DUNDAS.'
Page 223, line 8—scenes = glooms.
" " " 31, 32—*read*,
Ye dark, waste hills, and brown, unsightly plains,
To you I sing my grief-inspirèd strains.

Page 287.—'STRATHALLAN'S LAMENT.'

Verse 1, line 1—surround = o'erhang.

    "   " 4—*read*, Still surround my lonely cave.

    " 2,   " 1–4—(in draft MS.) *read*,

           Farewell fleeting, fickle treasure,

           Between Mishap and Folly shared !

           Farewell Peace, and farewell Pleasure !

           Farewell flattering Man's regard !

Verse 2, line 5—us = me.

    "   " 6—*read*, Nor dare a hope my fate attend.

    "   " 7—us = me.

Pages 327, 328.—'THE CHEVALIER'S LAMENT.'

Verse 1, line 3—hawthorn trees = primroses.

    " 2,   " 2—While = When ; wi' = by.

    "   " 3—*read*, No birds sweetly singing, nor flowers gayly

              springing.

    " 3,   " 4—the *omitted ;* but = tho'.

    " 4,   " 3—deeds = faith.

    "   " 4—*read*, Alas ! can I make it no better return !

Pages 352, 353.—'WRITTEN IN FRIARS-CARSE HERMITAGE, ON NITH-
SIDE.'

Page 352, line 9—As = When.

    "   " 10—star = sun.

    "   " 19—step = steps.

    "   " 25—As thy = As the ; When thy ; When the.

    "   " 31—*read*, And teach the sportive younker's brain ; *or*

              And teach the sportive younker-train.

    "   " 32—Experience' lore oft bought with pain.

    "   " 33, 34—*read*, Say the criterion of their fate,

              Th' important query of their state.

    "   " 34—*read*, The grand criterion of their [his] fate ; *or*

              The important query of their [his] fate.

    " 353,   " 3, 4—*read*, Wert thou cottager or king,

              Peer or Peasant ?—no such thing !

    "   " 5—and *omitted.*

    "   last line—of Nithside = on Nidside.

Pages 369-372.—'FIRST EPISTLE TO ROBERT GRAHAM, ESQ., OF
FINTRY.'

Page 369, line 3—various = mazy.

    "   " 4—*read*, She forms of various stuff the various Man.

    "   " 5—*read*, The useful many, first she calls them forth.

    "   " 13—strong = gross.

    " 370,   " 3—But = Yet.

    "   " 14—wages = homage.

Page 370, line 23—Pitying = Viewing.

        „   „ 25—And to support = In pity for.

        „   „ 26—*read*, She clasp'd his tendrils round the truly great.

        „   „ 28—bounteous = generous.

        „   371,   „ 6—owns = feels.

        „   „ 11—the = all.

        „   „ 16—ask = crave ; seek.

        „   „ 17—giving = bounteous.

        „   „ 18—tax = crave.

        „   „ 25—*read*, Seek not the proofs in private life to find !

Pages 379, 380.—'MRS FERGUSSON OF CRAIGDARROCH'S LAMENTATION FOR THE DEATH OF HER SON.'

These verses are entered in the volume known as the 'Afton MSS.,' now in The Cottage at Alloway. They are headed 'A mother's lament for the loss of her only son,' and are followed by this note (*not*, however, in the autograph of Burns)—'To the Memory of Alexr. Gordon Stewart, only son of General Alex. Stewart, M.P., and Mrs Stewart of Afton, who died at a Military Academy at Strasburgh on the 5th of December 1787, aged 16.'

Verse 2, line 1—cruel = savage.

    „   4,   „ 3—*read*, O, do thou come and lay me low.

Page 388.—'THE LAZY MIST HANGS FROM THE BROW OF THE HILL.'

The second last line of the poem reads in Currie's edition (1800)—

    This life 's not worth having with all it can give.

Pages 392, 393.—'AULD LANG SYNE.'

Verse 1, line 4—*read*, And days o' lang syne.

Chorus, line 1—my dear = my jo.

When sending these verses to Thomson (September 1793), Burns removed to the end the stanza which here stands second. It is so printed in Thomson's *Collection*.

Edinburgh :
Printed by W. & R. Chambers, Limited.